GATE-CR[...]

At the center of the open[...] circle and at one edge a m[...] behind the shed was a Gate! From the sound of pounding hooves and outcries others were coming. The elvensteed Miralys's speed had outpaced them.

Denoriel's heart leapt with mingled joy and rage. Harry was not yet taken. The boy and his horse were being herded from the south toward the Gate.

The Sidhe could not touch the boy because of the iron cross he wore, but they planned to drive him through the Gate and deal with him Underhill. There were ten following him, only five even vaguely human. His horse was wild-eyed and lathered, ahead of its pursuers only because it was so terrified of them.

At the front was a Sidhe whose eyes were mad—huge, his slitted pupils closed so tight that the eyes seemed all one glittering green; his mouth was open, the sharp teeth showing as if he wished to tear at his prey with them. In his hand he held a huge crook to hook Harry from his horse.

The elvensteed leapt forward, between Harry and the demented Sidhe. Denoriel's sword made a downward stroke with the full strength of his terror and his rage behind it. The Sidhe screamed.

An impossible twist, another leap, and Miralys was beside Harry's horse. Denoriel reached over and yanked the boy from his horse. Then the elvensteed seemed to fly across the clearing.

"Hold tight, Harry," Denoriel bellowed. Harry's body was between him and the iron cross. For now, but not for long, Denoriel could bear it.

The need to dodge trees and leap brambles prevented Miralys from using his full speed. The not-horses were virtually on Miralys's heels when the elvensteed found the grove and charged into the Gate. . . .

BAEN BOOKS by MERCEDES LACKEY

This Scepter'd Isle

Mercedes Lackey
Roberta Gellis

THIS SCEPTER'D ISLE

This is a work of fiction. All the characters and events portrayed in this book are fictional, and any resemblance to real people or incidents is purely coincidental.

Copyright © 2004 by Mercedes Lackey & Roberta Gellis

All rights reserved, including the right to reproduce this book or portions thereof in any form.

A Baen Books Original

Baen Publishing Enterprises
P.O. Box 1403
Riverdale, NY 10471
www.baen.com

ISBN: 0-7434-9889-5

Cover art by Larry Dixon

First paperback printing, February 2005

Library of Congress Catoging-in-publication Data: 2003022161

Distributed by Simon & Schuster
1230 Avenue of the Americas
New York, NY 10020

Production by Windhaven Press, Auburn, NH
Printed in the United States of America

CHARACTER LIST

The Sidhe (Shee)

Child of Dannac (Dan'-nay)—applied to all Sidhe; deathly insult to say one of the Sidhe does *not* deserve the name

High King Oberon (O'-ber-on)/Queen Titania (Ty-tane'-ee-a)—rulers of all Elves

King Huon (Hugh'-on)/Queen Melusine (Mel'-u-seen)—rulers of French elves

Hen Ne (Hen-knee)—man-chicken in Fur Hold

Eigg Oh (Egg Oh)—head on legs with arms; Humpty Dumpty blurred face in Fur Hold

Kitsune (Kit-su'-ne) Matka (Mat'-kah) Toimisto (Toy-mist'-toe)—fox-headed man in Fur Hold

Seleighe* (see-ly) *Sidhe, or Bright Court Elves

Denoriel (Den-o'-ree-el) Siencyn (Sen'-sin) Macreth (Mac-reth') Silverhair (Silver-hair)—known as Lord Denno Siencyn Adorjan (A-dor'-jan) in the mortal world; Christopher Atwood, name used when he was disguised as wine merchant

Aleneil (A-len'-ee-il) Arwyddion (Ar-with'-ee-on) Ysfael (Iz'-fay-el) Silverhair—FarSeer, extraordinarily gentle for a Sidhe; Mistress Alana (A-lan'-a) in the mortal world

Kefni (Kef'-nee) Deulwyn (Deul'-in) Siarl (See'-arl) Silverhair—father of two sets of twins; he was killed trying to rescue Pasgen and Rhoslyn.

Seren (Ser'-en) Teifi (Tee'-fee) Tynewedd (Tin'-weth) Silverhair—Denoriel and Aleneil's mother; she did not want to live after her lifemate died and faded away when her children became "adult"

Eirianell (Ay-ree'-a-nell)—Aleneil's eldest teacher,
  wears Atlantean dress
Rhonwen (Ron'-wen)—Aleneil's middle teacher, wears
  Greek dress
Morwen (More'-wen)—teacher who wears Tudor dress
Ieuan Hywyn (Ee-u'-an He'-en)—student of mortal
  history
Mwynwen (Main'-wen)—Denoriel's current lady friend;
  she is a dark elf (not in character, but dark
  skinned, dark eyed, with blue-black hair)
Ceindrych (Seen'-de-rich)—old, powerful healer
Treowth (Tree'-ow-th)—a Magus Major who had
  wanted Denoriel as apprentice. Superb skills and
  perceptions
Gilfaethwy (Gill-faith'-wee)—a Magus Major who
  specializes in Gates
Miralys (Mir-al'-is)—Denoriel's elvensteed; various
  colors
Ystwyth (Ist'-with)—Aleneil's elvensteed; in the mortal
  world she is palomino
Lady Aeron (Air'-on)—FitzRoy's elvensteed, silver-
  blue, silver mane

Unseleighe (Un-see-ly) *Sidhe, or Dark Court Elves*
Rhoslyn (Ros'-lin) Teleri (Tell-ee'-ry) Dagfael (Dag'-
  file) Silverhair—FarSeer in the Unseleighe court,
  creator of the not-horses and all kinds of constructs; in the service of Maria de Salinas
  (Catherine's maid of honor) she is Mistress
  Rosamund Scot
Pasgen (Pass'-gen) Peblig (Peb'-leg) Rodrig (Rod'-rig)
  Silverhair—a mirror image of Denoriel; in the
  mortal world a human mage, Fagildo Otstargi. In
  service as advisor to Wolsey he is Sir Peter Kemp
Llanelli (Lah-nell'-ee) Ffridd (Frith) Gwynneth (Gin'-
  neth) Arian (Ar'-ee-on)—the mother of Rhoslyn
  and Pasgen; she followed her twins into
  Unseleighe territory when they were kidnaped

and after their father was killed trying to rescue them, she remained with the Unseleighe. She is utterly devoted but also possessive

Prince Vidal (Vee'-dahl) Dhu (Dew)—current ruler of the Unseleighe Domain, Caer (Care) Mordwyn (More'-dwin). Thoroughly vicious

Aurilia (Awe-rill'-ee-a) nic Morrigan (More'-rig-an)— Vidal's lover and supporter

Torgen (Tor'-gen)—Pasgen's not-horse (clawed paws instead of hooves, tearing fangs, red eyes)

Talog (Ta'-log)—Rhoslyn's not-horse

The Humans

English

Henry FitzRoy—born 1519; earl of Nottingham, duke of Somerset, duke of Richmond; an extremely nice young man, not too clever (and he knows it); he does not want to be king

Kip Ladbroke—FitzRoy's groom, devoted and paid off too by Denoriel; first Denoriel's servant

Shandy Dunstan—FitzRoy's servant, like Ladbroke he first served Denoriel

Reeve Tolliver—boy from workhouse, now subgroom under Ladbroke

Dickson—one of FitzRoy's guards

Gerrit—one of FitzRoy's guards

Nyle—one of FitzRoy's guards

Shaylor—one of FitzRoy's guards

Commissioners at Sheriff Hutton:
  Henry Howard, duke of Norfolk (not in residence)
  Sir Edward Seymour (also FitzRoy's Master of Horse)
  Sir John Forrester
  Sir William Fenwicke
  Lord Henry Percy

Thomas Cromwell—Wolsey's aide who takes over from Wolsey after his fall

Richard Croke—FitzRoy's tutor

John Palsgrave—FitzRoy's tutor

King Henry VIII

Princess Mary—born 1516; innocent of malice toward Elizabeth in Book 1; she hates Anne

Margaret Pole—countess of Salisbury, devoted to Mary

Anne Boleyn—born 1507; Henry VIII's second queen. Anne is highly Talented, but she is terrified of it, very sensitive to being called a witch; thus her Talent is totally untrained and makes her emotionally unstable and very vulnerable to mental influence

Lady Lee—sister of Thomas Wyatt, Anne's only friend; Aleneil, called Mistress Alana, is her friend/ companion

George Boleyn (later Viscount Rochford)—Anne's brother, provides Denoriel's access to court

George Boleyn's friends known to Denoriel; favorites of the king:

  Henry Norris

  Thomas Wyatt—Denoriel likes him; he is intelligent and sensitive, a good poet; however Denoriel thinks he is hot-headed and impractical

  Francis Weston

  William Brereton

  Francis Bryan

Henry Howard—duke of Norfolk, FitzRoy's warden; deputy to FitzRoy when he was lieutenant of the Northern March: Under him were Henry Percy, duke of Northumberland; Thomas Fiennes, Lord Dacre (he had gout, his brother Christopher Fiennes was his deputy—kind of stupid, Denoriel runs rings around him)

Henry Howard (later earl of Surrey)—son of the duke of Norfolk; childhood playmate of FitzRoy when they both lived under the care of the duke of Norfolk

Mary Howard—also a childhood playmate of FitzRoy; he married her when he was fifteen or sixteen, she a year or so younger; she outlived him by many years

Princess Elizabeth—born 7 September 1533; in Book 1 a toddler of two or so; adorable, precocious, the object of Henry FitzRoy's devotion

Lady Margaret Bryan—Elizabeth's governess, truly fond of the child but unconscious of otherworldly influences

Blanche Parry—nursery maid (changes diapers and such). Was nursery maid to Anne, known as a witch, called in when strange things began to happen in the nursery. A strong witch but fearful of being burnt hides talent; she recognizes the intrusion of Rhoslyn into the nursery

Christopher Atwood—Denoriel in disguise

Catherine of Aragon—Henry VIII's first wife, Mary's mother

Francisco Felipiz—one of Catherine's Spanish servants

Maria de Salinas—favorite Maid of Honor to Catherine

Spanish

Inigo de Mendoza—imperial ambassador

Paco and Nacho—the two armsmen who tried to drown FitzRoy

Eustace Chapuys—Spanish ambassador, Emperor Charles's man

Basilio Carlomagno—servant

Enrique Porfirio

Martin Perez—a human mage; servant of Charles V; violent partisan of Catherine

PLACES

Seleighe (See-ly) Domain—Bright Court Elves

Unseleighe (Un-see-ly) Domain—Dark Court Elves, ruled by Vidal Dhu

Caer (Care) Mordwyn (More'-dwin)—the Domain of Vidal Dhu

Elfhame (Elf'-hame) Logres (Low'-gres)—home for Denoriel

Elfhame Avalon (Av'-a-lon)—"capital" of Elfhames; Oberon and Titania's palace; various training centers, including one for FarSeers

Academicia (A-cad-a-me'-see-a)—training place and workplace for the Bright Court mages

Elfhame Csetate (Ses-ta'-te)-Boli—the elfhame under Hungary

Elfhame Melusine (Mel'-u-seen)—the main French division of Underhill

Llachar (Lah-har) Lle (Lay) ("radiant place" in Welsh)—palace in Elfhame Logres

Gateways—a neutral domain which has unnumbered Gates; it is a dangerous place to remain in because its wild magic alters anything in it; dangerous even to enter because its Gates don't go where they should

Wormegay (Worm-gay) Hold—this is like a really bad shanty-town slum; drains power from anyone in it; the stronger the power the worse the drain

Fur Hold—a delightful place inhabited by human/animal mixtures and almost unimaginable beings (like Eigg Oh); the sky is painted blue; white clouds are painted on it; the sun looks like a sunflower with a face painted on it, the petals wave and sometimes the eyes wink. However the hold is not totally benign; unpleasant things can happen to visitors

CHAPTER 1

With red-eyed hounds wailing and horns sounding "the death," the Wild Hunt poured into the forecourt of Caer Mordwyn, the palace of Vidal Dhu. Rhoslyn Teleri Dagfael Silverhair reined in her black steed, feeling his flanks heaving beneath her legs, his muscles trembling with weariness. Automatically a sidelong glance measured the physical condition of her twin, Pasgen Peblig Rodrig Silverhair, and his mount, but his not-horse was no less tired than hers. It had been a long Hunt; their quarry had been a canny creature who had doubled and redoubled his track, trying to escape them. They hadn't expected that; it wasn't as if he was anything special, just a mere mortal boy out on the wrong moor on the wrong night.

He'd been a gypsy, though—perhaps that had had something to do with his cleverness.

Not clever enough, not by half. He'd finally gone to ground in a place he probably thought was safe, a churchyard—but elves weren't demons, no matter how many times mortals confused them, and the holy

1

symbols that mortals held powerful were of no use against them.

Cold iron now—if the fellow had remembered to keep even a single horseshoe nail about him, they might have cornered him, but they'd never have been able to touch him. The fool—going out at night, on the moors, without cold iron (and why hadn't he had a knife, at least?), a hawthorn sprig, or any sort of true protection against the Unseleighe Sidhe.

Perhaps he hadn't been a real gypsy then; a real gypsy wouldn't have been so foolish. A real gypsy would have had a cross made of horseshoe nails about his throat, and perhaps even a horseshoe in his pocket to boot. After all, a horseshoe was proof against mortal as well as Sidhe, when wielded in a fist.

The horses milled, the red-eyed hounds swarming about among their clattering hooves, the courtyard a seething sea of chaos and noise. Then Vidal Dhu, unmistakable in his ebon armor, rode his sweating horse halfway up the staircase, paused there, raised his hand, and a silence fell over all of them. Even the hounds cringed, and slunk away to cower beneath the hand of their houndmaster.

"Disperse," their leader said, the single word echoing against the obsidian walls that surrounded the court.

And, of course, they did.

The houndmaster left first, his charges surging about him in waves, but silently now, silently, for Vidal Dhu had made it plain that he was wearied of the noise. To their kennels they would go, to lick the mortal blood from their paws and dream of another such hunt.

The lesser members of Vidal's court left next, riding out, not through the Gate to the mortal world which was now dead and dormant until Vidal called it to life again, but through the ordinary courtyard gate into the Underhill realm in which Vidal Dhu held sole sway. The greater lords and ladies, those who dwelt here in Caer Mordwyn at the pleasure of their lord and master, dismounted as servants came to take their steeds. With the creak of leather or the soft susurration of silk, they slipped up the stairs to the Great Hall, and from thence, to their quarters.

Now only Vidal Dhu, Rhoslyn, and her twin brother Pasgen remained, still mounted, in the courtyard.

Vidal slowly removed the antlered helm he always wore when leading the Wild Hunt, a fearsome thing of blackened silver with a pair of antlers worthy of an Irish elk, and a grim, grated visor that permitted nothing of Vidal's face to show.

A servant appeared at Vidal's stirrup; literally. Such things were commonplace Underhill, depending on the strength of the mage, of course. Vidal handed the helm to the creature, which was black-skinned and looked rather like an elongated newt in Vidal's black-and-silver livery. With a jingle of harness and a creak of leather, the Unseleighe prince dismounted, and stalked down the staircase and across the courtyard to the twins.

He took Rhoslyn's hand in his, and bestowed a kiss on the back of it. Even through her leather gloves, his lips were icy.

"I believe that the FarSeers require your presence, and that of your brother, my child," he said, his voice a velvet purr over a blade of adamant.

Pasgen and Rhoslyn exchanged a look, and both dismounted. Rhoslyn had no idea how the Prince of Caer Mordwyn knew that his FarSeers wanted her and her brother—certainly no words had been exchanged between him and his servant. It was, perhaps, a measure of both his power and his control over everything within the bounds of his domain.

They were dressed alike, Rhoslyn and Pasgen, in

tight black leather breeches, thigh-high boots, and black silk shirts with billowing sleeves. Wide, waist-cinching black leather belts held their weapons, matching daggers and rapiers. They differed only in their headgear; Rhoslyn wore a flat cap over her silver-blond hair, while Pasgen, as long-haired and fair as his sister, went bareheaded.

While Vidal Dhu watched with cold, green, cat-pupilled eyes and more newt-servants came to take their horses, the two crossed the courtyard and climbed the stairs. When the prince of Caer Mordwyn spoke, it was wise to follow even an implied order.

Not everything was bedecked in black in Caer Mordwyn. Once past the doors, the entrance-hall was a blaze of red and gold, with brazen stairs rising right and left. Pasgen, with slightly longer legs, got a bit ahead of his sister, and preceeded her up the right-hand stair.

Vidal kept his FarSeers in a tower, which they never left. Why, Rhoslyn wasn't certain. It wasn't as if there was anywhere for them to go. They couldn't pass the established border of Vidal's domain. Vidal never took them with him anywhere. And she and her brother were rapidly overtaking their teachers in FarSeeing skills. There was no reason anymore to keep his old servants confined—unless it was to deprive them of all external stimuli so they would be more eager for their visions.

Rhoslyn shivered, glad Pasgen was ahead of her on the stair so he would not see her weakness, but a really horrible thought had just occurred to her. Would she and Pasgen be the next denizens of the tower?

The chamber holding the great Mirror was at the very top of the tower, in a round room with no windows. A plush black carpet covered the floor from edge to edge, black velvet draperies covered the walls, so that every sound was muffled. The Mirror, a round, shallow basin, black as the walls and filled with the clearest of water, stood directly on the floor. Around it were placed the stools used by the FarSeers. The lighting in this room, dim and subtle, came from the ceiling—the entire ceiling, which glowed like a moon, a flawless moon, a silver disk without a shadow on it.

The other three FarSeers, sexless elves, pale and willowy, were robed identically in black, like the robes worn by the occasional priestly mortal Rhoslyn had seen in the upper realms, equally sexless, equally pale. Those poor worms, however, were clothed in harsh wool, while the FarSeers were draped in velvet.

They waited already on their stools. Without a word, Pasgen and Rhoslyn joined them. The three elder elves raised their hands in silence, and a mist drifted down from the ceiling above, a mist glowing with latent power as it settled on the surface of the Mirror. Theirs was the power. As she thought it, the knot that had formed under Rhoslyn's breastbone, making it hard to breathe, loosened. She and Pasgen could not summon that kind of power—and by her will and her warning, they never would. However, it was Rhoslyn and Pasgen who would clarify whatever dim vision the FarSeers had sensed in the Mirror that had caused them to call for the twins.

The mist settled; the Mirror began to glow as the light within the room dimmed. Rhoslyn could not have pulled her gaze away from that glowing circle now if she'd wanted to.

But she didn't want to, not really, in spite of the price she knew she would pay. The power in the Mirror was like a heady drink, and filled her with languor and euphoria at one and the same time. She did not wish to look away, and although she forgot it when she left this chamber, the moment she took her place on the stool before the Mirror, she remembered, and longed for the draught.

Shapes formed in the shifting light, and she leaned forward, just as, on the other side of the Mirror, Pasgen did the same. She felt him, hot and strong, binding to her as she bound to him. Both drank the power, willing the shapes to become more.

"Ahhh," that was one of the three FarSeers, as shapes became figures, and figures became the images of mortals.

The mortal king of this island—Henry, eighth of his name—a red-haired infant in his arms. A deathbed, with a bloated, monstrous version of the same king upon it. A coronation procession, though who was being crowned, Rhoslyn could not make clear.

Then many images in rapid succession—green fields and fertile harvests, festivals, laden ships coming into port—musicians and players, poets and painters—faster and faster until they blurred together into a single impression of burgeoning and flowering—and blurred into the formless mist.

Inside herself Rhoslyn shuddered; it was a future Vidal Dhu would hate. He would not thank the FarSeers for such a vision. This future held none of the things that their prince treasured. Only when there was unrest and pain in the mortal world, did he reap a harvest of his own. Rhoslyn glanced quickly at the poor, pale things and was surprised that they were not weeping and groaning. They would suffer for what she had seen. But Rhoslyn herself? Deep within her something stirred . . . and she strangled it a-borning.

"That is one future," whispered one of the FarSeers. "Linked to the red-haired, mortal child."

Even as Rhoslyn thrust down that quiver of desire for light and joy, another image began to form. She knew at once that this was why the FarSeers were not aghast; this was what they had brought her and Pasgen here to See. She concentrated on a new potential, buoyed by a burst of will from Pasgen, on a future that did not hold the red-haired child or that golden coronation procession. Rhoslyn held to that thought, driving all others from her mind, as her brother was doing across the Mirror from her, and the shapes began to form in the mist again.

And this time—they were very different.

Linked to a woman, whose hair might once have been red but was now drab and dark; linked to a woman surrounded by those black-robed Christian priests, and beside her a man, hardly taller than she, pale and pasty fair, with a long, thin, melancholy face, softened only by too-full, too-red lips surrounded by a thin, sandy beard. His clothing was as black as the priests' and his small-eyed head was presented on his crisp ruff as if it were being served on a plate. And now images that would be much more pleasing to the prince passed like ghosts across the face of the mirror.

Fires, fires in the heart of which twisted the bound figures of mortals. Mortals trooping into churches beneath the eyes of priests, with fear in their eyes and bowed heads. More mortals, in the hands of those priests, screaming in agony, undergoing what the mortals drolly referred to as "the Question." More fires, more mortals, bound and shaven, some mere children, being marched to feed those fires. Books going on still more fires as well, and a pall of smoke covering the land. The smoke rose to obscure the fires, to mix with the mist, and then, as always, Rhoslyn felt Pasgen's strength withdrawn and her own drained out of her as the mist thinned and settled and vanished. She sagged on the stool and passed her hand in front of her eyes; when she looked again, there was only the Mirror, blackly reflecting the silver ceiling above, and across from her, the weary emerald eyes of her brother.

"Ahhh." This had the sound of satisfaction in it. "Well done, my lord, my lady. The prince will be pleased."

Rhoslyn could not tell which of the three had spoken, but the one nearest her clapped his hands, and servants, stick-thin creatures with fingers like gnarled twigs, parted the curtains beside her. They looked fragile, but as she knew of old, they were strong; they helped her down from her stool, as on the other side of the Mirror, they were helping her brother. After a moment, he waved them off unsteadily; she elected to lean on them. After all, what else were they there for?

"Your lady-mother is preparing your chambers for you, my lady," one FarSeer said, holding aside the curtains so that she and her escort could pass through. Rhoslyn wanted to protest—*not mother—she'll make such a pother!*—but it was too late. The decision had been made for her, and she was too tired to do anything other than go along with it.

She felt a moment of envy, when it appeared that Pasgen was remaining behind. Lucky Pasgen—he wouldn't have to listen to their mother's vaporings! And perhaps he would learn from the mouth of the prince himself what the visions all meant, and what parts, if any, the twins were to play in his plans. She would not let herself be left out of those plans this time!

But then the moment slipped away, for she was too tired to think about anything other than placing one foot in front of the other. Speculation could wait, and so could jealousy and rivalry.

For now—the sole center of her universe was the urgent need for rest. Everything else could wait.

❖   ❖   ❖

Elsewhere Underhill a far different hunt had come home, although here too the silver horns wailed the Mort. Their prey had well deserved his fate, for he had dealt death, and far worse than death, to many, and had grown so rich from his work that he had been flattered and courted instead of despised. The Sidhe had done what mortal law could not—or would not—and the swirling crowd of riders called cheerfully to each other as they dismounted from their elvensteeds and patted the dogs that leapt and cavorted around them.

Unwinking silver stars set in the illusory sky of Elfhame Logres burned down through the eternal twilight that shrouded the groves and meadows in misty blue. Denoriel Siencyn Macreth Silverhair turned away from the last of his companions of this night's Wild Hunt, leaving them to their revels and feasting under the shelter of the leafy boughs in the gardens of High King Oberon's Summer Palace. He had another appointment this night, one he would not break for a much higher price than wine and laughter.

"Miralys," he breathed, and the elvensteed was there, nudging him with a velvet-soft muzzle. He swung around the steed and mounted. Miralys had run all night, but he was ready and willing to run again. That was not necessary. Denoriel guided the silver-dappled, emerald-eyed elvensteed down moss-covered paths that led away from the sounds of music and laughter toward the Gate that joined Logres to Elfhame Avalon. As he rode, he made some significant changes to his appearance.

The Hunters were a fearsome group, whose fantastic armor, costumes, and weaponry were designed a-purpose to strike terror into the hearts of the mortal humans foolish enough to have earned their attention. Denoriel rode with the Seleighe Hunt, whose victims deserved their attention—those "whom the law could not touch," who made the mistake of venturing into places where the Wild Hunt rode freely, their power uninhibited by the taint of cold iron. There were men enough in England who committed the worst excesses, who left death and weeping in their wake, and escaped men's justice, either because of rank, wealth, or cleverness. But they could not escape the Hunt, once it was on their scent . . .

The Seleighe Hunt took only evil-doers; the Hunt of the Unseleighe Sidhe, the Hunt in whose ranks Denoriel's half-brother and half-sister rode, was not so discriminating. The wicked were much harder to separate from their fellows and lure or drive out where the Hunt could bring them their just reward, and the Seleighe Wild Hunt loved the challenge, sneering at the Unseleighe, who sacrificed poor careless innocents. Mortals, of course, could not tell the two apart, but that was their problem, not Denoriel's. He delivered justice, justice in the form of a slim, leaf-shaped blade and the bright silver arrows of elf-shot.

Nevertheless, his twin sister did not like to be reminded that he rode with any Hunt at all. Gentle Aleneil never caught sight of him in his batwing cloak and his night-dark armor without a shudder, so as he rode toward the Gate, he banished these accouterments, calling up the soft silks of courtly garb in Aleneil's favorite colors of green and azure to clothe himself anew. Denoriel was no Magus Major, but the elf who could not clothe and reclothe him- or herself with a single thought when Underhill hardly deserved the name of Child of Dannae.

He favored styles of an older mode than that current among the humans; the puffed breeches and short tunics, the lace ruffs and slashed sleeves seemed unreasonably silly, if not downright uncomfortable, to him. Let others ape the latest foppery of the mortals; he would keep to what suited him. His green tunic was beautifully molded to his body and at mid-thigh length exposed smooth-fitting azure chausses, cross-gartered in the green of his tunic, that displayed his handsome legs to fine effect. He could not change the obsidian hilt on his sword—and would not if he could—but the sheath was now soft silver rather than dead black.

Silver lanterns, like miniature moons, hung among the branches at intervals along the path, and he passed from light, into shadow, back into pearly light again. At length the path opened up into a round meadow, ringed with witch lights; the grass was studded with huge, white moonflowers, and at the center stood the Gate.

There was but one destination this Gate held—Elfhame Avalon, the mystic heart of Seleighe lands Underhill, and as a consequence, the Gate was guarded by Oberon's most trusted knights and warriors. Once, one of them had been Denoriel's father . . .

The knights on duty at the Gate to Avalon did not bear their usual arms and accouterments; they wore instead a uniform style of armor and the High King's livery. With their helms down and closed, Denoriel could not recognize any of them, but they recognized him.

Recognized who he was supposed to be, at any rate. The Knights of the Gate were also magicians of power and took no chances. Denoriel felt the shiver of a spell pass across his skin, like the caress of icy silk, as one of them cast a magic that would dispel any illusion over him.

"Welcome, and pass on, Denoriel Silverhair," said a hollow voice that sounded as if it came from some-where over his head, rather than from any of the knights. The two nearest him parted enough to allow him to take his steed between them, and onto the white marble platform of the Gate.

Gates took many forms, according to the whims of their creators. This one was an arched dome of opal lace, rising above the eight fluted pillars of chalcedony that supported it, its floor a platform of the whitest, blue-veined marble. Miralys's hooves rang on the stone as the elvensteed paced slowly across the marble to pass between the two closest pillars and under the arch.

And the moment that Denoriel reached the center of the dome, the very air shivered, he felt a moment of unsettling disorientation—

And he was no longer beneath opal lacework, but under the interwoven boughs of eight trees wrought of solid silver, and beneath the hooves of his steed, not marble, but a pavement-mosaic of an eight-pointed star, formed of thousands of pearly seashells, each smaller than the nail of a newborn baby's finger.

His twin sister, Aleneil Arwyddion Ysfael Silverhair, waited for him at the edge of the pavement, bathed in the blue twilight of Underhill, her eyes grave, but welcoming. Denoriel swiftly dismounted and strode toward her, hands outstretched to catch hers.

As always, he felt that shock of familiarity, that unsettling feeling of staring into a mirror that somehow inverted his gender. The same eyes, Elven-green with slitted pupils, were common to High and Low Court, Seleighe and Unseleighe—but hers were the exact shape of his. The arch of her brow duplicated his, the sharp curve of cheekbone was the same that his own fingers traced, the barely tilted nose, one he had lamented in his own features, but which her suitors called "adorable," was also the same. Differences— there were those. Her hair was longer than his; hers swept the ground behind her, unbound, covered only by a tiny, heart-shaped cap, while his was neatly trimmed at his shoulder blades. And she wore a gown, not a tunic or doublet, fitted in the bodice with a low, square neckline, spreading as to the skirts. Today she wore a gown, tomorrow it might be doublet and hose; Elven women were free to wear or not wear whatever they chose. But Aleneil not only chose the sweeping skirts, she chose them in the current human mode, not the antique garments of another century, nor the curiously wrought robes favored by the most traditional of their kin.

"I'm here, as you asked," he said, meeting her eyes and seeing trouble in them. "But you didn't tell me— have you asked me as sister, or as FarSeer?"

"FarSeer first; then as your sister. It is as FarSeer that I must show you something of grave import; it is as sister that I will then ask something of you because of what I will show you." Her solemn, almost fearful, expression gave him a chill of foreboding, but she said nothing more, though he looked at her with a hundred questions in his eyes.

She took his hand and led him away; Miralys they left to graze as he would near the Gate. The steed would come to no harm here, and if Denoriel needed to ride, Miralys would come to him at a thought, no matter where he was, Underhill or in the mortal world. Elvensteeds were not limited to passing by Gates.

They were all fortunate that the steeds would not travel into Unseleighe Domains in their unlimited journeys, or the ongoing skirmishing with their Unseleighe cousins would turn into something even uglier than it already was.

Elven FarSeers, Healers, and the most powerful of the Mages were trained here in Avalon, which was said to be one of the oldest Elfhames. Aside from the teachers and those in training, only a select group of

FarSeers actually dwelt here still. Avalon was small, but the very air hummed with power, and unlike any other Elfhame, there were no actual buildings here. Fragments of walls were melded with living trees and bushes, creating as much or as little privacy as the inhabitant or the use required. There were no roofs; where was the need for roofs where it never rained? Avalon's air was always that of a sweet and balmy spring night with a hint of a breeze, and if one wanted a little more darkness than the twilight, one could make one's dwelling in the deep shade of the boughs of a cascading cypress or a sighing willow.

In the time of Arthur, human mages and the novices in service to the ancient gods had come here too, to be trained, passing—if not "easily," then certainly at their will—across the boundary between mortal and Elven lands. But then Christianity had supplanted the ways of the gods and goddesses, and the humans came no more. No mortal had set foot in Avalon for a thousand years.

Which was, Denoriel reflected, just as well.

As Aleneil drew her brother deeper and deeper into the heart of Avalon, the signs of current and former occupants appeared more often along the path. The pathway itself was lit by moon-lanterns, and the pearly glow they shed showed the arch of a doorway here, the thrust of a tower there, a surprising burst of color from a stained-glass window framed, not in stone, but in the living trunk of a tree.

He knew where she must be taking him, although he had never seen the artifact himself—the great Mirror of the FarSeers. This was not only a vehicle for the FarSeers to use in seeing the possible futures, it had been enchanted to be able to capture those visions and show them to those who were not, themselves, able to FarSee. It was the only creation of its kind in all of the Seleighe lands; perhaps the only one in the world, mortal or Underhill.

When they came upon it, though, it was a complete surprise.

On the rare occasions Denoriel had thought about the mirror in connection with his sister, he had wondered idly whether it would be silvered glass or blackest obsidian? A still pool, rimmed with glowing precious stones? A giant ball of flawless crystal?

It was none of these things.

It was, however, set in the middle of a depression in the earth, a tiny bowl of a valley, carpeted with millions of minute flowers. They nestled among leaves no bigger than seed-pearls, which gave off a sweet, spicy scent as he trod on them. In the center of the bowl was a pedestal of alabaster; on the pedestal stood a silver frame, enclosing what appeared to be an enormous lens of crystal.

Standing beside the lens were three elven women Denoriel didn't recognize. One, like Aleneil, was gowned in the height of current mortal fashion, though her chosen colors were sapphire and sky-blue. One wore little more than draped silk gauze, pinned in the style of ancient Greece at the shoulder with bronze brooches and held to her waist with a matching belt. The third, gowned in a style not seen since Atlantis disappeared beneath the sea, wore silks in pastel colors that clung to her body, embroidered all over with vines and leaves, with trailing sleeves and a train that covered the tiny flowers for yards behind her. All three were blond, of course, for Seleighe Sidhe favored blond hair, but the first had hair like a ruddy sunset, the second like a field of ripe corn, and the third, like Aleneil, pale as moonlight.

"My teachers," Aleneil said simply. "Now come and look into the Mirror."

He stood where she directed, and she beside him. The three other ladies raised their hands, and a glow of power lifted about the crystal lens.

"Here is the nexus of our future," said the one in the dress of ancient Greece, and a mist seemed to pass over the surface of the lens. A moment later, the surface cleared, but within it, Denoriel saw the image of a human infant, red-haired and scowling, swaddled in fine, embroidered linen and lace . . . and glowing with power. The babe was being held by a figure that Denoriel recognized—the mortal king of England, Henry, who was the eighth of that name.

"And here are glimpses of the future when this child comes to reign in Great Harry's stead," said the lady garbed as a mortal of that court. The lens misted again, and scene after scene played out briefly before him— briefly, but enough to show him a future very bright for the mortals of England, a flowering of art, music, and letters, of freedom of thought and deed, of exploration and bravery. Oh, there were problems—twice, if Denoriel read the signs aright—Spain sent a great fleet against England, only to be repulsed at minimal cost. But the troubles were weathered, the difficulties overcome, and the result was nearly an age of gold.

"And this—" said the lady of the ancient ways, "is what will come to pass if that child does not reign."

Fires . . .

Image after image crowded the lens, and even Denoriel, not unaccustomed to pain and terror, winced away from the appalling scenes. Black-robed Christian priests, grim-faced and implacable, brought scores, hundreds of victims to the Question, torturing their bodies until they would confess to anything, then burning what was left in front of silent onlookers. Others, whose intellects burned as brightly as the flames, did not need to be tortured; they confessed their sins of difference defiantly, and were burned. In place of a flowering of art and science, came a blight. Darkness fell over the land, pressed there by the heavy, iron hand of Spain and the Inquisition.

Then the lens cleared, and the ladies stood quietly, watching him. "Interesting," he said at last, forcing his breathing to be steady and even and swallowing the constriction in his throat. "But I fail to see what relevance this has to us."

It was the last of the ladies to speak who addressed him, her brows raised, her voice patient, as if she addressed a particularly stupid child. "What happens to them has always been relevant to us, Denoriel. Britain is bound to Logres, and Logres to Britain; it has always been so, and will always be. Think! Have you never heard of Elfhame Alhambra, of Elfhame Eldorado, and what became of them when the hounds of the Inquisition were set loose upon the land of Spain?"

He stiffened; no elf liked to be reminded of the darkened, deserted halls of the great palace of Alhambra, of the silent gardens of Eldorado, both haunted by things it was better not to meet. If anyone had told him why the elves had fled those elfhames, it had not stuck with him. But the word had been enough to give him the clue . . . Inquisition.

The lady of the Greek peplos stared at him in rebuke. "If dark times come upon the mortals of Britannia, they will come to us. Death and cruelty feed our Unseleighe kin, as creativity and joy feed us. If that comes to Britain at the hands of the Inquisition—the gates to Logres will be open to the Unseleighe Underhill."

Her eyes flashed angrily at him, and he stepped back a pace, startled. "Your pardon, lady," he murmured. "I did not know—"

She sniffed.

"But, lady," he continued rather plaintively, "what has this to do with me?"

The lady in modern court dress answered him. "Imprimus, because the visions came to your sister, not to us. That suggests that, despite her youth and lesser experience, she is to have some part to play in this. Secundus, when my fellows and I attempted to scry further clues, we could see only you—you, and the red-haired child, together—in the visions of a golden future. So it seems that you, Sir Denoriel, are the key to all of this."

This did something more than merely take Denoriel aback; it shocked him to the core. He stood with eyes wide and mouth inelegantly agape, his gaze flicking from one to the other. However, it was Aleneil who came to him, and put her hand gently on his arm. He met her eyes eagerly, but she offered no escape.

"Brother, I am sure they are right. In every way, they are right. You are the key to all of this; the red-haired child of Great Harry of England must live, and thrive, and grow up to rule. You must go to it in the mortal world, and become its protector." Her emerald eyes held his.

"But I am a warrior, not a nursemaid—" he said, feebly.

"And perhaps it is a warrior that will be needed," the eldest of the ladies said, impatience and a touch of scorn on her lovely features. "In any case, you have no choice, Sir Knight. We are sworn to work for the good of High King Oberon and Elfhame Logres. We, his FarSeers, can and will order you to this task, if we must."

"That will hardly be necessary," he said coldly, drawing himself up and gathering his dignity. "I, too, am sworn to protect and defend my king and this realm. I will do what I must."

And with that, he turned on his heel and left, but he burned within. And not even Aleneil followed him.

CHAPTER 2

"I am a warrior, not a nursemaid."

The words rang heavy with irony in his memory as Denoriel regarded the child before him. It was very easy to see who the boy's parents were; the sweetness of the mother's temper was mingled with the mulishness of the father's. Even without Great Harry's red hair, it would be obvious to whom the boy owed that temper, too. But what the boy had to say rather surprised him.

"The very last thing I want is to be king," the boy said.

"King!" Denoriel echoed, gazing down at the child, who gazed fearlessly back at him.

That could have been a taught response, but the liosalfar did not think so. Truth was in the large eyes and the earnest expression. But surely this was not the red-haired infant of his sister's vision. Then a chill slowed his heart. Could this boy be the other ruler, the ruler who would bring the Inquisition to England? No. Impossible.

He was already very fond of this child, and had been drawn strongly to him from their first meeting. He had made some slight excuse to accompany one of the mortal friends he had cultivated on a ride to Windsor Palace. Sir George Boleyn had business with the duke of Norfolk, whom Denoriel knew had Henry FitzRoy, the natural son of the king, in his care. Boleyn was glad of the company, for it was a long ride from London to Windsor, and had not bothered to question Denoriel's reasons. Denoriel was fulfilling his duty to meet and measure all of King Henry's children.

This boy, Denoriel was sure had never been that red-haired babe. He was not even overflowing with those human characteristics that fascinated the Fair Folk. Henry FitzRoy had no wit, no brilliance, no great inventiveness, none of the things that marked the infant prodigy. He was one thing only, an innocent, and his goodness shone through him like a candle through a horn lantern. That would be the mother's contribution, Bessy Blount, who seemingly had not an enemy in the world. No small feat, in Great Harry's court.

Good and innocent. Denoriel's lips almost curled into a sneer. For good or ill, he was a warrior, not a nursemaid. He should be mounted behind Koronos, driving suitable victims to their well-deserved deaths, reminding the humans that the Fair Folk *were*. For a moment he burned with the desire for the Hunt—then, he sighed. No matter how much he thrilled to the Hunt, never, ever, would he take pleasure in the sacrifice of victims like Henry FitzRoy. The Wild Hunt of the Seleighe Court took down those who would not be missed; those who—although their own families and neighbors might mouth horror—were a relief to be rid of. So two purposes were accomplished: Underhill continued to waken fear and respect but no one was ever angry enough to seek an open confrontation.

"Because your father is king, does it follow that you should wish to be?" Denoriel said, and suddenly found himself squatting down so that he would be on more equal terms with the child, not looming over him; he suspected that far too many loomed over Henry FitzRoy threatening or demanding.

"Yes, but luckily I am not the son of the queen," FitzRoy said.

He spoke very softly, flicking a glance over his shoulder to be sure that no one was close enough to overhear, but his eyes gleamed with mischief. Denoriel could not help but grin in response. For the first time since he had met the child he felt there was something more in him than simplicity and goodness. Then he reproached himself. What did he expect from a six-year-old?

"What do you mean 'luckily'?" he asked, still grinning.

The boy giggled. "If I were the son of the queen, I would *have* to be king." Suddenly the smile disappeared. He sighed, his expression too adult for the rounded baby face. "I still hope to be spared that."

Denoriel became aware that the guards who were waiting at the gate of this secluded part of the gardens of Windsor Castle had begun to stir uneasily. He realized that, squatting as he was, the guards could see neither FitzRoy nor him. The boy had not yet noticed the guards' uneasiness, but Denoriel's hearing was particularly keen. He stood up.

"I think we had better stroll about or throw your ball or something," he said. "Your guards must be wondering why we are so still."

"Guards," the boy repeated, and sighed again. "Before I suddenly became a Knight of the Garter, and Duke of Richmond and Somerset, and Earl of Nottingham I could play in the garden any way I liked. Oh, my nurse or the tutor came with me. But usually they just sat on a bench. He read; she did her needlework. Now I have guards telling me not to go too far, not to lean over the pond, not to climb a tree . . ."

"They are concerned for your safety," Denoriel said, as he reached down and took FitzRoy's hand. "You cannot blame them. It is their duty to protect you."

"I know." The child allowed his hand to lie in Denoriel's and then curled it confidingly around one of the Sidhe's long fingers. "Still, it is irksome to have them always stepping on my shadow. The only time I am free of them is when . . ."

Denoriel made suitable sounds of sympathy and encouragement but he only half heard what the boy was saying. He was wondering again what he was doing here. FitzRoy seemed over- rather than under-protected. He wished the FarSeers could have been more specific about FitzRoy's role in the future. Why did he need to be involved with this child . . . although now he liked the boy so well he would miss visits with him.

Denoriel recalled how furious he had been when he was first told of his role as nursemaid. Swallowing anger as best he could—one did not vent a private frustration on a FarSeer—he had returned to where he had left his elvensteed when he arrived in Elfhame Avalon.

Miralys had been waiting near the Gate giving passage to Elfhame Logres, where Denoriel had a lavish apartment in the palace. Their majesties, King Oberon and Queen Titania, only occasionally graced Llachar Lle with their presence; they stayed when they wished to join the Hunt or settle some dispute that pertained particularly to Logres, but they lived mostly in Elfhame Avalon.

Denoriel did not need to speak or guide the elvensteed. Miralys stepped delicately up on the mosaic under the silver trees and was at the heart of the eight-pointed star when he was barely in the saddle. With his mind on his distasteful duty, Denoriel hardly felt the disorientation of passing through the gate and was only minimally aware of the steed trotting through Logres. When Miralys stopped, Denoriel dismounted. He did not look to see where he was; all he did was rub his face gratefully against the cheek of his elvensteed, who lipped his hair fondly and moved away.

Sighing, Denoriel turned to climb the broad marble steps to the wide portico. He did not try to enter by the huge brazen doors that were opened only to admit the king and queen. Beside them, deep inset into the thick wall of the palace, was a man-sized door, always open. As he passed he felt the slippery, icy feel of the recognition spell. Had he not been approved, an invisible wall would have formed before him, and if he had not retreated swiftly enough, that cold welcome would have changed to one hot enough to broil the flesh off his bones.

The corridor he faced when he entered, though short, was broad enough to permit passage to anything the great doors could admit. There had been times when that space was necessary, as when the Cern Abbas giant had come to complain that his worshipers were not being given free passage through the Gates of Underhill. Mythical beings were not common even Underhill but it was the expression on Oberon's face that made the visit memorable. Denoriel's own taut features relaxed a trifle as he recalled the sight of the enormous naked being, club in hand, with, even for his size, exaggerated private parts.

At the end of that broad corridor was another pair of closed doors, these of marvelously worked silver

depicting scenes of the founding of Elfhame Logres;
the doors opened onto the throne room of the king
and queen. Denoriel did not even glance at them but
turned right into a cross-corridor that looked narrow.
That, however, was only in comparison with the grand
scale of the center passage.

Once in, the cross-corridor was a comfortable size,
the walls glowing softly in opalescent mother-of-pearl
colors broken regularly by doors. These were as fanciful in color, design, and composition as the maker
of the private domain behind them wished . . . or could
manage.

Denoriel's door was an amusing trap. It looked like
an open way into the outdoors, showing a flower-starred
meadow with an elegant manor and some trees in the
distance. Many an uninvited guest had ended with a
sore nose and forehead from trying to walk through.
To any not sealed to it, the doorway was as solid as a
painting on stone.

Denoriel passed through and stopped dead. The
small antechamber opened left into a spacious dining
area with a huge window that looked out onto the same
meadow scene, except that the manor and the woods,
dark and tangled, were much closer. To the right a
broad arch showed a comfortable living space. The floor
was covered with glowing rugs, thick and soft. Chairs
covered in spider-silk formed two groups around small
marble tables; other chairs flanked a beautifully carved
lounge, also upholstered in dark red spider-silk, which
faced a handsome white marble fireplace.

The witch-lights in the chamber were all glowing,
but they would have lit as soon as Denoriel passed the
door. The give-away that his apartment was not empty
was the small but brilliant fire leaping behind a silver screen in the hearth.

For one heart-stopping moment Denoriel could not

remember whether he had forgotten to seal his doorway against one of his past mistresses, and then he saw the little, lithe orange-red creature cavorting and dancing in the flames. His breath whooshed out.

"Mwynwen," he said, walking forward as a tall, slender woman rose from the lounge that faced the fireplace.

He was pleased, flattered even. Mwynwen was no easy-come, easy-go light of love. She favored few males. He had been honored when she asked him into her apartment, delighted that she seemed to find his conversation engaging, and so surprised—and awed—when she invited him into her bed that he had been almost unable to perform.

Only almost. He suspected Mwynwen could, if she desired, stimulate a corpse. He had staggered home in the dawn and eagerly given her image to his door, the scent of her, the look of her, the essence of her magic, although he had never expected that she would come. And she never had come to him before, although they continued to be lovers.

"You were so angry," she said, holding out a hand.

He took her hand, his feelings split in two. He was thrilled that Mwynwen was so attuned to him that she had felt his anger across the Elfhame, for Mwynwen, a Healer, unlike most of the inhabitants of Llachar Lle, lived in a separate manor in the silver woods beyond the palace. At the same time her mention of his anger renewed it. Irritation, pique over the task set him, but more than that, a smoldering rage that he should be accounted of so little worth as to be set to be a puling infant's nursery-guard leapt up in him again, but he could not bear to be petty in Mwynwen's eyes and held his tongue.

"You are angry again," she said, great eyes growing greater with anxiety, "with me?"

"No! Not with you. Not ever with you," Denoriel said.

She folded her hand around his and drew him closer. "Then at whom?"

"Not whom either," he replied, beginning to smile a little. "One cannot be angry at a FarSeer. What they See is no blame to them. They do not make the future, only say what it might be."

"Ah!" Mwynwen seated herself again, tugging lightly on Denoriel's hand so that he sat down beside her. "You did not like the future a FarSeer predicted for you? But who had ordered such a Seeing?"

"Not for me . . . well, yes, of course for me, but it was not my future that was foretold. It was Aleneil—"

Mwynwen frowned. "I do not believe Aleneil would ever See what was not good for you."

"Oh, good . . . bad . . ." He wrinkled his nose. "It was cursed *undignified*, that's what it was."

"Undignified?" Mwynwen echoed, her perfectly arched brows rising until they nearly touched her gleaming black hair. She tightened her grip on his hand. "You are very young, my Denoriel, to grow so angry over your dignity."

"I am a warrior," Denoriel said, lifting his head proudly. "I am one of Koronos's best, and when they were brought to bay, I have fought men with steel blades and steel poniards without weakening. Yet my sister and her teachers tell me I am fated to be a—" he hesitated, then confessed it, flushing "—a nurse-maid." *Not even a proper Guardian to one of our own. . . .*

"To whom?" Mwynwen asked, not scornful but brightly interested.

He snorted. "I do not know! A red-haired babe! Some king's get, so they say!"

Mwynwen frowned. "I cannot recall any babe being born in any Seleighe domain. An Unseleighe—"

He shook his head. "No, a mortal. Some king's get, in the mortal realms, and they cannot even tell me which." His lip curled. "The mortals breed apace, and the kings are worst of all. How am I to tell *which* child it is supposed to be, even?"

But Mwynwen pursed her lips and looked very sober indeed. "Mortal? Then mayhap what you said about not weakening when you fought those who brandished steel weapons was why you were chosen. You know, Denoriel, that only a few of us can bear the mortal world with their iron fireplaces and iron pots and iron nails in so many chairs, even iron belts about their bodies . . ."

She shuddered and raised her free hand to look at it. Still, so many, many years later there were faint white scars where an iron girdle had burned her fingers when she tried to pull it away from a wound. Before she could find silk enough to shield herself so she could undo the belt, it had been too late. Arthur had not died, but he still lay in a deep sleep and might sleep forever.

Denoriel was frowning but more in thought than in anger now. "I had not thought of that," he admitted. "It is true that while I do not *like* iron—it roils my belly and makes my mouth taste like cat pi- . . . ah, sorry, makes my mouth taste foul—but I can abide it without much weakness, so long as it does not touch me direct."

"And if your charge was threatened by men with steel swords, you *could* fight." She sighed. "There are many who could not, no matter how great their desire."

"True." Denoriel pursed his lips thoughtfully.

The healer nodded wisely, and his temper cooled.

So, this lady, whose wisdom he respected, saw nothing to scorn him for—and now that he came to think of it, if Seleighe must needs go to guard a child in the mortal realms, well, perhaps he *was* the only one for the task. "So," she said, interrupting his musing. "Tell me of this red-haired babe and why you must protect it."

And when the tale of the two futures for England was told, Mwynwen sat quietly, watching her salamander dance in the flames. Very softly she said, "It was only two hundred mortal years ago, just about when you were born . . . I knew Alhambra and Eldorado before . . ." After a pause to swallow, she went on, "Denoriel, it is *important*—I cannot tell you *how* important—that the child survive and take the throne."

"Well, what should stop it, if it is fated to rule?" he asked testily, still unreconciled to the notion that he must needs waste his time in such a task. Truly, what could harm a mortal child in the close custody that *any* of royal blood must have that an elven warrior could defend against?

"Does it not occur to you," she said slowly, "that if Aleneil saw these futures . . . Rhoslyn and Pasgen would also see them."

"Good Lord Koronos!" Denoriel exclaimed, sitting upright suddenly. "How could I have forgotten my dearly beloved half-brother and -sister? No, I had not thought of it, but of course, nothing is more likely than what called to Aleneil also summoned Rhoslyn."

"And they are not likely to keep their vision from Vidal Dhu . . . ?"

"No, not at all likely. They are favored pets . . ." but he corrected himself before the Healer could. "No, that is unfair. They have their powers and they are very useful to Vidal Dhu. Still, they would not dare keep such a vision from him." But once again, his feelings got the better of his tongue. "And why should they wish to? They are as rotten—"

Mwynwen sighed, her expression full of melancholy. "Denoriel, give them the benefit of some doubt."

He did not argue, but the stubborn lift of his chin offered little hope that his opinion would change. Mwynwen sighed again. "Well, you are right in that they would not dare keep the tale of the vision from Vidal Dhu. And then even if they preferred the rule of the red-haired child, Vidal Dhu would not. Think you, would Vidal Dhu let matters progress as they will?"

It was now Denoriel's turn to sigh. "No, indeed, he will not." Then he frowned. "But even Vidal would not harm a child."

"He would not need to harm the child," Mwynwen pointed out. "He would only need to steal it away, leaving behind a changeling that would soon sicken and die . . ."

Denoriel's hand tightened on hers. "But how can I guard against that? The child will be in line for the throne and will be most carefully guarded. How could I make a place for myself in the child's household without betraying my true nature? And even if I could manage that, could I watch day and night for who knows how long?"

She narrowed her eyes in thought. "No, you could not. The Sidhe do not sleep, as do mortals, but even the Sidhe must rest. We will need to content ourselves with checking on the child every day or every few days to make sure its soul is whole. If it is not . . ." She leaned closer to him and Denoriel could feel her shivering.

"We will know that a changeling has been substituted, and that we will need to find the child and bring it out of whichever Unseleighe Domain it has been taken to. Probably Vidal Dhu's." Denoriel sounded nearly cheerful now, and indeed, felt a tingle of eagerness.

The thought of a battle with the Unseleighe set his blood racing. It was forbidden fruit—as mortal Christians would say. Queen Titania, and thus King Oberon, had ruled that there were to be no attacks on the Unseleighe Domains, but for a cause as worthy as the rescue of the red-haired babe, Denoriel was sure the rule would be relaxed.

Seeing the light in his eyes, Mwynwen sighed again. "Denoriel, please, remember. We lost your father and several more when we tried to wrest Pasgen and Rhoslyn from Vidal Dhu, and their mother Llanelli gave herself up to the Unseleighe because she could not bear to lose her children."

"But the Seleighe were half dead already from their battle to rescue Aleneil and me," Denoriel protested. "And—" he stopped abruptly and began to laugh. "We are making dire plans for dire circumstances . . . and we haven't the faintest notion who this child is, except almost certainly King Henry's get."

A soft chuckle added depth to his harsher laugh and the salamander, which had slowed its gyrations, began to leap and tumble again. "Well, you have a point," Mwynwen said. "I suppose then that the first order of the day is to find yourself an entrée into King Henry's court so you can examine his children."

"Ahhh . . . yes." He shook his head. "Oh, my poor ears!"

Mwynwen laughed and caressed those elegant members, whose long points reached quite to the crown of Denoriel's head. But then she frowned—and a moment later began to offer serious advice, first on a disguise. The Sidhe did not dare reveal their existence to mortals, who were as numerous as ants compared with their own limited numbers and, having found Underhill, could overrun it. It was one thing to appear as the Wild Hunt, which most men of education did not believe in, and which in any case was thought to be made up of ghosts and demons, not of the Sidhe. It was quite another thing for the Sidhe to appear in true form under the sun of the sons of Adam, for to reveal that the elves and their ilk were something other than the figments of fearful and superstitious country-folks' nightmares would be to invite trouble from those same men of education. Thus none of the Fair Folk ever appeared in his or her natural form among mortals.

"Make it simple," Mwynwen urged. "Leave the color of your hair and eyes alone. You are just a touch careless when you are challenged or hurried, my love, so the less you have to remember about your appearance the better."

He was a little bit hurt at being called careless, but since he did not expect to live constantly in the mortal world, it did seem too much a bother to recall exactly what color of hair and eyes he had last worn. There were mortals enough who were blond and green-eyed, so all he would need to remember if he kept his own coloring was to cast the illusion of small, round ears and round-pupiled eyes. He tried it out, and Mwynwen laughed.

"Very good. Very good, indeed. And we are fortunate in the hats that are being worn now." Suddenly a large floppy velvet hat with a fluffy, curled plume appeared in her hand. "Here, try this on," she said. "If you pull it over your ear on the left and let the plume curl over the ear on the right, they will be completely concealed, even if you forget the illusion."

Denoriel left the hat on because his thoughts had gone beyond clothing. "Who will I be?" he asked. "I need to walk among the lords of the land, and they are not so many that they do not all know each other or know of each other."

"Hmmm," Mwynwen murmured. "A noble exile . . . A very *rich* noble exile from far away," she began, and they settled down to make plans for a long-term stay in the mortal world.

"You will, Lord Denno, won't you?" the child asked anxiously, tugging at Denoriel's hand.

Jerked out of his memories, Denoriel smiled at the boy and gently squeezed his fingers. "If I can," he promised, carefully hedging his assurance because he had no idea what the child had asked. In the distance, he heard a man's voice calling his name and he lifted his hand and waved.

"Oh, Sir George will have to come to talk to His Grace of Norfolk again." FitzRoy pursed his lips solemnly. "His Grace is very stubborn and likes to consult others before he agrees to anything, even if he has made up his mind in the first five minutes."

Denoriel chuckled and pulled the boy against him for a quick hug. "That's very naughty, Harry—making fun of your elders. I wonder what you say about me."

FitzRoy's eyes went large and round. "I never say anything about you, Lord Denno, except that you talk a lot about gardens and it's very boring." A faint glisten of tears showed in the eyes. "You're a foreigner. If they think I like you too much, they'll find ways to keep me busy when you come . . . and you're the only one who *listens* to me." Denoriel suppressed a faint pang of guilt over his violation of the child's simple trust. "So you will ask to see me when Sir George comes again, won't you?"

"I will certainly ask to see you," Denoriel assured the boy. George Boleyn's voice, closer now, called his name again. Suddenly worried, Denoriel bent down. "I will find a way to see you if I am denied, Harry. I will meet you in the garden with the fish pond. Look for me there—sail a boat so you can stay a while— and don't worry," he said softly, and then, much louder when he had straightened up. "George! These gardens are just wonderful. I suppose it's because of all the rain you have in this country, and the child showed me several new paths today."

Sir George managed to smile and look faintly supercilious at the same time. He was obviously rather annoyed at having had to pursue Denoriel into the garden. Pretending not to notice, Denoriel returned Sir George's smile with mild amusement, noting that irritation did not improve the young man's looks. Boleyn could only be considered almost handsome when he was amused and being amusing. Glowering, he was somewhat too swarthy of skin and too prominent of nose, and his neat black goatee hid what Denoriel suspected was a weak chin. However, his lively dark eyes, abundant black hair, and considerable charm of manner—when he wished to exert it— redeemed him.

That famous charm was not particularly in evidence when Boleyn asked irritably, "However did a man who can ride and fence like you, Lord Denno, come by this womanish love of flowers?"

"By spending most of my life in a part of my country that is much harsher than England, where flowers do not grow so easily or in such profusion," Denoriel said smoothly, referring to his fabricated history, which made him an exile from Hungary, now under the heel of the Turks.

That claim made reasonable his occasional lapses from English manners, his occasional ignorance of current court gossip, and his faint accent. His English was totally fluent, marked only by the lilting intonation of the speaker of Elven.

"Well, if I can tear you away, we should get back. It will be a long ride."

Surreptitiously, as George Boleyn turned away, Denoriel hugged FitzRoy, then took his hand.

"Are you coming, Denno?" Boleyn called back.

"I must see the child to his guards first," Denoriel said, suiting his stride to the boy's.

"They can see him from here," Boleyn said impatiently.

"But I took him from them, and he is my responsibility until I return him," Denoriel said, and then added, "Tell the servants to call for our horses, George. I will be with you before they arrive."

Boleyn sighed as he turned to walk back to the palace, but he said no more. Denoriel continued his unhurried way to the guards, FitzRoy's little warm hand in his. He knew that Boleyn and his circle of friends considered Lord Denno's sense of honor far too exact to be reasonable, but it was a useful crotchet and, Denoriel thought, might serve him well in the future if he needed to do anything questionable.

Denoriel was, by Miralys's response to his sent thought, as good as his word. He left FitzRoy with his guards with another brief hug and many thanks for showing him this private garden, then set off for the front of the house. He did lengthen his stride to what was comfortable for him, but did not hurry unduly; Miralys would see to it that the horses arrived only after he himself did, by creating enough mischief to keep the stable-hands more than occupied.

Boleyn was muttering to himself about the inefficiency of Norfolk's stable staff when the groom finally came, rather breathless and mussed, pulling his forelock and apologizing for taking so long. "The devil got into this 'un for a couple o' minutes," he said, gesturing at Miralys with his head. "Wouldn't let me tighten the girth. And like you warned me, m'lord, wouldn't let me near 'is head to check 'is bit. Reared right up and threatened me with 'is 'ooves. Bit of an 'ellion, ain't he?"

"Yes," Denoriel agreed, smiling, "but what a ride. And he knows me and doesn't give me any trouble. Won't let anyone else ride him either, so I don't need to worry about having him stolen."

Denoriel stepped forward and took the rein from the man's hand. He stroked Miralys's soft nose, with care not to allow his hand to pass through the illusion of the bit with reins attached. The reins were real enough—they had to be for situations like this—but they were attached to a loose noseband that Miralys could discard if necessary.

Naturally Miralys wore no bit. Any head furniture at all had been a matter of considerable negotiation, but its lack could not be explained in the mortal world. Miralys either had to wear something or not take part in Denoriel's venture. That would mean Denoriel would have had to ride a real horse. Everyone, especially Miralys, considered that too dangerous, not so much because Denoriel would be unable to manage a stupid, mortal beast, but because he might forget he was riding one and expect from it things Miralys would do.

Actually Denoriel was rather grateful to Norfolk's groom because his innocent remarks confirmed the reason for one of Denoriel's peculiarities—unsaddling and grooming his own horse. It had rather horrified George Boleyn and his friends that Lord Denno would stoop to groom's work. They had been equally annoyed when Denoriel wouldn't offer to let them ride Miralys. Fortunately on such a brief visit unsaddling was not required. All that needed to be done for a horse's comfort was to loosen the girth.

Denoriel swung into the saddle and when Boleyn was mounted, moved off with him down the approach to the park gates. "And was your meeting with Norfolk successful?" he asked in a tone that was more polite than interested.

Boleyn laughed. "Sorry about Norfolk sending you off like that. We weren't really talking secrets. He's got an exaggerated idea of his importance and considers all foreigners dangerous. Well, if you'd been French or Spanish there might be some sense to it, but I doubt Hungary's in the least bit interested in the internal politics of England."

"Poor Hungary has little ability to be interested in anything with the Turks squeezing out her life," Denoriel said, "but I did not mind being sent away at all, to tell the truth. I cannot say that *I* am particularly interested in political squabbles in England. Oh, England is my refuge and I wish it to do well in every way. I will take up arms to fight for England if the country is threatened, but I have no knowledge and no influence so I could not help you in a political maneuver. And being sent away, ever so politely with young Harry, gave me a chance to look more closely at the gardens. Beside that I like the boy. He's a nice child."

"FitzRoy . . . oh, I mean Richmond. Yes, he is."

They paused to allow the gatekeeper to open one of the iron-bound leaves for them, Denoriel holding back until Boleyn was well ahead and then bolting through in one leap so he and Miralys would be exposed for as short a time as possible to the baleful influence of the black metal. Fortunately the area had been wide enough that the illusion of the bit in Miralys's mouth did not break. The elvensteed was beside Boleyn in two strides.

"Richmond," Denoriel repeated. "That seems so strange to me, to heap so many honors on a six-year-old child—Knight of the Garter . . . a six-year-old knight? Earl of Nottingham, Duke of Somerset, Duke of Richmond. Really, Boleyn, I thought I was coming to understand England, but this leaves me completely dumbfound."

George Boleyn sighed with complete sincerity. "It is because the queen could never give King Henry an heir," he explained. "And now—"

Now, as Denoriel knew well, she never would. Not with the king growing openly discontented with her company—and seeking other beds. Such as Elizabeth Blount, FitzRoy's mother, and George Boleyn's own sister, Mary.

"But the queen and king *do* have an heir, the Princess Mary."

No hesitation or inflection in Denoriel's voice betrayed his memory of the cold wash of revulsion that had passed through him when he had made his bow with others to Princess Mary. The reaction seemed dreadfully unfair. She was a sweet-faced child with a pleasant manner and a marked skill in music. She had even been a red-haired baby, although now her hair was a dull auburn. But Mary's face had never worn the engaging scowl Denoriel had seen on the infant in King Henry's arms, there was no power in her, as there had been in the babe, and the frisson of withdrawal from her hinted she was the antithesis of the ruler who would usher in a golden age for England.

Boleyn made a dissatisfied sound and Denoriel asked, "Why do you not like her? She is healthy and clever. She even has a royal air about her, young as she is. What is wrong with Princess Mary?"

If Denoriel had hoped for some light to be cast upon why *he* did not like the princess, he would have been disappointed. However, he had no such hope. He already knew that George Boleyn had no trace of Talent, although his father, Sir Thomas, did, and so did his youngest sister Anne. George would not have been responding to whatever repelled Denoriel about Princess Mary, but he could possibly explain just how much of a threat she was to the welfare of the Sidhe.

Boleyn's lips pursed. "She is a girl."

Denoriel frowned. "That is all? Is there some law in England as there is in France forbidding a woman to rule? Hungary had a queen once, and the country flourished."

That was not strictly true, but Denoriel had discovered that George Boleyn and his circle were profoundly ignorant of any history but their own, and not *too* proficient in that. To his mild consternation, for his knowledge of Hungarian history was superficial, Boleyn looked strongly interested.

"Is that so? Who did she marry? Did he influence her rule?"

"Marry?" Denoriel hastily sought through what he had been told by Jenci Moricz, who had been induced to come from Elfhame Csetate-Boli to Elfhame Logres to give him a quick course in Hungarian history and social customs. "It was a long time ago," he protested mildly. "I'm not very sure, but I think she married the man who had been betrothed to her by her father. Sigismond, he was called."

"Ah, yes, but what I really want to know was who ruled?"

Denoriel laughed. "It was some two hundred years ago. I did not live there then. They were called joint rulers, but I suspect that it was Sigismond that ruled because Queen Maria died after about fifteen years and Sigismond continued to rule for many years more."

"Ah ha!" Boleyn nodded vigorously. "That was what I thought and that is exactly what King Henry opposes. If Princess Mary becomes his heir she will have to marry a prince of a foreign country. To marry other than the reigning prince or the heir apparent, would be to demean England's honor. Yet, if Princess Mary marries the reigning prince, he will doubtless rule England as well as his own land and England would become no more than a conquered state, although no war had been fought."

So, Denoriel thought, *that is a way that Spain could come to rule England without war.* If Mary married a Spanish prince and the people came to accept him or were so cowed they could not rebel . . . and then Mary died. Then Spain might continue to rule.

"Then why could she not marry one of her own noblemen?" Denoriel asked. "Surely he would be less important than she, and she would hold all the power."

"That would also demean the crown of England, but there is another danger there," Boleyn said, and Denoriel was surprised at the shrewdness of his expression. "Wives often become attached to and dependent upon their husbands. King Henry fears that any noble house from which a husband was chosen for Mary would soon wield far too much influence over all the rest of us."

"Hmmm." Denoriel considered that while the horses began to stretch into a trot. "There is sense in that," he agreed after a moment.

They rode southeast now on a well-traveled road. Denoriel felt as if they were hardly moving. With some difficulty he restrained himself from urging Miralys faster, reminding himself that Miralys was pacing himself so as not to stress Boleyn's horse. He saw that Boleyn was staring ahead, chewing on his lower lip and decided to distract him. He really did not want to know what Boleyn's business was, as it could not concern the red-haired child.

"But George, I do not see what King Henry's dissatisfaction with his heir has to do with loading such heavy honors on a six-year-old child."

"FitzRoy . . . ah, Richmond, is male," Boleyn said. "When *he* marries, he will rule no matter what his wife's heritage."

"But he is not legitimate," Denoriel protested, not because that had any meaning to him but because he remembered the suppressed fear and passion with which the boy had announced he did not wish to be king.

Sidhe sometimes took life companions, but by and large they loved until they tired of one another and then parted. In any case, even if they chose to use the seldom invoked state of legal binding, which mortals called marriage, that had nothing to do with children. A child, no matter how conceived, was a blessing to be cherished more highly than any other thing in Underhill.

Boleyn nodded agreement with Denoriel's remark, then shrugged. "Well, there is good precedent for bastards ruling England, William the Bastard, who is now often called 'the Conqueror,' being the best known example. Still that is why the king is moving slowly, indicating what might be his preference by the honors but not yet naming the boy his heir. He wishes to discover how his people react to the idea."

Denoriel shook his head and then hurriedly put up a hand to stabilize the large, floppy hat that would hide his ears if some encounter with cold iron should break the round-ear illusion. He had had to abandon his favored clothing for garments that were fashionable at court. The stylish clothes together with his skill as a swordsman and the quality of his horses—Miralys in

several different colors and lengths of mane and tail—
had gained "Lord Denno" of Hungary a place within
the circle of Henry VIII's friends.

"I don't understand," he admitted, laughing. "I don't
think I want to understand. Let me enjoy riding about
the country and hunting with you, George, and looking at gardens. Do not trouble my head with politics."

CHAPTER 3

Several weeks later Denoriel came to Windsor again
on one of his regular, if secret, visits. He dismounted
and Miralys disappeared into the little copse opposite
a long-forgotten postern gate in the wall around
Windsor Palace's gardens. He listened for a moment,
but there was no human sound nearby. The gate
yielded to his touch—he had, at the cost of a sick
headache that resisted Mwynwen's best efforts at
Healing for three days—removed the iron lock and
substituted a blackened silver imitation that had only
an illusion for wards and was sealed with magic.

As far as the safety of Windsor, his substitution was
an improvement. No thief, no assassin, could open his
lock as, with patience and skill, such a man might have
opened the iron one. For his purposes, it saved the
chance of raising questions in anyone's mind about the
frequency of his visits to young Harry FitzRoy. Officially he had seen Harry once in the interval. That time
Lord Denno had again accompanied George Boleyn,
who had business with the Duke of Norfolk, to

Windsor—for the pleasure of the ride and Boleyn's company, he said. Lord Denno had then politely left Norfolk and Boleyn to discuss their business in private and had gone off to walk in the gardens.

Considering Lord Denno's fondness for flowers, it was not surprising to anyone that he should encounter the young duke of Richmond in company with his playmates Henry and Mary Howard. The children all liked Lord Denno, who had the wit to invent new twists for old games, and, since Harry FitzRoy never mentioned Denoriel when he met him alone, Norfolk believed the foreigner only saw all three children together.

This was a clever lie—without one false word being uttered—because over those weeks FitzRoy had insisted on sailing his boat in the pond every day. Sometimes Henry and Mary brought boats and sailed them too——Denoriel never appeared on those days—but most of the time the Howard children found something more interesting to do and left FitzRoy alone. The guards, knowing the garden to be safely walled, stayed at the entry from where they could usually watch all three children.

Denoriel approved heartily of the situation as it was. The official visits when he accompanied George Boleyn had made Norfolk familiar with Lord Denno's fondness for children—and Denno had provided a sad tale of young brothers and sisters lost to the Turks—but aroused no suspicions of any particular relationship with FitzRoy. Denoriel's other incursions, twice or thrice a week, went totally unnoticed by anyone.

No one even knew Denoriel had ridden out of London, since he had, with King Oberon's approval and the assistance of one of the Magus Majors of Elfhame Logres, created and set a small Gate to open from near the palace Llachar Lle to two places: Lord

Denno's private set of rooms in his rented house in London and a tiny wood near a crossroad about a mile from Windsor. Four other destinations could be set into the Gate, even though it was a small one, only able to take him mounted on Miralys, but for now the other possibilities were empty.

Actually when Denoriel arrived at Windsor today, he was not certain that he would find Harry at the pond. He had visited the boy only the previous day, and ordinarily would not come again for one or two days more; however, he had had news that he found unsettling after he had returned to his London house.

A message had been waiting for him. That was innocent enough, only being a pressing invitation to accompany George Boleyn, Thomas Wyatt, Henry Norris, and Francis Bryan to attend the theater that afternoon. Although Denoriel found the scenery and effects incredibly crude and unconvincing, he had great admiration for the plays themselves and George's friends were all devoted to art and literature, which made discussions of what they had seen fascinating. Wyatt was a remarkably fine poet, George somewhat less skilled but with a pretty turn of phrase. Norris and Bryan were musicians of considerable skill. Denoriel always enjoyed an evening with them . . . and sometimes picked up valuable court gossip too.

So it was after the play, when they had all settled at a favorite tavern. To Denoriel's surprise the men did not discuss the entertainment, even though it had been thought provoking. They were too full of the fact that King Henry had named Princess Mary Lord Lieutenant of Wales and ordered that she be sent with a great household to Ludlow Castle—a traditional appointment for the heir to the throne.

That should have settled the confusion about who

King Henry would name his heir . . . except that the king, with clear intent to obscure the issue, had ordered almost the same honors for Henry FitzRoy. At the time he had been elevated to the peerage and given precedence over all other nobles, except those of the king's blood, he had also been named Lieutenant General North of the Trent. Now the king publicly reconfirmed him in that position and named him in addition keeper of the city and castle of Carlisle. Finally the king decreed that FitzRoy would be sent, with a household every bit equal to that of the princess, to rule—through his council—the north.

Denoriel had no idea why that news made him immediately uneasy. It would be some weeks, possibly even months, before FitzRoy's household could be assembled and the move begun. However, when he parted from George and his friends and reached his London house—ostensibly to go to bed for the night— he had naturally Gated to his apartment in Llachar Lle. There he found a bright, nearly transparent little creature flitting about his living room. It flung itself at him as soon as he entered the house, twittering with delight. It was a nearly mindless, but very affectionate, spirit of the air and, in contrast to its own happiness, carried an uncomfortable message from Aleneil.

Aleneil had waited for him for some time, the bright little thing burbled, but had to leave for a session with her teachers. She, too, had had presentiments of danger—not a true Seeing, not even a hint of what kind of danger, only danger and soon. Possibly with the assistance of the more experienced FarSeers, she would learn more, but she had wanted to warn Denoriel.

Danger. But from where, for whom? Denoriel reviewed his recent movements and realized he had hardly interacted at all with the rest of the Sidhe of

Elfhame Logres—other than Mwynwen. He had been with Mwynwen frequently, either in his own chambers or her house, resting and leaching out of his body the subliminal aches and slight sickness that extended exposure to iron caused . . . because most of his time was spent in the mortal world. So the danger must come from there, but the only change in the situation was the renewed emphasis on the elevation of FitzRoy.

Did he dare wait to hear again from Aleneil, Denoriel wondered? No, he did not! FarSeeing was more a nuisance than a help, he thought, sending a thought for Miralys. Soon. What did soon mean? Within minutes of when Aleneil had the presentiment? Within hours? Within days?

Anxious and exasperated, Denoriel Gated to Windsor, left Miralys to conceal himself in the copse, and let himself into the garden. Having slipped sidelong through the barely opened gate, he stood with his back to the wall, hidden in the shadows, and listened. Aside from the normal sounds of night, insects and some peeping of frogs from the pond, there was utter silence.

Carefully Denoriel worked his way through the gardens, slipping from hedge shadow to tree shadow, to where he could see the palace itself. The bulk of the huge building was dark and silent—no flickering of light from window to window as if someone were rushing around, no sounds of excitement. Torches flamed at the front door and guards stood to each side of it, but from their stance, there had been no trouble recently nor were they expecting trouble. There were other entrances to the palace, but those were all locked and barred every night. He did not believe any of them could be breached without considerable noise.

Denoriel allowed a soft sigh of relief to ease past

his lips. Whatever Aleneil had felt had not happened
yet. But despite that assurance, inside he was as taut
as a bowstring. It would happen . . . soon. How soon?
Denoriel stood in the shadows, staring out along the
road that led to the outer gate.

It took a moment for his eyes to recover from that
glance at the torches and he had to restrain an impulse
to "tch" with irritation and shake his head. What in the
world could those guards expect to see if their eyes
were accustomed to the light of the torches? And
mortals were near blind at night anyway. But that was
irrelevant.

The road was empty and silent. Denoriel shrugged.
No one would be admitted to the palace at this time
of night, at least not without considerable fuss and
bother. So either the danger was already within or it
would arrive in the daylight tomorrow . . . or the next
day, or the next.

He felt like howling with frustration. Within. He
sighed. Yes, he could get within. He had witched a
window—fortunately that had had only a small metal
catch—near FitzRoy's apartment during his "official"
visit to Windsor, when he had asked the children to
see their wing of the palace. But if he were caught,
there was no explanation he would be able to give.
Lord Denno would have to disappear, and it would
be very much harder to find a new identity . . . and
still harder to re-win Harry's confidence.

There was no way, he told himself, that anyone could
get the child out of the palace, but to slip into his
bedchamber and smother him . . . Denoriel's breath
caught. No one would! Surely no one would harm such
a small, sweet child!

Even as the thoughts passed through his mind, his
clothing turned a dull, dusty black and he was slipping
from shadow to shadow across the open ground. His

footsteps made no noise and his movements, a short rush when a cloud passed the moon, and an utter stillness in which his dark form could easily be one more ornamental tree or bush, would deceive most watchers. He reached the wall of the building that held the children's quarters.

Here there was shadow enough between the towers that beetled out from the wall. Beneath the witched window, Denoriel stopped, put his back to the wall, and stood, hardly breathing, listening. Nothing. Silence. It was too far from the pond to hear the frogs and there was nothing to attract insects. The walls were rough, unfinished stone blocks. Denoriel pulled off his boots and attached them magically to his back where they would not get in the way; there were plenty of places for his long, thin fingers and toes to grip.

He went up and was inside quickly enough to be sure that no one could have come on the scene and noticed him. Inside the silence was even more profound. Several of the chambers were vacant, reserved for visiting children of friends and relatives. Denoriel passed silently along the corridor, his heartbeat increasing with his fear of what he would find—but all he found was peace.

In the outer chamber of FitzRoy's apartment, a fat night candle in a corner near the door lit the room as bright as day to Denoriel's night-sighted, dark-adjusted eyes. In the next room, a manservant or a guard was asleep on a settle. That made Denoriel tense and he hurried past to the next door. The innermost room was FitzRoy's bedchamber; that was also well lit with a night candle.

The boy's nurse slept on a truckle bed pulled out from beneath the high four-poster, but not with sodden flaccidity as she would had she been drugged. Her fingers twitched very slightly on the coverlet and she made a tiny whistling snore. Although the lightness of her sleep threatened discovery, Denoriel's pulse began to slow as he circled around and approached the bed on the side opposite the truckle bed. If Harry was safe, he could deal with the nurse if he must.

Silently, careful not to rattle the rings, Denoriel pulled the curtain back a bare inch. He heard FitzRoy's peaceful breathing, saw his face, the cheek resting on a familiar silk kerchief clutched in one hand; Denoriel remembered wrapping that kerchief around FitzRoy's wrist when he had hurt it in a game. He swallowed. The truckle bed creaked. Denoriel froze. When the sound was not repeated, he dropped the curtain and eased to the edge of the bed, then around the bottom until he could see; the nurse was quiet now, seeming more soundly asleep.

A few strides took Denoriel to the far wall where he skirted a heavy wardrobe and a chair. The door was open as it had been. Half in, half out of the room, he paused and listened. The guard/manservant was asleep as deeply as when he entered; still, it seemed to Denoriel that he did not breathe again until he was out in the corridor. There he paused. The boy was safe and well, but the feeling that something ill was brooding all around was even more intense.

What had he proved, Denoriel wondered. Harry was safe in his bed, but someone else could do just what he had done with a far less innocent purpose. He thought of searching the area for strangers and then realized how very silly such a plan was. For one thing, that was just asking to be caught. For another, how would he know who was a stranger and who belonged in the castle? He had no roster of all of the servants, nor of the noble guests who might be staying at Norfolk's invitation.

Across the corridor was a door. Denoriel went and listened. Silence. He tried the latch. The door was not locked. He opened it, listened again, then slipped inside, leaving the door barely ajar. He would watch. If anyone tried to enter FitzRoy's apartment he would . . . what? Denoriel sighed. What could he do without betraying his own presence?

Eventually the answer came to him and Denoriel sighed again. Magic was *very* hard to do in the mortal world and he was already depleted by having changed his clothing to black. Still, the spell he needed, the Don't-see-me spell, was very simple and required very little power. Telling himself to listen all the more carefully, he closed his physical eyes and began to look around with inner sight.

The ability was not common to the Sidhe; when as a child he described it to one of the Magus Majors, the magus wanted to take him as an apprentice. He had refused because he wanted to be a warrior, an armored knight, like the father who had died fighting the Unseleighe . . . Denoriel's lips twisted. Now he was a nursemaid. Or, perhaps not; the very air seemed heavy with threat.

To Denoriel's surprise he could "see" a very faint palely glowing haze. There *was* power in the mortal world, it seemed. He mentally shook his head at himself. Of course there was power in the mortal world; there were mortal mages and more humans than they themselves knew were born with Talent. With his inner sight, Denoriel stared at the haze of power, but it seemed so dispersed as to be useless. No, not entirely. There was a bright thread in the glow for which Denoriel "reached." It was thinner than a spider's web, but when he "caught" it, he gasped with shock.

It was as if the power that smoothly filled Underhill, as the spirits in good wine blended perfectly in the body of the liquid and could not be separately tasted, had been distilled into a thin but powerful stream of brandy, almost pure spirits. It burned along the power channels in his body, making him aware of them as he never was in Underhill, but his weariness dissipated and he was prepared to watch for the rest of the night without doubting his alertness.

He even hoped for a few moments that the replenishment would remove the sense of dread that hung about him, thinking that the feeling of sharp anxiety and heavy threat was a result of the iron in his surroundings. Far from relief, he felt even more anxious. Something was coming, something evil.

It did not come that night, however. No assassin slipped down the dark corridor. No peak of warning hinted at anyone with ill intent entering through a window as he had. When false dawn passed and the sky began to lighten again, Denoriel made ready to slip from the room and make his way out of the building. Although he was not familiar with the morning activities, he assumed no one would attack the boy for the next few hours. Too many servants would be in and out, bringing water for washing and breakfast and generally making ready for the day. Then FitzRoy would be in the schoolroom with the others.

His suppositions soon became fact. Doors began to open and shut on the floor above, steps sounded on the tower stairs, there were low voices giving greetings, issuing orders. Denoriel made sure the corridor was empty, invoked the Don't-see-me spell, which barely drew on the power he had taken in, walked calmly down the main staircase, and waited near the doors for the guards to open them. When they did, to allow a clerk or some upper servant to enter, Denoriel stepped out.

During the long dark hours, he had considered

remaining with FitzRoy but he had finally decided the attempt would be useless and might well be dangerous. He could not be close enough to Harry to protect him from an attack by a long-trusted servant, and if he could leap on the attacker in time he would have betrayed himself. Besides such an attack seemed utterly impossible. Henry Howard and Mary Howard would be there as would their servants; guards would be at the door. And, although he did not trust the feeling, his sense of threat was somehow . . . outside, not within.

The place where Harry might be alone was after nuncheon when the children were free for some hours of play. On any fair day, they all made for the garden. Denoriel did not know whether he hoped the boy would stay with his friends, in which case Denoriel thought no attack would be made and the tension he felt would continue, or would go by himself to the pond to sail his boat. If he did that and the guards saved themselves the walk to the pond by remaining at the gate, as they usually did, FitzRoy would be alone and vulnerable.

And the threat might not even be directed against FitzRoy, Denoriel thought, walking toward the garden that held the little pond. He felt it and felt it urgently, but perhaps that urgency was a signal that he should be elsewhere watching and warding. He ground his teeth with helplessness and anxiety and then suddenly realized that Aleneil might well have an answer by now. She had not sent any message, but it would be hard to reach him in the mortal world. He had several hours before FitzRoy would not be surrounded by friends, guards, and teachers; he would Gate to Llachar Lle.

That was not quite as easy as usual this early in the morning. Cartloads of supplies, meat, vegetables, milk, and cheese, were coming in from the surrounding farms. Messengers were leaving the castle. Bailiffs and other clerks were traveling toward it to make their reports to Norfolk who, Denoriel realized, must be in residence. Perhaps the threat was directed at Norfolk; he was a proud, hot-tempered man and had enemies in plenty. Denoriel could not guess why a threat to Norfolk should make *him* uneasy . . . All the more reason for him to speak to Aleneil.

He could not simply call Miralys as usual; he had to cross into the copse and find the elvensteed, and then they had to wait some time for the road to clear. When they reached the small wood that held the Gate to Llachar Lle, Denoriel almost cursed aloud. There was a seemingly endless train of horses and carriages following a most elegant hearse. Denoriel could do nothing but ride on past the wood; because the copse was so small, there was scarcely any reason to enter it—and if he did so and did not emerge, someone was sure to notice.

By the time Denoriel reached his apartment, he was utterly enraged. That Aleneil sprang to her feet and rushed to him as soon as he entered did not assuage his temper.

"The boy," she cried. "They are going to kill the boy."

"Kill!" Denoriel echoed. "Even the Unseleighe would not do that. Surely not Rhoslyn and Pasgen! Not even if Vidal Dhu ordered it."

"No, no. The Sidhe are not at fault," Aleneil said. "I hope Rhoslyn and Pasgen do not even know about FitzRoy . . . or if they do, they think him of no account. I do not know why he *is* of account."

"He will not come to rule?"

Aleneil shook her head. "I do not believe so, and if he should, it will be for only a few years and will not affect the rule of the red-haired child. There is a boy of his seeming who *will* rule, but . . . but he seems to be much younger than FitzRoy, although in a Seeing, time . . ."

She sighed and walked back into the living quarters to seat herself on the lounge. Denoriel followed and sank into one of the red-silk-covered adjoining chairs. There was no fire in the hearth; of course, there was no need for one, except as a decorative effect. The temperature everywhere in Llachar Lle was comfortable.

Denoriel wanted to let himself rest. The channels in his body still burned slightly and those that did not ached. But he could barely lie back in his chair although he knew there was no hurry; he could return to Windsor and arrive at any time he desired. Then he realized it was Aleneil, who usually was a pool of serenity, that was transmitting tension to him.

"You *must* save FitzRoy," she said.

"Of course I will," Denoriel assured her irritably. "I got into his apartment last night to make sure all was well with him—and it was. It was no changeling in his bed. Then I watched by his door to make sure no one entered or left. He is safe now with his friends and teachers."

"But the danger comes soon," Aleneil insisted, her face creased with anxiety. "Perhaps it is already there or on its way. I feel it pounding within me like the beat of my heart. I do not know why, but if FitzRoy dies, the red-haired child will never rule and we . . . we will go down the same path as Alhambra and Eldorado."

Denoriel repressed a shudder and stood up. Mwynwen had showed him those two, sad realms herself, and told him in great detail what had happened to them. He could not bear for such a fate to come upon his own home. "Comes from within?

From among his friends? Those who are supposed to be his guardians? Comes from without?" His voice was higher than usual. Fear was so unaccustomed an emotion to him that he did not recognize it and covered it with anger.

"I don't know!" Aleneil wailed, and then, suddenly her breath was coming quick and short and she whispered, "Now! Go now, Denoriel."

Considering the emotions that had been generated in his chambers, Denoriel was not surprised to find Miralys waiting. He flung himself into the saddle and less than a quarter hour later out of it in the copse across from the magicked gate. There was no one in the road. Denoriel ran across, ran in through the gate . . . and realized that he had not willed his time of arrival to be the same as that when he left.

He heard a child's shrill cry of shock and fear, and he ran as he had never run before, tearing his sword from its scabbard, bellowing "Harry! Harry!"

He burst through the hedge that surrounded the pond and saw two men, one standing guard, the other leaning over the water, cursing, reaching for FitzRoy. The boy had apparently torn himself out of his attacker's grasp when it loosened at Denoriel's shout. But Denoriel could only hope FitzRoy could keep out of reach because the man standing guard had drawn his sword and struck at Denoriel's lighter blade.

Denoriel twisted his wrist, rolling his blade along and around his opponent's. He was trying to catch the other sword and tear it loose, but the ruse failed—in fact, he almost lost his own weapon as an icy, burning chill ran up his sword and his arm, spread across his chest. He was not as resistant to steel as he had believed; at least not when he actually touched it through his silver blade.

It was his opponent who saved him because he

disengaged to feint high and thrust low. Denoriel parried, gasping, realizing that this was a more skilled swordsman than the noble-born dilettantes with whom he had practiced. Desperate not to touch the other's blade, Denoriel slashed right and left, advancing on his opponent, smashing his blade down on the attacker's arm with all his strength when the man tried to thrust through his wild swings. He was aware of movement behind the man he fenced with, aware that he could not prevail against two fighters of the same caliber.

"Run, Harry!" he shouted, wondering why the guards had not yet arrived.

With the boy's cry and his shout, they must have heard. From where they stood at the gate to the garden with the pond, they should have seen him fighting. Why did they not come? He needed the help. He was a fine swordsman, and he had fought men bearing steel before—but never alone, never two against one. And he had not repeatedly had to touch the steel as he parried. He was chilled and shaking. His guts knotted tighter and harder with each touch of his weapon against the other's and sickness clogged his throat, making it hard to breathe.

Then the other man cried out, not in pain but in shock and disgust. There was a thud and a splash. Denoriel's opponent was distracted—no more than a twitch of the head and a flick of the eyes to see what had happened behind him, but it was enough. Denoriel's blade slid up then pierced the man's sword arm, his silver blade carrying Denoriel's spell of pain and poor healing. The attacker howled and dropped his blade but made no attempt to retrieve it or to run, either of which Denoriel guessed he feared would have been fatal. Instead, he flung the poniard he held in his left hand at Denoriel's face.

Aware of the damage a scratch from the weapon

could do—even a glancing blow could raise a dangerous welt—Denoriel staggered back. The attacker took the chance he had made for himself; Denoriel could feel him dart past and thrust at him but missed. He could not see well enough to stop him. From the sound, he had run for the garden gate. Then Denoriel knew the guards would not come, that they had somehow been disposed of. He started forward as FitzRoy shouted a warning, whipping his blade back and forth although his vision was so blurred he could not see the other man's weapon.

A shriek and a shock told Denoriel that his blade had connected and he drew and thrust, still without really seeing his opponent. An oath gave evidence of the accuracy of his strike, but his blade did not penetrate. He struck hard armor under the man's doublet and another terrible shock ran up his silver blade to his arm. Denoriel bit back his own scream and, completely blind with sickness, thrust again, lower, at the man's belly where he would not wear armor. The thrust did not connect, yet the man screamed again.

Through tear-filled eyes, to which vision was returning, Denoriel saw his opponent go down on one knee, body twisted to look behind. His sword was still up, guarding, but for that moment the man was nearly immobilized. Then a gleam of sunlight caught his moving blade and through blurred eyes Denoriel saw it. He stepped inside its reach, praying his silk tunic would protect him if he were hit, and thrust violently at the hand, not the sword.

One last shriek as the weapon dropped from the bleeding hand, the spell generating far more pain than the piercing blade. Then the attacker leapt to his feet and, limping badly, fled wide around Denoriel in the direction the other had taken. Denoriel sank to his knees on the muddy ground, gasping, cried out as his bare fingers touched the fallen sword.

It was pulled away. Denoriel's eyes widened; there must be another man. He tried to rise but could not; he could not even raise his sword. But his half blind eyes could see no man shape and no burning, killing stroke came. He heard the scrape of metal on the ground and the nausea induced by the continued nearness of the steel diminished.

"Here, quick, put on your hat."

FitzRoy's voice, breathless, anxious. Denoriel had not even realized he had lost the hat, and then he also realized that in his anxiety and haste, he had not invoked the illusions that hid his ears and the slit pupils of his eyes. He knew, with a sinking heart, that all disguise had failed, that his long hair, wildly disordered, must no longer conceal his ears. And the boy was so close, staring into his face, seeing his cat-pupilled eyes.

Despair all but overwhelmed him, but still Denoriel drew a gasping breath, trying to think of an explanation. Only FitzRoy showed no surprise or fear. His hands, cold and wet, thrust Denoriel's hat onto his head, cocked it at the right angle, adjusted the plume, and tenderly tucked the long ears into shelter under it.

"Do you know what I am?" Denoriel whispered.

He was holding back tears as he contemplated needing to bring the child to Elfhame Logres and subjecting him to the torture of having his memories destroyed. That was a dangerous thing, even with the best of the healers and a Magus Major working together. Too many memories might be lost. The child's mind could be damaged.

His vision had cleared and he saw FitzRoy's smile. "Of course," the boy said. "You're my fairy knight, my guardian. The Elf-Queen must have sent you to protect me. She's supposed to like little boys."

Denoriel nearly fainted with relief, clutching the boy in his arms for a long moment, indifferent to the wet from FitzRoy's clothing soaking into his own. Then he held the child at arms length and smiled broadly at the innocent face so near his own. Harry had found the perfect concealment. If the child said he had a fairy guardian, everyone would think it just a childish fancy. No one would argue that it was impossible or laugh at him so that he would try to defend his assertion with facts that might betray the truth. The adults who cared for him, particularly the nurse who told him fairy tales, would hide their smiles and nod. To be a fairy guardian was safe.

"I knew who you were the very first day when you knelt down to speak to me and kiss my hand," the boy continued, bright-eyed with happiness. "No one else ever did that; they just talked down at me, laughing inside when they called me 'Your Grace.' I saw your eyes. They aren't people eyes. Nurse told me about the fairies, only she calls them the Fair Folk, how they take care of children, how the fairy knights drive away nightmares and hobgoblins, and how sometimes a fairy knight will be guardian to a child if his Queen sends him—"

Mwynwen had been right to call him careless and to urge him always to wear a hat. Apparently he had forgotten to invoke his disguise the day he had first come with George Boleyn to meet Harry. And the nursery stories—a lucky accident . . . or Dannae was supporting him more openly than usual—were why the child had accepted him so easily, so quickly.

"Is there someone who is cruel to you, Harry?" Denoriel asked anxiously.

The boy considered Denoriel's question and looked

a bit shamefaced. "No," he admitted. "Norfolk means well. He really does, even when he shouts and gives orders that spoil things." He sighed. "And Henry can't help being seven years older so he wins all the time. And I love Mary . . . even if she is a girl. But—but you came to *me*. You came to me when the others weren't near, so I knew you were *my* fairy knight in particular. Was it because of my father that you came?"

"You're quite right about that," Denoriel said, finally finding the strength to get to his feet. "I'm your fairy knight and I was sent by our Queen to watch over you." What a relief! He didn't even have to lie, which the child might have sensed. "I was sent because—" now what was he to say? "—because you needed me, and because of your royal blood." He winked, and FitzRoy smiled wanly back. The boy already knew about the privileges of rank, even in the sinister line; he found nothing unusual that the elven Queen should send one of her knights to guard the offspring of the mortal king. In his world, kings and queens, when they were not at war, exchanged such courtesies as a matter of course.

He started to reach for FitzRoy's hand and realized he was still clinging to his unsheathed sword. His vision was now back to normal and he saw the dark stains on the blade; he could not sheathe it as it was. He extended his arm and asked FitzRoy to find the kerchief in his sleeve so he could wipe the weapon. Instead the boy removed his own fine linen kerchief from his belt and held it out.

"Take mine. It's wet already." As he said the words, FitzRoy's eyes widened. "And I guess I do need watching over. That man," he said, his voice now tremulous and unsure, "he was going to *drown* me."

"What did he do?" Denoriel asked.

"He pretended to be interested in my boat—he

called it *una barca*—and when he came close, he pushed me into the water. And he was trying to push my head under when you yelled. He kind of jerked around and I went lower and pulled free. He kept grabbing for me, but mostly he was watching the fight so it was easy to keep out of his way. And when I thought he was going to stand up and join the fight against you . . . I threw two handfuls of muck from the bottom of the pond into his face."

Denoriel burst out laughing. "Good for you, Harry!" Then he sobered. "I'm your fairy knight, true enough, and I am a good warrior, but I'm not all powerful. If you hadn't helped me . . . I would have been killed."

FitzRoy nodded wisely. "Because fairies can't stand cold iron, and those men's swords were iron. Nurse told me about that too, but I forget the name of the story. I remembered about the iron though, how iron burns fairies. That's why I dragged the swords away from you."

"Clever Harry! The swords were making me weak."

"I knew that. That was why I hit the man in the back of the knee with the mast of my boat. You're magic, I suppose, but you aren't God. Only God is all powerful." The boy sighed. "But God's a lot like my father. He's far away and He must be busy with more important things than me." His eyes brightened and he smiled again. "I guess that's why there's fairies and fairy knights."

Denoriel bent down and embraced the child quite fiercely. "Yes. That's why there's fairy knights, to make sure children are protected."

FitzRoy hugged him back. "When he pushed me, I was afraid, but I knew you'd come. I've wondered ever since you came why I was so lucky as to get a fairy to help me. Now I know. Except . . . I don't know. Why should he try to drown *me*?"

"You didn't know them?" Denoriel asked. And when FitzRoy shook his head said, "How did they get past the guards?"

"I'm not sure." The boy frowned. "I saw them come into the garden . . ." He hesitated and then said, "But you're right. I didn't hear them talk to the guards at the gate. I didn't think of that then because I was very annoyed with the men. I knew you wouldn't come if they were here. I know no one is supposed to know about fairy guardians, which is why you only come when I'm alone."

"That's true, but we're going to have to confess that we are special friends. You see, you are going away—"

FitzRoy clutched at Denoriel's hand. "I know. I'm to be lord lieutenant in the north. It won't matter, will it?" he asked fearfully. "If you're my fairy knight, and you have magic, you can come to me up north, too, can't you?"

"Yes, I can," Denoriel assured him, smiling. "But we agreed I'm not all powerful. I'm not all knowing, either. I'll need to see the place where you are living in the north so that we can arrange where to meet or so that I can get to your apartment. I won't have the excuse of coming with my friend Boleyn."

"Oh, yes." The boy nodded. "I can ask for you—not as if we've been friends all along, but because you saved me from those men. I can say I don't want to go to a new place if you can't come too."

"We can try that first," Denoriel agreed. "If it doesn't work . . . don't worry yourself, Harry. I will find a good reason to visit Yorkshire . . . wool, probably. And once I am there, it is only reasonable for me to come to call. But until I can find a way to you, be careful. Don't be alone."

"No, I—" FitzRoy began, only to be interrupted by

a high girl-child's shriek, echoed by an older boy's shout.

Denoriel snatched FitzRoy up in his arms and set out for the sound, cursing himself for forgetting that, foiled of one victim, the men he had driven off FitzRoy might have decided to seize another child.

CHAPTER 4

Mary Howard's shrieks redoubled when she saw Denoriel come tearing down the path to the pond, FitzRoy clutched under one arm and his bared sword in his hand. Her brother, Henry, bravely thrust her behind him and drew his small knife. Denoriel skidded to a halt.

He looked around wildly. No attackers. No one even in sight, although Denoriel's keen ears caught the sound of alarmed voices in the distance. He set FitzRoy down on his feet.

"Henry, Mary—be calm, at once!" he took an authoritative tone with them, assuming that they would react to it appropriately. And, in fact, they did, Mary stilling her cries, and peering doubtfully around her brother. "Enough. There were men here, who attacked FitzRoy. When you cried out, I thought the two of you were in danger, but you are not. All is well." He sheathed his sword.

"Someone tried to drown me," FitzRoy said, his voice holding excitement and pride now rather than fear.

"You mean you fell in the pond and don't want to get scolded for it," Henry said, turning his lips down in a pout, as soon as he got over his momentary fright. "Who'd want to drown *you*?"

"No, I was pushed. I—"

A rustling and thumping in a group of ornamental bushes off to Denoriel's right made him draw his sword again and gesture to the children to go out onto the lawn where the oncoming servants and guards could see them. The sound grew more desperate and the bushes quivered but no one emerged to attack. Denoriel approached cautiously, listening, then rushed around the bush only to stop and sheathe his sword. He had found the missing guards. At least they were not dead, and could verify his part of the tale!

Almost simultaneously the forefront of the wave of rescuers arrived, led by Norfolk's steward, a grizzled man in a fine suit of black.

"Here!" Denoriel called. "Gentleman, there has been much mischief and misadventure! Richmond's guards are here, bound and gagged."

Two more guards pushed through the gate. At the steward's gesture, one threatened Denoriel with his pike. FitzRoy tore free of someone attempting to hold him and rushed over, interposing himself between the pike and Denoriel.

"It's not Lord Denno's fault," he cried. "There were two men. One pushed me into the pond and Lord Denno came and saved me."

Denoriel held up his hands, placatingly. "Patience, Your Grace," he said to FitzRoy—because these were formal circumstances and the boy was duke of Richmond. "The . . . ah . . . steward has no way of knowing whether I was in league with the others and just pretended to be your friend." He turned his attention to the steward, drawing himself up. "His Grace has been attacked, and I came at his call to help; near the pond there are two swords and a poniard . . . and a fair amount of blood to show there really was a fight. Someone should look there. Also, I think this is a tale that should be told to His Grace of Norfolk. And these men should be released."

Eventually, but not without considerable argument—the steward indignant over a foreigner giving orders—the weapons near the pond were collected. Then a tactful message was sent to Norfolk and FitzRoy was taken to his rooms to get dry clothing—which he refused to do unless Denoriel went too. After another considerable delay while Norfolk finished his business with the Imperial ambassador and Mendoza was seen off, all three children, FitzRoy's two guards, Denoriel, the steward, and a guard from the main gate were assembled in the room in which Norfolk conducted business.

Denoriel retained his sword and was not bound because of FitzRoy's stubborn and, in the end, screaming defense. Later, when he knew Norfolk better, he would be surprised at FitzRoy's understanding of his uncle's temper, and grateful that the child was so perceptive as well as brave enough to risk the duke's anger. If Norfolk had seen him arrive bound and disarmed, the duke would have assumed him guilty, and once Norfolk assumed something only the king's command could change his mind. And Norfolk exploded when he heard the true cause of their request for audience, bellowing at the steward and everyone else that his business with Inigo de Mendoza had been trivial compared with an attempt on his ward's life.

When Norfolk calmed, it was Henry Howard who told his part of the tale first, how he and Mary had gone to summon FitzRoy to tea. "You know how he is, Father," the boy said, smiling rather fondly at

FitzRoy. "When he starts sailing that boat of his on the pond, he seems to forget everything else."

Norfolk chuckled. "We'll have to get him appointed Lord High Admiral," he said.

Henry Howard frowned as if the mild jest did not please him, but did not respond overtly. He said, "Mary was first. She went through the gate, and then I realized there wasn't any guard and I started to call her and say that Harry must have gone back to the house—but she screamed, and when I rushed over to her she pointed and said she'd seen a foot under the bush. Then the bush shook, and I shouted, and the next thing we knew Lord Denno was pelting along the path carrying Harry in one arm and a sword in his other hand."

"Was Richmond struggling?" Norfolk asked.

"No, sir, not at all, and anyway, as soon as he saw us, Lord Denno put Harry down and sheathed his sword. Then Harry started to tell us about being pushed into the pond and Lord Denno saving him, and the bushes started to shake again. Lord Denno told us to go out on the lawn to the people who were running from the house and he went to look behind the bush."

"How long was he there, Henry?"

Henry Howard considered. "Scarcely a moment?" he said doubtfully. "He shouted almost at once that he had found the gate guards."

Norfolk looked at the steward and the guard who had followed him. "Could Lord Denno have tied up the guards in the time he was behind the bushes?"

"No, Your Grace," the steward said, reluctantly. It was clear that in his mind, this Lord Denno was a foreigner and therefore untrustworthy and likely to do unorthodox or even evil things. Nevertheless, he was an honest man, and could hardly deny the testament of his own eyes. "I could see him the whole time," the steward admitted. "He was standing up behind the bush. He never bent down at all, and he had his sword out in one hand. The guards were lying on the ground, bound and gagged. I don't see any way he could have done that."

Norfolk turned his eyes to FitzRoy's guards, who recoiled slightly at the expression upon the duke's face. Denoriel felt a little sorry for them; Norfolk was no easy master, and he did not accept excuses for failure. "And how, may I ask, did you get into that condition? Did either of you see Lord Denno today?"

"N-not till he found us, Your Grace," one man answered.

"I don't know how it happened," the other man said, his voice shaking. "I don't remember anything except standing by the gate. I'd been looking over the hedge, watching the boy . . . I mean His Grace of Richmond . . . getting ready to put that boat of his in the water. Then Dickson said to look, and I turned around and did, and saw a party coming up the long drive and then . . . then . . . I don't remember anything."

The man sounded desperately frightened. It was entirely possible he was frightened of the punishment Norfolk would mete out for his dereliction of duty, but Denoriel did not think so. He suspected the man was fighting a deeper and more elemental fear, having looked into his own memory, and finding there—nothing.

Now, a blow to the head could cause such memory loss, but surely the men would not have been so easily taken unawares. Not with two of them there.

Denoriel extended his senses, "feeling" around the man, who was swallowing nervously. Perhaps . . . perhaps there was the faintest "stench" of controlling magic. His lips tightened with self-disgust.

Warrior was he? Today he had been unprepared for everything. Only Dannae's mercy had let him arrive before Harry was killed and they were all plunged into a nightmare of pain and terror from which they might never waken—all because he had forgotten to set the time to which he wanted to Gate. Worse, he had endangered the secret of Underhill by pure carelessness, by forgetting his disguise. Harry, the child he was supposed to protect, had saved him.

Now he was late again. If he had felt for magic when he first found the men, perhaps he could have sensed the spell clearly enough to identify the maker. Now he could not even be sure the guards had been felled by magic.

That seemed more and more likely, however, when Dickson's tale confirmed that of the first guard. Dickson had listened to the first man with a slight expression of contempt, and he started confidently enough, relating his watch over the lawns and road from which the garden in which Richmond played could be reached. He continued with the arrival of the visiting party, even mentioned recognizing the banner of Inigo de Mendoza, the Imperial ambassador, and thinking that only a Spaniard would bring half an army to ride thirty miles from London to Windsor . . . and then his voice faltered and he stared at the floor.

"Well?" Norfolk urged impatiently.

The man stared at him, cheeks blanching. "Then I heard Lady Mary scream, and I tried to get up." He began breathing shallowly, as the same fear crept into his voice and his eyes stared into space with an expression of disbelief. "And I was lying on the ground tied up and gagged. Then Lord Denno came around the bush with his sword in his hand and I kicked and squirmed, but I couldn't get loose, and then he called out that he'd found us."

It must be, Denoriel thought, that they had been bespelled. But if so, why were they bound and gagged?

Denoriel barely heard the sharp questions Norfolk addressed to the guards; he was thinking, hard.

If the two attackers had carried a spell that felled the guards so they could get into the garden and drown Harry, they would have wanted the spell to wear off naturally. They would assume the guards would not report themselves as having fallen asleep on duty. And after the boy had been found drowned, they surely would not admit that they could not remember what happened—instead, perhaps they would have made up some tale of fighting several foes and being overcome, and of course, whatever they fabricated would not have matched the descriptions of the true attackers. Or perhaps the bonds had only been intended as a temporary measure, to ensure that the murderers could do their work without interference, and the men would have been released as soon as the deed was done. Then they would have been left to awaken naturally, and to find FitzRoy—and it all would have been supposed to be a terrible accident.

But who would bespell them? The minions of Vidal Dhu? Would even Vidal Dhu give orders that a child should be drowned? Denoriel felt almost as chilled as when he touched the steel of the attackers' armor and swords. And with that thought he knew he had the evidence that he had not fought Unseleighe Sidhe. Those were mortal men with the weapons of mortal men. And that provided a kind of answer to why the guards were both bespelled and gagged and bound.

Because the mortal men did not trust the spell. They could have been given some artifact and told how to release the enchantment. Perhaps they had not been told how long the spell would last, or they did not believe what they were told. And the spell had not lasted very long. His fight with the attackers had seemed interminable, but truly it had taken less than a quarter of an hour. Perhaps an equal interval had been spent by the men themselves, finding the pond and attacking FitzRoy. And the guards were kicking and struggling by the time he had run to the gate in answer to Mary's scream. Less than half an hour.

Not a Sidhe spell then . . . or was it a spell cast by a magus who was not familiar with the mortal world? A moment's thought convinced Denoriel that was unlikely. Vidal Dhu, whatever else he was, was not a fool. He would not make that kind of mistake. Denoriel did not know whether he was more relieved or more horrified. He was pleased that not even a member of the Unseleighe Sidhe would empower anyone to kill a child, but to know that a mortal mage was involved . . . that was not at all good. He had not heard of such mages in—well, in fact, he had *never* heard of such mages, except as tales. He had assumed that mortals had lost their magic as they grew more "learned."

His attention was recalled by a discreet tug on his hand and he realized Norfolk was addressing him directly.

He riveted his attention on the duke's craggy face. Norfolk was frowning, but not, it seemed, over anything Denoriel was responsible for. "So, it seems that not only are you innocent of any attempt to harm Richmond, Lord Denno, but we all must be grateful for your defense of him."

Demoriel bowed, slightly, but Norfolk was not done with him.

"But what I do not understand, my lord, is how you came to be near the pond when the gate guard here says you did not enter Windsor through the main gate." Norfolk riveted him with a stern gaze that had likely cowed lesser men than Denoriel.

Confident in the renewal of his mortal disguise while Harry was changing his clothing, Denoriel met Norfolk's gaze squarely and said, "I came through the postern gate in the wall, Your Grace."

"Postern gate?" Norfolk looked confounded.

Denoriel pressed his advantage. "Yes. I had come across country, for the road was dusty from the passage of some party that had traversed it before me. As a consequence, I was riding alongside of the garden wall, when I came to the postern gate. It was open and I was sure that could not be right. I knew the garden with the pond was beyond that stretch of wall and that His Grace of Richmond often played with his boat in the pond—all the children joked about his fondness for it. And it seemed to me—"

Norfolk's face was turning a dangerous color. "Open? A postern gate was open? I know nothing of any postern gate there!"

With some effort, Denoriel did not permit himself to sigh. "Yet the gate is there, and it was open. If you will come with me, Your Grace, I will show it to you." He saw Norfolk flush, remembered he needed a favor from the choleric human, and added placatingly, "Truth to tell, my lord, I had never noticed it either, until I saw it open, and I have accompanied the children to the pond once or twice."

With Norfolk steadily insisting that he had never heard of any postern gate in the wall, they all trooped out of the palace, across the lawn of the inner bailey, and through the gate of the garden that held the pond. FitzRoy's boat, its mast broken and its sails in shreds, lay sadly half in and half out of the water. The child picked it up as they passed, turning it in his hands, while Denoriel led the way down the overgrown path, now showing broken twigs and crushed plants where he had run through. At the end of the path, he gestured to the low door, overhung with ivy and the branches of a weeping willow. "Here you see it, my lord. It is easily overlooked from this side. I am only glad that I saw it when I did."

"I cannot believe my eyes!" Norfolk exclaimed. He turned an accusing gaze on the guards who had accompanied them. "Who knew of this?"

They all shook their heads, muttering equivalents of "Not I, Your Grace," until the steward cleared his throat.

"I did not know of this gate, Your Grace, but Windsor is very old," he said. "It was begun by the first William. It has been much changed, but parts of the old structures remain. It is possible that that piece of wall dates to the Conquest. I can have the clerk of the muniments check."

Norfolk grunted at him irritably. It was clear that he didn't care how old the wall was. "It's closed now," he said to Denoriel.

"Yes, Your Grace," Denoriel agreed meekly. "When I came through, I closed it behind me. I was sure it was wrong to have a hidden gate like that open."

While the steward was speaking, Denoriel had walked to the gate. Now he shook its "fastenings" until no one could doubt they were secure. He sent up a brief prayer to his goddess that no one else would want to test it, but Norfolk was staring at him, not at the gate.

"You should not have come through—"

He bowed his head, and allowed distress to enter his voice. "Forgive me, Your Grace, but I explained to you why I am so very fond of the children. I always fear for children, for they are very vulnerable, and I knew they played in that garden. What if they found it, and in childish mischief, slipped outside? Anything could have happened to them then. I could not leave that gate open while I rode around to the front and argued with a guard about a gate he did not believe existed being open. And there was no way I could close that gate from the outside. I had to enter the grounds to close it from within and then I heard Richmond cry out and I ran."

Norfolk grunted again, and said, "I will yield you so much, Lord Denno, that your entry, however wrong, was very necessary and had the best result. Nevertheless, I must admit I am very puzzled as to what you were doing at Windsor at all. I am sure I have no appointment with Boleyn today nor do I remember your name as requesting an interview."

"No, Your Grace," Denoriel agreed, having no intention of trying to prove Norfolk wrong again. "I had no intention of visiting Windsor Palace. I was simply riding past on my way to . . ." He hesitated and brought a faint flush to his pale cheeks, then continued uneasily, " . . . ah, Your Grace, I would rather not say. It is a private matter, an . . . ah . . . an appointment with someone I met when I rode here with Sir George . . . a lady, one I am sure is not of your acquaintance, but . . ."

"I see." Norfolk's expression became less severe and his lips twitched. "Very well. I need not pursue the matter further."

"Thank you, Your Grace."

Then Norfolk frowned again. "But how did you get here? Your horse . . ."

"Probably in that copse, Your Grace; I believe I mentioned that I was riding here. Miralys is very well trained. The countryside—" Denoriel recalled an image provided to him by Jenci Moricz "—near my home was not . . . not so tame as yours. Miralys knows not to stand in an open road but to seek shelter when I dismount. He will come when I call as long as he can hear me."

FitzRoy openly tugged on Denoriel's hand and he

looked down at the boy. "What is it, Your Grace?" he asked.

"You promised," FitzRoy said. "You promised you'd ask."

"Ask for what?" Norfolk said, his voice hard again.

Denoriel pretended to look embarrassed. "The child was frightened," he said softly. "He asked if I would be able to protect him when he must move north. I assured him he would not need my protection, that he would be well guarded . . . ah . . . but at that moment he was not willing to trust his guards." Denoriel shrugged. "I promised I would ask you if I would be received if I requested to visit His Grace in the north."

Norfolk looked both baffled and a trifle annoyed. "You would come all the way to Yorkshire to visit a child, Lord Denno? That seems a great deal of effort to go to merely to indulge the boy."

Denoriel smiled, and contrived a little more embarrassment. "I know it may seem soft and womanish of me, but I am so very fond of children that I find it harder to deny them than to indulge them. I grieve, deeply, for my brother and sister." Well, that was true, although it was not for Pasgen's or Rhoslyn's death. He sighed. "And it so happens that it would be no true effort, as I have business in the north. Wool brings me there, wool for the carpets that are woven by my family's retainers in the Middle East. The Turks took everything in Hungary, but the businesses of my family were far flung, and I am now the heir to everything outside of my native country."

"A substantial business," Norfolk remarked, with a touch of the hereditary noble's contempt for mere "business."

"Very substantial," Denoriel said flatly, as if he had taken offense at Norfolk's words, then added stiffly, "And as I no longer have my lands and properties, I must concern myself with it if I am to prosper. Once, I was a prince as well as a merchant; if I must become all merchant, and prince in name only, then I shall do what has been laid before me by God and even though others may forget that I bear the blood royal, I, at least, will not." Norfolk had the grace to look a little shame-faced. "I must visit my factors in Yorkshire some time. To me it would not matter if I went soon after His Grace of Richmond arrived there. Then I could redeem my promise to him and assure him of his safety."

"Please, sir?" FitzRoy begged, looking toward Norfolk but pressing himself against Denoriel's leg. "If Lord Denno says I will be safe, then I will be. No one here could help me today, only Lord Denno."

"But that is ridiculous—" Norfolk began.

Denoriel shrugged his shoulders and smiled. "He is a child, Your Grace," he said softly. "If you agree and I come once or twice, he will soon forget and feel secure. Life is, I suspect, difficult for a child in his peculiar position."

Norfolk made no response at first, his eyes fixed on Denoriel's face and Denoriel held his breath, fearing for a moment that his disguise had failed and that the duke had noticed his strange eyes. But obviously the duke's mind had been elsewhere for he nodded suddenly and said, "Turkey carpets? Your family makes Turkey carpets?"

"Not my family, Your Grace," Denoriel replied, his voice cold and stiff. He sounded strongly indignant, which he meant to do, but much of the ice in his tone was from choking back laughter at the opening Norfolk had given him. "My family are not, nor ever were, weavers. We were noble when the ancient Britons were painting themselves blue and capering about naked except for half-tanned animal skins. I can trace my ancestry to—"

"I beg your pardon, Lord Denno," Norfolk said, raising a placating hand and looking embarrassed. "Of course I did not mean to imply that you did the weaving yourself. Do you import the carpets here to England?"

"I have not been doing so yet," Denoriel replied. "My usual port is Marseilles, but my original purpose in coming to England was to determine whether it would be worth my while—"

Now, though Norfolk attempted to conceal it, he was as interested as any Flemish importer at the prospect of new revenues for himself. "It would. Indeed it would be worth your while to have the carpets come directly into London or Southampton. I could arrange—"

But Denoriel allowed his tone to hold a touch of frost. "I said my *original* purpose. To my surprise I have found friends here and lovely, clever women, and I like the climate. I had thought recently to buy property and live in England, but if I am to be . . . ah, rejected . . . because of my connection with business—"

"Not at all!" Norfolk exclaimed. "Not at all!" He laughed. "Whatever gave you that idea?"

He raised an eyebrow. "It had seemed to me that you were not precisely enthused with my offer to visit the duke of Richmond after I mentioned my wool factor."

"Do not take offense where none was intended, my lord," Norfolk said. "That had nothing to do with your business. I—" he hesitated, frowned, then continued in a rush "—I hope you will not take umbrage, but I would speak plainly. You *are* a foreigner, Lord Denno, and . . . ah . . . depending on Richmond's future, which is too uncertain to speak of now, it might not be wise for him to be too attached to you."

Now he shrugged, judging it wise to point out to Norfolk that of all of the people with whom FitzRoy might be in contact, he was the only one without a long list of personal interests. "To me, Your Grace? I am the safest kind of friend for His Grace. Remember, I am a man without a country. My poor nation has been swallowed by the Turks. I will do nothing to benefit those conquerors, and I am connected with no party in England by family or tradition. And as for my business interests—they are without borders. My wares can be sold—or not—in any civilized country. I have, as the saying goes, *no* ax to grind. In fact, I care only for him in that he is a fine young lad, who reminds me greatly of my own, lost sibling." Then suddenly he laughed. "The boy is six years old, Your Grace, and his father in the best of health, thank God. The question of who might or might not influence him need not be considered now, surely?"

Norfolk rocked back on his heels as he pondered Denoriel's words. "I suppose not. Very well, Lord Denno. If you should come north, you will be welcome at Sheriff Hutton or Pontefract—Richmond will not be going to Carlisle Castle although he has been named its keeper."

"Hurrah!" FitzRoy shouted.

Norfolk looked down at him and frowned, then transferred the expression to his own children. "Henry, Mary, take Richmond off to have his tea, and see that you do not leave him alone again. Nor do I want you to leave the house. I will have Croke sent to you."

"Will you come up to my rooms to say good-bye?" FitzRoy asked, turning to Denoriel.

"There is nothing to be afraid of now, Har— I mean, Your Grace." Denoriel said. "You heard His Grace of Norfolk give orders that the entire palace be searched and that extra guards be assigned to your corridor and room."

"I heard," FitzRoy muttered, "but there were guards at the gate and those men got in. You *knew* something was wrong. I want *you* to come look at my rooms." He clutched tight to Denoriel's hand, his tone growing shriller, his face pinched. "Look at my boat. If you hadn't come, I would be dead. I'll tell everybody! I'll tell everybody!"

"Go up to his rooms, if you don't mind, Lord Denno," Norfolk said hurriedly, stemming what he feared would be a hysterical outburst and now convinced that Lord Denno would calm the child.

"No, of course I don't mind," Denoriel said with his arm around FitzRoy. "Thank you, Your Grace. He will be calmer tomorrow, I am sure."

CHAPTER 5

"You fools!" Vidal Dhu snarled. "Or are you traitors?"

Pasgen and Rhoslyn stood shoulder to shoulder. Often enough they competed with each other, but not when Vidal Dhu was threatening; then it was best to present a united front. Both stared at their master—green cat-pupilled eyes glaring back at their prince's.

Vidal Dhu had called them to stand before him in his ebony throne-room. That had been a bad sign. It had been worse that he had sent guards to bring them. But worst of all was that he had kept them waiting, cooling their heels in the antechamber, for nigh onto an hour before he had them brought within.

"You will have to be more specific, my lord," Pasgen said, reaching out to Rhoslyn as he spoke, gently pushing power at her. "About what were we fools?"

No communication accompanied that gentle probe of power; Pasgen did not dare form a thought of what he wanted for Vidal Dhu to pick out of his mind. The small finger of power would, he hoped, be lost in the general surge in Underhill and the roiling currents around Vidal stirred by his mood. Pasgen took no chance with the prince in so foul a temper; he never knew how deep the prince could read him.

However, he had not underestimated Rhoslyn's understanding. Her strength met his, and together they began to spin a web that could catch and dissipate any strike Vidal Dhu launched against them. The prince was unfortunately prone to striking first and thinking later. Likely he would regret it if he blasted those so useful to him, but then it would be too late for them. If they foiled his strike, he might even be grateful.

"You Saw the wrong child," Vidal roared. "You have spent months insinuating yourselves into Princess Mary's household, and she was never the one who is critical to the future we desire."

Now both Pasgen and Rhoslyn looked dumbfound. "But that can't be true, my lord," Rhoslyn protested. "Princess Mary is the ruler who will bring the Inquisition to England. She is already fanatically devoted to her religion. She has been taught by her mother to be almost as devoted to Spain and its causes. Moreover Queen Catherine will not conceive again—I have made certain of that. It would be unlikely that the child would live, as no others have, but I could see no reason to leave such a chance alive. That makes Princess Mary the legal heir to England."

"Legal heir," Vidal Dhu snarled. "In England the legal heir is who the king says is the heir."

"But there is no other he could name," Pasgen said, raising his chin stubbornly. "Why should you call us traitor? We have done all that was required to ensure Mary's coming to the throne—"

"There *is* another," the prince bellowed, springing to his feet. "And you did not See him or mention him. Was that apurpose? Are you so warped by that mother of yours that you secretly crave playing with the mortals and for that idle pleasure would deprive us all of the power that comes from their pain?"

At the sneering mention of their mother, Rhoslyn's release of power to the net surged so strongly that to Pasgen's eyes it took on a soft glow. Rhoslyn might often be impatient with their mother's clinging, cloying affection, but she would hear no other criticize Llanelli. Pasgen touched her arm.

"If Rhoslyn and I missed an heir to the throne, it was not by intention," Pasgen said with seeming calm. "For certain there is no red-haired infant—not even a distant cousin."

"A son." Vidal Dhu sat down again, now his expression as he looked down at the twins would have been suitable if they were excrement left by one of his creatures on the carpet. "A son," he repeated. "And you missed him. Henry FitzRoy—"

"We did not miss him," Rhoslyn said, flatly. "The son is nothing. I went with Mary's servant to bring him a little gift and I examined him." She shrugged. "He is six years old, and no infant. He is a bastard, and thus, not in the line of succession. And furthermore, he has none of the power that was hidden in the red-haired babe. He isn't specially clever. He isn't even specially pretty. He lives in obscurity—luxurious, well provided for, but with no hint of favor or special interest by his father."

"True enough," Pasgen agreed. "I made an occasion to talk to the Spanish mage . . . ah, Martin Perez is his name. He is a servant of Charles V, sent to England to keep the Emperor informed of everything political. Perez told me that the king displayed FitzRoy widely when he was born to show that he could engender a live son, but then he swiftly lost interest in the boy. It would take a miracle before England would accept a bastard as the heir to the throne."

Vidal Dhu's face had grown colder, more frozen, with each word they uttered. The twins fell silent.

"Stupid! Lazy, stupid fools!"

His voice was soft now and Rhoslyn and Pasgen braced themselves, but what he sent at them was not the massive blow of power they half expected or the ball of balefire, both of which the net would have caught and dissipated. What flowed from the gesture he cast at them was a shower of tiny threads of brilliant colors—sick green, dirty yellow, virulent blue, bloody red—that wriggled through the spaces in the net and struck at any patch of bare skin.

There was enough of that. Rhoslyn's gown exposed her neck, her shoulders and arms, and her chest down to the cleavage between her breasts. Pasgen wore only a sleeveless tunic, open in the front to his navel, to expose his well-muscled shoulders and arms and the smooth swell of pectorals. Rhoslyn screamed and beat at her body. Soon tears poured down her cheeks and she whimpered. Pasgen hissed between his teeth, but made no attempt to wipe away the writhing threads. Instead he spoke three words, and the fire-worms faded. And when he raised his eyes to Vidal Dhu, there was that in them that made the prince gesture at Rhoslyn, who was instantly free of her torment.

"That was to teach you not to think you can avoid my punishment," the prince said to them. "And I see that you have not yet dismissed that useless barrier."

"My lord," Pasgen said, his voice flat. "We are aware of your infinite variety of punishments and did not intend to avoid your righteous wrath. What we intended was to avoid being struck down without true cause. Your wrath is fearsome, and when you are angry, it is difficult to reason with it. We have always and will always do our utmost for you, but there are others in your court who are jealous of your regard, and may persuade you of misdeeds on our part that we had not even thought up, much less performed. " He gestured broadly. "So we protect ourselves. Fire-worms—indeed, anything that can get through this net—I can deal with. If you had chosen to blast us with power or burn us with fire, the net would protect us. I would find it hard to reverse death."

Vidal Dhu looked at Pasgen for just a moment as if he were considering the meaning behind Pasgen's remark that he would find death "hard to reverse." The prince then turned his glance to Rhoslyn, but from his expression seemed to find little satisfaction in what he saw. Pasgen was aware of the growing coldness beside him. He had no idea what Rhoslyn was thinking, but knew that even Vidal Dhu's probes would be unable to penetrate the shields she had erected.

They had been careless, Pasgen thought. They should have known the prince would sense the concentration of power in the net. Each of them should have added some subtle shielding. But it would have been necessary to react as if the fire-worms were effective anyway, and Rhoslyn's reaction was the best thing for both of them . . . though she would not thank him for seeing benefit in her suffering.

"The price you will pay for your neglect—to put the most innocent interpretation on your dereliction of duty," Vidal Dhu said, seeming to have dismissed completely not only what he had done and his previous bad temper but also Pasgen's refusal to dismiss the defensive net, "is to bring here to me Henry FitzRoy, the bastard son of King Henry VIII."

Rhoslyn shook her head. "You have called me stupid and lazy, my lord. Perhaps I deserved your chastisement for the latter, but I am *not* stupid. Anyone could have made off with the child I visited. He was hardly watched, except by a nurse who seemed more interested in her knitting than in her charge. Thus, the price, according to all I know, is too low to repay our carelessness. " She frowned. "Therefore, something must have changed that makes the deed more difficult. Something has made FitzRoy more difficult of access, and you call us lazy because we were not aware."

"Exactly! You see how a little discomfort stimulates the brain?" Anger returned to Vidal Dhu's expression. "While you two played in your hidden fastnesses—" the prince smiled with chilling sweetness as he informed them that he was aware of their experiments in the unformed regions of Underhill "—Henry FitzRoy has been given honor upon honor. He is now duke of Richmond—in case you did not know, that is the title the king himself bore before he came to the throne. And Richmond has precedence over every nobleman in the kingdom except King Henry himself and the other heirs of the king's body."

"But the princess has been sent to Wales with a great household in the traditional role of the heir to the throne," Rhoslyn pointed out.

"And FitzRoy has been appointed Lord Lieutenant of the Northern March, given the same kind of household, and sent to rule in the north," Vidal Dhu spat. "The king has not yet named his heir, but to so favor a bastard could have only one purpose."

Pasgen's mouth formed a thin, bitter line. "My informant will suffer for not telling me this! I'll see that none of his spells work for a month."

"You should have applied the punishment earlier," Vidal Dhu snapped. "Or do you not know that he has been acting in your absence? He gave a spell to a pair of cutthroats who barely missed drowning FitzRoy."

After a shocked silence, Rhoslyn asked, "By your will, my lord?"

"No, of course not," Vidal replied, unconsciously rubbing his hands along his arms as if the ice in Rhoslyn's voice had touched him physically. "Why should I order the child's death when it would be so much more amusing to have him here?" He paused, then looked from one twin to the other and whispered, "Bring him to me."

That was the last thing he said, nor did he trouble to bestow so much as another glance at them. A contemptuous gesture of one finger dismissed them, and they wheeled around each other, still shoulder to shoulder so the web would continue to protect them, went down the three steps from the dais on which Vidal's throne reposed, and started down the long aisle lined with Unseleighe creatures.

Neither would have been surprised if Vidal had launched a blow at them once their backs were turned. It would be no attempt to kill, not now once he had given his orders, but it would amuse him no end to see them fall on their faces. That sign of his disfavor would invite the sly minor torments of the boggles, the goblins, the small trolls and half-grown ogres that lined the aisle. Both kept their faces totally expressionless but seethed within. It was typical of Vidal Dhu that he did not reprimand in private but did his best to shame anyone who had displeased him before the entire court.

They passed the Unseleighe Sidhe—not so many of those, but a few true elves were born on the dark side, and their number was swelled by emigrants from the Seleighe Court. Tastes in amusement and occupation among the Sidhe varied. A few found themselves made uncomfortable by the disapproval of their neighbors and sought welcome among others who enjoyed pain and misery; fewer had gone so far that Oberon had cast them out. But Rhoslyn and Pasgen knew they were safe enough passing the Sidhe; those dark elves would be quick enough to leap on them if torture to the death was their fate. To trip them or pinch them or squirt them with foul-smelling liquid, however, was beneath Sidhe dignity.

Beyond the Sidhe was a mixed mass of repulsive beings of all sizes. First a thing with the head of a frog, a long, pronged, snakelike tail and slimy-looking leathery wings darted across their path, spraying a noxious liquid that dripped down the web of the net. Rhoslyn ignored the imp; Pasgen kicked out as he took a step and caught it on its soft belly so that it flew into the grip of a troll who was just reaching out for a sly push or pinch. The troll popped the creature into his mouth and looked gratified.

Most of the Unseleighe creatures were not very clever, and a Hag, seeming to think that the sacrifice of the frog-faced creature to the troll had been to pacify it when it threatened Pasgen, reached long, clawed fingers toward Rhoslyn to tear at her. Without even looking at the creature, Rhoslyn sent a burst of power through the net that burned the Hag's fingers to blackened stumps and followed that with a spray of the same fire-worms that Vidal had loosed upon her. Glancing in that direction at the Hag's howls of agony, Pasgen just saw the outflow of fire-worms. He grinned. No one could say that Rhoslyn was a slow learner.

They had not quickened or slowed the pace at which they were advancing, but the fate of the frog-face and the Hag seemed to have made an impression. No further attempts to annoy the twins were ventured, and in a few more moments they reached the doors. Those did not open automatically, even resisted momentarily when Pasgen applied pressure, but when the black material of which the doors were constructed began to turn bright red where Pasgen and Rhoslyn were facing them, they swung apart.

Behind them was silence. Pasgen and Rhoslyn wheeled around again, still inside the net of power, and faced into the throne room, looking down the aisle of creatures toward Vidal Dhu's throne. In unison they began to raise their right hands. The doors slammed shut.

Pasgen breathed out a long sigh and Rhoslyn closed her eyes for a moment and drew in a deep breath. Their glances met, and the net around them dissolved. As it did, it became obvious that the construct had been almost dissolved before each reabsorbed part of the small amount of power that remained in it. Unwilling to deplete themselves too much while in Vidal Dhu's presence, each had drawn on the net—Rhoslyn for the surge that burned the Hag and created the fire-worms, Pasgen for his assault on the closed doors that Vidal had tried to use to make them look weak and foolish.

"Your place or mine?" Rhoslyn asked.

"Mine," Pasgen said. "Mother might be at your place, and I don't want her to hear about this."

Rhoslyn nodded and they hurried down the black marble steps to the courtyard where, off to one side, the two not-horses were tied. The coal-black steeds turned their red-eyed heads toward their oncoming riders. One lifted its lip to hiss, showing teeth that were as large and strong as those of any horse, but pointed into tearing fangs.

One of the things Rhoslyn and Pasgen bitterly envied their Seleighe half-twins was their elvensteeds. Barely in their teens, they had invaded Seleighe territory for the single purpose of getting mounts for themselves. But elvensteeds, they discovered, could not be accustomed to many of the sights and sounds in the Unseleighe Domain of their master. They were restless and unsettled, even when the Domain was quiet, and unless confined, which was virtually impossible without the expenditure of enormous amounts of power, they would flee the place and not respond to their riders' summons. Perhaps in another realm or Domain, a quieter one, they might prove to be reliable and tractable mounts, but not here.

An alternative was clearly necessary, and Rhoslyn had sought for and found an Unformed region where the mists of formative stuff were particularly thick and sensitive. There she had worked over many years, gathering, forming, strengthening, and transferring crude sentience until she had created two beasts, not horses, certainly not elvensteeds, but something she and her brother could ride. The not-horses were stronger and cleverer than the mortal animals and far more vicious, but they could be controlled. One important aspect of the elvensteeds that Rhoslyn had not yet been able to duplicate was their ability to travel Underhill or reach it from the mortal world, and vice versa, without a Gate.

The twins mounted, after cuffing the restive mounts. Pasgen led, since it was his private domain—or one of them; Rhoslyn was not sure how many he had—to which they were going. He rode past the elaborate Gate Vidal Dhu had built outside the palace courtyard, straight ahead until the manicured lawn began to disappear into a tangle of trees and bushes. Only, when they came really close it was apparent that these were not well-defined constructs but blurred and ill-formed figments.

"He called us lazy," Pasgen muttered. "I wouldn't leave a dog-kennel in this half-done condition."

"It makes it easier to know where we are," Rhoslyn said, applying a sharp mental prod to the not-horse, which started to shy at the approach to the edge of reality.

Pasgen snorted and Rhoslyn recognized the strange mixture of awe and contempt: awe for the enormous power that could create the semblance of a large forest, probably with one careless gesture; contempt for the sloppy indifference that would then leave the work half done. Rhoslyn wondered as they passed through the ill-defined border and out into nothingness, how long it would be before Pasgen was tried too far and challenged Vidal. She shuddered, knowing she would be standing beside Pasgen when he tried. She could not help it; despite their differences, loyalty, and yes, love, bound them.

Her brother paused, Rhoslyn holding in her mount beside him; he lifted his head and swung it slowly right to left, his nostrils flaring slightly as if he were a scenting hound. After a moment, he set out at a slight angle to the direction in which they had crossed into the unfinished part of Vidal's domain.

Rhoslyn gathered power from the swirling mists in case she had to drive off something inimical. Vidal had left behind some very unpleasant things when he grew bored with creation. Perhaps he had intended them to be guards of his lands or denizens of the forest with which he had planned to surround his palace, but he had never finished his work so the creatures roamed free, taking what life force they could for their sustenance.

Defense was not necessary, however. They soon came to the end of Vidal's Domain and passed into another area of swirling mists and erratic breezes. Here Pasgen paused again, his body tense as he seemed to listen, but Rhoslyn knew he was feeling, sending out all his senses. She would have done the same, except that she did not know what Pasgen was seeking. In any case, she would not have had time because he nodded almost immediately.

"It's here. I came a different way, but I thought if we went off at that angle that we would avoid Wormegay Hold."

"Urgh!" Rhoslyn said. "That's a place I really hate. Why in the world did you set your Gate there?"

There were, of course, a number of Gates in and around Vidal Dhu's palace. Neither Rhoslyn nor Pasgen used them, unless they were going to the mortal world or to some place with a group to make merry or make mischief. Neither wanted Vidal able to trace where they had built their own private Domains, so the Gates that had those destinations were always built in Unformed areas that were not easy to find. Moreover they never worked or remained longer in those areas than necessary to reach their Gates.

Pasgen laughed at Rhoslyn's reaction as he set off at a quick place, quite sure of his direction. "I don't have a Gate in Wormegay," he said, "but except for this one finger that touches Vidal's domain, it's the only way into this area. Most people don't like Wormegay, but it has outlets into about twenty Other places." He was silent for a little while, then said thoughtfully, "I wonder if Wormegay is a sink of some kind, if all the oddities without power drain down into it and then can't get out."

"You do have weird ideas," Rhoslyn said, keeping her mount right on Pasgen's heels. She did not want to become separated from him in the formless mists and either need to call for help or spend who knew how long sensing for a Gate which he, doubtless, had hidden well.

Rhoslyn never did see it. She only knew they had passed through by the brief sense of disorientation, which made her not-horse hiss, and the fact that she was suddenly on the outskirts of the Bazaar of the Bizarre.

Rhoslyn sighed, knowing Pasgen would not let her stop.
She envied him his self-control as they rode into the
market and were deafened by every creature known and
unknown crying his/hers/its/their wares, assaulted by
such a variety of odors in such quick succession that one
could not enjoy the delectable or reject the obnoxious,
and the sights . . . they were en masse indescribable.

Without hesitation, Pasgen wove through the
crowds—here even the not-horses received no particular attention—and darted down this alley and that.
Eventually he opened a shabby but not noticeable gate
and passed through to what seemed the backyard of
an inn. He rode into an empty stall of the stable . . . and
disappeared. Rhoslyn rode in on his not-horse's heels
and rode out into another Unformed area.

Here at last they came to the Gate that debouched
into Pasgen's Domain, although Rhoslyn admitted to
herself that she probably would not be able to find it
again. That wasn't significant. Pasgen had provided her
with her own path to his domain, but that, equally
devious, started from her own and all the Gates were
keyed to her and "called" her.

Anyone who knew Pasgen would instantly know they
had arrived in his home place. It was quite beautiful,
but wholly and completely unnatural. There were trees,
but they were perfect, with exactly symmetrical
branches that bore perfectly shaped leaves exactly
spaced on each branch. And those leaves glittered and
tinkled when they touched each other in the very
slightly perfumed breeze that blew gently, first one way
and then another. The bushes were equally perfect,
some low and rounded, some squared, some taller,
shaped gracefully from a wider base to a peak. They
glittered too, and rustled musically.

The not-horses walked quietly along the soft lavender graveled road that wound gracefully through the

outer lawns to the inner gardens. Rhoslyn sighed. Not a flower was out of place, not a leaf wilted. Even the bees flew in perfect patterns, and the butterflies danced predictably in defined groups to gentle music. Perfection. Peace. Stagnation!

"You don't like it?" Pasgen asked.

He always asked the same question, as if a short absence would have changed her mind. Rhoslyn shook her head. "I like a little disorder."

"Don't we have enough disorder in our lives?" Pasgen's voice was edged and rough.

Rhoslyn looked away and her voice was so soft only a Sidhe's ears could catch it. "A little happy disorder."

If Pasgen heard, he did not respond and around the next bend the house came into view. It too was beautiful, if stark. Pure white marble with black accents to mark the graceful curves and outline the many windows. There were no fanciful towers or turrets. The house was low, only two levels . . . at least only two levels above ground. What was below Rhoslyn did not know and did not want to know.

They went left when they entered through the gates, which drew apart as soon as Pasgen approached. Large, smooth-bodied servitors came forward to take the not-horses to a stable that complimented the house without obtruding. Servitors were constructs, beautifully made, neither handsome nor ugly. They were incredibly strong, totally without volition although capable of carrying out instructions, and mindlessly devoted to Pasgen, although they would obey and protect her too, Rhoslyn knew.

Entering through the side door brought them to a small room where one could wash one's hands and change one's shoes if earth from the garden clung to them. They exited into a wide but not intimidating corridor with neutral, pleasant walls and rugs. A few doors down were two arches open onto the public rooms of Pasgen's house. On one side was a handsome dining parlor, all stark black and white: white walls, black floor; white marble table, ebony chairs. It was too familiar for Rhoslyn to give it more than a single glance.

On the other side was the room in which Pasgen entertained guests. The color scheme was the same, except for colored cushions here and there, but the colors were muted. Rhoslyn sank into a corner of a white leather—settle, she supposed, although it was heavily padded, not like the settles she knew at all, with the padding covered in the leather. She was surprised as she always was at how comfortable it was. Somehow despite frequent visits to her brother's dwelling she always expected the rigid-appearing furniture to be uncomfortable as it looked; instead it was smooth, enveloping, soothing.

"Something to drink? Eat?" Pasgen asked.

"Wine, I think, after that session." Rhoslyn watched Pasgen make a sign in the air and, after a moment, one of the servitors came in carrying a tray which held a bottle and two crystal glasses. "How could we have so overlooked the boy?" she wondered as the servitor set the tray on a clear glass table set on ebony legs. Pasgen lifted the crystal bottle and poured. "How could we have neglected to check up on him? He *is* the king's only living son."

"I'm amazed you need to ask," Pasgen said, handing her a glass into which he had poured a delicate pink wine. "What could it be except an arrangement by our dearly, dearly beloved half-sister and -brother." His fine, clear skin flushed slightly. "Can you believe a Seeing came to you and to me about the fate of this sceptered isle that did not come to Aleneil and Denoriel? Our powers are mirrored; we are two edges of the same sword. They could not interfere with that, and, of course, they would not put the child Mary at risk, but they must have layered on misdirection spells. . . ."

Rhoslyn nodded slowly and sipped the wine. Like everything else in Pasgen's Domain it was delicious, gentle, soothing. She had to fight the effect, and her voice was sharper than usual when she said, "That wouldn't be Denoriel. He's never paid much attention to magic and I don't think he has much Talent." Her mouth turned down in disdain. "He only wants to be a mighty swordsman, a brave warrior, and nothing more."

"Possibly." Pasgen, who had finished his glass of wine and was pouring another, had regained control of his temper. "Does it matter who covered that child with spells? Aleneil could have done it. She's pretty strong. The point is that we now know. What are we going to do about it."

"Snatch the boy, of course."

Pasgen shook his head at his sister. "Not so easy now that an attempt has been made on his life." He flushed again with rage. "That fool! That incompetent! I'll have the skin off Martin Perez for trying to kill that child and not telling me about him."

Rhoslyn laughed. "No, don't do that. Mortals tend to die without their skins unless they are Underhill. And he might be useful in the future since he is apparently a mage. How good is he, Pasgen?"

"I never bothered to test him." He sighed. "You know, Rhoslyn, Vidal was not so far off the mark when he called us—me, anyway—careless and lazy. I knew Martin Perez had Talent, but I had no idea he knew how to use it." He was silent for a short time, but Rhoslyn saw he was thinking hard and did not speak. Then he took another sip of wine and said,

"I wonder if that was more work by dear Aleneil. Is it possible that she is bespelling us so that we will not take this situation seriously?"

"Who knows what Aleneil and those teachers of hers will do. Liars . . . Hypocrites . . . Power is nothing, they say, but they use it. Oh, how they use it, sucking it from the air, from the ground, and blaming us for taking it from pain and death."

Her voice was hard and louder than usual as she fixed her attention on blaming the Seleighe Sidhe, on not remembering, not *ever* desiring, the music and laughter and applause in a certain theater in London when the red-haired queen ruled.

Pasgen looked at his sister, surprised by the angry passion in her voice. Usually Rhoslyn was the milder of them when discussing their Seleighe kin. He did not want to come right out and ask if their present project for seating Mary on the throne and bringing the Inquisition to England was making her uncomfortable. It was not knowledge he wanted in his mind when he came before Vidal Dhu again.

"We are wandering from the point," he said. "I agree that we must somehow take the child, I merely meant to point out that he will be far better guarded now that Perez made such a disastrous mistake."

"Against a nun? One single, small nun? A nun vouched for by Princess Mary's governess?"

CHAPTER 6

Denoriel was not simply able to say "Good night," to FitzRoy and leave, as agreed with Norfolk. Even though he had taken the precautions of looking in the cupboards and under the bed—in fact anywhere a frightened little boy could believe a person might conceal himself, when he gave the boy a last hug and turned away, FitzRoy burst into tears. His guards tried to intervene—not, of course, the same guards who had been at the garden gate—these two knelt and assured the boy that they would guard his door with their lives. On the whole, the poor child had been amazingly brave up to this point; small wonder that he gave vent to his feelings now. One, at least, of these guards must have had a young child of his own; without losing a particle of his deference, he looked into FitzRoy's eyes, and redoubled his assurance that the boy was safe.

What about the windows? Denoriel thought. He had come through a window. More uneasiness rose in him when he recalled how soundly the guard had slept when he had visited FitzRoy's rooms the previous night.

Doubtless these men would be more alert tonight because of the aborted attempt on the child's life, but the killers had not been found and might make another attempt. If they were hiding somewhere in the palace and still had the sleep spell, these guards might be no more successful at protecting FitzRoy than the first pair.

So Denoricl lifted FitzRoy in his arms and promised to stay until Harry was completely sure it was safe. That stemmed the tears; the guards were relieved and made no protest, and Denoriel hoped that Norfolk would never learn how far his permission to accompany FitzRoy to his room had been stretched. At least FitzRoy's nurse, who Denoriel suspected knew more than most others, would not inform the duke. She smiled and nodded a welcome.

FitzRoy was soon in bed, but Denoriel made no move to leave. In fact he climbed the steps and sat down beside the child. Although he had no real presentiment of danger, no sense, as he had had the previous night, of approaching evil, he felt incomplete, uneasy, as if there were something he should do and had not. He spoke softly to FitzRoy, assuring him of protection—and with the words he knew one thing, at least, that he could do for the boy's safety.

The nurse had moved to the other side of the room where she was examining clothing and dividing what needed to be laundered from what could be used again. Denoriel whispered two words and FitzRoy's eyes closed. Then he closed his own eyes and sought for the thin white lines of power in the diffuse cloud that floated everywhere Overhill. He drew a sharp breath as he drew one to him and the line of light seared his power channels; then he put the pain aside and began to build a shell of protection around the sleeping boy.

When he was done he sighed with satisfaction although he felt as if thin streams of fire were burning within him. Still, the pain of his body was worth the peace in his mind. No one would be able to touch FitzRoy and no spell would penetrate that barrier. Until the child woke in the morning and got out of bed, he would be invulnerable. Denoriel rose and went to the nurse.

"I've got him asleep," he murmured. "Please don't touch him or speak to him so that he wakes. Let him sleep off his fright. By the morning it will be far away, more of an excitement than a terror."

"Certainly, m'lord," the woman agreed. Then tears filled her eyes. "Who was it, m'lord? Who could be such a monster as to wish to hurt so sweet a child?"

He heard his voice roughen with anger. "If I knew, I would hunt them down, and you may be sure they could never try to harm him again. Alas, there were two and aside from seeing that they both had black hair and dark eyes, I was too busy looking at their swords to look at their faces. Surely there are many who match that description, and men that are black of hair and dark of eye could be of any nation."

The nurse nodded, though he noticed that she narrowed her eyes in thought at his minimal description. "Of course, m'lord. God bless you for saving him."

Denoriel nodded and patted her on the shoulder. Outside the apartment, he headed down the stair. Everyone knew him now and all the guards he passed acknowledged him with nods and smiles. As he crossed the great front hall, a servant hurried to meet him and ask if he wished a mount and an escort to be brought from the stable to take him as far as the gate. Denoriel accepted and within the half hour was at the gate, where a whistle and a mental "come" brought Miralys from the copse. The groom that had accompanied him widened his own eyes at that.

Remounted, he rode west along the road that surrounded the palace as if he had been coming from London in the southeast so that he would have passed the postern gate and the garden with the pond. He had no particular destination, but turned south on the nearest road, which took him, just as dusk was falling, to the small town of Winkfeld. There to his relief he found a decent inn. He took Miralys to the stable himself, and when the ostler showed surprise and approached to remove the "horse's" saddle, Miralys threatened him with teeth and hooves.

Denoriel laughed. "He will let you fill his manger and the pan for oats and bring water, but if you try to touch him or his gear . . ."

"Never mind, m'lor'!" the man said, goggling at the elvensteed. "I can reckon well enough!"

Denoriel laughed again. "As you can imagine, I find it quite safe to leave him anywhere." He flipped the man a coin. "Here. Warn anyone away from him if you will. I am tired of threats and complaints when he turns on fools who won't leave him be."

The common room was bearable, at least no worse than those he visited in London with George Boleyn and his friends. The rushes on the floor were not trodden into a slimy mass stinking with decaying food and spilled ale and wine, and the tables, if stained, were not wet and filthy. He ordered ale from the landlord who sat behind a counter that protected the barrels of wine and beer, and then went to sit at a table back in the shadows.

It was a relief that the place was tolerable. Denoriel knew he would have to wait until dark before he could ride back past Windsor to that copse at the crossroad. And he still had no idea of how to protect FitzRoy for tomorrow and tomorrow . . .

As he sat waiting for his ale, a new and horrible result of the attack on FitzRoy occurred to him. Until now neither he nor Aleneil, who was making her own contacts among the queen's women and the few noble ladies who had leave to attend the court, had detected any Unseleighe interest in FitzRoy. Certainly there was no trace of Rhoslyn and Pasgen around Norfolk or Windsor. Denoriel could only hope they were ignoring the boy, thinking him of no account.

Possibly their Seeing had been somewhat different than that Aleneil and her teachers had. And, of course, Vidal Dhu and his FarSeers would have been concentrating on the second vision, the coming of the Inquisition, in which the Princess Mary was so prominent. Doubtless Rhoslyn's and Pasgen's first purpose would have been to make "friends," as he had made "friends," so that they could occasionally be near the girl to be sure all was well with her. They might not have learned immediately about FitzRoy's elevation. It was not impossible that Mary's servants, trying to ignore a threat they could do nothing about, did not mention the boy. And it was actually likely, seeing that he represented an indiscretion on the part of the queen's beloved husband, would *never* mention FitzRoy under any circumstances at all.

Denoriel's lips thinned. Not all of Mary's servants or supporters were ignoring FitzRoy. When Harry had related the attack on him to Norfolk, he had again mentioned how one of the men called his boat *"una barca."* Although he tried to hide it from the boy, to Denoriel's eyes the duke had been visibly disturbed, cursing the Spanish under his breath. Later he had said something to the steward and the guard from the front gate about the assassins probably having gained entrance *and* escaped by hiding themselves among Mendoza's entourage. Next time he came, Norfolk ordered, he was to come in alone; his army of guards could wait outside.

One tiny mouse-hole plugged. Denoriel was reasonably sure that no other direct attack on FitzRoy would be attempted. What he feared was far more insidious. Pasgen could take on the seeming of anyone; he could even mimic the duke himself. Oh, not for long. The duke's servants and guards would soon know something was wrong, but Pasgen would only need a quarter of an hour. In that guise he would be able to approach FitzRoy, dismiss the boy's guards . . .

Suddenly Denoriel froze, smelling/sensing/recoiling within from something burning cold, inimical. Shifting his eyes cautiously first to the door of the inn and then over all the others within, he sought the source of the evil. But no one new had entered. Had one who had been there recognized him and now was seeking to seize him? There were not many. Two old men on a settle near the low-burning fire, two men dressed as drovers near the doorway so they could look out and keep an eye on their beasts, three or four men back near the far wall of the inn crouched over a table.

None of those was even looking at him, but the terrible hot/cold was approaching. The barmaid? Denoriel could hardly believe his eyes, but the woman was the only one coming closer. Denoriel slid his stool back so he could spring to his feet without catching his thighs under the table. His hand drifted down to his sword hilt. He could not imagine what would happen when he plunged that silver sword into a seemingly innocent woman just doing her ordinary work . . . And then he saw it!

Around the barmaid's throat was a black ribbon, and from that ribbon hung a black cross—long as Denoriel's thumb, its cross arms just the right width for a graceful

form, and thick as a sliver of wood—not steel but a
cross of true cold iron. It was not, of course, the cross
that affected Denoriel—that symbol only warded off
creatures of true evil—it was the cold iron. Now that
he knew what had affected him, he was able to brace
himself to bear the discomfort. It would do him no
harm unless he actually touched it or tried physically
to force the girl . . .

Denoriel's thoughts stopped dead and then began
to race. "That is a beautiful cross," he said to the
barmaid as she set the mug of ale down on the table.

She smiled at him. " 'Tis 'tisn't it? M'brother made
it. He's blacksmith here."

She lifted it in her hand held it out as she spoke
so Denoriel could see it better. He cringed back against
the wall, shaking his head.

"I've trouble seeing things near-at-hand," he said,
swallowing hard. "Makes it cursed hard to read—but
then, what's a clerk for but to read to a gentleman, eh?
Do hold it away from me so I can better see it."

Evidently the barmaid had heard of folk with the
long-sight. She smiled agreeably. "Ay, there's those as
can't see what isn't right by their noses and there's
those that's arms ain't long enough to hold summat they
want to see."

But she drew the cross back the width of the table
and Denoriel let out his breath. "Yes, that's a lovely
thing. Is it the only one your brother ever made? Could
he make another?"

She looked at him quizzically. "If'n he made one,
surely he could do more. Why, d'you want one, sir?"

"Well, yes, I do, but I am only traveling through on
my way . . . ah . . . to visit a lady." Now, how to get her
to part with this cross, now? "She'd be pleased with
such a well-made ornament."

The barmaid cocked her head. "A lady what would

be pleased to have a cross like mine? It's only iron, sir, not silver, and sure not the good gold."

"Because it's iron. You know, there are tales of such things holding particular virtue." Denoriel hesitated and then said, "I know this was a gift from your brother, but if you would be willing to part with it and ask him to make you another . . . I would pay well. I've never seen a cross of iron before. I'll . . . I'll give you a golden boy for it."

"Oh, sir!" The barmaid's eyes went wide and she started to reach up to untie the ribbon as if she could not give him the gift quickly enough.

"Wait—" he said. "I don't want to make any trouble in your family. Why don't you run over to your brother and make sure he will not mind your selling a gift he made especially for you."

The girl shrugged, and looked at him as if she thought he was a little simple. "He sells his work all the time, sir. That's how he lives. 'Course he wouldn't mind! 'Nd he ain't in Winkfeld, today. He's in Ripplemore. He won't mind, I swear it."

While she spoke she was struggling to undo the knot in the ribbon and Denoriel was wildly seeking a way to take the cross without seriously injuring himself. Fortunately the knot refused to yield and with several frantic pleas for him to wait, she rushed off to find someone to untie the ribbon.

Meanwhile Denoriel had pulled two large silk kerchiefs out, one from his sleeve, which was for elegance and show, and one from an inner pocket where he kept it for wiping splashes, tying around scrapes, and other mundane chores that arose while keeping company with a six-year-old. He laid them out on the table, folded into generous quarters, the stained one right in front of him and the other near his elbow. And when the woman came running back, breathless with fear that he had changed his mind, he took a golden guinea from his purse and laid it on the table beside the stained kerchief.

"Put it on the cloth, if you please, so that I may do it up for her," he said, gesturing for her to take the coin. "And will you bring me some bread and cheese?" That would get rid of her so that she would not see he didn't dare touch the iron cross.

"Wouldn't you like a whole dinner, sir?" the barmaid urged, tucking the golden coin down between her breasts. "I'll bring you the best, and no cost either."

"No." Denoriel laughed. "There will be a full meal waiting for me at my lady's house. Just the bread and cheese, if you will."

The woman almost ran to the kitchen, drawing the small amount of attention that had turned on Denoriel when he offered for the cross, and he quickly drew the silk over the cold iron. Holding it gingerly so his fingers did not come in contact with the metal, even through the layers of silk, he moved the packet to the other kerchief and covered it even more thoroughly. Finally he transferred the wadded silk to his purse. The worst was over, although he could still feel a kind of bite near his thigh and a general unease from the shielded cross.

Unwilling to wake the smallest suspicion about what he had done, Denoriel slowly ate his bread and cheese—which he noted, grinning inside, had been brought by the landlord; the barmaid had apparently decided to keep well out of sight in case he should change his mind—drank his ale, and finally made his way leisurely out of the inn and back to the stable. Miralys snorted and fidgeted as he neared, but Denoriel entered the stall and told the elvensteed to be quiet.

The ostler walked over, his face mirroring surprise

in the light of the lantern he carried. "Be full dark, sir," he said. "When you didn't come right out, I thought you was staying at the inn. Not safe to ride in the dark. Moon's not even up."

What was dark to the ostler was like early evening to Denoriel, but he merely smiled and pretended to check Miralys's girth and the nonexistent bit. "I'm not going far and I know the road. Besides, there's a lady at the end of it," he said, earning a knowing laugh from the ostler, then led Miralys out and mounted.

As soon as they were on the road, he reassured Miralys, who was quivering with anxiety, that the sense of discomfort was not any oncoming danger but the cold iron he was carrying. He could feel the steed's unspoken protest and chuckled.

"I'm not going to keep it," he assured Miralys. "Certs, I could hardly keep it Underhill for long! It's for FitzRoy—he's mortal; cold iron won't bother him. And I'm afraid he'll need it. I think Unseleighe attention will be drawn to him after that attack, and I cannot stay with him day and night. I put a shield on him tonight, but I don't dare trust to shielding which he can't sense and couldn't renew. If the shield failed, all would be lost. But cold iron . . . no one could take him by force if he were carrying cold iron."

Reluctant approval from Miralys. Denoriel sighed and said, "Go around behind Windsor where the gate guards won't see us, Miralys, and let's Gate back Underhill. I can't bring this to FitzRoy tonight. I'd have to break the shield to give it to him and that would be a waste of work and magic."

Once home, he headed for the dining room. "A decent evening meal," he said into the air. "I don't care what."

Instantly a place setting, goblets, a decanter of wine

all appeared before his favorite seat, one which permitted him either to look out through the windows at the woods and meadows or call up a clear panel on the far wall that would show the outside corridor. He did neither, staring sightlessly down at the delicate porcelain plate until, a few moments later, he became aware that it was still empty. He looked around, puzzled, and then laughed at himself.

The cold iron, even muffled at it was, was keeping his servitors away. Sighing, he rose and went into the living room. There, he deposited his prize in a shielded box he used to keep odd trinkets he had taken from the victims of the Wild Hunt. They were all things with some feel of power to them, things Koronos said should not be left for others to find but that no one else wished to touch. Nor did anyone else have any suggestions about how to dispose of the objects, so Denoriel, the least affected, kept them.

He looked down at them: an odd little knife, mostly of bone but with an ugly hook and serrated edge of steel; a whistle that had almost defeated the whole Wild Hunt because it sent the dogs howling and groveling in agony and brought all the elvensteeds to their knees; three matched steel coins with sharp edges connected by short thin chain to . . . Denoriel had no idea for what those coins were used, but there was an ugly feeling about them.

Shaking free of the recurring question, he put the well-wrapped cross in the box on top of the lot, and closed it. When he returned to the dining room, his meal was on the table. He began to eat without tasting. There was no doubt that the cold iron cross would keep any lesser Unseleighe creature away from FitzRoy. A determined Sidhe might force him or herself to come near the boy, but to seize him would cost pain, even injury.

That raised another question. He rubbed his thigh, where the ache caused by the shielded cross he had carried in his purse was just beginning to diminish. How could *he* touch Harry if the boy was wearing the unshielded cross? FitzRoy was used to being hugged; Denoriel shuddered at the thought of pressing Harry to him with that cross hanging on Harry's chest. He could do it if he had to, but . . .

He pointed to his wine goblet, which was refilled, and sipped from it while he pondered the problem. Harry had called him a fairy knight, and was aware that fairies could not abide cold iron. And therein lay his solution. He would only have to tell the child to pull a protective silk pouch over the cross when he arrived. But layers of silk had not been enough to keep the thing from hurting him, though it was merely some discomfort and not real injury; still, he didn't want to wince every time he embraced the boy. Perhaps a magic shield more effective than those he knew would help. Mwynwen might know . . . or Aleneil.

Aleneil first. She would be anxious about what had happened after she sent him off to the mortal world in such a hurry. He gestured at the table, which was instantly cleared, and sent a call to Miralys. Then he went to get the cross. When he opened the box, an aching unease stole out of it like a miasma. Denoriel set his teeth and reached for the cross, then hesitated. If he took that with him as it was, he might upset the patterns of the Gates. Denoriel shook his head. All the Magus Majors in Underhill would be out hunting his hide. He closed the box again and took the whole thing with him.

The FarSeers had their own place within Elfhame Avalon, comprised of the learning place and a number of separate cottages. It was tucked away by itself across wide meadows and buried in a gentle shadowy wood of flowering trees. A narrow grassy path approached it, passed under an archway in the featureless, round, white school building, and opened onto a placid lawn through which ran a very small tinkling stream. A number of cottages were arranged around the lawn; they were indistinguishable one from another, but Denoriel knew that his sister's house was the last to the left when exiting the arch, closest to the woods.

He sent a thought out to her, and the door opened at once. A moment later Aleneil was standing in it, a hand stretched in welcome. Denoriel dismounted, the box firmly clutched under one arm. Miralys dropped his head to the grass of the lawn.

"What happened?" Aleneil asked as she gestured him to come into her sitting room. "I scryed the fight, but who were the men? Why did they try to kill FitzRoy?"

"I'm not sure who the men were, but you were right about them not being Unseleighe, even though they used a sleep spell on FitzRoy's guards. They were purely mortal. Their weapons were steel."

"A sleep spell?" Aleneil echoed, then said, "Sit down, brother, and take some ease. You have had no rest in a long time. Are you hungry?"

It took Denoriel a moment to remember that he had eaten, so distracted had he been during the meal, but he said, "No, I ate at home—though I have not the faintest idea what."

Aleneil nodded acceptance and waved toward the chairs that flanked a well-padded settle. Denoriel sat in one, delicately carved and inset with mother-of-pearl, which luminously gave back the greenish blue of the double-thick soft cushions. He set the box on his lap. Aleneil looked at it, but seemed to decide to put that question aside.

"You said the assassins had a sleep spell?" she said, sinking down into a corner of the settle herself.

Denoriel's lips tightened. "There's a mortal mage involved."

"A mortal mage," she repeated, her expression reflecting distress. "I thought the coming of Christianity, or at least, of all this 'New Learning,' had done away with them. All the years of hunting and burning because some fool wrote down 'Thou shalt not suffer a witch to live.' If the witch does no harm, why not?" She sighed and shook her head. "Of course, there still were born those who could *become* mortal mages. Men and women are born with Talent all the time, but I didn't know anyone would dare train one or that any were strong enough to give a spell to another to use." She tapped her finger on the arm of the settle. "Perhaps one of those men was a mage, himself?"

He shook his head. "I cannot say, except that I think not. Both were too skilled as swordsmen to have spent much time studying magic. And neither tried to use magic on me when we were fighting, nor against FitzRoy. My guess is that they had an amulet with a release word but had no personal knowledge of or trust in magic." He told her about how the ensorcelled men had been tied and gagged, finishing, "And they did wake within a time that I felt was too short for safe completion of the purpose."

His sister frowned a little. "But it would not have been too soon if you had not come. It would not have taken long to drown the boy, perhaps five minutes. Then they would have fled, and the guards would have wakened very soon, all but eliminating the chance that someone would find them asleep."

Denoriel scowled. "Do you really think a human mage could judge the duration of a spell that finely? I cannot."

"I don't know," Aleneil admitted, "but I don't want

you to underestimate your opponents. So, you believe that the men were only hire-swords?"

He thought back to his encounter. "Possibly hire-swords, but not, I think, men off the London street. Norfolk seemed to think that they were Spanish and had come in the entourage of the Imperial ambassador, Inigo de Mendosa, and then, after I wounded them, got away by hiding themselves among his numerous guardsmen."

"Spanish." Aleneil shivered gently. "That is from where the Inquisition will come if we do not manage to enthrone our red-haired babe, but why should the Spanish attack FitzRoy?"

So Denoriel told her what George Boleyn had told him about the succession to the throne. When he had explained the importance of a *male* heir, she sighed and nodded.

"They wish to make sure the path is clear for Princess Mary who, in her innocence and piety will bring in the Inquisition." She shook her head. "Cruel, so cruel! I cannot understand these mortals. But how can you possibly protect FitzRoy from mortal attacks? You cannot be with him constantly."

"I'm no longer much worried about direct or physical attacks." The more he thought about it, the less likely another direct attempt at the boy's life seemed. "I don't think poor FitzRoy will be allowed to enter the jakes alone. He will be better guarded—the men right with him, not standing at a gate some distance away—and the other children will be with him too. And since strong suspicions have already been aroused by this past attempt on him another, even if successful, would be fruitless."

His sister blinked at that. "Why?"

He smiled humorlessly. He grew better acquainted with the machinations of mortals every day. Perhaps, when all this was over, he should consider a position as advisor to the Seleighe king. "Because King Henry would be so outraged that he would likely expel the Spanish from the country and make sure that all Spanish influence is removed from around the princess. She is still young enough to be taught to hate them, specially by her father, whom she admires and loves. And for her mother to try to excuse them . . . What could Queen Catherine say, that the Spaniards murdered her bastard nephew to smooth her daughter's way to the throne?"

Aleneil nodded slowly. "She would soon abhor Spanish influence. I have heard something about her, and apparently she is truly good at heart but narrow of mind. So is young FitzRoy safe?"

Now came the tricksy part. "From death, I hope he is, but more endangered than ever of being stolen away to the Unseleighe Court. Until now, as you said to me, they have overlooked FitzRoy. Mary is the legitimate heir, and Underhill we do not think so little of our women as they do in the mortal world. Unfortunately this attempt on him by the Spanish will point out that *they* fear him and draw Vidal's attention."

Aleneil interrupted. "But to steal him away would result in the same outrage and suspicion against the Spanish—"

"Not if a changeling was left in his place."

"But how can they make a changeling?" Aleneil asked. "None of them has ever seen FitzRoy, have they?"

"I don't know," Denoriel admitted. "I never felt any touch of the Unseleighe on him, and I know the people who are always around him. But Windsor is a busy place, especially when Norfolk is in residence. Many come and go—those assassins did."

"I see." Aleneil bit her lip. "A changeling! How can you protect him? There is no way you can be constantly in his company. I can help you set a shield that will protect him from being ensorcelled or being fooled by a glamour, but if they simply muffle his cries and carry him away . . ."

Denoriel shook his head and grinned. "I have the answer to that." And he opened the box he had set on his knees when he sat down.

Aleneil gasped and shrank away as far as she could get. "In the name of Dannae, what have you there?"

"Cold iron," Denoriel said, his voice a bit rough despite having braced himself against the baleful influence of the thing. It was hard to believe that it wasn't a thing of evil in and of itself, that it was just that it was poison to his kind. . . .

"Put it away," Aleneil said, somewhat breathlessly. "Why did you bring it here? For what will you use it?"

"This is what will protect FitzRoy," Denoriel said, dropping it back into the box and closing it. "He is mortal. He can wear it without harm or discomfort. But no Unseleighe creature will be able to approach it. A determined Sidhe might seize him, but not for long. The cross was muffled in more than eight layers of silk."

"A cross? I have never been affected by a cross before," Aleneil protested.

"The cross is made of cold iron—pure cold iron without any admixture of any other metal. What I have come for, sister, is help with a shielding spell to muffle it."

Aleneil shook her head. "But if you shield it, it will no longer protect the child."

"The spell will be on a pouch I will provide, a triple-thick, tight-woven silk pouch. I hope the silk will shield the spell from the iron and the spell will shield *me* from it. Harry is used to being touched by me. He holds my hand and expects me to hug him—and I am glad enough to show him all the affection he wants because he's a sweet child . . . but I cannot touch him if he will be wearing that cross, unshielded."

As he spoke, Denoriel was already envisioning the kind of silk pouch he wanted, the tightness of the weave close enough to make the silk waterproof. He decided on three layers bonded together with the substance the silkworms used to seal their cocoons, which made the silk almost as stiff as wood but more flexible. That bonding substance might even provide additional shielding.

He envisioned the pouch the length and width of the cross then added a touch more space so the cross would slip in easily. But how would it stay in? Denoriel thought of the easiest thing for a still-clumsy child, a simple flap. No, a flap with a hole in it for the gold chain he would provide to go through. When the cross was pulled out, the pouch, still held by the chain, would drop behind, leaving the cross exposed. To *ken* such a thing was a small matter, easily done.

As he saw it, so it appeared on his hand a little while later. He noticed as he called in and wove power and air and mist from the Unformed places together with atoms of earth from the lawn that he could feel the channels throughout his body as if they were a little bruised. They were not painful now; the power Underhill seemed to soothe away the too-hot lightning power he had drawn into him in the mortal world, but he was aware of them, aware of other things in his body. When he had time, he must speak to a Magus Major . . .

He held out the pouch to Aleneil and she touched it with one finger, then cocked her head to one side. "Is that suitable to a child?" she asked. "That solid black?"

Denoriel sighed at his oversight and fixed his eyes

on the silk. Silver and gold threads began to crawl over the surface; then the interstices filled with color. When the pattern was complete, they both smiled. Denoriel had imitated an image he had seen frequently, a sweet-faced woman in a blue mantle with one hand raised in blessing.

"Yes, that's just the kind of thing that would be given to a child," Aleneil said, and began to build a spell, gesturing for Denoriel to follow the creation in her mind.

When she was done, he repeated the process, layering one shield over the other. Then he drew a deep breath and opened the shielded box to lift out the silk-swathed cross. Aleneil rose and withdrew. Denoriel set his teeth and began to unwrap his prize. His teeth were gritted and sweat beaded his forehead by the time he was able to lift the cross by its ribbon and slide it into the pre-pared pouch.

The violent sickness that had made him think he was going to lose the dinner he couldn't remember was instantly gone. The feeling of malaise, the subtle ache in his bones . . . all gone. Denoriel took a deep breath and called for his sister, who peeked warily around the doorway, then smiled and came in.

"I see we were successful," she said.

He nodded. "I just hope we weren't too success-ful. You see how I made the pouch so the cross can hang inside it or outside. I was afraid if I just gave the pouch loose to the boy he would lose it. He's only six, after all. Now I am concerned that he will for-get to take the cross out again when I leave him."

Aleneil shrugged. "I can bespell you to remind him to take the cross out whenever you leave him. That is no great problem. More important is how you are going to hide the cross from his servants and any-one else who might see him take off his clothing and how you are going to explain to him what it is for, that he needs to put it in the pouch in your presence, and *always* wear it."

"There will be no need to hide it from his servants. I am not going to give it to Harry directly . . . at least, I hope I will not need to do so. I am going to tell a tale to the duke of Norfolk that will induce him to give the cross to Harry. He need not know that the boy will always wear it because the nurse will not tell him. She is superstitious. If she believes the cross to be a good-luck charm, she will help the boy hide it. For now, that will be enough."

CHAPTER 7

Pasgen examined himself with near-black, round-pupilled eyes, staring into the full-length reflecting glass. Tight black curls framed his swarthy-skinned face and fell to his shoulders, hiding his ears although those were bespelled by illusion into the stupid round ears of a human. A tightly pleated white ruff encircled his throat, relieving the stark black of his doublet. But the buttons were gold and gold piped the seams. Gold also clocked his black hose and showed through the slashes on his puffed breeches.

He was richly enough dressed, Pasgen thought, to affirm his position to the man he was about to visit. His only variation from the Spanish norm was that he was taller and stronger than any of the Spanish men that he had yet seen. *Too bad,* he thought. He was not going to diminish himself into pathetic mortal stature. If Martin Perez remembered him and described him, it would not matter. Inigo de Mendoza would deny the existence of such a servant—and Perez would be even more sure of his importance if he did not know Pasgen's master. He would probably assume anyone dressed with this much wealth and with such physical presence reported back to a very high churchman at the least—or perhaps, had been sent directly from the king of Spain.

Besides, his strength would serve as an additional weapon to terrify the fool who had betrayed him.

A thought sent one of his blank-faced servitors for a horse, a *real* horse, not Torgan the not-horse, because he could not take a beast with clawed paws instead of hooves, blazing red eyes, and predator's teeth into the mortal world. When frequent visits to Overhill had become necessary, Pasgen had purchased mortal horses for himself and Rhoslyn. He rode a handsome brute as black as his not-horse with a temper even worse than Torgan's; Pasgen did not mind the temper, but the beast did not have the strength of the not-horse.

By the time Pasgen reached the door of his manor, the horse was saddled and waiting. He rode to the Gate that would take him to the Bazaar of the Bizarre, and then, as if he had come to shop, through the market to a second Gate that debouched in the mortal world just outside of London.

It was black night to mortals, but barely twilight to Pasgen. The horse jibbed at first, misliking the need to ride out into darkened streets, but Pasgen simply gripped its feeble mind and rode it through the night. He did not force the animal beyond its limits, however, so it was late afternoon when he passed the gates of Windsor and disappeared into a small wood just off the road. From there he watched, and when he saw the guards demand that every person who came to the gate be identified, and then be searched for weapons, he knew that things had changed at Windsor. Drastically. This was not the time to force a confrontation, particularly when he saw that if the person insisted on going to the palace, he found himself accompanied by a guard.

Pasgen did not attempt to enter.

Instead he rode on to the little town that had grown up to service the needs of Windsor Palace. At the inn he complained bitterly that he had come all the way from London at the request of the steward and that he had been turned away. What was going on? Pasgen demanded. Half a dozen patrons rushed up to the serving counter to tell him.

It took some time to sort out all the different tales, but when he was sure enough of what was fact and what was assumption, Pasgen grumbled that the steward could go hang, that he would return to London. He paid for the meal he had ordered and several rounds of drink for himself and a group of those he considered best informed about the events in the palace the previous day. Then he went out and demanded his horse.

It had not been a satisfactory journey—except that he had learned that what Vidal had claimed was true, that there *had* been an attempt on FitzRoy's life.

As he rode back toward London, he considered whether he should create a Gate near Windsor. He was surprised that he had not sensed one nearby because it seemed likely to him that the so-called foreign Lord Denno who had saved FitzRoy was really Denoriel. He snorted lightly with contempt when he realized there was no Gate nearby. Just like his stupid, overcautious half-brother. Denoriel was so fixated on keeping the secret of Underhill that he probably rode the whole way from the London Gate each time he paid a visit to the boy.

However, if Lord Denno was Denoriel, Pasgen

thought, that added another layer to his problems. The moment Denoriel saw the changeling they intended to substitute for FitzRoy, he would know what the creature was. A local Gate would make his escape with the real FitzRoy quicker and safer, but Gates left traces that Denoriel might well be able to read and follow.

Well, Pasgen thought, he had time to consider whether to build a Gate. It would take Rhoslyn some days, perhaps even a week, to create the changeling. Perhaps she could make it real enough to fool Denoriel for a while. She would have a good image of the boy because she would wrench that image hair by hair out of the minds of the men who had been sent to kill him.

Although he had not pressed the horse and had even lent it a little strength, the animal was very tired when he passed through the Gate to the Bazaar. But of course, his journey was not even close to being done. Instead of returning to his domain, he simply turned around, and passed through the same Gate again, this time arriving in London midmorning of the day after the attack on FitzRoy. Pasgen knew exactly where he was going, although he had never actually been in London before. He had a mental grip on that treacherous mage's aura and the man could not escape him no matter where he hid himself.

Reminded by this of precisely why he had spent a day riding to Windsor and almost another riding back, Pasgen was suddenly furious.

When he noted that passers-by were looking at him in startlement, then quickly shying out of his path, he damped down his rage, lest he attract too much attention. Then he took the moment to be sure that the aura wasn't moving—just in case the wretch might be, say, on a ship on his way back to Spain. . . .

But no. There was nothing to indicate that Martin Perez knew his deception had been discovered. He was unlikely to be hiding, and unlikely to suddenly decide to take himself elsewhere, unless he felt Pasgen's anger. And although Pasgen didn't think Perez was a good enough mage for that, it wouldn't do to alert him at this point. Another reason to throttle his own anger— for now.

The road was perfectly straight and would bring him past Whitehall Palace and onto The Strand. Down a lane south from The Strand was a small house not far from the manor rented by the Spanish to be their embassy. That was his goal, and Pasgen knew by the strengthening sense of Perez's aura that his path would lead him there. He gave his mind to just what he would do to Perez, and after losing himself in the pleasurable contemplation of taking full measure of his vengeance, wakened with a start to shrill imprecations.

Pasgen looked around with considerable shock. The road was now overfull of people on foot, ahorse, driving carts and wagons, pushing bushels by hand, and his tired and nasty-tempered brute of a horse had shouldered aside a handcart, tipping it over so that what it carried had been spilled into the mud of the road. Instinctively Pasgen lifted a hand to blast the mortal fool who had got in his way, but hearing curses rise all around him, thought better of the impulse. Instead he fished a gold coin out of his purse.

His lips curved up in a travesty of a smile. He could blast them all, but that would betray the kind of power he wielded and even Vidal Dhu would not condone that. Better to let them tear each other apart. It was far more satisfying when the mortal scum did his work for him. He called an apology, and flipped the gold piece into the air toward the woman who had been pulling the handcart but made sure it fell just short of her reach. She flung herself forward, but others had seen the glint of gold in the air. Pasgen wrenched his horse left, away from the converging crowd, and then drove it forward. Behind him he heard screams and shouts, then louder howls of rage and pain. No matter who won in that tussle behind him, there would be many more losers than winners. He did not look back.

That had been amusing, but he realized that he could not afford to cause riots all along his path, and he gave his attention to managing the horse, cursing it under his breath because it did not have the wits of a not-horse. Torgan, instructed by a mental command, would have picked its own way through the crowd and with a minimum of fuss. The damned horse seemed bent on causing as much havoc as possible.

The attention he was giving to where he was going also opened him to a variety of other unpleasant experiences. The sun was too bright; it hurt his eyes. The road was growing more and more crowded, and the people did not draw aside respectfully. They shook their fists at him when he tried to force a passage, and shouted curses at his back. Worse, everything stank! The odor grew worse and worse as he approached the city, and all kinds of filth appeared in the ditches alongside the road.

There were Unseleighe domains that were as disgusting, he supposed, but ordinarily the denizens of those places were summoned somewhere less noxious if one of the Sidhe wished to give it orders. If messages had to be delivered to such a domain, mortal slaves were sent, or constructs, or even lesser Unseleighe. Here he could not avoid the miasma; he could not even eviscerate the mangy dogs that barked at his horse, ran at its legs, and made the stupid beast shy so erratically that Pasgen, who was a superb horse-man, was twice nearly unseated.

Rage grew in him, and the need to keep it inside made it worse. And when he realized that the aura he sought had peaked and was diminishing, he sat for a moment on his horse perfectly still, fighting the urge to destroy, destroy anything. Then, slowly, carefully, to keep himself from lashing out all around him with balefire and thus clearing the area, he turned the horse—no easy thing in the crowded street—and retraced his path. When he felt the aura peak again opposite the lane between Somerset House and the Savoy Palace, he rode south. At least this small street was less crowded, mostly servants afoot and a few liveried riders.

About a third of the way down the street he felt the aura begin to diminish again and turned back. A grand manor occupied the whole corner. The next house was a more modest structure of dull-red brick with black door and window frames. There was a rail to the right of the front door; that was where he rode up, and stopped, sure that he had, at last, tracked his quarry to its lair. Pasgen waited a moment, but no servant darted out to take his horse and finally he dismounted and tied it to the rail himself. It was just as well, he told himself. He would not be inside long.

He applied the knocker to the door thunderously, and when it was flung open by a startled and angry servant, threw a compulsion spell at him and demanded to be taken to his master. Pain contorted the man's face, and a mewling cry escaped him as the spell pierced his mind and froze his faculties. Then he turned about and began to walk woodenly across the small entrance foyer toward the stair that rose to the second floor. Unable to do anything except lead the way to his master, he left the door open. Pasgen growled but took the time to shut the door, being disinclined to cope with unexpected intruders.

Silent, although his eyes showed horror, the servant opened the door to Martin Perez's bedchamber. He had not knocked; Pasgen had not told him to knock. Pasgen did not knock either, simply walked in. Perez was just allowing a second manservant to button his breeches. He gaped at Pasgen, who had walked past the ensorcelled servant.

"How dare you!" he cried. "Out! Out of my bedchamber!"

He recognized Pasgen, of course. The fool. He clearly was under the misapprehension that he, and not Pasgen, was the master here.

"Be still, little man," Pasgen snarled. "Be grateful that I did not decide to lesson you in public."

"Lesson me? For what? Do you think you can?" There was assurance and contempt in Perez's voice.

Pasgen saw the mage's fingers move, heard the subvocalization of some spell. He wondered whether he should let the fool cast it and break it so that it would backlash, but in the end, he was too angry and impatient. He gestured. Perez froze. For one moment Pasgen simply stared at him, allowing him to struggle to free himself, and grow more and more frightened as he realized that he could not.

"You betrayed me. You lied to me."

A tiny finger gesture freed Perez's mouth. He cried, "No." Pasgen cut him off.

"You never told me about the king's son FitzRoy. You concealed the fact that the king is considering naming the boy his heir instead of Princess Mary."

Perez's eyes, the only things that could move beside his lips, slid desperately from side to side. "No! I did not tell you because I did not wish to waste your time.

FitzRoy is nothing and nobody. King Henry will never name him heir. He will never place a bastard on the throne."

Pasgen twisted his hand and Perez screamed. The servant who had been attending his master and had been shocked into paralysis by what had happened, now drew a knife and leapt at Pasgen. Without even turning his head, Pasgen drew his sword, and with a single gesture, pulled the man onto the blade without ever releasing his magical hold on the master. Perez screamed again in horror, as did the dying servant.

Pasgen allowed the man to drop to his knees, hands clasped impotently around the blade, then pulled the sword free as he toppled over sideways, eyes glazing with pain and encroaching death.

"FitzRoy is no longer the boy's name," Pasgen said, ignoring the servant and the spreading pool of blood around him as a thing of no moment. He did wonder, though, at Perez's look of horror. This was hardly a gentle age; the mayfly mortals died brutally as a matter of course every day. But perhaps Perez was horrified, not by the servant's death, but by the realization that Pasgen was far more powerful than the Spaniard had guessed. "He is now earl of Nottingham, duke of Somerset, duke of Richmond, the premier duke of the kingdom as well as Lieutenant of the Northern Marches. He has more honors than the princess, has been given an equivalent household and his household holds equivalent power—"

"Nothing. It all means nothing," Perez gasped, his eyes on the bloody sword in Pasgen's hand.

The weapon came up; the tip just touched Perez's throat. He could not flinch away. He began to weep.

"It means so little that yesterday you gave two men a sleep spell to be used on the child's guards so that they could—" Pasgen hesitated; even the Unseleighe Sidhe would not kill a child "—drown him."

"That was not my doing!" Perez's voice was so high with fear that he sounded like a gelded man. "I thought it was nonsense, only King Henry's ploy to win some more points in his negotiations over Mary. I said to draw attention to FitzRoy was a mistake. But the Imperial ambassador demanded the spell—"

He stopped abruptly as Pasgen's sword inched forward and pricked him. The spell held him so rigid that he could not tremble, but tears ran down his face.

"The attempt failed," Pasgen said, contemptuously. "Both men. . . ." He sneered. "Oh, brave! Oh, how noble! How truly in the tradition of the El Cid! So clever, to imagine sending two men to drown a child! Your noble *hidalgos* . . . were wounded, and fled."

Perez was white under his natural skin-tone, which had the effect of making him look pasty and sallow.

Pasgen drew little figure-eights in front of Perez's nose with the tip of his blade. "There was considerable confusion concerning who was guilty of the attack. Sometime later, Inigo de Mendoza and his retinue left Windsor. Then the attempt on FitzRoy was reported to Norfolk and the palace and grounds were carefully searched. The gate guards swore that no two wounded men had gone out, but the men could not be found. They went out with Mendoza's retinue. I want those two men."

"They were not my men," Perez protested. "How can I—"

"I do not know. I do not care," Pasgen told him in a tone that brooked no argument. "I want those men. I will return here tomorrow evening. I will find them here . . ." he smiled " . . . or I will take you."

Pasgen then turned and left, ignoring Perez's cries

to be released. The spell would wear off after a while, and Pasgen did not want the mage to try to follow him. He retrieved his horse and returned to The Strand, but instead of turning back to find the Gate he had used, he turned right at the corner and rode further east.

Somewhere ahead, Pasgen sensed a Gate, and he was curious. He could not tell whether it was a very small Gate or simply far away, but he intended to find it if he could. If it were Denoriel's Gate, it would be well worth the time spent to know it. Pasgen smiled thinly again. A neat ambush could be set at a Gate if they needed to neutralize Denoriel for a while. He would not kill his half-brother . . . no, not kill, but he would be delighted to disable that righteous prig.

As he rode along Watling Street, he passed St. Thomas's church. His head lifted and turned when he felt a tiny quiver of power, but he did not rein in the horse. He had often felt a similar touch of power in mortal churches. Another thin smile bent his lips as he rode past; that power had not been nearly enough to save the wretches who thought they could shelter there from the Wild Hunt. Besides, there was a surer, stronger source of power somewhere ahead and to his right.

He rode down Watling Street and then into the East Chepe, one of London's larger markets. He shuddered. Entirely too many things here were made of iron and steel. He kicked his tired horse, feeling it trembling with weariness beneath him. At least now the brute was so worn out that it wasn't fighting him. Probably he should not have come this way; if he did not soon find a Gate the animal might collapse on him. He pushed a little power into it, and to his right felt an answering silent bell.

Down Fish Street . . . *faugh,* what a smell came up from pools of filth holding decaying scales and skin and fish guts, from heaps of heads and tails and fins! And the stink of the river was not much more salubrious, but at last he was out on the bridge. In its way it was worse. His horse could barely make a way through the buyers and sellers, who came right to his side and thrust trays of goods, often pins and needles of steel, into his face.

There was nowhere to go but ahead. Both sides of the bridge were filled with stalls. Several were armorers who sold steel swords and knives; there were even blacksmith's shops (although at least the forges were off the bridge) that exhibited nails and hinges and handles and Dannae knew what else—all made of iron. Although he touched nothing—he had pushed away the peddler of needles and pins by shoving his shoulder with a boot-clad foot—the evil cold beat at him. Pasgen's gorge rose and he regretted the little strength he had given the horse as his own faltered. Still, ahead, the bell-tone held steady and it seemed that a drift of cleaner, purer air flowed out toward him.

He found the Gate only a little way down High Street, right—he had to laugh—in a tiny grove of trees in the graveyard of St. Saviour's church. The tone he "heard" and the "scent" in the air told him that the Gate would lead into Seleighe territory, but his horse was too tired to go back to his own Gate and unless this was one of the guarded portals, he could pass for Seleighe. The graveyard was empty. Pasgen dismounted and led his horse into the shadowed grove.

He did not recognize any of the six destinations patterned into the Gate and chose one which felt the least "sweet" at random. The choice was fortunate; Pasgen arrived in a neutral area now mostly inhabited by spirits of the air. This lot were cheerful, babbling things which happily directed him to an adjoining Unformed area.

He had remembered to change his somber black to some frivolous combination of rose and blue and the silly creatures were delighted with him. Several wished to accompany him, and he had to turn quite nasty and hurt a few of them to discourage them, but he really could not have them tagging along into Unseleighe territory or marking his path to his own domain. For one thing, they'd quickly become meals there for whatever happened to catch them. . . .

He left the exhausted horse and collected Torgan at his home. From there it was only moments until he completed the tortuous path and went through a last Gate into Rhoslyn's domain. He wrinkled his nose as he looked around. Untidy, that's what Rhoslyn was— a patch of woodland here, a meadow there, a babbling brook following a wavering course over stones of every size and shape, flowers here and there.

Not that there was even the smallest hint of carelessness or laziness. Every stone was a perfect stone, every flower a perfect flower, but like those in the mortal world they were uneven, of different textures, colors, and sizes. Why should she do that when it would have been even less effort to make them all the same or of complementary shapes and colors that fit together in ordered masses to soothe the eye? He sighed. Rhoslyn was Rhoslyn.

Even the path meandered, going off toward one side of the domain under overarching shade trees and then wandering the other way, out into the undappled light of the silver sky where a wide vista of lawn spread to display Rhoslyn's castle. Pasgen sighed again. The castle was not large, not even grand, but it was right out of a mortal's romance, with turrets and pennons, even with a drawbridge over a moat. At least only black swans floated on the water.

The bridge was down and Pasgen rode across. At

the open gate one of Rhoslyn's servants was waiting to take Torgan. The construct looked like a wisp of a girl, too large-eyed, with long, thin hands that seemed hardly able to clutch the reins. But those fingers, thin as they were, could cut like razors, not only through flesh but through bone.

Once when Rhoslyn had brought a girl servant with her to a meeting where Vidal Dhu had promised physical rewards that must be carried away, an ogre had tried to seize the girl. The ogre had been torn apart, swiftly and efficiently. The servant had not lingered over the dismemberment to enjoy the ogre's pain, Pasgen remembered, but in general Rhoslyn's servants were more expressive than he would permit in his own constructs, readily speaking, laughing, and crying.

In fact, the girl smiled at him and said shyly, "How nice to see you here again, Lord Pasgen. Please go right in. Lady Rhoslyn is aware of your arrival."

Pasgen did not reply. He knew that if he had not been recognized and approved, the construct would have seized him. But to his surprise, the seeming girl actually looked hurt when he ignored it. Was Rhoslyn going too far in animating her constructs? Perhaps, but if she was practicing that kind of animation, it would be very useful in making the changeling.

He was just turning into a very cozy parlor when Rhoslyn came down the stairs. She gestured him quickly further into the room and closed the door behind him. Pasgen felt a sealing spell and raised his brows at her.

"Mother's here," she said, eyes bright with tears. "Vidal gave her something again. I don't know what it was this time, but she's a right mess."

A "right mess" was an understatement; Rhoslyn had been nursing her mother for the better part of the day, and cursing herself for not having the skills of a Healer. For a long moment Pasgen made no response, but Rhoslyn could see the pulse beating in his throat. He always pretended a greater indifference to their mother than she did, but Rhoslyn was sure he cared for Llanelli deeply, perhaps more deeply than she.

Then he said softly, "I am not yet strong enough."

"No." Rhoslyn put a hand on his arm. "Even together we could not destroy him."

Pasgen shook his head. "That we might accomplish if we put our minds and strengths to it, but I could not hold the domain together."

It was Rhoslyn's turn to be frozen into stillness. She had not sensed her brother's ambition previously . . . or she had denied it to herself. "Would you want to?" she breathed. "Would you want to rule the ogres and goblins and hags?"

"Would you want to set them loose without any control? Or see them in the hands of someone weaker and more vicious than Vidal Dhu?" His tone was savage, however, she knew it was not aimed at her but at their "guardian" and master.

Again Rhoslyn was silenced, but she reached out and put her hand on Pasgen's arm. She had not understood his sense of responsibility. She had not even thought of anything beyond the chance of being free of Vidal Dhu—and really, that was unlike her. What Vidal was doing to their mother had shaken her. She took a deep breath.

"You are right, of course, and this is no time to be at odds with our master. We must make sure that Princess Mary comes to the throne, but is there anything we can do for Mother?"

"What do you want me to do?" Pasgen asked, his voice grating. "I can get enough of that disgusting drug to send her into Dreaming—"

"No!" Rhoslyn cried. "That would be forever. I . . . I don't want to lose her. When she's free of it, she is of great use to me. I will see her through this recovery as I have in the past. At least she has enough sense to come to me when she is overcome by craving."

"Yes, but you won't have time to attend to mother just now," he said, dismissively. "I'll take her to her own place and care for her. I've done it before."

Rhoslyn looked at him with anger and distrust. "The last time you nearly let her go into Dreaming. No. There's nothing so important—"

"That was a mistake." Now that he saw she was angry, he softened his own attitude a trifle. "I meant her no harm. I thought it would be kinder to wean her away from the stuff slowly. I know better now."

She sniffed, and gave him a warning look.

But he was too full of his own matter to pay much attention to her warnings. "What's more important is that I'm going to bring to you the two men who were sent to kill FitzRoy. Both of them saw him. One of them even touched him. You can wring out of them everything you will need to know to make a changeling."

Rhoslyn looked down at her fingers and deliberately stopped them from knotting and unknotting. Her lips thinned. She wanted to say that the making of the changeling could wait, but she knew the men's memories would fade with time. Still, the need to care for Llanelli and her distaste for what it would cost to extract memory in such detail drove her to protest.

"I don't need to pick over two humans' dirty minds to build a changeling," she said. "Surely you can find a sprite or some kind or a brownie that could give me a visual image—"

He shook his head firmly. "That will not serve in this case. Unfortunately a likeness on a mindless construct will not be sufficient. The person who saved FitzRoy from being drowned was a Lord Denno. He is my height, white-blond hair, green eyes, to humans he seems incredibly strong, for he fought off two skilled swordsmen. Who do you think that is?"

"Denoriel!" Rhoslyn spat, flushing in annoyance. Always it was the other twins! Was she never to be free of them? "You are right. He would not be fooled by a simple construct for five minutes, and he would know how to make it fall to pieces, which would prove magic to be at the core of FitzRoy's disappearance." She hesitated and then asked, "Is Perez known to be a magician?"

She actually heard her brother's teeth grinding in anger. "I'm afraid so. The man is a fool and must whisper about his powers."

"Then if FitzRoy's disappearance is known to be connected to magic, the Spanish would be blamed." Rhoslyn sighed. "But no matter how good my changeling, Denoriel will 'smell' the magic in it."

As was often the case, Pasgen was ahead of her. "Yes, but he will take time to try to discover whether FitzRoy has been bespelled before he begins to use harsher magic. What will turn a construct to dust will cause considerable pain to a mortal. If the changeling acts and speaks like FitzRoy, we may have days, even weeks, to hide the child."

"Very well," Rhoslyn said wearily, "take Mother back to her own domain, but I will send two of my servants to be with her. You will have to destroy the constructs that are serving her now. I am sure they have been corrupted; Vidal has probably made them into his creatures, and it is no longer safe to allow them to continue in her service. Then you can bring the men to the Unformed place where I made the not-horses. There is no direct Gate to my domain from there, and I found the mists rich and ready for development."

CHAPTER 8

The morning after the attack on FitzRoy, not too early but at a time carefully calculated to be before Norfolk would be ready to begin the business of the day, Denoriel rode up to Windsor Castle from the west rather than the east. This time he stopped at the main gate and asked if the duke of Norfolk was still in the palace and, if he was, whether the duke could spare him a few minutes. His exploit of the previous day being well disseminated, as he had hoped, Denoriel was waved ahead to the entrance of the palace itself.

From there a servant was dispatched with his request and in a flatteringly short time returned with an invitation to the duke's apartment. However Norfolk did not greet him with open arms.

"I hope you have not come to see Harry," Norfolk said. "His guards say he seems calmer this morning and I would prefer not to wake up unpleasant memories for him."

"No, indeed, Your Grace," Denoriel said. "I hope most sincerely that he will soon forget . . . well, no, I cannot believe he would forget what happened but that it will recede in his mind. However, I have been unable to put out of *my* mind the way he clung to me before he finally fell asleep. I have been concerned that the poor child would continue to want me near him and be frightened. This would be inconvenient for all, and, I think, of no great good for the boy."

"Well, he must learn to conquer it," Norfolk said, but Denoriel could tell he was not happy about what he had said.

Without even probing Norfolk's mind, Denoriel knew that the duke was deeply worried about King Henry's reaction to the news of the attack, which would reach him this morning. If the king also heard that Harry was miserable and had not got over his fright, it was possible that King Henry would appoint another guardian. Denoriel hoped to make use of Norfolk's anxiety.

"Yes, of course," Denoriel agreed, "but it occurred to me that anything I could do to give His Grace confidence might be a help." He bestowed on the duke his most charming smile.

And as he might have predicted, Norfolk misunderstood. "Forgive me, Lord Denno, but I cannot permit the duke of Richmond to become dependent—"

"No, no." Denoriel raised a hand in protest. "That the boy should constantly crave my company would not be acceptable either to you or to me. I love the child— I will admit that—but obviously I have a life of my own to live; I certainly cannot live with him. It would ill befit my status or his. Moreover, I understand that His Grace is too important a person to form such a close bond to a foreigner. However, young children believe easily in wonders and marvels. I think if the child had a talisman that he believed was a good-luck charm . . . it might give him the courage he needs and confidence enough to learn to stand on his own, as a man. And—as it happens, perhaps this particular talisman does bring protection."

While he spoke he had been drawing the cross in its protective pouch out of his purse. He had also been casting the very lightest of spells on Norfolk, a spell of confidence and acceptance. Inwardly steeling himself, Denoriel flipped up the silk flap and drew the cross out of the pouch by the heavy gold chain he had "kenned," created, and connected to the cross—at the cost of burnt fingers that Mwynwen had to heal. He held the cross up, hoping Norfolk would be looking at it rather than at his dry lips and sweat-beaded brow.

"This was my younger brother's. It was said to be an ancient relic, taken from the grave of one of the disciples of Christ. It was said to give protection and good fortune. I would like His Grace of Richmond to have it."

Norfolk shook his head slightly. "It doesn't seem to have helped your brother."

"My brother did not have it when the Turks overran Hungary—or I would not have it in my possession now." Denoriel's voice was shaking and he swallowed and swallowed again, grateful that Norfolk would almost certainly put his sickness down to emotions over his losses. But he could bear no more and slipped the cross back into the pouch. "I was going on a long voyage and my brother gave the cross to me, to keep me safe." Tears of easing pain came to his eyes and he drew out his kerchief and openly wiped them away. "I was safe," he whispered. "Only my brother died."

Norfolk reached out for the cross and took it from Denoriel, who suppressed a sigh of relief. A moment later the aching nausea returned as the duke pulled it out of the pouch and examined it closely, turning it this way and that. Finally, he returned it to the pouch and seemingly rather reluctantly, held it out to Denoriel.

"A true relic is too precious a thing to give to a six-year-old child," he said.

Denoriel smiled and reinforced the spell of belief. "I cannot prove it is a true relic—I only believe it myself. However, you can explain that it is a precious possession of mine to His Grace's nurse. She will take good care of it."

Norfolk's hand closed around the pouch and drew it back, away from Denoriel. "But why should Harry believe that this will truly protect him?" he muttered, frowning.

"If you will promise not to tease the boy or laugh at him," Denoriel said, "I can give you a reason that only a six-year-old would believe but no one else will argue about."

"What is that?"

Norfolk was still looking at the cross in its pouch. Now he drew it out again. Denoriel stepped back a bit and forced color into his face. He cleared his throat awkwardly.

"I am afraid that His Grace of Richmond thinks I am . . . ah . . . I am—"

"Yes?" Norfolk's gaze was now keen and wary.

"His fairy guardian," Denoriel got out in a rush. "A fairy knight sent to him by the Fairy Queen to protect him."

"What?" The duke burst out laughing.

Denoriel made a helpless gesture and offered a sheepish smile. "Children!" He gestured toward the cross. "Put it away, please. I will be content when I know young Richmond is wearing it, but it makes me sad to look at it now."

Norfolk slipped the cross into its pouch and then tucked it into his purse, but he had not been distracted from his surprise and amusement. "Fairy gaurdian?" he repeated. "Why did you tell him that?"

"I never did, Your Grace," Denoriel protested. "It is ridiculous. It was because of a series of accidents. One day when His Grace was playing by the pond I came through that part of the garden. His boat had got away, but I didn't know that. I only saw the children running up and down the shore of the pond and I waved at them. It seems that a breeze came up and blew the boat back."

"Didn't you tell them it was an accident?"

"I never spoke to them at the time. Then another time it was a kite. The string broke and he was crying over losing it. I saw it caught in a tree and climbed up and brought it down. He insisted that the kite was loose. That time I did tell him the string was caught on a branch but he said he hadn't seen me climb the tree, just call the kite down to my hand." He shrugged. "Children! They see magic where there is none. Who knows what else he believed. And then when the men attacked him and I happened to see the open gate, that seemed to be the finishing touch." Denoriel sighed heavily.

Norfolk, however, was no longer looking so amused. His expression was uncertain, both wary and relieved. "So if I tell him this cross is your way of protecting him when you cannot be with him," Norfolk mused, "you think he will believe that."

"I suspect so, my lord." Denoriel shrugged but then frowned. "But, Your Grace, I beg that you *not* believe it. I beg you to keep a close watch on him. Perhaps that cross is a true relic, but perhaps it is not. You and I know that God helps best those who help themselves. As the boy grows into his manhood, he will leave such childish fears and beliefs behind."

"But that he should believe you to be something wonderful—" Norfolk cleared his throat. "I do not wish to offend you, Lord Denno. You have been most understanding and helpful, but to have so much influence over the premier duke in the country . . ."

"While he is a child of six?" Denoriel chuckled. "I doubt he will remember the idea for very long, and if he should remember it some years from now, he will be greatly embarrassed by it."

Norfolk snorted, then laughed. "I suppose you are right. Very well. Do you want to give it to him?"

Denoriel gave a quick thought to being able to explain the real purpose of the cross to FitzRoy but then realized that Norfolk would probably come with him. He shook his head.

"I have not the time today, Your Grace. I must be back in London before night. I would be grateful if you gave it to him and told him I could not stay today but that I would come to visit him in three days? If you will give me leave to come in three days, that is? I have business in Maidenhead and I could stop in Windsor on my way back toward London because I will be . . . ah . . . spending the night with a good friend who lives not far from here. I think three more days will give young Richmond time to settle and come to trust his 'charm' without my presence."

Norfolk pondered it, and Denoriel waited for his tiny spell of influence to work. "Hmmm. I will not be here then, but yes, I will leave word that you should be made welcome, Lord Denno. And I will see that Harry gets this before I begin my day's business."

When Pasgen arrived at Rhoslyn's summons, having followed a spirit of the air, he found her standing over two bodies. One was lifeless; the other was stirring slightly, its eyes empty and drool slobbering its chin. Rhoslyn's face was as white and translucent as the mists that swirled around them. Her eyes were sunken, her cheeks hollow.

"I have what I need," she said, her voice flat. "Get rid of the remains."

"Why me?" Pasgen protested.

Rhoslyn trembled with some emotion Pasgen could not identify and said, choking, "I was the one who had to wade through the filth of their minds. I will have the labor of building a changeling . . . a child that I know cannot live. At least you can clear out this offal!"

"What do you want me to do with them?" Pasgen asked irritably. "What's left isn't even good as bait for the Wild Hunt."

Rhoslyn closed her eyes. "I don't care what you do with them so long as they are gone from this place. What's left of them is muddling my image."

"Did you bring one of your servants?" Pasgen asked, looking around, but the thick, almost palpable clouds of . . . whatever . . . were too dense.

"I never bring my servants here," she said, "and you should not either. The mists attract them. I lost a girl some time ago. Perhaps she let herself lose form and be a part of what is here, but it is equally likely she has gone feral and preys on what passes through."

"How did you lose control of her?" Pasgen was amazed.

Rhoslyn shrugged. "She was the construction to whom I had given the most free will. She was my personal servant and managed the others."

"I've told you and told you that giving them free will is dangerous."

"Yes."

The single word was flat, but behind it Pasgen sensed a well of loneliness. He almost put out a hand to take his sister's, but he knew that despite their being twins he could not fill her need. Rhoslyn needed other women as friends, as confidants, and had none. The Unseleighe Sidhe could not be trusted. Rhoslyn had found that out the hard way. So she had tried to create a friend as well as a servant, and that had failed.

"Mother is much better," he said, offering oblique comfort.

"I'm glad," she replied, "but she's not safe. As soon as *he* lays hands on her, she tells him everything. She can't help it. Now take these things and go."

She gestured vaguely in a direction from which Pasgen could feel the power of a Gate. It was not the Gate by which he had entered this Unformed domain, but it was much closer than the one he had used.

Pasgen opened his mouth and closed it. As far as he knew there was nothing he or Rhoslyn were doing that should be concealed from Vidal Dhu. Their master had demanded that they remove Henry FitzRoy as a threat to Princess Mary's eventual elevation to the throne, and that was precisely what they were doing. But if Rhoslyn was in addition doing something she did not want Llanelli to divulge to Vidal Dhu . . . he didn't want to know about it.

So he swallowed his questions and doubts, shrugged, and looked hard at the drooling idiot. At his gesture, it rose to its feet, stumbled to the corpse, and lifted it. Pasgen mounted Torgan. The idiot staggered along in the not-horse's wake. Fortunately the Gate was not far. Pasgen drew the shambling thing beside him so he could touch it and bring it through the Gate with him.

They came out in Gateways!

Pasgen drove his wavering charge off to the left to leave the Gate clear, and sat for a moment looking around. He had been here before, but never on purpose, and it shocked him that Rhoslyn would direct him here. He felt a chill that had nothing to do with the strangeness and danger of the place. If Rhoslyn was using Gateways to reach the area in which she was creating, she was desperate to hide her trail. But why?

Pasgen heard a thud and turned quickly to find the cause, his sword half drawn. Very few, if any, lived in Gateways for the place was strange and beyond Sidhe magic. Gateways was awash with enormous but resistant power, true wild magic. Spells cast here or built here had far greater power than spells worked anywhere else, but all too often, in fact most of the time, the outcome of the spell had nothing to do with what the mage had intended.

Nor could the power of the domain be used in any ordinary way. Many mages had tried to mold and hold the place, but anything formed in Gateways, no matter how careful or how powerful the original working, slowly *trans*formed . . . and no one could predict into what. Sometimes a palace would slide into formlessness and disappear; doorways and windows could come alive and snap open or shut, trapping, maiming, or killing anyone unwise enough to enter a building formed in Gateways. Plants could become mobile, animals root to the ground, and the nature of each and of any being who remained was as unpredictable as its form.

Despite the dangers some, stubborn and foolishly unwilling to give up trying to control so much power, had remained too long. Often what Gateways had made of them was inimical. However the sound that had startled Pasgen was only caused by the idiot, who had dropped his burden and tumbled down atop the corpse when Pasgen's absorption in his thoughts had relaxed his will.

Now Pasgen uttered a small sigh of relief. He had suddenly perceived a more logical reason for Rhoslyn to send him to Gateways than a need to conceal her location. She had thought, he supposed, that he could leave what was left of the mortals here. Pasgen considered the idea briefly. It was not such a foolish idea, because it would rid him of the mortals without leaving any trace. It was unlikely that they would be able to pass through any of the many, many Gates and they would soon either die or be altered beyond recognition.

Perhaps he should leave them here. It would be much simpler than the notion that had come to him when Rhoslyn said to get rid of them. He could just turn Torgan around and go back through the gate. Not that there was any danger of being trapped in Gatways for a Sidhe or any other creature able to pass through a Gate. The domain had been given its name because for eons nearly all those who came hoping somehow to force the domain into submission had built a Gate to get there. And the Gates had remained . . . in a way. Each Gate was there and rooted firmly, immovably, in Gateways. The destination they sent one to was another matter entirely.

One time a Gate might take you out into your chosen destination, another time it might drop you into Wormegay Hold, or Elfhame Avalon—right in the midst of King Oberon's elite Magus Major guards—or the Bazaar of the Bizarre . . . or some nameless domain that seemed unconnected to any other place Underhill. The power tones of the Gates, so many, were a cacophony in his head.

Having sat for a little while staring at the inert forms of the mortals, Pasgen shrugged. Leaving them seemed like the waste of a fine opportunity. He still wanted to drop what remained of the guardsmen on Martin Perez's doorstep. He doubted that he would need to expend another spell to make the man obedient after that.

By the time Pasgen had accomplished that purpose,

he had regretted his decision many times. If the first part had not been so easy, he would have reconsidered and left them in some Unformed domain. But—ah hubris!—it was easy. He had roused the mortal reduced to idiocy and forced him to carry his dead companion to the closest Gate. Since there was no way to tell where any Gate would deliver one, the closest was as good as any other. In the Gate Pasgen fixed his mind on the London exit—and to his intense surprise that was where he arrived in the late afternoon.

Both mortals dropped to the ground again as the force of Pasgen's will was diminished by the weakness of the power in the mortal world. Torgan squealed in dismay as its strength also ebbed. The sound was horrible, more like the death cry of an enormous rat than any sound a horse could make. Pasgen silenced the creature, dismounted, and led it just past the Gate, which was concealed in a seeming tangle of brush in a wooded area north of Westminster Abbey. He then rolled the human bodies into the brush too.

Not far from the Gate was an overgrown lane and Pasgen walked down that to Tothill Road where there was a livery stable. While he walked he changed his clothing to decent but ordinary merchant's garb, complete with hat and belt and purse with silver and gold coins. He had to lean on a tree to rest when he was done because of the drain on his strength, and he ground his teeth with rage until he feared he would damage them and consciously relaxed his jaw. He *hated* the mortal world, purely hated it.

He had recovered most of his physical strength by the time he reached the livery stable, but he hoped most sincerely that he would not need to do any more magic. Like getting to London, the first step—renting a horse and carriage—was easy; driving the carriage

up the miserable lane was not, and binding the will
of the stupid horse to do it drained him again, but not
so severely.

When he felt able, he carried the two bodies—one
was still breathing, but barely—to the carriage. Turning the thing was a trial and a torture, but it was done
at last. Driving down the lane was easier, and then he
was out on the road. From there he had no trouble
until he came to the lane on which Perez's house stood.
There to his horror he found that the large manor on
the corner was all lit up and the lane was clotted with
carriages.

In time he was able to make his way past the
arrivals at some celebration, time not completely
wasted because he came to realize that he could not
simply roll the bodies out of the carriage and leave
them. People were getting out of their carriages well
within sight of the front door of the modest brick
house, and even if the high-born guests did not
bother to look at Perez's house, the eye of any
coachman who was idly sitting and holding his horses
steady might well be caught by what he was doing.
Even if no one marked him moving the bodies,
which was unlikely, leaving them lying across the
front door could not escape notice for long as the
coachmen drove down the street to find a place to
turn and then lined up along it to wait for their
masters.

Pasgen sought desperately through the ambience of
the mortal world for power that he could tap. Nothing! Well, not totally nothing. He could feel a kind of
thin soup eddying about that would take more time and
effort to gather than it would lend strength in use.
Denied a more elaborate and elegant solution, Pasgen
then did the simplest thing he could; he spread the
illusion of large sacks over the two bodies.

When he had recovered from that drain he carried both men to Perez's doorstep and left them there. The illusion would last for some hours, but by dawn it would be gone. Then it would be a matter of luck whether Perez's servant opened the door and found the bodies or whether the Watch or anyone else that passed saw them and enquired why two dead men were lying on the magician's doorstep.

It was Pasgen's misfortune that the latter was the case, and long before dawn. The Watch had been more assiduous in its attention to the lane in which Perez's house was because of the gathering of nobles at the Spanish embassy. They had swept through several times, driving away any who were not servants of those who attended the affair so that the high-born guests would not be troubled by beggars or, far worse, assaulted by thieves or cut-purses.

Not long after midnight, when the hardest drinking guests—thus those most prone to attack—were still staggering out of the building and waiting for their carriages, one of the watchmen saw two men in dark garb seeming to crouch in Perez's doorway. He called to the fellows in his troop to assist him in the apprehension of those he assumed to be planning evil—or why would they be hiding in an adjoining doorway?— and ran forward holding up his torch and brandishing his cudgel.

He was followed immediately—not, as he expected, by his fellow Watchmen but by several giggling and inebriated young men, who had been guests at the grand affair in the embassy. The Watchman had reached his prey before he realized it was not his fellow Watchmen who were on his heels, and he turned and cried out, "Lud ha' mercy. They're dead!" before he realized to whom he was speaking.

"And they're wearing m'lord the ambassador's livery!"

the foremost young man said, steadying himself on his companion's shoulder. He giggled and shook his head. "Delivered to the wrong place. They belong next door."

"They're not *both* dead," the other man said. "See, George, one's wriggling."

"George, Francis, come away," urged a very tall, very blond gentleman, who had followed the others more slowly and seemed more sober than his companions. "We don't want to make more trouble for the Watch than they already have."

"No, look Denno," George Boleyn said, somewhat sobered by shock. "I swear they're embassy guardsmen, and one *is* dead. What's going on here?"

Denoriel felt a sudden wash of dread pass over him as he looked over George Boleyn's shoulder and saw faces he knew too well despite features relaxed in death and idiocy.

"Those are the men I fought in Windsor's garden two days ago," he breathed.

"Fought? Didn't know you'd been dueling, Denno," said Francis Bryan, who had keener ears than Denoriel expected. "How come you didn't ask me to second you?"

There was a touch of reproval in his voice. Francis Bryan fancied himself an expert swordsman and a master of all the proper forms in dueling. In the interests of being accepted by the group, Denoriel had not disabused him of the notion about his swordsmanship.

"Dueling? Can't have been dueling," George Boleyn protested. "One doesn't duel with guardsmen. Denno's a bit ignorant about the proper thing sometimes, but he's got better style than that!"

"Yes, of course I have," Denoriel said, repressing his panic and gently pushing George and Francis to the side so the rest of the Watchmen could get past them.

In the light of the Watch's torches, the area was bright as day to Denoriel. He could see there was no new blood or bruise on the dead man, only the wound his sword had made in the hand; the eyes of the other . . . Denoriel swallowed. The thin power of the mortal world also made more conspicuous the residue of the spells that had drained out one man's life and left the other mindless.

The men he had fought in Windsor garden had died by magic, and it could not be Perez's magic—although Denoriel had discovered that he had provided the sleep-spell amulets—or the bodies would not have been left on his doorstep. That meant the assassins had been dealt with by the Unseleighe Court. And that meant that Vidal Dhu was taking an interest in Harry FitzRoy. But why kill Harry's attackers? Not to punish them. Vidal Dhu had no reason to want to protect FitzRoy, who could be considered a rival to Princess Mary. Why those men? And why had their minds been so ruthlessly, so minutely, torn apart?

Denoriel knew the only answer to that which made sense. Because both of them had seen Harry and one of them had even touched the boy. Between them they could describe Harry clearly enough for the making of a changeling!

As the answer came to him, Denoriel's hands closed on George Boleyn's shoulder and Francis Bryan's arm. Both men cried out, and Denoriel released them with an apology. They both stared at him, sobered by the pain and surprise.

"God's Blood, you're strong," Francis Bryan said, rubbing his arm.

George Boleyn blinked, looked back over his shoulder at the Watchmen clustered around the dead man and his witless companion, and turned again to stare at Denoriel. "But I did hear you say you'd fought those two," he said. "Did you do that to them?"

"No!"

Denoriel's voice was choked and his muscles quivered with the need to grab both men, carry them to Bryan's carriage, and bid the coachman gallop all the way to his house so that he could get back to Windsor through the Gates. Instead, he stood still and made his lips form a slight smile. He could not leave without the pair because he had come in Francis Bryan's carriage. Nor did he think he would be able to reach Miralys, who was Underhill, and would not want to wander amidst so much cold iron in the city, and to set off on foot would take too long. He told himself that whoever was building the simulacrum could not complete it so quickly. But he still burned to get to Windsor to make sure Harry was still there, not some changeling in his place.

Then he wavered on his feet, clutching at Boleyn and Bryan for support. Oh, Dannae! If Norfolk put that cold iron cross into a hurried and ill-made changeling's hands, it might dissolve into dust and mist.

Horrible as the thought was, it was also an instant comfort. If Harry had suffered no damage from receiving the cold iron cross—even if the simulacrum was so well made that it would not dissolve, it would be horribly burnt by the iron—Harry was truly the human boy, not a changeling. Any sign of harm to the child would have sent a troop of Norfolk's men after Lord Denno and there had been nothing, not even a message canceling his proposed visit the next day.

"Hold steady, man," Bryan urged as Denoriel sagged against him.

"Time to get Denno back to his bed," Boleyn said.

Mentally Denoriel thanked the goddess for his momentary weakness and gladly allowed his friends to steer him to the front of the Spanish embassy and signal urgently for Bryan's carriage. Bryan hesitated as they were about to climb in to ask if Denoriel was about to be sick, but he assured them he had only been dizzy momentarily. They watched him warily for a few minutes, but by the time they were turned around and on The Strand headed east, they relaxed, no longer fearing they would have to open a door and hold his head outside.

Convinced that Denoriel was not about to spew, George—his residual drunkenness making him stubborn—reverted to the question of Denno having fought the two victims. It was clear to Denoriel that the pair would never let him out of the carriage at his house by St. Thomas's Church if he did not satisfy them. And since the king must already have received Norfolk's report of the attack and so many others knew of it already, he told them the whole story about seeing the open postern gate, going in, hearing FitzRoy calling for help, fighting off the two attackers, and their escape.

There was a long moment of silence, and then Boleyn looked back over his shoulder at where they had come from, although the Spanish embassy was long out of sight. "And now," he said, "one's dead and the other will not be telling any tales. And left on Perez's doorstep. Probably that means he didn't kill or maim them, but I suspect he had something to do with the attack on FitzRoy . . . I mean, Richmond. And leaving his tools at his house dead and mindless was a warning to him." Boleyn looked sick, and yet avid at the same time. "Torture, maybe. I've heard it said that the Inquisitors know tortures that will wring a man's soul from his body, but leave no mark. Mayhap the magician failed—and his masters have left him a warning."

Bryan burst out. "God's Death! Why should anyone want to hurt Richmond? He's no more than five years old—"

"Six," Boleyn said, "and a very nice, clever child."

"So?" Bryan persisted.

"So, m'father says—and you know he's in the king's confidence—that Henry's feeling out the nobles and trying to nerve himself to name the boy his heir." Boleyn shrugged. "There's reason enough for you."

Bryan shook his head. "Oh, I know that. Everyone knows that. But what if Henry does name Richmond heir? There's years and years for the king to change his mind."

"Not if he marries Mary to a French prince."

Francis Bryan let out a long, low whistle. "Damn Wolsey, that must be his idea. He's the one who wants to cozy up to the French. I didn't think about that. And he's had the French ambassador here looking the princess over, listening to her play her music. You're right, George. If Wolsey gets Mary married to a French prince, Henry will move heaven and earth *not* to have her come to the throne. The thought of a Frenchman ruling England would make him turn over in his grave."

"Doesn't want a Spaniard ruling in Mary's name either," George Boleyn pointed out, then looked at Denoriel. "You did us all a favor, Denno."

Denoriel shook his head. "I only wanted to protect the boy. I've got quite fond of him."

"He's a nice boy," George Boleyn repeated, "but there's no reason you shouldn't profit a bit from being a hero." He poked Francis Bryan who was nodding off in his corner of the carriage. "We're going boating with Henry tomorrow, aren't we, Francis? Don't you think the king ought to know *exactly* what happened?"

"Norfolk'll have to report it," Bryan mumbled. "Sounds to me as if half the servants and guards at Windsor know."

"Wake up, Francis!" Boleyn said, poking him again. "Of course Norfolk will report the attack, but how much credit do you think Denno will get for the rescue, eh?"

"Please," Denoriel said, "I don't need any credit. Especially if it will annoy Norfolk. I've . . . ah . . . made a friend quite close to Windsor, and it suits me very well to be able to claim I've come to the area to visit Richmond."

"A friend eh? Now who—"

"Oh, no," Denoriel said, forcing a laugh as the coachman slowed the horses when they passed St. Thomas's. "No guesses about my friend. Luckily here is where I leave you. Thank you for the ride, Francis. And for heaven's sake *don't* come calling or send messages before noon. I won't be awake."

He slipped out of the carriage before they could protest, and gave the coachman a signal to move on. And he managed to walk indolently toward his door trying to look tired and just a little drunk, in case they looked back at him. Inside he galloped right through a large reception room into a smaller, more private sitting room behind it. This had a discreet door at the back, almost invisible in the paneled wall, which was locked by magic. It swung open under his hand into a handsome, if small, stable with two stalls and a tack room.

That door was also locked by magic, and the side wall of the room was bare wood. Denoriel walked right through it, caught his breath, and was at the Gate in Elfhame Logres. A mental cry brought Miralys and he leapt into the saddle, picturing the exit Gate at Windsor.

Sensing his need, the elvensteed covered the mile to Windsor in moments, and Denoriel dismounted at the postern gate, opened the magic lock, and entered the garden with the pond. Miralys took himself to the copse right across the road to wait. Denoriel did not bother to waste magic on changing his clothing. He was dressed lavishly for the embassy affair and he did not expect to be seen anyway. As he ran through the garden, he gathered what power he could from the general ambience, hoping he would not need to sear his channels with the mortal world ley lines.

At the gate to the pond garden, Denoriel paused and looked toward the palace. Two guards stood at the door. Denoriel cast the Don't-see-me spell and ran across the lawn to the place between the towers where the magicked window was. He climbed up, went through the window, and walked very softly out of that room and into the corridor.

There were two guards at Harry's door and both of them were wide awake. Denoriel sighed. He was glad and also annoyed. It would be necessary to put both guards to sleep because the Don't-see-me spell was not enough. If the door to Harry's apartment opened the guards were sure to raise an alarm, even if they didn't see him. The spell did permit him to walk right up to them, murmur the sleep spell under his breath, and touch each. He left them rigid as ramrods, standing at their posts although they saw and heard nothing. If anyone should pass in the hall, all would seem well . . . provided no one spoke to them and expected an answer.

Another two guards inside the room. Both turned toward the opening door and leveled halberds. Denoriel closed the door behind him, holding his breath, hoping they would think someone had opened the door, looked in, seen the threat and closed the door again.

"Who was that?" one whispered to the other.

"Don't know. Didn't see anyone."

Denoriel stood still, breathing as silently as possible. The guards lifted the halberds to rest, and Denoriel's hopes rose, but he had rejoiced too soon.

"I don't like that," the first guard said. "Nyle, go over

and stand in front of the bedroom door. I'm going to ask Gerrit whether he opened the door and why."

That did it. Denoriel invoked the sleep spell and touched the guard just as he reached for the door. He covered the room in three long leaps and touched the second man before he realized it was taking a long time for the first to open the door. Then he had to cling to the doorframe to keep from falling. He was freezing and utterly hollow inside, drained so far that it was an effort to breathe. His vision was fading, but bright against the gray of dimming sight was a brilliant thread. Denoriel reached, drank it down, welcoming the searing shock.

CHAPTER 9

Once Denoriel had made sure that the nurse would not wake, he approached the bed. Halfway there, he had to grit his teeth to force himself close enough to lift the bedcurtain. On the boy, the cross seemed to have even more power. He dared not touch Harry, but called softly to him until the boy turned and then sat up in the bed.

"Put the cross into the pouch," he whispered. "The cold iron hurts me."

Rubbing his eyes, but unquestioning, the boy did as he was told. For some reason that made Denoriel's guts lurch, but he didn't try to examine his anxiety at the moment. His mind was fixed on the unpleasant explanations he had to make. He dreaded telling the child about the need to wear the cross all the time and only put it into its pouch when he himself was near. But as soon as he said that, Harry looked at him with eyes that seemed much older than six and nodded. It was amazingly easy to explain about the use of the Iron Cross to FitzRoy.

"Evil fairies," he said. "I know about evil fairies.

157

They're in all the stories too. As soon as Norfolk gave
me the cross and said you had sent it, I knew. Do
you think . . . is it because my father wants to make
me his heir that the evil fairies are interested in me?
Princes always have trouble with evil fairies and
magicians."

"Likely," Denoriel said. He wouldn't lie to the boy.

Harry sighed. "I hope I never get to be a prince.
But even if I do, you'll take care of me, won't you Lord
Denno?"

"I'll do my best," Denoriel promised. "But you've
got to watch out for yourself too. You have to wear
the cross—you can wear it under your clothes so no
one will ask why you're wearing an old iron cross every
day. The only time you put it in the pouch is when
I'm with you . . ."

As he said the words, Denoriel suddenly realized
why his bowels had knotted when without a doubt
Harry had put his cross away at his request. With a
feeling of sick helplessness he saw that Harry's knowing
him might be a fatal trap. His half-brother Pasgen
looked enough like him to be a twin. That semblance
could get Pasgen past the guards at the palace gate,
and Harry's own guards would be relaxed and careless.

Unfortunately Pasgen was a tool of Vidal Dhu.
Denoriel did not believe that his half-brother would
harm a child, but at Vidal's order, he would certainly
replace that child with a simulacrum and carry the child
off to Vidal's domain. If Harry saw Pasgen, he would
assume it was Denoriel, put his cross away, and become
completely vulnerable.

"There's one problem," Denoriel said, and then his
voice faltered. He could not say his own brother was
an evil fairy. "Evil fairies can put on a seeming. You
mustn't put your cross away just because someone looks
like me."

Harry's eyes widened and filled with moisture. "If I can't trust you . . ." he quavered.

"That part is easy," Denoriel said, sitting on the bed beside him and giving him a hug. "We'll have a secret signal. Before you put the cross into its pouch, you will say 'Where were you on Tuesday?' and I will say 'At the docks, looking for my ship, *The Nereid*.' "

"But what if it *is* Tuesday?" The boy's eyes had brightened at the idea of playing this game.

"Ah, then we need two more passwords. It's a very good idea to have two or three things to say so people won't hear you ask me the same question each time I come to see you."

"I know. I can say 'Is that a new sword?' and you can say 'No, it's the one I had the day your ship got broken.' "

"That's good, Harry!" Denoriel grinned as he offered the heartfelt praise. "If you ask if the sword is new, someone who doesn't know the game would probably say yes. And saying it was the day the ship got broken . . . Hey-a-day, that's wonderful. Everyone knows about the fight, but the ship getting broken was only important to you."

"One more," the boy said.

"Will you be able to remember them all?"

FitzRoy sighed and screwed up his face. "After all the lessons Master Croke sets me to learn by heart. Yes, I'll remember."

Denoriel laughed. "Ah, yes. I'd forgotten that joy of childhood, learning lessons by rote. So, a third secret exchange . . . hmmm. Ask 'Which horse did you ride today, Lord Denno?' And I'll answer 'I rode Miralys.' I don't think anyone else knows the name of my horse"—Pasgen certainly did not know it—"so that will be safe."

FitzRoy grinned happily and repeated the three exchanges a couple of times. The last time, however, the smile disappeared from his face and his eyes rounded with worry again.

"But what do I do if the answer is wrong?" he asked.

"Leave the cross bare, be sure you stay far enough away so he can't grab you, but don't panic if he does because he'll let go right away—the cross will hurt him and he'll be surprised—and then you can run away."

"But if I run away from you . . . from someone who looks like you . . . I can't tell the guards it was an evil fairy, can I?"

Denoriel laughed. "No, you can't. Even if they didn't laugh, it would make them suspicious of me the next time I came. You can call back that your belly is grinding and you must go to the jakes . . . or any other excuse for leaving quickly. Then send down a message that you don't feel well and don't go out again."

FitzRoy thought that over, his face sober but no longer frightened. Denoriel was saddened. It wasn't right that a child should be so accepting of danger, so prepared to endure it. Mentally he cursed King Henry for endangering his son, and then laughed at himself. If Harry hadn't been involved in the succession, he would never have met the child. Had it been so short a time that he had railed at being a nursemaid?

"How will I let you know if the evil fairy comes?" the boy asked.

"By Our Lady, what would I do without you, Harry? You've got the wisdom for both of us. A poor fairy guardian I seem to be!"

FitzRoy giggled. "You're a very good fairy guardian— at least I'm sure Master Croke would say so. He is forever telling me I must apply what I learn. You don't do everything for me. You let me think up things for myself." He shook his head. "But I can't think of an answer to that question."

He smiled, glad that he was finally able to think of something else to add to FitzRoy's protections. "Aha! That's where fairy guardians have an advantage. We do have some helpful magic. Do you think your nurse would let you have a mouse as a pet?"

The child blinked at him. "A *mouse*?"

"Don't you like mice? Most boys do."

"*I* like mice, but nurse . . ." He shook his head. "No. Not a mouse. One got into the room and she screamed and screamed, even after it was caught."

Denoriel laid his hand on FitzRoy's shoulder, about to say he could manage the nurse but a dull ache started in his hand. Even shielded, the cold iron troubled him on close contact. He realized the boy had saved him from a serious mistake again—although this time without intending it. If Denoriel had brought a spirit of the air enchanted to look like a mouse and FitzRoy had touched it while wearing the unshielded cross, he might have killed the poor thing.

"All right," he said, "no mice. Do you think I could talk her into a kitten?"

FitzRoy wrinkled his nose again. "Her, sure. She'd like a kitten, but kittens are for girls!"

"That doesn't matter," Denoriel urged. "You won't be able to touch it while you're wearing the cross anyway, so you can pretend it's Nurse's kitten and just has taken to following you around. That will be all right, won't it? Norfolk won't be here tomorrow, so I'll come up to your room and talk to Nurse. I'm sure she'll keep the kitten."

"You're going to magic her, aren't you?"

The boy had a face full of mischief, and Denoriel suddenly had the feeling that he was going to request his nurse be enchanted into allowing him greater freedom. "That's enough of that, young man," he said, trying to look severe when he really wanted to hug the child tight for his quick mind and his courage. "What if someone heard you?"

"But what good will a kitten do?" Harry's eyes were bright with anticipation.

"Kittens can vanish—even quite ordinary kittens disappear whenever you want them for something— and my special kitten can not only vanish but it will be able to find me."

"Magic," the boy breathed, his eyes bright as stars. "But what if the bad fairy comes where I'm not allowed to take the kitten?"

Denoriel raised an eyebrow. "Kittens can get in anywhere. Just pretend not to see it—if you do see it. And tell Mary not to mention it either. Probably Lord Henry won't see it at all."

After a moment FitzRoy nodded and after another moment, he said softly, looking down at his fingers, "I know I'm a duke, and I'm supposed to be very clever and brave and protect my people, but will you give me another hug, Lord Denno?"

Denoriel swallowed and quickly shifted his position on the bed so that he could pull the child into his arms. He held the boy very tight for a moment and then loosened his grip but continued to hold the child against his shoulder, ignoring the ache the cold iron started in his bone and muscle. His throat was tight with tears. He knew FitzRoy was well cared for, but did anyone ever hold him, tell him he was loved? The nurse probably loved him dearly, but she probably also believed it would be presumptuous of her to tell her high-born charge that she loved him.

"I love you, Harry," Denoriel whispered.

His vision blurred. Holding the boy was almost like having a child of his own—a joy he would likely never know. His arms tightened and he kissed the child's silky hair.

It was as if the boy melted into his arms. FitzRoy rubbed his face against Denoriel's chest, sniffled a little, then sighed. Denoriel stroked his hair and, although the mage channels in his body burned and throbbed, he whispered a small spell of easy sleep and sweet dreams. But even when he knew Harry was asleep, he could not let go of the child. He himself almost fell into the resting state that served the Sidhe for sleep, holding the warm little body, but finally he stirred. He still had much to do if he was to finish the protections for FitzRoy.

He laid the boy down, broke the spell he had put on the nurse, restored the Don't-see-me spell on himself and stepped out into FitzRoy's sitting room. The guards still stood where he had left them, one guarding FitzRoy's bedroom door and the other just about to reach for the handle on the door to the corridor.

Although his mage channels were already raw and sore, Denoriel sought and found another ley line. Lightning coursed through him when he drew the power, and he bit a bloody gash in his lower lip to hold back a cry of pain. If only the Sidhe could endure the ravages of the magic of Overhill, they could be as strong in the mortal world as Underhill.

Strength had flowed through him with the pain, but he could not use it at first for it was almost as painful to use Overhill power as to drink it in. He thought it was worse this time than it had been the last. A sane elf would forget that power existed. Denoriel sighed. He could not chance that his strength would fail and his nighttime visit to Harry be exposed.

When he was steady, he opened the door to the corridor and stepped out, leaning back into the room to break the sleep spell on the guard near the bedroom door. As that guard blinked, he closed the door enough so that the hand of the guard reaching for the door just touched the handle. Quickly he touched both the outer door guards as he stepped between them to the other side of the corridor.

The door opened all the way. The inner room guard leaned out, saying, "Gerrit, did you open this door a couple of minutes ago?"

The man called Gerrit looked puzzled. "Of course not. Why would I . . ." He cocked his head. "Hmmm. I thought I heard a noise just before. Maybe I did open the door and look in."

"Good! That's a relief. I could swear I saw the door open, but no one came in. Right. Keep alert."

Denoriel sighed gently with relief and made his way to the room of the magicked window, then out the window and down the wall, across the garden, and out of the postern gate. Miralys, having sensed him coming, was waiting right there. And then they were in the copse at the crossroad and through the Gate where Denoriel chose the pattern that would take them to Elfhame Avalon.

The guards at Avalon Gate looked amazed at his finery, but the cold prickle of the identity spell acknowledged him. He asked if Aleneil had left and was told that she had not. In moments Miralys had him at his sister's door, and she was opening it as he dismounted, her eyes wide with worry. He realized then that it wasn't just his clothing that made the guards stare, it was the way he looked—exhausted at the least, and possibly in pain. One did not often see a Sidhe in pain Underhill.

"Are you hurt, Denoriel?" she cried the moment she saw him.

"No. Yes." He shook his head. "Oh, not seriously, I believe. I am just weary and aching from using Overhill power."

"Overhill power?" She stared at him, dumbfounded. "There is virtually no power in the mortal world."

Denoriel blinked. "Yes there is. You don't see it?"

She had backed away while he spoke to let him through the door and now she shut it behind him and gestured him through into her sitting room. Denoriel dropped into his favorite chair beside the settle; the luminous blue-green cushions reflected the delicate mother-of-pearl design and together seemed to cool and soothe his aching body.

"I never looked, and I am not so often in the mortal world as you."

"Most of the power is like a thin soup, but there are these bright lines within the soup and those . . ." He made a sound like someone who has taken a too-hot mouthful. Then he frowned. "I think they may be dangerous, and more dangerous the more you use them. I hurt more this time, and Underhill has not soothed me as well. I think I will have to go to Mwynwen. But that can wait. I must finish the protections for FitzRoy."

"Denoriel," she said very softly. "Do not . . . love him."

Denoriel looked down at his own long fingers, winding together. "It's too late," he murmured. "I held him in my arms, like my own child . . ."

She bit her lip. "That way lies only grief. An elf-child is forever, or nearly forever. A mortal is like the flower of a brief summer, he blossoms and is beautiful . . . and dies. Save only if he is brought here and kept here, with us, and that—you cannot do. He is the mortal king's son. To bring him here would be impossible."

There was a silence, after which Denoriel said, "I know, but right now my purpose is to keep him from being abducted and held prisoner in the Unseleighe Court."

She sighed. "I thought the cross would protect him from that."

"If FitzRoy is not befooled into covering it," he said doubtfully.

He told her quickly about visiting FitzRoy to explain about always wearing the cold iron cross unshielded, except when he was there, and his sudden realization of how easily Pasgen could be mistaken for him. He explained, too, the device they would use for recognition.

"But it is not enough," he said. "I think we need to know if an attempt is made to abduct the boy, and I cannot be there all the time. We need a messenger that can be disguised as a pet—I thought a kitten, a very elegant one who would wear a silver collar. Kittens are very clever about hiding, and it would be large enough and strong enough to follow the boy around without being carried."

Aleneil nodded slowly. "An air elemental would be best. They do not need Gates and they are merry-spirited."

"Also flitter-witted," Denoriel said dryly. "How long do you think an air spirit would stay with the boy?"

"Oh, I will put a spell in the collar that will keep it steady, and of course I will use one of the more sober ones and gain its interest and approval." She looked at Denoriel and shook her head. "Enough. You are starting to look transparent. Go to Mwynwen and let her heal you. I will let you know when the kitten is ready, and you can Gate to the proper time."

"No," Denoriel said, "I must go back and keep watch."

"For what?" Aleneil protested. "You say the attack on FitzRoy was not from the Unseleighe Court. We are not even sure they are aware of the boy."

"Yes, they are!" He explained about the Watch finding the attackers, one mindless and the other dead, on the front steps of the magician's house. "That can only mean someone stripped their minds to discover all they knew about Harry. They will build a simulacrum, abduct the boy, and leave the changeling in his place."

She was getting annoyed with him, something that rarely happened. "But what good can you do, exhausted and hurt as you are? I will find the proper air spirit and build the collar and the spell. Whatever they do in the time that takes will not matter because you will Gate back to before they acted."

"That doesn't help. You know it doesn't help. If I change the circumstances to prevent what they did, they will do something different, but the end result will be the same. I must go back at once!" he said, feeling tension building unbearably within him. "I cannot bear the thought of Harry held by Vidal Dhu."

"Denno," Aleneil cried.

In her distress she used the name of their childhood when she could not form all the syllables of Denoriel, but he only shook his head and levered himself out of the chair. The truth was that Denoriel did not know what he could do to prevent Pasgen from seizing Harry; in fact he could not imagine any way his half-brother could make the exchange of simulacrum for boy. However, he knew he could sense the presence of magic as Harry's guards could not and be prepared to protect the boy when they would not know he needed protection. He would do *something*.

Passage through the Gates seemed a bit more disorienting than usual, but Miralys carried him safely to Windsor. Denoriel was able to open the magicked postern gate, cast the Don't-see-me spell, and make sure that Harry was Harry by the simple expedient of being unable to approach the boy closer than about two feet. That meant he was wearing the iron cross.

He was safe with Henry and Mary Howard and with his guards still close and alert, so Denoriel was free to make a round of the palace and the grounds where he could detect no Underhill influence.

At dusk, something did try to enter with a dark-clad messenger, but the crossed halberds of the gate guards—meant only to stop the messenger until he identified himself—drove it away. It was a harmless thing and nearly mindless, only meant to record what it saw and heard, so Denoriel did not pursue it. What it had seen and felt was just the information Denoriel wanted the Unseleighe Court to have—that Windsor was closely guarded. He followed the messenger into the palace, but the man only delivered his sealed packet to the steward and departed promptly.

Denoriel was now certain he did not dare leave Windsor, but he was growing more and more uncertain of his ability to protect Harry. The constant use of the Don't-see-me spell was draining him and the use of even that very small amount of magic was increasing the pain in his power channels. However, if what accompanied the dark-clad messenger had been an Unseleighe Sidhe and not a lesser thing, it would not have been driven away by the halberds. He shuddered, leaning against one of the trees that lined the long avenue, at the thought of confronting an Unseleighe Sidhe. But if he had to drink lightning again, he would, rather than risk Harry.

At full dark he abandoned the gate. When Norfolk was not in residence the gates were all locked at night and no one was permitted to enter. No matter how urgent the message, there was no one in Windsor with the power to act. Denoriel had realized he could not patrol all the walls. If something came over them, he could not stop it. The best place for him to be through the night was with Harry.

It was easy enough for Denoriel to get into the palace when the doors were opened for servants. He wandered through the many chambers and corridors, feeling for magic, but all he sensed was his own work on the window of the chamber near Harry's apartment.

His timing was good. Denoriel flattened himself against the corridor wall. Harry was just coming along with Henry and Mary and his guards to have his bread and milk and go to bed. He watched the children say their good-nights, and then followed the guard called Nyle into the outer room. The nurse was there, just pouring warmed milk into a bowl and crumbling in some soft, white bread. She smiled when the boy came in and asked some question about his day's activity, but she did not give him a welcoming kiss or smooth back his hair as a mother might have done . . . as Denoriel would have done, if he could have touched the boy.

He slipped into the bedchamber when the guard opened the door and watched, standing in a safe corner where no one would run into him, until the child was settled in his bed. When the nurse had finished her nightly chores, pulled out her trundle bed, and settled herself to sleep, Denoriel sank into a chair to watch and wait. He tried to rest but could not, partly because of the need to sense for magic and partly because, even this far from Harry, the ache of cold iron froze his bones. After a few hours, he moved the chair further from the bed.

The sun was just rising when a fluffy white kitten suddenly appeared in his lap. "Ah, you found me," he whispered.

:Found. Always find. Boy?:

Denoriel carried the kitten closer to the bed, but paused when it began to squirm in his arms and merely reached out to pull the bedcurtain aside so the spirit could see FitzRoy.

:*Why hurt?*:

"He must wear a cold iron cross to prevent any Unseleighe creature from touching him." Denoriel smiled. "The cross doesn't hurt him. He's mortal." He dropped the bedcurtain and moved away. "You don't have to go near him, only follow him and watch for any Unseleighe being—or any Sidhe. If you sense *any* Sidhe, come for me." After all, *he* had been assigned at Oberon's orders to guard this boy. There was no reason for any other Sidhe to come near Harry.

Most of the time it was not easy for the lesser creatures of Underhill to determine whether an elf was dark or light. The magic of the guardians of the Gates in Elfhame Avalon could identify the Unseleighe, but Denoriel doubted that the spirit of the air could do so. It did not matter. No other Sidhe of the Seleighe Court was involved with FitzRoy and if someone who was merely curious came, he wanted to be here to make sure no harm was done by carelessness.

Relief followed by more anxiety swept over Denoriel. The more sensible part of him told him all that was left for him to do was to deliver the kitten. Deep within cold fear lingered. Those men's minds had not been racked apart without purpose—and that purpose was to build a changeling to replace Harry FitzRoy. Denoriel found himself trembling so violently he had to sit down and fight to control the pain that tore at him. *Fool*, he said to himself, *what protection could you give the child weak and nearly blind with pain as you are*.

So he waited impatiently for the sun to rise, for the nurse and the guards to take up their morning duties and move around so he could get out. He told himself over and over that it was impossible for anyone to abduct Harry any time during the morning. His schedule was too fixed and he was continuously in the company of many besides his guards. Henry and Mary would be with him as well as Master Croke, his tutor, who knew of the attack and was no fool. Denoriel slipped away when the night and day guards exchanged duties. Miralys was waiting and he had only to Gate to Logres.

A good meal and a few hours of rest Underhill restored him enough to look like his usual self when he arrived openly at the main gate of the palace in late morning, carrying a large wicker basket. Although the gate guards were about to let him pass, he opened one of the wooden flaps that closed the basket to show the fluffy white kitten.

"For the nurse," he said. "She is still sadly shaken and reluctant to allow poor Richmond to go out at all. That is bad for the boy and reminds him of the attack on him. I hope the little animal will divert her attention. But do pass the word so if anyone sees the kitten they won't put it out of palace grounds."

Not that being put out would have kept the air spirit out, but Denoriel did not want any attention fixed on the seeming animal. If it were known to be a resident of the palace and free of the grounds, no one would notice it and remember its doings or talk about them. The last thing Denoriel wanted was for his half-brother to learn from gossip that an animal with strange abilities was following Harry around.

He was still hero enough in the guard's eyes to gain instant agreement and he rode on to the stable where he put Miralys in a stall. The stable boys were aware of the horse's supposed foul temper and would leave the elvensteed alone. The house guards also welcomed him, but told him he was too early and that Richmond was still with his tutor.

Denoriel nodded, and said he knew it, that he had come with a present for the boy's nurse. He showed the kitten, which now opened its blue eyes and stared at the guards, and he asked them not to lock it out if it got outside. Both laughed and agreed that it did not seem to be much of a threat and promised not to bar its entrance.

"And I hope it catches any mice that get into His Grace's rooms," one said. "Last time that nurse nearly screamed the whole building down. She'll like to have a kitten as long as His Grace of Norfolk don't object."

Denoriel smiled. "I think I have credit enough still to gain permission for her to keep a kitten. And it will not be here very long. Do you not move to Yorkshire soon?"

"Don't know if we're goin', milord. His Grace keeps his own council."

He nodded sympathetically and moved across the entrance toward the stair. The men returned their attention to the outer paths to the door. His interview with the nurse about the kitten was very short indeed. She welcomed the advent of the little animal and accepted without any question his assertion that he had brought it because FitzRoy had told him of her fear of mice.

Having to brace his body against a shudder of pain when he reinforced the small spell that would keep her from ever questioning FitzRoy's wearing of the cold iron cross, was a reminder of his vulnerability. He settled deeper into his chair, ostensibly to wait for FitzRoy but really because he was not sure he could stand. However he soon realized he could make use of his weakness, and began to extract from the nurse all the information she had about when they would leave for Yorkshire and how they would travel.

She did not yet have a definite date for their departure or certain information about who would be in charge of the move, but he did learn enough to be able to plan arrangements to meet with his northern factor at a time when it would be most safe and convenient for him to travel with FitzRoy's party. He had a whole variety of excuses. It was cooler in the north in July. He wished to examine the flocks himself so he could fix a price in advance. He would be carrying gold to seal his bargains and would need the protection of the boy's guards.

To his delight, when FitzRoy returned to his room for a nuncheon after his lessons, the boy said accusingly to Denoriel, "Where were you on Tuesday, Lord Denno? I thought you were coming to see me then."

"I was down at the docks, looking for my ship, *The Nereid*," Denoriel replied. "Did I forget to tell you that His Grace of Norfolk is interested in my carpets? I thought if the ship was in, I could bring some for him to look at, but it hasn't arrived."

"Business," FitzRoy said with a sniff, turning away so he could slip the cross into its pouch. When he turned back he added, "Power is in the land, Master Croke says."

"Yes, Your Grace," Denoriel agreed, laughing, "but money can buy land . . . and power."

"Look, Your Grace," the nurse put in, pointing to the basket in a safe corner, "Lord Denno brought me a kitten to keep away the mice."

The little white cat obligingly popped its head over the edge of the basket, but came no nearer. FitzRoy looked at it and then up at Denoriel; there was a darkness behind his eyes. Denoriel understood. The boy thought that having his guard in place, Denoriel would leave him in its care.

"Kittens are for girls," Harry said.

The nurse laughed. "I'm a girl," she said. "And since he was so kind as to bring me a present, would you like to invite Lord Denno to have a nuncheon with you?"

"Yes!" FitzRoy exclaimed, his eyes lightening a little. "Can you stay, Lord Denno?"

It was an effort for Denoriel not to groan aloud. His nearness to the cold iron, even for only a few minutes, was still an icy pain in his bones, in his gut, everywhere under his skin—except where his power channels burned and throbbed. He needed to get to Mwynwen, but he could not let Harry think he would be abandoned.

Denoriel nodded, trying to reassure the boy that there would be more hugs, more assurances of affection, when they were alone. But all he could say in the nurse's presence was, "Until dusk, at least. I have promised to visit a friend in this area tonight, but I am free until then. Shall we go out into the garden?"

"No," Harry said, "let's stay here. We can play some games—and, and it looks like rain."

Denoriel did not think it looked like rain. He thought Harry just did not want to share his company with the other children. He suspected that Harry had had some sad experiences as assigned guardians of whom he had become fond were transferred to other duties. He could not tell the poor child that fairy guardians could not be reassigned—because, well, he was there to protect Harry because there really *was* danger, and Denoriel might be hurt and another sent in his place. If he were forced into a confrontation with Pasgen or some other denizen of the Unseleighe Court, he might be long in healing.

The nurse had this and that to do in the bedchamber so there were times when he and Harry were alone except for the guards. Sotto voce, Denoriel promised that the kitten was only an extra safety factor, that Lord Denno would visit as often as Norfolk would permit. And once, when Harry made a very clever move in the game of backgammon they were playing while the nurse was in the bedchamber, he was able to lean across and say, "I *do* love you, as if you were my own little brother, Harry. I'll not desert you, and I shall come whenever I can."

The child lit up like a stage at performance time, and the assurances seemed to have taken hold. When Denoriel finally rose to go as the light started to fail, FitzRoy saw him off with a cheerful wave, to the evident satisfaction of the nurse.

However, the extra hours in close proximity to the cold iron, even shielded, had done him no good. Denoriel needed all the power of his will to move with his usual grace instead of creeping about bent and trembling like an old man. Fortunately once he was astride Miralys he needed to make no further effort. The elvensteed took him directly to Mwynwen where he fell off his mount into the healer's arms, barely conscious.

Later—he did not know how much later—Denoriel became fully aware. "The spirit!" he cried. "Did the spirit come for me, the little white kitten?"

"No one came for you," Mwynwen snapped. "And I would like to know what you think you could have done in the state you were?"

Denoriel sat up in bed and breathed . . . without pain! Of course, that was not all Mwynwen had to say.

No, indeed, she had quite a bit to say on the subject of how he had abused his body. At length, and in detail, truly leaving him with his metaphorical tail between his legs and his ears pinned back. Still, he considered the cost of a sound scolding a cheap enough price for Mwynwen to draw the ache of cold iron from his body.

The searing of his power channels, however, was to prove more difficult to remedy than his exhaustion.

And it took longer than he liked.

For one thing, Mwynwen had never seen—or rather,

felt—the condition before, and withdrew from him in haste when she touched the burning pain. For another, Denoriel was unable to describe exactly what he had done to absorb the power or what it was like, beyond telling her it was like being struck by lightning. She persuaded him to remain with her for another day or so only with the greatest of difficulty.

Finally she consulted one of the oldest healers, one who had helped in the founding of Elfhame Logres, and loved her work so much she was not tempted to drift away into Dreaming. Ceindrych remembered when the Magus Majors who had built the domain out of the chaos of the unformed drew too hard and fast on their power and that of Underhill and burnt themselves. From her Mwynwen learned the techniques and spells for restoring burnt power channels.

But even so, the healing took time and Denoriel did not feel that he could afford that time. He fought her spells—injuring himself further—so he could visit FitzRoy to be sure the boy was safe, to be sure the kitten had not lost interest and flitted away.

Exasperated, Mwynwen bespelled his anxiety to subside. It was stupid, she thought, for him to delay his recovery by constant fear. If the air spirit brought word that Denoriel was needed, she would break the spell. Until then, she would keep him with her.

They enjoyed each other's company . . . yet it was not the same as it had been between them before Denoriel had taken on his mission to the mortal world. He found that the light gossip about dress and changing relationships within the Elfhame, the news of minor outrages committed by the Unseleighe and the plans to punish and prevent further mischief, no longer had the power to bind his attention. Despite Mwynwen's spell, although with lesser intensity, he worried about Harry and longed to hold the child again.

Although Mwynwen warned him even more straitly than Aleneil of the danger of caring for a mortal, she could not resist listening hungrily to his descriptions of the boy. She even shared his anxiety about keeping FitzRoy safe and suggested warding spells he could use. However, it was only the child that interested her, and nothing else in the world of mortals. Beyond asking Denoriel to be sure to record any healing spell he came across, Mwynwen found the doings of humans coarse and dull.

But even Denoriel's delight in Mwynwen could not now diminish his interest in life in the mortal world. At first what he had done had only been to give verisimilitude to his cover story about a great trading empire. Thus, he had purchased a ship and trade goods through his connection with Elfhame Csetate-Boli. Through Elfhame Melusine, he had hired factors in France. In England, he had personally hired factors, sold a cargo, considered what new cargo to purchase for trade through connections he was making with Elfhames near Persia and India where rugs and tapestries such as he had discussed with Norfolk were made. He was immersing himself more and more in the affairs of mortal men.

And so, inevitably it seemed, distance began to come between Denoriel and Mwynwen—not a coolness; they were still fond, the union of their bodies still brought joy to each, but neither was so absorbed in the other as he and she had been in the past. And one day, Mwynwen did not protest when Denoriel said he must go and visit Harry. Partly that was because she had done all she could and Denoriel was almost totally recovered, but partly it was because she felt just the faintest shade of relief to hear no more about Overhill and be alone in her house again.

Before he left, Mwynwen warned Denoriel that his

fear about the use of Overhill magic had been correct.
He could use it, but he would suffer for it, and the
more he used it, the longer and more uncertain his
healing would be. At best he would be in considerable
pain for a long time—at worst he would burn out his
power channels and be dead to magic, even
Underhill—perhaps he would even be reduced to a
mortal.

Even so, just before he turned to go out the door
to mount Miralys, who was waiting, she put a hand on
his arm and bade him bring her news of FitzRoy—
so sweet a child, she said, longing in her eyes, for with
all her lovers and all her healing powers she had never
conceived. Then she broke the spell that had dulled
Denoriel's fear.

Terror seized him again and anger too as he realized what she had done. Denoriel hardly thanked her
for her care. He was free of physical pain and able to
use magic again without agony, but his anxiety for
FitzRoy tightened his throat and knotted his gut. He
remembered that he had checked on the spirit of the
air, but had he checked often enough? Had some
Unseleighe Sidhe deflected or even destroyed the white
kitten? There was no time Underhill. Had the boy felt
he was forgotten? *How long had he been under
Mwynwen's care?*

CHAPTER 10

All that anxiety, all that terror, and nothing at all had happened! In its abbreviated manner, the kitten reported that there had been no manifestations of Unseleighe magic in the palace or the grounds and no Sidhe had paid any visit in any guise.

To Denoriel's horror, that news only intensified his fear. It was impossible that human questioning had rendered the men who attacked Harry mindless and dead without a single mark on their bodies. That was Sidhe work. Unless he was mad, Harry was somehow the target of that work.

He was relieved when he found that only a bit over two weeks had passed in mortal days. And he calmed down when it finally occurred to him that a really good simulacrum was just not that easy to make. Possibly the changeling was not yet ready, and that was why the kitten had nothing to report.

Fortunately, he was still *persona gratia* with the guards, officials, and servants of Windsor, and he had no trouble being admitted to visit. Harry was delighted to see him, but not resentful or forlorn at Lord Denno's extended absence, because the child had been distracted by the preparations for going north, which were now in full swing. The boy was perfectly willing to accept Denoriel's excuse that he, too, had been making preparations so that he could accompany the cortege. Harry jumped up and down with joy.

Since Norfolk continued to be absent on some other duty, Denoriel took the liberty of coming to visit FitzRoy every day. He had been nervously sure that the child was being watched by someone from the Unseleighe Court, although he could not get the faintest hint of any dark creature—nor could the white kitten. Still, the time for completing the most elaborate simulacrum was surely over and Denoriel hourly expected some new move on the part of the minions of Vidal Dhu.

After a few more days, Denoriel began to suspect that Pasgen—or whoever was assigned to try to seize FitzRoy—was prepared to wait for him to give up his watchfulness. In an effort to trigger an attempt on the child while he was alert for it, Denoriel explained to FitzRoy that a ship (not *The Nereid*) had come in and he had to be away for a few days. He rode off to London, Gated back, shielded his magic and himself, and waited. And still nothing happened.

Did the Unseleighe believe that it would be easier to make the exchange of children during the confusion of the journey north? That really raised a problem and made it essential that Denoriel accompany the cortege and be in close attendance on the child. For that, he would need to obtain Norfolk's permission.

The duke was still absent, but Denoriel had heard that he would return to Windsor after the twenty-second of July, when FitzRoy would receive a commission as Warden General of Scotland. Norfolk would then examine the preparations for travel, probably the Privy Council that would actually govern in FitzRoy's name would gather, and within a week FitzRoy would go north to Sheriff Hutton. Until they left, it would be impossible for Denoriel to spend much time with FitzRoy. The duke disliked any suggestion of FitzRoy's steadily increasing attachment to a foreigner; if he knew the truth of things, Denoriel would never be allowed near FitzRoy again.

Denoriel set about laying a fog of misinformation around himself. He made his visits briefer and openly arrived in the late afternoon so he could seem to go somewhere else in the early evening. Actually he came soon about the time FitzRoy ate his nuncheon and remained concealed about the palace for most of the day. He hinted to guards and nurse that he was in the throes of a love affair, trying to fix his interest with his lady before he had to travel north on business. The nurse and the guards believed FitzRoy was serving as Lord Denno's excuse for being in the area, in order to see his imaginary light-o'-love. They smiled and covertly promised not to mention his frequent visits to the duke of Norfolk unless specifically asked.

Meanwhile Denoriel had stolen some morning time, when he was sure Harry was safe—making doubly sure by the device of Gating back to Windsor shortly after he had left it—to visit Aleneil. He needed to enlist her help in obtaining servants who would be able to live in his London house while he was gone. Low Court elves, if he could establish a Node in his garden, and if they could bear the amount of iron in the house, would be ideal.

Aleneil was very relieved to see him well again and satisfied by his report about the air spirit attending to its duty. She suggested he send the little creature back while he was with FitzRoy to have its spell reinforced, and said she thought she would be able to shield the Low Court elven servants so that they would be comfortable.

"Will I need to teach them English or French?" she asked as an afterthought.

Denoriel thought a moment and then smiled. "No. Let them use Elven, and we'll let it be thought that they are from Lord Denno's native country. If I ever come across anyone who can speak Hungarian, I'll say they speak an obscure mountain dialect. That will ensure that the servants can't tell my visitors, who I'll stake high odds are curious as monkeys, anything at all."

Aleneil sighed. "Alas, I fear that is the only way to keep them from chattering. They are curious as cats, addicted to gossip, and I dare swear, only a little less flitter-minded than children."

"Ha," he replied. "They aren't the only creatures as curious as cats and as gossipy as any old woman. Boleyn and the others have been asking how I was managing in a house with no servants and offering to find staff for me so I could give entertainments and live in comfort. I told him I was waiting for my own people to come from Hungary." He laughed. "I'll teach them just enough English to say 'Wait here,' 'Master will see you now,' 'Master gone away. Leave message?' and they'll have to understand when the guests order wine or ale."

"Only women?" Aleneil asked. "Won't that rouse some nasty suspicions? I think you ought to have at least as many menservants. I know I can find enough who have magic sufficient to keep mortal guises on themselves."

"Oh, can you? Good." That was a relief; the Low Court elves had varying abilities with magic, but none of them could ken and replicate objects without a great deal of effort, and not all could hold a *glamorie* upon themselves for any length of time. "If you can find enough who wish to help, I'll be glad to have . . . ah, four men and four girls. A couple will have to be in the house all the time, but the others can Gate back and forth to Logres through the Gate in the tack room." It wouldn't matter that the faces would change; the elves playing servant would never leave the house, and he knew from experience that nobles and the wealthy never noticed the faces of those who served them.

"That makes things easy, but didn't you say you were going to ride north with FitzRoy's cortege?" his sister asked, with a frown. "Won't it look funny if you ride alone?"

"It will, but I can't take Low Court elves so far from their home trees. I suppose I'll have to take Boleyn's or Bryan's offer of a couple of menservants. I hate to do it. Their loyalty will be to Boleyn or Bryan, and if they see odd things . . ."

"Don't do that yet," Aleneil said. "Let me ask around the High Court. It seems to me that I heard there were some children grown who wanted to go back to the mortal world, or at least, to try. You would be the ideal intermediary between life Underhill and that much harsher life. And they could come back Underhill with you if they felt they could not bear the filth and crudity."

She would bring the servants, she assured him, and explain their duties to them. And she would teach them the phrases he had suggested as well as how to say "Don't speak English. Pardon, please."

He in turn taught her the pattern in the small Gate in Logres that would take her direct to the tack room in the stable of his London house and he gave her a spell to open the magic-locked doors that would let her into the house. Then he Gated back to Windsor, his heart in his mouth . . . but nothing had happened in his absence.

Norfolk returned. Denoriel made sure not to be visibly in Windsor that day although he skulked around after FitzRoy under the Don't-see-me spell. Once the boy was in bed, while the kitten (spell renewed) kept carefully watchful guard in the boy's room, he went Underhill to restore himself, anxious but realizing how foolish he had been to render himself helpless.

The next morning, when Harry was still at his lessons, he arrived at Windsor with a baggage mule carrying five exquisite Turkey carpets, *The Nereid* having arrived safely on the fifth of July. Of course, if the ship had not come in, Denoriel would have asked Jenci Moricz to obtain carpets and Gate them through from Elfhame Csetate-Boli, but he was glad the ship was there and the whole cargo in a rented warehouse.

It was Norfolk he asked to see, telling the steward that he had with him the Turkey carpets in which the duke had expressed an interest. He was admitted to Norfolk's presence promptly and he was unsurprised but gratified by the duke's pleased astonishment over the quality of the carpets.

Denoriel then explained his notion of having rugs of similar patterns made of English wool, which would considerably reduce the cost. Norfolk received that information with enthusiasm, since it meant another market for English wool. But, Denoriel said, he had not been able to explain to his factors exactly what he needed in the fleece. He would have to travel north and see the flocks himself, and when he found what he wanted, he would like to set a price in advance and pay part of the price to bind the deal. That meant, he added, that he would be carrying a substantial amount of gold and silver. He had no private army of retainers. Could he travel north with His Grace of Richmond's cortege?

With his eyes on the carpets, Norfolk agreed without the slightest hesitation. Then Denoriel thanked him, but not nearly with the relief he actually felt, and offered the five carpets as a gift of thanks. Norfolk demurred, protesting over the value of such a gift . . . which might be taken as a bribe.

"For what?" Denoriel asked, gesturing negation. "What have you to offer me, other than the safety of your guards on my way north? I have no political aims, no desire for any royal appointment, certainly no wish to evade importation fees or duties, nothing to ask of you as an official of the realm. But I do have many more rugs to sell, and giving these to you will be of great profit to my man of business—I hope. I hope you will be willing to display them where guests and those who come to you on business will see them. And when they ask where you came by such beautiful carpets . . . I hope you will speak the truth and send them to my man of Siencyn Adorjan—that is the name of my business enterprise—to buy carpets of their own."

"Well," said Norfolk, after a moment of thought. "They are a gentlemanly, a princely gift. And I can see no conflict in accepting them—"

"Even my man of business is one of your own English," Denoriel assured him. "For I have him upon my good friend Boleyn's direction."

"George Boleyn?" Norfolk's brow cleared. "A good choice. And you have my thanks, Lord Denno."

Now Denoriel had yet another reason to be grateful for his acquaintance with the young Boleyn—that card in a pocket in his elegant doublet, carefully inscribed with the name and direction: on Watling Street, west of St. Thomas's Church. *Ah*, he thought, *that, at least, was a servant I could accept from Boleyn. A superior man of business, who would not think of mixing with the common servants, but will show and sell my rugs and other goods.* Taking the man on freed him from the tainted appearance of being a merchant himself, yet permitted him to have a visible means of support. Now he could play the lordling without having to account for the torrent of money he spent—or, at least, appeared to spend. The thought flitted through his mind as he rose and bowed, signing away Norfolk's renewed thanks as he left.

He did not appear to linger, riding away from Windsor in the direction his "friend" was supposed to live, but he slipped off Miralys at the postern gate and reentered the palace to watch over Harry through another eventless day.

Denoriel's anxiety was almost gone. There were only four days before they began their journey north and he was almost convinced that the attempt would be made while they were traveling. He could not imagine how an exchange could be made, but he intended to ride right beside Harry all the way and watch by his bed all night. Just because nothing had happened yet did not mean that the danger was over. But the longer an attempt was put off, the more difficult it would be for it to succeed.

The next morning he was able to examine and make sure the servants Aleneil had brought would be able to care for his house and carry on while he was gone. He liked the Low Court fay that she had chosen, for they seemed steadier than most of their kind, though they did look upon all of this sojourning Overhill as some sort of grand adventure. Still, they were willing and intelligent, and Aleneil promised to return periodically while he was away to continue their training.

He gave more time to the three mortals that Aleneil

brought to accompany him on his journey. One, Edward Trace, did not remain a candidate for a retainer very long. He had been taken by the elves after his cruel and drunken father became a toy—and then a dead and broken toy—of the Wild Hunt. Perhaps "taken" was not the right term, for poor Edward had practically been given to the Seleighe Elves of Logres.

When his mother had come looking for the husband she assumed had fallen down drunk again and had found the dead man, she had stared down at the mutilated corpse for a while and then begun to laugh. Finally she went back to the half-collapsed hut which had sheltered them and brought the infant Edward to lay beside the dead body. What had been going through her mind at that moment, no Sidhe could fathom. Perhaps she had been driven mad by her husband's abusive behavior; perhaps she had simply decided that she could not bear to look on the child of a man who had been so cruel to her. Maybe she assumed someone would find the dead man and living child before the latter died of exposure; perhaps she had not thought at all, except that she could not support herself and a child, and had laid the latter aside as an encumbrance. She had then shrugged once and walked away.

Edward had been snatched up by one of the lingering Sidhe and raised Underhill. No matter what he was told, he clung to the conviction that the mortal world was more real, more perfect . . . more *something* than the world of the Sidhe, and that he would be more than a mere servant in the real world. He had insisted that he wished to return Overhill.

Because she felt Edward needed to understand why most Sidhe avoided the mortal world and that he might settle better into his life Underhill when he had tasted Overhill, Aleneil took him to her brother's establishment. It did not take him long to realize his mistake.

He had been taught English as well as Elven and as his first lesson Aleneil gave him a few coins and sent him to the market. The rutted, muddy street (and that was a main road through London) awash with all kinds of debris—from offal to excrement in its gutters—that led to the East Chepe was a shock. The crude market, the yelling, pushing peddlers, the loud, cheating merchants, who groaned of being beggared when he protested their inflated prices, and the goods themselves, rough fabrics, crude furniture, blemished, half-ripe or overripe fruits and vegetables, sickened him. No heaven here.

Beyond that, there was no magical breeze to waft his purchases back to the house. He had to carry them himself through the noise and the filth. Muddy water fouled with Dannae alone knew what spattered his hose, and he knew there would be no near-mindless, faceless servitor to wash them. He would need to do by hand menial tasks done Underhill by spells or those mindless servitors, for he had no magic to perform them as the Low Court Sidhe did. The mortal world no longer seemed like a place of endless glorious possibilities from which the Sidhe had been keeping him. He elected to go back Underhill with Aleneil.

The other two men, Kip Ladbroke and Shandy Dunstan, were different cases. Both had also been snatched up after a Wild Hunt—Denoriel even remembered Kip—but they had been much older, Dunstan nearly fifteen and Ladbroke twelve. In each case, but at separate times and places, they had been traveling, not willingly, in the company of an older male. Dunstan had been bound and bruised, beaten so severely that he could barely stagger along; Ladbroke, tethered by the neck like a dog, had been bloody and weeping.

Both had been caught up by the Sidhe, separated from the target of the Hunt, judged innocent but as having seen too much, and delivered to Elfhame Avalon.

Both Dunstan and Ladbroke knew the mortal world well and the bottom of it to boot. Both knew what they would be losing by leaving Underhill. Even for servants of the Seleighe Court life was easy, safe, beautiful. Both knew they would still be servants in the mortal world and that in many ways life would be much harder.

On the other hand, both were mortal and clever and bored to death by the sameness of life in Elfhame Avalon. Both wanted to go places and do things, to find wives and marry and have children; both hoped for adventure and excitement, and the chance, maybe, to help some other young lad in dire straits, if only by calling on their own elven rescuers. Neither was foolish enough to wish to "escape" Avalon, to try, penniless and without friends or relatives, to build a life in a hard world. So they had remained Underhill; however, when offered a place in the retinue of a Sidhe lord who was masquerading as human, both seized the offer with joy. This would be the ideal chance to insinuate themselves back into the world of men—if Denoriel's task came to an end, he could and would easily find them employment in the retinue of one or another of his noble friends. And if it did not—they were assured of a continuing place in *his* employ.

Denoriel accepted both and left them to make themselves comfortable in the house, to find quarters for themselves, to buy horses and tack for the journey, and, most important of all, to construct stories of who they were, where they came from, how they had come into Denoriel's service. When they—and Denoriel—were satisfied by the tales, the Sidhe would arrange to have some papers prepared that would support their claims. It would not need to be much—

parish birth-records, and a forged letter or two of recommendation.

Having Gated back to Windsor, Denoriel spent another totally unproductive day guarding Harry. The white kitten was just as bored as he, so it was fortunate that the newly reinforced spell in the collar kept it fixed to its duty.

Now only two days remained until the party left Windsor. Denoriel, again refreshed by a night Underhill, came directly to the London house in the morning. He checked on what Dunstan and Ladbroke had done and was well satisfied. As Aleneil had assured him, these were clever, resourceful men.

Despite having been away from the mortal world for respectively ten and twelve years, they had chosen excellent horses, sturdy cobs without much beauty or speed but with considerable endurance; respectable tack, worn but in good order and repair; and they had each concocted a solid tale.

Each kept his native birthplace, fearing to be caught speaking in the wrong accent. Ladbroke claimed he had been an orphan and was picked up in the street and sold to a shipmaster. Dunstan said his father had sold him, having too many children and not enough to feed them.

Eventually they had come to the same ship and become friends, risen to be marines, and when they came to port in Southampton had decided they had had enough of ship life. Their shipmaster, sensibly not wanting disaffected fighting men aboard, not only released them but told them of having heard, through a fellow shipmaster, of a foreign gentleman who needed servants who could also wield a blade. A dispatched message had received a favorable reply, and here they were.

Denoriel pronounced himself well satisfied and promised to arrange identification for them. Then he handed over another purse and bade them go out and buy clothing sufficient for a journey of at least a month and a pack mule that could carry their baggage and a tent. They would leave for Windsor the following morning to be sure to be ready whenever Norfolk gave the order for FitzRoy's cortege . . .

And just as he was giving them the last of their instructions, a white kitten landed on Denoriel's shoulder.

:Black Sidhe!: It shrilled at him. *:Come now! Black Sidhe! Great power!:*

Denoriel did not even finish his sentence. He fled to the stable, leapt on Miralys, who formed a saddle beneath him as he struck his back. They burst through the wall between the worlds as only an elvensteed could, setting off alarms as they passed into Elfhame Logres. But Denoriel and Miralys were known; the guard set no magic barrier and without waiting to explain, he Gated to Windsor.

He arrived at the main gate of the palace looking enough disordered to make the guards smile. "Busy night? Slept late did you?" he asked.

For once Denoriel did not echo the smile. His mouth was thin and grim, but he forced himself to look pleasant, though cool—as indeed, he should, for the guard's comment was presumptuous. "I—needed to say good-bye; it took some time. May I enter? I need to ask some questions about the journey."

The guard nodded. "A'course, milord."

The guard looked and sounded chagrined, as if he knew he had overstepped even the foreigner's affability. The gate was opened wide and Denoriel and Miralys passed through. He was tempted to ride the elvensteed right up to the palace door so he could ask questions, but Miralys went toward the stable and the white kitten suddenly appeared again in his lap.

"Where is Harry?" he asked it in a frantic whisper. :*Tutor:*

Denoriel breathed again and ceased pulling at the reins, a useless enterprise since they were not connected to a bit. Miralys continued toward the stable. "Where is the black Sidhe?"

The kitten promptly disappeared. Still anxious but less so, Denoriel looked around and saw that the doors of the carriage house as well as those of the stable were open. Just within them was a very handsome coach, a more elegant design even than that of Francis Bryan, and on the seat Denoriel caught a glimpse of something very strange. He hurriedly stabled Miralys and told the stable boys to leave his horse saddled.

"I don't expect to be here long. I just came to confirm the date of departure. Oh, whose is that most elegant coach in the carriage house?"

"Princess Mary's. She is departing for Wales very soon and sent a nun with a gift for His Grace of Richmond."

A nun! Black Sidhe! Denoriel had been too alarmed to wonder at what the air spirit had said, but now he remembered the creature could not tell liosalfar from dark elf. So what the air spirit meant was a Sidhe clothed in black.

Controlling his urge to run from the stable, Denoriel nodded his thanks at the boy who had answered his question, and tossed him a coin. The other boys promptly converged on the recipient to claim a promise of sharing, which was what Denoriel had hoped they would do, and he stepped out and slipped into the carriage house.

He hesitated near the doors for a moment, extending his senses, but the coach itself was of ordinary mortal stuff and there was no coachman. Likely the man was in the stable with the horses. Denoriel walked closer, came right up to the window, and finally opened the door to look inside.

A large toy ship that reeked of magic! A ship exactly like the one that had been damaged when FitzRoy hit his attacker with the mast. Cold coursed up and down Denoriel's back. Someone had wrenched the description of that ship from deep within one of the attacker's mind. Neither man would have consciously remembered all the details. Could the ship be bespelled?

He had no intention of allowing Harry to touch that thing until he had examined it more closely. He raised a foot to step into the carriage so he could take hold of the large ship and his toe hit something soft. He looked down and barely prevented himself from screaming "Harry!"

The naked child lay on the floor of the coach, wrapped only in a heavy black cloak. He was so exact an image of Henry FitzRoy that Denoriel blinked and bit his lip. But it was not Harry. The child stank of magic and more magic; it was the child, not the ship, that was bespelled, which was why the boy had not wakened when prodded by Denoriel's foot.

Sent to seek for the black Sidhe, the white kitten had first appeared in Master Croke's apartment, one room of which had been set aside and fitted out as a schoolroom. It was a moderately large room with two small tables and chairs for Mary and FitzRoy and two normal-sized tables—one much larger than the other—and covered with books and pamphlets. One served for Master Croke and the other for Henry Howard. A large and handsome globe stood in one corner; in the other was an unusually large and smooth slate fitted upright into a wooden frame. Against the wall behind Master Croke's table was a short bookcase holding more books and loose papers.

Unfortunately Mary had seen the kitten and cried out, "Oh, you cute little naughty. How did you get in here?"

Whereupon Master Croke went to open the door and let it out and Mary protested and jumped up to catch it and set it on her lap. The kitten ran away to avoid her. Master Croke ordered her to her seat but then started to look for the little cat himself to be sure he had evicted it. He knew it would cause more disruption if he had not.

The kitten did not dare actually vanish, so there were another few minutes of delay while it appeared, disappeared, and finally scuttled from behind the globe stand to whisk through the door and out.

To go from chamber to chamber, even as an air spirit could travel, would take too long. The kitten listened and felt, sending out diaphanous probes, but it did not dare open itself fully for fear the Sidhe would sense it and seize it. Thus its search was slower than it could have been, but eventually it perceived the Sidhe aura, followed it, found it . . . felt a flicker of recognition.

Rhoslyn, wide-wimpled and garbed in lustrous black—a nun of wealth and family—stood with her head modestly bowed while the duke of Norfolk waved away his servants and clerks and gestured for his guards to go out too. She read his expression easily enough and had a little struggle with herself to keep from smiling. She had asked to speak to him alone and a moment later saw him dismiss her as a threat. After all, what harm could one small nun do him?

But Rhoslyn only wanted privacy because she could not bespell a room full of people, and Norfolk's clerks, guards, and servants would see what she was doing to bind him. Bind him she must; she couldn't take the chance that he would refuse to allow her to take FitzRoy to the stable. It was an odd request; she should, of course, have brought the present to the house.

Actually she intended Norfolk no harm at all—at least no physical harm. After the changeling he believed to be his charge sickened and died, he would lose the profitable sinecure of being FitzRoy's guardian and he would certainly consider *that* harm, but it was nothing his clerks and servants and guards could have protected him from, so—

A twinge of magic, the briefest scent of Underhill, made Rhoslyn wince and glance around. If her information had been wrong and Denoriel was near . . . But the sense of intrusion, the flicker of white, was gone.

Startled by her sudden movement, Norfolk said, "Yes?"

She looked up and simpered. "Beg pardon, Your Grace. It was a little prick. A flea bite perhaps."

Her eyes held his. He moved a hand uncertainly and began to frown. "You are from the Princess Mary's household and need private speech with me?"

"It is no great matter, Your Grace. Because she is leaving very soon for Wales, the princess wished to send to her half-brother a little gift."

Rhoslyn's fingers made a gesture and Norfolk looked down to where they were now drawing invisible symbols on the table that stood between them. Norfolk's eyes were beginning to glaze but he was a strong-willed man and he had been disturbed by the idea that someone in Mary's household felt that secrecy was necessary to deliver a small gift.

"Why . . . Why . . ."

He meant to ask why news of a gift from the princess to Richmond need be kept secret, why he needed to dismiss even his guards, but the words clotted on his tongue and he did not remember what he had intended to ask.

"I would like to talk a while in private to His Grace of Richmond. I wish to show him the princess's gift and remind him of her prior claims, remind him that the will of God is more binding than the will of kings. We could sit for a few moments in my coach. His guards may, of course, accompany us. You will have to give an order that he be taken from the schoolroom to speak to me. I will wait for him in the entranceway, and I will bring him back to the entranceway."

Now Rhoslyn flicked her fingers up and Norfolk's eyes rose following them, their gazes locking together once more. Norfolk's expression became less wooden. He licked his lips and shook his head. She snapped her fingers softly and he blinked and rang the bell that stood on the table.

The door swung open. His guards stepped quickly into the room, hands on their sword hilts, but seeing their master and the nun in the same positions and perfectly calm, the guards merely took their places by the door and stood waiting. The duke's clerk followed them in. Norfolk crooked a finger at him and the clerk hurried forward.

"Go up to Master's Croke's apartment and tell him to send Richmond down to the entryway. His Grace of Richmond is permitted to go to the carriage house with this nun. She has a present for him in her coach."

The sharp anxiety for Richmond's safety that had made everyone in Windsor overcautious about him right after the attack had waned in the weeks that followed without any alarms, but enough remained to make the clerk ask doubtfully, "His Grace of Richmond is to go alone?"

"No, with his guards, of course," Norfolk said.

There had been a look of stress under the duke's bespelled calm that had made Rhoslyn tense, but the mention of the guards seemed to relieve that. Rhoslyn was grateful that she had remembered to permit the guards to accompany them. A single touch could make them walking sleepers, able to follow their young master but incapable of really seeing or doing anything.

Rhoslyn thanked the duke for his courtesy, curtsied, and followed the clerk out of the room. He turned left in the corridor and went toward the back of the building; Rhoslyn turned right and walked the short distance to the wide staircase that led down to the entrance hall. There she stopped, signaling the servant who waited to open the front doors that she was waiting for someone. The man stepped back, Rhoslyn turned to watch the stairway, holding her breath.

Vidal Dhu had commanded that they bring Henry FitzRoy to him, but he had no real interest in the child. It was she who had made the changeling, hair by hair, to be perfect, not only in face and form but close enough in mind so he could take up FitzRoy's place in the schoolroom, in his games with the other children, in his relationship with his nurse.

She had almost come to love that simulacrum. It had wrung her heart that the poor little thing must wither and die in the mortal world as the magic which fed and sustained him slowly faded and ebbed. Certainly she would not deliver his mortal model to the untender mercies of Vidal Dhu. It was enough that she was sacrificing her creation, that in the mortal world, Henry FitzRoy would die and be no rival to Princess Mary for the throne of England. Underhill, for her labor and her pain, Rhoslyn intended to keep the real Henry FitzRoy for herself.

Her eager waiting was not disappointed. Within a quarter hour, two tall guardsmen came down the stairs, one before and one behind a child whose features she

knew better than her own. Her breath quickened with
eagerness. For once, she would have a real reward,
something she valued, in return for her labor in the
service of Vidal Dhu. She would have a child, a child
of her own!

CHAPTER 11

Gasping with fear, Denoriel caught the changeling up in his arms and drew the cloak more completely around him so that he might appear to be a large and unwieldy bundle. He backed out of the coach, nudged the door closed with his shoulder, and stood for a moment, his heart pounding wildly. If whoever had brought the simulacrum came now . . . He could not fight with the child in his arms and a magical attack or defense . . . he had no idea what effect it would have on the changeling. Denoriel looked frantically around the carriage house for a place to hide what he held.

In the next instant he realized he could not hide the boy—no! the construct—here in the carriage house. Whoever had brought him—it—would feel its presence. Denoriel stared down at the bundle in his arms, feeling the warmth, the steady breathing, the relaxation that felt like trust. He knew that what he should do was draw the magic out of the—the *thing* and let it crumple to nothingness. His gorge rose and he swallowed hard, clutching the little boy closer in his arms.

He would bring it to Mwynwen. Perhaps she could save it, set a spell on it so that it could draw power from the rich flow Underhill. No! He dared not leave Windsor to carry this—this changeling Underhill. The black Sidhe, whoever it was, might seize Harry, might abduct him even if it could not leave the changeling behind. And there was the ship, too. What if the ship carried some spell that could make Harry docile or even do him harm? Where? Where could he hide this simulacrum that the magic in it would not call out to its creator?

Could Miralys take the boy to Mwynwen without him, bursting through the wall between the worlds right from the stable? What if the stable boys noticed the elvensteed's absence? And first he had to get to Miralys . . . Miralys. Miralys had a huge magic aura that, likely, would swallow up the magic presence of the changeling. And Miralys could protect the boy too. It would take a strong and determined Sidhe to get past the elvensteed.

Now he had to get to Miralys. He could not simply walk back into the stable with a large bundle in his arms. He would have to use the Don't-see-me spell, but he hated to deplete his magic when a confrontation with the black Sidhe was imminent. He glanced down at the simulacrum he held, knowing he could increase his own store of power greatly by sucking power out of the boy. Denoriel shuddered and cast the Don't-see-me spell. If he needed it, he would drink lightning. Crippling his magic was better than killing a child, even if it was a construct.

It was no trouble after that to walk through the stable to Miralys's stall. He laid the bundle down in the straw right under the small trough affixed to the wall to hold grain. He could see the straw flatten, but the bundle did not appear even when he withdrew his arms. He wondered if the spell on the changeling would break when he broke the spell on himself . . . if the sleep spell would break too . . . Would the child cry out? Would Miralys be able to keep him from running to the stable boys?

Biting his lips, Denoriel drew his knife, cut strips from a horse blanket, bound the child lightly, folded his kerchief and gagged him; then he drew straw over him. Poor child, how frightened he would be if he woke. Denoriel prayed the black Sidhe's sleep spell would hold and then bit his lip again. If it did, would that mean that the black Sidhe was stronger in magic and spell casting than he?

He turned to Miralys. "This is the changeling," he whispered. "It is . . . it is the image of Harry. I cannot harm it, but I cannot chance its being found and mistaken for Harry. Keep it safe for me, Miralys."

And there was a white kitten in the empty grain trough.

:With sour man:

What? Denoriel thought, but he did not say it aloud. He searched his scattered wits for what the air spirit could mean. Then he remembered he had sent it to look for the black Sidhe. Sour man?

"Norfolk?"

:Big place. Many servants. Bespelled sour man . . . maybe. Nearly caught. Ran away:

Denoriel swallowed hard. "Find Harry!"

He did not raise his voice above the whisper he had been using, but the force in it sent the air spirit out of the stable like a pebble from a slingshot. He stared after it until Miralys nudged him with his nose and then dropped his head to gently nose at the child. Denoriel wondered if the spell affected the elvensteed; he thought not, because Miralys had not seemed in the least surprised when he spoke, but, of course, the elvensteed could smell him . . . And then he uttered a soft sound of contempt for himself and rushed out of the stable and back to the carriage house.

Beside the coach door, Denoriel drew a long breath and dismissed the Don't-see-me spell. Imagine standing there in the stable and wondering about Miralys's abilities when the black Sidhe could have arrived and given Harry the ship! No, the kitten would have come to warn him. But that thought could not cover over the fact that he had been idling in the stable near Miralys because he was afraid!

Denoriel could feel his skin heat with embarrassment. He was no coward—he had raised his sword against both men and Sidhe—but he was aware of his weakness in the use of magic. What a young fool he had been to refuse the teaching offered by Magus Major Treowth and assume that his skill with a sword could answer all threats.

No matter. He would not let Harry be taken. He opened the coach door, stepped in, and took hold of the ship. The ambience of magic was very much diminished and what he felt from it had a flavor that Denoriel recognized. He breathed a sigh of relief. The ship was only radiating the residual magic of being a kenned object; that magic would fade steadily until the ship was only a real thing of wood and cloth and string.

Sure now the ship was harmless, Denoriel wondered why it had been left in the coach—and then felt like a fool again. The ship was the excuse to bring Harry here. Of course the black Sidhe would bring the child to the coach! That was where it expected to clothe the changeling in what Harry was now wearing, put a sleep spell on Harry, and cover him with the cloak. It would then send the changeling, now wearing Harry's clothing, out to Harry's guards, who must be bespelled not to notice the exchange, and drive out of the gates as innocent as an angel.

Would Harry also be bespelled? Denoriel's breath caught and then sighed out in relief. Not unless the child had for some reason shielded his cross. Denoriel felt a chill of apprehension, but the black Sidhe could not know the secret exchanges and Harry had never failed to use one before he put the cross into its pouch.

Denoriel picked up the ship and backed carefully out of the carriage, again shutting the door with his shoulder. Despite his suppressed anxiety, he had a wicked smile on his lips. *Just how angry will the black Sidhe be*, Denoriel wondered, *when he sees me coming out of the carriage house to present the ship to Harry?* Angry enough to be off balance and less able to throw spells? His smile disappeared. Angry enough to forget the need to keep the child safe and throw levin bolts about?

Rhoslyn would certainly have bespelled the child if she could have gotten close enough to FitzRoy to touch him, even right there in the entryway. She had carefully prepared a spell that induced a state of utter compliance. In its hold, a person could walk, possibly even answer a direct question, but be no more aware than one who slept and be perfectly obedient. All she had to do was touch the person she wanted to bespell and say, "*Fiat.*"

Unfortunately for her, as the two guards and the boy reached the level floor of the entrance, the guards fanned out to either side, shepherding the boy safely between them. *Once caught, twice shy*, Rhoslyn thought, remembering the attack on FitzRoy, so she said nothing and nodded to the servant to open the doors.

To her chagrin, the taller of the two guards bowed slightly and gestured her ahead. However, perhaps it was just as well. If she had put the spell on them immediately, one might have stumbled going down the stair, or his posture or expression might have changed enough to alarm the two guards who stood outside the door. She followed patiently until the road that led to the stables and the carriage house curved out of sight of the front door. Then she stopped, turned, and curtsied.

"It is not right for me to precede the duke of Richmond. You all know where the carriage house is. That is where I am going to show His Grace the surprise I have for him."

The boy looked brightly interested now. When he had first seen her nun's habit, his expression had held a mingling of anxiety and mild resentment. He had not been told why he was sent for, apparently, and expected a lecture of some kind. He was an adorable boy, his expression keener and more changeable than that of the changeling. Still, her heart ached a little at the thought of that innocent victim.

FitzRoy started to say something and the taller guard said, "Very well, Sister."

"Why can't we all walk together, Gerrit?" FitzRoy asked.

"It's safer this way, Your Grace," Gerrit said, smiling down at his charge. "No matter which way anyone runs at us, Nyle and me can be right around you. If the good Sister was between, she'd be in the way, and she might be in danger too. Before or behind, she'd be out of the way and safe."

Rhoslyn could have done without that explanation, but it was easy enough to think of a reason why the guard's logic was no longer valid. She let the three pass her and followed for a little while without any protest.

When she knew the carriage house would soon be in sight, she stepped closer, touched each guard lightly on the back of the neck, and murmured, "*Fiat.*"

A few steps later—the open doors of the carriage house were now quite near—she said, "Wait, please." Everyone stopped, but only FitzRoy turned to look at her. The two guards stared straight ahead. The child looked up, first at one and then at the other. His eyes widened a trifle and his lips parted.

Hastily Rhoslyn said, "Please let me and His Grace go ahead together now. You can see the carriage house so it is quite safe. There cannot be any attack from the palace carriage house."

That was utterly ridiculous. The carriage house with its stored carts and coaches and wide doors was an ideal place to lay an ambush—assuming the ambushers could have got into Windsor . . . and at least one set of attackers *had* got in before. Still, the guards said nothing. FitzRoy looked from one to another again, puzzled and beginning to show signs of suspicion, but Rhoslyn had already come around in front of them.

"Come," she said, holding out her hand. "Take my hand. You will be perfectly safe holding the hand of a Holy Sister. Your guards are overcautious. No one would attack a nun."

The last sentence seemed to reassure the boy and he stepped out from between his guards, holding out his hand. Rhoslyn bent forward a trifle and took it, the word "Fiat" ready on her tongue. Instead she screamed and snatched back her hand. Simultaneously the child shouted, "Lord Denno!" and leapt past her before she could muster the strength to resist the burning pain and seize him.

"Rhoslyn!" Denoriel exclaimed, shocked, although he did not know why he was surprised.

He had heard that Rhoslyn was a master fabricator, that it was she who had molded the not-horses out of the unformed stuff of the chaos lands. But it was Pasgen who was the greater spell caster. Somehow he had expected a Sidhe who could attack and defend with spells, even though he knew the black Sidhe could not have been Pasgen because it was dressed as a nun.

His half-sister's name was all he was able to say, however, because as Harry came close, the cross he wore was driving into Denoriel spikes that burned with cold.

"Is that a new sword?" Harry cried, his eyes round with excitement.

"No," Denoriel got out, swallowing pain. "It's the one I wore the day your ship got broken. And here is a new ship to replace the old one." He held it up for Rhoslyn to see, but to Harry he said urgently, "Get behind me! Don't cover your cross!"

The boy slipped behind him and grabbed at his doublet, his fingers brushing the back of Denoriel's thighs. Denoriel hissed with pain, but the heavy silken cloth of his hose saved him from the worst of the burning. Warily, he watched Rhoslyn, wondering if she would tell the guards to attack him.

The guards . . . if they attacked, he could shout for help from the stable boys. No, he couldn't. They would come out, but they were more likely to help the guards than to help him. Still, if the guards attacked him, they couldn't grab for Harry on Rhoslyn's command. Bespelled as they were, they could only follow one order at a time. He could give Harry the ship and tell him to take it to the palace to show Norfolk. But Rhoslyn seemed to have forgotten the guards completely. She stared at the ship Denoriel was holding.

"You've been inside the coach," she whispered. He could barely hear her. "You found . . . You found . . ."

Her eyes were enormous and shining with tears—and they were a deep, warm brown, as were the brows above them. Denoriel wondered if he would have recognized her if the wimple had not covered all but the central portion of her face. If he had seen her dark-eyed, dark-haired, round-eared and dressed as a court lady, would he have known her?

But the tears! Denoriel could not imagine Rhoslyn weeping over anything at all. Death and pain fed her power. Could she care for the changeling she had made? The simulacrum was as much her own creation as a child born of her body, and to pass as Harry it would have had to have the same sweet, sunny nature. Had she fallen victim to her own creation's charms?

For a moment Denoriel was strongly tempted to tell her that the changeling was safe. Then he realized that her show of emotion was likely a trap for him. There was little chance that she could fashion another simulacrum; the knowledge she had drawn from the attackers had been transferred bit by bit to the changeling that now lay under the straw in the stable. However, if Rhoslyn knew that it still lived, attempts would be made to seize it and complete the exchange another time. Harry would be in continued danger.

"It is beyond your reach now, Rhoslyn."

The tears spilled over and ran down her cheeks. "Murderer!" she breathed. "Murderer!"

"Whatever I have done, it has made what *you* wished to do impossible. Tell Vidal Dhu that we guard our charge well."

"Oh, I will tell him, Denoriel Siencyn Macreth Silverhair, I will tell him! I will tell all of Underhill that you murdered a helpless child. I will have your heart's blood for it."

She whirled past him, Denoriel backing away and turning so that he was always between her and Harry.

But she did not look at them. She ran into the stable, and Denoriel could hear her calling an order for the princess's coach to make ready to depart. Denoriel bent down to hand the boat to FitzRoy, gritting his teeth against the effect of the cold iron cross.

"Did you murder a child, Lord Denno?" Harry's eyes were enormous and his voice trembled.

"No, of course not! I just hid him from her." He thought about trying to explain to Harry what Rhoslyn had intended, and realized at once that there was no time. "She must not know, though! Now run back to the house, Harry, quickly, and show His Grace of Norfolk the lovely ship that Princess Mary sent to replace the one that was broken."

"Will you come with me?"

Fortunately the boy's hands were both busy holding the ship and he could not reach to take hold of Denoriel.

"No, I cannot. Not today." Nonetheless Denoriel began to walk back toward the palace with the boy, past the guards who were still staring into space. "I . . . I must watch to be sure the Sister truly leaves Windsor. I will not harm her, but she must not stay."

There was a moment of silence while FitzRoy first stared up at his motionless guards and then at Denoriel. He thrust the toy ship back at the elf.

"No, no. Keep it, Harry. It's nothing to do with the nun. It's a gift from your sister, Princess Mary. It will not harm you, I swear."

FitzRoy clutched the ship to his chest, began to smile, lost the smile as he glanced at the guards again. Then he asked softly, "Did my cross hurt her? Was that why she yelled? She was a bad fairy, wasn't she? What did she want to do to me?"

"Nothing," Denoriel hastened to assure the child. He didn't want Harry to have any more nightmares of being drowned or otherwise killed. "She wouldn't have hurt you, Harry."

Denoriel would not go so far as to say Rhoslyn would have been kind. The Unseleighe Sidhe enjoyed pain and fear, physical or mental, and drew power from a variety of violent emotions. He wouldn't say that either because he didn't want to frighten the child, but he had to tell FitzRoy something to keep him wary of those who could not abide cold iron.

"I think she intended to take you away. But if you had not been wearing your cross," he continued, "she would have done to you what she did to the guards and would have taken you away where I could never come to see you. Worse than that, she would have kept you from your father, the king. Now I know you don't much care for being a duke and being responsible for a lot of people, but it is your father the king's will, and truly, Harry, although you don't want the burden, it is for the good of England. The bad fairy doesn't understand that, and wanted to put someone else in your place as duke, someone who would not have understood that he must do his duty."

"I know," the boy said, sighing. "His Grace of Norfolk tells me my duty over and over." But then he smiled. "Anyway, I wouldn't want to go anywhere that we couldn't be together sometimes, even if I didn't have to be a duke any more." The smile disappeared. "Why did my sister Princess Mary send a bad fairy to me? Does she hate me?"

The last thing Denoriel wanted was for Harry to show fear or hatred toward Princess Mary. That would be dangerous politically.

"Of course not," he said, keeping his voice steady with an effort as the cold iron wore away at him, "I don't think Princess Mary knew anything at all about Rhoslyn being a bad fairy. I think Rhoslyn made someone the

princess trusted ask to borrow a coach for a nun. You
know how much the princess loves the Church. She
would agree to that."

"And the ship? How did Mary know my ship was
broken?"

"Oh, Harry," Denoriel sighed. "Sometimes I wish you
weren't so clever. Likely the princess didn't know about
the ship. But she might have been told that the nun
wanted to visit you at Windsor. If so, she would have
told the nun, or maybe the servant who asked for the
loan of the coach, to bring you a present in her name.
Princess Mary surely wished to give you a gift, for she
cares for you. The ship, I'm sure, was Rhoslyn's idea,
but the idea of a gift was Princess Mary's."

"You know her, don't you? You know her name."
FitzRoy looked up at the guards. His lips trembled and
tears came to his eyes. "What . . . what did she do to
Gerrit and Nyle?"

Behind him Denoriel could hear the clop of hooves
and the coachman talking to the stable boys or maybe
to the horses. He had about a quarter of an hour while
the coach was drawn out of the coach house and the
horses were backed along the shaft so the traces could
be fastened. Denoriel urged FitzRoy around the curve
in the road and toward the trees and shrubs that bordered it. He had realized that he couldn't send Harry
back to the palace without his guards.

"I'll take care of Gerrit and Nyle," he said, praying that he could. "Just you wait here—don't move
because I'm going to make you a little invisible house
of protection."

He cast the strongest shield he knew around
FitzRoy. As the shield formed—a thin, shining mist to
his inner sight, not much more dense than the thin
ambience of Overhill power—he breathed a sigh of
double relief. First that the shield had formed at all

around the boy wearing cold iron, and second because the aching, burning cold caused in him by the cross had disappeared. That meant that the shield, no matter how diaphanous it looked, was whole and strong.

Now he put a finger to his lips to warn Harry to silence and then ran back toward the carriage house. The coach had been drawn out into the cobblestone-paved yard and with the help of two stable boys, the coachman was completing harnessing the glossy and well-fed horses to the vehicle. Rhoslyn stood waiting near the door. He walked wide around the horses and carriage, unnoticed by the busy men, and came close enough to speak too low to be heard by them.

"I think you had better break the spell on Richmond's guards," he said, smiling as sweetly as he could.

She looked at him and her lip lifted like that of a snarling bitch, but she made no reply.

He held steady under that glare of hate. "I will lay whatever odds you like that somewhere in speaking to Norfolk you mentioned Princess Mary. Richmond has already been attacked by men who came with the Spanish ambassador and are suspected of using magic. That could only have been done to remove a rival to the princess. Do you now want a nun from the Princess's household to be associated with ensorcelling Richmond's guards?"

If hate could have been launched from a person's eyes like a spear, Denoriel would have lain dead at his half-sister's feet.

"I will not meddle with the boy's memory," he said. "He will surely, sooner or later, mention how you cried out at his touch when he was wearing cold iron. Together with the mindless guards at whom the stable boys are already casting uneasy glances . . . Is that not coming close to exposing what you are?"

She raised her hand.

Denoriel's smile broadened. "I do not think this is the time to be casting levin bolts about—not with the coachman and the stable boys so close—"

Rhoslyn spat at him. Denoriel jerked back, barely avoiding the gob of saliva, but he would not have cared if it hit him, because Rhoslyn had walked past him to confront the staring and frozen guards. He could not see what she did or hear the spell words, although he enhanced his already keen hearing as much as he could, but both guards looked down between them and then looked at her with horror on their faces. Rhoslyn flounced away, as if she had been scolding them for dereliction of duty.

Denoriel hurried up to them while they were still staring wild-eyed at each other. "Richmond is quite safe," he said. "I was just coming out of the stable when you both stopped dead in your tracks and he walked on with the nun, so I stayed with him while the Holy Sister gave him his present from Princess Mary. It was a ship, like the one that got broken, and he wanted to run back to the palace to show his little friends and His Grace of Norfolk, but I told him to wait for you. He's just around the curve—"

They were off, running. Denoriel was very glad they had not waited for any further explanation from him because he was running out of ideas. He sighed. He hoped he would not have to plant false memories in them—and he hadn't the faintest idea of how to do it—because they were good men. If he could not convince them that worse would follow any confession on their part of their failure to stay with FitzRoy all the time, they would certainly report themselves. But Denoriel did not want them replaced. Gerrit, Nyle, and Dickson were all truly fond of Harry; they told him stories, were willing to play games with him, and made their constant surveillance as pleasant as possible, whereas most of the other guards just stood about glowering.

Oh, sweet Lady Dannae, he had forgotten the shield! If they tried to touch Harry . . . Rhoslyn had gotten into the coach; the coachman whistled to his horses, cracked his whip; the vehicle began to roll forward almost on the heels of the guards. Denoriel hastily cast the Don't-see-me spell, raced around the coach to where he could see Harry, dropped Don't-see-me, and dissolved the shield the moment the coach passed.

Fortunately neither man had dared reach out to touch Harry and encountered the shield before he dissolved it. Denoriel himself arrived just in time to hear Harry greet the guards with genuine joy. The boy was clever enough not to ask what had happened to them, but he was only a child and his relief at seeing them made clear he had known something was wrong. Denoriel caught at Gerrit's arm and drew him a little back from Harry.

"Take the child back to the house and let him show Norfolk the ship. Don't say anything to Norfolk about what happened. No harm was actually done—I swear it—and the boy would be heartbroken if you and Nyle were punished or removed from caring for him."

The last sentence brought an even more anxious expression but no agreement. Denoriel continued desperately. "If you will just wait until your stint at guarding is over before reporting to Norfolk. The nun is truly gone and I do not believe will try to return, certainly not today. Richmond would be so upset if he heard Norfolk dismiss you or assign some harsh punishment."

"But we—we did not guard him. If you were not here, who knows what would have happened!"

"Nothing at all," Denoriel lied. But truly if the

exchange with the simulacrum had been made, the guards would not have been aware that anything had happened. "The Holy Sister only has a temper, and an exaggerated idea of her own importance in the princess's service. She only told His Grace of Richmond of his half-sister's affection for him and that he must not agree to being a rival to Princess Mary. And then she would have given Richmond the ship. I happened to be here and saw the ship in the carriage so I took it out and gave it to the boy. She was angry at my presumption and ordered her coach and left."

"His Grace of Norfolk should know," the man said, weakly.

"Know what? That for a moment you were bedazzled by something you cannot explain and Richmond was out of your sight? No harm came to him. And Norfolk will not be happy to hear that Princess Mary—or her household—was involved."

Gerrit bit his lip.

"Only get Nyle to agree to wait until your day's duty is finished before you report to Norfolk," Denoriel urged.

By then he hoped to be able to return with Aleneil, who would be able to spin a memory for them that fit with what he had told Gerrit. The man nodded uncertainly and then, watching FitzRoy who was excitedly pointing out the beauties of his new toy to Nyle, he nodded more certainly. Nyle smiled at the boy, then turned toward his fellow guard.

"Gerrit."

"I'm ready."

"Lord Denno," Harry said. "I have to go back to the palace now."

"I know. If he's not too busy, show His Grace of Norfolk your new ship." He caught Harry's eyes, and held them for a moment, trying to impart more than he was saying aloud. "But maybe the less said the better about how you got it—except, of course, that it was Princess Mary's gift? Hmmm?"

He glanced at the two guards; saw FitzRoy's glance in turn; saw him look back, soberly. Bless the child! He was beginning to understand. "Maybe you shouldn't mention me or Gerrit or Nyle at all? Hmmm?"

Harry nodded; Denoriel sighed silently with relief. "Anyway, I'll see you tomorrow. You remember I'm riding up into Yorkshire with you."

FitzRoy jumped up and down. He couldn't clap his hands because he was holding the ship. "Will you be riding the dapple horse? He's easier to see."

Despite the pain coming so close cost him, Denoriel could not resist walking up to the boy and bending down to kiss his hair. Harry had remembered not to use the name of Denoriel's elvensteed, so their third exchange of recognition would remain a secret between them.

"Dapple it is," he forced through swelling lips.

"Come along, Your Grace," Nyle urged. "Are you sure you don't want me to carry that ship for you?"

Denoriel waved and turned away as he heard FitzRoy say, "Oh, yes. You can carry it for me now." And he wondered as he walked into the stable whether that clever child had held the heavy ship all that time just so the guards would not wonder why he did not ask "Lord Denno" to hold his hand.

CHAPTER 12

While the coach rolled away from Windsor Palace,
Rhoslyn was so torn among grief, fury, and fear that
at first her mind could not fix on anything. She cursed
Denoriel, hardly able to believe he had appeared at
Windsor so early. He had been watched from afar for
weeks while she worked on the changeling, and
although he was known to visit Windsor at frequent
if irregular intervals, he *always* arrived in the afternoon,
sometimes quite late afternoon. Had he known she was
there? How had he known?

There was something, something she should remember, some sense of faint magic, but not mortal magic—
no, this had the delicate feeling of Sidhe magic. When
had she felt it? While she was bespelling Norfolk? Had
there been a flash of white at the same time?

But she could not hold the thought. Instead, she
wept, muffling her sobs in the veils of her habit,
grieving over her poor little changeling, so sweet, so
good. It was not fair. It was not fair. Denoriel had
destroyed it—

Yet she had always known it had to die. Once in the mortal world there would not be power enough to sustain it. It would have wasted away in a few weeks or at the most a few months, and it would have been tormented by stupid, ignorant mortal physicians. They would have been trying to cure it, but nothing could cure it as the power she had used to build it faded away.

She shivered and wept harder, hating herself for the fate she had known was in store for the child she had created. And then, hiccupping with grief, she comforted herself with the thought that it had probably never known pain or fear. Her sleep spell was strong and Denoriel would have sucked out its poor little store of life while it still slept. At least he would not have waked it; Denoriel took no pleasure in fear or pain.

Damn him! Damn him! Why was he in the wrong place at the wrong time? Let him be accursed by the Great Evil. Rhoslyn shivered again, now with fear. Wishing Denoriel to be in the hands of the Great Evil brought her own master to mind. Vidal Dhu would be *furious*. He would send her to the seventh plane of demons to be tortured for a thousand years.

No, Pasgen would not allow Vidal Dhu to do her real harm. But . . . she could not stop shivering . . . that would bring a confrontation between Pasgen and Vidal Dhu too soon, and she was in no condition to help her brother. She was depleted, depleted of some deep inner force by the strength she had expended to make her changeling. She had surface power enough, the power that one drank in from Underhill; she could cast sleep spells and obedience spells, but the deep, inner energy that was natural to her was fragile and worn.

She began to weep again for the false child's death, to curse Denoriel again, to swallow terror as she thought of Vidal Dhu's reaction to her failure, her thoughts going round and round from grief to rage to fear as the coach rumbled toward London. Somewhere in the back of her mind that other Rhoslyn, the one who had coldly cast the sleep spell on the simulacrum, who had come running to meet her with open arms, and carried him through the Gate to his eventual death, noted that this time, this little time, was all she would have to indulge herself. And she wept even harder for that other Rhoslyn who would all too soon choke off grief and tears.

Eventually Rhoslyn felt the coach slowing. She dried her tears, willed her eyes and nose and skin to show no sign of the weeping, and sat up straight. Here was where she must change places with the nun who had been sent to put the fear of God into FitzRoy if he dared think about replacing his legitimate sister. That so-called Bride of God had brought no pretty toy from a loving half-sister; if FitzRoy had truly encountered her, he would have been left in terror and tears. Rhoslyn hissed faintly between her teeth when she thought about the time, the effort, the elaborate planning that had been brought to naught by that demon-spawn Denoriel.

How had he known? Again the memory of a flash of white, a hint of Seleighe spirits . . . and then she knew. Air spirit! He had had an air spirit watching for her and had Gated to Windsor to intercept her attempt to take FitzRoy. Air spirit. Roslyn's teeth ground together. If she caught one, she would tear it to pieces with her bare hands and drink its agony with joy.

She drew back the leather curtain and peered out the window of the coach. Yes. This was the place. About halfway between Windsor and London, was a small inn and a large stable at which horses could be hired. Out beyond it, Pasgen had built a temporary Gate for her. Roslyn's jaw set in a new spurt of rage.

Pasgen was no less depleted than she. A Gate was no easy thing to create and hold, but they had thought it would be necessary since she was to bring FitzRoy with her. She bit her lip. Now it was all for nothing.

The coach came to a halt so that the hired horses, which had made the second half of the journey to Windsor, could be exchanged for the those which had drawn it from London and were now fed and rested. Rhoslyn alighted from the coach supposedly to use the jakes, to refresh herself with a plate of bread and cold meat and a cup of ale while the harness was transferred from one set of horses to the other.

There were other travelers in the inn, but after a word and a coin offered to the landlord, Rhoslyn took her bread and meat and ale through the public room to a private one in the back. She closed the door behind her, set her hand on the latch and whispered two words. Satisfied that no one could enter, Rhoslyn set the food on the table and walked to a far corner of the room, which was unnaturally dark.

As she approached, the corner brightened. By the time she reached it, she could see a woman with oddly cropped hair, wearing nothing but an undershift, who sat with closed eyes, supported by the walls on either side of her. Rhoslyn sighed and stripped off the nun's habit she was wearing, which she replaced with the sober but elegant gown resting beside the woman on the bench.

When she was dressed, except for the final lacing of her gown, she gestured for the ensorcelled woman to rise, finish lacing her gown, and don the nun's garb. Then Rhoslyn gathered her will, took a deep breath, bit her lip, leaned forward, and put her hand on the woman's forehead. Fortunately the false memories she had to impart were simple: the nun had to remember herself requesting permission from Norfolk to speak to Richmond and give him a gift—it was a prayer-book, not a toy, full of admonitions—delivering the lecture she had already fixed in her mind while walking with the boy to the coach, handing over the gift, and leaving.

The nun would report her interview with FitzRoy to Maria de Salinas, Queen Catherine's favorite maid of monor. Maria would be sadly disappointed in what the nun said, as would the queen, because the nun would have to admit that FitzRoy had not reacted at all to her urging that he refuse any precedence over his sister. Rhoslyn had no sympathy to waste on them. It was largely Catherine's fault that she had so underestimated the threat FitzRoy was to Princess Mary's inheritance of the throne.

The queen had publicly professed herself shocked and disgusted when her husband began to heap honors on his bastard son. She had protested to Henry and been soothed by his assurances that he was merely providing the proper status and income for a child of royal blood. From then on Catherine refused to hear anything about FitzRoy, which she never failed to call him, ignoring the titles that had been bestowed upon him.

Rhoslyn, who had established herself as a dear friend and advisor to Maria de Salinas, had assumed Catherine understood her husband and had accepted the queen's attitude toward FitzRoy. Once Rhoslyn had learned different, she had set about rectifying the queen's deliberate blindness. She had conveyed to Maria de Salinas a strong anxiety about the possibility that FitzRoy would be preferred over Princess Mary. King Henry was very prone to telling soothing lies. Maria conveyed the anxiety to Queen Catherine, and pointed out that it was dangerous to keep ignoring the boy.

Catherine was too proud and too stubborn to reverse her disapproval and recognize FitzRoy, but Maria de Salinas, via Rhoslyn, had an answer to that. It would be most natural for ten-year-old Princess Mary, a lonely only child, to be curious about her half-brother and to wish to be in contact with him. It would be kind of the princess—and would probably please King Henry—if Mary were to send FitzRoy a gift before she and FitzRoy were farther apart. Mary had chosen a prayer-book; Maria de Salinas had chosen the prayers, which Mary had copied into it in her own neat hand. The child was already so steeped in the gloomy Christianity of her mother's Spanish priests that she saw nothing out of the ordinary about a book of prayers begging frantically for God's forgiveness for unspecified (but presumably heinous) sins being sent to a child of six.

The conveyor of the gift would be a nun. Rhoslyn skillfully discouraged the idea of sending a priest by hinting that male visitors might be suspect after the attack on FitzRoy by members of the Spanish ambassador's retinue. The nun would bring Princess Mary's gift, explain to FitzRoy that his sister loved him and make clear his duty to that sister was to refuse to usurp her place. If he agreed, the nun would shower blessings on him; if he insisted on being his father's heir, he would be accursed of God.

Rhoslyn thought the idea ridiculous, but she certainly did not discourage Maria de Salinas; replacing the nun would be Rhoslyn's passport into Windsor, where she had to go to exchange FitzRoy for the simulacrum. Naturally, she had made no attempt to say anything about Princess Mary to FitzRoy, nor did she regret that she had not.

First of all, she had expected to take the FitzRoy with her; the changeling would die; and all threat to

Mary's precedence would be removed. Secondly, even though the abduction had failed, Rhoslyn was sure that no remonstrance would have the smallest effect on Harry FitzRoy. No doubt Catherine and Maria de Salinas had conceived the silly notion because the lecture might have been effective with Mary, who had been imbued with a deep love and reverence for the Church. FitzRoy had not. Nor was it likely that he would be given any choice in his actions. It was Norfolk and the king to whom these remonstrances should be addressed, not the child, who would do as he was told by his keeper and his father. The women of Catherine's court were living in a dream-world in which men of ambition and greed would somehow be turned from their path by tears and prayers.

Those thoughts Rhoslyn shielded from the nun's mind. With a final suggestion that the woman eat and drink what was on the table and then complete her journey, Rhoslyn unspelled the door and slipped out of the room. Down a side corridor was a back door leading to the jakes in the yard. She hurried out, knowing no one would look at her or find the action noteworthy. Still, she made sure the yard was empty before she slid around the side of the privy into a tall hedge behind. An opening, visible only to eyes that could look through illusion, took her to the Gate.

The disorientation was terrible, worse than Rhoslyn had ever felt before. She had not realized how magically depleted, how physically exhausted, she was. Rage, grief, and fear had filled her completely. Now, facing the end, the necessary admission of total failure, even the negative emotions that had upheld her sank into a black depression. She staggered, went to her knees, her eyes closing.

A painful grip on her arm yanked her forward, out of the Gate area, pulled her upright. She stared around

at Pasgen's windowless but brilliantly lit workroom.
Because the Gate was only supposed to exist for less
than a day, Pasgen had set it up in one of his work-
rooms. He been waiting for her, eager to collapse the
Gate which was a constant drain on him. He shook her
so that her teeth rattled, and shouted at her.

"Where is FitzRoy? I thought we had agreed that
you would bring him here where there was the least
chance of tracing him!" He shook her again, his voice
rising with anger. "*Where is he?*"

Rhoslyn opened her eyes; it took as much effort as
to climb a mountain. "The changeling is dead, and I
don't have FitzRoy," she said flatly.

He snarled. "Dead! What in the lowest plane of
demons ails you? How could you make a simulacrum
that would not last at least a few hours?"

Anger gave Rhoslyn strength again, and enough
energy to wrest her arm out of Pasgen's grip and stalk
through the door of his workroom. It was a Gate, and
nearly brought her to her knees again, but it left her
in the short corridor between his bedroom and his
living room. Steadying herself against the wall for a
moment, she turned into the latter, and sank down on
one of the uninviting looking but comfortable sofas.

"The changeling was murdered," she said to Pasgen,
who appeared in the doorway moments later, face
stormy with rage.

But that brought him up short. "Murdered?"

It was her turn to snarl. "Blast you, can't you do
anything but repeat what I say? Go and shut down the
Gate. There's no need for you to feed it. We won't be
going back to Windsor again."

Pasgen's mouth dropped open. Rhoslyn could not
tell whether it was surprise at her vicious tone or a
prelude to shouting at her, but clearly he realized that
first things should come first, and he went back out

presumably to the Gate that would take him to his workroom so he could close down the Gate to Windsor. Rhoslyn closed her eyes again. She did not yield to her first impulse, which was to run away and cry until she slept; she did rest and draw in power from the ambience of Underhill.

First her fear faded. It was clear that Pasgen would not abandon her. Despite her assurances to herself, she had always wondered whether, if she made a serious enough blunder, he would walk away and leave her to her fate. Then her rage settled from a boiling hot turmoil into a kind of hard determination to repay Denoriel—with usurious interest—for what he had done to her. That determination, like hardened lava, covered her grief, although somewhere deep inside she was bruised and torn.

"What do you mean the changeling was murdered? Is a changeling enough alive to be murdered?"

Rhoslyn's eyes snapped open; she sat straighter on the sofa. "Mine was!" she spat. "He was as much a child as any mortal living, and he would have passed as Harry FitzRoy for however long he lived . . . but Denoriel sucked out the power that gave him life and cast the husk away."

"Denoriel?" Pasgen cleared his throat as he realized he had again repeated what Rhoslyn said. "Denoriel was not supposed to be there. It cost me five servants to watch for his movements. Having them pass as human ate their energy so fast I could not always save them."

"I will make you more," she promised wearily.

Pasgen shrugged, as if her offer was of no account. "Denoriel never came to Windsor before two of the clock and often not until four or five. Twice—no, three times he came secretly in the night, or it might have been another Sidhe—the servants do not see as well as we do at night. Whoever it was entered through a magicked door and climbed the castle wall to enter through a magicked window. Denoriel *never* came to Windsor in the morning. That muscle-bound sword swinger had not brains enough—"

She interrupted him with a snort. "That muscle-bound sword-swinger outthought us from the moment he took on the care of FitzRoy. I was wrong about him. He is more, much more. Even if Denoriel had not been there to interfere, my plans were in ruins." She thrust out her right hand which was still reddened and slightly puffy. "I could never have touched the boy to change his clothes with the simulacrum. I do not know whether I could even have cast a sleep spell that would hold him. FitzRoy was wearing cold iron in a form that was deadly! And he had been wearing it on his flesh for a long time."

"Cold iron? But then how could Denoriel . . ."

Once again she interrupted him. "Pasgen, we have always underestimated him. Do not, I pray you, do so any longer. I have discovered to my sorrow that he is more than a simple-minded warrior. He is cleverer than I would have believed. He saw the boat in the coach and must have guessed I left it there to induce the child to climb in. He went to get it, saw my poor little changeling . . ."

Her mouth trembled and she steadied it with an effort and continued, "And he is strong! He bent over FitzRoy as if the aura of cold iron did not exist. I had to walk at arms' length and I could barely keep my gorge from rising or resist the pangs in my arms and legs. *He* stood right beside FitzRoy and handed the boat to the child. I think their fingers touched and he did not even wince."

Pasgen stared at her, then said quietly, "Let us not go overboard the other way and start to believe Denoriel invincible. He has a resistance to the devil metal . . . I had heard that. I think mother told me. And of course he knew the child was carrying it so it did not take him by surprise, as it took you. What troubles me much more than any strength Denoriel has is that he thought to arm FitzRoy with cold iron . . . and that he somehow knew you were in the palace that morning."

Rhoslyn sighed. "I think I know the answer to how he knew I was in the palace. A very strict watch is kept over FitzRoy since those stupid Spaniards attacked him. No one is allowed to approach him at all, so I had to get permission from the duke of Norfolk to speak to the boy. And I wanted him called out of his school-room before Denoriel could possibly arrive. While I was . . . ah . . . convincing Norfolk to call the child from his lessons to go with me I . . . I sensed something of a Seleighe spirit and . . . and there was—I did not see it with my eyes but there was a flash of white."

"There and then gone?"

"Yes."

Pasgen's lips thinned. "An air spirit set to watch. But for what? For you? For me?"

She thought about that, thought about the limited thinking ability of an air spirit. "I would say for any Sidhe. That tells us that Denoriel was the only one who was attending to FitzRoy, but that is of no benefit to know now. FitzRoy is leaving for Yorkshire tomorrow, and Denoriel is riding with the cortege."

"And the air spirit, too, which means that if we approach the cortege, Denoriel will be warned." He frowned. "Still, air spirits are notably inconstant. I can think of more than one device that would confuse it or draw it away. And there should be some easy way to distract Denoriel. Along the roads the cortege will travel in a long drawn-out party. Surely we should be able to separate FitzRoy from the others."

Rhoslyn had begun shaking her head as soon as Pasgen mentioned the air spirit and distracting Denoriel. "You will not draw away or distract this air spirit. I suspect Aleneil's fine hand is on the creature. Doubtless she has bound it in some way to its task. And nothing will distract Denoriel. Any threat to the cortege would clamp him to FitzRoy's side like a stickfast. Not to mention the boy's own guards, who remember clearly what happened to those whose failure of attention permitted the attempt to drown him. Don't even think of it, unless you mean to call out the whole Wild Hunt."

Pasgen shook his head. "Not that, nor to do anything else that might call Vidal Dhu's attention."

She shuddered at that reminder. "I doubt I will need to *call* his attention after I tell him—"

But Pasgen cut her off. "You will tell him nothing. He did not know when we intended to make this attempt. There is no reason for him to know that we failed."

"I failed, not you," she said despairingly.

"I as much for not thinking and planning better." Pasgen's face contorted into a grimace of irritation and dissatisfaction. "It is too bad that the changeling was lost, but it will matter much less in the wilds of Yorkshire. We may need to wait a few months, but I believe that our first plan was too complicated. I will have to discover where Denoriel has his Gate placed, then I will create one for us. Sooner or later it will be possible for us to herd FitzRoy through that Gate, and never mind substituting anything. Why should we have bothered with creating a substitute at all? He will simply be lost, and they will not know where, and when he is gone, the future that Lord Vidal wanted will come to pass."

Rhoslyn sat up straighter and her eyes brightened.

"But first we need to be rid of that accursed air spirit. I can bind a few minor Unseleighe creatures to follow and watch the cortege. Inside Windsor using hobgoblins and the like was impossible, but their auras will be less apparent out in the countryside and Denoriel may not associate them with himself or FitzRoy if I use a different one each day. As soon as they discover what form the air spirit has taken for watching FitzRoy, I will devise some constructs whose single purpose will be to kill it."

Pasgen shrugged. "That would be a waste of time and effort. It will be replaced quickly and to repeat the killing will betray us. Anyway, do not have it killed on the journey to Yorkshire. That will tell Denoriel too much. Let him try to guess what we intend to do and wear himself out watching. And, despite Vidal's hysteria, it will be years in the future before we need worry about the boy usurping Princess Mary's place. A month more or less—a year—more—it would not matter. We have time to watch and wait until after the Gates are set. Then we can take him."

Rhoslyn said nothing, afraid that Pasgen would read in her words how much her arms ached to curve around a small, warm body, to hold a child that wriggled and laughed and cuddled against her for comfort. She made herself shrug in response to Pasgen's reasoning, but inside she reaffirmed her determination to have FitzRoy. She would rub Denoriel's nose in the foul mess of defeat. And she would tell no one, not even Pasgen, that she had the child. He would be hers, all hers, for as long as she wanted him.

This new place in Yorkshire to which FitzRoy was going was far more rural than Windsor. It was far from the court in London, from the Spanish embassy, and from the minions of the Emperor Charles. The vigilance around FitzRoy would soon relax. Denoriel could not *live* with the boy, and he too would often be absent keeping up with his friends in Henry VIII's court.

Another idea occurred to her. Pasgen had a fine hand with Gates. Surely he could do something that would make Denoriel's personal Gates answer her. Or if he could not do that, perhaps he could repattern the Gate so that it would dump Denoriel into Vidal's Court or just lose him completely in the Unformed chaos lands. And if Denoriel was out of the way, she might not have to wait so long before she had FitzRoy in her arms. This time she would leave no changeling behind with half her heart. She would snatch FitzRoy and let the blame fall where it would.

CHAPTER 13

The white kitten was in the grain trough when Denoriel reached Miralys's stall, and the straw was still mounded up slightly where he had covered the changeling's body.

:Out gate:

Denoriel nodded wearily, acknowledging the air spirit's report that Rhoslyn was gone. The bone-deep ache of exposure to cold iron was fading, but he felt cold and exhausted. His power channels were sore too, and he had not touched mortal-world power. He supposed it was from setting and releasing the Don't-see-me spell so often and from casting that strong shield around Harry. And his work had barely started.

"I don't think anything more will happen," he said in a low murmur to the air spirit, "but since this is the last full day Harry will be in Windsor, I'm not sure. If this is a good location for the Unseleighe for some reason, they may be desperate and try again to take him. You had better stay close to Harry, and

come for me no matter where I am or what I am
doing if another Sidhe enters Windsor."

:*Done:*

The little creature giggled happily and was gone. It
had plainly enjoyed all the chasing and finding, but
Denoriel hoped never to have another morning like this
one. He slipped down to his knees and brushed the
straw off the simulacrum.

The Don't-see-me spell had faded—Denoriel had
not put much power into it because he expected to
dismiss it shortly—and his breath caught at the likeness to Harry. Rhoslyn was a maker of rare skill. If it
had not been for the aura of magic that imbued the
child . . . construct . . . he would have been fooled.
Denoriel shook his head, but then he reached out and
smoothed back the little boy's hair.

What was he to do with this . . . this creature? He
leaned closer, frowning. Surely the . . . the child's breathing was shorter and shallower than it had been, his little
face paler? Denoriel's throat tightened. The spells!
Could the sleep spell and his own Don't-see-me spell
be drawing on the changeling's small store of power?

Denoriel snatched up the child, trembling with
panic. But even as he was about to mount Miralys and
tell him to breach the wall between the worlds, he
realized he did not know what such violent transmis-
sion would do to the already fragile being he held in
his arms. Would that be worse than another Don't-see-
me spell? But the Don't-see-me spell would only be
in effect for minutes.

Swallowing nervously, Denoriel cast it, and walked
out of the stable, leading Miralys. He knew he looked
awkward with one arm cocked across his chest as if
he were carrying something—which, of course, he
was—but he walked quickly, scowling, and none of the
stable boys approached him.

Mounting was not easy, but Miralys helped, and then they were gone from the stable area and just rounding the curve that would take them to the front gate. And as soon as they were out of sight of the Windsor guards, Denoriel dismissed the Don't-see-me spell. He looked down into the child's face, which was surely paler and more pinched, and clutched the boy to him—but he didn't know how to send power into the child.

"Miralys," he breathed . . . and they were at the Gate to Elfhame Logres, and then Miralys stopped at Mwynwen's door.

Denoriel could not remember having decided what to do with FitzRoy's changeling, but Miralys was often wiser than he. This was obviously the best answer to the problem. He sent an anguished mental call to Mwynwen, and struggled out of the saddle. The door opened. Mwynwen stood in it, but there was no welcome in her face and little concern for what had forced that plea from him . . . until she saw the bundle in his arms.

"FitzRoy?" she gasped.

"No, his changeling. And it is dying, I think."

"Come in. Come in quickly."

The walls were all a soft and soothing white with moldings and borders of a pale, grayish blue that radiated calm. Denoriel had never paid much attention to this part of Mwynwen's home. Mostly he had come in through the garden to her private quarters and was not seeking calm but excitement and pleasure. If the effect had worked on him while he was ill, he did not remember it. Now he was grateful as the pain in his throat and chest eased and his bowels unknotted.

She led the way past two modest-sized reception rooms and a parlor to a cross corridor that had several closed doors. She turned left and went to the end of the corridor where she opened the last door. Denoriel's breath drew in with surprise. It was a small room, but the walls were painted with lively murals, scenes of childish gaiety—there were children rolling hoops, chasing each other, hiding behind bushes, playing with dogs and lambs.

The wall opposite the door held two large bay windows, each of which had a window seat that looked out—one onto a farmyard with ducks and geese, chickens and calves; the other onto a near meadow in which colts were at play. Against the right-hand wall was a small sofa, just large enough for a child and another person to sit side by side. Against the other was a small bed with a gay counterpane. In the center of the room was a table on which were blocks and some small figures.

Denoriel was stunned into silence. Magically cleaned and aired, how long had this room stood ready for the healing of a child?

"On the bed," Mwynwen ordered.

He laid the boy down, his arms loosing the child reluctantly. Mwynwen pushed past him, running her hands up and down from the simulacrum's head to his toes, whispering to herself, biting her lip and shaking her head. Denoriel stood back, wringing his hands in silent anxiety. He tried to think that what he felt was stupid; a changeling could not live long in any case. But all that line of reasoning accomplished was to bring back the pain in his chest and throat, the grinding in his belly, and tears to his eyes.

But then, Mwynwen drew a deep breath and laid her hands on the child's head. Now her voice rang out clear and Denoriel felt a tingling as some spell disintegrated and then a sort of rushing, as if a strong breeze blew past him, only the air did not move.

"Good morrow, sweetheart."

Denoriel blinked. He had never heard that tone in Mwynwen's voice, no matter how sweet, how intimate their caresses had been.

"Who are you?"

FitzRoy's voice. Denoriel swallowed hard.

"I am the lady with whom you are now to live, dearling."

Denoriel's lips parted to protest and then closed. Someone would have to watch over the changeling for signs of failing and if possible repair the fault. The best person to do that was Mwynwen. Aleneil could, but she was not principally a healer. And there was no need to ask if Mwynwen was willing; her eyes, her voice, the way she bent toward the child . . . construct . . . Denoriel recalled Aleneil's warning to him, but Mwynwen would know without telling. Even so, she would have fought him if he tried to take the changeling away.

"I am not to live with His Grace of Norfolk any longer?" The child looked worried and his voice was tremulous.

"You would not have done so in any case," Mwynwen said in a comfortable, matter-of-fact tone. "The move to Yorkshire changed all the plans. Do you know who you are, my love?"

"Of course. I am Henry FitzRoy, duke of Richmond and Somerset and earl of Nottingham."

"Oh, my," Mwynwen said, a smile in her voice. "That's rather a large mouthful isn't it? But since you are to live here with me, could we make it a bit shorter? Could I call you . . . Richey—short for Richmond?"

"I am not to be a duke any more?"

"Will you mind very much? Perhaps—"

"I won't mind at all," the changeling said. Suddenly

his brow creased in a puzzled frown. "Someone was always telling me how I must act and . . . and . . . I suppose it was my guardian, but it was so hard to remember . . ."

"That's all done with. You don't need to remember any of it. Only remember that your name is Richey. Mwynwen is my name, and if you call me, I will always be there to help you. Now do you feel well enough to have some bread and milk?"

"Have I been ill?"

"No, love, not really. But you were taken on a long journey and that tired you. Are you still tired?"

The construct sat up. "Only a very little," he said. "But I don't feel like sleeping any more."

"No, indeed," Mwynwen agreed. "Come along with me now, Richey, and have a nice nuncheon."

Behind her back, Mwynwen made dismissive gestures at Denoriel. Again he felt like protesting and again swallowed the protest as he realized that Mwynwen didn't want Richey to see him. Likely she was afraid seeing him would wake some confused half-memories in Richey of what had happened since Rhoslyn brought him into the mortal world and Denoriel carried him back Underhill. So, very quietly, Denoriel backed away and stood quite still while Mwynwen maneuvered the little changeling out of the room. When they were gone, Denoriel made his way to the front door where he found Miralys waiting.

"Where now?" he mumbled to himself.

He leaned against the elvensteed, cold, empty, and exhausted, trying to dismiss his sense of loss and unable to decide whether the loss of Mwynwen or that of the changeling was the most painful. The elvensteed snorted gently, managing to convey a sense of disdain over folly. Denoriel sighed as he mounted, but his lips soon parted in silent laughter at himself.

How could the changeling have preferred him? It *wasn't* Harry. It had never seen him or known him. Even if the minds of the attackers had yielded images of him fighting them, Rhoslyn was unlikely to have transmitted those images to the changeling's mind. She would not want the simulacrum to feel any affection or dependence on him and the attackers would not have been aware of his relationship with Harry. And he wasn't as pretty as Mwynwen . . . even a six-year-old would notice that.

Was he piqued because Mwynwen had not been aware—or cared if she were aware—that he was hurt and depleted? Ridiculous when the changeling was in so much worse condition. No, he had to stop thinking of Richey only as Harry's simulacrum. They would grow in different directions now, no matter how long Richey lived. In a few months or a year—if Richey lived that long—they would not even look much alike, even though their features were similar, because life in the mortal world and Underhill was so different.

Harry's face would grow older faster with the need for wariness both physical and emotional. All stress would be absent in the bland, protected environment Mwynwen would provide for Richey, and the child . . . yes, child. Richey *was* a child, no matter how he had come to life. He would look young and innocent, probably for the whole short term of his existence. And how foolish it was to envy Mwynwen the care of him. He had Harry, and would have him for many years.

He was aware then of a shock of disorientation. If Miralys had not somehow held him to his saddle, he would have toppled to the ground. Which Gate, he wondered, and then did not need to wonder as Miralys came to a halt in front of Aleneil's cottage. Of course. He needed to tell Aleneil what had happened. His head was so thick right now; it felt as if it were stuffed with silk floss. Maybe she would have a better idea than he about what he should do next.

He managed to dismount and get to the door. It opened but Aleneil was not there. Denoriel knew he was always welcome in his sister's home and went through to the parlor where they usually talked. He felt a stirring in the air around him and understood that he could ask for food or drink and he would be served. He could not remember the last time he had eaten, but he wasn't hungry and just shook his head.

He sank into his favorite chair, leaned back and closed his eyes. His fingers traced the inlaid patterns of silky, cool mother-of-pearl and he felt calmer, but his thoughts still would not come clear. He kept seeing the tears on Rhoslyn's face. He had not known that she *could* cry. He wondered if she had put too much into the changeling. His eyes opened slowly and he stared across Aleneil's room. The walls were white but with the faintest rose tint, which made them warm and somehow cheerful. The ever-changing pictures were of sylvan scenes of exquisite beauty. His eyes closed again.

"You look as if you had been dragged backward through that precious Wild Hunt of yours. What have you been doing with yourself?"

Denoriel yawned and sat up, putting up a hand to rub the back of his neck, which was twisted. Elves did not sleep, but he must have been close to that state. Perhaps he was catching it from so much time spent in the mortal world. At least he felt better than he had when he arrived. He was not as cold or as empty, perhaps not as exhausted either, but he surely did not want to do anything yet.

"Preventing Rhoslyn from putting a changeling in Harry's place," he replied in answer to her question.

"A changeling!" Aleneil looked around as if she expected to see the construct lying about somewhere in her room.

Denoriel chuckled a little. "He was fading fast, poor little devil. I brought him to Mwynwen. She restored him and will keep him safe."

"Him?"

"She named him Richey, and I think she means to keep him alive as long as she can," he explained. "I can understand why. He is not like other constructs. He is truly a child. He talks and thinks and feels to a remarkable extent—if I had not known better, I would have mistaken him for FitzRoy. He knows who he is and has 'memories' of his earlier life. Rhoslyn intended him to pass for Harry without raising any doubts so that his death would be accepted as the end of any threat of a male to supplant Princess Mary as heir."

Aleneil looked troubled. "Was it wise to restore him? If Rhoslyn can snatch him back—"

He rubbed his chin uneasily. "She believes I killed him. She called me a murderer, and I did not contradict her. She . . . she wept."

"Oh, poor Rhoslyn," Aleneil sighed. "To make a changeling so real, she must have invested a huge amount of herself in the creature. Oh, dear. She would not have done that unless she felt it truly important that FitzRoy be removed from the world, and I suppose that means that she and Pasgen *have* seen the image of the future that we have. Tell me what happened."

So Denoriel described the entire morning to her, beginning with his summons to Windsor by the white kitten and ending with the scene in Mwynwen's house. That last made Aleneil's lips compress, but she said nothing, clearly feeling that Mwynwen was more than old enough to know how she should and should not bestow her time, energy, and heart.

All she said was, "I do not need to warn you to keep a close watch on FitzRoy. I am glad I was able to renew the spell on the air spirit only a little while ago. It will be attentive, especially because there was an attempt on the boy. And do not allow *yourself* to be distracted. The most likely device they will try is to attack some innocent and helpless member of the party traveling north. Do *not* go to rescue the innocent or you are likely to lose FitzRoy."

He nodded. "I had thought of that already. Fortunately Norfolk is not going with us. He is needed in London and may go to France on some diplomatic mission. Northumberland has gone ahead to be sure all is ready. Lord Dacre was supposed to accompany the cortege, but his gout is crippling and he has sent his brother Sir Christopher Fiennes. That one is not the most perceptive of men and Norfolk seems not to have warned him about preventing my closeness to the boy. I think there will be no trouble if I actually ride beside Harry. I know his guards will not object; they are aware of my skill with a sword."

Aleneil still looked concerned. "You will not be able to share his quarters at night."

"Yes I can, if I use the Don't-see-me spell." He sighed. "But it drains me, Aleneil, and Mwynwen warned me not to use mortal-world power . . . and I am tired."

She looked at him with concern. "I think you need to come back Underhill every night, once FitzRoy is settled in his bed. Surely his guards will be alert, and the air spirit will summon you."

"To where?" Denoriel asked, a touch bitterly. "There are no Gates between here and our destination, and I am not even certain which route they will take. Once

Harry is established in Sheriff Hutton, I can ask Master Treowth to construct a Gate for me, but to build one each night . . ."

"No, that is too much to ask," she admitted. "And I cannot now see how you could return here every night. But instead of exhausting yourself, perhaps we should try another way. Surely a gold coin or two to whoever arranges quarters should make it possible for you to be lodged near the boy. If you are in the same building, you should be able to respond quickly enough to the air spirit to foil any attempt on him." She nibbled on her lips for a moment and then said, "Arrange for the guards to tell the servants of this Sir Christopher about how you rescued FitzRoy and have the boy ask for you to be near him."

He nodded; that was a much better idea than trying to lurk unnoticed in Harry's room. "I can do that. We will have to hope that Sir Christopher is less suspicious of a foreigner binding Harry's affection. Still, since I will have no baggage train—"

Aleneil looked aghast. "No baggage train? You cannot be serious, Denoriel. How can you travel from Windsor to Sheriff Hutton without a baggage train? Do you intend to wear the same clothing for a month or more?"

He waved dismissively. "Of course not. I have gold enough to pay for whatever needs I may have other than clothing, and I can make a new suit every day, or even two, if I must dress for dinner."

Aleneil sighed. "And precisely how do you intend to explain your wardrobe with no baggage train?"

Denoriel opened his mouth, then shut it, then said, "Oh."

Aleneil grinned and shook her head at him. "I will see to the making of five suits suitable for dress wear, three for daily riding and two for private comfortable wear after a day's riding, with suitable undergarments, hose, boots, and shoes. And each servant you bring with you will also need a change of livery. You will need a packhorse. No elvensteed is going to carry baggage."

They both giggled at the thought. Then Denoriel remembered that he had told Ladbroke and Shandy Dunstan to buy a packhorse for their clothing and a small tent in case there was no room in the cortege's lodging for servants. Perhaps his goods would fit on that horse. He shrugged. It was not important; he had gold, and packhorses were easy to come by.

There was again a stirring in the air and then a stirring around Denoriel. He assumed Aleneil's servants were taking his measure. He did not ask about the style. Aleneil herself dressed in the highest of courtly fashion copied from the mortal world. If she did not already know what a gentleman should wear, she would find out without trouble. And then Denoriel wondered again why she chose to wear such uncomfortable clothes— and promptly felt like a fool. Aleneil was a FarSeer. She must have some idea that there would be a need for her to have an identity in Henry VIII's court—or at least, among the ladies-in-waiting about the queen—and was accustoming herself to the garments.

He was about to ask her about that when the servants were gone, but Aleneil forestalled his question by inviting him again to eat. Denoriel was surprised to find that he was feeling much better, and quite hungry, so he agreed.

But then, he began to wonder why she never spoke about what she was doing any more, and he realized at that moment that of late, Aleneil told him only what she thought he needed to know and nothing more. He took a sidelong glance at his sister, and it came to him with a feeling of shock that it was she, and not he, who had always been more involved in what he lumped under the general heading of "politics." As a FarSeer, of course, she would be—which meant that if anyone knew what all the repercussions of what he—and by extension, Pasgen and Rhoslyn—were doing, it would be Aleneil.

For a moment he was annoyed; and then it came to him that before he had begun to nursemaid Harry, he had not *wanted* to know about the sometimes delicate maneuverings between Under- and Overhill. He had been satisfied to go and fight wherever he was told or to hunt whoever was chosen as the quarry for the Wild Hunt. It was not fair to blame Aleneil for not telling him everything she knew, nor to think she was trying to conceal anything from him, yet now he wanted to know the very things he had wished to avoid before. Thus when they moved to Aleneil's dining room, he began diplomatically by asking why she had such a passion for uncomfortable Tudor clothes.

She demurred. "Well, they are very elegant, are they not?"

He snorted. "I think they're miserably uncomfortable. How can you bear that tight bodice? And that stupid corset flattens you. You could be a boy!"

"Not in this skirt," Aleneil said, laughing. "It takes long practice to learn how to move at all without tripping or catching one's heel in the hem or the train."

"For men it's that stupid gown! It's always in my way. Those huge padded shoulders and the sleeves that hang down behind . . . And the shirt and the doublet and the jacquette—"

He stopped speaking suddenly and a look of horror came over his face, just as a plate of food appeared in front of him. There was an indistinct sound, an agitated swirl, and the plate rose in the air and began rapidly to float away.

"Hi!" Denoriel called. "Where are you going with my dinner?"

Aleneil was laughing heartily. "It's the face you made. My poor servant thought you were horrified by the food."

"No, no. Put it back," Denoriel said, waving at the plate which was hanging uncertainly in the air. As it settled, he said to Aleneil. "When I was describing the clothes, I realized I would actually have to put them on and take them off during the trip instead of just calling them into existence on my body. I'll need to find out if Ladbroke or Dunstan can serve as a valet. If not, I'll have to see if Boleyn can recommend one."

"Boleyn?" Aleneil repeated, looking very interested.

"Yes, George Boleyn." Now was the time, Denoriel thought, to make clear to Aleneil that he wanted and needed to be alert to the politics and relationships in the mortal world. "George is the son of Sir Thomas Boleyn, who is one of King Henry's favorite diplomats. Sir Thomas gets sent all over Europe and was elevated to Viscount Rochford when Harry got all those titles."

Aleneil smiled at him. "So you *do* understand that just being a watchdog is not enough. My dear brother! I am extravagantly pleased with you!"

He laughed. "Oh, yes. A rich merchant would be interested in politics, so I must be. And of course, what happens between England, France, and Spain affects Harry."

"Good." Aleneil sighed. "I was worried about how to make you aware of problems around FitzRoy that don't seem to touch him now, but may in the future."

He sobered, seeing the worry in her eyes. "I could see that. I've managed to insinuate myself into George's group of friends—Francis Bryan, Thomas Wyatt, Francis Weston, Henry Norris . . . a couple of others. They are close to King Henry, play tennis with him, gamble with him, and could provide an introduction if I should ever need one." He knitted his brows when she showed some surprise at his comment. "I'm a Hungarian nobleman whose family were all killed by the Turks, but who's rich as Croesus because of a wide-flung trading empire the Turks couldn't touch. Didn't I tell you all this?"

She shook her head, and he could not imagine how he had failed to tell her of his plans. But then, he had been very angry at being sent to watch over a child. . . .

"I don't think you did," she admitted. "But your connection with George Boleyn is very, very convenient. I am also acquainted. Not with George himself but with his mother, who is Elizabeth Howard—"

He caught that name as one familiar to him. "Howard? Related to Norfolk?"

She nodded. He thought he saw approval in her glance. "His sister."

"Ahhh. What made you interested in the family?" So she was going into the mortal world on her own! Presumably she was in search of that elusive child who would bring the age of gold to the mortals.

"The women, of course," she said reprovingly. "The elder daughter, Mary, may still be the king's mistress, although he seems to be losing interest."

He raised an eyebrow. "And the likely mother of the red-haired babe?"

"I hope not!" she exclaimed. "The red-haired baby must be in the royal line with no doubt attached to its parentage. Mary is married to William Carey, and if she bears a red-haired child it will be acknowledged by Carey as his own. He has already acknowledged her first child—"

"The king's get?" he asked, a little crudely.

She shook her head. "I think not. The child was not fair, but dark. The boy was named Henry . . . but that might not mean anything; many children are named for the king, and Henry, who is starving for boy children, never acknowledged this one."

"I suppose because Mary does also lie with her husband, and he could not be sure." Denoriel speared what looked like a pink rosebud and conveyed it to his mouth. "Ah . . . this is excellent! I thought it would be sweet, but it is pungent and delicious."

"Smoked fish," Aleneil said, absently. "No, it is the second daughter in whom I am interested. She is very young now, just fifteen, and when it looked as if there might be war between England and France, she was called back from France where she had been one of Queen Claude's women."

Yet another woman grown. "Did *she* appear in a FarSeeing about the red-haired babe?"

Aleneil sighed in an exasperated way. "Nothing clear enough to make it worthwhile to warn you, and I am almost sure that the child is not yet born. *But* the red-haired babe *is* associated with a dark-haired, dark-eyed woman—a very clever woman . . . a woman who has the makings of a witch . . . which would make sense, given the power we sensed around the babe."

Perhaps the girl might be of interest after all. "And George Boleyn's youngest sister matches this description?"

"I think so, but I am not certain, although she does have the nail of a sixth finger on her left hand." He sensed Aleneil's discomfort; like many FarSeers, she was uneasy when she could not foresee the future clearly.

"Are you going to try to teach her magic?" he asked,

with interest. Now that would be a fascinating prospect—especially if she chose to pit herself against Queen Catherine for the legitimate affections of the king.

"No!" On that point Aleneil was certain. "She would reject me utterly and probably report me to the nearest witch-hating priest she could find. She is terrified of her Talent and seeks only to deny it, but she uses it unconsciously . . . on men. She is already welcome at court and has attracted attention . . . of Wyatt for one."

"Wyatt is married," Denoriel pointed out.

Aleneil laughed. "It seems to matter as little to Henry's courtiers as it matters to us."

"Hmmm. If she is to be Henry's mistress and the mother of the red-haired babe, I had better see to it that Wyatt does not despoil her," he said, with just a touch of callousness. "We want no doubts about her to rise in the king's mind."

"That would be useful," Aleneil agreed—just as callously. She could, he reflected, be just as ruthless as anyone when it was mortals who were being discussed.

"Do you want me to try to meet her?" he asked, thinking it might be amusing to see the little fifteen-year-old coquette attempt to use her wiles on him.

"No, certainly not," his sister said firmly. "If she developed a taste for you, she might refuse King Henry's advances, and we don't want that to happen until we are sure who will be the mother of the red-haired child."

Denoriel was silent for a while, giving his attention to the many-flavored delicacies on his plate. When it was empty and had floated away, he looked at Aleneil, frowning.

"I don't like the fact that her Talent is so strong and

untutored and that she is using it. That use could attract unwanted attention, and she would be defenseless against any attack on her, against any idea a dark Sidhe wished to implant in her."

"I am aware. I will try to protect her, but she is a very high-spirited girl and I doubt will accept a duenna, as a Spanish girl would." She made a moue of distaste, and added, "Her father and mother are too well aware of the advantages Mary brought them while she was the king's favorite. Now that Mary's allure seems to be fading, they do not wish to restrict Anne too much. If not King Henry, she is like to snare a powerful suitor."

He raised an eyebrow. "At least then we will not need to worry about an untutored witch being the mother of the red-haired babe."

Aleneil shrugged and shook her head. "Let us forget all this for now. The child's birth is some years in the future."

Denoriel smiled and the talk turned to small personal matters. After the meal, considerably refreshed, although with a new worry at the back of his mind, Denoriel Gated to his house in London. He arrived shortly after the white kitten had appeared on his shoulder and he had rushed off, but Ladbroke and Dunstan did not appear in the least surprised and neither mentioned the miraculous appearance of the white kitten. Having lived so long Underhill, they were well aware that the kitten was some spirit the Sidhe was using and that hours or even days might have passed for Denoriel between his previous departure and his seeming arrival only some quarter hour later.

To Denoriel's relief, Dunstan pronounced himself capable of attending to a gentleman's needs. Fortunately one of his masters Underhill had affected the highest mode of mortal dress. It was not quite as elaborate as that popular in the Tudor court, but Dunstan knew how to tie, hook, and button. Only, he pointed out that becoming Denoriel's valet would mean he must wear different clothing than he had bought for himself and that doing so would leave Ladbroke as the only groom.

"Get what clothing you need," Denoriel said to Dunstan, and, turning to Ladbroke, "Take on a boy. Pick one out of one of the workhouses, one who can ride. That should make the poor creature grateful enough to close his eyes to a few peculiarities of his master and to keep his mouth closed about them, too. You can hint, I suppose, that my disappearances and reappearances are owing to my business and I don't like that business discussed. And I won't be coming and going quite as much while we're on the road . . . no Gates."

Another thing that long residence Underhill had induced in Ladbroke and Dunstan was self-reliance and resourcefulness. Partly out of curiosity about what they would do, partly out of envy over the human ability to create new ways to deal with problems, Sidhe masters would often drop their human companions—adult ones, anyway—into difficult or dangerous situations and watch them squirm out. Not all survived.

Denoriel had had no human servants but was sufficiently familiar with the practice and with the evidence of what Dunstan and Ladbroke had already accomplished to be sure they would find a way to do anything he asked. He said only, "Some trunks with clothing for me will be Gated through from my sister in Avalon. See if it will fit on the packhorse—"

"Mule, m'lord," Ladbroke said. "Mules are better for carrying packs."

"Fine. If my trunks will overload the beast, get

another. And set out for Windsor as early tomorrow morning as you possibly can. You can bed down in the inn in Windsor if they have room for that night; if not, you have your tent. I will meet you at the main gate of Windsor at dawn day after tomorrow. The cortege is due to leave at dawn."

"Will it, m'lord?" Dunstan looked surprised.

Denoriel grinned. "It won't, of course; probably won't leave until nine of the clock or even later. Still, we should be there—that is, by the principal gate to Windsor—so we can choose our places."

"Very good, m'lord," Dunstan nodded. "You'll be riding right by his young Grace's carriage or alongside his horse if he's allowed to ride. Where do you want me and Kip? Should we be together or spread out in the line of march?"

"You need to be as near as possible to where I am so you can see where I'm lodged." He considered his tactics, deciding that he would order his little force as if he expected attack at any point. "You'll also need to see where Ladbroke goes so you can run messages to him if it's necessary. As I said, I'll meet you at Windsor, but if that white kitten should come to you, follow it and be sure to carry your weapons . . . steel weapons, not silver."

"Steel, m'lord?" both men echoed in chorus.

He nodded grimly. "Yes. You'll have to set them aside when you actually serve me, Dunstan, but I am not as badly affected as some. Sword, poniard, bow. No armor, though, nor helms. Armor may be too much iron for me."

"Outfitted as you say. Day after tomorrow at dawn at the main gate to Windsor," Ladbroke repeated.

Denoriel smiled and clapped him on the back. "I know I can depend on you two."

"That you can, m'lord," Ladbroke replied. "Leave

the journey to us, and keep your mind on seeing the boy stays safe."

"Oh, do believe me," Denoriel replied. "That is what is uppermost on my mind. . . ."

CHAPTER 14

Denoriel's party met as planned at dawn outside the great gate of Windsor. Within the gates, those who were traveling from Windsor should have been forming up in some kind of order, considering the number of supposedly trained and disciplined royal guards present. After all, nobles of the great houses went on Royal Progress with the king all the time, and they themselves changed their habitations twice yearly, between London and their own estates. But—Denoriel had to swallow his urge to laugh—the royal party was rapidly mirroring the large and disorganized mass of servants, luggage, guards, and pack animals that accompanied his courtier friends when they traveled.

Not that Denoriel's entourage was disorganized. Shandy Dunstan, attired in plain, serviceable black worsted garments headed the procession on a handsome, sorrel cob. Kip Ladbroke, in brown homespun and leather, followed on a larger, nondescript bay. Behind him was an emaciated boy with a dazed look of wonder on his face. He was also attired in decent homespun, mounted on a sturdy pony, and holding the lead rein of a glossy, well-fed mule, to whose pack saddle was attached another mule as like the first as could be a twin. Despite the dazed expression, the boy sat his saddle as if he were glued to it, and his head turned to check the mules each time one of the animals shifted. Clearly he knew horses and their ilk; Denoriel wondered what his tale was.

Time passed. The light, which had been dim, brightened gradually, promising a pleasant morning. More and more people arrived, most on foot. Denoriel thought that most of the inhabitants of the village had come to see the party off. They stood by the road, waiting to see the cortege go by, hoping that the lords who accompanied it would scatter largesse. Two groups, however, were on horseback. A discreet signal from Denoriel sent Kip Ladbroke back toward those. Denoriel scanned those who waited by the sides of the road, opening himself to sense for magic of any kind. There was nothing.

The crowd inside the gates thickened and Denoriel could hear a rising volume of sound, pierced once in a while by a female shriek or a masculine bellow. The sun came up over the trees. More servants and lesser personages were thrust down the entrance avenue. The noise rose. Denoriel was sure it must be deafening near the palace.

He approached the open gate. One guard leveled his pike and then said, "Oh, it's you, Lord Denno." Then he looked uncertain, glancing from Denoriel to the slowly revolving mass of men, horses, mules, and carts near the palace and trailing down the long entrance avenue. After a moment, he said, "If you want to go in, you can, m'lord, but . . ."

"Since I'm quite sane," Denoriel said, chuckling, "I *don't* want to go in. But I promised His Grace of

Richmond that I would be traveling with the cortege and I am a little concerned that if he does not see me, he will be distressed."

"That's all right, m'lord. His guard Nyle was down here not long since. Maybe he'll be down again and can carry a message back."

Denoriel's lips thinned. He would lay strong odds that Nyle had been sent to the gate to look for him, but he had been back down the road concentrating on those waiting to see Harry pass and had missed the guard. He was just about to ask how long ago Nyle had been there, when the noise reached a new peak and a double column of Royal Guards drove their horses down the avenue, pressing those already in it to the sides, except for one cart, whose driver whipped up his mule and careened out of the gate before the guards reached him.

Shandy Dunstan rode past Denoriel, his sturdy gelding blocking the road so that the smaller mule was forced to turn aside and draw the cart southward. The driver cursed fluently, but not in English. Shandy retorted, loud and strong, in Elven. Denoriel grinned, knowing that Dunstan would say he was speaking Hungarian if anyone asked. Then the grin grew rigid as the pony pricked up its ears and put on a sudden burst of speed.

Aleneil had chosen better for him than he had suspected. Apparently Dunstan, at least, had a thread of Talent. What he had shouted in Elven was addressed to the beast, bidding it to run away—and so it had, carrying the small cart rapidly toward London, with Spanish curses trailing more and more faintly behind.

What had the Spaniard planned to do? Surely he had not intended to attack Harry in the midst of a substantial armed guard. And why in a cart? If he had wanted to lay an ambush from the side of the road, he should never have appeared in Windsor at all. An informant? Seeking news and gossip among the servants?

Denoriel put the questions in the back of his mind as the guards came through the gate, two, four, six, eight, ten. Behind them came a gorgeous coach. Denoriel felt his eyes widen. It was nearly as elegant as anything mage-built Underhill from its decorated, spoked wheels to its domed roof.

The side panels were carved, gilded, and painted with Harry's coat of arms—ridiculous crotchet, that, the poor child was hardly of an age to bear arms, much less need an escutcheon, but the arms went with the title, and he'd been given the title of a man grown. The posts that supported the roof were elegantly turned and had elaborate gilded finials. More carved and painted wooden panels about a foot wide were suspended from the roof. Behind those, Denoriel did not doubt were rolled-up leather curtains that could be let down to keep out the dust or the rain. The dome of the roof, which provided room for one or two of the occupants of the coach to stand up, was also gilded and topped with a gilded finial.

On this fine, mild morning, the curtains were raised and Denoriel could see four occupants, one very small who was twisting and turning in his seat, one plump motherly figure beside the uneasy child, a hand on his shoulder as if to keep him from launching himself out of the coach, and sitting back to the horses, two men Denoriel did not recognize. Denoriel pushed to the forefront of the mounted groups, but he could not really see any way to approach the child.

That problem was soon solved. Behind the coach were four more guards, who divided two by two as soon as the coach passed the gate, and rode quickly to take up positions to each side. Gerrit, the forward man on the near side of the coach, called out immediately in surprise and relief.

"Oh, Lord Denno, there you are. His Grace has been asking for you."

At his words, FitzRoy let out a shriek of joy and bounced to his feet, twisting out of his nurse's grip on his shoulder. She grabbed at his arm, but was unable to keep him from leaning so far over the side of the coach that he seemed in danger of falling out.

"Harry! Sit down at once!" Denoriel shouted.

The dark-haired, black-bearded man seated on the far side of the coach, had leaned forward to grab at FitzRoy, as did the large, fair-haired one beside him, but the child had already popped back into his seat, only waving energetically and shouting, "Here I am, Lord Denno. Here I am."

The black-bearded man then asked the nurse a question, which she answered volubly. Meanwhile ten more guards rode out of Windsor to form up behind as the coach came nearly to a dead stop while the groom, who rode the front near-side animal, maneuvered the four horses around. Sharp turns had to be negotiated carefully because the coach wheels did not turn and too hard a pull at right angles could topple the vehicle.

Black-beard then spoke to Blond-hair, and he called out to Gerrit to ask Lord Denno to ride around the coach so he could speak to Black-beard. Denoriel wasn't sure whether he should be overjoyed or annoyed, but it turned out that FitzRoy had done just the right thing.

Sir Christopher Fiennes (Black-beard) was quite ignorant about dealing with children and, moreover, had not the kind of authority over his charge that Norfolk had. He had not the faintest idea of what to do when at the hour of departure FitzRoy began to scream and declare he did not want to go to Sheriff Hutton; that he had not known that Henry and Mary Howard were not going with him; that he had to talk to Norfolk—which was impossible, the duke having removed to London as soon as Sir Christopher arrived.

One does not beat the son of a king, even a bastard son, or drag him along kicking and screaming, not when that son is obviously being groomed to follow his father to the throne. Children can have surprisingly long memories. Sir Christopher compromised by calling for the boy's nurse. Ordinarily she would have ridden in the large char full of women servants that was to follow the coach, but she was able to calm the boy— Sir Christopher, not the most perceptive of men, did not bother to learn how—so he kept her with them in the coach.

Actually the nurse had told FitzRoy that Lord Denno was a man of his word. If Denno said he would be in the cortege, he would be. Perhaps business had made him late and he would need to catch up. They would send Nyle or Gerrit to look for him once they were out on the road. That had sufficed to get FitzRoy into the coach, but he had been very restless, peering this way and that in the hope of seeing Denoriel and when he did not, obviously trying to delay the departure by demanding to get out to piss, complaining that he had forgotten some toy that he could not live without, and other such ploys.

No command from Sir Christopher or plea from his nurse had been able to quiet him, so his prompt obedience when Denoriel shouted for him to sit impressed his unhappy deputy warden. The nurse's further assurance that FitzRoy was always quiet and obedient to Lord Denno and that Denno was a man to be trusted completely, having saved FitzRoy's life at the risk of his own, was a further insurance atop the glad and relieved way the boy's guard had called out to Denoriel.

Furthermore, it seemed to Sir Christopher, who knew little about foreign affairs, except those with Scotland, that it was much better that Lord Denno should be a Hungarian merchant, even if he claimed noble status, than that he be one of a voracious English family seeking advancement. After all, if Denno sought tax relief or trade advantages through the king's bastard's influence, that was less important than seeking political advantage. How much damage to the Treasury could one rug merchant do, after all? One man, granted a miniscule relief from import levies—insignificant.

Thus, in short order of his being summoned to speak to Sir Christopher, Denoriel had permission to ride beside the coach and keep FitzRoy occupied. Denoriel gave grateful thanks. Sir Christopher nodded and turned away, but Denoriel was sure for a little while, at least, Sir Christopher was likely to pay close attention to what an utter stranger to him said to the king's son.

That was no problem. Denoriel was happy to keep the conversation to matters of childish interest. Besides, since he had no intention of confiding to a child his worries about the purpose of the Spaniard in the cart or his fears of ambush on the road, he had nothing to say to FitzRoy of which Sir Christopher could disapprove. Still with Sir Christopher's suspicions in mind, Denoriel kept his voice audible.

He played some word games with FitzRoy and then urged the child to correct his English usage, because he occasionally made errors in idiomatic speech. He sent FitzRoy into gales of laughter by confusing "press" a person to do something with "squeeze," as in "Can we not squeeze the young lady to play another tune on her virginals."

They had covered all of a league and a half by then, the horses straining and the coach bumping and banging over the deep, hard-dried mud ruts. Sir Christopher and his guard had had enough. When the coach hit a particularly bad bump and came to a stop until a wheel could be freed, he shouted to the driver to hold up until he dismounted. He would ride for a while, he said, to save himself from being battered to a pulp.

"And what about me being battered to a pulp?" FitzRoy asked, watching with disfavor as Sir Christopher's man ran off to bring forward their horses.

"I'd take you up on Miralys," Denoriel said, "but—"

"Oh, please! Please!"

"But I'm sure it wouldn't be allowed." Denoriel shook his head warningly at FitzRoy. "Still, we can make the ride easier, I am sure. Mistress Bethany, if you could bear riding pillion behind my man Dunstan for a little way, he could take you back to the char and you could bring back pillows and bolsters to make His Grace and yourself more comfortable."

"It's an angel you are, Lord Denno," the plump nurse said, smiling. "I'll do just that. It will make me feel like a girl again." She got down from the coach, and as Ladbroke lifted her to Dunstan's cob's broad back, she said to Denoriel, "I was surprised that Sir Christopher didn't have pillows brought, but it isn't my place to speak unless I'm asked."

"I doubt he's ever traveled by coach before," Denoriel said. "Or, at least, not on country roads. I'm sure he rides when he travels."

Mistress Bethany sniffed, getting across a definite sense of disdain without saying a word. Dunstan cautioned her to hold tight, and rode off down the line of the cortege.

"Why can't I ride?" FitzRoy asked. "I know they brought my pony. I like to ride. I'm a good horseman."

"Yes you are, Your Grace," Denoriel said, smiling despite the cold shiver that ran down his spine.

Nothing could be more dangerous. Even if the guards closed tight around the pony, Denoriel could envision a hundred ways to spook all the horses and send them galloping off in every direction. Maybe he could freeze the pony and snatch Harry off onto Miralys, but he and Miralys might be kept busy fending off an attack. Nor could he tell Sir Christopher the truth about what kind of dangers threatened them on this journey. And the man might just give in if Harry whined and carried on about wanting to ride. Anything was better than that.

"But the pony would soon tire and you would be back in the coach," Denoriel continued. "I have a better idea. Tomorrow, you show your bruises to Sir Christopher and tell him you will be seriously ill if he makes you ride in the coach all the way. Ask him to take you up before him."

FitzRoy's eyes widened and began to glisten with tears. "But I don't want to ride with him. I want to ride with you, on Miralys."

"Oh, you will. You will." Denoriel smiled a truly wicked smile. "It is possible he will refuse to take you with him, in which case you will begin to cry and threaten to write to your father about his cruelty. If he suggests that you ride with one of the guards, become haughty. Insist that only a nobleman can carry you. See if you can get your nurse to suggest *me* to carry you."

"Oh, good!" FitzRoy giggled. "Bethy will do that. She likes you. She loves the kitten you gave her." But then the boy frowned. "But what if he agrees to carry me?"

Denoriel laughed aloud. "Ah, then you must become an actor. You must talk, and talk, and talk. And ask questions and more questions. And if the poor man tells you to be quiet, you can sniffle a little and say he does not care for you and he does not wish you to learn anything. I suspect you will be given over to my care soon enough."

FitzRoy giggled and held out a small hand. "You don't mind if I talk and ask questions, do you?"

Denoriel bent from Miralys to squeeze the little hand.

"You do love me, Lord Denno, don't you?" he whispered

"Indeed I do, my heart," Denoriel whispered back.

The wheel was freed. Mistress Bethany returned followed by a packhorse loaded with cushions and bolsters and tied atop, the white kitten's basket. FitzRoy was seated on a cushion and padded back and sides by bolsters, the nurse turning her head as she tried to armor her charge against the jolting to tell Denoriel that she had had a terrible fright about the kitten. Someone had opened the basket, it seemed and found it empty. She shook her head.

"That little devil. I don't know how she does it, but she can manage to hide in that basket. Anyhow, when I looked she was there, fast asleep."

Denoriel smiled at her and sent a mental warning to the air spirit not to appear on his shoulder or in his lap where anyone could see. He received in reply an uncertain warning. The air spirit sensed something foul, but it was not close. Denoriel decided that one way or another, tomorrow he would have Harry on

Miralys with him, even if he had to bespell Sir Christopher to get him to agree.

It was easier than he expected. Despite pillows and bolsters, more bruises and two nasty scrapes were added to poor Harry's collection of injuries. The road between Windsor and Maidenhead, where they would stop for the night, was heavily traveled and it had rained the previous week. That meant that wagons and carts had worn deep ruts in the mud, and when the rain stopped, those ruts dried hard. The ridges had been broken down somewhat, but that made the road worse yet, where a ridge had been smoothed only to meet a harder, higher ridge.

Harry was twice thrown to the floor of the coach and once jounced up so hard that his head hit the edge of the seat. He was not rendered unconscious, but had a scrape and a decided bump to show for the experience. After that Denoriel dismounted and sat in the coach holding the child in his lap.

Sir Christopher found them that way and was appalled when he saw FitzRoy's swollen and bleeding forehead. He explained to Denoriel and FitzRoy that the road improved further along, but the expression on Denoriel's face and the fact that FitzRoy burst into tears did not imply any confidence in what he said. Whereupon he asked angrily if they expected him to somehow smooth the road, and FitzRoy immediately said he wanted to ride too.

To Denoriel's eternal gratitude, Sir Christopher vetoed that notion immediately, saying it was too dangerous, that the pony was not accustomed to the open countryside, only to the confines of Windsor park and might shy or bolt. Then the nurse said that Lord Denno had offered to take His Grace up before him on his horse. Pillion was too dangerous, she said, the child could be shaken loose or slip off; but astride on

the front of Denno's saddle, with the pommel to grip
and Lord Denno's arms to either side, His Grace would
be safe.

Denoriel said only that he would be glad to do it.
Having Richmond in front of him in his saddle would
be a far less painful way to travel than having the
boy on his lap and riding in the coach. Denoriel
found it interesting that Sir Christopher did not offer
to carry Harry himself. He swallowed a smile, deciding that if he had not the keenest mind in the kingdom, Sir Christopher had a strong sense of
self-preservation. He was at least clever enough to see
that if there were an accident in which the child was
hurt, he could blame Denoriel, the nurse, and the boy
himself.

For everyone except Denoriel, the remainder of the
afternoon was delightful. The nurse went back to ride
in the char with her friends. That vehicle, although also
without springs, was much wider than the coach so that
its wheels avoided most of the ruts. In addition, being
more heavily laden, it bounced less and there were
many bodies to brace oneself against. Mistress Bethany
was well pleased.

The groom in charge of the coach was overjoyed.
Because he no longer had to keep the horses to a snail's
pace while he tried to avoid the worst of the ruts, the
whole cortege was moving faster. That pleased both sets
of guards and Sir Christopher.

FitzRoy was in seventh heaven. Perched on the
back of Miralys, he could see much more, even
though his four guards had closed up around him.
And his beloved Lord Denno's arms were around him,
tighter than they had to be to keep him safe, holding him in a warm embrace. He was secure and loved
and *important*, because, little boy though he was, he
still knew a great deal more about England's nobles

and court gossip than did foreign born Lord Denno, and with no Sir Christopher to listen, Denno could ask and he answer.

Denoriel had been as happy as everyone else as they made another league and a half. Harry had shielded his cross as soon as Denoriel took him into his lap, and with the boy's body between him and its baleful influence, he was only minimally aware of discomfort. And that was wiped away by being able to hold Harry in his arms, occasionally to bend his head and kiss the child's hair, to have Harry rub his cheek against him.

Besides that, the boy's prattle was very useful indeed. Master Croke instructed the children about what lands and territories each great power controlled so that Denoriel learned things that were too common knowledge among his courtier friends to be mentioned. And Harry picked up this and that from hearing Norfolk talk. One thing Denoriel learned that answered a lot of questions he had not dared ask—hints and meaningful glances but never any direct remark—was that Cardinal Wolsey—Harry wrinkled his nose in distaste— was the real king of England.

Denoriel had just parted his lips to ask Harry another question about Wolsey and his policies when a shriek holding absolute horror burst into his mind.

:Goblins! Goblins!:

The air spirit was terrified, and rightfully so. A goblin could see an air spirit and was often quick enough to seize and crush it, absorbing the power that gave it life energy. Truthfully, Denoriel was terrified also. He was less afraid of the goblins themselves— he had fought them several times when something had aroused them to try to invade one or another Elfhame—than he was of their effect on the humans he accompanied.

If they fled, leaving him alone with Harry, he could be overwhelmed. Goblins never came by ones or twos, but in swarms. Would Harry's cross protect him against them? Denoriel found he could not remember whether goblins were sensitive to cold iron but he thought that even if they were not, they would still shrink away from the religious symbol itself. Should he tell Harry to take the cross out of its pouch and display it on his chest? But if the boy did that, Denoriel himself would be incapacitated or partially incapacitated so that he could not defend them properly.

And why were goblins here, now? Why would Vidal Dhu break the concord that bound Seleighe and Unseleighe to secrecy? What could be important enough to make the Unseleighe prince bring a host of goblins into the mortal world and expose the existence of Underhill and its unearthly denizens? The Wild Hunt was one thing. Those who saw it close and clear did not live to speak of it. Those who caught a single glimpse of it before hiding, were only half believed, just enough to keep the fear of the Sidhe alive without rousing the mortals to concerted action. And anyway, most thought the Wild Hunt to be a troupe of ghosts and demons, not the Sidhe.

Could King Henry have suddenly named Harry his heir and died? Be on the borders of death? Surely that was the only eventuality that could force Vidal Dhu to be indifferent to an act that would bring Oberon—and, indeed, all the Sidhe rulers, Seleighe and Unseleighe, and in France and elsewhere—down upon him.

Nonsense. Vidal would never take such a chance. More likely he would begin to plan how to destroy Harry, and make way for Mary.

Denoriel took a deep breath and dismissed his panic. Panic would gain him nothing—and how could a horde of goblins come down on them here?

As for postulating that Harry had suddenly become king, that was absurd. Had Henry named the boy his heir and fallen on his deathbed, twenty riders would have been sent galloping on Harry's trail. They would surely soon have overtaken the slow-moving cortege. And even if Vidal had scryed the king's illness and knew of it at once, it would take time to gather an army of goblins and build a Gate to send them through.

And why would Vidal set goblins on the cortege on the well-traveled road between Windsor and Maidenhead instead of waiting until they reached the wilds of Yorkshire?

Another question suddenly occurred to Denoriel. Miralys had been plodding steadily along in the wake of the first ten guardsmen without a sign of nervousness. Denoriel knew that Miralys was no more afraid of goblins than he was, but the elvensteed was no fool either, and would not dismiss the warning the kitten had given without intense watchfulness.

So, was the air spirit mistaken? About goblins?

He sent out the thought, :*Are you sure about the goblins?*:

:*Goblins! Goblins! Hundreds! Thousands!*:

:*You are safe in your basket. The goblins cannot reach you. Where are they? Why cannot I sense them?*:

:*Many! Many! Little. Little. Like mice.*:

Denoriel's first impulse was to burst into laughter. Goblins the size of mice did not seem much of a threat, particularly as goblin power seemed to be proportional to goblin size. Then there was an echo in his mind of his own thought that the best way to seize Harry would be somehow to startle the horses of the guards and other gentlemen riders so the cortege would disperse. It did not take much power to scurry under the horses' feet, to climb up their legs, their tails, and claw and bite. Hundreds of the tiny creatures could surely send the horses wild. It would have been easy enough then to gallop a horse free of goblin attack up to the carriage, seize Harry, and ride away.

Despite his concern, Denoriel almost smiled. There would be no seizing Harry off Miralys's back and out of his arms. A shield would easily ward off such tiny pests. But surely Pasgen and Rhoslyn—he assumed it would be Rhoslyn trying to redeem her previous failure—were watching and had seen Harry riding with him instead of in the carriage. They must know Harry was out of their reach, so why go ahead with the attack? Denoriel thought he knew the answer: because it would be nearly impossible to dismiss all those goblins.

His apprehension returned, and then a deeper fear. Perhaps Harry was *not* out of their reach, after all. Enough goblins, however small, could overwhelm anything.

As to why here rather than in the wilds of Yorkshire? Probably no one among the Sidhe would notice what sort of tiny beastie was attacking the horses. The concord would not be violated. And because this road was often traversed by patrols guarding against outlaws, the guards would not be expecting trouble. Their reins would be loose in their hands, their weapons seated solidly in their sheathes. They would scatter when their horses were panicked.

No, Harry was *not* safe. And neither was he.

:*Where?*: Denoriel sent with considerable force, hoping to pierce the air spirit's terror.

:*Near! Near! Near! Let me go! Let me go!*:

:*I cannot reach you to take off your collar. Stay in your basket. You will be safe.*:

Near? How near? Denoriel was afraid to open his mind fully for fear Rhoslyn would sense it and launch a violent strike at him. He thought he could resist her alone, but if Pasgen joined with her . . . Gingerly he extended his feeling for magic and more rapidly closed it down. There was a foul stench, a disgusting miasma all along the ground.

Now! Now Miralys was uneasy. The elvensteed's steady pace did not vary, but Denoriel could feel the tension in his mount's body.

"Harry," he said urgently, "if the other horses run away, don't be frightened. Just hold on tight and if I have to draw my sword, try to lie down alongside the pommel and curl around it."

"What's the matter?"

"I'm not sure, little friend. I just . . . There's something nasty in the woods. I . . ."

Then it came. The ground seemed to heave—black, brown, gray—at the edge of the woods that bordered the road and roll forward over the green grass verge. Denoriel shouted a warning. Harry's four guards looked wildly around, drawing their weapons, but they were looking for men charging out of the woods.

"Look at the ground," Denoriel shouted. "Hold your horses hard."

"Rats!" Nyle yelled. "A plague of rats!"

They looked like rats only if you didn't look at them too closely. Those were tiny hands, not foreclaws, and wizened faces beneath cowls of dirty hair, but their mouths were full of needle-teeth, and those fingers ended in talons. Whoever had called them up must have forgotten how little power was available to them in the mortal realm—that was why they were so tiny—

Denoriel only cried out to beware, that the creatures bit, but chaos had already engulfed the rank of guardsmen ahead of them. Horses screamed and plunged. Others bucked and leapt sidelong. Still others

ran across the verge and burst through the brush on
the side of the road into the field beyond. The troop
of ten was scattered in moments.

Clutching Harry to him, Denoriel called up the
strongest shield he had. Unaware that he was protected, the boy clung to the pommel with one hand;
the other lay on his chest, ready to pull his cross out
of its pouch.

Meanwhile, panic had cleared the road immediately
ahead. Miralys suddenly made a gigantic leap, right over
the squirming pall of brown, black, gray that covered
the road ahead of him. Denoriel turned and cast a
spray of levin-fire behind, sure it would not be noticed
in the panic. However, even as the power flowed out
of him and cold weakness flowed in he knew it had
been wasted. Oh, possibly a few dozen of the horrid
little beasts had been destroyed, but they had not been
following Miralys. They were streaming down the road,
sending all the horses mad and even attacking the
riders and those in the char.

He patted Harry's arm. "It's all right Harry," he said.
"They won't bother us."

The boy let go of his cross. "Nyle? Gerrit? Dickson?
Shaylor?" he asked anxiously.

"Here they come now."

And so they were, controlling their frantic horses
and forcing them forward through the thinning tide of
goblins to close on their charge. One stubborn goblin clung to Dickson's breast, trying to gnaw through
the leather and he swatted it hard with one hand.
There was a moment's resistance as the tough skin held
against the pressure and then the creature burst. All
the men cried out at the terrible stench.

Denoriel backed Miralys a little farther up the road
so he could watch both sides. Usually ambushers
would follow after an initial attack, but sometimes

they would wait on the opposite side the better to surprise their victims. Only no one burst out of the woods on either side of the road. Although Denoriel half drew his sword, he was not really surprised by the lack of a second charge to follow the first. If the purpose of the attack had been to seize Harry, those who sent the goblins must already have realized they could not succeed.

"Should we go see if we can help?" Dickson asked doubtfully, watching the chaos spread back down the cortege.

"What could you do?" Denoriel asked, holding Harry tight against him. "Sword or bow, even a knife, can't be used against them. You'd do more harm than good, getting in the way of people driving them off. Besides, God knows what started them. Your duty is to stay by His Grace and protect him. What if outlaws should chose this time to rush the cortege?"

The men began anxiously to scan the road ahead and both sides. Denoriel himself no longer had the smallest desire to laugh at the tiny, nearly powerless goblins. He swallowed.

He and Harry were in no danger because Miralys could easily outrun the little horrors and his shield protected them, but for those whose horses had become uncontrollable a multitude of dangers loomed. A man thrown from his horse could be badly injured by the fall, swarmed over in moments and badly clawed, probably could be eaten alive in a quarter hour if he were knocked unconscious and could not defend himself. The horses would be slashed and bitten; some might succumb to the poison in the goblins' claws and bite. That might happen to the servants in the char, too.

He thought of Mistress Bethany and gritted his teeth. There was nothing he could do. The largest

shield a Major Magus could cast could not cover the
entire cortege, particularly as it scattered in panic. And
he could feel his own power draining; he should never
have tried to use levin-fire against the goblins.

All he could do was watch—as helpless as any mere
mortal!

And hope that the worse was not to come.

CHAPTER 15

It took hours to reassemble the cortege, which dragged itself into Maidenhead after the sun had set. Long before that, Denoriel and Mistress Bethany had settled FitzRoy in the very best chamber of the best and largest inn of the town. Without argument, Denoriel took possession of a tiny servant's room that opened into FitzRoy's bedchamber, the nurse having elected to sleep in a trundle bed right beside her nurseling. All with approval of Sir Christopher.

Even while most of the cortege was fighting goblins and the disorder was spreading, Sir Christopher and his guard had forced their way to Denoriel. Both were bleeding, as were their horses. However, Sir Christopher's relief at seeing FitzRoy no worse for the event, not even badly frightened, was enormous, and ensured Denoriel's continued supervision of his precious charge. And Denoriel's suggestion that he go ahead with FitzRoy's four guards and another four of the guardsmen who had regained control of their horses and returned, also obtained instant approval. In fact,

Sir Christopher nearly groaned with pleasure at having one burden removed so he could attend to reordering the cortege.

Denoriel sent Nyle and Shaylor to collect Mistress Bethany—if she were in condition to ride pillion behind one of the men. She too was bitten and bleeding but came, perched determinedly behind Nyle, utterly furious, and the white kitten's basket was fastened behind Shaylor.

"What were they, Lord Denno?" she asked as soon as she was close enough to speak without shouting. "Those weren't no rats I've ever seen before. And they were after my kitten. Ten of them I squashed, I swear, trying to get into her basket. And the others in the char must have took out near fifty. We all nearly fainted from the smell."

"I have no idea," Denoriel answered mendaciously. "I never saw one close enough. Miralys here didn't like them one bit and he's got a mighty jump. He just sailed right over them, and then they went down the road so we didn't see any more."

"And you're all right, Your Grace?" she asked looking at FitzRoy. "You weren't bitten or scratched?"

"No, Mistress Bethany. Lord Denno took good care of me."

"He always does," the nurse said, with a warmly approving glance. "Still, the sooner we're under a tight roof the better I'll like it. And better still if we can get a priest to come bless us! Those weren't no natural rats, that I'll swear!"

That was true enough. She obviously relaxed when they arrived at the inn and were welcomed with every honor and grace the innkeeper could devise. Even so, when Denoriel said he would like the servant's chamber, she was clearly glad. The kitten was released. It had recovered from its panic and investigated every inch of the chamber, even darting out the door when an inn servant came bringing warm water for washing. It soon returned, calming the nurse's anxiety, and settled in her lap.

Fortunately for Denoriel, reaction from the excitement soon overtook everyone. Someone managed to find a priest, a little mendicant friar of one of the begging orders, who looked greatly perplexed at what he heard, but obediently went around signing the cross, muttering Latin, and splashing holy water over everything. That settled the nurse further. FitzRoy ate well, but with half-closed eyes and he barely managed to finish his sweet before the eyes closed completely. Mistress Bethany was little better off. Denoriel urged her to go to her bed also, promising that he would keep watch.

She accepted his assurance with heartfelt thanks, but when both were asleep, he swathed one hand in layers of silk and pulled the boy's cross from its pouch, arranging it to lie naked on FitzRoy's chest. Then he gathered the last remnants of his strength and cast a shield over FitzRoy and most of the bed. Afterward, he clung to the bedpost, eyes dim, shaking, drained nearly to his core.

For a while he simply breathed, eyeing the glittering white lines of power that alone were clearly visible to him and seemed to waver toward him seductively. *Not yet,* he thought. *Some day I may be desperate enough to take the chance of burning out my magic completely, but now I have Harry to guard.*

As some purely physical strength slowly came back to his muscles, the temptation receded; however, he knew that keeping watch in his present condition would be useless. He must go Underhill. Perhaps Mwynwen could do something to restore him or teach him how to absorb power a little faster.

He left the room, saying to Gerrit and Dickson, who

were on guard by the door in the corridor, that he needed to catch a breath of air. He knew they were tired, he added, but he begged them to be extra alert, at least until he returned. And then he walked around the side of the inn.

Miralys was there, which was just as well because his shaking knees might not have carried him much further. How he got into the saddle—not the mortal-world leather and wood construction, but something Miralys himself created to hold him—he never knew. He had barely enough consciousness to tell the elvensteed to take him to Mwynwen. Freed of the restraints of looking or acting like a mortal horse, the elvensteed sped across the distance from Maidenhead to the nearest Gate in less than an hour.

She greeted him with reservation, even with guarded hostility, blocking the doorway.

"And what is it you want now?" she asked coldly.

Tears stung Denoriel's eyes at the icy rejection. He would have retreated, but his need was too great; also he doubted his ability to leave with dignity. "My lady—" he faltered, in a voice like a croak. "—I fear I need your help—"

Then she seemed to recognize his debilitated state and softened, reaching out to help him into the house.

When she had told him to lie down on the bed in a small room well away from the chamber to which he had carried the changeling, she asked what he had been doing to so deplete his reserves. He told her of the goblin attack, watching her eyes widen in dismay.

"If I had not had the lad with me—it would have been desperate. As it was, nothing came of it. But when we came to shelter, I had to shield Harry," he finished wearily. "I still have to. But I am—spent."

She nodded vigorously to that but then bit her lip

and stood staring down at him as if she wished to sieve out his soul.

After a while she sighed and began to pass her hands over him repeatedly, from the crown of his head to the soles of his feet, murmuring softly all the while. Denoriel knew it was a spell, but he could not make out the words no matter how closely he listened. And then she bound the spell to him so that it sank into flesh and bone, becoming part of him.

Denoriel gasped in surprise at the flood of warmth and power that seemed to ooze from everywhere into him. He sat up, restored, and stared at her.

"What? What did you do? I am filling with power like a well that has reached an underground river!"

She smiled, but her eyes were sad. "It is indeed an ill wind that blows no one any good. That is a mortal saying—the child is full of mortal sayings. What I have given you is a spell I devised to feed power to poor Richey."

"The child!" Denoriel exclaimed. "Oh, wonderful. Can it save him?"

There was a little silence and then, her voice grown harsh in a way Denoriel had never heard, she said, "You cannot have him."

Denoriel drew a sharp breath. So that was why she had nearly refused him entrance. She thought he had come for the child.

"No," he said. "My lady, I have no wish for him. I have Harry. And I know Richey must stay with you. I fear even with the spell you have devised that he will never be strong—but I was saddened by the thought that he was made to be more fragile than even a mortal child, and that this would bring you sorrow."

"No," she sighed, and her eyes filled with tears. "Even with the spell, I do not know how long . . ." Then she smiled. "But he is happy. He is like a bright-feathered bird, always chirping merrily, filled with one clever notion after another. The toys he loves best are those from which he can build other toys, and what he creates is wonderful."

That gave Denoriel an idea for a present for Harry when it would be time to leave him . . . if he dared leave him. He stood up.

"Would you like to see him?" Mwynwen asked. Her voice was uncertain as if she desperately wanted to show off her prize but was afraid seeing it would make Denoriel wish to seize it.

"I do, but I daren't take the time," Denoriel said. "Later, perhaps. And it will be better when he is more settled with you, anyway. Let him know he is cherished by you first, and become secure in the knowledge. Then I will see him."

Mwynwen nodded, but she did not move away from the door. "I hope you will not misuse what I have given you," she said. "An unlimited and quickly renewing source of power . . . That will give you a great advantage over most other Sidhe."

"I am not a quarrelsome sort," Denoriel said, smiling, knowing that he had said exactly the right thing about the poor little changeling. "And most of my time is now spent in the mortal world where even this spell cannot gather power very well." He shook his head. "I must go back at once. Can you tell Aleneil about the goblin attack for me? If the Unseleighe are so desperate to seize poor Harry, I had better be there to defend him."

"Yes, go," she urged, now looking anxious. "I cannot bear the thought of your Harry, so much like my Richey, in the hands of Vidal Dhu. And don't worry. I don't forget that they might be seeking Richey too. He is guarded by the strongest protections I can devise."

They parted better friends, but Denoriel knew the special bond they had had no longer existed. He wondered, feeling his ears grow warm as he mounted Miralys, whether Mwynwen had wanted his loving or his youth? He was *very* young for a Sidhe. Had he been desired as a lover or as a substitute for a child? It was an embarrassing question, and Denoriel pushed it aside. He had not felt this well and strong since he had started visiting the mortal world. He should be grateful for what he had, not whining over what he had lost. There were elven women enough who would look on him with favor—and anyway, he had always known that one day she would lose interest in him. Few elven passions lasted forever—nor, in truth, would most Sidhe wish them to.

He and Miralys took the Gate from Logres to Windsor, set to arrive just at the time he had left the inn. The elvensteed covered the distance from Windsor to Maidenhead in less than a quarter hour, so when Denoriel came round the corner of the inn, just enough time for a leisurely walk had passed.

Even so, the guards were glad to see him. No one had tried to enter His Grace's chamber, they reported, but one man they did not recognize had passed down the corridor. He had not paused, only glancing once at them.

Denoriel's teeth set for a moment. What had seemed to them a man passing without pausing could have meant they were blocked by a spell—but there was no lingering remnant of magic around either man. Although he was impatient, Denoriel thanked them for their alertness and urged them to let him know at once if the man passed by again. Then he hurried inside, but the shield he had set over FitzRoy showed no sign of tampering and the sleeping nurse was simply sleeping, not bespelled. He took the most comfortable chair in the room, gave it some extra padding with a pillow Harry had knocked to the floor, and sat down to watch out the night.

No further disturbance troubled Denoriel that first night, but over the weeks it took them to reach Sheriff Hutton, he had cause again and again to thank Mwynwen and the spell she had bound to his being. The tiny-goblin attack was only the first of many dangers that struck their cortege.

They found the students in Oxford rioting when they arrived in the town and had to fight their way to the castle. It was pure accident that Harry had been on Miralys with Denoriel when they entered Oxford. The road had been dull, but much less rutted than the stretch between Windsor and Maidenhead, so Harry had been riding in the carriage, playing games with his nurse. It happened that a game ended just as the town came in view, and Harry begged to be taken up on Miralys so he could see better.

Mistress Bethany was nearly injured when a group of students surged over the coach. Had FitzRoy been riding in it, worse might have befallen. As it was, she boxed the ears of one so soundly that he shrieked and let go of the white kitten's basket. She kicked a second where he was most sensitive and shoved him over the coach's low side as he howled and curled over on himself. Then FitzRoy's guards converged on the vehicle and drove the students off with the flats of their blades while the air spirit shrieked into Denoriel's mind, *:Possessed. Some are possessed:*

It was not afraid of mortals, however, and was merely amused by their attempts to seize it. That was just as well because it was willing to roam ahead of the cortege and a few days later warned Denoriel of caltrops scattered on the road. Denoriel promptly told

Nyle a sad tale of a wool trader going north with a full purse who had lost it and several members of his party to outlaws who played that kind of trick. Nyle rode forward to warn the guardsmen. If he looked a little strangely at Denoriel when the caltrops were discovered, that was a lesser problem than having half the horses disabled.

North of Leicester they were attacked by outlaws, but that might have been a normal hazard of traveling because the air spirit gave no warning. Even with Harry on his saddle, Denoriel managed to disable three. Other guards did as well. All those captured had their hands tied behind them and a rope around their necks by which they were dragged back to Leicester by four of the guardsmen.

Two more attempts were aimed at the air spirit. One was foiled by the stubborn determination of the nurse not to part with her pet for any threat or blandishment and a second by Denoriel's untrained but genuine mage sight, which disclosed some near-invisible thing's stealthy approach. Denoriel's silver sword made quick work of the formless construct, which could whip out tentacles or extend itself to envelop and draw the not-quite insubstantial air spirit into its maw.

To FitzRoy's guards, who were the only ones close enough to notice him stabbing and slashing at nothing with his sword he said he was doing some esoteric exercises. They all exchanged glances and then nodded, but they were particularly jumpy all the rest of the day and Gerrit twice asked the nurse if she felt cold or a breeze when the leaves were not moving.

As they entered Nottingham, they lost two guards from the tail of the cortege. Without explanation, the chain holding the portcullis slipped off its hook and the heavy iron gate crashed down. It killed both horses and one man and took the arm from another. Denoriel was furious. Such an attack could not result in seizing Harry. The cruelty and wastefulness was typical of the Unseleighe, but he could only clutch Harry tighter and use his strength more lavishly to create shields. After Nottingham, one man was assigned to gallop through the gates of any town or castle where they were scheduled to stay and stand guard on the portcullis winch.

No one was bored—that was for sure. The guardsmen were keenly alert, watching the road underfoot, the sides of the road, the branches of the trees overhead—from which, in a heavily wooded section past Doncaster a troop of rag-clad wild-men had dropped. FitzRoy's guards and Denoriel had borne the brunt of that attack, which was clearly aimed at the boy, but Nyle, Gerrit, Dickson, and Shaylor had given a good account of themselves and put six beyond doing any harm. Denoriel's knife put paid to another two, and Harry valiantly used his little knife to stab the hands of the one who tried to seize him.

All the attacks ceased when they reached York. Possibly that was because by then, although they were all very tired, every man and woman was prepared to fight. Sir Christopher had grown more and more wary and now rode up and down along the cortege, watching for any oddity and urging even the servants to be prepared to defend themselves. And they were prepared. Denoriel thought gratefully that it would take a full-scale army to accomplish anything against them.

Sir Christopher was not swift of wit, but once he got an idea he used it to the uttermost. At first, he had told Denoriel, as they sat over their wine one evening, he had accounted the attempts on the cortege as the natural result of riding through the overpopulated south with what was obviously a rich caravan;

later, he said, he had come to realize that the attacks were aimed at the little duke of Richmond.

With that fixed in his mind, he began to wonder whether his charge would be safe in Sheriff Hutton. It had been known for months that that was where Richmond was going; what if the servants and guards of the castle had been bribed to allow the child to come to harm? Sir Christopher felt he could trust no one except the members of the cortege, who had proved themselves faithful. But the members of the cortege could not garrison a whole castle. So, from York Sir Christopher sent a message to his brother, Lord Dacre, desiring him to change the entire garrison of Sheriff Hutton.

Whether that precaution had foiled any further attempts on the boy or the Unseleighe had decided for reasons of their own to desist, Denoriel did not know. Of course when they first arrived, Harry was strictly confined to the castle itself and its immediate grounds. That was no hardship because the castle was very large.

Very, very large; even Denoriel was impressed as they rode up to it, with Harry in the coach with Sir Christopher, in order to present the proper dignified approach.

"It's big!" Harry exclaimed in surprise.

"It was built," Sir Christopher told Harry, "in 1379 by Lord Neville of Raby on the site of a twelfth-century keep built by Bertram of Bulmer. And now it is yours, and it is my opinion that a lord ought to learn every inch of the properties in his possession."

Possibly because he had learned something about FitzRoy or possibly by accident, Sir Christopher had said just the right thing to intrigue a child. Denoriel could see that Harry would be happy for weeks exploring. Not only would he have the four great towers, each four stories high, and the interconnecting buildings full of galleries, passageways, and chambers, some of which held ancient furniture; in addition he could look for the remains of the earlier keep, including the base of its donjon, which was said still to exist.

The southwest tower was given over to the boy. The top level housed his guards so that no one could come through the roof to attack him. FitzRoy's own apartment was on the third level, which was high enough for the windows to give a fine view of the countryside. They were true windows rather than arrowslits, but firmly barred with elaborate wrought iron grates. Denoriel sighed faintly as his bones began to ache and his stomach churned. However, no Sidhe was going to come in through those windows. There were two rooms to the apartment, a bedchamber and a small parlor in which the boy could eat.

Servants quarters were on the ground level, which had no entrance and no windows. The servants and everyone else had to go through the gatehouse of the main building into the garden where an outer wooden stair rose to the second level. Normally that level would not have been living quarters at all, but assigned to guards on duty, who would examine anyone who entered. However, after some negotiation with the other members of the council—who were *finally* convinced that a Hungarian lord could have no interest and no influence on the Scottish border—Sir Christopher had arranged that Lord Denno and his personal servants, who had shown themselves as good as any guardsmen in the many attacks during the journey, should occupy those rooms.

Within the four towers was an inner bailey that held the small garden. In any attack that won through the gatehouse, the guards would destroy the four flimsy wooden stairways and leave any intruder faced with

unscaleable walls from which arrows and other lethal
materials could be rained down.

Outside the castle was a large outer bailey within
a formidable stone wall and beyond the wall, a substantial moat. The outer bailey held the stables, the
pens for animals being fattened for the table, the coops
for chickens, the dovecot, the kennels, a smithy, the
laundry, the kitchens, many sheds for storage, and many
small cottages for the army of servants needed to
support the establishment. Swans and geese floated in
the moat, available for dinner and a first warning and
early defense against any invasion.

For the time being, FitzRoy was confined to the
castle itself and the small inner garden. That suited
Denoriel perfectly. He spent two weeks examining
every chamber and corridor from the top of each tower
to each cellar below. He took Harry and whichever two
guards were on duty through all the public places in
the castle; the private rooms he checked with even
greater care at night. Nowhere was there a hint or a
smell of magic. The air spirit also flitted through the
castle and agreed—Sheriff Hutton was not tainted with
magic.

After two weeks, Denoriel felt his excuse of lingering
until FitzRoy was settled into his new residence was
growing a trifle thin. He told Sir Christopher, who was
still in charge of the castle and FitzRoy while the other
commissioners attended to legal and political affairs,
that he must be about the business that brought him
to Yorkshire and left Sheriff Hutton, ostensibly to
purchase wool. He rode with his men as far as
Aldborough and then bid Miralys to look for a Gate.

The senses of an elvensteed were much keener than
those of a Sidhe when it came to finding Gates. As he
had suspected, there *was* one, long abandoned, in a
Node-grove a quarter-hour further on by elvensteed's

swift pace. Marked by druidical signs, he knew immediately it would take him through the wall between the worlds to Avalon, as most Gates that had been used by druids did. It would not do if he was to travel regularly from Sheriff Hutton, but it would serve for now.

Aleneil was very glad to see him. She had been worried about him because she had been scrying their journey and was aware of how often the cortege had been under attack. She was amazed that he was not worn to a thread as he had been while guarding FitzRoy in Windsor. Unwilling to give even Aleneil Mwynwen's secret without her permission, Denoriel bypassed discussing his unusual reservoir of power by asking urgently whether his sister knew the whereabouts of Magus Major Treowth or any other Magus Major who would be willing to build a Gate for him.

"Treowth is gone," Aleneil said. "No one knows for certain where or why but a persistent rumor has it that he has moved to the Bazaar of the Bizarre." She closed her eyes a moment in thought, then brightened. "Gilfaethwy is at the school, however, and *he* specializes in Gates. I'm sure he'll help you, to keep the boy safe!"

Denoriel gave her a hug and turned to leave, but she held him back, saying she presumed he had not seen his mortal court friends since he had been on the road.

Denoriel shook his head, impatient to get negotiations for his Gate going.

"You had heard that the Emperor Charles has refused to join Henry in tearing France apart and had finally decided to marry a Portugese princess and not wait for Mary?" she asked.

"I heard enough wild talk by George and his friends about how they would grow rich on French lands, and yes, they were furious that Charles would not accommodate their greed, but that was in March or April while I was just beginning to win my way into their circle. As for Charles marrying the Portugese woman, thank God for that," Denoriel by habit used the Christian God in his speech. "The last thing we need is Charles's Spanish or Imperial notions driven into Mary's head. She's Church-ridden enough as it is. What are you trying to tell me, Aleneil? This is all old news."

"Yes, but it is becoming new again because Wolsey is urging on the king a peace treaty with France. And that may be good news for you in that Rhoslyn and Pasgen may be so busy keeping Wolsey from tying the king too tightly to France that FitzRoy may become less important to them."

He made a face. "Or more important because of the king's reluctance to have a French prince rule England through his wife."

"I did not mean you should be less vigilant on FitzRoy's behalf," she protested, "Only that however little King Henry may want a French prince on the throne, Vidal Dhu would want it even less. Remember, the Inquisition was never allowed to take hold in France as it did in Spain, and the French are more addicted than the English to making merry. I think Pasgen and Rhoslyn—who are the most likely to serve Vidal's purpose— will be making mischief in the King's Court and you should not bury yourself in the north, but cultivate your courtly friends and pay attention to the gossip about England's balancing between French and Imperial interests."

"Hmmm." Denoriel gnawed gently on his lower lip. "That may be possible. Fortunately Sheriff Hutton is too far north for casual visits by Boleyn and his set and they are not much interested in Scottish affairs. Well, except for Percy . . . It might be possible for me to be in two places at once, or very nearly. I can Gate from Sheriff Hutton to London . . . Ah, yes. By any chance, have you discovered what mortal guises Pasgen and Rhoslyn have taken?"

"Yes." His sister pulled a face of her own. "It is fortunate that Lady Elizabeth is watching politics closely, because her husband is so often sent abroad by the king, and she has found me a good confidant when he is gone. Rhoslyn is Mistress Rosamund Scot, fervently religious, which makes it possible for her to go on retreat frequently; she is a close friend to Queen Catherine's favorite maid of honor, Maria de Salinas. Pasgen is Sir Peter Kemp. He is supposed to be related to the wife of George Cavendish, who is Wolsey's gentleman usher. He is apparently a welcome guest at all times to Wolsey. I can only believe that both Rhoslyn and Pasgen meddled with their patrons' minds."

Denoriel's lips curved down in distaste. "Very likely. I will do what I can to avoid both and listen hard for those names. Anything else?"

Aleneil cocked her head at him. "Yes. When you have leave to do so, please tell me how you are managing to drink power as a sponge drinks water."

So he had not succeeded in throwing her off that scent. Well, he should have known better—in her place, he'd not have been distracted, either. "Good God, will everyone in Underhill see it? Should I try to shield it?"

She thought, looking hard at him for a moment, then shook her head. "It is clear to me because I know you so well and you are different from what you were before. Close friends might notice but not someone who does not know you passing well. As to the shield, to build one would prevent you from drinking power. But there is a danger. You will be like a beacon light to anything that eats power—so have a care if you go into the chaos lands."

He raised his brows. "Anyone who goes into the Unformed places needs to have a care. But I will remember what you say. If I cast a shield, I will lose my ability to take in power." He frowned. "Oh, bitterly do I now regret thinking my sword could solve all problems. I will study magic, I swear it . . . as soon as I find the time."

She laughed at him and sent him on his way. A few heartbeats later Miralys brought him to the soft, glowing white, apparently featureless round building that housed the Academicia, often just called the "School" or the "Place of Wisdom." He dismounted and asked permission to enter. A door promptly manifested just in front of him. It looked invitingly open, but Denoriel—whose own door always looked open—did not attempt to enter. He came closer and thought clearly of who he was, that his sister was the FarSeer Aleneil, and that he wished to consult Magus Major Gilfaethwy.

A moment later a tall and surprisingly portly elf stood in the doorway. His hair was more white than blond, his ear-tips inelegantly short, and his expression was not inviting. He stared at Denoriel, taking in the round ears, the round-pupilled eyes, and the court clothing.

"What do you want, mortal?"

"I'm not mortal, magus," Denoriel said without heat, although he had already identified himself and the mage would have had that information if he had bothered to listen. It also surprised him that the mage had not bothered to send a probe that would differentiate between mortal and Sidhe. Still, mages were sometimes *other*; Treowth certainly was. So he went on, "I am Aleneil, the FarSeer's twin, Denoriel. I am wearing mortal guise because I am now working to protect a mortal child who my sister Sees is of importance to the well-being of Underhill. That is why I have come to you. To protect the child, I need a Gate to a place in the mortal realm."

The mage frowned. "Gates to the mortal world are not easy to build."

"I am willing to offer compensation, if there is something I have that would be pleasing to you," he said, humbly—remembering the adage, "It is not wise to anger a wizard, for you would not enjoy the taste of flies."

"What could you have—" the mage began, and then suddenly stopped and smiled.

He pointed at Denoriel, who immediately felt the odd quiver of being moved a short distance by Gate. And he had been. He was now in an incredibly cluttered workroom. Books lay on shelves, on benches, on the floor. They were atop of and under sheets of parchment and paper; other sheets were stuffed between the pages. Among the books were all kinds of vessels, mostly of glass but some of silver and pewter, even gold. Around a few, tiny salamanders danced, and within the vessels liquids bubbled. A few had fallen and spilled their contents onto the books and papers. The spills looked dry, most of them, as if they had been long ignored. At least the odors in the room were pleasant.

"You said you were often in the mortal world?" the mage asked, and gestured vaguely at a stool.

Since it was covered with papers and two squashed scrolls, Denoriel made no attempt to sit. "Yes, magus."

"Good! There are some things I desire from the mortal world. I will build your Gate, and from the mortal world you will bring me . . ."

Denoriel's lips tightened, ready to refuse to abduct a child, although from what he had learned about the life of the boy who was now assisting Ladbroke, there were many who would be better off Underhill. But to his surprise, the mage reached out and fingered the hanging sleeve of his gown, then snorted disparagingly.

"Kenned," the mage said. "I want the real thing and the first thing I want is wool."

"Wool?" Denoriel echoed unbelievingly.

"Yes, wool. That stuff that grows on one of the mortal world animals."

"I know what wool is," Denoriel said. "I was just surprised because I am supposed to be buying wool right now. But I had no idea that there was any difference between a kenned artifact and that from which it was kenned. I will get all the wool you want . . . er . . . For what do you want wool, magus?"

"Never you mind," Gilfaethwy said. He then raised his hand and snapped his fingers. When he opened his hand, a silvery amulet lay in his palm. "Take this and set it where you want the Gate to open."

He was about to gesture, which Denoriel was sure would deposit him outside the door of the Academicia, but an idea had come to Denoriel and he raised a hand. If all Magus Gilfaethwy wanted was artifacts from the mortal world, he could afford to have an extra Gate or two.

"Ah, magus . . ." Denoriel said hastily. "I will bring you anything you want from the mortal world. Could you build two Gates, one inside the castle of Sheriff Hutton and one about a mile outside it? And another two some months from now in Pontefract castle?"

The mage pursed his lips. "Not everything I ask for will be as easy to obtain as the wool. And it must be real, and from the mortal world. Blood, for example. I need mortal blood that has never been Underhill and has never been touched by a magic spell."

Denoriel was just about to say he did not need the extra Gates when he remembered the ridiculous mortal practice of bleeding themselves. He could easily bribe a chirurgeon or a barber to save blood for him . . . but he would have to remember to go as someone besides Lord Denno. If people heard of Lord Denno of Hungary buying blood, they would think he wanted to drink the stuff and call him an evil spirit, or suspect him of sorcery. That was the last thing he needed!

"Very well. I can bring you blood, but you know it does not stay liquid very long."

"No trouble. I will give you a spell of stasis, that will keep it fresh."

Stasis. Denoriel suddenly remembered FitzRoy's guards standing like statues. Had they been breathing? He could not remember.

"Magus, I have another problem. The boy I must protect is a target of the Unseleighe Courts. They seek to abduct him. He has mortal guards, but they have already once been made helpless by magic. Do you know of a spell that can ward a mortal against magic, either mortal or Underhill magic?"

He was thinking how much safer Harry would be when he could not be with him if his guards could not be turned into statues or automata. Awake and aware, with their steel armor and steel swords, they could protect the boy against any Sidhe attack.

"There is still mortal magic?" Gilfaethwy asked, his eyes lighting. "I had thought that idiotic Christianity they stupidly embraced had destroyed both the magic and those able to use it. It was said, but that was even before I was born, that mortal spells were much stronger than Sidhe magic because the spell had to work on so much less power. Do any books from those ancient days survive?"

"That I do not know," Denoriel confessed, "but I can certainly find out."

"If such exist, get me a true grimoire and I will build

as many Gates as you desire. Here—" He snapped his fingers again and opened his hand to show half a dozen silver medals. "As an earnest of my goodwill. These amulets will ward off most spells of compulsion."

Denoriel accepted them gleefully. "Gilfaethwy, my thanks! I had not expected such generosity!"

"It is not generosity," the mage said, bluntly. "I expect a full recompense. And if you are going to start on fulfilling your bargain, you had best get on your way."

It is not wise to anger a wizard, he reminded himself, and hastily did just that.

CHAPTER 16

Denoriel spent a really busy two weeks gathering up the materials he had promised to Magus Gilfaethwy. Surprisingly the least expensive and most satisfying to obtain was the grimoire. Denoriel had guessed why the mindless and dead assassins had been deposited on the steps of that particular house. When the king's men had taken away the fool that dwelled there for questioning, he had entered it, smelled out the secret room in which the magician worked, found the grimoire, and took it. If the theft crippled the magician, it was, he thought, an entirely appropriate punishment for the attack on Harry.

The wool was, of course, no problem. He purchased two fleeces from a Yorkshire wool merchant, thinking that Gilfaethwy might want the wool in its most raw form, as well as a bale of sheared wool, and several skeins of yarn, both dyed and in the natural state.

The blood was the most difficult because of needing a reasonable explanation for the chirurgeon. He had no trouble finding the man, simply presented himself at his own house in London in disguise. He called himself Master Christopher Atwood, and said he was a wine merchant. He wore decent merchant's dress, was dark-haired, dark-eyed, and asked to speak to the business manager he had employed on George Boleyn's recommendation. When he was admitted by the Low Court servants—who recognized him but who were silenced by a gesture—he asked the manager for the name of George's doctor. His own had died, he explained, and he liked to be bled regularly.

The chirurgeon had his doubts when Denoriel asked him to save the blood. He very nearly refused when Denoriel gave him three bottles, although he did not know, of course, that they were bespelled to keep anything within in stasis. However, a heavy purse of gold and an assurance that Denoriel did not want to know the names nor care from whom the blood came soothed the doubts away.

He Gated back to Avalon and delivered his prizes, then took a day to cover on Miralys the distance the cortege had traveled in a month so he could set Gilfaethwy's devices for creating Gates. One he placed under the stair that led into his own apartment in FitzRoy's tower; the other he set in a tiny glade, shielded by a particularly dense patch of woods. The spot was well away from the road but near a trail used by huntsmen that led to Sheriff Hutton. He spent that night masked by the Don't-see-me spell anxiously checking Harry, the nurse, and the four guards and then roaming the castle smelling for magic. He found nothing and the air spirit assured him that it had sensed neither Sidhe nor demon.

By the time he had seemed to travel among the wool merchants and go out to examine the flocks themselves, which were regrowing their fleece, the Gates were in place. Denoriel tested them both and both delivered him to or from Avalon or Logres, from which points he could Gate to London or to Windsor, and to the stair under FitzRoy's tower or the glade in the forest. There was something odd about the transit, a kind of roughness, perhaps a heartbeat longer of disorientation, but Denoriel accepted that as a difference in the kind of magic Treowth and Gilfaethwy used. He was so glad to be able to Gate from one of his responsibilities to another, that he had no inclination to question the means.

He returned to Sheriff Hutton openly, followed by his three servants and the pack mules now loaded with samples of wool of all kinds. Sir Christopher was glad to see him. FitzRoy, now thoroughly familiar with the castle, had nearly given him and everyone else a fit by playing hide and seek. He had tried to explain why such an action was dangerous, Sir Christopher said, but the boy was only a bit over six and he thought Lord Denno's remonstrance added to his own might have more effect.

Denoriel promised fervently to do his best to check that kind of mischief and rushed off to see Harry. He was intact, truly Harry, wearing his iron cross, and the air spirit, also intact, swore he had been with the boy and no magic had come near him. FitzRoy was a little resentful of having his amusement curtailed, but when Denoriel reminded him of the attempt to abduct him, he sighed and said he wouldn't do it again.

In compensation, Denoriel got permission for the boy to go into the outer bailey, accompanied by his guards—now all wearing "holy medals of St. Ursula," which would protect them from any chance of bedazzlement. Just before he left to return to London, Denoriel found the remains of the twelfth-century keep. There was a stair down into a cellar, which was in very good condition and still held some dented pewter cups, some wooden platters, a broken knife, warped barrels, and beyond a crumbling door a smaller chamber that was furnished with manacles, chains, what might once have been whips, and the knotted cords that were twisted around a victim's head to crush his skull by degrees. An unsettling discovery, which reminded him that the Unseleighe were not alone in their ability to invent horrors.

Denoriel Gated two Sidhe who specialized in structure into the castle one night so they could put the strongest spells of support on the old donjon. It would hold up, they assured him, for another hundred years without shifting a single pebble. Then he told Sir Christopher, who promised to allow FitzRoy to investigate with suitable attendants.

He then left, to bring his wool to London, promising Harry he would come to visit in the autumn when he would need to check up on the flocks whose wool he had preordered. He kept his word, found some fault in the treatment of the sheep, and lingered for nearly a month—or seemed to linger. It was no problem for him to Gate to London after FitzRoy was abed and spend a convivial evening, drinking, gambling, and whoring with George Boleyn and his friends.

This was necessary as the turn of political events might have been the reason why no further attempt had been made on Harry. A peace treaty had been signed between France and England on thirtieth August. Since Francis, the king of France, was still a prisoner in Emperor Charles's hands and King Henry was still hoping to convince the emperor to join him in dismembering France, the treaty was not regarded too seriously. However, the emperor persisted in refusing to join Henry in the rape of France, and the king grew more and more resentful and estranged from

Imperial purposes. It did not help that he grew more and more estranged from his queen, Catherine, at the same time.

Eventually Denoriel returned to London, but after a period of good weather in December when he might have ridden north, he Gated to the woods outside Sheriff Hutton. There was snow in Yorkshire and when Sir Edward Seymour, the commissioner now in charge of FitzRoy, marveled at his hardiness, he laughed and said the weather was very mild compared to the mountains of his home. However, when it snowed again, it was a good excuse to stay for a while and celebrate Christmas with Harry.

Denoriel was back in London when the news came that Emperor Charles had liberated Francis in January 1526. The terms of the treaty trickled back to England and were so severe that no one believed Francis had any intention of fulfilling the provisions. By early spring new French overtures were being made to England; Francis, a widower, offered himself as a husband for Princess Mary.

Resentful as he was of the Emperor's rejection of his daughter and refusal to cooperate with him, Henry seemed about to get the French territory he wanted through marriage rather than war. Wolsey, however, was sidetracked into making a league against Charles with a number of Italian states.

Denoriel was in Yorkshire again in May, ostensibly to examine and collect the sheared wool for which he had contracted, but really to celebrate Harry's seventh birthday on the seventh of June. Any dealing with the Italian city-states was slow and complicated and there had been no FarSeeing that indicated the league was of any great importance. Denoriel stayed for a month and a half. To mark his birthday, Harry, who was growing noticeably, was given permission to ride out into the area around Sheriff Hutton. He was a very good horseman, and no one was at all concerned about his ability to control his pony.

FitzRoy would be accompanied, of course, by his own two day guards and eight others, but leaving Sheriff Hutton seemed to Denoriel to make Harry very vulnerable. He found reasons and excuses to linger in Yorkshire for several more weeks and warned the air spirit to accompany the boy whenever he was out of the keep. Even after he had officially departed, Denoriel Gated back to Sheriff Hutton every few days to watch secretly for any sign of Unseleighe magic.

However, the Unseleighe Court had more to worry about than a bastard prince whose father seemed to have put aside his intention of making him heir. Fortunately for Denoriel's peace of mind, Wolsey's negotiations with the Italian states were progressing very well and the League was actually formed—but then Wolsey would not commit England to any real participation. He even drew back somewhat from the marriage proposal, having it worded so that one of Francis's sons, now hostage to Emperor Charles in Francis's place, would be accepted as a substitute for the French king. Marrying Princess Mary to Francis's son would be a much weaker tie than if she were the king's own wife.

Denoriel suspected Pasgen's fine hand in Wolsey's wavering, but so long as no Imperial prince was put forward for Mary's hand—and in truth, there was no Imperial prince—Denoriel was satisfied. A new Imperial ambassador arrived in England in December 1526, but he had been arrested in France and detained for six months. His orders were long out of date and he could not prevent King Henry's gradual leaning toward France. Pasgen, and presumably Rhoslyn, too, were probably busy trying to prevent a fatal breach between

King Henry and the Emperor and for the moment, Harry was safe from them.

Meanwhile Aleneil was spending much more time than she previously had in the mortal world. She had moved from being simply Lady Rochefort's friend to a wider acquaintance among the wives and daughters of Henry VIII's courtiers. She was still a welcome guest in the Boleyn household, however, and was doing everything she could to divert Unseleighe attention from the fact that King Henry's affections did seem to be fixing on George Boleyn's younger sister.

Mistress Mary Carey was completely out of favor and had retired to her husband's estates in the country. Anne herself had not yet seemed to realize that Henry was interested in more than light dalliance and flirted with him throughout 1526 in the same witty, lighthearted manner in which she flirted with Wyatt and young Percy.

Aleneil was concerned. Her Seeing had hinted that this woman might be the mother of the red-haired babe, but that would not do at all. The red-haired child *must* have an undisputed claim to the throne. Another bastard, even if it was male, would not be a candidate for the throne. For a time Aleneil was afraid to do anything. To touch Anne, she thought, would leave a mark of magic on her that any Sidhe could read. She carried her troubles to her sister FarSeers, and was given an answer.

Anne, if she married the king, would indeed be the mother of the red-haired child they all awaited, but no one could See how that could come about because the king was already married and notably fickle. The only hope for marriage was for Anne to stay pure. As for helping her keep that resolution—did not Anne already have Talent? Did she not use it, if unconsciously, to draw men to her? Would that not hide the barest touch of magic influence?

Aleneil had burst out laughing when those questions were asked. Even if Rhoslyn did notice Henry's interest and examine Anne, Rhoslyn would far more likely attribute Anne's resolve to remain virgin until married to priestly influence than Seleighe magic. Quite a few of the good and great priests were unconscious magic wielders and some of the prayers they used worked quite well as spells.

Certainly Anne's resolution held firm all through 1527, and the more she resisted her royal suitor, the more fixed he became on having her. Both Rhoslyn and Pasgen were now aware of Henry's passion for the girl but found that they could do almost nothing. Rhoslyn could not reach the king at all, and Pasgen, who could reach him through Wolsey, found Henry's determination so fixed that he would have needed virtually to wipe the king's mind to remove it.

Both arranged to meet Anne and found her well protected. Aleneil had presented the girl with a tiny but exquisite cross, solid gold and set with precious stones—each one of which carried a warding spell. The gift was a charming novelty, and because it was so small Anne wore it constantly, as an earring, as a bangle on a bracelet, as a sparkling accent in her night-dark hair.

Beyond the efficacy of the spells and more important was Anne's own awakened ambition. She had seen her sister . . . and several others . . . used and put aside. Henry, she realized, was not of a constant nature. Likely soon after he got what he wanted, he would lose his taste for it. Thus, as long as he was *not* able to satisfy his desire for her, he would remain fixed in his pursuit. And if he were utterly determined to have her . . . then he would have to marry her. She would accept nothing less.

Whether it was his desire for her that put it into his mind or whether the idea had long been there but without focus, in 1527 King Henry began moves to free himself of his marriage. In May 1527, a tribunal was summoned to test the validity of the king's marriage. If Henry thought these preliminary steps would bring Anne to his bed, he was mistaken. She remained adamant.

Moreover, Wolsey suddenly developed Pasgen-inflicted doubts and insisted that the secret tribunal was not sufficient. They needed the opinions of more notable theologians than he. However by then it was too late for a tribunal to pronounce on the marriage and then quietly obtain the pope's signature and seal on the annulment. Imperial forces had attacked and sacked Rome two weeks before Henry's tribunal had met. The pope was Charles's prisoner and it was obviously useless to try to get the pope to invalidate the marriage of Charles's aunt.

Virtually indifferent to these early moves in what was to become the king's "great affair," Denoriel continued to watch Harry grow and to be delighted. He had been afraid that as the boy approached young manhood his own interest would wane, but that was not true. He loved the growing boy as much or more than he had loved the child and took even greater pleasure in his company.

Harry's eighth birthday passed and then his ninth. The air spirit was released and replaced by another. This one could put on the cat's guise if necessary, but mostly simply remained invisible. Denoriel found a small white cat and bespelled it to love Mistress Bethany—who had graduated from FitzRoy's nurse to mender and caretaker of His Grace's undergarments—reason enough to be in His Grace's bedchamber whenever he wanted the only mother he had ever known.

The commissioners' intention to dismiss Mistress Bethany when His Grace no longer needed a *nurse* brought Harry his first taste of power. His grief on being told of Bethy's dismissal alarmed the air spirit, who summoned Denoriel. Having only left a few days earlier, he came secretly at night. He looked at Harry, bravely holding back tears, and at Mistress Bethany, who was weeping freely and said, "You are duke of Richmond, Harry. In so small a thing as your personal servants, you may make your own choices"—and proceeded to suggest ways a royal child could enforce his will.

Thus, when Mistress Bethany was summoned by Sir John Forrester, FitzRoy accompanied her and flew into such a rage that Sir John was taken aback. He had not known that the little duke, usually so biddable, was capable of such fury, and discovered that although the boy loved his horse and the hunt far better than his books, he was very clever and listened with both ears. He had learned enough about the way the northern march was administered to blacken Sir John very thoroughly in the king's eyes, and he made that very, very clear. Sir Edward listened in horror; he was an honest man and fond of the boy he served as Master of the Horse.

Various expedients, such as finding some way to compel FitzRoy's silence (a difficult proposition in the face of four well-armed and fanatically devoted bodyguards), preventing any contact between the king and his son (even more complex when every messenger from the court requested an audience with the boy), and culling his letters—were all abandoned very quickly as being impractical.

Sir John, who had mentioned interfering with FitzRoy's correspondence shuddered on second thought. FitzRoy wrote a great many letters: to the king himself, to the duke of Norfolk, to Norfolk's son Henry Howard, to Mary Howard, even to Lord Denno, although Denno was still a frequent visitor—but in this case unwilling to oppose His Grace's will—and every one of those letters was answered promptly. Any silence on Richmond's part would call forth considerable concern and immediate investigation.

Sir John, Sir Edward, and Lord Henry Percy also discovered that Richmond could hold a grudge far beyond what any of them had expected of the usually cheerful and compliant child. He, who they had hardly known was inhabiting Sheriff Hutton with them until they crossed his will, began to make their lives a hell by constant complaints and demands. If Mistress Bethany was to be gone, he pointed out, they had better get accustomed to hearing that his bathwater was too cold, that his shirt was too starched or not starched enough, that his breakfast did not please him, that he could not sleep and wished to be read to ... A page carried that message to all three commissioners in the castle at three of the clock in the morning.

Moreover, the commissioners said in hasty consultation the next day, what the boy asked was very little. The nurse's pension would have been nearly equal to the stipend they now paid her, so no real savings were involved in dismissing her. Let him have his way; it was not worth the struggle to break his will—and the truth was that none of them was sure who would win and all were sure that long-lived and bitter hatred would follow.

The next test of FitzRoy's power came when he was deemed capable of riding a horse rather than a pony. He attended closely to Sir Edward's choice of five mounts—two hackneys and three hunters—but he did not interfere. However, Sir Edward quickly recognized Richmond's tone of voice when he stated flatly that the animals chosen were in remarkably fine condition and he would like to keep the grooms attending them.

Although he did not really recognize them, Sir

Edward thought the grooms looked familiar; they must have come with some regular guest, he thought. Fortunately no other commissioner had actually promised the positions to any client's stable-hands, and when the grooms professed themselves willing and honored to serve His Grace, Sir Edward agreed. Grooms had no influence.

Thus Kip Ladbroke and Reeve Tolliver came into FitzRoy's household and Harry knew his connection with Lord Denno was assured—if he could get out to the stable no matter where he went. When the dismissal of Mistress Bethany had been contemplated, Sir John had selected a valet from his hangers-on. FitzRoy had never allowed the man to touch him or his clothing, and some weeks after Kip and Reeve had been appointed, he sent for Sir John, accused the valet of theft, and asked that Shandy Dunstan be employed in his place.

Sir John was outraged. Dunstan was common as dirt, a low friend of Ladbroke and Tolliver. He tried to draw the line, refusing to replace his choice with a commoner. Valet to the premier duke of England was a position of power and influence. It must be a political appointment, reserved for a gentleman.

A very regal Richmond informed him coldly that the creature he had selected was a thief and no gentleman, whatever his birth. He was drunk and dirty. Sir John sent furious messages. Several other commissioners arrived to argue and explain, to offer their own candidates.

After a tantrum that covered the dining parlor and the commissioners with thrown food and broken crockery, Richmond was confined to his apartment as a punishment with the valet to watch him. Sir Edward made sure that the valet could do the boy no harm, warning Nyle and Shaylor, who were on guard duty that night to listen for any outcry and succor their master. But they heard no outcry, no suspicious sound of any kind.

Still, right under the nose of the valet, FitzRoy disappeared entirely. The valet spent the whole following day searching for him, having locked Mistress Bethany in her chamber to keep Richmond's absence secret.

When the valet finally confessed, Sir John was terrified; he ordered the valet imprisoned and sent for his fellow commissioners. They began yet another search of the castle and its grounds but found nothing and no guard had seen the boy, including FitzRoy's own four, who were half crazy with rage and fear. They demanded that the valet be given into their hands to have the truth squeezed out of him.

Sir Edward, with Sir John's violent approval, calmed them with promises that the king's torturers would do a better piece of work on him. Then he and his fellows spent the night trying to compose a letter to explain the loss of his son to the king.

They were still at it when Mistress Bethany, coming to grieve and pray in Harry's room among his toys and little precious things, found FitzRoy asleep in his bed, with Shandy Dunstan just entering the room with his hot water. She ran, shrieking with joy, to tell the commissioners that the lost was found. If they suspected that Dunstan was somehow involved, they kept it to themselves. The boy's smile told the commissioners that worse might befall them than a day's anxiety in another contest between them. Nothing more was said about gentleman valets. Let the king appoint Richmond's servants himself if he wished.

Everyone, including Lord Denno who had stage managed the disappearance in a nighttime visit to Harry's chambers, breathed a sigh of relief. FitzRoy's

personal household was now fully staffed with men who
were safeguarded against Sidhe tricks and otherwise
incorruptible. It would be impossible for Pasgen to
insert an agent of his own among them. Lord Denno
then arrived openly to celebrate Harry's tenth birthday; Harry went back to being a most good-humored,
obedient child, and the spring of 1529 began to slide
into summer.

Although by no means scholarly, Harry was wide
awake on the subject of politics. Over the years he had
listened with deep interest when the commissioners
discussed the rising and falling fortunes of King Henry's
attempt to obtain a divorce from his wife of nearly
twenty years so he could marry Anne Boleyn of the
light laughter, the witty tongue, the dark eyes and night-
dark hair. Harry pleased his commissioners by saying
openly and most sincerely that he wished the king well.
Nothing could please him better, he swore, than a
healthy, long-lived legitimate brother. He did not wish
to be king.

By the summer of 1529, however, it seemed more
and more likely that his fortunes were again rising. The
chances of obtaining the divorce seemed doomed to
failure. The pope could not be brought to sign a bull
ending the marriage. Wolsey, driven by the king's
urgency, convened an extraordinary legatine court to
pronounce the marriage invalid and present the pope
with a fait accompli, but Wolsey was unable to force
the court to come to any decision. The pope's legate
adjourned the court and Queen Catherine sent an
appeal to Rome.

That Rome would rule against Henry was a foregone conclusion, which meant that Catherine, who
could bear no more children, would remain his wife
and Princess Mary would be his only heir. It again
began to seem that, deprived of the chance to marry

again and try for a male heir, FitzRoy might be brought forward and established in Mary's place. The commissioners became more and more accommodating to FitzRoy's every desire; several took the time to explain their function and the meaning of the parchments he was asked to sign.

Other attempts were made to please the boy. He loved to ride and listened avidly to every tale of hunting, so he was included in a hunting party for which deer were driven close to the castle. He acquitted himself so well that a second hunt, less confined, was arranged. The boy kept his seat when others of the party ended up on the ground.

Denoriel was not happy with any of this; not with Harry's growing importance as a possible heir, nor with the freedom the boy had been given. He was made aware of any stranger who came to the castle, but who knew who or what might be lurking in the woods. He took his worries to Aleneil, but she did not think the threat to FitzRoy was great. FarSeeing had shown nothing more than the general danger of abduction that had hung over FitzRoy from the beginning, and she was distracted by her need to protect Anne around whom Unseleighe threats were gathering.

Mwynwen, to whom he also brought his worries, was not much more helpful although she sympathized with him. Richey, who was still alive and actually seemed less frail, was also demanding more freedom. He could no longer be confined to the house; he had Mwynwen's servant guardians, but they were vulnerable to many kinds of attack. She could only shrug and suggest that Denoriel ride along with the hunt unseen. Whether his presence deterred attack, Denoriel could not be sure, but there was none and the air spirit never sensed any magical presence.

After riding to several increasingly long and hard

hunts, it seemed ridiculous to confine FitzRoy to traveling in a carriage when the entire party moved to Pontefract—which they had done several times without attack over the years. FitzRoy begged to ride, and permission was granted.

Unfortunately Denoriel could not find any reason to accompany the party and the commissioners were growing just a little wary of FitzRoy's long attachment to him. He elected to follow through the woods. Twice the air spirit came to him; somewhere magic was being worked, but it was not Sidhe magic, maybe only some wise-woman. It had no definite warning to give.

Meanwhile FitzRoy enjoyed the journey immensely and behaved so well that Lord Henry and Sir Edward promised he should ride whenever they traveled. Henry Percy, who had not been on that disaster-cursed journey from Windsor to Sheriff Hutton, was sure traveling was safe. FitzRoy was perfectly willing to remain well within the protections of his small personal Household, which was further surrounded by the royal guards.

Gerrit and Nyle rode ahead, behind the royal guards who rode ahead of the commissioners. Dickson and Shaylor followed just behind FitzRoy and ahead of another contingent of guards. On their heels came Reeve, leading Harry's extra horses. On FitzRoy's right rode Dunstan, now wearing half armor, sword, poniard, and pistol; Ladbroke rode to his left, also, surprisingly, in half armor with, if one looked carefully, knives peeking out of his boots, both sleeves, and behind his neck. He also carried a sword.

They arrived at Pontefract without incident and remained there until the second week in October when three of the commissioners, Lord Henry Percy, Sir William Fenwicke, and Sir John Forrester received notice of the election of a new parliament. In the same mail pouch was an urgent letter from Lord Denno's business manager. He left Pontefract with the commissioners who were going home.

Sir Edward did not like Pontefract, which had been built in 1086 by Ilbert de Lacy. It had been somewhat modified by later de Lacys but was still very uncomfortable compared with Sheriff Hutton. The hunting was better at Sheriff Hutton too. Sir Edward decided to move his charge back to Sheriff Hutton. FitzRoy, pleased by the idea of a journey, made no protest.

Near dawn on the third of November, the same day the new parliament assembled, the duke of Richmond, his servants, bodyguards, and the household in general set out to return to Sheriff Hutton, a little more than eight leagues away. It was a long day's ride, but Harry was sure he could manage and they planned to do it in one day.

Denoriel almost did not Gate north to follow them, even though he had a letter from Harry telling him when they would leave. His attention was also now fixed on Anne as the threat to her grew more intense. Ordinarily the most graceful of women, Anne had twice tripped—seemingly on her own feet—and nearly fallen down a flight of stairs. She had taken the sweating sickness, when no one else nearby had it; Mwynwen had to come from Underhill to cure her, in the guise of an old herb-woman friend of Anne's old nurse, Blanche Parry.

Although it frightened Anne very much because she could half see, half sense them, Aleneil had warded her around with invisible servants. It was tedious and exhausting; the servants could not long endure the mortal world and had to be replaced very often so they had to be watched constantly. Denoriel was forced to take watches with his sister.

George Boleyn had been attacked when he was accompanying his sister Anne home from Whitehall

Palace. Neither he nor Anne had been injured, but Anne was frightened even more, sobbing that she had seen demons urging on the attackers. Later she denied that, assuring everyone that it had only been her fright that made shadows take horrible form. Aleneil, however, had been certain Anne's witch-sight had exposed the truth. For the next few days, Lord Denno had accompanied George to safeguard his sister, but then Anne was offered an apartment in the palace.

Aleneil left some air spirits on guard, but she was sure that no attacks on Anne would take place so close to the king. The Unseleighe knew better than to wake suspicions of their existence so close to the heart of mortal government. George was also delighted; he had been tied to Anne's apron strings and had given up many of his own amusements. There was a horse race scheduled for the fourth of November. He invited Denoriel as a thank-you for his help.

Meanwhile several uncanny accidents had happened to Denoriel's house in London. The workroom there, which Aleneil used, was wrecked when a wall collapsed, and a Low Court servant was injured so badly that he had to be sent back Underhill for healing.

Watching the slow progress of the moon across the sky on November second, a sudden anxiety seized Denoriel. After all the hue and cry in and around London, nothing had been accomplished. The damage to his workroom was superficial; no Unseleighe traps were found in it. No harm had come to Anne or George, but threat hung about them. Could all this rather open and pointless damage and threat have the purpose of diverting him from guarding Harry?

Thus when the cortege left Pontefract just after dawn on November third, Denoriel was about a mile ahead, back in the woods where he would parallel their course. He had Gated from London to Logres and then from Logres to Pontefract. He felt oddly sick when Miralys stepped out of the Gate area at Pontefract but was distracted by hearing the scouts for the cortege gallop by.

Harry's party rode until the horses were tired, then stopped for a picnic and to change their mounts and rode on. By midday Denoriel felt foolish. He was much tempted to ride back to Pontefract and Gate back to London to accompany George to the race. Then he sighed and decided to go all the way to Sheriff Hutton. Since he would have to adjust the Gate anyway to deliver him to London in time to meet George for the race, it made no difference whether he Gated a few hours earlier from Pontefract or a few hours later from Sheriff Hutton.

The ride was totally peaceful and Denoriel spent most of his time thinking about Anne. She was not truly beautiful, even by mortal standards, although her face had a most lively and intriguing expression. Her eyes were gorgeous, though, large and lustrous and so dark they looked black, as did her hair, which was also exquisite, hanging to her knees in a shining curtain when it was not demurely covered by a coif, cleverly lighted here and there with a gold chain and a twinkling jewel.

Aside from the small Talent she had, which Denoriel could hardly sense, Denoriel could not for the life of him see why King Henry should be so enamored. True, Anne was very intelligent, very well read, able and willing to discuss religion or politics. She was also not so slavishly subservient as most of the other women that Henry had been interested in, or even the male courtiers that he favored most. She laughed and teased, denied the king any physical satisfaction while assuring him she adored him, and very often scolded—but never about anything she desired for herself. Denoriel would credit her for cleverness; she never asked for anything . . . except for marriage, and even that she said was for the king's good, not her own.

Denoriel sighed and dismissed the thoughts. He was not the only one who wondered at Mistress Anne's grip on the king. He looked around and saw that the woods were familiar; he was quite near the glade that held his Gate. Good. This duty was very nearly finished. The sun was westering, but there was still plenty of light. Another quarter hour's ride would see them safe at Sheriff Hutton.

:Magic! Magic!: the air spirit reported, landing on his shoulder. *:Across the road. Coming near.:* And then suddenly it uttered a wail of pain and terror and disappeared.

CHAPTER 17

There was no sense in trying to gain control of the air spirit to ask where Harry was. Without urging, Miralys leapt toward the road. Denoriel's sword was drawn, but even before they burst past the brush that lined the road, he saw that Harry was safe, mounted on his sturdy cob. Three of his guardsmen were clustered around him; the other, ably assisted by Dunstan and Ladbroke, was driving off a huge gray-skinned monstrosity.

What hellish thing was this?

Nothing Denoriel recognized. Miralys hesitated and Denoriel swallowed when he saw the toad face—only toads did not have glowing red eyes nor long, yellow fangs that dripped something vilely green protruding from their lipless mouths. Gray skin, harder than boiled leather, Denoriel knew. There were only a few places on that body that a sword could pierce.

Vaguely Denoriel was aware that the guardsmen who rode ahead of and behind Harry were fighting other beasts, driving them away from the wagons filled with supplies and servants. His business was with the one threatening his boy. He watched the long, scaly arms, waiting for one hand or the other to rise in an attempt to seize one of the men attacking it. Miralys would leap forward and he would strike under the arm . . .

But alarms were thrilling up and down his body! Something was terribly wrong! For all their size, creatures like this were quick and agile. This . . . thing . . . was roaring and waving its arms, striking at the men, but it was not really fighting and it was terribly clumsy . . . and there were cuts on its arms and body where the men's swords had struck it, but there was nothing oozing from the wounds.

He glanced again at where Harry sat, passively waiting to be defended on his cob. A cob? Harry did not ride a cob! Illusion! That was Reeve the men had formed up around. Denoriel realized why Miralys had hesitated. The elvensteed was not afraid of any Unseleighe monsters—no more than sensible caution required—Miralys had stopped because he sensed that what was fighting Harry's men was not a threat and that Harry was not with them.

With a despairing oath, Denoriel turned back into the woods and reached for the air spirit. Now he knew what had happened. When the "monsters" attacked, the horses had been terrified and the cortege had scattered. Harry's gelding, faster and higher spirited than the others and with Harry not strong enough to control it, had carried the boy across the road, away from the apparent threat, and into the woods. In only a few minutes Harry's guards and Dunstan and Ladbroke had mastered their horses and formed up around their charge—only it was Reeve, bespelled to look like Harry.

Rhoslyn . . .

She might not have retained enough of Harry's mind and spirit to build a second changeling, but his appearance would be branded into her brain. She could cast an illusion good enough to fool even those who knew Harry well.

:Where?:

Denoriel put all the force of his mind and will into that demand. He knew that Rhoslyn and her Unseleighe group had launched some kind of attack on the air spirit and to force it near its enemies might spell its death. He was not ordinarily cruel, but he had to find Harry. He prayed that he was not already too late. Even if the air spirit were wounded and dying, he thought that Aleneil's spell would hold. It would know where Harry was.

:Here: came faintly back to his mind. He had been right. The air spirit, drawn by the spell that bound it to Harry, had somehow followed. He had a direction and Miralys had it too. The elvensteed seemed to leap from where it was to one of those open, low-brush-filled areas found in any wood. Denoriel knew the steed had passed through the trees, leaping and dodging but at such speed that it seemed one single stride had brought them to their goal.

:Here: but more faintly, as if the spirit were retreating . . . or dying.

At the center of the open area was a large blackened circle and at one edge was a moldering shed of some kind. Gate! In or behind the shed was a Gate! But Denoriel had no time to try to discover anything about it. The air spirit's call had brought them to the Gate, not to Harry himself; however from the sound of pounding hooves and outcries others were coming. Miralys's speed had outpaced them.

Denoriel's heart leapt with mingled joy and rage. He still had a chance. Harry was not yet taken. He urged Miralys to the northwestern edge of the clearing. Harry was being herded from the south toward the Gate in the shed on the northeast edge. The Sidhe could not touch the boy because of the iron cross he wore, but they planned to drive him through the Gate and deal with him Underhill.

Harry burst out of the trees, still firmly in the saddle, although he had let go of the useless reins. There were about ten following him, only five even vaguely human. His horse was wild-eyed and lathered, ahead of its pursuers only because it was so terrified of them.

At the front was a Sidhe whose ragged hair flowed in the wind. His eyes were mad—huge, his slitted pupils closed so tight that the eyes seemed all one glittering green; his mouth was open, the sharp teeth showing as if he wished to tear at his prey with them. His horse trailed streamers of blood-tinged mucus from its mouth, probably nearly dead but driven on by the Sidhe's will. And in his hand he held a huge crook with which he intended to hook Harry from his horse.

Behind, screaming at the mad Sidhe to stop, their fanged and red-eyed not-horses striving to overtake the ravening Sidhe, were Rhoslyn and Pasgen. Behind them were two more dark Sidhe, beautiful still but with lips twisted into cruel smiles. And ranging them to either side were beasts on other beasts. Denoriel's eyes caught twiglike arms with huge hands finished with shining claws, something with bat-ears and a long, curling tongue mounted on an emaciated pig as big as a cow . . .

Miralys leapt forward. Two strides put the elvensteed between Harry and the demented Sidhe. Denoriel's sword made a downward stroke with the full strength of his terror and his rage behind it. The Sidhe screamed. Arm and crook flew to one side as Miralys hit the foundering horse with his shoulder and threw the dying creature aside.

An impossible twist, another leap, and Miralys was beside Harry's horse. Somehow since the first warning from the air spirit, Miralys had undone the spell that held his head furniture together and rid himself of it and the reins. Denoriel had both hands free; he held his bloody sword in one hand and with the other tore off his heavy double-lined silk cloak and twisted it around his arm.

Braced for pain, as Miralys slowed to match pace with Harry's tired horse, Denoriel reached over and yanked the boy from his horse onto Miralys. Then the elvensteed seemed to fly across the clearing.

Behind him Denoriel heard Rhoslyn scream with fury. In the same instant, he felt the flickering pain of a near miss with elfshot.

"Hold tight, Harry," Denoriel bellowed, and then lower but still clearly. "My horse's name is Miralys."

With those words, the boy, who had been struggling, threw his arms around Denoriel's neck. The Sidhe gasped with pain, but there was enough clothing between him and the iron so that he was not totally incapacitated. He managed to lift and turn Harry so the boy's back was to him. Harry swung his leg over Miralys and Denoriel drew a sharp breath of relief. The arm with which he clutched the boy—right across the chest where the cross lay—was shielded with layers of insulating silk; Harry's body was between him and the iron cross. For now, but not for long, Denoriel could bear it.

The not-horses had been behind the bespelled mount of the mad Sidhe and had been driven sideways when the poor creature fell and began to convulse in dying or Denoriel would have been overtaken when Miralys slowed to pick up Harry. Now the elvensteed really stretched, but the need to dodge trees and leap brambles prevented Miralys from using his full speed.

The not-horses were also fast and powerful. They were virtually on Miralys's heels when the elvensteed found the grove and charged into Denoriel's Gate.

When Miralys and his burden disappeared, Rhoslyn shrieked with rage and despair. She drove Talog forward at the Gate, hoping to enter so close on their heels that she would arrive at their destination with them.

Pasgen shouted a warning and almost simultaneously, because it was clear she would not listen, uncoiled a long black whip. He had brought it to drive FitzRoy's horse if necessary—or to drive FitzRoy himself— through his Gate, but he used it now to snake forward and coil around Rhoslyn's waist.

He almost pulled her from Talog's saddle, and she was so beyond herself that she turned, screaming, hand raised to fling a levin bolt at her brother. But before she could act, the whole grove lit with a terrifying burst of light and energy.

Talog and Torgan were thrown backward and nearly flung to the ground. Their clawed feet won them a purchase no horse could have maintained and they remained erect. Rhoslyn and Pasgen, armored by the nasty tricks Vidal Dhu too often played on his followers in the Hunt, stayed in their saddles.

For a moment they sat in stunned silence, staring at the blackened and flattened brush where the Gate had been. In the distance they could hear the rest of their party following, but only the not-horses could approximate the speed and agility of the elvensteed. The others would be a little while reaching them.

"You killed him!" Rhoslyn spat. "You murdered my boy! I will—"

"No!" Pasgen protested. "The collapse of the Gate was none of my doing. I did meddle with it, but only to wipe out its old terminus at Logres and—"

"You told me you couldn't touch Denoriel's Gate in London!"

"This was different. That London Gate was made for Denoriel, fitted to him. Close as we are in essence, brothers, that Gate knew I was not Denoriel. This one and the one at Pontefract are different. They are good Gates, but designed for general use. It was easy to repattern them. I swear I did the Gates no harm."

"Liar!" Rhoslyn sobbed. "You didn't want me to have the child. How often did you tell me not to scry to watch him. If you didn't prime that Gate for destruction, why did you hold me back from entering?"

Pasgen grimaced. "Because there would hardly have been room for you and Talog as well as Denoriel and Miralys and the boy where I had the Gate set to go. You would have opened my trap because my domain is keyed to you."

"Your domain?" she breathed, and then, breathlessly, "There was a little time. Do you think they could have got through before . . ."

"I don't know," Pasgen said, taking a deep breath. "Let's get back to my Gate and find out. No, we can't. We have to disperse those accursed monsters of yours."

"No need. As soon as they are killed, they will begin to dissolve. There will be nothing to carry back to Sheriff Hutton or to bring others to see. And I doubt if anyone was even hurt. Even if they don't die in the fighting, they will fall apart as they wander in the woods."

"Very clever," Pasgen said.

Rhoslyn shrugged. "Cleverness had nothing to do with it. I wanted to use the least power and expend the least effort. But what are we going to do with the Hunt you brought?"

"I have a leash on them. The Gate will draw them to it and close when the last goes through."

But they did not find Denoriel in the trap Pasgen had set. Both stood staring at the chamber, mockingly set out as a welcoming guest room. There was a handsome sideboard, fitted out with plates and cups. On it stood several covered dishes and three pitchers, holding ale, wine, and milk—all untouched. On the opposite wall was a comfortable settle and two chairs. A beautiful Turkey carpet covered the floor. All that was missing were windows and doors.

There was no smallest sign of disturbance . . . not that Pasgen had expected Denoriel to touch the refreshments provided or to permit the boy to sample them. More telling was the absence of any smell or feel of magic, and if Denoriel had spelled his way out of the trap, he would have had to use powerful magic.

"Then they are dead," Rhoslyn whispered.

"I don't know." Pasgen shook his head. "I have never heard of a Gate collapsing on anyone. It seems to me that anyone within would be thrust out. Of course they might have been killed by that blast of power . . ."

"Would it happen on both sides of the Gate?"

"I don't know," Pasgen repeated. "I will send out some finders, but I have no idea where to tell them to seek, except Logres—and my creatures cannot go there."

Rhoslyn was not to be denied. "You can send an air spirit to Logres. They will not examine any air spirit."

Pasgen hesitated, then shook his head again. "No air spirit will work with me or for me. I had to go through one of their domains, and they would follow me and play about me no matter what I said. I . . . I killed one and injured others."

"Air spirits?" Rhoslyn's tone was neutral, but inwardly Pasgen winced. After an almost imperceptible pause she went on, "Very well. I will try to set the air spirits to look in Logres and Avalon, but you will have to give me a binding spell to hold them to the task."

"You had better do the spell yourself," he said glumly. "They might well sense me in it and flee you. I will tell you what to do. Come down to my workroom."

She followed him through the indoor Gate that brought him to his workroom—one of them anyway; Rhoslyn suspected that there were others that were not open to her. While he was assembling the materials for a spell that could be impressed upon an amulet of some kind, Rhoslyn asked what they were going to tell Vidal Dhu.

"He isn't going to be pleased," she said, sighing. "He had some choice remarks about our inability to snatch FitzRoy when he first demanded that the child be brought to him."

"But all he made were remarks. I don't think he is much interested in FitzRoy any more, even though he insisted that we abduct him. We have Aurilia nic Morrigan to thank for that." Pasgen raised one eyebrow significantly.

"Aurilia nic Morrigan," Rhoslyn said thoughtfully. "She is certainly the most beautiful Sidhe I have ever seen. Did you ever discover where she came from? You know, I've been avoiding the court. I felt that the less Vidal saw of me the less he would be reminded of FitzRoy, but I had to come to the summoning for pledging. That was the first time I saw her."

"I don't know where she came from. One day she was just—there, looking like the *perfect* embodiment of all that is the Sidhe." His eyes softened just a trifle, and he began to wax poetic. "Her hair was that pale golden blond like the earliest sunshine at sunrise. Her eyes were truly emerald green with such perfectly oval pupils . . . nose, mouth, skin, everything perfect. I started to feel for the spell. I couldn't believe anyone could really look like that. And she just let me look and smiled at me."

"I'll bet she did," Rhoslyn said with a snicker. "Eat you whole, that one would."

He sighed. "Maybe. She looked so cool, so clean. Most of the she-Sidhe here . . . I nearly . . . but Vidal came over and just stood with his hand on her arm. I'll fight him some day, but not over a female." He shook himself briefly, and lost that vague dreaminess. "And not over one with what I saw in her eyes when I looked again."

Rhoslyn grinned. "So she's going to eat Vidal. Good. But I had no idea that she was interested in anything beyond her face and body, more jewels and more servants."

"Oh no. Don't ever underestimate her." He nodded when she pursed her lips in speculation. "Vidal's the better magician and she knows it and won't challenge him—she'll use him instead—but she's the brains. The whole domain has run smoother since she came. Of course, it's bad for anyone who has taken her spite, but there's less chaos."

Rhoslyn tilted her head slightly to one side. "I wondered how she had kept Vidal so interested."

"Oh, he's strayed a couple of times, but he still hops when she says 'frog.' Even more interesting is that he doesn't seem to know it." He chuckled. "She keeps up the pretense of being totally dominated by him, not empty-headed, but passive. As if all the ideas are his."

"If she can do that, she's *very* dangerous." Rhoslyn wasn't half as amused at the situation as he was.

Pasgen nodded. "Oh, yes. I still try to look as if only my fear of Vidal is holding me back from trying for her; the best way to stay on her good side is to let her think I'm besotted. I hope she hasn't seen through it. But right now she is very useful in keeping Vidal so preoccupied that we are one of the least of his concerns. She is certain that Anne Boleyn is the key to the red-haired child, and she *wants* the child to be born. She believes Anne can be perverted and disgraced, the child disinherited; then, when it is no longer carefully guarded, it can be abducted and brought here."

"No longer carefully guarded?" Rhoslyn echoed. "What does Aurilia think the Seleighe Court will be doing? That accursed half-brother of ours has successfully thwarted every move we have made to snatch FitzRoy. Do you think he will be less alert for the red-haired babe?"

His eyes glinted with thoughts she could not read. "Right now I am quite content for Aurilia to dream her dreams. She would not thank me, or you, for trying to open her eyes. When she is certain of something, she is very certain—it is a weakness we need to remember—and I would rather Vidal concentrated on something other than FitzRoy."

Rhoslyn sighed. "You're right about that. So what do we tell him?"

"We will tell him the exact truth," he replied firmly. "The Sidhe we brought will stand witness that we killed the air spirit, but not quickly enough. That Denoriel appeared, took the boy through a Gate, and that the Gate collapsed. Let Vidal think FitzRoy is dead. In a few weeks, mortal time, I believe the matter of the divorce will begin moving again. With Aurilia urging Vidal to let Anne marry the king, he will lose interest in FitzRoy again."

Rhoslyn sighed. In her heart there still lived an image of a six-year-old child with wide, trusting eyes and chubby little arms outstretched to her. She would have given everything she owned to have him in her arms.

But the boy clinging with such determination to his bolting horse, his jaw set and thrust forward, fear in his eyes but also rage and hate . . . She was not so certain she wanted *that* boy.

CHAPTER 18

It was fortunate that Denoriel was carrying his naked sword in his hand when they were thrown out of the Gate with force enough to stagger Miralys. Something with bat wings and a great many teeth leapt at them. It was so vicious and stupid, that it impaled itself. Sick with pain from the iron cross and a much worse disorientation from traveling by Gate than had ever struck him before, Denoriel was in no condition to fight.

The violent failure of the Gate had another advantage. Miralys's stagger brought the elvensteed's adamantine silver hooves down with some force on something like a short, fat, slimy snake, also with a great many teeth, every one of them dripping with venom. The feel of the creature beneath his hooves made Miralys leap sideways off the Gate platform. And now it was FitzRoy's death grip on the pommel and the elvensteed's mane that kept Denoriel in the saddle.

A short dash away from the Gate to the far side of what might have once been meant as a park around a fountain drastically reduced the number of attackers. Miralys needed only once to kick out hard backward—none of them ever knew what his hooves connected with because it crawled away cursing and whimpering—to ensure them of some needed quiet and privacy.

After some little period, FitzRoy's hands began to relax their hold on mane and pommel, enough at least so he could turn his head. "Are you all right, Lord Denno?" he asked.

His voice, a little thin, a little tremulous seemed to recall Denoriel from his daze. With an expression of disgust he shook the dead bat-winged thing off his sword and looked at the blackish stain on the blade. Then his left arm made an abortive movement as if to reach for something, but it was still tight around FitzRoy.

"The cross," he muttered. "The iron cross must have collapsed the Gate." For a moment his grip on the boy tightened even further, so that FitzRoy grunted in pain. "God's Blood, my stupidity could have killed you."

"Should I put the cross away, Lord Denno?" FitzRoy asked.

"I . . . I don't know," Denoriel admitted, wiping the blade off on the skirt of his doublet. "It's a protection to you in one way and, well, the failure of the Gate shows that in other ways it's a danger. Sorry, Harry, my head's full of uncombed wool. I'm not thinking very clearly."

The boy had been looking around while they spoke and his nose wrinkled with distaste. "I don't think we should be here, Lord Denno. I've never been, but I've heard Reeve and Ladbroke talk. This looks like the worst slum in London." He hesitated and then added, "Except I don't think there's anything like that—" he gestured toward the corpse Denoriel had shaken off his sword "—even in the worst slum in London."

"No, we're not in London," Denoriel said, sick and dizzy and hurting, wondering how much he dared tell the boy.

He knew Harry loved him dearly and he guessed that Harry knew there was something a bit uncanny about his Lord Denno. However, well on the way to eleven years of age, the boy no longer had the easy belief in fairy knights that he had had at six. He was well educated, and a great deal of that education was aimed at ridding him of childish fancies.

Still, Harry had not been totally overset by plunging into a small grove in the woods around Sheriff Hutton, feeling as if he were being turned inside out, and emerging in what was obviously a badly decaying city. Nor had he screamed or struggled when one monster attacked them from above and another from below. Moreover, there was now a glint in his eyes that made Denoriel want to smile.

Fairy knights might be for babies, but Harry wanted to believe in magic. He would tell the boy the truth, he decided. Well, actually, he didn't have much choice since he couldn't think of any lie that Harry would believe. And the child was remarkably trustworthy. In the more than four years since he had first been exposed as not an ordinary human, Harry had never once slipped by accident or shown any desire to boast of an uncanny friend. In fact, whenever anything Denoriel did was noted or remarked upon, Harry would shrug and say, "Foreign. He's Hungarian. They're strange."

The most urgent thing was for the boy to be prepared for anything so that he would not freeze in terror or become hysterical—not that his behavior so far indicated he would. However, he would be best prepared by being told the truth.

Meanwhile the hopeful glint in Harry's eyes was replaced by concern. "Lord Denno, I think we better get off Miralys and give him a chance to rest. He's shaking."

Denoriel started. The child was right. The elvensteed was shuddering. Denoriel looked around but saw no sign of danger; he let Harry down from the saddle, following immediately. When nothing struck, he sheathed his sword.

"Turn your back to me, Harry," he said through gritted teeth, hoping to minimize the growing aching and weakness the iron cross was causing.

His next action was to reach for the girth of the mortal-world saddle. They would not need it here; once recovered, Miralys could provide a far more comfortable saddle from his own substance. A buckle caught on the heavy double-lined silk cloak Denoriel had wrapped around his arm to protect it from the cold iron. He had been wearing a cloak because the weather Overhill was turning cold and raw in November. He didn't need the cloak, but he always wore what was common among his friends to fit in.

Recalling that silk helped reduce the effect of cold iron, he turned and flung the cloak over Harry's shoulders, crossing it in front. The child looked surprised.

"I'm not cold, Lord Denno. If you are, you can have the cloak."

"It's never cold Underhill," Denoriel said, "nor too hot either. The silk shields me from your cross. Keep the cloak closed, Harry, and keep a watch out for me. If you see anything, anything at all, tell me. I'm going to try to find out what hurt Miralys."

Now Denoriel removed the saddle and set it on the ground, then examined Miralys to make sure he was not cut or bitten anywhere. There was no sign of any injury, but when the elvensteed rested its head on his shoulder he had an immediate impression of heat and light billowing, almost engulfing them, held off by some force emanating from the elvensteed.

The Gate. The Gate collapsing. Then the force Miralys had used to hold off the ravening energy of the failing Gate began to wane. Denoriel could feel the elvensteed's fear . . . and there was a wrenching, a last terrible effort, and then they were spilled out into . . . ah, now Denoriel at least recognized where they were . . . Wormegay Hold.

Denoriel stroked Miralys, trying to pass into him some of his own power, but that attempt failed. Possibly the elvensteeds used another source of energy than that which powered elven magic, one that was as rich in the mortal world as Underhill. He had never known the source to fail, but now he felt Miralys's desperate effort to gather strength. Had the collapse of the Gate damaged the steed?

"It's all right, Miralys," he said, stroking the silky hide, caressing the steed's head. "You don't need to carry us. Harry and I can get around Wormegay on foot. It's not that big. And we can stay right here for a while. I don't think anything's noticed us. Maybe I can raise a shield—"

The thought was interrupted by FitzRoy asking anxiously, "Is Miralys all right?"

As shock receded, Denoriel was better able to think. Harry's voice seemed to bring together the cloak, the reduction in his pain now that Harry was wearing it, Harry's need for protection, and the idea of a shield, which had come to his mind. It occurred to Denoriel that he could build a shield onto the cloak, which, hip-length on him, covered Harry from neck to ankle.

As long as the boy kept the cloak closed, most of the invidious effect of the cold iron would be eliminated. If there was some threat in which the cross could protect the boy, he would only have to fling the cloak back. That would not break the shield and when the threat was gone, Harry could just close the cloak and the worst would be over.

Settlement of the first question the boy had asked him—whether or not to cover his cross—somehow made Denoriel more sanguine about solving all his other problems.

"Miralys is just exhausted, Harry," he said. "Are *you* all right?"

"Oh yes," the boy said brightly but still watching all around. "But this place is a *mess*. Just look at this park. Half the trees are dead and the weeds are just growing over everything. The statue fell off that fountain in the middle and it's all black and slimy. I think there's a dead animal under the bushes over there. And there's a bench here, but I think someone . . . er . . . shit on it."

Denoriel looked at the bench and shuddered. A gesture of his hand swept it clean. Another gesture sent the dead thing—he was grateful Harry had not seen it more clearly because it was a Dreaming Sidhe, not a dead animal—to a different corner of the area.

"And look at those houses just outside the park. They're all falling down and *mold* is growing on them. Ugh! What's more, this place smells." FitzRoy glanced up at him before returning his attention to the area surrounding them. "I was never in a park that *smelled* before. I don't think this is where you expected to take me. Do we have to stay?"

Denoriel saw Miralys fold his legs and sink down to rest. He put his hand on Harry's shoulder and drew the boy to the bench.

"We have to stay for a little while, until Miralys feels better. Let's sit down, Harry. I have a lot to explain."

"That would be good, Lord Denno," the child said solemnly. "I am much older than when we met and I . . . I don't really believe in fairy guardians any more. But some of the things you do . . ." He shook his head. "I never dared ask you, not even when we were riding out because I was so afraid someone would hear. What are you, Lord Denno?"

Denoriel laughed weakly. "Actually, fairy gaurdian is pretty close to the truth. Do you know anything about the Sidhe?"

"One of my tutors told me something about them, I think. We were studying the legends of the Welsh and Scots and Irish. When the Milesians defeated the Tuatha de Danaan, the Tuatha de Danaan went down into the sidhe . . ."

He gestured wearily for the child to stop. "Yes, well, the story is a bit more complicated, but never mind that. The sidhe are not in Ireland alone. They . . . they are everywhere in the whole world. And it was not only the Tuatha who built or went down into them."

"Are you of the Tuatha de Danaan?" A wide-eyed stare.

Denoriel shrugged. "Some mortals call us elves. Some call us Faery. Some call us the Fair Folk." A smile twitched at his lips. "Some call us names that it is better a youngling like you doesn't hear. But as you call yourselves English, from the name of your land, England, we call ourselves Sidhe from the place we made for ourselves, the sidhe. Now, because many, many other folk than the Sidhe live in that place, we keep the name Sidhe and call the place where we live Underhill. Thus sometimes we call your world Overhill or the mortal world."

FitzRoy clasped his hands. His eyes were enormous but bright with pleasure and excitement, not fear. "Oh,

Lord Denno are you truly my own personal elven knight?"

Denoriel flicked the boy's nose. "Certainly not! I am my own personal elven knight, as you are your own personal boy. I am not a pet or a toy and do not belong to you. When you are older, I will be able to explain why certain mortals are of great importance to the Sidhe. For now it is enough for you to know you are one of those mortals, and I am assigned to protect you. So, in a sense, I *am* your fairy guardian."

The boy giggled, nervously. "But if you are my guardian, I fear you have fallen short of the mark this once! You saved me from those creatures that attacked us true enough, but I suspect that you have driven us from one peril to another."

Denoriel sighed. "Well, this certainly isn't where I intended to take you. But I believe it was your cross that made the mess and wrecked my plan. Underhill we have a swift means of travel, which we call called Gating."

The boy blinked. "Is that why we went into that dark place in the forest and of a sudden we were here?"

Denoriel tried to scan the area around them for trouble and answer the boy's questions at the same time. "Yes. Exactly. But you know that your iron cross won't let any Sidhe nor many other Underhill residents touch you. It has a power of its own. And that power . . ." He searched for an explanation. " . . . ah, interfered with the magic power that lets a Gate move folk who are magical from one place to another. Look, you—" he pointed. "Look to that blackened place, there. That is—or was—actually the Gate where we came in. I'm afraid the cold iron collapsed the Gate where we entered so we can't get back by entering that Gate again."

"But you saved us!" the boy exclaimed.

Oh, how he wanted to take credit for that! But honesty forbade him. "No, I didn't. I didn't even know what was happening. Miralys saved us, which is why he's exhausted. There is a Gate there—" he pointed to the ruined fountain. "But I do not know where it goes, and I do not know where we can find another one."

Harry bit his lip. "Then I'd better put my cross away."

He shook his head; the motion made it ache. "No, you might need it. This place not only looks worse than the worst slum in London, it's more dangerous. You might need your cross for protection. The magic hereabouts is no help to us; I had rather see it disrupted."

Harry put one hand on Denoriel's arm. "But it hurts you, Lord Denno."

He managed a wan smile. "Yes, but I think I can solve that problem."

Denoriel then told Harry about putting a shield on his cloak and how he could hide or expose the cross very quickly. In fact, he built the shield while he was explaining, and when Harry wrapped the cloak tight around him, Denoriel sighed with relief.

"Yes, that does it. I feel much better—"

He left the sentence unfinished and turned around sharply to look at Miralys who was heaving himself to his feet. Denoriel exclaimed wordlessly with concern. The elvensteed was in a sorry state. His coat was dull and there was a sort of insubstantiality about him.

Before he could protest and urge Miralys to continue to rest, FitzRoy said, "There's someone coming. It's only a little girl, but she looks very strange."

Denoriel whirled around, his sword coming out of its sheathe. Underhill little girls were often anything but harmless. He swept Harry behind him and faced a starveling child, huge-eyed, pallid, dressed in limp tatters that were soiled with dark stains. Her hair was white and trailed behind her, the strands that brushed the ground tangled with twigs and dirt. A ribbonlike, pale tongue slipped out between her thin lips and licked them. And a sense of hunger welled out of her that nearly drew a cry of pain from Denoriel.

"Pretty Sidhe," she whispered. "I can give you what will make Dreaming worthless. Give me that sweet and tender enchanted boy."

"Go away," Denoriel said. "I will give you nothing, and of a certainty I do not desire anything you can give me."

The huge eyes grew even larger. It needed all of Denoriel's strength not to fall into them. "If you will not give him to me, I will suck *you* dry and then I will have him anyway."

Denoriel curved his lips in what was not a smile. "You would have already if you could. Go away and I will not hurt you."

She laughed. "Even pain is power," the sultry whisper began again. "You did not bring that tender morsel here and bind it with spells for nothing."

"What I do is none of your business," Denoriel snapped. "I said to go away and I meant it." He slashed at her with his sword.

It did not touch her, but she shrieked anyway and opened a mouth that seemed to split her head in two, exposing long pointed teeth. Her hands came up, the fingers suddenly sprouting shining claws. Denoriel lunged forward and slapped his sword down hard on one hand. She screamed and staggered back, her hand blackening where the silver sword had touched it.

Denoriel breathed a sigh of relief and stepped forward again. There were those that could not abide cold iron and those that could not abide silver. The creature, for it looked far less human now, retreated, spitting. But the sense of hunger that was sucking at him did not diminish, and Denoriel's long-sighted eyes saw other movement coming from the streets around the park.

He heard Harry cry out, "Miralys!" and whirled. The elvensteed had just brought his front hooves down on a crawling thing that looked like an armored fish with the head of a tusked boar. Behind it something squirmed along the ground, the snakelike body creeping forward on thousands of tiny legs . . . no, hands . . . lifting the most exquisite Sidhe face toward him. An enormously long tongue suddenly snapped out of that face and flicked toward Harry. Denoriel cut it off and then severed the head from the body.

"Behind you!" Harry gasped.

Denoriel turned again, fearing that the ten or twenty creatures he had guessed were coming from the street had all arrived at once. Fortunately it was only the swiftest among them, a winged being that any mortal would have taken for an angel, so fair was its face, so glistening its multicolor wings, so pure a white its fluttering robe. Only a mouth gaping wide to expose long, pointed teeth and clawed hands outstretched to seize did not match the image.

This time the silver sword did not blacken the hand it struck, but the scream from the faux-angel was just as heartfelt as that of the wraith because Denoriel struck off its hand. It groped with the other hand, stretching its neck, elongating it like a folded ribbon, its teeth snapping. But that was a fatal mistake, for Denoriel turned the sword and struck at that impossibly thinned neck. It severed as easily as the hand. The head flew off to his right as the body thudded into the ground.

He heard the boy cry out in a brief triumph behind him and heard, too, Miralys's anguished groan as the steed raised his body and struck out backward with his hooves.

"The Gate!" Denoriel cried. "Wherever it takes us will be better than here."

He caught up the saddle, afraid to leave anything of theirs behind. Harry grabbed the trailing sleeve of his gown—the first time Denoriel had known the cursed things to be of any use. They made it to the rim of the fountain before anything else reached them.

Harry leapt lightly up over the stone rim and on to the plinth, but he did not enter the dark haze that seemed to rise out of the black slime that covered it. Denoriel dropped the saddle beside him and turned back to urge on Miralys, who he thought was lagging behind to guard their rear, but he saw with horror that the elvensteed's mouth gaped open, foam dripping from his lower jaw, while his ribs worked like bellows. The steed was struggling to raise his legs over the fountain rim.

Denoriel leapt down, not knowing what he could do to help, the elvensteed being many times his weight and beyond even elven strength to lift, just as a thing—like an antelope with a huge penis hanging down below its belly and, stuck on its neck, the head of a bird with bulging eyes and a serrated beak— struck at Miralys. The elvensteed shrieked and leapt over the fountain rim and up the two steps, shying back from the Gate itself only because Harry had his steel knife in hand.

The bird-antelope struck at Denoriel. He struck back, and the creature was beakless. And before he could strike again and kill it, three other things—one like a bent-over old man but with the head of a vulture;

a second four-legged creature with a toad's warty skin and wide mouth but with a crocodile's teeth and, incredibly, human-looking shoes on its four feet; and the third a bat-winged something with human breasts but a spider's head—leapt on the struggling bird-antelope and began to devour it alive.

Denoriel raised his sword to plunge into the creature's throat in mercy, but Harry shouted at him, "Lord Denno, hurry! Miralys is falling."

Turning to run to Harry, Denoriel himself almost fell. His arms felt like old, wet dishrags and his knees were shaking. He was cold and hollow, as he had not been since Mwynwen bespelled him. As he staggered up the two steps to the plinth he noticed that the air was empty. The horrors of Wormegay Hold were clearer to the eyes than the beauties of any other domain Underhill because there was no faint, near-invisible mist in the atmosphere.

No time to wonder. Miralys was, indeed, sinking. With a cry of fear, Denoriel put his arm around the neck of the steed and heaved, kicking the saddle ahead of him. He grasped for Harry with his free hand as he pulled as hard as he could. He should not have been able to support the elvensteed, but Miralys was so light, as if he was only an illusory image of himself. The push should not have moved Miralys at all, but the whole entangled group staggered forward into the dark haze of the Gate.

For a moment nothing happened and Denoriel gasped with fear. Had this Gate also collapsed or been damaged by the disaster at the other Gate? As the thought came, his strength was drained even further so that he fell to his knees. Indeed, he would have fallen flat on his face if Harry had not supported him.

Then came the darkness of transition, the horrible feeling of being wrenched inside out. Usually that lasted so short a time that it was not significant. Now it went on and on. There was no sound. He thought Harry was shouting at him, but he couldn't hear. He could no longer feel Miralys. Lost? Could they be lost in the void through which the Gates made contact, terminus with terminus?

Would they spend eternity in this hell?

CHAPTER 19

Almost mindless with terror, Denoriel finally recalled that there were open Gates, Gates that would take you anywhere you were strong enough to chose as a terminus, if there was a Gate terminus there. He fixed his mind on Logres . . . on Gating to Logres . . . blessed Dannae, how he wanted to get to Logres! . . .

. . . and spilled out into a swirling mist so thick that he could barely make out Harry and the larger bulk of Miralys.

The elvensteed, solid again, dropped to his knees, bearing Denoriel down.

But a moment later, he shook himself, and then got to his feet. Denoriel no longer felt cold and empty. Mwynwen's spell was working again. He heard Miralys snort—a nice energetic snort.

"Where are we now, Lord Denno?" Harry asked cheerfully. "I don't think this is where you wanted to go either—but it's almost like home. London has fogs like this. Are we back in London?"

"I'm afraid not, Harry." Denoriel picked up the

338

saddle. "Here, let's just step down—careful, there should be a sort of platform. Now hold on to me and don't let go. A foot away and I couldn't see you in this mist. We're in what's called the Unformed lands. If I were a strong enough magician, I could build a whole world in here."

"Are we going to stay here while you build a world?" the boy asked.

Denoriel sighed. He wasn't cold and empty, but he was so tired his knees felt soft. He bent them and felt around. Behind him there seemed to be a low platform of stone—he bruised a knuckle on it. That must be the Gate. Ahead and to each side, however, the ground seemed firm and dry. No one had even bothered to make grass. That was hopeful. Some mage had been here or there wouldn't be a Gate, but perhaps he or she had only wanted to mark an Unformed place for future work. He set the saddle down.

"Let's sit down while I catch my breath."

Harry sat down on the saddle. "After that are you going to built a world?" he asked with the typical persistence of a child.

"No—no!" He sighed. *Ah, the boundless confidence of the young.* . . . Harry clearly thought he could do anything, and as flattering as that estimation was, he was going to have to disabuse the boy of it. "Unfortunately far stronger mages than I use these lands, and sometimes they are not kindly mages. Sometimes they create unfriendly beasts and leave them as guards."

Harry patted his arm. "They couldn't be much more unfriendly than the beasts we met in that other place," he said, sounding forlorn. "Lord Denno, why did they attack us like that? We weren't threatening them in any way."

"They were hungry," Denoriel said before he thought.

Harry drew in his breath sharply. "They wanted to *eat* us? They are cannibals?"

Denoriel was surprised into a thin chuckle. "I don't know that you can call them cannibals," he said, aghast at the horror he had suggested to the child and wanting to make light of it. "Cannibals eat their own kind. I'm not sure there were two of any kind in Wormegay Hold."

"Cannibals or not, they wanted to *eat me*," Harry replied, indignation overriding fear. "That girl said I was sweet and tender!"

Although actually he wasn't at all sure about it—the dark stains on the wraith's tatters could easily have been blood—Denoriel said, "No. I don't think they wanted to eat our flesh. What they were hungry for was the power I put into the spell on your cloak and the power that is part of your life force and mine."

There was no need to mention that the way the attackers would have got their life force would have been to tear them apart in the most painful way possible. The threat—at least from those in Wormegay Hold—was gone now, and there was no need to frighten a child. Denoriel himself was not really horrified; the draining of life force by the Unseleighe was a fact too long known and recognized to hold his mind. What he kept thinking of was the clarity of the air in Wormegay; it stank, but there was no mist . . . There was no mist of power!

"I didn't realize it at first," Denoriel said slowly, "but Wormegay is completely empty of power."

"How can you tell?" Harry asked, sounding eager and interested. "You said you put a shield on my cloak, but there's nothing there that I can see or feel."

"That's because you don't work with magic." Denoriel smiled at him, and in case he couldn't see the expression in the thick fog, he bent down and kissed the boy's hair. "That's a good thing, Harry. Mortal mages are only trouble for themselves and everyone else."

"Well . . . maybe." The boy glanced back over his shoulder at where the Gate might be; they were sitting not far from it. "Maybe we should move father away from here. In case a few of those things decide to follow us?"

"Follow?" Denoriel repeated tensing, but then he shook his head. "None will follow us. If anything in Wormegay Hold could use the Gate to get out, that creature would have done so already. They're all trapped in there, so stripped of power that the Gate doesn't recognize them as magical."

That was *very* strange. Denoriel had never heard of anyplace Underhill that did not have a flood of ambient power. Oh, some places had more and some less; the air and substance in some was more malleable than in others. Most of the great realms like Logres and Avalon were specially rich . . . but a domain that sucked the power out of those in it? Denoriel had never heard of such, and felt that he should warn the Magus Majors of the Seleighe Court. Harry tugged his hand, drawing his attention.

"I'm not magical and I got through," he said.

"You were holding on to me."

Denoriel shuddered, suddenly remembering how drained he had been; how he had almost fallen when the Gate drank power from him. He realized then that even the Gate at Wormegay was not powered; it needed to draw power from anyone who wanted to use it. Denoriel restrained another shudder.

Had he been a little more empty, perhaps they would have been trapped in Wormegay Hold. And Miralys—the Hold had been drinking from Miralys as if he were an open well. Yes, the magi had to be warned with a particular caution for elvensteeds. Denoriel could feel Harry looking around, and after another moment the boy spoke.

"This fog isn't clearing at all. We'll have to think of a way not to go around in circles when we start to move."

"I think I'll try to find out where this Gate goes before we set out across an Unformed domain."

After a little silence Harry said, "I'm not sure I want to travel by Gate again if that's what it's going to be like each time. I didn't have my knife out and I was holding the cloak closed over my cross, so I don't think it was my fault this time."

"No, it wasn't, Harry. It was mine." He sighed. "I wasn't strong enough to hold to the thought of where I wanted to go, and now we're here . . . and might as well be on the other side of the world."

"This is not such a bad place, Lord Denno," the boy said comfortingly. "But it surely is the worst fog I've ever seen. London suffers from dreadful fogs some-times, but I don't think this thick. What did you do wrong?"

Denoriel rubbed one temple; his head was starting to ache again—or else, now that he wasn't fighting for their lives, he had finally noticed the ache. "The Gate is what is called an open Gate. That is, if a Sidhe just thinks hard about where he or she wants to go, the Gate will take them there . . . if there's a terminus there. The reason we were stuck in the Gate so long was that I didn't remember about open Gates right away. There are so few Gates like that any more—they're really hard to make—that I was just waiting for the Gate to take us wherever it went. I wasn't thinking about any place in particular that I wanted to go."

There was a momentary silence and then Harry said, "And this was the place you wanted to go? Why?"

The elvensteed stamped and snorted. Denoriel said, "Not me. Miralys? Was it you?"

A silken nose touched his cheek then prodded more firmly, as if to show that the elvensteed's strength had returned. His certainly had, Denoriel realized. And then he understood. The flow of power, and probably of whatever energy the elvensteeds used, was most plentiful—one might even call it overwhelming—in the chaos lands. His spell had restored him completely in moments; likely the same was true for whatever means powered the elvensteeds.

"The *horse* brought us here?"

"Miralys isn't a horse any more than I am a man," Denoriel said. "He is an elvensteed. Although I have never heard him speak to me, I am sure he could if he wanted to. And he is as clever—if not more clever— and far more powerful than any man and most Sidhe. In fact, Miralys might be able to take us where I want to go without the Gate."

Miralys backed away a little and Denoriel sighed. "Either he can't or he isn't yet strong enough to do that," he said to Harry. "Stay here. Don't move off that saddle; it's human made and I can sense it even in the fog. I'm going up to look at the Gate more closely. Maybe—"

"There's something coming, Lord Denno!"

Denoriel jumped to his feet and drew his sword. A head poked through the fog, which thinned around it. It was an adorable head, with bright dark eyes peering through curled white wool, and crowned with tiny horns. Denoriel watched tensely as the fog thinned further, as green grass appeared below the feet and around the little creature, which opened its mouth— Denoriel lifted his sword to center on it. But no teeth showed . . . and it said, "Baa baa."

"It's a lamb," Harry said, also on his feet.

"It *looks* like a lamb."

Denoriel had not sheathed his sword. The mist was clearing steadily, the grass spreading. Trees began to appear in the distance. Miralys moved forward and stepped onto the grass. To Denoriel's relief, the elvensteed had regained his solidity, and his coat was its normal, shining dappled silver.

Miralys sniffed the lamb. It uttered a startled *baa* and shied away, but didn't run. A moment later it had arched its back and stiffened its legs and came bouncing back toward Miralys. Harry laughed aloud and Denoriel's sword dropped. The gait was so typical of the young—sheep, goats, deer, cattle, horses—all bounced on stiff legs in playful approach. Finally it bounced right into Miralys and butted him with its tiny horns.

Denoriel's sword came up again, but Miralys only snorted at the lamb and lowered his head to the grass to graze. Denoriel bit his lip. The lamb danced off to join other sheep, which had appeared in the near distance. The scene could have been lifted out of any rich grazing meadow in England, except there was no shepherd. Could Miralys have been bespelled by stepping into the scene?

He lifted a foot to follow the elvensteed and then put it down. If he, too, were bespelled, what would Harry do?

"Harry, just step out into the grass. Don't walk far away. Stay about where we saw the lamb."

The boy glanced at him, suddenly smiled, and stepped onto the grass. He walked a little way toward Miralys, put his hand on the elvensteed's shoulder. The lamb—or another lamb—jump-hopped over and baa'd; Harry touched its head and it shied away. Miralys lifted his head. Harry turned toward Denoriel, walked back, and stepped out of the scene to the Sidhe's side.

"I think it's just a meadow with sheep. Miralys seemed just as usual, and the lamb felt like a lamb. It didn't try to bite me. Do you think it could all have been there all along and we just didn't notice because of the mist?"

"I don't know," Denoriel said.

The truth was that he didn't think so. He believed their presence had either triggered the creation or carried it from wherever it usually manifested to this area. He examined Harry with mage sight, but could see nothing beyond the blinding glare of the shield on the cloak. The boy's face and hands seemed normal; no sign of magic flickered on them.

"I guess it's my turn," he said, and stepped into the shepherd's paradise.

The words had come unbidden to his mind, but now that they had, he recognized that what was all around him was exactly and precisely that—a shepherd's paradise. He listened and looked with every sense he had—and again cursed himself for being so young, so foolish, so arrogant as to turn his back on mage training. He could sense nothing inimical at all. There was even a sense of peace pervading the scene, but not an enforced peace. However, Denoriel knew he might be unable to sense something slow and subtle that any visitor might carry away with him.

If so they had all been infected already. Miralys was grazing steadily. Harry had run ahead toward four or five lambs playing together. Denoriel sighed and sat down on a convenient—too convenient?—fallen log. The bark had been cleaned and the trunk hollowed slightly to make a seat. He tried to look totally relaxed and unaware, even closed his eyes for a while. Nothing happened.

The mist had cleared off so completely that one could see a blue sky above, dotted with natural-seeming clouds that moved. It all looked so real that Denoriel felt anxious. Could they have been cast out into the mortal world? Then he remembered the mist so dense the place could only be part of the Unformed lands. He glanced up again.

Just now a cloud was obscuring the sun, but it passed. Denoriel's pupils closed to slits, and he needed that protection; however this was not the real sun of the mortal world. He could look right into it.

Safe. This was a safe place. Denoriel let his muscles loosen. They would stay a while—he could always make up the time, and perhaps he would not need to; time ran slower Underhill—until they had recovered from the shocks of the blasted Gate and Wormegay Hold.

Harry was playing among the lambs as he had probably never been allowed to play before. The little creatures, accustomed to him now, allowed him to embrace them. Then, impatient of restraint as all young creatures are, butted him away. Sometimes two or three vied for his attention and they all went down in a tangle.

Denoriel called him, and he came at once, flushed and bright-eyed, but he begged to stay a little longer, and Denoriel could not find it in his heart to deny him his joy. Poor Harry had so little lighthearted joy. So they stayed, recovering from the shocks they had had, until the artificial sun was actually dropping in the west. Denoriel thought it probably moved faster than the real sun did, but not fast enough to disturb anyone accustomed to the mortal world.

Finally—to Denoriel's relief—Harry returned to his side on his own, breathless and rather grubby. Denoriel thought that his costly silk-lined cloak could never be restored, but it was a small price to pay for the boy's pleasure.

"Lord Denno, is there anything to eat here?" Harry asked, making clear the reason for abandoning his play.

"It's been a long time since the cortege stopped for a nuncheon."

"Miralys," Denoriel called, his throat tightening as he realized he had not seen the elvensteed for some time. However, before his anxiety could rise any further, Miralys was there, as beautiful and vibrant as he had ever been. "Shall we try the Gate, Miralys, or will you leap us across to Logres?"

For answer a saddle formed on the elvensteed's back. A double saddle, really, for there was room for Harry just behind the pommel. About to mount, Denoriel remembered the mortal-world saddle. He was less anxious about leaving that here. He could not believe the mage who had constructed this shepherd's paradise would mind their having used it for a little time or trace them through the saddle to do them harm.

Still, the thing was mortal-made, not elven kenned; Denoriel remembered how Gilfaethwy insisted on mortal-world artifacts untouched by elven influence. Perhaps the saddle would be worth something to someone. Denoriel ran back to the Gate to retrieve it and heaved it over Miralys's croup, where linen bands suddenly appeared to fasten it.

He mounted, grasped Harry's hands and pulled him up. The boy had scarcely swung his leg over Miralys when they were plunged into an icy darkness that gave way almost instantaneously to the gorgeous, otherworldly garden outside the palace of Llachar Lle. Miralys carefully trod the narrow path that skirted a quiet pond surrounded by moonflowers and nightlillies. The long, silver leaves of Underhill's willows trailed over them, a welcoming caress.

Beyond the pond the path widened and then debouched onto a close-cropped lawn. Harry gaped upward at the shining, unveined, white marble walls of the palace, rising two stories to a battlemented wall above the huge bronze doors. To either side of the central building were slender round towers, showing many wide windows above the second floor. Pennons flapped from each tower.

Denoriel also stared upward. Oberon and Titania? Here? Why? Did the king and queen know he had been involved in the destruction of a Gate? Or were they here to chastise him because he had apparently abducted a mortal boy of great importance? And he had allowed Harry to see and understand far too much of Underhill.

"Those towers," Harry said with an odd note of disapproval in his voice instead of the wonder Denoriel had expected, "a cannon would take them down in an hour. Even a trenchbut . . ."

"We don't have cannon Underhill," Denoriel said, but a cold chill ran up his back.

It was true that the Unseleighe were unlikely to assault a palace, but if those of the mortal world were sufficiently frightened or angered . . . or driven by greed . . .

The mortals had mages. A human mage, particularly one not too particular about how he gathered his power, could open a portal into Underhill, could bring in those terrible brass cannon, could turn Llachar Lle to rubble, to less than rubble, in an hour.

He shook off the horrifying vision and gestured for Harry to dismount and follow him.

The mortals had a saying: *Sufficient unto the day are the troubles thereof.* And if the presence of the High King and his Queen was anything to go by, he had troubles enough for now.

CHAPTER 20

FitzRoy had some initial nervousness about sleeping alone in a room—he had never been without a nurse or, now, his valet Shandy Dunstan on a truckle bed by his side. Denoriel solved the problem by pointing out that there were many servants listening for his smallest wish, and proving it by telling Harry to ask for anything he wanted . . . within reason.

"What's not within reason?" the boy asked at once.

"Twenty naked dancing girls," Denoriel replied and then blushed. The bed brought only one thing to his mind.

FitzRoy blinked. "What would I want with *twenty*?"

Blushing harder, Denoriel said, "You're a naughty boy! What would you want with one?"

The boy tried to swagger; the effect was enough to make Denoriel suppress a grin. "Don't know, but I'd like to find out."

Denoriel laughed. "Not tonight. You're too sleepy. Take it from someone who does know. Being too tired takes the fun out of it. No. Ask for a glass of water or more cider or a sweet."

He then went out of the room. After a little while, he heard a giggle and, eyes wide, rushed back in. There was, to his relief, no dancing girl, but Harry did have a large glass of water and what looked like marchpane sweets in a golden dish on the table beside the bed. In addition, he was attired in a clean, white nightshirt and a small nightcap.

He sighed sleepily when Denoriel came in and said, "You're right, Lord Denno. Your servants are paying close attention to me. But it is passing strange to have my clothes taken off and a nightshirt put on when I can't see what's doing it."

"As long as it was done right," Denoriel said, coming to the bed. "I'm glad they didn't have any trouble with your cross." He eyed the pouch in which the cross was concealed, but the shield spell over the enshrouding silk seemed strong and solid. Then he bent down and kissed the boy on the forehead. "Do you want me to stay until you fall asleep?"

There was no need to ask. Harry's eyes were already closed and his breathing deepening. Denoriel stood by the bed for a few moments longer, mentally commanded the servants not only to serve but to watch and protect, and left the apartment.

As he crossed the great corridor of Llachar Lle, he felt a Thought brush him—a Thought he knew could rip away all his protections, could seize and rend him soul and body if it desired—and his step hesitated. A moment later the touch was withdrawn. Denoriel breathed again and hurried out. Miralys was waiting, trembling, at the foot of the steps.

When they arrived this time, Denoriel did not even need to speak to whatever guarded the Academicia. Magus Major Gilfaethwy was waiting at a doorway and bellowed at him before he had even dismounted.

"You meddled with my Gates! How dare you! You asked for simple Gates that would take you from one place to another. You tried to cheat me by changing the patterns!"

With a considerable effort, Denoriel got control of his jaw, which had been hanging open in shock. He had no idea that Gilfaethwy could have known of the collapse of the Gate near Sheriff Hutton—or how he could have learned of it so soon.

"I did not meddle apurpose, magus, I swear to you," he said as soon as he was able. "I was fleeing an Unseleighe attack, and the child who was the intended victim of that attack was wearing a cold iron cross, which seems to have disrupted the Gate."

The mage scowled, and Denoriel wondered if he was about to find out what flies tasted like. "That, too, I felt Denoriel Siencyn Macreth Silverhair. But if you had not first meddled with the Gate, it would not have failed so catastrophically, and I would not have nearly been rendered witless and useless."

"I am so very sorry, magus, but I didn't do it!" Denoriel protested, dismounting and approaching the fuming mage. "I swear I didn't. I don't know how, and there wasn't any other place I wanted the Gate to go."

"Liar!" Gilfaethwy roared. "I sensed your aura caught in the patterning. Do you think me such a fool that I do not leave safeguards on my creations? You aren't the only half-baked, untaught, untalented half-wit to try to cheat me! I sensed your aura . . . and the foulness you had hidden beneath your so-young, so-innocent . . ."

The mage's voice faded and Denoriel felt an assessing touch sweep over him. Denoriel had done this and that of which his too-gentle sister disapproved, but he was sure he had never done anything that a fellow Sidhe would consider foul and he raised no shields, except those that already existed on his very inmost being.

Then his mind caught on the idea of an aura very like his but tainted with foulness. Pasgen. Pasgen had meddled with the Gate!

"It was not I," Denoriel insisted. "I have a halfbrother . . ."

"Eh?" He caught the mage quite off-guard with that.

He hurried on. "Surely the tale is known to you! I have an Unseleighe halfbrother . . . We are contending with one another over this child. It is not impossible that he tried to set the Gate so that if I escaped into it, I and the child would be transported to . . . likely to his domain or to his twin sister's."

The mage blinked. "Twin sister?"

"Yes. There are two sets of twins, myself and my sister, and Pasgen and his." The double births were so extraordinary—quite unheard of—he could not believe that the mage had never heard of them.

"Silverhair . . . twins. Aha. Now I remember, of course. Two sets of twins."

Gilfaethwy paused, stared hard at Denoriel, and snapped his fingers. When they had arrived in his overcrowded and even more disordered workroom, he nodded.

"Now I remember." He spoke absently, and Denoriel suspected, mostly to himself, for the words came slowly, as if he was pulling memories out of some corner of his mind that had not been looked into for a very long time. "Yes. Llanelli Ffridd Gwynneth Arian craved children to the point of madness, and had a great magic worked and caught in it your father—not that he knew what she had done because he went innocently from Llanelli to the bed of his current lady . . . ah, yes, your mother . . . and enough of the spell was bound into him that she, too, conceived. And also twins. And then the

Unseleighe learned of you, and came to take you. You and your sister, we saved, though at cost. And one set was stolen away by our Unseleighe kin—and Llanelli followed her children into the halls of shadow."

Denoriel made a wordless sound of agreement.

"So you are innocent of playing with my Gates. And your half-brother is a magician of considerable ability." He paused, making chewing motions with his mouth as if he had an sour unripe fruit in it that he had to swallow. "He understands Gates. He made it a little unstable, but likely if the child had not been wearing the cold iron cross, the Gate would have placed you where he wanted you."

"That gives me no great joy, magus," Denoriel said.

Gilfaethwy shrugged.

"Can you take the Gates down and replace them with new Gates?" he asked, urgently.

The mage gave him a withering look. "To what purpose, you idiot? Do you think your brother is not aware of what happened? Do you think he would not repattern any Gate you used?"

"Even the ones in London and at Windsor?" Denoriel persisted. "Can you sense his meddling there also?"

"I cannot even sense the Gates at this distance. Those are Treowth's Gates. He uses a completely different system than I do. If you want those Gates tested, he must do it himself."

Denoriel sighed. He had been told that Treowth had moved to the Bazaar of the Bizarre. There were three great markets Underhill—Elves' Fair, Goblin Market, and the Bazaar of the Bizarre. Denoriel had never been to any of them. He was young enough, still, to enjoy his life filled with music and dancing and making love and the Wild Hunt for excitement and danger. He had not yet needed to seek for toys in the market—any of the markets, where it was said that making a bargain for what you wanted might cost your life or your soul or both.

Elves' Fair catered to those who were so weak in magic that they could not build their own servants. Constructs of every variety were available there, as well as bound monsters, bound elementals, and, very occasionally, mortal slaves. There were no guarantees given with that merchandise. Goblin Market sold mixed wares, toys, spells, devices—mortal, Sidhe, and from the other planes—as well as information, but it was said that you could take nothing away except what you already had and did not want. Bazaar of the Bizarre was what it said . . . except that what was bizarre to elves and the denizens of stranger realms was bizarre indeed.

The question was how to get there. Denoriel drew a deep breath and said, "I know that Magus Treowth is said to be in the Bazaar of the Bizarre. I paid you for Gates, but I do not have them and you say you cannot replace them. Your contract is not fulfilled Magus Gilfaethwy."

"I *can* replace them," Gilfaethwy snarled. "Out of my good heart, I have warned you—"

"That you cannot make me a Gate proof against my halfbrother's meddling," Denoriel snapped back. "Very well, I accept that. Instead, tell me how to get to the Bazaar of the Bizarre and how to find Magus Treowth when I am there."

Again Gilfaethwy seemed to chew on that sour mouthful, but then he shrugged his shoulders. "It is easy enough, only four Gates from Avalon."

"Four Gates?"

"Oberon is not inclined to favor the notion that the Seleighe Sidhe become enamored of 'foreign' toys or uncanny slaves. Thus, he does not make the path to the markets easy." He made a grimace. "The High King is right, too. The Sidhe get lazier and lazier. With a little thought and a little labor they could make anything they can buy at the markets."

"I am not going there for toys," Denoriel pointed out. "The child I am protecting must be returned to his own time and people. The good of the mortal realm of Logres as well as that of Elfhame Logres, and perhaps Elfhame Avalon, rests on him somehow. I *must* have a safe Gate."

The mage heaved a theatrical sigh. "Very well. Very well. The first Gate is from Avalon to the Hall of the Mountain King."

"The Gate from Avalon only takes me to Logres!" he protested

The mage gave him another withering glance. "You *are* an idiot! The Avalon Gate has six termini. Pick the one to the Mountain King's Hall."

"How?" Denoriel roared, his hand going to his sword.

A flash of light flew from Gilfaethwy's index finger. As swiftly Denoriel's shields were up and the light splashed harmlessly on them. Gilfaethwy's eyes opened wide.

"Not such an idiot after all," he said, grudgingly.

"Shields I know," Denoriel said. "My duty is to protect the child. Shields have been necessary."

Gilfaethwy sighed. "Very well. In every Gate there is a power point." He gestured and a small Gate appeared in the air between them. "Look for that." When Denoriel nodded, his brows went up, but he only said, "Feel within for the nodules—"

As Denoriel "reached" within the Gate, the mage waved a frantic hand at him. "Aieee! Do not touch them or think at them. There is only the Void on the other side and no Gate back."

"Sorry," Denoriel said, contritely.

Gilfaethwy paused, and gave him a measuring look. "You are very quick to learn. How is it that you are so disgustingly ignorant of magic?"

"Because I am just what you said, Magus Gilfaethwy . . . an idiot!" Denoriel replied feelingly and sincerely, full of disgust at his own ignorance and hubris. "I thought my skill with a sword could answer any trouble I might find and I refused to learn. Of course I was terribly wrong. I know it now."

"Hmmm." Gilfaethwy eyed him with speculation. "It is not too late."

"I know that, magus," he said earnestly. "And I have sworn that I will learn magic as soon as I have time. But right now what is most important is the safety of the child I guard and his return to his own time and place."

"Yes, yes." The mage waved dismissively. "You said that already. Very well, when you have arrived at the Hall of the Mountain King, *do not* leave the Gate. Find the power point and chose an Unformed domain as your next stop. There are only one or two in that Gate and both of them are safe enough if you do not look for trouble."

"An idiot, but not that much of one," he said, quietly.

"The Gate in the Unformed domain, either one, will have a terminus in Furhold. Go there."

Denoriel smiled involuntarily as he thought about Harry in Furhold. What a shame they could not linger.

"Furhold is the only real complication. You must cross nearly the entire domain to find the second Gate. It is at the back of the Badger's Hole. That Gate goes direct to the Bazaar."

"Thank you, magus," Denoriel said. Gilfaethwy raised

a hand, but Denoriel did too, and said, "Wait. What will it cost me to have you keep a watch on the Gates, the one from Logres to Sheriff Hutton. I know the one in the wood is gone, but there is another in the palace itself—"

"I know. I placed it there." Gilfaethwy's voice was dry.

"Yes, of course. Sorry. But I would like to know . . . and about the two Gates one in, the other near, Pontefract."

Gilfaethwy was silent for a moment and then his lips pursed outward, folded in, and he said, "I would like to know, too. I will keep watch. As to the price . . . I will not make it too onerous. Another book, perhaps."

"Thank you."

Denoriel did not know whether the magus heard him since he was outside beside Miralys before the words were out of his mouth. He mounted slowly, rethinking his reaction to Gilfaethwy's mention of Furhold. Harry would enjoy it, but was it safe to take him through so many Gates, several of which Pasgen could have reached? And even the neutral, Seleighe-leaning, domain of Furhold had its dangers.

But how could Pasgen know he would go to the Bazaar? And could there be a greater danger than to leave the boy alone without anyone to explain why he was there in Llachar Lle? With Oberon and Titania and their taste for mortal playthings so close?

Miralys's response to Denoriel's sudden anguished sense of urgency was to return to the Gate in what seemed like a single leap and virtually levitate to the center of the eight-pointed star under the interwoven boughs of the silver trees. Denoriel caught barely the slightest touch of the recognition spell and the faintest shiver of disorientation before they reappeared under the dome of opal lace of the Gate at Logres.

The steed was not quite so quick about reaching the steps up to the portico of Llachar Lle.

Denoriel felt Miralys's reluctance, and when they reached the steps to the palace portico, he slid down and hugged the elvensteed, thinking it would be safer to take Harry with him. Then his arms froze around the steed's neck as the Thought touched him and what he had been about to say to Miralys caught in his throat. Under his hand, the elvensteed shivered. And again the touch was gone.

"I'm going to wake the boy and take him with us," Denoriel said to his steed. "I can't leave him here."

To his intense surprise Miralys broke from under his hand and disappeared into the sort-of wilderness beyond the pool. Fear rose in him. Had Miralys felt something in that Thought he had missed? Would he be unable to wake Harry? To leave with the boy? Heart pounding in his throat, Denoriel hurried up the steps and to his apartment.

He expected disaster, but found nothing amiss. However, it seemed that time for a mortal passed even more swiftly Underhill than he had believed. While he was with Magus Gilfaethwy, Harry had slept himself out and wakened. He was in his seat at the table, happy, if slightly anxious over Denoriel's absence, eating a typically English breakfast.

"Did you sleep well?" Denoriel asked, thinking that Harry would probably retain the experience as a bad dream if Oberon had snatched him to examine him and then replaced him. Replaced him . . . "Harry, take out your cross, just for a moment."

The malaise of being in the vicinity of cold iron hit Denoriel at once. A servant coming into the dining room not only dropped a plate but disintegrated. The cross was real. Harry was real.

"Right. Put it away, please."

"Why did you wish to see my cross?" Harry asked around a mouthful of porridge.

"I just wanted to be sure the cross was working." He rubbed his hand across his forehead surreptitiously, wondering if *he* was going to have a chance to rest any time soon. "We're going to have a busy day out and around Underhill."

The boy dropped his spoon and clapped his hands. "Oh, good! You *are* going to let me see more."

"It is not an excursion for pleasure. You remember those bad faeries that were chasing you?" The boy nodded over a piece of bread slathered with jam. "It was partly their fault that the Gate was destroyed. So now I can't use the other Gate because I'm afraid it's been changed. We have to find Magus Treowth and find out if he can fix the Gates or build a new one."

"And if he can't? Will I have to stay here with you?" There was no mistaking the eagerness in Harry's face.

Denoriel laughed, ruefully. "Don't look so happy about it. No, I'm sorry to say there are other ways to reach the mortal world, but those will take much longer and we would have to explain where you've been all this time . . . and lots of other things. If Magus Treowth will deal with the Gates, that will be easiest. And don't pout. You're going to see the Bazaar of the Bizarre."

"Is it *really* bizarre?" FitzRoy swallowed two spoonsful of porridge in a hurry, crammed the remainder of his jam-covered bread in his mouth, and washed the whole down with milk. "I'm ready," he said.

Denoriel laughed again. "Not in those clothes. You look like trade goods in those clothes."

Harry shivered slightly. "They'll think I'm a slave? But I don't have any other clothes."

"Don't worry about that. Just take off what you're wearing—"

He gave a mental order to the servants *not* to clean

the clothes. Then when Harry stood before him in undershirt and small clothes, he gestured. Harry gasped.

On his feet were square-toed, open-work shoes of polished leather. Through the cut-outs and then up to mid-thigh one could see long, bright blue tights and over them in successive layers, a brilliantly white linen shirt with a smooth, round collar; a square-necked doublet of darker blue than the tights, lavishly embroidered in bands with a twining vine pattern in gold; a sleeveless jacquette of gold satin striped in the dark blue of the doublet, which showed through the widely open front of the jacquette.

The jacquette came together to a tight-fitted waist and extended down in a full skirt to mid-thigh, concealing the bottom of the doublet, but the sleeves of that garment were visible past the short, puffed sleeves of the magnificent gown. This was enormously full and completely lined with ermine so that the deep turned-back collar and lapels showed the shining white fur in contrast to the gown's rich gold-on-blue brocade.

"Oh, my," Harry said. "This is full court dress, isn't it? Won't I be hot?"

"No," Denoriel said, smiling. "The weather Underhill seems to adjust to one's clothing—except, of course, for those domains like the arctic tundras or the deserts where the temperature is part of the making."

In another moment he was attired much as FitzRoy was, except that he was wearing black and gold with red embroidery and sable fur instead of ermine. Another gesture created two hats, one of blue velvet, one of black, each decorated with a single ostrich plume. Both put on their hats, nodded at one another to indicate they were on straight, and stepped out into the antechamber.

"Not the cloak too," Harry protested.

Denoriel looked down at the small figure so enveloped in clothing that it looked tubby, which Harry was not. "No, I suppose not," he sighed. "Just take the cross out where you can slip it out of the pouch easily if you need to or I tell you to."

The boy sighed with relief. Denoriel smiled at him and picked up the mortal-world saddle. Perhaps it would be enough to trade for information about Treowth's lodging. He went to the door, looked out, saw no one in the corridor, and gestured for FitzRoy to step out.

The boy checked so suddenly, right in front of the door, that Denoriel almost leapt after him, fearing that Harry had seen some danger previously concealed. The corridor was empty, but the loud thrum of voices coming from the wide, main corridor was a shock, and Denoriel could see a crowd of Sidhe where his corridor entered the main corridor.

Denoriel hesitated for a moment, wondering whether he should retreat to his apartment. In the next moment he had decided that the large crowd would be the best concealment for him and the boy, and he took Harry's hand and tried to turn sharply left to make his way to the front door. That proved impossible; there were simply too many Sidhe moving toward the throne room. Harry, small and light, was swept up immediately. Denoriel, unwilling either to release his hand or pull his arm out of its socket, perforce followed inexorably toward the wide open doors.

Once inside the throne room, however, it was possible for Denoriel to move sideways along the wall. Most of the crowd was eager to go forward to be as close as possible to the dais on which were the thrones of the High King and Queen. He did not move far, hoping when the crowd diminished to be able to slide out before the doors were shut.

He did not succeed in that either. Indeed, he was just congratulating himself on his cleverness, guiding Harry toward the door with a hand on his shoulder, when he was accosted by a very High Lord Sidhe, a Sidhe he knew—Lord Ffrancon—standing directly in his path.

The elf was a half a hand taller than Denoriel, straight as a pine and supple as a willow. His hair was pure silver and cascaded down his back like the foam of a waterfall. The points of his ears stood proud, a hand span above the crown of his head, but his green eyes were light, silvered over, betraying his age. He wore a leaf-green tunic with a high collar that fanned out behind his head over silver tights and an undertunic of darker green, which showed at his neck and in the tight sleeves that were exposed below the full, dagged sleeves of the tunic. A wide silver band holding one single emerald as large as a pigeon's egg confined his hair and the long arm-guard of an archer, chased elaborately in solid silver, on his right forearm were his only ornaments.

"Denoriel Siencyn Macreth Silverhair?"

Denoriel swallowed. "Yes, my lord?"

"Come forward with me. A place is prepared for you and the mortal boy."

Denoriel swallowed again. The High Lord Sidhe began to walk forward, the crowd parting before him. Denoriel gave Harry a tiny shove to follow and himself walked almost on the boy's heels. It was just as well that he maintained his grip on Harry's shoulder, because the boy was staring around in such wide-eyed amazement that he twice tripped over his own feet.

At first Denoriel was not certain whether it was the chamber itself or the folk in it on which Harry's attention was most centered. Then he realized it was the room for now; Harry was tripping because he was

trying to walk forward while his head was tilted back
looking at the ceiling and the walls. The roof was high,
but Denoriel thought no higher than an English cathedral. Only this roof was midnight blue and filled with
brilliant stars, which shone between the vaulting beams
of silver.

From the beams hung banners, and more banners
were displayed from poles along the walls. Each pen-
non was brilliantly woven of silk and each commemo-
rated one of Oberon's or Titania's victories. Dragons
reared in challenge against the High King; huge ser-
pents coiled, trying to envelop him; a herd of lamia
twisted their snakelike bodies and lifted their viciously
toothed female human heads against Titania's lightnings;
and again and again images of fallen dark Sidhe
appeared, fruitlessly confronting the High King and
Queen, celebrating the defeat of those who wished to
tear rule of Underhill from Oberon's and Titania's
hands.

The beams were supported by two rows of pillars
slender enough not to obscure the view of the dais
and so set that one's eyes were almost forced to
center there. The pillars were of pale marble through
which ran bright glitters and brilliant streams of light.
Harry almost bumped into one and Denoriel pulled
him closer. He could see the direction of the boy's
attention; it was no longer fixed on the chamber but
upon the dais.

Harry's fascination was no surprise. The High King
and his Queen were a wonder even to those they
ruled. Titania was pure High Court elf, except that
she was taller than most male Sidhe. Her body was,
of course, absolute perfection. Her hair was a rich
gold, elaborately dressed in a high confection of tiny
braids and curls, which showed off her ears; those
reached high above her head, delicately shell pink,

almost transparent—but the tip of one ear was bent, which tiny imperfection made her somehow more perfect.

Titania's eyes glowed a bright, pure emerald. Denoriel knew she was older even than Lord Ffrancon, but there was no silvering of *her* eyes and they looked deep enough to fall into and drown. Her lips were pale rose and through the ethereal pale blue and white silk robes she wore, she looked . . . translucent, as if she were lit from within.

The High King. Denoriel only glanced and looked away. He did not want to draw Oberon's attention and, besides, one needed only one glance to remember. The High King was a dark contrast to his glowing wife. He could appear pure liosalfar—Denoriel had seen him in that guise—golden-haired, green-eyed, dressed all in white silk and cloth of gold and strewn with diamonds, but when he came to Logres, most often, as now, Oberon seemed more dark Sidhe than bright.

His hair grew from a deep peak on his forehead and swept back in gleaming black waves, the points of his ears showing through, well above the crown of his head. His brows were equally black and high-arched over dark, dark eyes—black, bottomless pools. In contrast his skin was white, not pallid and sickly, but with the hard, high gloss of polished marble. He towered over all other Sidhe—and not by enchantment—and formidable muscles in shoulders and thighs strained the black velvet tunic and black silk tights he wore. He was all in black only lightened by silver piping on every seam and the silver bosses on his belt and on the baldric that usually supported the long sword which now leaned against his throne.

Lord Ffrancon pointed and two chairs appeared an ell back from and to the right of the dais. Denoriel put his arm around Harry's shoulders and led him to the chairs. Although many noble Sidhe still standing watched, the boy sat down in one without question; Denoriel put the mortal-made saddle on the floor and sat beside Harry. The High Sidhe lord stepped up on the dais and whispered in Oberon's ear. Oberon leaned over and spoke to Titania. She looked briefly at Harry, then at Denoriel, and then shook her head.

Denoriel had never been so glad of anything before in his life as he was that Harry was nothing special. He was a most ordinary looking boy, with sandy hair, pale, nondescript eyes, blunt features. Even his older, thinner face retained the look of sweetness he had had as a younger child, but there was nothing in that to attract a Sidhe's attention.

One would think that the High King and Queen would be primarily interested in the good of Underhill, Denoriel thought, and to a certain extent they were. However, too often their own pleasure—or their quarrels with each other—took precedence over the common good. Not forever, which was why they remained High King and Queen, but they were prone to indulge themselves. Of course, when they were finished with their amusements, they were powerful enough to bring everything back to where they had begun . . . Only sometimes the plaything had terrible—or wonderful—dreams and could never again find contentment.

A Thought—not as terrifying as the one Denoriel had felt earlier, but equally strong—brushed by Denoriel, and Harry's look of pleased wonder blanked. He still sat in his chair and still looked at the dais and its occupants, but his eyes were empty. Denoriel gasped and jumped up.

"I have done him no harm." The Queen's voice was rich and very sweet, pure music in the mind and heart. "It would be better if he did not remember what was said here."

"Which leads me to ask why you brought the child Underhill?" Oberon asked. "I sense that you love him far more than is sensible for a Sidhe to feel for a mortal. Do you plan to keep him?"

Denoriel remained standing and managed to meet Oberon's eyes. "No, Your Majesty, of course not. I brought him here to save him from an Unseleighe Hunt. You are, I am sure, aware of the FarSeeing that concerned the red-haired child."

"Yes. Is he the red-haired child?"

"No, Your Majesty, but he is essential to the preservation of that child. My sister, Aleneil, a FarSeer, has Seen that much, but no more. She charged me to watch over Harry."

"Has he needed watching over? And never mind the 'Majesty.' Oberon or Lord Oberon will do."

"Yes, Lord Oberon. He has needed watching over." Denoriel's lips thinned, and at a gesture of invitation he told the whole story of his guardianship of FitzRoy. He began with his defeat of the two swordsmen who had attempted to drown the boy, described Rhoslyn's attempt to replace him with a changeling, mentioned Pasgen's and Rhoslyn's attacks on the cortege traveling to Sheriff Hutton.

Oberon stopped him there and asked for a better description of the mouse-sized goblins and a confirmation of his estimate of their numbers. There were sounds of indignation from the crowd of attending Sidhe. A raised finger silenced them but Oberon's eyes were blacker than ever and bleak.

"They nearly had him this last time," Denoriel went on. "It has been so long in mortal years since the last attempt that I almost did not accompany the party. The Council have been traveling back and forth without attack since they settled in the north and it is no great distance, but I—oh, it was an excuse to see Harry so

I did go. This time the Unseleighe used man-sized monsters to scatter the party—"

"The same pair? Your half-brother and -sister? To whose domain do they belong?" Oberon already knew, of that, Denoriel would have been willing to stake his life—but he wanted his court to know, too.

"Yes, Lord Oberon, the same pair. Vidal Dhu rules the domain but they have some power there. I am not sure how much, but enough this time to call out the Unseleighe Hunt. They knew they could not touch him, you see. He wears a cold iron cross, pure cold iron, not steel—"

"Here?" Oberon bellowed, leaning forward, hand raised.

Denoriel stepped in front of FitzRoy. "My lord! It is safely warded in silk and spells."

"I thought there was something uncanny about the child," Titania said. "It does not trouble you, Denoriel?"

"Without the spells, it does, Your Majesty." He shrugged. "My bones ache, but I can bear it. I am somewhat resistant to cold iron."

"Silverhair—his father—was, too," Oberon remarked to his wife and then looked back at Denoriel. "And his uncle has the same gift—if gift it is. Go on—and sit down. I won't hurt the boy. So, if your half-brother and -sister couldn't touch him how did they plan to seize him?"

Denoriel shrugged. "I am not in their confidence, my lord, but believe the plan was for the Hunt to drive him into a Gate. My half-brother is quite skilled in Gates. I suppose they thought once they had him Underhill that they would be able to get him to take off the cross." Denoriel smiled grimly. "I doubt they would have succeeded; Harry is a most determined child." Then he shivered. "But they might have killed him with their attempts."

Now Titania leaned forward, examining Denoriel speculatively. "Did you fight off the whole Hunt?"

Denoriel felt like a bird confronted by a particularly beautiful and especially venomous snake. To waken Titania's interest in him as a male—it was not unknown for her to favor the odd elf who seemed heroic—would be a disaster. Though Oberon was more often amused by her escapades than jealous, Titania's favors could leave a drained wreck behind.

If Denoriel could have backed away, he would have. Held motionless by the chair, he managed to say, "No, Your Majesty. I am no hero. I snatched Harry off his horse onto Miralys and ran like a frightened rabbit to my own Gate—only Pasgen had meddled with it—"

"How do you know that?" Oberon snapped.

Denoriel then explained in detail his interview with Gilfaethwy and the magus's conclusion that Denoriel must find Magus Treowth to get Harry back home. When he stopped speaking, the High King nodded and leaned back in his chair.

For quite a long time Oberon said no more, his eyes going from FitzRoy to Denoriel. Denoriel would have been frightened out of his wits, if he had not noticed an occasional twitch of the High King's lips. The crowd of Sidhe behind him was sympathetic too; he heard a number of hisses when he spoke of Pasgen and a muted cheer when he described his unheroic foiling of the Unseleighe Hunt. Denoriel tried not to show his relief at that sign of support. Oberon ruled his people, but he was not above noting their feelings.

Finally Oberon said, "We must discount the attack by the human mage, but that still leaves three attempts to get control of . . . who is he, Denoriel? Who, precisely, is this child who is so crucial to our future?"

"His name is Henry FitzRoy, and he is Earl of Nottingham, Duke of Somerset, and Duke of Richmond.

He is the first duke in England, having precedence over all other nobility except those of the king's own blood, and he *is* of the king's blood, being King Henry's natural son."

"Natural? Of course he is natural. Unless . . ." Oberon looked eagerly interested. "Have mortals learned to create unnatural children that are real and survive?"

Denoriel shook his head. "Not that, my lord. These humans marry, as do we, but it is forbidden to them to couple outside of that bond—"

Oberon and Titania both laughed raucously.

"No doubt a rule more honored in the breach than in the keeping." Titania giggled.

"Yes, Your Majesty." Denoriel smiled. "Very much so, and flagrantly in the case of their king, whom his subjects call familiarly 'Great Harry.' But any child born outside of such a union is counted somehow lesser and punished by not being in the succession for goods or lands. I must admit I do not understand why the child is punished for its parents' sins, unless perhaps it is to make the parent sorry. Such children are called 'natural.' "

Oberon shook his head. "Clever as they are, what fools those mortals be! As if one's birth is of any moment." He laughed. "Vidal Dhu was as high a blood line as Lord Ffrancon here, and your half-brother and -sister even share your blood. Their tastes, their way of gathering power, that is what divides Seleighe from Unseleighe Sidhe."

"It is not all Pasgen and Rhoslyn's fault, Lord Oberon." Although he had no love for them, Denoriel felt bound to offer some defense. "My half-brother and -sister were raised Unseleighe. They were taken as infants to the Unseleighe Court. My father died trying to rescue them."

"I remember," Oberon said. "Impatient and passionate, Silverhair was. Yes."

"A noble fool. If he had waited . . ." Titania shrugged and sighed.

"Which Vidal Dhu is not, although he is equally impatient. He has once again allowed his greed for power to push him too far. He should never have meddled with this child, who is too important, too close to the real power in Logres. Still, I did not interfere. He has had a fair chance to catch the child. Three times they have attempted to seize him and three times they failed. That is enough."

"That is more than enough!" A delicate flush dyed Titania's cheeks and her eyes were almost too bright to meet.

Oberon glanced at her and shook his head. "I am High King of all the Sidhe. Except for very special circumstances, I will not stretch out my hand to favor the Seleighe over the Unseleighe Court, but failure that brings Underhill close to exposure must be punished."

"It must indeed," Titania snapped. "You expend too much effort to cozen the Unseleighe. A good lesson is what they need."

"*Gentle* lady," Oberon's irony was palpable, "I am not ready to go to war over who rules a mortal kingdom."

Titania lowered lids over her gleaming eyes. "Who spoke of war? However, if you do not deal with Vidal Dhu, I will. Even though I can use it, I do not like the foul taste of the power that drains from mortals in misery. *I* favor the coming of the red-haired babe, and any who will see it to the throne."

Oberon did not answer her directly. Denoriel wondered if sometimes the dark High King liked a flavoring of agony in his power source. He buried the thought deeply as Oberon rose from his throne and stepped down from the dais.

"We do not need to go to war over one child. However, Vidal Dhu has gone too far." Oberon's lips tightened. "There must be other ways to further his cause. Your Harry FitzRoy is too high on the mortal ladder of importance to meddle with so openly. The use of goblins and monsters in daylight when there were so many to see, was a violation of the pact of secrecy. There are too many mortals who will now cry of uncanny forces. I think I must put FitzRoy beyond Vidal Dhu's reach."

The High King had stopped before Harry's chair. Now he leaned forward and pressed his thumb into the center of the boy's forehead. It seemed to Denoriel that the finger sank deep into the flesh and right through the bone of the skull; he leapt to his feet again, drawing a frightened breath, but stood frozen. And when Oberon withdrew his hand the skin was unblemished . . . except that a brilliant blue six-pointed star blazed on Harry's forehead.

Oberon stepped back and Denoriel could move again, but the High King did not look at him. He turned and resumed his throne, saying to Titania, "He is protected now from any Sidhe and likely from most of the lower planar creatures. Vidal Dhu cannot touch him. That is as much as I am willing to do." Then he faced forward again and gestured at Denoriel. "You, like your father, are a fool. In the mortal world, he will grow old and die and break your heart."

And all that Denoriel could do was to bow his head, for in his heart, he knew that his king was right.

But it was, of course, nothing that he could, or would, do anything about.

CHAPTER 21

As Denoriel sat down, sense returned to Harry's eyes. And when Oberon gestured to him, he rose quickly and went to the foot of the dais. There he removed his hat and swept it, the ostrich plume brushing the ground, into a full, elegant bow. Titania smiled at him and, as unable as any she-Sidhe to resist a child, beckoned him closer. He bowed again, then mounted the dais. Titania drew him near, bent and kissed his cheek.

"So you seek a way back to the mortal world?" she said. "Do you not like Underhill?"

"Oh, Your Majesty, I love Underhill," FitzRoy said and then he sighed. "But I owe my service to my country and to my father, the king. I must go home and do my duty."

"And will you tell all your friends and servants about the wonders you have seen here?" Oberon asked.

"No, Your Majesty. At least, not unless you order me to do so. No one would believe me, I think." He cocked his head to one side, his expression thoughtful.

"Besides that, Lord Denno, my . . . my protector, has told me never to speak of such things. Although I do not know why, I do know that it is dangerous for him. When I speak of him it is as a Hungarian nobleman, who sometimes acts a little strange because he is a foreigner."

"Ah! That is very good. Very good indeed." Oberon lifted his head and looked over FitzRoy at the assembled Sidhe. "And so I say to my people here assembled that Harry FitzRoy is under my protection, and that you and . . . ah . . . Lord Denno have my permission to seek through Underhill for a Gate that will take you home."

Oberon reached out and lifted the hand that Titania had left resting against FitzRoy's cheek, folding it into his own. The boy thanked him sincerely, bowed once more, and began to back away from the thrones. Denoriel grabbed the saddle, jumped up, and steadied Harry as he stepped backward off the dais. Together they continued to back away along the aisle toward the great doors.

The distance was magically much shorter than it had been as they walked toward the thrones, and the doors opened for them and then closed behind them. Denoriel let out a huge sigh of relief, watching the doors nervously. After a moment he closed his eyes and gripped Harry's shoulder.

"You were perfect, Harry," he said, and laughed, opening his eyes to look down at the boy. "I nearly swallowed my heart when Oberon beckoned for you to come to him, but you knew exactly what to do and say."

Harry grinned at him. "I am my father's son, and it is expected that I will soon be summoned to court. You may be sure my tutors have drilled me in bowing, walking backward, and being *very* careful of what

I say to royalty. But, oh, my, what a *beautiful* lady the queen is!"

"Yes, she is," Denoriel agreed. "And as clever and powerful as she is beautiful. But we must avoid her if we can. She has a great desire for little mortal boys; she likes having their innocence about her."

"I would not mind staying with her . . ." Harry sounded a bit dreamy, but then he shook himself. "No. It is my duty to go home."

Denoriel was relieved. "Yes, it is, and I fear that we may have to walk to the Gate, because—"

"But Lord Denno—" Harry interrupted, "Miralys is here, and oh, look!"

Denoriel had started down the steps still looking at FitzRoy. He stopped suddenly when the boy spoke, looked down, and then stood transfixed, mouth agape. Miralys, as Harry had said, was there, waiting. But with him was a second elvensteed, much smaller, exquisitely beautiful, with a silvery blue coat admirably set off by a flowing silver mane and tail. She—the steed had to be female—craned her head coyly to look at FitzRoy with large, dark eyes.

Before Denoriel could move, the boy had run down the steps and flung his arms around the smaller elvensteed's neck. "Oh, you're the most beautiful creature I've ever seen," he cried. "Oh, have you come to carry me? Will you? Oh, please! I'll sit as light as I can, I promise."

Denoriel took the first four steps flying, then slowed and sighed with relief as he saw the elvensteed nuzzling Harry's hair. The steeds were elegant and dignified; they did not appreciate unmannerly behavior, and could be quite unpleasant about rebuking it. However, it was plain that the mare had taken no offense. Once again, the child's charm had won over another elven ally.

Harry was still burbling to her. "And I'll brush you

and comb you all you like. Oh, I know you can take care of yourself, Lord Denno told me so, but grooming, that's for being together, for love. You'll let me brush you, won't you, Lady Aeron?"

"Aeron?" Denoriel breathed.

It was not that he was surprised that Harry knew the steed's name. He had known Miralys's name when the elvensteed first came to carry him. He was surprised *by* the name. Aeron was Cymric for the goddess of slaughter.

When she heard him, the mare lifted her head and looked at Denoriel; in that moment her eyes burned red. Denoriel choked and looked at Miralys, who whickered softly. Denoriel had the strong impression that if Miralys could, he would have shrugged. Denoriel sighed. When your steed laughs at you, you are in a bad way. Naturally, knowing the dangers threatening Harry, Miralys would have arranged for a steed capable of defending herself as well as the boy.

He put the saddle on Miralys; it was easier than carrying it. Aeron made a saddle for FitzRoy and Denoriel gave him a leg up. They were barely mounted, when they were at the Gate. Denoriel looked into it, willed, and the plaque with its nodules appeared, each bearing a miniature image. Once under the opal roof, Denoriel extended a thread of power to touch the image of a huge, dark hall.

The reality made Denoriel choke again. The "huge," dark hall was, perhaps, some four ells long, three ells high, and two wide—not even as large, although higher, than his bedchamber in London. In every other respect it was what one would expect of the hall of a mountain king—a dark cave lit by flaring torches and by myriad gleams in the rough-hewn walls and ceiling, which hinted of precious gems. A fire, huge for the size of the hall, burned redly in the center.

Beyond the fire was a throne chair, forged of some dark metal and decorated with skulls. More skulls sat on the benches, which also served as tables on the other three sides. To each side of the throne was a table, and on that table lay heaps of stones that caught the light of the fire and winked and shimmered. On the benches, in the jaws of the skulls, were more stones. Some jaws held more jewels, some fewer.

"If those are precious stones—" Harry began from beside Denoriel.

"A trap," Denoriel said. "Gilfaethwy warned me not to leave the Gate."

There were people . . . manikins, perhaps a half a foot tall . . . all turning to look at the Gate. And suddenly the figure on the throne chair seemed to see them. He leapt up, grabbing from the side of the chair a war hammer almost as large as himself. The men (for they were men despite being so small) on the benches also rose, drawing swords and unloosing war axes. Other figures, (likely women for they wore full-skirted gowns) backed away toward the walls. The sound the warriors made in shouting was more a screech than a roar, but their intention could not be mistaken.

Hastily Denoriel called up the floating plaque and directed his will at a nodule that showed only a white mist.

The Gate here was nearly as formless as the swirling mists, four pillars that wavered and shrank, threatening to dissipate. There was a roaring cough in the distance and a growling shriek. Harry watched the mist, one hand wound into Lady Aeron's mane. The elvensteed also watched the mist, and Denoriel could see her eyes gleaming red. He willed the plaque and it formed, but then it distorted and he found it almost impossible to make out what was on the nodules.

More menacing sounds rose from the mist and

seemed to come closer. Then something shrieked in death agony. The plaque was twisting and writhing, the pillars of the Gate seemed more tenuous by the moment. Something long and thin began to creep out of the mist. Miralys snorted and stamped his feet. Denoriel caught a glimpse of bright yellow surrounded by blue and he selected that nodule.

They arrived on a raised platform surrounded by a low, white-painted fence. The platform had a roof shaped rather like half an onion with the stems at the top replaced by enormous ostrich feathers. The inside of the roof was also painted white and the floor the elvensteeds stood on was very clean red brick in a herringbone pattern. Then there was a burst of applause. Harry gasped. Denoriel sighed. They had arrived at Furhold all right, in one of its more playful moments.

Arranged before the stand upon which . . . obviously . . . performances occurred were a dozen rows of chairs set in a semicircle. All of the chairs were occupied by beings—that was the closest Denoriel could come describing the audience—and all of the occupants of the chairs were applauding and looking eagerly at the platform.

"Harry, can you play? Sing?"

Harry was staring at the audience, his eyes round as tennis balls and giving the definite appearance of being ready to pop out of his head and bounce. He took a deep breath and swallowed.

"Yes," he said.

"Which?" Denoriel asked, dismounting from Miralys.

"Both," Harry said, then blinked, but his eyes remained fixed on the persons regarding him. "I guess I sing better than I play," he said, shrugging and beginning to grin. "One doesn't really have to learn how to sing."

Lady Aeron moved—the closest Denoriel could come to the motion was to say that she flexed her back—and Harry slid down to stand beside Denoriel. The elvensteeds both leapt over the low fence behind Harry and Denoriel and seemed to disappear. Neither Harry nor Denoriel turned to look for them. They would be there when they were needed.

Meanwhile a being suddenly rose from beside the performance area; its head and body to the waist were those of a handsome Oriental man, but it had large multicolor wings attached to its back, and from the waist down the body of a large speckled hen. It bowed gravely to Harry and Denoriel and mounted the two steps from ground level to the platform, its chicken claws clicking audibly on the brick.

"The High Court Sidhe and the mortal boy will now grace us with their art."

"I am not so sure what we will do will be art," Denoriel said, chuckling, "or that we will even perform with grace, but we will do our best. I need a lute. I did not know I would need an instrument."

The being gestured and Denoriel noticed that low chests had appeared along the fence surrounding the platform. When he looked again, one of the chests was labeled LUTES.

He opened it and took out a lute that looked suspiciously like the one he occasionally picked at when he was home alone and bored. He sighed again.

"Do you know the 'Maiden in the Moor?' " Harry whispered.

"Hum a line or two," Denoriel murmured back.

As he had hoped, it was a rather generic tune that almost any rhythmic verse would fit. He began to strum the lute. When he got to the chorus, Harry nodded. Denoriel began again and Harry began to sing:

Maiden in the moor lay
     In the moor lay
Sennight full, sennight full
     Maiden in the moor lay
Sennight full and a day

Good enough was her meat
What was her meat?
The primrose and the——
The primrose and the——
Good enough was her meat
The primrose and the violet

Good enough was her drink
What was her drink?
The chilled water of the well-spring
Good enough was her drink

Good enough was her bower
What was her bower?
The red rose and the lily flower
Good enough was her bower

Maiden in the moor lay
     In the moor lay
Sennight full, sennight full
     Maiden in the moor lay
Sennight full and a day.

The boy's voice was not only high and sweet but
strong. Denoriel gazed down at him with considerable surprise. If it wasn't the silliest song he had
ever heard, it was close to it, but it didn't matter
at all. The audience was enchanted. They stamped
their feet—those that had feet—and clapped their

hands, and beat their wings, and jumped on and off their seats, and honked their horns, buzzed, waved their trunks and tentacles. Denoriel bowed. Harry bowed.

"A most worthy entertainment," the man-chicken said. "Will your boy sing again?"

"I am very sorry," Denoriel said. "We are pressed for time."

"This Gate is one way," the man-chicken remarked with a sly smile. "You can only enter Furhold here. You cannot leave from it."

"I know," Denoriel assured him, mendaciously.

Actually he had *not* known that he could not leave from this Gate at all. That was another bone he had to pick with Gilfaethwy, who had made the transits to the Bazaar of the Bizarre sound so simple. He began to wonder if the magus was so deep in his work that he had made connections with the Unseleighe. Was he paying off favors by exposing Harry to his enemies? What had Gilfaethwy wanted the human blood for?

"Well, for only one song, the reward cannot be great. We hoped for some extended entertainment. Three songs at least."

"Our need for reward is not great. Only direction to the Badger's Hole."

"Oh, Hen Ne, don't add pig to your mixture. You've had more than you expected when you made that drunken bet with Eigg Oh."

The speaker made Harry's eyes widen with delight and made Denoriel smile. He could have been a boy of twelve or fourteen. He was a bit taller than Harry, dressed almost identically, although his colors were red and gold . . . except he had the head of a fox. Denoriel bowed slightly—acknowledgment, not respect; Harry made haste to do so too.

"Thank you, kitsune," Denoriel said, picking his

words carefully. The kitsune, which were fox-spirits, were well known for being tricksters. "Will you take us to the Badger's Hole? And what will I owe for your service?"

"I'm Matka Toimisto and you won't owe me anything. I assume if you want the Gate at the Badger's Hole that you're going to the Bazaar? I'll just go along with you. A High Court elf and a boy marked with Oberon's favor seem like good company for the Bazaar of the Bizarre."

Meanwhile Hen Ne had been joined on the platform by a being that made even Denoriel blink. It was a head, just a huge head with rather blurred features half buried in folds of flesh. It had arms sticking out from about where its ears should have been— the ears were near the corners of its eyes—and two short, sturdy legs under its chin.

"No, I won't," the head was saying. "And it wouldn't matter if they sang and played for the next week. You need three acts—three different acts—not three songs by one act."

"You are totally unreasonable, Eigg Oh," Hen Ne protested. "Who knows how long it will be before someone else comes through this gate. I need the—"

"Excuse me, gentles," Denoriel said, almost succeeding in hiding his smile, "but my ears are not only long but keen. I hear from what is being said that the boy and I cannot be of further service. Being that is true, we thank you for our welcome to Furhold and will be on our way."

The man-chicken looked very disgruntled, but he made no active protest and the head's folds of flesh rearranged themselves somehow into an expression of satisfaction.

Denoriel returned the lute to the chest and took Harry's hand. The boy looked a bit startled, but Denoriel said, "It's very easy to get separated in Underhill. Furhold is reasonably safe, but there is the occasional trouble-maker even here. Unless you're mounted on Lady Aeron we should maintain contact with each other."

"Oh, I'd find him for you," the kitsune said.

Denoriel raised his brows. "How obliging you are. *What* did you do at the Bazaar that you need our company so desperately? If you drew a weapon . . ."

"No!" Matka Toimisto exclaimed. "No, I never! But there was this girl and her man took exception . . . I was only *talking* to her . . ."

"I can imagine," the Sidhe remarked under his breath and Harry giggled; he was old enough now to recognize sexual innuendoes.

The kitsune sighed, but all he said was, "I hadn't finished my business. I really need to go back."

"You are welcome to come with us," Denoriel said, "but I can't promise you my protection. We are not shopping at the Bazaar. I must find Magus Treowth—"

"Magus Treowth? But that is the person I want to see also!"

Denoriel hesitated, then asked, "May I ask what business you have with him?"

"It isn't a secret. I want to learn how to pass between the worlds unGated. The elvensteeds do it."

The kitsune's eyes gleamed, Denoriel suspected with a mixture of mischief and avarice. He wondered if he were doing the right thing in allowing Matka Toimisto to accompany them. It would save time and effort if they could get to the Badger's Hole without a dozen stops for directions and misdirections, but letting loose a kitsune on the unsuspecting mortal world seemed an unnecessary addition to its problems.

Then again, so long as a kitsune could find a Gate, he was loose on the mortal world anyway.

They had all stepped down from the platform while they were talking. As soon as they were clear of the semicircle of chairs, the elvensteeds appeared. Denoriel asked if it were worthwhile to mount and the kitsune shook his head.

"You can't go any faster than me," he pointed out. "And I'm afoot."

His smile was very cheerful and he started out across the parklike lawn with apparent confidence. Denoriel decided his shoulders were not broad enough to support the problems of the mortal world. Magus Treowth was no fool, and knew what the kitsune were. Likely he wouldn't give Matka Toimisto what he asked for without some safeguards—if what the kitsune wanted was possible at all.

Their progress across the lawn was by no means direct. It was necessary to stop and dodge the myriad of playing children who were running and jumping, sometimes on two legs, sometimes on four, sometimes on more, occasionally rolling themselves along like hoops. Blankets were spread and every variety of animal-human mix seemed to be indulging in games, picnics, and foreplay for lovemaking. Denoriel didn't know whether to tell Harry not to look or just hope he wouldn't notice. At the moment the second choice seemed safe enough. The boy was staring up into the "sky."

"Lord Denno," he said, sounding bemused, "that can't be a real sky. Look at the sun. Oh! It winked at me!"

The sun was a round, bright yellow saucer with a face painted on it, except that the features were mobile. It was surrounded with petals, which occasionally waved as if in a breeze and also occasionally gave off bright sparks. The blue sky surrounding it made no attempt to seem real. It looked painted, and the white clouds visible here and there did not move and looked painted too.

"No, it's not real," Denoriel said, and laughed. "I think it was a committee that made Furhold. One of them must have had a sense of humor."

Harry squeezed his hand. "It's nice here. Really nice. The people are so friendly."

He waved at a party of bearlike beings wearing short leather pants with straps over their shoulders. They were playing some complex game laid out on a board between them, but they looked up and waved back at Harry as he passed.

A group of boys—well, none were wearing obviously female dress, although it was hard otherwise to tell gender or even kind—ran past rolling hoops. Harry looked up hopefully.

"Could I ask if they'd let me play?" he asked.

"I suspect we're going to have to explain how you were out all night as it is," Denoriel said. "I'm not sure I can think of a way to explain your being 'lost in the woods' with nothing to eat or drink for a couple of days. Somehow I doubt Sir Edward would believe primroses and violets . . ."

Harry laughed and they walked a little faster. Soon a darker rim to the lawn appeared, which resolved itself into buildings as they came closer. Matka Toimisto pointed off to the right and they turned in that direction.

CHAPTER 22

Vidal Dhu had summoned his court—every single being that owed obedience to him was present in his huge black-pillared throne room. The floor was the red of blood, and sometimes those who needed to cross it felt as if they were wading in blood; the walls were red-patterned gold. Mage lights glowed from skull holders affixed to the pillars and walls; heads, huge things not remotely human but with some recognizable features that made them more loathsome, hung from the ceiling burning green and purple, the mouths working in silent agony.

At the forefront of the repulsive mixture of creatures were straight golden chairs with bloodred cushions on seats and backs. In those sat the Unseleighe Sidhe, some as fair as and nearly indistinguishable from their Bright Court kin, others as dark as night—hair and eyes and sometimes even skin. Right at the front Rhoslyn and Pasgen sat rigidly erect. This prominent positioning could not harbor good news; they knew that in their bones.

In knowing that, they were better informed than Vidal Dhu himself. He had not admitted it to anyone, even to Aurilia, who now sat beside him—in a slightly smaller throne, but a throne, not merely a chair, nonetheless—that he had not the faintest idea of why he had sent out the summons. When she had asked, he had shaken his head at her, as if he had a secret he did not wish to divulge. Now, however, he had nothing to say to the assembled horde—

And just as he was wondering if he should concoct something, the great black doors to the hall slammed open.

Every head turned, and from most came gasps and grunts of surprise, of fear, of anger. A brilliant light put to shame the witch-lights in the skull holders and the ghastly colors of the burning heads. In the center of the clear brilliance stood Lord Ffrancon, the waterfall of his white hair interwoven with chains of diamonds, his white tunic and trews embroidered in gold, and sprinkled with more diamonds.

"Well, well," Vidal Dhu said, his lips curving into a sneer, "the messenger boy from the High King. All alone, are you?"

"Messenger, yes," the High Court lord said, smiling very slightly, not in the least discomfited by his reception. "Boy . . . ah, alas, it is a *very* long time since I was a boy. At about half my lifetime, I can remember you as a puling infant, Vidal Dhu. And alone . . ." He paused a moment, significantly, his smile broadening. "I am never alone. The Thought follows me."

Before he could control it, Vidal's breath sucked in. Now he knew why he had summoned his court. The Thought had touched him, ordered him, and he had obeyed, without even being aware of it.

Aurilia laid a hand on his arm. "We are here assembled. What message do you bring us from High King Oberon?"

"First, that the mortal boy, Henry FitzRoy, Duke of

Richmond, is under King Oberon's personal protection and may not be harmed or abducted." A single elegant eyebrow lifted, awaiting Vidal Dhu's reaction.

"A High King who is not just, who is not impartial, does not deserve his honors!" Vidal spat.

"Take them from him then," Ffrancon's voice was soft and smooth as if it had been oiled, his faint smile betrayed no real emotion. He paused, waiting for some reply and when none came, shrugged and continued. "Three times you tried to take the child and failed. And twice you used other-planar creatures, chancing exposure of our existence here—"

"Three times!" Vidal exclaimed, looking past Lord Ffrancon to where Rhoslyn and Pasgen sat.

"None of the tiny goblins we used were captured. Most of the mortals thought they were mice or rats," Pasgen said. "Your watchers failed us, Lord Vidal. We were told the boy would be in the carriage with his nurse. The plan was to have her carry him away. But he was not in the carriage. He was mounted before my half-brother on an elvensteed."

"You cannot call it a failure when the High King sends one of his minions to foil my servant's plan," Vidal said to Lord Ffrancon.

Pasgen's teeth snapped together when Vidal called him a servant, but he had no chance to speak because Lord Ffrancon laughed heartily.

"That was no doing of King Oberon's. He and the queen have only just returned from a very long journey. He knew nothing of this boy over whom you are quarreling or he would have put an end to the quarrel sooner." Now Lord Ffrancon showed a little—a very little—emotion. A cold, clinical anger, and a hint of distaste. "In the name of Dannae, Vidal Dhu, the boy is the king's *son*. Did you think he would not be missed, sought after, questions raised if he were not found?"

"I had a changeling . . ." Rhoslyn began. "And Denoriel killed it! How did he know I was coming? How?"

"Yes, how did Denoriel always 'happen' to be there when we arranged to capture the boy?" Pasgen added.

"I am not sure." Lord Ffrancon was smiling, now rather sadly. "Nor do I—or more importantly, the High King—care. It was none of King Oberon or Queen Titania's doing. It is, I think a mortal thing, one of the results of a mortal . . . ah . . . sickness called love. Denoriel is bound to the boy, and the child to him, I believe. Denoriel senses when the boy is in danger. Surely you have seen that before?"

Vidal snarled softly. He had seen it before. It was not unknown, although it was not common, for the Hunt to be disordered, sometimes even driven away, by those who loved the victim coming out with crosses and weapons of cold iron. He made no other reply, however, and the High Court lord shrugged.

"In any case the boy FitzRoy is now off bounds. Feel glad that you did not succeed in taking him and making it needful for King Oberon to retrieve him and cover your blunders." Again, that cold, elegant look of disdain. "Attempting to meddle with so valuable a mortal child would have been costly to all the Sidhe, Seleighe and Unseleighe alike. The High King might well have visited a worse punishment on you for using Unseleighe minions to attack the traveling party. Your underling-creatures can be slain. What if one had been?"

"They were not true Unseleighe!" Rhoslyn exclaimed. "I am no fool. They were constructs, good for only a few hours, and if they were killed they fell to dust immediately. No one would be able to bring an otherworldly corpse as evidence of an otherwise unbelievable tale. The High King is being unfair. He is tilting the board toward the Bright Court."

Lord Ffrancon turned slightly, and fixed her with a chilly gaze; she paled beneath it, and the unspoken rebuke. "Child, do not presume to instruct your elders in the matter of—politics. The High King does not mete out his judgments lightly. And do not presume that what you have seen in your visions is unknown to him. He knows that the boy FitzRoy will never rule—and yet interfering with him further endangers all of us. In any case the High King is not pleased by your meddling so close to one of the thrones of the mortal world. His order is that *none* of those close to King Henry, or the king himself, of course, are to be physically harmed or abducted. You have been fortunate, in that the mortals have not sought to discover the truth behind their legends. There will be an end to them."

Vidal Dhu started to rise, but Aurilia held tight to his arm. Her nails dug into the black velvet sleeve so deeply that she cut the cloth.

While Vidal was still choking on his rage, she said, "We hear and obey."

And the brilliance that had enveloped High Lord Ffrancon winked out, leaving the whole throne room by contrast, dark, and those in it blinking.

The High Court emissary gone, Vidal turned on those at hand. "Three times!" he roared, staring though the dimness to where he had seen Rhoslyn and Pasgen. His anger lanced out in physical form, hot enough to burn.

"That was very wrong." Aurilia's voice was as smoothly cold as Vidal's had been hot. "You should have told Lord Vidal of your attempts and failures."

"Three failures!"

Vidal lifted his hand; Aurilia pulled it down again. "But Vidal, in a way, they did us a favor. They fixed the High King's attention on physical removal or damage. Thus, all is not lost, my love. No, indeed." She smiled placatingly at Vidal Dhu. "We will, as I said, obey to the *letter* the order of King Oberon."

He looked at her at last, and she murmured softly, "Dismiss the court, my lord. Order them to stay out of the mortal world, unless they Hunt with you, for the time being . . . until Oberon sticks his nose in someone else's business. One day . . . one day he will anger enough lords so that—"

Vidal's hand came over her mouth, and she dropped her head. He rose to his feet and virtually repeated what she had said, only omitting the remark about King Oberon. Obediently, still somewhat dazed by a power that had not permitted even the most unruly of them to make any kind of attack on their visitor, though some had tried, they began to leave. Vidal looked at Rhoslyn and Pasgen.

"Not you two," he said. "I am not finished with you."

Aurilia smiled and nodded. "You are so clever, my love. They can be used and punished at the same time. But before we get to that, tell us how the Princess Mary progresses."

A nasty refinement of cruelty to make them wait and waste power by needing to support full shields lest Vidal lash out at them while Aurilia was occupying them. Aurilia's doing, that; Vidal could never wait to apply a torment. She could not only wait, but be interested in what you said, while she made *you* wait.

"I have not seen the princess in several months," Rhoslyn reported. "One of King Henry's ways of tormenting Queen Catherine to make her compliant to his desire for a divorce or an annulment is to forbid her to see her daughter. I used to go with the queen quite frequently when she visited Mary, however, and at that time the princess was shaping just as we desired."

"I have no direct contact with the princess, but I am in the confidence of Chapuys, the Imperial ambassador. He knows me as the human mage, Master Fagildo Otstargi, a Christianized Turk. After that disaster perpetrated by Mendoza—the previous ambassador—and his mage Martin Perez, I felt that I had better be available to direct any plans for the use of magic. Perez has returned to Spain." Pasgen's lips twitched. "His grimoire was stolen."

"There is some point to all this digression, I presume," Vidal said.

"Let him talk, love," Aurilia purred. "This and that idea has come to me. When you have heard them, of course you will decide what would be best to do."

Pasgen kept his face blank, but he felt uneasy. He had forgotten for a moment that Aurilia was not the perfectly exquisite and perfectly empty-headed she-Sidhe she appeared to be. To cover his anxiety, he made a half bow.

"To come to my point. Chapuys visits the princess regularly, sometimes bringing letters, sometimes bringing verbal messages from the queen. I attend him as often as I can. I would say that the princess has continued in the correct direction. She admires, almost reveres, anything Spanish; she thinks her great-uncle, the Emperor Charles, is the most perfect of men and a perfect example of the best ruler. Her faith in the Church is absolute—" his lips twisted "—but only when the Church agrees with her mother."

"Then you think she will be a suitable instrument for bringing the Inquisition to England?" Aurilia's voice was soft, almost dreamy and her tongue slipped out between her pointed teeth to moisten her full, red lips.

"Her only fault as far as I can see is that she is very soft-hearted," Pasgen said thoughtfully. "Her nature is gentle and kindly. She really cannot bear seeing anyone suffer without wishing to relieve that suffering. She will need to be taught more strongly that to save the body, to relieve the physical suffering, will condemn the soul."

Aurilia turned toward Rhoslyn and smiled. Rhoslyn thought that was a mistake. It damaged the image of perfection she otherwise projected; her teeth were jagged and pointed like a shark's. Fleetingly Rhoslyn wondered how she managed not to stab Vidal Dhu when she kissed him.

"So, Rhoslyn, there is your next task. Find a place close to the princess. It must be a position of respect and one in which your advice will be attended." Aurilia's tone left no mistake that this was an order. "There should be little difficulty in putting steel into Princess Mary's spine since she already believes in the Church, and that to reject the Church and all that it stands for is to bring damnation."

"I can arrange it for you, Rhoslyn," Pasgen said. "I've already gotten into Chapuys's mind. Just say who you want to be and he'll introduce you to Vives, Mary's tutor."

"Good enough," Rhoslyn said. "I will deal with Vives. He's an idiot who thinks females are improved by harsh treatment. I'll have him put me in charge of Mary's religious training. It will be easy enough to convince her that faith is everything and triumphs over all small vanities. I'll pander to her love of music and fine clothing as long as she *believes.* Then, I will convince her that torment of a sinner's body is nothing, so long as the soul is saved—that the only thing that matters is confession of sin and heresy, and if death follows, not only is this no tragedy, it will enable the soul to go to heaven without repeating the sin with a recantation. Which, of course, will mean that anyone who does not believe as she does, believes wrongly and must be forced to accept her belief."

Aurilia smiled again and stroked Vidal's cheek. "See. See how we obey the High King. No harm will come to Mary. I'm sure Rhoslyn will defend Princess Mary from abduction or any other physical harm with all her skill and strength. And she will shape our tool—"

"*If* she comes to the throne," Vidal said, lips twisting. "How are we going to keep the red-haired babe away from it without abducting the child?"

"By making sure the mother is so disgraced that the red-haired babe is removed from the succession irrevocably. When the child is no longer of any interest to the powers of Logres, *then* we can set a changeling in its cradle. *Then* no one will care or think of witchcraft. And then *we* will have the child, we will have the use of the mind that would have ruled a realm and raised that realm to great heights."

There was a momentary silence as all four considered that. Rhoslyn and Pasgen had Seen the glory that was England, and the prosperity of Logres, under the rule of the one who had once been a red-haired babe. The creativity that welded a nation of self-seeking, squabbling nobles together and brought peace and prosperity could as easily be turned to the aggrandizement of the Unseleighe Court. What Vidal Dhu was thinking was not clear, but must have been something similar, because his tongue briefly caressed his upper lip, but then his mouth thinned with anger and anxiety.

"Easily said," Vidal remarked, "but the mother-to-be my FarSeers now say is Anne Boleyn, the absolute center of the king's love and attention. No matter what she does, what she says, the king holds her without fault. By your agreement, Aurilia, we cannot meddle with her; she must be inviolate."

Aurilia laughed softly and Pasgen stiffened his muscles to restrain a shudder. She looked at once smug and cruel—and satisfied. "Inviolate from physical hurt or abduction *only*," she said, voice purring. "That was what the High King ordered and to which I agreed. And remember that King Henry is as fickle as any pretty maid. Who knows how long he will think diamonds and pearls drop from her lips with each word, no matter how sharp. If the king casts her away, no one will care what we do with her—or the red-haired babe."

"Do not count on that. The Seleighe will be watching," Pasgen said. "Nor would I count on Boleyn losing the king's interest. I've heard Chapuys, the Imperial ambassador, speak of her."

Despite himself Pasgen was growing interested. He was not certain how powerful a sorcerer Aurilia was, but she had a brilliant and devious mind.

"And this Chapuys says what?" she asked, mildly.

"That Anne is very clever—infernally clever is the way he puts it. And he calls her a witch, who has ensorcelled the king."

"I wonder if that can be true?" Aurilia murmured. "If Mistress Anne Boleyn is Talented . . . Oh, if she is Talented and untrained, I have a plan that will destroy her and no Sidhe of the dark court need go near her to bring it about. No spell will be cast on her. We—" Aurilia giggled; Rhoslyn shivered "—we will not be to blame for what damage the girl does to herself."

"But how?" Vidal asked, pulling her hand away from his face as if he had suddenly become aware that her stroking caress was muddling his mind.

"Ask rather when than how," Aurilia said. "If she yields to Henry and he casts her off, we can exchange the child at any time. However, if she can manage to hold off the king until he is ready to marry her—if he can get her no other way—we will need to work more carefully. Once she is married and with child . . .

Then—" Aurilia closed her eyes for a moment, savoring her plan "—then Anne will get a little gift from an old friend, an adorable little puppy."

"But if it is bespelled—" Vidal objected.

"No spell will be on it, nor will any spell manifest unless the dog is in Anne's own hands." Aurilia's smile made Pasgen shiver. "While she holds it and caresses it, her Talented mind will be prodded into an urgent need to express her pride, arrogance, and ill humor. And since those are natural to her, no one will suspect meddling."

"I hope not, but those accursed half-siblings of ours are likely to be somewhere around Mistress Anne watching and listening," Pasgen pointed out.

"Aleneil has already given Anne a safeguard, a small golden cross—" Rhoslyn began.

"A cross is no impediment," Vidal said.

"No, not the cross," Rhoslyn continued impatiently, "the spells set into every gemstone on the cross. The old Imperial ambassador wanted to cast some kind of spell on her, but his magician's attempts came to nothing. I understand you are not setting a spell, just an urging into her mind, and it may pass the wards, but if Aleneil is anywhere near Anne, won't she feel the effects of the dog?"

Aurilia shrugged. "That is a worthwhile warning. Half your pains will be remitted. It will be easy enough to make the dog shy of Sidhe. If Aleneil comes to call, the dog will go hide somewhere."

"And what are our pains to be?" Pasgen asked.

The Badger's Hole was just what it said, a very large hole in the ground, large enough for Miralys and Lady Aeron to pass through as well as Denoriel, Harry, and Matka Toimisto. The first few feet were pitch dark and forbidding; Harry tripped over some roots in the ground and would have fallen if Denoriel had not caught him and taken his hand.

"Sorry," a high-pitched voice with the hint of a chitter in it rang out. "Thought you were all from Underhill. Didn't notice the mortal among you."

And lights came on. The place, now visibly an earth tunnel with root tendrils hanging down from the roof and showing in the walls, thicker roots making the floor uneven, remained essentially a badger's hole. It widened out noticeably ahead, and the witch lights clustered and following them grew noticeably fainter as they drew nearer what should have been the badger's den.

So it might have been, if badgers, even mortal human-sized ones, furnished their chambers. Ceiling and walls remained much like those of the tunnel, except that the walls all had torch-holders with blazing torches in them and a huge root shaped into the form of a candelabra holding lighted candles hung down from the ceiling. Still the place was rather dim. FitzRoy craned his neck to see all around.

There were tables in the center of the room, rough-hewn, as were the benches and a few chairs that surrounded them, some of which still wore the bark of the trees from which they had been made. On them were quite an assortment of animals, some with manlike heads, some with the upright posture that permitted them to sit in humanoid fashion; some sat on their haunches, which was a bit less convenient for leaning over the table, but all had grasping hands with opposable thumbs. Most of them looked up at Denoriel's party, but not one looked surprised, even by the elvensteeds.

A five-foot-tall badger approached. Aside from his size and his hands—one of which held a tray with a bottle and a glass on it—he seemed to be an ordinary badger, black with white stripes and short powerful arms and legs. The kitsune stepped ahead and something passed from the kitsune's hand to that of the badger.

"Gate to the Bazaar what you want?" the badger asked Denoriel, casting a suspicious glance at the kitsune.

"Yes, thank you," Denoriel replied. "If you would be so kind."

The badger gestured at them to follow and wove his way among the tables, stopping about midway to deposit the bottle and glass. Denoriel saw that the walls at the sides of the room were undercut so that there were booths sheltered from the light of the torches in the deep shadows. Surely at the very back of one of them eyes gleamed just above the table and a dark form seemed to hang down from the booth ceiling. Some light from the suspended candelabra showed a very fair Sidhe sitting at the table to the front of that booth.

"Want to watch out for the boy," the badger said.

"He has King Oberon's mark," Denoriel pointed out. "Surely that will be protection enough."

"From those who come from Underhill." The badger snickered. "The Bazaar of the Bizarre didn't get its name for nothing. That's the fair attended by those who come from other worlds, and mortals who are strong enough in sorcery to find their way. Some of the otherworlders care nothing for King Oberon's commands."

Denoriel shrugged. "If they are forced to obey the rule of the Bazaar and commit no violence, I can hold my own."

"But can the boy?" the badger persisted. "Some of the inducements that will be offered to him will be hard to resist."

"Well, Harry?" Denoriel looked down at the boy who was still holding his hand.

"I don't believe I will be tempted after . . . after . . . I have my duty, after all."

The boy's eyes widened as he heard the words that came from his lips and he clutched tighter at Denoriel's hand. Lady Aeron stretched her neck forward from where she walked behind him and lipped at his hair comfortingly.

"Ah, duty." The badger chuckled. "Mortals and their duty. Duty brings them Underhill and duty gets them into trouble here. Never heard of duty keeping a mortal *out* of trouble."

"Harry means he must return to the mortal world," Denoriel said.

As he spoke they came to the back of the chamber, which was closed by double wooden doors, rather like those of a barn in the mortal world. The doors opened as they neared.

"Good luck," the badger said, pointing across the backyard at what seemed to be the roots of an enormous tree.

Six roots stood out of the ground, each as large as a mighty tree trunk, joining together some ten or twelve feet above the ground. Both Denoriel and Harry stared upward at the colossus, which reared out of sight into a silvery twilight sky.

"Where's the funny sun?" Harry asked.

Denoriel shook his head. "It may be that those doors we passed are a Gate in themselves. I don't know."

He was speaking slowly, examining the openings between the great roots. They were designed, he saw, to admit only one being at a time. Lady Aeron and Miralys could go separately; they would arrive anywhere they wanted to arrive when they wanted. The kitsune could presumably take care of himself, and in any case

Denoriel felt no responsibility for him; however, Denoriel was damned if he was going to allow Harry to step through that Gate himself. He bent his knees.

"Up on my back, Harry," he said. "I'm not taking any chance on a Gate whisking you away."

The boy giggled, then obediently climbed up on Denoriel's back. Even through the pouch and the spells and all the clothing, Denoriel could feel the cold ache of that accursed cross. He thought with relief that Harry could now take it off whenever they were together. Oberon's mark would protect Harry from the Sidhe.

He stepped between two of the roots, but had no time to seek the power points. The faint shiver of dislocation passed through him immediately, and he found himself under a wooden arch with a decorative curved trelliswork that spelled out BAZAAR. Harry slipped down from his back but intelligently took his hand.

On each side of the arch, attached, brightly colored banners waved. Directly in front of the archway was a large sign so placed that no one emerging from the Gate could possibly avoid seeing it. In fact one had to walk several steps right or left to pass the notice.

The words, in beautifully calligraphed Elven, said, NO SPELLS, NO DRAWN WEAPONS, NO VIOLENCE and below those words ON PAIN OF PERMANENT REMOVAL.

Denoriel stared at the sign for a moment. A feeling, gut-deep, assured him that the threat was real; something would remove . . . remove? remove to where? . . . any being that cast a spell, drew a weapon, or committed violence. He sighed. Then what did the kitsune fear? Resolved to watch that sly little fox closely, Denoriel stepped around the sign. Just on the other side he saw the kitsune standing between Miralys and Lady Aeron.

"Let's go," Matka Toimisto said, craning around Lady

Aeron's shoulder to look. "The elvensteeds have generously offered to walk with us right to the entrance. I'll be safe once we're inside the Bazaar."

So, Denoriel thought, the prohibitions against violence only apply inside the faire itself. In this . . . he looked around frowning at the huge area stretching out to his left in which an assortment of vehicles and animals that even he found straining his belief were tethered? bound? settled? Never mind, he would think about that later.

"You're sure you were just talking to that girl?" he asked.

The fox didn't answer, merely shook his head as if a fly were buzzing around it, but he was so obviously nervous that Denoriel took pity on him and started for the entrance. This was a narrow passage, blocked by another large sign on which two words in letters even larger than those of the previous warning appeared.

CAVEAT EMPTOR!

"Buyer beware?" Harry said.

Denoriel looked down at him. "You can read the sign?"

The boy blinked in surprise. "You know I can read!" he said indignantly. "And the Latin is very simple."

"Latin? But it's in Elven," Denoriel began, and then laughed. "What a fool I am. Of course, the sign appears in whatever language the reader knows. And yes, the buyer must beware at these faires. The only thing a vendor can't do is hit you over the head and steal your purse. Every other form of stealing is acceptable."

"Can I buy something?" the boy asked eagerly, ignoring both the sign and Denoriel's confirmation of its warning.

As they moved to step around the sign, the elvensteeds backed off. Denoriel looked at the sign again. Below the CAVEAT EMPTOR were lines in smaller letters. "If you can't walk, hop, crawl, roll, slither, or whatever, on your own, you can't come in!"

No transport inside the Bazaar. That seemed unfair to Denoriel. The elvensteeds were as much people as most residents Underhill and more so than many. Why should they be excluded just because they were generous enough to carry the Sidhe? He received a feeling of reassurance from Miralys and a touch of humor. He shrugged. It was true enough that the elvensteeds weren't interested in buying or selling. And then, looking back at the large area they had passed and seeing some of the beasts and vehicles there, he could understand the reason for the rule.

Denoriel sighed, transferred Harry's hand to his gown, and removed the mortal-made saddle from Miralys. It was about all he had to trade with, except for the gold coins in his purse, and the Sidhe traders at least could make their own. Then with the boy's hand firmly clasped in his again and the saddle on his shoulder, he stepped around the sign . . . and realized the kitsune was gone.

A flash of rage was followed by resignation. He should have expected it and the mischievous fox had at least got them to the Bazaar quickly and without trouble. Furhold was rarely evil, but its denizens were great ones for playing games.

His suspicion was unjustified, however. Just beyond the passage into the Bazaar Matka Toimisto was waiting, backed against the wall that enclosed the faire, watching the movement of the motley crowd. Denoriel began a step in his direction and was caught short by Harry, who had retained a firm grip on his hand. The boy had stopped dead in his tracks, mouth agape.

CHAPTER 23

Pasgen looked into the mirror one last time to assure himself that his disguise as Fagildo Otstargi (close, if little known, advisor to Thomas Cromwell, Cardinal Wolsey's steward and legal expert) was perfect. Despite the exotic name and the fact that Cromwell believed him to be a subtle and powerful magician, Master Otstargi showed no outward sign of his uncanny abilities. Not for him spangled robes or tall, conical hats. So garbed, no sensible man in political service would dare public association.

He nodded at the nondescript figure that nodded back at him from the mirror. His ears were round, his eyes a soft brown as was his hair, most of which was confined under a moss-green velvet cap. He had a well-trimmed mustache that grew down around his small pursed mouth into an equally neat goatee. His clothes were of fine cloth but muted color and very conservative style; his doublet the same moss green as his cap, his gown a darker green. A modest amount of slashing saved his doublet from being dowdy although the slashing showed only a glimpse of a very white and delicately embroidered shirt.

Aside from the sword that was belted over his doublet under his gown, he wore no jewelry except the two rings on his left hand. Even they were subdued, dark stones that occasionally sparked a sharp glint of red or gold set cabochon in very simple gold settings. He was the picture of a wealthy man with no desire to call attention to himself.

Such discretion should be a pleasant change for Cromwell, bound to the cardinal, who loved display. Even so, and although he was responding to a summons from Cromwell, Pasgen was not looking forward to this meeting. He was going to have to warn Cromwell that he must leave the sinking ship that Cardinal Wolsey had become and look out for himself.

There was no further advice, no additional clever expedient that even a magician as skilled as Otstargi could suggest to save the man who had virtually ruled England for fifteen years. Unfortunately Cromwell did not yet see that Wolsey's time had run out. Cromwell believed that Wolsey had been very clever in managing King Henry's last demand to be freed from his marriage. The cardinal seemed to be obedient to the king, convincing the pope to allow the court examining the king's marriage to be held in England.

However, the delay after delay in convening that court, which was supposed to give ample time for the king to grow disgusted with Mistress Boleyn's sharp tongue, had not worked as expected. Henry had grown impatient, but not with Mistress Anne, and the delays had been seized upon by Cardinal Wolsey's enemies.

That party, headed by the dukes of Norfolk and Suffolk, had long hinted to the king that Wolsey's loyalties were divided. Now they seemed to have proof that Wolsey did not really support Henry's purpose of divorcing his wife to marry Mistress Anne Boleyn. Look, they said, at how the cardinal was more fearful of offending the pope than eager to do the king's will.

The dukes of Suffolk and Norfolk pointed out that the court summoned to examine the validity of Henry VIII's marriage was presided over by two cardinals—Wolsey and Campeggio. Campeggio was an old man and very sick. It had taken him months to make the trip from Rome, which most churchmen accomplished in six weeks and a messenger could do in less time. And when he had arrived, Campeggio had taken to his bed for another few weeks. Surely Wolsey, who had dominated everyone else, could have seen to it that the sick, old man gave the desired verdict—that Henry's marriage was null and void.

Instead, proceedings had been dragged out for more than another three months, and then Wolsey had permitted Campeggio to adjourn the court, which virtually guaranteed that the case would be remanded to Rome. In Rome, still dominated by the influence of the Holy Roman Emperor, Charles V, Henry's case was hopeless. Since Charles was Catherine of Aragon's nephew, he would never agree to any expedient that permitted King Henry to marry again.

The Emperor looked forward to seeing Princess Mary on the throne of England, possibly married to a suitor he would provide, which would put England right into his hand. Charles was taking no chance that his cousin Mary would be superceded by a male born of some subsequent wife. The pope had his orders; Henry's marriage was not to be dissolved.

Pasgen was as eager as Charles to see Mary on the throne, welcoming the Inquisition to England, but somewhat to his surprise Aurilia had convinced him that the Unseleighe Court could have their cake and eat it too. If they allowed the red-haired child to be born and abducted the babe, Mary would still rule, still set the fires of the Inquisition burning. Meanwhile, the babe could be raised at the Unseleighe Court, and they would control one of the most protean and inventive mortal minds that would exist for a hundred years.

Contrary to everything they had tried to do before, now Pasgen needed to see that Anne climbed into King Henry's bed. It would be best, for his purposes, if she yielded her body without managing to seduce Henry into marriage. But to watch or influence either event, Pasgen needed to have access to the court.

Until now his access had been through Cromwell and Wolsey, which had conveniently kept him well clear of Alceneil and her connection to Anne's family as well as FitzRoy and Denoriel. However Pasgen was sure Wolsey was about to lose his grip on the king and Pasgen did not want Cromwell to go down with his master.

Cromwell was actually a human Pasgen enjoyed. He had a remarkably ingenious mind and could reason black into white. In addition he had a most captivating manner—even to a hired inferior, which was what Pasgen was pretending to be; Pasgen was well aware of the cruelty masked by the charm, but that only made Cromwell more attractive. Moreover Pasgen did not relish the idea of needing to establish a new "human" identity, so he had determined to save Cromwell from being destroyed with Wolsey if he possibly could.

Fortunately Pasgen did not need to travel far; Cromwell was currently housed at York House in Whitehall, which was a short ride. He left the bedchamber, which he locked behind him, and went down the stairs. A servant bowed, his glazed eyes betraying that he was capable only of following specific orders. Pasgen told him to send for his horse and while he waited, mounted, and rode to his destination he again rehearsed in his mind what he would say to Cromwell.

The first part of the interview went just as Pasgen expected, with Cromwell paling, denying, arguing, and slowly coming to recognize the horrible validity of Pasgen's prediction. He was driven at last to the feeble protest that the king could not be so ungrateful after all the years of Wolsey's devoted service.

"Devoted to whom?" Pasgen asked rather nastily. "Undoubtedly the cardinal has managed the affairs of the realm reasonably well, but as much or more to his own benefit as to the king's." Pasgen's mouth twitched. "He is probably richer than the king—and Henry is aware of it. Moreover in this latest matter, he has failed most disastrously. You know, too, that in ruling in Henry's name the cardinal has made many enemies, enemies far more supportive of the king's desire than Cardinal Wolsey."

"But the king and even Mistress Anne's father, Lord Rochford, were pacified over the adjournment of the divorce trial when the revenues of Durham were signed over to them." Cromwell knew, even as he made the argument, that it was a hollow one.

"Yes, but that was before Wolsey's blindness to the true import of the treaty of Cambria and his deliberate misreading or misremembering of articles."

"Because his spirit was so disordered over the king's displeasure." Cromwell rose from the chair he had been sitting in, opposite that he had invited Pasgen to use. "But that was in August. Why now?"

"Have not Mistress Anne and her father been constantly in King Henry's company while the cardinal has been denied access to the court?"

Cromwell paled at this reminder and sat down again. "Perhaps if I—"

Pasgen shook his head. "It is too late to do anything except to save yourself. If I were you, I would go to the king with a tale—"

"No!" Cromwell looked appalled and then suddenly less frightened and very thoughtful. "Betray my master in his time of need?" he said slowly. "No, indeed."

"Will it make it any better for Cardinal Wolsey if you are destroyed with him?" Pasgen snapped.

"Certainly not." Cromwell's lips, which had been tight with tension, softened somewhat. "I will speak to the Cardinal as soon as he returns and see what arrangements can be made to mitigate the blow, if a blow must fall."

Pasgen permitted a very faint hint of disbelief. "What arrangements will stand against King Henry's will?"

"Oh, none," Cromwell agreed, "but this is England, and even the king cannot swallow Wolsey and his possessions without raising protest from the people."

"But the people will be overjoyed to see Wolsey fall," Pasgen pointed out. "He is greatly hated. And though the people may protest, it is the king who rules."

Cromwell made a disdainful gesture, but at the same time bit his lower lip. "That may be true, but no man in this land will like to see any other—even one much hated—stripped of his rights and possessions without some account of the reason therefore."

Pasgen laughed. "Well, there are surely reasons enough to send Wolsey to the gallows, and the people more than willing to see him there and believe any ill of him. It is time to think of saving yourself by—"

Cromwell shook his head. "Perhaps I cannot save his power, but great wealth can be used to good purpose aside from making a fine show to impress the mighty. And given time to recover, who knows what the cardinal can do?"

Pasgen paused, and allowed his eyes to catch and

hold Cromwell's for a moment, willing him to recall
every moment when he had seen the king panting
after Mistress Anne like a dog after a coy bitch. "I
do not think even Wolsey's wealth will buy back the
king's favor nor any time, no matter how long. Not
unless Wolsey has been concealing a decree of annulment about his person."

"I wish he were," Cromwell said, "but unfortunately he has no such bribe. But for others . . ." He
seemed to make up his mind about something.
"Look into your crystal, Master Otstargi, or your
wreathing smoke or whatever means you use to
foretell the future and tell me who should have
pensions settled on them."

"Pensions?" Pasgen repeated, bewildered.

Cromwell stared at him meaningfully. "Unless stipu-
lated in a will as a charge on the heirs and the estate—
and Wolsey has no heirs, beyond a few minor bequests
to servants, except the king—a pension ceases with the
life of the payer of the pension."

"Ah, I see," Pasgen said, "I can see why the pen-
sioners would do what they could to protect the cardinal and his estate. But if you are the one who
arranged the pensions but are not tainted with failure
in the matter of the divorce and yet have done what
you can for your master . . ." This was a truly clever
ploy.

Cromwell nodded and gestured the end of the subject, then smiled winningly. "So, Master Otstargi, I thank
you for your warning, but I called you here for another
matter entirely. I have just been looking over some old
reports about the young duke of Richmond and have
come across some instances of his exerting his power.
I had always believed he was a good-natured and rather
stupid child, but these reports show him to be surprisingly clever, and one case shows that he can be

quite . . . ah . . . ruthless, or shall I speak more plainly and say 'vicious,' in order to get his own way."

"The child is not important," Pasgen said, dismissively. "He will never be king, of that I am quite certain."

"Oh, I am certain of it too. The king will end his marriage, one way or another and take a new wife, whether or not it is Nan Boleyn. Still, there is no doubt that the little duke's father is fond of him, and he is the premiere duke of the realm." Cromwell knitted his brows thoughtfully. "He will have influence, especially as the king grows older. I am afraid my master did not pay enough attention to the men appointed as his council. He thought more of their ability to govern the north than about Richmond, but now I believe it time to show the little duke we are his friends. I am thinking of having the boy brought back to court—"

"There is no time," Pasgen said through clenched teeth, getting to his feet.

"No time?" Cromwell rose too, frowning. "Perhaps you have seen true and the king may be contemplating a dismissal, but the cardinal is even now at a council meeting where all is as usual or a messenger would have been sent to me."

Pasgen shook his head. "I cannot tell you the day or the hour, although I have strained my abilities to the uttermost—"

That much was true; he and Rhoslyn had pushed their ability to FarSee without the mirror and the power provided by the wan Sidhe of the tower to the limit.

"So." Cromwell shrugged. "Likely nothing will happen until the divorce case *is* remanded to Rome—"

"No!" Pasgen exclaimed. "I can tell you it will be soon, very soon. I have seen the cardinal at the head of the table in the council once—perhaps that would be today—or, perhaps twice. But then, I saw him in an empty room where I think he previously held court, and officers came to call him to the king's bench to answer some charge . . ." He shook his head, and loaded his words with warning. "Master Cromwell, I would not delay making whatever arrangements can be made."

When Harry stopped dead and stared around with wide eyes and open mouth, Denoriel's breath caught and he sought wildly for danger. After what the boy had seen during his time Underhill and the calm way he had accepted the High King and Queen and the creatures that inhabited Furhold, Denoriel could not imagine what horror could stop him in his tracks.

But, as it turned out, it was fortunate he was holding the saddle on his shoulder or he would have had his sword in his hand.

There was nothing! Could Oberon have given the boy enchanted sight as well as protection? Or the gift of presentiment, to warn him of danger?

"What it is, Harry?" he asked, forcing his voice calm.

"There can't be a faire this big," the boy said, breathlessly. "There can't be. I've been to faires. I've been to the markets in London. They were streets long, but this is as deep as it's wide. It's as big as a town. It's as big as London!"

"I thought you'd seen something that frightened you," Denoriel said, breathing out in relief. "It *is* a big market, but don't believe everything you see. Remember the sign. I would bet, though I'm not sure, that half of what we think we see is illusion."

"I' faith?"

"Yes, truly."

The boy shook his head. "It doesn't stink either. Is that an illusion too?"

Now Denoriel laughed. Of all of the things that had been difficult to get used to in the mortal world, the stench was the hardest. Eventually, he'd placed a spell on his own nose, to filter out the odors. "No, I don't think so. I suspect whatever it is that 'removes' those who don't obey the rules also removes the garbage."

FitzRoy giggled and squeezed Denoriel's hand. "Will you buy me a fairing? I would have somewhat to remember this by."

"Ah . . . do you remember? How we came to Underhill?"

"The monsters that pursued me? And how you swept me off my poor foundering horse and . . . and saved me?" His eyes grew wide with recollection. "How could I not remember?"

"And where we went and what we saw?" Denoriel persisted.

The boy was quiet and then he whispered, "I cannot say it. It is all clear in my head, but I cannot say it." His lips trembled and he firmed them. "I am sorry you do not trust me, Lord Denno. I promised I would not speak of what I saw, and I think I have been good of my promises in the past. I . . . I am ashamed that you do not trust me."

Denoriel dropped to one knee before the boy. "Not I, Harry. It was not I. The king or queen, perhaps. Likely the queen, since she touched you. It was for your good; so that none should say you were mad. Also they do not desire that where we live comes to the notice of your people. You are so many and we so few, you see, and you have cold iron."

"You think I would ever do anything to hurt you and yours, Lord Denno?" Now the wide eyes were filled with a world of hurt. "After all the good you have done me?"

Denoriel stood up again. "No, of course I don't, but the High King and Queen do not know everything that is between us, and do not really know you. And they have done you little harm, only made it impossible for you to betray their secret."

FitzRoy frowned. "I didn't say they did me any harm, but they most surely insulted me by their lack of trust. I *said* I would not speak of what I saw."

Denoriel sighed, but before he was able to think of a way to salve the child's hurt feelings, Matka Toimisto touched Denoriel's arm.

"Are we going to stand here all day?" the kitsune asked.

"No, we are ready to go. Shall I ask—"

"No need to ask. It took me five visits to track Master Treowth down, but I have him now, and the faire does not shift like so much of Underhill." The kitsune all but preened at his own cleverness. "Go straight ahead until you reach that very large blue-and-gray pavilion."

They walked as directed, but not exactly straight since Harry was continually crying, "Oh, look!" and tugging Denoriel off to the left or right to look at some displayed item. None were anything that Denoriel wanted FitzRoy to have; one that sent the boy into fits of laughter was so obscene that Denoriel pulled him away and scolded him.

FitzRoy looked up at him, totally astonished. "But it was only a fat jester slipping and sliding and doing tumbles. What is wrong with that?"

Denoriel could feel heat rising in his face. It was time, he thought, to find a woman. Apparently the toy was one each person saw as something different. What he had seen did not speak well for the state of his mind.

"I don't think that would work at all in the mortal

world," he said. "Or, if it did, it would certainly cause a great deal of trouble. You can't have that one, Harry."

"I don't really want it." The boy glanced sidelong at him and grinned. "Well, if I could see what you saw, I might, but I suspect after the second or third time I saw the jester I would grow tired of him. That's why real jesters are necessary. They make up new things all the time."

The kitsune urged them on impatiently, and groaned each time Harry stopped, but he did not seem as anxious now as he had before. They were making reasonably good progress, only two or three items on the booths having drawn FitzRoy's attention, until suddenly the path was blocked by a corpulent Sidhe who reached for Matka Toimisto's arm. Denoriel and FitzRoy stopped and stared, neither having seen an overweight Sidhe before. The kitsune dodged around Denoriel.

"Where's the girl you promised me, kitsune?" the Sidhe growled.

"I didn't promise her to you," Matka Toimisto said. "All I said was that I would get her to talk to you."

The Sidhe glowered, and Denoriel sensed something that he did not like. "But you never brought her, did you?"

The kitsune's ears were flat to his head. "She was on her way, I swear it, but her father and two brothers grabbed her and . . . and I didn't see her again."

"But you had what you wanted from me, and it's not something you can give back, is it?" The stranger's smile held no humor in it. "So, you owe me a debt, kitsune."

Matka Toimisto cast a glance at Denoriel and sighed. "All right, I owe you, but no blood, no life, nothing that's a mortal danger. I would have found that turn on my own. Well, what do you want?"

The Sidhe laughed softly, "Half share of whatever you get from Treowth."

"But it isn't the kind of thing—" Matka Toimisto began, then stopped and frowned. "All right," he said, "half share."

"And don't think I won't find you. I—or my friends—will find you wherever . . ." He started to turn away then swung back to Denoriel. "What will you take for the boy?" he asked. "He isn't very pretty, but—"

Vaguely Denoriel was aware that Matka Toimisto had slipped away, but he was not concerned. He was reasonably certain that he would find the kitsune waiting for them at the blue-and-gray pavilion. For some reason Matka wanted his company, or Harry's. He shook his head at the Sidhe, and frowned.

"The boy is not for sale or trade, and you should be able to see that he has King Oberon's protection." He didn't understand this fellow—he wasn't precisely Unseleighe, but he wasn't Seleighe, either. In fact, Denoriel was beginning to wonder if he was Sidhe at all.

He certainly had an unpleasant smile. "Well, I'm not going to do him any harm, am I? He'll enjoy himself, I promise. Come, name a price. I have toys and joys you cannot imagine—"

"No!" Denoriel said. "And he isn't 'mine' to dispose of in any case. He is his own person."

"Oh, is he?" The Sidhe turned his attention to Harry. "Poor boy," he said. "I see that your protector is either poor or unkind. Here we are in the greatest faire in any world and he has not bought you so much as a stick of candy. I will buy you anything you want if you will come with me."

"Thank you kindly, sir," Harry replied, shrinking a bit closer to Denoriel, "but I cannot accept your offer. I am required to return to the mortal world as soon as I can. There are those there who will be anxious over my absence if I overstay the time."

Denoriel bit back a smile. Anxious was a miracle of understatement about what Harry's council must be feeling right now. He missed most of what the fat Sidhe was saying, however, because he suddenly realized that Harry had understood what was being said. And now, listening carefully, he realized that the language was not Elven. It was like the message boards at the Gate and the entrance. Whoever saw them saw them in his own language. Whatever language was spoken, each being understood in his own language. There must be a powerful spell set over the entire faire so that no one could misunderstand anything that was written or said. It might be the single most powerful spell Denoriel had ever heard of!

His attention was recalled when Harry shook his head and pulled gently on the hand he was holding. He turned the shoulder that held the saddle toward the fat Sidhe and began to walk toward him at a pace that showed he would walk right over him if he did not give way.

"The boy says no," he said firmly and clearly. "No it is. Let us go now. We have business with Master Treowth."

The corpulent being—Denoriel truly was no longer sure it was a Sidhe; it had not reacted properly to his mention of Oberon's protection and probably had not been able to see the glowing star—shrugged and walked away around a nearby booth. Denoriel watched for a moment, but it did seem to be going away, and he went toward the blue-and-gray pavilion again, stopping here and there to let Harry look at various displays. As he expected he found Matka Toimisto waiting.

Before he could speak to the kitsune, the proprietor of the part of the pavilion near where they had stopped came forward. He, or rather it, was apparently made of metal, its overlapping plates flexible enough so that it could move fluidly. Around the oval sitting atop its shoulders, which Denoriel assumed was its head, was a circular dark band within which bright sparks danced. Denoriel stopped to stare and found it was holding out an exquisite golden lap harp. About to shake his head, Denoriel remembered that Mwynwen occasionally played the lap harp. He put the saddle down on the ground between his feet and reached out, only to have the kitsune knock the instrument to the ground.

"You owe me again, kitsune!" the metal creature snarled.

"I don't owe you *anything* now," Matka Toimisto snarled back. "I've just saved your metal skin. Talk, that's one thing. Harm's another. That's iron under the gold."

"Well, and so what? It's up to the buyer to watch out. If he can't see that it isn't solid gold, that's his problem not mine."

"Iron *hurts* Sidhe, you fool. Our debt's cancelled. I told you I've saved your worthless carcass. If he took that and was hurt or died, you'd be *removed*."

"Ignorance isn't violence," the metal being retorted. "How was I supposed to know?"

But Denoriel thought the thing did know, thought he recognized the sound of the voice as that of the corpulent Sidhe. It was very hard to read malice in a band of sparkling darkness on an otherwise featureless metal face, but he felt malice. And he wondered whether the metal being had hoped to incapacitate him and somehow snatch Harry. He wasn't sure whatever it was believed in *removal*.

The kitsune picked up the lap harp and replaced it on the sales counter. Denoriel shrugged and turned away. The boy was tugging on his hand. He picked up the saddle.

"Look." Harry pointed at an object another of the metal creatures was holding out. "That's what I want, Lord Denno, please?"

"What in the world is it?" Denoriel asked.

It was made of a silvery metal, somewhat like the bodies of the metal beings, but like them it caused Denoriel no discomfort. It had a curved handle obviously meant to be held in the hand attached to what seemed to be a narrow pipe above which was fixed a small, flat, rectangular box, little wider than the pipe. On the underside, where it could be reached by an extended finger, was a curved trigger like that of a crossbow.

Wordlessly, the metal being pulled the rectangular box out of the thing revealing a long open slot in the pipe. It reached into a leather pouch and withdrew five darts, which it dropped in before it replaced the box atop the pipe. Then it unscrewed the curved handle, fitted to it a pumping mechanism which forced open a valve and proceeded to pump nothing into the handle. When the pump would no longer depress, it was pulled free, the valve closed, and the handle was screwed back into the pipe.

The being then turned, pointed the whatever-it-was at a target at the back of the pavilion, and pulled the trigger. There was a sharp hiss and one of the stubby darts appeared in the target, sunk right up to where it widened. Denoriel gasped. Harry crowed.

"Please, Lord Denno, please?"

"What is it called?" Denoriel asked.

"A gun," the metal being said.

Gun. Denoriel was familiar with the word; it referred to various instruments of iron that threw out metal pellets, expelled with great force by the explosion of black powder. That was a mortal invention that the

Sidhe wanted no part of. It was one of the reasons that they were so determined to keep their very existence a secret from mortals. But those guns were huge. This one . . .

Denoriel put the saddle down again and held out his free hand. The metal thing put the gun into it. Denoriel turned it this way and that, careful not to touch the trigger, which he now saw was caught by a hook that would prevent it from being pressed back and allowing the gun to fire. There was nothing at all about the object to suggest it was Sidhe work. The thing had a rather crude appearance, the metal rather uneven and unfinished looking, like a casting that had not been polished.

"It isn't like any gun I've ever seen, and it doesn't use black powder," Denoriel muttered.

"So it isn't against the rules," Harry said eagerly. "I'm not allowed to use black powder yet. Sir Edward thinks I'll blow myself up or set fire to my apartment. I'm not such a fool. But this doesn't have black powder."

"How will we ever explain it?" Denoriel asked, unable to resist the pleading in the boy's eyes.

"I'll hide it unless I need it. Anyway, I can always say you gave it to me—that would be true—and that I had no idea from where you got it."

"And what do you think you'll need it for?" Denoriel asked, fighting a rearguard action against total yielding.

The boy's face grew surprisingly hard. "I'll have iron darts made for it, cold iron. I can bring one of these to the blacksmith and he can copy it. I'll say it's a game piece. And if anyone chases me ever again, *I'll shoot them with cold iron.*"

And Denoriel remembered that he had seriously considered not following the cortege this time, and Harry could have been taken. Likely there was no need any more, with Oberon's blue star blazing on Harry's forehead, but there were non-Sidhe threats to the boy too. He glanced at the dart in the target. It looked as if that would have gone right through a mortal.

"What will you take for the gun?" he asked.

The first metal being had been sidling closer. Now he spoke urgently to the second.

"The boy?" the second metal creature said tentatively.

Denoriel glanced at the first being and laughed. "I have said several times that the boy is not for sale or trade. He is a free person. I do not own him. Besides which, it is the boy for whom I want the gun."

"Come with us, boy," the first metal being said. "I will give you all the guns you like, far handsomer than this one, which is a cheap thing only made for trade. Come, I will show you—"

Whereupon the second metal being swiftly touched the first on a silvery knob on one side of the sparkling band that ran around its head. For an instant the sparkles blazed into a solid band of light; then the band went dark and the creature stood still.

Had the second harmed the first? If so, the removal spell did not recognize what the creature had done as violence. Interesting. Denoriel shrugged, put the gun down on the counter, and picked up the saddle.

"Lord Denno?" Harry's voice was small and pleading. "Even if it is just a cheap thing, I'd like to have it. If we were going to stay long and could look around, maybe we could find a better one, but if you're going to take me home right away, we won't have time to look. Please."

Denoriel sighed like one much put upon. "So, how much? I have ears. I heard what your fellow being said—a cheap item for trade."

"That." The metal being pointed at the saddle on Denoriel's shoulder.

"The saddle? You want my saddle for the gun?"

The disbelief in Denoriel's voice at the offer to exchange something that was rather wonderful for so mundane an object as a saddle must have come across to the metal creature as shocked rejection at the thought of giving up his precious possession. It put a possessive finger—there were only two and a gripping thumb Denoriel noticed—on the gun, nodded decisively, and leaned forward to touch the saddle.

Harry had not attended numerous chaffering sessions with Mistress Bethany without learning something. He was going to be the stupid, eager buyer, careless of the value of what was traded. He tugged at Denoriel's hand.

"Oh, please, Lord Denno. Please. I'll get you another saddle. I promise I will, and it will be just as fine as this one that you've insisted on carrying with you wherever we've gone. Please, Lord Denno. I'll have a special saddle made for you when we get home, if you'll get me the gun."

Denoriel allowed the saddle to slide from his shoulder to where he could clutch it against his chest. He started to shake his head. Harry began to plead with him again. The metal creature began to curl its hand around the gun. Harry snatched it from the being's hand and held it up. Denoriel turned his head toward the gun and saw from the corner of his eye that sparkles were beginning to light the darkness of the band around the head of the first metal being. It had not really been harmed then, just temporarily silenced. He had better finish this business and get the gun before that one woke up completely.

As if he were doing something he already regretted, Denoriel released a great sigh and let the saddle slide further down right onto the counter. He kept one hand on it, however, the fingers curved around one edge as if he was ready to snatch it back into his arms.

"Everything goes with the gun, right?" he asked. "The pump thing, the bag of darts, and an extra square part."

Harry yipped and clutched the gun to his chest. Denoriel told him to be careful lest he shoot himself. The metal being began to expostulate about the cost of the pump and the darts. Denoriel noticed more sparkles dancing around the headband of the immobilized metal creature and that one of its hands was twitching. He shrugged, reached into his purse, and threw a golden guinea onto the table.

"Take the pump and the pouch, Harry," he said. "Unless the trader wants more. In that case, just put the gun down and let me take my saddle back. I'm sure we can spare the time later to look for another gun."

Silently the trader handed over the pump and the pouch. Denoriel stroked the saddle. Harry tucked the gun into one of the capacious pockets of his gown and followed it with the pouch. Then he took the pump in hand and started away from the pavilion, tugging at Denoriel, who gave the saddle one last stroke and then followed the boy's lead.

At the next side alley, the kitsune appeared and gestured for them to follow him into it. When they reached him he was shaking with laughter.

CHAPTER 24

"That's the best example of biter bit I've ever seen," Matka Toimisto gurgled. "You two should set up a booth here. You'd be rich in no time. What with the boy's wide-eyed wonder and you looking as if your heart would break over that stupid saddle . . . That was the slickest piece of trading I've seen in a long time. And why in the twelve planes of Hell have you been carrying that thing around anyway?"

"There aren't twelve planes of Hell," Denoriel said absently, counting steps and turns and fixing them and whatever landmarks he could spot in his mind as they worked their way through the narrower, back alleys of the faire.

The kitsune frowned. "*Was* there something special about that saddle?"

"No, nothing at all. I'm glad we're taking such a circuitous route. I have a feeling there'll be a metal army on our heels soon."

"Maybe not." Toimisto shrugged, and seemed singularly unconcerned. "One thing this market does teach is that what's waste to one being is precious to another. So, why were you carrying it?"

"For the purpose it served. As an item of trade. And, kitsune, I'm not blind. This is the fourth time I've seen that weapons booth." He frowned. "We've been going in a circle of sorts."

"That's right," Matka said, agreeably. "Once passed widdershins, once deosil, then once more widdershins. Fourth time a square should open . . . ah, there it is."

Denoriel noticed that the kitsune sighed slightly with relief. Perhaps the complicated path they had taken had not been purposely to confuse him. Not that it had. Denoriel was one of the most skilled of the Wild Hunt and he could track and remember the hiding places of the slyest of mortals. He would remember the way to Magus Treowth's lodging.

This, however, did seem to be the end of the road. They crossed the square, which looked surprisingly like any square of houses of the wealthy in mortal London, and came to a tall, narrow building. Matka Toimisto knocked on the door.

A large eye opened in the wood. A mouth formed below it. "You again," the mouth said. "Go away."

"But I brought someone I know you want to see," Matka said urgently. "Look behind me." He stepped aside, but not so far aside that he could not get through the door if it opened. "Here is Lord Denoriel and the mortal boy he is guarding. They need a path into the mortal world."

There was only silence. Denoriel stepped closer. "Magus Treowth," he said. "I am sorry to trouble you, but two Gates that Magus Gilfaethwy made for me were meddled with. One destroyed itself. I did not dare try the other. I need to know if the Gates you built for me are safe to use. I cannot risk this mortal boy. He is precious."

The door popped open. The kitsune slid inside and seemed to disappear. Magus Treowth appeared halfway down a steep flight of stairs, and he was in a temper. Denoriel braced himself, but did not have a chance to warn Harry.

"Who would dare meddle with my Gates?" he roared.

Harry winced, wide-eyed, and shrank behind Denoriel.

"I don't know whether your Gates were changed or not," Denoriel said. "That's what I came here to find out. I do know that Magus Gilfaethwy blamed me for trying to repattern his Gates—which I had not done— and told me that both the Gates he had built for me had been damaged. As to who . . . I have no proof, but I believe with near certainty that it was my half-brother."

The mage glared at him, as if he suspected a trick. "Why?"

An unhappy frown creased Denoriel's brow and— somewhat to his own surprise—he felt a surge of emotional pain. "I think he wanted to kill me." He shook his head, and swallowed. There had always been an intense rivalry between himself and Pasgen, but there had been an unspoken agreement between them, or so he'd thought. After all, they were blood-kin. . . . "I knew he didn't like me—well, I don't like him—but kill me?"

But the mage snorted. "If he thought he could kill you by damaging a Gate, he's a fool and knows nothing about Gates. It's true that the Gate anchor itself would explode and burn, but anything or anyone inside the Gate would just be cast out, usually into the chaos lands."

"Truly?" Denoriel felt his frown fading. "Of course, you must know, no one knows as much about it as you do. Pasgen knows a great deal about Gates, about magic in general, much more than I do. But he couldn't have known that I'd have Harry with me, so I thought he wanted to destroy me." He smiled, feeling a great deal of relief—though for the life of him, he couldn't have told why. "My dear half-brother just wanted me to be lost for a while so I wouldn't interfere with exactly what I *did* interfere with."

"Maybe that makes sense to you," Treowth said, and sighed. "All right, come up to my workroom and I'll see what I can discover."

Meanwhile FitzRoy had been tugging at Denoriel's hand, and when Denoriel looked down at him he said plaintively, "Breakfast was a long time ago, Lord Denno. I'm hungry."

"Of course you are," Denoriel said. "I am, too." He looked up at the Magus Major. "Magus Treowth, I must feed my young charge here. Can you recommend a safe food stall, and can I purchase something for you as well as for the boy and myself?"

"Boy." Magus Treowth looked down at FitzRoy. "Yes, we can't starve the child." His head swung, his gaze fixed on the fox-man. "Kitsune, go out and bring food enough for all of us—even you, you worthless toy."

Then he gestured for Denoriel and FitzRoy to come up and opened a door on a room full of books. However, there was a table and some chairs in the center, and a gesture and muttered word sent the books spinning back onto the shelves. Another gesture brought a most peculiar thing to the table, a snarl of golden wires that offered several ends and loops which seemed to promise that if you pulled the right one the whole device would unfold into something fascinating.

"Yes, yes, boy," Treowth said in answer to FitzRoy's inquiring glance, "go ahead and try to unwind that while we wait for out dinner."

FitzRoy narrowed his eyes and tucked the pump away in one of his hanging sleeves to free both hands. He did not do the obvious thing, which was to pull a loose end. Instead he grabbed a loop and carefully pushed it back through the strands of wire that were holding it. The tangle of wires began to unfold, but only the part where the loop had been seemed straightened. The remainder looked even worse. FitzRoy took his lower lip between his teeth and began to look for another likely spot to work on.

"Now," Treowth said to Denoriel, "he won't hear us— oh, he'll know we're talking but won't make sense of what we say. How and why did Oberon mark the child?"

"You know of the FarSeer's prediction about the red-haired babe?"

"If I knew I've forgotten." The mage shook his head. "Tell me again."

So Denoriel gave a swift and abbreviated version of what the coming of the red-haired child would produce and what the failure of that child's acceding to the throne would produce. Treowth winced now and again, but didn't interrupt except to ask why, if FitzRoy was not the red-haired child, he was so important. Denoriel admitted he did not know, only that it was his duty to protect the child. "There is something about him that is important to the welfare of the babe, but we have been unable to FarSee what it is."

"Then with Oberon's mark on him, you can keep him Underhill," the mage observed, clinically.

He sighed. Life would be so much easier, if only that were true! "I wish I could. Poor Harry wishes so too, but he is too near the seat of power in England. If he went missing, so ferocious an investigation would be carried out that the very secret of Underhill would be in danger and his father, who is king, might launch an attack to regain him."

"Then he must be returned," Treowth said. He pulled on his lower lip, and muttered something under his breath. "Well, it will not always be the case that we must go in fear of mortal discovery. Some day I will have the secret of how to resist mortal weapons."

Denoriel looked at him in surprise, and for the first time, the irascible mage smiled. "That is why I am here, where stranger things than those of the mortal world are available. There are certain weapons . . . but they need a power we do not have."

"Weapons?" Denoriel asked unhappily.

The mage gestured vaguely. "To use as a shield, something that will turn their cold iron red hot and make it impossible to hold, or to change it into some other metal that cannot harm the Sidhe."

Denoriel shook his head. "But if they are defenseless, will not they be abused?"

The magus looked at him and sighed. "As many of them as there are, they could overwhelm us by sheer numbers. We must have *some* protection. Gilfaethwy is working on the same problem, but he thinks he can find a way to make the Sidhe resistant to cold iron. He thinks it is something in the blood."

"In the blood of mortals?" Denoriel was pleasantly surprised. That explained Gilfaethwy's desire for mortal blood in a most innocent manner.

"No matter." Treowth waved a hand. "You need passage to the mortal world to return the child. I will add a pattern to your Gate to take you the same distance as but in a direction opposite to where the destroyed Gate was anchored."

"But I think my half-brother will be able—"

"He will be able to do nothing, nor will his master, no matter how powerful. No one will meddle with *my* Gate." He smiled, ferally. "At least, anyone who does meddle will get a very rude surprise."

As if time had been somewhat suspended while he and Treowth spoke, when the Magus Major finished, Harry pulled a new strand of the golden wire and the whole mass unfolded and reformed itself into a narrow shape, rather like a small whale but with enormous outstretched flippers. The boy crowed with delight and the door opened showing the kitsune carrying a large tray with many bowls and covered containers on it.

"Eat," Treowth said, and promptly disappeared.

They were just finishing their meal, having put aside a portion of each dish for the magus, when Treowth walked in the door. He came to the table and smiled at FitzRoy, who touched the golden creation and said it was beautiful.

"Unfortunately it will not work in the mortal world so I cannot let you take it with you," Treowth said. It appeared that not even Treowth was proof against Harry's charm.

"Oh, no, sir, I couldn't take it anyway," Harry demurred. "It's too big to hide and . . . how would I ever explain it? I'm supposed to be lost in the woods."

"A most sensible child." Treowth patted FitzRoy on the head and the boy grimaced, but the magus did not seem to notice. To Denoriel he said, "If you are ready?"

Denoriel stood up and Harry did so too. Denoriel took the boy's hand.

"I will send you to the Gate at Logres," Treowth said.

"If you please, magus, we need to leave the Bazaar afoot," he demurred. "Our elvensteeds are waiting at the entrance to the Bazaar. We cannot abandon them."

Treowth shook his head, and chuckled. "Fool. They know. They will meet you at the Gate."

"Thank you," FitzRoy and Denoriel said in chorus, but found they were talking to the chalcedony pillars of the Gate.

FitzRoy bounced off the white marble dais and ran to Lady Aeron who was, as Treowth had promised, waiting. Denoriel gave the boy a leg up into the saddle Lady Aeron produced for him and then mounted Miralys. They were back at the palace of Llachar Lle in moments. Denoriel was very happy to see that the great gates were closed and the wide corridor was empty.

In Denoriel's apartment, FitzRoy changed back into the soiled clothing he had been wearing when he had first arrived. The sleeves and pockets were not as capacious, but the gun, pouch, and pump were tucked away. Denoriel then dirtied the boy's face and hands and finally stood with his head cocked to the side.

"How about a few tears, Harry?"

"I'm too big to cry," the boy replied indignantly.

"Even if you were lost in the woods?"

"Well . . ." FitzRoy hesitated. "You know, I don't think I can say I was lost in the woods. They'll have had the whole castle guard combing the area and they'll have found my horse. I'll have to find a place to hide. There's charcoal burners' huts in the wood. If I was locked into one of those and maybe tied and gagged—"

"That's very clever, Harry, but you can't be tied and gagged. It wouldn't be comfortable for you, and they'll expect to see marks on your wrists and face after all these hours. Just say whoever dragged you in there held your nose and poured something down your throat. If you were drugged, you'd have been asleep and unable to call for help. Then when you woke up and started calling for help . . . I'll see that Ladbroke or Dunstan is there to hear you."

The boy grinned with delight at the idea of being the hero of such an adventure, but Denoriel shook his head. "Don't be so pleased," he said. "I doubt there'll be any hunting for you this autumn. In fact, I will give odds that that's the last time you go out riding for a long time."

The grin disappeared and FitzRoy sighed. "I know, and they'll probably watch me in the keep nearly as carefully as outside if I say I was snatched off my horse. It can't be helped, and I'll have my gun to practice with and . . . and a lot to think about." He hesitated and then said, "You'll come to see me, won't you, Lord Denno?"

"Of course I'll come," he assured the boy, "although God only knows what excuse I can conjure up in order to come up here in the autumn. Don't worry, I shall manage."

They went out then, and remounted the waiting elvensteeds. When Denoriel thought about a destination, a glowing oval appeared with four dark spots. One, Denoriel knew was the Gate under the stair in Sheriff Hutton; mentally he rejected it and it disappeared. A second was his house in London; that, too, vanished, as did the mark that represented the copse near Windsor. The one remaining spot became blacker and then larger and larger. When it would accept her, Lady Aeron stepped through; Miralys followed.

The blackness did not lift, and Denoriel was momentarily panicked. Then he realized that the darkness was simply full night in a moonless wood. His eyes soon adjusted and he saw they were in a thicket that had grown up around the stump of a huge tree that lay on its side so that the enormous roots formed almost a small cave. Lady Aeron's pale hide gleamed a few feet ahead. She was already walking toward a rather overgrown opening that had long ago been cut through the thicket so the charcoal burners could harvest the tree branches.

A very short, also badly overgrown path, led to a much more used trail. This showed not only ruts made by the wheels of a cart, but footprints too. Fortunately the marks were not fresh. It looked as if the charcoal cutters had passed through a week or so earlier. Perhaps they had been checking on their ovens, making ready for the busiest burning season, just before winter.

Denoriel looked back and gestured. Hoofprints and tiny signs of the elvensteeds' passage, like broken twigs and torn leaves, disappeared. The opening from which they had come was now more overgrown. Denoriel nodded and followed the direction of the footprints on the trail, listening intently, but there were no sounds beyond those of a normal night.

When they reached the woodcutter's hut and FitzRoy had to part with Lady Aeron, Denoriel got the tears he had wanted. They weren't for fear of being locked up in the dark but for parting with his elvensteed.

"I might never see you again," the boy sobbed into her mane.

The steed nuzzled him with her soft muzzle and lipped at his hair. Miralys came near also, and nudged FitzRoy's shoulder. Denoriel hugged him too.

"I can't promise," the Sidhe said, "but if there's an opportunity—if there's a time when your absence won't be noticed—I'll come for you. There are places to hunt where we were, we could . . . but don't think about that now. You need to look scared." He hugged the boy again. "Don't be. Not really. I won't be far and no one is really hunting you."

Denoriel was as good as his word. It took him less than half an hour to find Ladbroke, whom he led to the charcoal burners' hut. He looked meaningfully into Ladbroke's eyes for a moment, then turned Miralys and rode away.

Ladbroke shouted FitzRoy's name and inside the shed, the boy heard him with relief, shouted back and ran to pound on the door.

Pausing only to summon Reeve Tolliver and Dunstan by the use of a shrill whistle, he pushed up the crude wooden bar that kept the door closed and FitzRoy tumbled out into his arms. Ladbroke held the boy tight, weeping with relief and FitzRoy patted him comfortingly on the back, also shedding a few tears, partly for the lost Lady Aeron and partly in relief, because a half hour is a long time for a boy to be alone in the dark.

When Reeve Tolliver arrived, gasping more with terror than with effort, and saw his master, he did more than weep; he knelt on the ground and kissed FitzRoy's feet. Only a few years separated Reeve from the starving boy Ladbroke had found abandoned in a church yard; no one wanted the stable ostler's son when his father died. Tolliver knew that FitzRoy was the source of his food, his shelter, all the stability in his life.

Dunstan also embraced his charge, but he immediately proffered a flask of water and a roll, which he had been prudently carrying. FitzRoy drank the water eagerly and then began to pick at the roll—he had eaten very well at Treowth's table but he would not speak of that. Instead he reminded himself of Lord Denno's story about the drugged drink and complained of a foul taste in his mouth.

Finally Ladbroke ran down the charcoal burners' track, shouting for FitzRoy's personal guardsmen. They were the only ones still searching; the others had given up when the light failed. Sir Edward had then sent out summons to the other councilors with appeals for more men, for a veritable army of men, intending at dawn to search outward from the road foot by foot.

Ladbroke shouted "Found! Found safe!" as he ran down the road, and soon roars of joy drifted back.

Meanwhile Dunstan and Tolliver had offered to carry FitzRoy, which he refused, saying he was eager to walk after having slept for so long. He asked if his horse had escaped, and was assured that it had, although it had been found in a completely different part of the wood. Two of the guardsmen soon met them on the track. The other two had gone running back to Sheriff Hutton.

There, even Sir Edward enfolded FitzRoy in his arms and wept with relief and joy as he stuttered questions about what had happened, where the boy had been.

Mistress Bethany cried out in protest at the questions. She wanted FitzRoy to have a meal in bed and then sleep. The boy patted her but shook his head.

"Been asleep," he said. "Don't want to go to bed. And my mouth tastes foul so I'm not very hungry."

"What happened, Your Grace?" Sir Edward asked. "Where have you been all this time? We searched. God knows we searched and called for you."

"Happened? Well, those things—monsters? demons?—scared my horse—" He shuddered, then looked defiantly at Sir Edward. "Scared me, too, but I didn't fall off. Only I couldn't stop the horse from running away. And then I realized two men were chasing me. My poor horse was so tired, and they caught up. One of them grabbed the horse, the other grabbed me and dragged me out of the saddle. Threw a cloak or a blanket over me. I couldn't squirm free and . . . and I could feel the horse was moving pretty fast. I didn't think it would be smart to try to jump."

"No! God's grace, no. You could have been hurt . . . killed. But did you see them? I've got men hiding near the charcoal burner's hut. Surely they intended to come back for you as soon as the search died down. Thank God your guards and servants wouldn't give up. If we catch anyone, would you be able to say they were the ones that captured you?"

FitzRoy shook his head. "I don't know. They were

behind me most of the time and when we were in the hut and they made me drink that stuff that put me to sleep, it was too dark to see much. They were dark-haired and dark-eyed, I think, and one had a neat beard. And I didn't understand the language they spoke. It sounded a bit like French, but it wasn't French. I can speak French."

FitzRoy described the men who had attacked him years ago in Windsor; their appearances were burned into his memory. He knew they were dead. Lord Denno had told him that they were dead not long after the attack, when he had expressed a fear of being attacked again. It was safe to use their faces and the way they spoke, so he wouldn't by accident describe someone he had seen around the castle or village and get an innocent person into trouble.

By the time Sir Edward had asked all his questions at least three times, FitzRoy was drooping. He claimed to have been in a drugged sleep all day, but actually he had been wide awake and having some very exciting adventures—singing in Furhold and passing through the Bazaar of the Bizarre. Eventually Mistress Bethany got her way and he was escorted back to his apartment by his own people and another ten guardsmen.

He ate a little of the meal Bethy brought and then dismissed her. He thought about sending Dunstan away too, but then decided he needed at least one ally, and without speaking brought out the gun, the pouch, and the pump. Dunstan stared at them, open-mouthed.

"We need to hide them," FitzRoy said.

"Where *have* you been, Your Grace?" Dunstan breathed, but he didn't wait for an answer, gathering up the gun and its accoutrements.

Staggering with sleepiness now, FitzRoy followed him and saw him stow everything away in a bottom drawer of a chest in the dressing room that held odd

tools and rags for repairing chains and settings for
jewels and other decorative metal adornments on
clothing that might be damaged by wear. The gun
itself he partially concealed under a rag in a far back
corner of the drawer; the remainder of the objects
he simply tossed into the drawer and left in plain
sight.

FitzRoy breathed a sigh of relief. If anyone looked
into the drawer, those odd parts would draw no curiosity. They seemed to belong among the odd tools.
Before Dunstan closed the drawer, however, FitzRoy
removed one of the stubby darts from the pouch.

"I need to get the blacksmith to copy this—only in
cold iron," he said to Dunstan. The valet's eyes widened, and FitzRoy knew that Dunstan understood and
breathed another small sigh of relief.

His confidence was justified. Dunstan was surely
aware that magic had been used to try to abduct
FitzRoy. He must have known, or learned, that Reeve
Tolliver had been disguised by illusion to look like his
master. Dunstan and everyone else had seen the
monsters attack. Cold iron was a defense, at least
against some of the creatures.

"I'll see to it, Your Grace," Dunstan said, face and
voice grim.

The valet put the dart away in his pocket and began
to remove FitzRoy's clothing. Now FitzRoy recalled that
Dunstan and Ladbroke had been recommended to his
service by Lord Denno. He felt warm and protected,
almost as if Lord Denno was there. He was quite sure
that Dunstan and Ladbroke knew what Lord Denno
was. Likely they knew about, possibly even had been
to, Underhill.

Tears came to FitzRoy's eyes. He would so have
liked to talk about it, to tell someone about Lady Aeron
and how riding her was a whole new thing—but he

knew he could not and he suspected from Dunstan's expression that he could not either.

Here they were, trapped in silence, and yet—he exchanged another look with Dunstan, and the latter nodded. "Fostering, m'lord," the man said, quietly. "We've been fostered 'mongst Lord Denno's folk."

That was all he needed to say. FitzRoy sighed, and smiled. "Wonderful," he said softly. The spell upon him allowed him that much.

"Oh, aye, Your Grace," Dunstan said, with a smile that reached and warmed his eyes. "Every bit of that."

CHAPTER 25

Having waited long enough to see Harry safe in his servant's care, Denoriel directed Miralys to take him back to the Gate, back to his apartment in Logres. Elves did not sleep, but Denoriel felt sorely in need of that human restorative. He was not sick with draining of his power; that seemed, as Mwynwen had promised, to be restored as fast as it was used—and he had used virtually no magic anyhow.

It was the responsibility of caring for Harry, he decided, as he dismounted by the steps of Llachar Lle, the tension of watching for danger and being constantly ready to protect the child. But it had been wonderful too. All of Underhill was new to his eyes, bright and beautiful, funny and terrifying.

He thanked Miralys, and the elvensteed nuzzled him before trotting away. Lady Aeron was already gone. She had disappeared as soon as Harry was locked in the hut. Denoriel smiled, thinking of how that pair had bonded. When this was over, Denoriel promised himself, when the red-haired babe was safe on the throne, he would bring Harry back Underhill to ride Lady Aeron and explore its wonders with him. In such company, Denoriel knew he could never suffer the ennui that brought too many Sidhe to Dreaming.

At the door of his apartment, he suddenly wondered what had happened to the kitsune, and he chuckled as he entered. Clever as that little devil was and absent-minded as Treowth seemed to be, he did not think Matka Toimisto would get the magus to invest him with the powers of an elvensteed—if even Treowth could do that.

He was allowed about three steps into the antechamber, still grinning and wondering what the kitsune wanted to do in the mortal world that would require the ability to escape to Underhill without a Gate, when his amusement was wiped away by his sister's voice calling his name. Frowning—not because he didn't wish to see Aleneil but because he knew this was more trouble—he entered the living room.

"What happened?" Aleneil asked, jumping to her feet.

"When?" Denoriel asked, feeling stupid; but so much had happened and he was too tired to want to recount everything.

"The boy! Did the Unseleighe seize him?"

He snorted; sometimes Aleneil could be so—

Well, she was his sister, and he loved her, but there were times when she just gave way to fear and even hysteria, and forgot to *think*. "Would I be here, strolling into my apartment if Harry was in Unseleighe hands?"

Aleneil put a hand to her head, and the tension simply ran out of her. "No, of course not. I know you care far too much for the boy to accept his loss so calmly, but I was frightened."

Denoriel sighed and sat down, waving at Aleneil to do so too. "You were right to be frightened. George

Boleyn had invited me to watch a race with him . . . Oh, heaven, I'll have to Gate back to London—"

"Never mind that. It will be hard on you, but you can Gate back in time if you need to. Nothing will happen at the race that will cause any paradox. Your presence or absence won't matter." She looked up at him with question in her eyes. "Why was I right to be frightened?"

"Because I almost didn't go to accompany Harry's party from Pontefract to Sheriff Hutton. They'd ridden that distance so often without the smallest threat . . ." He shook his head. "Thank Mother Dannae that I *do* love Harry. It was more the urge to see him than any fear for him that made me Gate north." Then Denoriel frowned. "What do you mean you were frightened? Did you FarSee the attempt to take him?"

"I learned about it, but too late. I was in the mortal world, visiting Lady Lee—she is Thomas Wyatt's sister, and about the only female friend Anne Boleyn has. It was Eirianell. She suddenly saw a vision of monsters attacking FitzRoy's cortege. The Vision was so strong—she wasn't even at the Mirror."

Denoriel winced. "It was probably happening just as she Saw it."

Aleneil nodded. "But Eirianell couldn't ignore it. She sent a messenger to warn you, but it couldn't find you. Then she sent for me, but she thought I was Underhill. By the time the air spirit reached me in the mortal world it was probably too late. Still I sent messengers to you everywhere I could think, and none could find you. What happened?"

"I was just barely in time to save Harry. Someone, Rhoslyn probably, had put a glamour on the boy groom to look like Harry and all the guards, even our own people, were clustered around him ready to fight off the monsters. Meanwhile Harry's horse had been driven into the woods and Pasgen had called out the Wild Hunt to take him."

"You fought the Wild Hunt?" Aleneil's voice scaled up in disbelief.

"I? Never." He laughed, wanly. "I simply seized Harry, pulled him off his horse and then ran like a rabbit . . . only the rabbit hole was no safe haven. Pasgen had meddled with my Gate and instead of bringing me to Logres, it destroyed itself and threw me and Harry out into Wormegay Hold."

"That was probably just when the air spirit was looking for you," she said, nodding. "They won't go into Wormegay. But later? Or did you decide to hide there?"

"Not there!" Denoriel's shoulders tightened and drew in as he remembered the horrors in that place. "There was another place we could have stayed—" he described the shepherd's paradise and Aleneil smiled "—but my first purpose was to get Harry back before anyone noticed he was gone." He sighed. "If I could have done that—"

"It wouldn't have explained away the monsters anyway," she pointed out

"Just as well." Denoriel smiled. "Vidal Dhu is about to discover that he has overstepped this time, and Harry is safe from the Unseleighe for good."

"The cross?" she asked, wonderingly.

He smiled, recalling Oberon's expression. The High King was not happy with Vidal Dhu. "King Oberon."

Aleneil gasped, and echoed the king's name, and Denoriel told her about his summons to the throne room of Llachar Lle.

"Titania was there too?" Aleneil breathed. "How was it between them?"

"Better than usual, I think, but I suspect that Titania is growing restless." He raised an eyebrow, and Aleneil nodded, knowingly. "She was looking at *me*, but that passed when I described my less-than-heroic rescue. And Harry, thank Dannae, is the most ordinary boy. Nothing beautiful or lissom about him, and the Tudor court dress made the poor child look like a small ale keg with a head and skinny arms and legs."

Aleneil giggled at the description, but sobered quickly. "Do you think Oberon wants to see the red-haired child rule Logres? Sometimes I think he leans more to the Unseleighe way than to ours. He has a temper—and he can sometimes be so very cruel."

He had to shrug. "I don't know. To read him is impossible—at least for me. But one thing is sure. Oberon is utterly determined to keep Underhill a secret from mortals. He marked Harry to protect him, saying the Unseleighe had tried three times and twice come close to exposing our existence, so they were forbidden to try again to take the child. But he also made it impossible for Harry to speak of Underhill."

"Well, if Oberon marked him, the Unseleighe will leave FitzRoy alone, so he is safe," she concluded. "And I cannot see the harm if the child cannot speak of Underhill. Who can truly trust a child to hold his tongue at all times? I think it a small price to pay for his safety."

"But he is only safe from a threat from Underhill," Denoriel reminded her. "Unfortunately there are mortals who wish to be rid of a continuing threat to Princess Mary's accession to the throne, and I suspect that after this attempt on him, his councilors may advise the king that Harry would be safer in court, under Henry's own eye." He sighed. "I don't think Harry will be safer, but Sir Edward and the others were all terrified of what would happen if they lost him. They want the responsibility back where it belongs, with his father."

She pursed her lips in thought. "And Henry is not

so careful of his son as he should be. . . . However, that may not matter." She fixed him with a look that told him that she wanted him to pay attention to what she was about to tell him. "I have been doing my best listening-in-corners. It is now quite clear that the failure of the divorce trial to produce the result the king wanted has not diminished his determination to have Anne. I believe even the Imperial ambassador realizes that as long as King Henry is young enough and healthy enough to breed a legitimate son, he will not name FitzRoy his heir."

"I hope so." He looked away from her for a moment, at the illusory fire in the fireplace. "In spite of what Treowth said, Gating makes me anxious now, and with Harry in the north, I was Gating constantly. If he is with the court, I can just stay in the mortal world."

"We may both be living most of the time in the mortal world," Aleneil said. "The reason I was waiting for you is that Eirianell has been consulting a student of mortal history, and she wishes to talk to both of us."

Eirianell met them at the Place of Learning. She could not invite them into her house; she apologized gracefully to Denoriel, explaining that the auras of others lingered and disturbed her with undesired Visions of their lives and doings. Aleneil had known, of course, and had arranged for one of the gardens near the Place of Learning to be kept free for them, and she led them there to a bower under thornless roses.

There was a small ivory table painted with a long blue lake surrounded by mountains. Sandalwood chairs inlaid with ivory, added their scent to that of the roses, keeping it from being overpoweringly sweet. Eirianell seated herself in the deepest, most shadowed, part of the arbor, gathering her long train around her feet. Her silk gown's pastel colors flowed and blended with each movement of her body to which the gown clung, and the embroidery seemed to move and change on her trailing sleeves.

"There have been ill portents since last we spoke Lord Denoriel," the eldest of the teachers began. "It finally occurred to Rhonwen and myself that having Aleneil with us when we tried to FarSee Logres was totally disruptive. She knows—or thinks she knows—what is happening. She is too much involved with the people. Her 'knowledge' and hopes and fears were all tangled with our Vision. So we did not summon her . . . and we learned."

"I am very sorry," Aleneil whispered.

Eirianell stretched a long arm and delicate hand and touched Aleneil's cheek. "Child, how could you know if we did not? The fault is ours, mine and Rhonwen's and Morwen's. And Rhonwen and I excluded Morwen also. She is much taken with the ways of the mortals, even if she has not been living with them."

"If Harry is in danger, I will bring him Underhill—" Denoriel began.

"No! He has a role to play and to remove him will condemn us all." She saw the mulish, rebellious expression on Denoriel's face and sighed. "The danger is not immediate. It will not touch him until he is a man, so you will have time to consider."

"Denoriel," Aleneil murmured. "Remember how angry you were when the charge of FitzRoy was first laid on you? Now listen before you leap to conclusions."

"Let me tell you the worst first," Eirianell said. "We have seen that the fires will come. There is no avoiding them, but if the red-haired babe is born and is in the succession for the throne, that period of torture will be short. If there is no successor, worse will befall England, not only a search for heretics but the full Inquisition."

"Then what we are doing is useless?" Aleneil asked, faintly.

"By no means," her teacher said decisively. "The boy must be protected into his manhood for in some way that is not clear, his life stands between the red-haired child and destruction. And the child must be born legitimately and recognized as King Henry's get, or it will not come to the throne and the priests of the Inquisition will whip the mortals into a frenzy that will destroy Elfhame Logres. It will be as dead and empty as Alhambra and Eldorado."

"If my life can protect Harry's, I will lay it down," Denoriel swore.

"Only do not throw it away. Think before you act," Eirianell cautioned. "Fortunately I have some practical suggestions. Aleneil, you must keep Mistress Boleyn out of the king's bed."

"She has shown no signs of yielding to Henry's importunities," his sister replied—but there was a hint, just a hint, of doubt.

"Not yet, but now that the easy path to her body has been blocked, the king will try to buy her. He will make her father a double earl, her brother a viscount and give her material gifts. When there is enough to make life good even if he does abandon her, she might yield—she will in the long run, but not yet. Not for four long years."

"Four years!" Aleneil exclaimed in tones of despair. "I do not think even Anne's wit and her perfect purity can hold a man for four years."

"Perhaps not, but there is something else that will fix him to the idea of marriage to her." The FarSeer had a certain look of satisfaction about her. "I told you I had consulted with Ieuan Hywyn. He says there is something at the back of the king's mind that possibly he does not remember is there. He must be reminded. Almost fifteen years ago Henry's attention was drawn to an affair in which an anti-clerical reformer named Richard Hunne was said to have committed suicide when a prisoner."

Aleneil looked puzzled at the statement. Well, so was Denoriel! "What in the world has this to do with—"

The teacher chuckled. "So young. So impatient. Listen. Our joy, perhaps our lives depend on this small thing. This Richard Hunne read the Bible, which the clergy forbids; he annoyed the clergy when his child died by refusing to pay the customary fee for the winding-sheet. He held on to the winding sheet and was imprisoned and tortured by the clergy. The common folk and burgesses were angry when Hunne was arrested. When his suicide was announced they became infuriated and refused to believe he had killed himself. They accused the bishop of London of condoning Hunne's murder."

"Likely enough," Aleneil sighed. "Most will condone anything for a gold coin or two."

"The bishop was enraged, and Hunne's *body* was tried for heresy and burned, if you can imagine it. The citizens were even more outraged. They pursued the matter by raising in Parliament the question of whether the murderers in Hunne's prison had been protected by a clerk's right to be tried even for civil offenses by his own clerical tribunal. And this is where the king came into the affair. This is what must be recalled to Henry's mind."

"What?" Denoriel was totally confused.

"That at the time of the Hunne affair, King Henry recognized clearly that the Church was the greatest rival to his own domestic power." She nodded when she saw the dawning understanding in both their expressions. "Ieuan Hywyn says that although King Henry enjoys being called Defender of the Faith and fulminating against heresy abroad . . . he will brook no rivals to his absolute power within his own realm. The king summoned all the parties to Blackfriars—"

"Where the divorce trial was held," Aleneil said.

"Yes, but in the Hunne case the king won." The FarSeer steepled her fingers together in her lap. "He surrounded himself with his own lay judges, and the Lord Chief Justice, well aware of Henry's resentment of any man of the cloth being able to escape the king's justice, of the feeling of the nobility, the burgesses, even the common folk, ruled that indeed a clerk could be summoned before a lay tribunal for a lay crime. His soul could be judged by the Church, but his body must answer to the courts of the land. Thus, the Chief Justice ruled, the clergy in the case of Richard Hunne had been guilty of *praemunire*—of asserting papal jurisdiction in England against the king's right—and were guilty of a crime."

"Oh!" Aleneil exclaimed. "Oh, my!"

"A bit more than 'oh my,' I think," said Denoriel, who was, at this point far more educated in the ways of mortal politics than he would ever have dreamed of being four years ago. "I do not believe that any king has so asserted himself against the Church since the murder of Thomas à Becket."

"The entire Church, including Wolsey, went down on their knees and assured Henry they had no intention of doing anything prejudicial to the Crown and Henry replied—I have his exact words from Ieuan Hywyn." Eirianell closed her eyes to recall the memorized statement. "He said, 'The kings of England have never had any superior but God alone. Know well, therefore, that we will ever maintain the right of our crown and of our temporal jurisdiction.' Which means that for cases tried in England, Henry did not recognize the right of the Church, which means the pope, to decide a legal case."

"But how can we . . . I don't think I even know a priest," Denoriel protested. He had avoided the clergy as much as possible, being fearful that a Talented priest might "smell" his magic.

"Anne," Aleneil said. "Anne has become very interested in theology, and particularly in any theology that challenges the power of the pope." She cocked her head at Denoriel. "And you can work through George. Hungarians are bound to have a different view of the pope in Rome . . . what with the Moslem heathens breathing down their necks all these years. You might sound puzzled about why the king is so subservient to the pope—and perhaps, why the pope seems unable to respond to the needs of his flock. Not suggesting the king not be subservient, just asking why."

Eirianell nodded. "Once King Henry gets the bit of the Church interfering with his right to rule between his teeth, the marriage to Anne will be as much of an excuse as it will be a matter of passion. *But* the girl must stay out of his bed until he has committed himself to her so publicly that he cannot back away without looking an ultimate fool."

Although it was now true that Seleighe and Unseleighe were united in desiring the birth of the red-haired babe, opinions on how to get the child started differed widely. Aurilia nic Morrigan believed it would be easiest to steal the child if it were a bastard. Pasgen and Rhoslyn agreed with her, but Rhoslyn, tied to Queen Catherine and Princess Mary was in no position to approach Anne—and would not even if she could.

Even Vidal Dhu would not challenge King Oberon's direct prohibition against harming anyone close to the king. So while Anne remained the center of King Henry's attention she was safe from any direct interference. Plans were being made for a very indirect means of influencing Anne in the future, but those were not yet ripe. At present, the best Pasgen could do was to prevent the divorce from taking place and find devices that would convince Anne that it was time to yield her body to the king. Possibly Henry could buy her with favors to her family.

Pasgen's credit as the magician and fortune teller Fagildo Otstargi had been substantially increased by the accuracy of his predictions of the fall of Cardinal Wolsey. Just as Otstargi had foreseen, on the ninth of October when Cardinal Wolsey went to Westminster Hall, the king's servants who usually preceded him were absent and he found that a bill of indictment had been preferred against him. On the tenth the dukes of Norfolk and Suffolk arrived at York House to informed him that the king had dismissed him from his position as chancellor.

They asked for his seal of office; Wolsey refused and demanded either to be told in person by the king that he was dismissed or to receive an order in the king's own hand demanding his seal of office. Wolsey had counted on Henry's known aversion to writing anything and hoped for a personal interview. It was a forlorn hope, Cromwell told Master Otstargi. On October nineteenth the written demand had arrived and Wolsey had handed over his seal of office to the outwardly concerned but inwardly triumphing dukes of Norfolk and Suffolk.

Partly by his own wit and partly because he had accepted Pasgen's prediction that Wolsey *was* ruined, Cromwell had survived the fall of his master; however he had not taken Pasgen's advice to abandon Wolsey. In fact, when the Parliament met in November, he had pleaded Wolsey's case so well in the House of Commons that the bill against him was dropped.

Cromwell had impressed the whole court by his loyalty and care of Wolsey's affairs while obeying every royal order to the letter. And by the most unlikely avenue of opening himself to attack by one of Henry's courtiers, Cromwell had brought himself to the notice of King Henry. As yet he had no royal appointment, but his influence was growing. Still, Pasgen knew that whatever his outward demeanor, Cromwell hated Anne Boleyn . . . which, as if Pasgen's thought had drawn it forth, Cromwell promptly confirmed.

"That witch-bitch Boleyn poisoned the king's mind against the cardinal," Cromwell spat. "I heard she warned the king not to allow any meeting with the cardinal lest he fall under Wolsey's spell again."

"The cardinal has great persuasive powers," Pasgen said mildly.

"Spell!" Cromwell snarled softly. "She's the one who casts spells. She's got every mark of a witch—that extra finger on her left hand and a black mark like a star on her breast, and—"

"Master Cromwell," Pasgen said soothingly, "I don't believe Mistress Anne is a witch. I have detected no magic on or about her . . ."

That, of course, was not true; Pasgen knew of Anne's Talent and knew how she used it unconsciously. He also knew it was totally untrained and unguarded. That was the basis of Aurilia's plan for Anne's destruction and he did not want Cromwell, whom he hoped to guide into considerable power—which would, of course, be directed by his personal magician—to think of Anne as a witch.

At least—not yet.

"Besides," Pasgen continued, "it is not safe to . . . to speak ill of her. She . . . the picture is not so clear to me as that of the poor cardinal's downfall—there are still some uncertainties—but I believe unless Mistress

Anne Boleyn soon yields her body to the king, she will be queen. Of course, the longer the divorce can be delayed, the more likely she will yield. But some hope must be held out to the king or he might take matters—and by this I mean in terms of the divorce—into his own hands."

Cromwell hissed between his teeth, then seemed to conquer whatever emotion had gripped him. For a moment his face was blank, then it relaxed into a kind of interested thoughtfulness. "To keep the king hoping but move no further forward toward the divorce . . . ah, yes. There is a cleric, one Dr. Cranmer, a fellow of Jesus College in Cambridge, who mentioned to the king's secretary, Dr. Gardiner, that what should be done was to take the opinions of the divines at the great universities in Europe as to whether or not King Henry's marriage is valid."

Pasgen smiled. "If I know the habits of divines at universities, it might take a year or more to gather those opinions."

"Giving Mistress Anne more time to hang herself." Cromwell nodded. "But what if she does not? Are you *sure* she has not ensorcelled Henry? He seems positively to relish her scolding."

"It is a novelty," Pasgen pointed out. "Queen Catherine was nearly always agreeable or submissive. Every other leman that the king has desired has flung herself into his bed almost before he could ask—why, even Mistress Anne's own sister! It is forbidden fruit; what he is denied, he must needs want. How long the novelty will last, I cannot read, but nothing in the near future shows change. The best way to be sure the king will rid himself of Mistress Anne is for her to grant his desire." Pasgen bit his lip. "Do you not think it time for the king to try to buy her?"

"Unless he turns a county over to her," Cromwell said dryly, "I do not see how he can give her more. He has showered her with jewels and money."

"No, no, I meant something more permanent." He inclined his head toward Cromwell. "Her father has always yearned for the earldom of Ormonde. Why should he not have it? And that would make the son . . . George, isn't it? . . . Viscount Rochford. Mistress Anne is very fond of her brother, I understand. When she has their nobility to support her, perhaps she will care less for being the cast-off mistress of the king. She took fright at her sister's banishment to the country, but with her with father an earl, she would still have a place at court."

Cromwell shook his head and then laughed. "Yes, she could come to court, but everyone there would snicker behind their hands. Still, her father, Lord Rochford, has only known me as an enemy. If I suggest this expedient to the king . . ."

By the eighth of December, Boleyn had his earldom . . . earldoms in fact, for he was not only named earl of Ormonde, to which title he had some family claim, but earl of Wiltshire as well. Pasgen laughed to himself when that news came to him. It seemed that Master Cromwell was eager to impress his tame magician. Boleyn's elevation was too quick, too pat, for it to have been a result of Cromwell's urging. Doubtless he had learned of it at court and pretended to be an instigator of the idea to increase Pasgen's belief in his power with the king.

Well, let the clever little clerk work to impress Pasgen. That would only make Pasgen's work easier.

However, to Aleneil's relief, Anne's father's and brother's elevation had little influence on her. She was at best a self-centered creature, and, though mildly

pleased that she now had a right to be called Lady
Anne rather than Mistress Anne, she had her hopes
firmly fixed on a far more exalted title. Earl and viscount had no direct advantage for her; she was still
precariously balanced on the knife edge of simultaneously tempting and refusing the king.

Nor did Anne have much support, Aleneil thought.
Oh, her mother and father and brother all petted and
praised her, but now, having their desires fulfilled and
fearing that too much resistance might sour the king's
affection and make him turn on those he had only
recently given so much, none urged virtue as strongly.
There were even hints that perhaps King Henry should
be rewarded for what he had done.

In Anne's opinion, however, Henry had done nothing
for *her*. *Her* dreams were not fulfilled. Aleneil sighed.
She had heard a great deal of Anne's opinion recently,
for what support Anne did have came from Lady
Margaret Lee, Thomas Wyatt's sister, and Anne's only
female friend. Lady Margaret had come to know Anne
before her marriage when Wyatt had been courting her
at the same time that Anne had first aroused Henry's
interest. Although Lady Margaret's intention had been
to warn Anne off her brother, who was already married, she had been fascinated by Anne's wit and grace.

Admiration was always a path to Anne's regard,
which was why her relationships were nearly always
with men, but this time it fixed her attention on Lady
Margaret. The least clever of the Wyatt family, Margaret was only barely pretty in a pallid way, which also
made her acceptable to dark and vivid Anne. And, as
Margaret was disposed to continue to admire, to listen and agree with Anne's opinions, she soon became
necessary to Anne.

In like manner, Aleneil, under the guise of Lady
Alana FitzWilliam, distant kinswoman of Sir William

FitzWilliam, treasurer of Henry's household, became the attached friend and companion of Lady Margaret. Lady Alana was even plainer than her mistress. Although her features were neat and pleasant, she had a sallow complexion and muddy eyes and hair.

There was simply nothing about Lady Alana that attracted notice; one could look away from her for just a moment and forget her face. However, no one ever forgot Lady Alana's clothing. Her sense of fashion and instinctive knowledge of what color and ornament and what styles would best become her friends soon made her indispensable to both Margaret and Anne. Just at this time, dress was desperately necessary to Anne, who had to balance her somewhat limited purse, her status as the king's acknowledged favorite, and the necessity of looking at one and the same time interesting, magnificent, and never tawdry.

Thus Aleneil was admitted to an inner, inner circle free of any influence except Anne's will and pleasure. She said little for some time, confining her conversation and advice to the color and fit of Anne's gowns. However, after Cranmer and others left to obtain opinions on the king's marriage at various universities, Aleneil managed to introduce, somewhere between the placement of silver lace and the cloth-of-gold stomacher, a book by William Tyndale—who had been exiled for his translation of the New Testament into English. The book was called *The Obedience of the Christian Man and How Christian Rulers Ought to Govern.*

Anne only glanced at the book cursorily until she realized from what Lady Alana was saying in her soft, apologetic voice, that *The Obedience of Christian Man* set out to prove that a king governed by divine right; thus, the ruler was answerable only to God. The pope had no power over a monarch and there could be no distinction between the clergy and the laity. Church affairs and temporal affairs were all under the sole control of the king.

When Aleneil left to accompany Lady Margaret home, she no longer had the book. When and where it came into Henry's hands Aleneil never asked, but by the late summer of 1530 he had thoroughly absorbed the ideas. These theoretical notions found a more solid basis in the *Collectanea satis copiosa,* put together from the opinions Cranmer had garnered in Europe. The collection of scriptural, patristic, and historical arguments justified Henry taking into his own hands his matrimonial affairs. What the *Collectanea* offered Henry was the demonstration that he was already head of the Church, all he had to do was behave as such. The question that remained was how.

Aleneil devised Anne's New Year gown for the beginning of 1531, a magnificent affair of crimson-colored velvet embroidered in gold and trimmed in sable. Her hair, loose and flowing to her hips, was a glistening shadow against the vivid gown, moving as if it had a life of its own. Aleneil felt there could be no doubt from the king's reaction that he was still and even more enslaved, but Anne's wit rang brittle and Henry's laughter was overloud.

In private after the feast, Lady Margaret burst into tears, fearing that her idol had fallen at last. Aleneil comforted her; she did not believe that anything was wrong between the lovers. In fact, she assured Margaret, the way they touched and watched each other implied that they were planning together something important . . . and uncertain.

What that was soon became apparent. Parliament and a Convocation of the Church were summoned for the second and third weeks in January. The entire court knew that Henry planned to extort a substantial sum from the Church to relieve his ever-present financial need. There was no surprise about the demand and no doubt about the response. To avoid various prosecutions for their involvement in Wolsey's schemes, the Convocation quickly offered a hundred thousand pounds.

To the relief of the prelates, the amount was accepted. The pardon that was offered, however, was a shock. It was not a pardon for involvement in Wolsey's crimes; it was a general pardon for the illegal exercise of the Church's spiritual authority in the past, and it described Henry as "protector and highest head" of the Church and clergy. Aleneil now understood Anne's and the king's tension—and it was not without cause.

However, the king had the bit well within his teeth and was determined to bolt from the old, well-trodden paths of the relationship between Church and ruler. When the Convocation did not immediately accept this pardon and made protest, Henry sent them another on February seventh. The king had not backed down an inch. Not only was the pardon again for the crime of exercising the Church's authority illegally, but it went even further in describing King Henry as "sole protector and supreme head of the English Church and clergy." It was clear that resistance would not bring compromise, only drive the king to greater radicalism.

Further argument ensued, but the outcome was a foregone conclusion. As a sop to the Convocation, Cromwell, now officially a royal councilor, suggested that Henry allow "so far as the law of Christ allows" to be added to the phrase "sole protector of the English Church and clergy" . . . and it was done. That Henry and clergy read Christ's law far differently did not matter to him at the moment, the first wedge had been driven.

Anne's joy seemed to mount to seventh heaven. She was sure that the king only needed to recall Parliament and they would pass a bill of divorcement. Henry, knowing the English Parliament better, was not so sanguine. Through Cromwell the king soon learned that his own council had broken into violent factions over his claim to be head of the English Church. Until he could pressure them to speak with one voice he would make no further move. He delayed the recall of Parliament from October to the following January.

That news conveyed from Cromwell to Pasgen to Rhoslyn brought from her a sigh of relief. Rhoslyn had not been idle but her efforts produced few results. Maria de Salinas, the queen's favorite lady in waiting, was always eager to pass to Catherine any idea that might forward her cause. But Catherine was not much of a partisan. She *knew* she was right. She had been a clean maiden when she and Henry had wed; thus her marriage was legitimate and God would protect her claim.

Her stubbornness was like a great granite cliff. She clung to her position as queen, regardless of the slights offered her or of Anne's presence. Nothing, neither threats nor promises nor strong urgings from the pope that she retire to a convent, thus protecting her daughter's position, would move her. She was Henry's true wife, she always had been, and always would be. Nothing that a man—even a king—could say would make that untrue.

Even after Henry left her in July 1531 she remained immovable with regard to her position. As late as November of that year she attended state occasions, although she was never allowed into the presence of the king. After a few abortive attempts to offer advice, Rhoslyn realized that her place in the queen's court was essentially useless.

There was no way without bespelling the king—and that was specifically forbidden—that Henry's affection could be drawn back to Catherine. Thus, there was really no point in her dull role as a nun in Maria de Salinas's household. Rhoslyn knew that she and the queen were already at one on the point that there should be no marriage between Anne and Henry.

Their reasons differed: Rhoslyn wanted Anne's child to be a bastard so that no one would care what became of it. Catherine wanted her husband as well as the world to acknowledge the legitimacy of her marriage; she wanted her place as queen back and to ensure that there would be no legitimate rival for the throne to her daughter, Princess Mary. Rhoslyn had no fear that Catherine would weaken under any pressure. She told Maria de Salinas that she had been recalled to her convent and left the queen to her own devices.

Her job there was over. It was time to find a new task.

CHAPTER 26

Lord Denno was a frequent enough visitor to Thomas Boleyn's London residence that he was shepherded into the lower parlor without question. There he loosened the rich, wine-red, sable-lined cloak he wore as he approached the settle and two chairs that flanked the fireplace. A huge fire roared on the hearth and its light blinded him so that he swung the cloak off his shoulders before he realized that the chair closest to the hearth was occupied.

"Good afternoon," he said, bowing slightly, and then more deeply as he recognized the duke of Norfolk and added, "Your Grace, what a pleasure to meet you again."

"Meet me again?" But the querulous tone only lasted until Denoriel had thrown back his hood and exposed his face. "Oh, Lord Denno. Yes it is a long time since we last met." He smiled suddenly. "That was when you delivered to me the fruit of that little speculation of ours into Turkey carpets. Hmmm." He came more erect in his chair and stared at Denoriel. "You haven't by any chance come to offer a similar speculation to Lord Wiltshire?"

Denoriel laughed heartily. "No, I am sorry to say. Truthfully it has been a bad time for carpets. I have lost my workshop. The people were all scattered by a new local conqueror. Until peace is made, there will be no carpets woven for me."

"A social call?" Norfolk's eyebrows went up.

Denoriel Smiled. "Yes and no. After our business is done, likely Lord Rochford and I will continue on to social pleasures, but I do have business with him. One of my ships is in from France and Lord Rochford has an interest in the cargo."

"Ah. You did not think I would be interested? Did I not say you would be welcome to me whenever—" He stopped when he realized Denoriel was shaking his head.

"It was Lord Rochford who came to me with an opportunity for investment," Denoriel said quickly. "He had wind of a cargo of fine wine from Bordeaux but could not hire a ship and was unable to take full advantage of the cargo because of a temporary embarrassment. I offered my ship *Neptune* and to cover any charges he could not meet, and we split the cargo between us. This morning I had news that *Neptune* had come to port, so I sent a message to George, who asked me to meet him here so he could ask his father if he wanted any wine."

"Bordeaux wine?" Norfolk's interest increased. "A good red?"

"Unfortunately I have not yet had a chance to taste it and will not for perhaps a week until it is transported to a stable place and allowed to rest." He smiled when he saw Norfolk's avid gaze. "However, if it is as good as George hopes, would you like some wine, Your Grace?"

"He can't have any," a strong voice said.

Denoriel turned to meet the eyes of Thomas Boleyn, earl of Ormonde and Wiltshire and, more importantly, father of Anne. He was a man of middle height, what could be seen of his hair under his flat velvet cap still dark. His eyes were large and dark also, like his daughter's, but his nose was stronger. Little could be seen of his chin under his beard, and that, unlike his hair was graying.

Nonetheless, Boleyn's shoulders under doublet and gown were still broad. He had been one of Henry's companions during his youth, before Henry's older brother Arthur had died. In those days, Henry's father had been desirous that his younger son be more interested in the pleasures of life than in politics, and Henry's companions had been chosen for their addiction to sport. Thus, Thomas Boleyn had been a champion jouster, a wrestler of note, and a bowman who took many prizes.

Since George was laughing as he walked beside his father and Wiltshire was grinning, Denoriel understood his remark to the duke of Norfolk was a joke. He bowed again to all three and shook his head.

"I beg you gentlemen, do not embroil me in a quarrel with His Grace of Norfolk, who has always been most gracious to me." He made a piteous face. "It is he whom you must convince about the wine, because if he asks it of me, I will give him what he desires."

"Oh, he will yield his share readily enough."

Wiltshire bowed to Norfolk, who had politely stood up to greet him. There was, of course, no need for Norfolk to rise. He still outranked Wiltshire, but Norfolk was not the kind to forget the benefits of being polite to the father of Anne Boleyn.

"Ah," Norfolk said, jocularly, "You know the wine

is bad and wish to save me from wasting my money."

"Grace of God," George said. "I hope not! Aside from what it would cost me, it would never do to serve bad wine at the Christmas celebrations."

"Christmas? But that is two months—" Norfolk stopped speaking and nodded. "Yes, I remember. You are in charge of the entertainments. Two months is short enough for making those arrangements." Then he sighed. "I do not envy you."

"Why?" Wiltshire looked suddenly anxious. "Have you heard bad news?"

"No." Norfolk hesitated and then seemed to make a decision. "I hope you will not take this amiss, Wiltshire, and it is no reflection on Anne, but I have been troubled about Christmas. This will be the first for the king without Catherine and his daughter."

"And a fine relief it will be!" George snapped.

"For you. For Anne . . . yes. But for the king? Catherine was like an old shoe, ugly but comfortable." Norfolk was clearly not comfortable with this situation, though he was not about to protest it. "And the king is really very fond of Mary. He will miss her, her music, her adoration, her joy in being with him . . ."

"Anne will keep him busy," Wiltshire said, and then added, "Pardon me, gentlemen, let us all be seated and let me send for some refreshment."

Norfolk dropped back into the chair he had been sitting in, George and Denoriel took the settle, and Wiltshire seated himself in the second chair, after signaling to a servant to bring wine and cakes. When each had a filled glass in hand, Norfolk cleared his throat.

"It is true that Anne can occupy the king, and while she is with him, he will not repine. But you know and I know she cannot be there every moment. There are times when her presence at his side would not only be politically provocative but would strongly reinforce the scurrilous rumors that she is Henry's mistress." Denoriel listened with intense interest, for there was no one who was as skilled in the delicate movement of the court as Norfolk. "When the Lord of Misrule comes in, and the Mound opens on its surprise, and on a dozen or more significant moments during the celebrations, Henry will be alone. There will be no adoring face for him to look into . . ."

"Why not?" Denoriel asked.

All the men turned to look at him with shocked faces.

"There are proprieties that cannot be ignored," Wiltshire said. "Much as I would like Anne—"

"Not Lady Anne, my lord," Denoriel said, "the king's own dear son, who loves his father near to worship and can see no fault in him, who will look as adoring as any man could desire, and enjoy without criticism everything presented."

"God's grace," Norfolk breathed, "I had forgotten Richmond. How did you happen to think of him Lord Denno?"

Denoriel laughed. "Because His Grace of Richmond and I are very good friends. Wool. You remember the wool I needed for the carpets I wished to have made? Well, there are no carpets at the moment, but there are fine Holland woolens, and I still buy wool from the north. And what better and safer lodging could I have—at no cost, too—than a chamber at Sheriff Hutton? I have visited His Grace of Richmond at least twice a year and sometimes much more often since the boy went north."

"I had no idea," Norfolk said, not entirely pleased.

"There was some talk about bringing Richmond south after an attack on the cortege coming from Pontefract, but for some reason that was put off," Wiltshire remarked.

That vagueness about the cause of putting off Harry's return to court probably meant that Anne had opposed the idea. Denoriel was not certain whether it was because she wanted no rival for King Henry's attention or because she feared the boy might speak against her. Denoriel knew Harry would not do that. And the king must not be allowed to be lonely and unhappy. Anne might think it served her purpose by reminding him she would have been with him if she were his wife, but Denoriel wondered if the diminution of his pleasure might not make the king wonder whether his long pursuit of Anne was worthwhile.

Beside that, Harry would love a Christmas at court. He was nearly thirteen and growing restless. Although the hard strictures against his riding out had been relaxed, he was now at an age that wanted to see and experience new things. Several times he had asked Denoriel if they could not "take a little trip together," his eyes saying what his lips could not. And Denoriel had been sorely tempted to take the boy Underhill again. But encouraging his desire for Underhill was not healthy. This would be better, fixing his mind on the delights of his own mortal world.

"But do you not all think that Richmond will make a happy substitute for Mary?" Denoriel insisted. "He is not so musical . . . well, if he sings right now he will provide amusement of another sort. He will have his father in fits of laughter because his voice is breaking . . . but he adores the king and he has no objection at all to Lady Anne."

"What can he know about her?" Wiltshire asked harshly.

"What I told him," Denoriel said flatly. "That Lady Anne is a good and gracious lady, that the king loves her dearly, and that her only wish is to make King Henry happy and, if God wills, give him an heir to his throne."

"But if she gives the king an heir, that would exclude Richmond." Wiltshire looked skeptical.

"Yes, indeed, and nothing could make Richmond more happy than to be excluded from the succession forever," Denoriel countered. "I cannot speak for the future, of course, but right now, and indeed, for as long as I have known him, the very last thing he wants is to be king. He is a very good boy, my lords, but he does not love his book as well as he loves his horse and he regards the council sessions that he must attend as a form of penance—good for him but dull and painful. To him, kingship is only more, much more, of the same penance. I assure you that Richmond will welcome Lady Anne with goodwill and every courtesy he can devise. And you know, I am sure, that neither Catherine nor her daughter Mary have ever regarded him with favor."

Norfolk and Wiltshire looked at each other. "Should we broach this to the king?" Norfolk asked. "But what reason can we give that does not mention the absences at court?"

"A very simple reason, and a true one," Denoriel offered. "That the boy is near thirteen years of age, that he feels isolated and confined in the north. That he misses his father and greatly desires to show how much he worships and honors the king. That he yearns for adventure and new sights."

"Good enough," Norfolk said. "I doubt the king will object . . . if there is no opposition."

Wiltshire nodded. "I will speak to Anne. I will point out that the boy writes to his father frequently and that if he asks to come, Henry would not wish to refuse. So why not make a necessity into a gracious welcome . . ." He turned to George. "And since we are back to the Christmas festivities, the matter of the wine, or most of it, being settled, is there anything else you need from me?"

"A list of those suitable to be named Lord of Misrule, if there are men you would like to see so honored," George replied promptly. "I can use my own friends . . . well, some of them. The last thing we need is sly innuendo or coarse jests. But because of . . . of the lack the king may feel, we need some startling entertainments for times when he must be on the dais alone. I have in hand players for several masques and the usual tumblers and jugglers, but I would like something special."

"You need a conjuror," Denoriel said. "For when the Mound comes in, for example. If there were a great cloud of colored smoke when it opened and the duke of Richmond stepped out of that—"

"Magic?" Norfolk and Wiltshire exclaimed in chorus.

"Not real magic," Denoriel said, "mountebank tricks that the mountebank will himself expose for the amusement of the court. He could even allow some of the courtiers to use his devices and perform a trick themselves. Thus all the court can see no true witchcraft was involved."

"Do you know of such a conjuror?" George asked eagerly.

"Not here in London, no," Denoriel replied sadly. "I knew of one in Hungary, but he is long since fled . . . or dead. I thought you would know."

"No magician in London would admit he was a fake and show people his fakery. They all wish to be thought true wonder-workers." George looked disappointed. "How did you know this one you speak of was willing to expose his tricks?"

"Because he taught many of them to me," Denoriel said, smiling. "Since I know I have no more magic in me than my scullery maid—" That was true enough; Denoriel's scullery maid was a Low Court Elven maid with considerable power. "—and I could do the tricks as well as he, after some practice, I knew there was no true witchcraft in it."

"You can do magic tricks!" That was no question; it was a demand. George turned toward Denoriel, who slid back into the corner of the settle.

"That was long ago," Denoriel protested faintly. "I am long out of practice. I could not . . ."

"Oh yes you can," George said emphatically. "You will make an ideal Lord of Misrule. You have two months to practice, and I swear I will murder you if you try to refuse."

"Hmmm, yes," Norfolk said thoughtfully. "You are not English, but you can be trusted. I am not so sure that I would wish to trust any common conjurer with an open entrée into the court."

Denoriel swallowed hard so all the men could see his uneasiness—which was, of course, entirely feigned. "Very well, I will see what tricks I can muster and practice them, but I truly am not fit to be Lord of Misrule. I have no idea what to say . . ."

"Make no pother about that," George assured him buoyantly. "I will write out several speeches for you. You need only commit them to mind and say them entire or in parts when the Lord of Misrule must speak."

"And what do I wear?" Denoriel asked pathetically.

George Boleyn leapt to his feet and extended a hand to pull Denoriel out of his seat. He bowed quickly to his father and to Norfolk. Guessing his intention, Denoriel also bowed and caught up his cloak from the back of the settle.

"We will devise something, never you fear," George said as he hurried toward the door. "And you will be masked, you know, so you need not worry about your customers recognizing you and accusing you of magicking their accounts."

Although he continued to protest, Denoriel could not have been more satisfied with the outcome of the morning's meeting. Not only had he finally arranged for Harry to come to court, but he had arranged for his own attendance too. He would be able to watch over Harry, to protect him against any physical, mortal attack, and to counsel him about sycophants and flatterers who would try to take advantage of his good nature or those who might slyly hurt his feelings.

In fact, of all the Sidhe directly involved in the affairs of England, only Denoriel had been enjoying himself over the years between 1529 and 1531. True, Denoriel had to Gate back and forth between London and Sheriff Hutton, but all the Gates had the feel of Treowth about them now, and he soon shook off his anxiety. His confidence had been buoyed up too by the king's frantic efforts to find some path to a divorce; as long as Henry's intention to marry Anne remained fixed, Harry was no longer important.

The boy was a delight to him, growing, as he passed his twelfth year, into the fine stripling his childhood had promised. If he was no great scholar—his Latin was sadly rudimentary, his Greek nearly nonexistent—he could speak good French and his manners were exemplary. He had other skills, honed by Denoriel, mostly in private. He was a good swordsman, a superior horseman, a decent bowman for his age and size, and a remarkably fine shot with the strange gun he had brought from the Bazaar.

He was learning politics too, from Sir Edward and his other councilors, but Denoriel was not polishing his ability as a sportsman without purpose. The Sidhe had given some thought to what was to become of his beloved ward. Was Harry to be no more than another useless bored and idle popinjay of a courtier? And if he were that and the king never had a legitimate son, would he not be a danger to whoever held the throne? His Harry could not sink into obscurity because of the blood in his veins and the status of premier nobleman in the kingdom which King Henry had fixed upon him.

It would not do. To live safe from royal suspicion, Harry must become an honored and trusted agent of the Crown—preferably with his duties set outside England. With his calm and humorous disposition and his closeness to the throne, Denoriel could foresee for Harry a long life of satisfaction and usefulness as a diplomat. And for that his skill as a sportsman would be as important in many cases as his knowledge of politics.

Now Harry's suitability for that life seemed about to be tested. He must please his father, charm Anne Boleyn, and manage not to offend a flock of jealous courtiers looking for offense.

During the second week of November, Denoriel arrived in Sheriff Hutton carrying the duke of Norfolk's command that Richmond come to court for the Christmas celebrations. No one could be certain of the weather at that time of year, and plenty of time had been allowed for travel. Even so they were nearly late.

It rained two days out of three, and in many places the ditching and draining being half-done or totally neglected, the roads were foul pits of mud. To add to the difficulty, the law that roads be fifty feet wide was largely observed by ignoring it. In far too many places there was hardly twelve feet from verge to verge, and those verges—again contrary to law—were overgrown with bushes so that travelers were forced into the rutted and fetlock-deep mud in the center of the road.

The overgrown verges also left the travelers open to attack from outlaws hidden in the brush. The constant rain and aching cold—and the number and obvious armed strength of their party—saved them from that, but at some point in the journey, they knew they would not make London in time. FitzRoy and his guards and servants with Denoriel and Sir Edward simply left the baggage carts behind and made for London at the best speed of the saddle horses.

Denoriel did not dare express surprise or complaint since he was supposed to have traveled this way many times. To his relief and amusement, FitzRoy thought it great fun. He never seemed to mind being cold and wet, which Denoriel alleviated with a little spell for warmth as soon as he noticed his Harry shivering, and the boy positively delighted in the small, dark, dirty alehouses where they often had to stop for shelter when it became impossible to reach the elegant lodgings Norfolk had arranged. Harry slept on the floor without protest, stamped on roaches and other nameless creatures that tried to invade the bedding, and squashed lice with only a sigh.

That forbearance was doubtless partly inspired by the fact that in the mean hovels where there was no other entertainment and no one to tell tales to the court, Denoriel practiced his feats of legerdemain. Sir Edward was uneasy . . . until Denoriel rubbed Sir Edward's own hands with two different powders, and Sir Edward himself made smoke by clapping his hands together. It was nowhere near as dense or strongly colored as the smoke Lord Denno made, but that, Lord Denno said, was a matter of practice.

Entertainment aside, Denoriel mentioned to Harry

that he would make a fine diplomat, as a great part of a diplomat's time seemed to be taken up in traveling—in the greatest discomfort—from place to place. The idea enchanted Harry, who had only recently regretfully given up the notion of being a merchant like Lord Denno. He had finally come to accept the fact that his being a merchant could never be permitted. A foreign lord was not important enough to disgrace his title by mercantile activity, but the premier duke of England could not so embarrass his good name.

By the time they reached London, no one would have guessed—except for the fine horses they rode— that Harry was the premier duke of England; they looked more like beggars come to town. All the changes of clothing they had been able to carry in their saddle-bags were so mud-stained and filthy that it was impossible to tell Tolliver, the lowest of the grooms, from Harry himself.

Obviously they could not present themselves at court in this condition—not that Denoriel knew where the court was. Nor could they spend too much time seeking shelter, as the short winter day was coming to a close. Denoriel would have taken the party to his house, except that he was sure Norfolk would disapprove of such familiarity without permission. The duke now seemed resigned to Lord Denno's relationship with Harry, but Denoriel did not want to take any advantage that might raise the duke's doubts again. He asked Sir Edward to lead them to Norfolk's London residence.

If Norfolk was not there, then Denoriel would offer the house on Bucklersbury. But the duke was at home—it was, for a change, pouring rain mixed with sleet, and he had cancelled several appointments. He came running down the stairway himself to greet his guests with cries of relief because they were already more than a week behind their estimated arrival and he had been worried. Relief soon mingled with horror when he learned they had no baggage and had no idea when it would arrive, if ever.

Servants were sent scurrying for changes of clothing, although the duke said, apologetically, that he did not think the servants would find anything to fit Lord Denno, who was so tall. Denoriel promptly eliminated that concern by reminding Norfolk that he had a home in London and would have no trouble changing his clothing.

He realized too late that being rid of him had been Norfolk's purpose, but he left forthwith. It would be worse to make excuses to stay than to leave Harry to his own devices. He couldn't be with the boy every moment; Harry would have to manage on his own. Later he learned he had missed the perfect confirmation of his idea that the boy would make a diplomat—if he lived.

Taking advantage of their condition, Norfolk sent his ward's servants off to be cleaned and reclothed. He summoned his own valet and dressers to his son's apartment, in which FitzRoy would temporarily be accommodated because it was warm while another apartment was prepared for him. FitzRoy was stripped and a bath brought up. When he was clean and wrapped in one of Henry's bedgowns, Norfolk invited him to sit down to a belated meal and himself joined him.

After commonplaces about the trip and FitzRoy's health and what he was currently studying, Norfolk got to what he really wanted to know and asked about Lord Denno.

"I' faith, we are good friends now," FitzRoy said.

"Since I went to live in the north, Lord Denno has been coming several times a year to see about his wool—actually I think he may own the sheep from which it is sheared. He is very particular about the wool."

"Wool is sheared in the spring," Norfolk remarked. "Why would he need to come north several times a year?"

"I said he was particular. He comes to inspect the sheep in the summer and autumn, sometimes even in winter. Whenever he comes, he stays at Sheriff Hutton. He says it is because the accommodation is free, but I think he doesn't care a bit for that. He's very rich, you know. Very rich."

"Then I suppose he need not ask you for any favors." Harry was very good at reading nuances of expression. Norfolk was probing, and Harry was happy to give him an answer of which he would approve.

"What kind of favor could I do Lord Denno?" he asked, innocently. "He'll take nothing from me, unless it is a keepsake of some sort—one of my poems, or suchlike. I wish I could think of something. I'd do it quick enough. He's saved my life twice, you know, once at Windsor and once when something . . . a plague of tiny things like mice or rats gone quite mad, attacked my cortege when we were first going to Sheriff Hutton."

Norfolk frowned. "Lord Denno shouldn't remind you of that. It's enough to give you nightmares."

FitzRoy laughed. "Lord Denno has never mentioned either rescue—except to tell me that the men who attacked me in Windsor were dead. That was because I asked him directly whether they would try to hurt me again."

Norfolk was still frowning, but now it was in puzzlement. "Then what do you talk about when he comes to visit you? I assume he does spend some time with you when he comes to Sheriff Hutton."

"Talk? About wool and his accursed sheep." FitzRoy laughed again. "And about gardens. Lord Denno has a passion for flowers and plantings. Sometimes we talk about books. He likes Caesar and Herodotus. But mostly we fence or shoot at butts or ride out hunting." For a moment the boy's eyes grew misty, but all he said was, "He's a capital horseman, Lord Denno. And he tells me about the court. He admires the Lady Anne very much, I think, for making my father happy."

Nothing to fear there . . . yet, Norfolk thought, so when a servant came in with some of Lord Henry's outgrown clothing, Norfolk wished his charge a good and quiet night's sleep and left, presumably to allow the boy to try on the garments in private and then go to bed. Actually he made his way to the room assigned to Sir Edward to probe further.

First Norfolk thanked FitzRoy's master of the horse for bringing the boy safely to London. He received a smiling denial, a reference to the passionate devotion of FitzRoy's servants and guardsmen, and a laughing encomium of Lord Denno's ability to find some hovel or other to shelter in when all hope seemed lost.

That gave Norfolk his opening. "I had no idea that Lord Denno was such an intimate in Richmond's household," he said rather coldly. "Is that wise?"

"It used to worry me," Sir Edward admitted, "but in the beginning none of His Grace's councilors wished to add any more grief and anxiety to him. He was upset enough at losing his playmates, your son and daughter, and the familiar servants of Windsor. Lord Denno's presence did him much good."

"And he took advantage of that to enlarge the intimacy. Richmond will be a *very* rich and very powerful man when he comes of age." Norfolk came directly to the point. "So, what do you think Lord Denno wants?"

Sir Edward shrugged. "We all waited, of course, for the bill to be tendered . . . but there has been no bill. The man has never asked for anything—except his lodging and food—in all the years he has been coming to see His Grace."

There was another opening for information; Norfolk took it. "Then he does come to see Richmond, not to examine his sheep or his wool?"

"I think so," Sir Edward said thoughtfully. "No, I am sure so. Although he does go out and ride about the farms. He often takes His Grace of Richmond with him."

"Inspecting sheep farms?" Norfolk was not certain whether or not to be offended. It was not unheard of for a nobleman to take direct interest in his holdings, but it seemed very "rustic" an occupation.

"I do not think it can do the duke any harm to know where wool, which is so much the wealth of England, comes from." Sir Edward sounded defensive.

"Perhaps not. But what *does* Lord Denno want that is precious enough for him to spend so much time with a child?" Norfolk did not understand this, and he did not like things he could not understand, "It isn't as it was at first, when it looked as if the king might name Richmond his heir. There's no chance of that now, and yet Denno pursues this relationship with the boy."

Sir Edward smiled at him. "Believe it or not, I will swear that it is just being with the boy himself that Lord Denno wants. I made some enquiries, Your Grace. Lord Denno does not need money. He could probably buy his bankers. He pays all tariffs and taxes promptly. He has never asked any of Richmond's councilors for any favor at all and has never been in any trouble with the law."

"So?" Norfolk persisted.

"So, I stand by what I said." Sir Edward smiled to soften the defiance. "I know Lord Denno has no one in the world to call his own. His own family is all dead, and I think because of the terrible pain that caused him he hesitates to marry and have children. I think what he wants from Richmond is . . . the feeling that he has someone. There is no doubt in my mind that he sincerely loves the little duke, that he would lay down his life for the boy."

"Hmmm. I like him myself, you know," Norfolk confessed. "It is only the thought of a foreigner having such a grip on someone as powerful as Richmond will be that makes me uneasy. And Richmond admits he would do Lord Denno any favor he could but that he cannot think of any—which means Denno has put nothing in his head." He still didn't understand it— and he wished devoutly that the foreigner would do or ask for something so that he would at least know where the man stood! Still—it all seemed harmless enough. "So, for now it seems safe to allow all the access to Lord Denno that Richmond desires."

"You relieve my mind," Sir Edward said. "Cheerful and pleasant as Richmond is, he has a will of his own— and when it is crossed he can be vicious and of long memory."

Now this was something that Norfolk understood. Richmond had his mother's sweet and biddable manner most of the time—but cross him, and it seemed, you got Great Harry in a rage. "Ah. And he will have the king's ear . . . So, the servants and guards . . . you say they are fond of him and he of them? I had no time to look at them—not that there would have been much I could see under the mud. Are they fitting to attend and guard the duke in Greenwich?"

Sir Edward nodded. "The guards are the same ones

you yourself appointed in Windsor. They love that boy like a son. When he was lost, only his servants continued to search the forest in the dark, which no one else would do for fear of the terrible creatures that had attacked us. Nor did they fear they would be faulted. Everyone else had quit the field. They are devoted."

Devoted was precisely what Norfolk wanted. "Good enough. They know the ways of the court, too, having been royal guards. The others?"

"The grooms will be fine, although there are only two," Sir Edward replied. "They know horses and are quite capable of holding their own with other servitors. If the king offers Richmond more horses, he may need one or two more under-grooms, which will not be a problem. The valet . . . most interesting man. Although he is common born, his speech is fine, and I have never known him to be at a loss in any situation. When we ride, he wears a sword, and he can use it . . . I have seen him do so. His sense of style seems good, too, but as you know we have little occasion for full court dress at Sheriff Hutton or Pontefract. You might want to appoint an under-valet with knowledge of what will be needed."

"Good. Good." Norfolk's brow cleared. Whatever else was going on, Richmond was going to be presentable, it seemed. "As I said I do not wish to upset Richmond if it is not a dire necessity. I want him happy."

"I, too," Sir Edward said, smiling. "He is a wonderful boy, when he is not crossed—so good at heart, so true and loyal. One cannot help caring for him."

Satisfied, Norfolk rose and bid Sir Edward a good night. He had a good night himself, relieved that he would not need to come into conflict with Richmond about his friend and servants just before the boy was restored to his father. From what Sir Edward said,

Richmond would not be easy to cow. Norfolk did not want the king to hear complaints about his son being deprived of trusted servants.

They were to be trusted, too, Norfolk thought with satisfaction when Richmond came down to breakfast, shepherded by his valet, who wore a remarkably long knife at the back of his belt, and two of his armed guards.

The boy was bright and wide-eyed, dressed sensibly for riding. Richmond said a polite good morning and then begged to be allowed to see a little of London before being sent to Greenwich. It had been raining so hard when they arrived, he complained, that he could see nothing.

Since Norfolk knew the king was at Hampton Court and would be engaged with the French and Imperial ambassadors, he was about to agree to allow Richmond to explore London when a page with very wide eyes entered and bowed and said, "Lady Anne Boleyn is come and asking for you, Your Grace."

Anne! At this hour of the morning? Norfolk rose, waving at FitzRoy to go on with his breakfast and went out with the page. Anne was waiting in the great withdrawing room, standing before the blazing fire, one hand raised to loosen the pin on her cloak. As he bowed, Norfolk noted that even that common gesture was invested with a kind of special grace.

"My lady, welcome. Please, let me take your cloak and seat yourself. Can I offer you some mulled wine?"

But Anne was not to be so easily pacified with courtesy and formality. "You can offer me some explanations, uncle. I have heard that Richmond has arrived and is your guest. Why?"

"My dear Anne," Norfolk said, "this was no secret plan of mine. It was discussed with your father and your brother over a month ago, and your father assured me that he would explain to you why we all felt it necessary that Richmond should come."

"So he did, but I—"

Anne stopped speaking abruptly in response to a timid scratch on the door. She looked furious, but Norfolk had already cried out, "Come," delighted that anyone else should bear the brunt of Anne's wrath.

The door opened little more than a crack, and FitzRoy peeped inside. "Please do forgive this intrusion," he said, "but I heard that Lady Anne was here. I am so desirous of meeting her. I was afraid she would leave without my having any chance to greet her."

Both adults stood staring at the opening too surprised to speak. Since there had been no rejection, FitzRoy took this as an invitation, opened the door wider, and poked in a smiling face.

"May I come in?"

"Yes," Anne said, recovering from her surprise, but not so far as to put on a cool manner. "Do, indeed, come in."

FitzRoy slipped inside, closed the door behind him, and made a handsome bow to Anne, murmuring, "Madame, I am very happy to meet you."

"Are you?" she asked, directly. Norfolk held his breath. What would the boy make of such rudeness?

"Yes, truly," FitzRoy replied earnestly, "For I have heard how happy you make my dear father, and anyone who brings him joy is very welcome to me, indeed."

Anne regarded him skeptically. "But if his joy is made complete, and God wills it, you may have a brother who will stand between you and the throne of England."

Norfolk drew in a sharp breath at the brutal directness, but FitzRoy only continued to smile, his eyes fixed in sweet innocence on Anne's face.

"I will pray with all my strength for that happy outcome," FitzRoy said. "Daily. Perhaps that is unkind, praying for a burden I myself fear to fall upon another, but I do not feel myself fit to carry that burden. And to give my father a legitimate prince would make him the happiest of men as well as the most blessed of kings."

Anne dropped the cloak she had removed but had been holding on to the chair nearest her and advanced over the broad-beamed, shining floor toward FitzRoy. She held out her hand, and the boy put his own into it without hesitation. She drew him with her back toward the fire. Norfolk backed away slowly and carefully so as not to draw any attention.

"Do you know what you are saying, Richmond?" Anne asked, gesturing him toward one end of a dark wood settle cushioned in crimson velvet and seating herself at the other end. There was a very faint smile on her lips, and she cocked her head in a charming look of doubt. "Or has someone been telling you what to say to me?"

FitzRoy sat and looked at her soberly. "No one even suggested that we might meet, madam, and no one has ever talked to me about you, aside from Lord Denno, who said you were a good, fair lady who has brought my father joy he has lacked in other company. But I do have ears—even if my councilors seem to think all children are deaf—and so I have heard them talking."

"About me?" Anne's voice was sharp and Norfolk held his breath.

"No, madam, about the king's concern for the succession," he said forthrightly—and correctly. "I have become aware that for me to come to the throne would cause strong protest, perhaps even war between those who favored me and those who favored Princess Mary."

Anne settled herself more comfortably against the cushions. "Ah, Princess Mary. She has no stain of bastard birth, so why should she not be her father's heir?"

"Because she is a woman," he replied on the instant. "Please do not frown at me, Lady Anne. I mean no shame on women in a general way nor do I support what my councilors call the Salic law in France, but to secure the next generation on the throne, the princess must marry. Only a reigning prince or his heir would be a suitable husband, and having taken such a husband, who will rule England?"

"Who, indeed?" Anne replied, making a little moue of distaste. "We would likely be an Imperial province or a French one."

"And so my father seeks a legitimate son to rule after him to ensure the peace and independence of this realm." He hesitated, then smiled broadly and a little brashly at her. "And I think he has chosen a very pretty lady to furnish that heir."

The hard glare in Anne's black eyes had softened some minutes earlier and she smiled at the boy who looked hopefully at her. "So you would not feel deprived if I were to marry your father and give him a son?"

"Not at all," FitzRoy said heartily. His nose wrinkled. "There is *nothing* duller than listening to petitions or measuring complaints against the law. You know what I would really like?" His eyes brightened from their usual dull light brown to a sparkling hazel. "I would like to be the king's ambassador and go to Paris and Madrid and Venice and Rome. No one could have his majesty's interests or those of England more to heart than I—and I could travel and see new things."

Anne was chuckling softly now. Suspicious and self-centered as she was, even she could see the naked truth in a child's eyes. She knew that in the future this child might change his mind and grow to be a danger, but for now he would do her no harm, and he might do her good.

"Well, you may count on me, if I have the power, to forward your desire in every way I can," she said, magnanimously. "I have had great pleasure in meeting you, Your Grace. And I hope we may meet again."

She rose and the boy rose also, putting out his hand and saying, "Surely we will, Lady Anne. I look forward to it. And you will tell my father of my wishes? I look forward also to hearing from you what he will say."

"You will be able to ask him yourself," she said, reaching for her cloak.

"Of course. But I will have a better hope of a sympathetic hearing if my wish comes from you, my lady." He gave her a sly look, and Norfolk smothered a chuckle. If the boy was no scholar of books, he was certainly well read in human nature.

She laughed and said, "Flatterer," but as Norfolk came forward to take the cloak from her hand and place it on her shoulders, he could see she was pleased, and then she bent and kissed FitzRoy's cheek and a notion came to him.

"Anne," Norfolk said, as he closed the door behind them and walked with her into the central hall where her two women waited, "I had a thought and I wonder if you would tell me what you think about it."

"Yes?" Anne Boleyn had come here angered, and had not expected to leave charmed and soothed. And by a little boy! In that, he was entirely like his father, who could charm the birds from the trees when he chose. Yet she could not doubt his sincerity; he might know how to charm, but he was not yet skilled enough to dissemble.

Her Uncle Norfolk, on the other hand . . .

The black eyes flashed. Anne knew her uncle wanted
to see her married to the king to ensure his own future
influence, but Norfolk never hesitated to use her at
any time. She always needed to measure what he asked
against what was best for her. This time, however, he
seemed more thoughtful than sly.

"Richmond," he continued, "is, of course, very eager
to see his father, but we have been racking our brains
for a suitable 'surprise' to come out of the Mound this
year. You remember that last year it was Princess Mary
and those girls, all playing instruments. What if this
year we make that surprise Richmond? Would that not
remove any regret Henry might feel over Mary and her
musical ladies?"

For a moment Anne stood quite still. She had been
wavering pro and con a plan to come out of the Mound
herself, although she knew that would arouse strong
objections. She had wondered whether the new enemies
she would make and the reinforcement of older angers
would add up to an advantage or disadvantage toward
binding Henry to her. Yet, dared she allow someone else
to take that place, someone who could turn the moment
against her?

Now she said, more to herself than to Norfolk, "Yes,
I remember that, and that chosen gentlemen the king
wished to honor came and took the ladies' instruments
and then danced with them—Henry with Mary."

"So do you think the king would enjoy the surprise
of having Richmond come out of the mound?" Norfolk persisted.

Anne raised her head slowly to look Norfolk right in
the face. "Yes," she murmured. "It is a very good idea,
but instead of Henry coming forward to welcome the
boy, when he comes out, Richmond will have to say
something suitable, and then choose me for a dance."

Norfolk had not expected that, and she could see from his expression that her suggestion was not welcome. Still, he must think that it was better than having Anne come out of the Mound herself, which he must have known she had been planning. "Done," he said, "only won't you look silly dancing with a child?"

She smiled up at him. "Oh, FitzRoy is quite tall enough, taking after his father as he does. That will suit me admirably."

CHAPTER 27

Norfolk courteously saw Anne and her ladies to the door. He was well pleased when he returned to the breakfast parlor, to which Richmond had also returned, and he readily gave permission for the boy to see something of London. He was less pleased when, just as he was suggesting that FitzRoy rest for another day until his old friend, Norfolk's son, Lord Henry, could guide him, Lord Denno was announced.

Richmond's face settled into a decidedly mulish expression and he said, "I am no longer six years old, Your Grace. And I am in the best of health, capable of a full day's hard hunting without fatigue. I do not need another day's rest. I wish to start seeing London today."

Norfolk opened his mouth to order the boy to his room, and remembered that he was being addressed by the premier nobleman in the kingdom who would soon be clasped hard in the king's arms. He saw that to insist Richmond spend a day tapping his toes while he waited for his own son Henry would ensure

Richmond would hate Henry on sight when he saw him again.

"Well . . . well . . . Let me think who would be suitable to guide you if you will not wait for my son," he said, temporizing.

"A guide is ready," Richmond said, his voice hard and uncompromising. "Lord Denno will show me everything. He lives in London, you know, and conducts his business from here."

"Lord Denno is not sufficient escort," Norfolk said, trying to sound reasonable and at least provide some buffer against the foreigner.

Richmond laughed, but not pleasantly. "I will lay odds that Lord Denno is a far better swordsman than Lord Henry, but that doesn't matter. Gerrit and Shaylor are on duty and will ride with us, and likely Dunstan and Ladbroke too." He spoke around a grim smile. "I am never unprotected, Your Grace, and—" He patted the sword Norfolk had not noticed he was wearing "—I am not unable to protect myself."

Which left Norfolk to curse himself for forgetting that Richmond was *not* six years old, was, indeed, entering that age which begets rebellion in the best-trained boy. Hastily he tried to retrieve Richmond's good opinion by offering fresh mounts. The young duke's good humor was instantly restored. He accepted Norfolk's offer with thanks, only remarking blandly that the horses might need another day's rest. They had carried riders, after all, while the riders merely sat in the saddle.

Whereupon, before Norfolk could reply, Richmond was on his feet, bowing, and in another instant out the door. No, Norfolk thought, he would not be easy to cow—say, instead, impossible. And Sir Edward was right. There would be no separating him from Denno or his servants, at least not until his confidence was won. Winning Richmond's confidence, Norfolk foresaw, signaling a servant and giving the order about the horses, would take time and very careful handling.

He would need to have a serious talk with Henry about dealing with Richmond. Or maybe he should keep the boys apart? Henry's temper . . . But surely he would understand that Richmond was far his superior in status and was at that touchy stage between childhood and manhood which needs to be treated with respect. Norfolk sighed. Henry wasn't out of that stage yet himself.

At least for today he need fear no disaster. Denno would protect Richmond and probably raise no political problems in one day. And the boy would be safe, Norfolk thought, as he came out of the breakfast parlor and saw that Richmond's two guardsmen were now planted firmly in front of the door of the small withdrawing room. They were talking to each other, but he saw that one pair of eyes had fixed on him and the other pair watched the front door.

A few moments earlier, a page had directed FitzRoy to the small withdrawing room. He had found Denoriel there staring thoughtfully into the fire. The Sidhe turned as he came forward, and smiled.

"I did it!" FitzRoy said, softly, but his eyes were bright with triumph. "I rolled right over Norfolk. He was going to send me to my room to play with my toys and wait until tomorrow for Henry to show me London."

Denoriel's high-arched brows rose even further. "Hmmm? I myself would prefer that you not see the parts of London Lord Henry might show you—at least, not until you are a few years older."

"I' faith?" FitzRoy giggled. "Maybe it would have been worth while to wait for him. *You* aren't likely to satisfy *that* curiosity."

"Not for a year or two more anyway." Denoriel grinned. "Did you remember to order the horses?"

"Norfolk is doing that—to coddle my temper after treating me like a child. Oh. I don't know whether he'll order a horse for you. Is Miralys—"

Denoriel laughed. "Miralys is just fine and would probably throw me off and jump up and down on me if I dared ride another horse."

FitzRoy sighed, but he could not say anything about Lady Aeron. Instead he asked where they would go, and Denoriel offered a number of destinations. "Actually I hadn't intended to use the horses today. I had thought of taking a boat on the river—but we can do that tomorrow."

"Will I be free tomorrow?" FitzRoy asked, quietly. "I thought I would see my father right away, but Norfolk says he's at Hampton Court busy with ambassadors."

FitzRoy looked down as he spoke, but Denoriel heard the hurt in his voice. "Do you want to lay odds that no one has told the king that you have arrived?"

He looked up, surprised. "But why not?"

"Of that, I cannot be sure," Denno said, not wishing to betray the plans that George Boleyn had bruited about, "Only that Norfolk would want to present you in a way that will redound to his credit and possibly would wish Lord Henry to accompany you into the king's presence. Also, remember, you have no clothes."

"Ah. Yes." FitzRoy sighed gustily. "Dunstan has summoned tailors. But would my father care about my clothes?"

Denoriel laughed. "Likely not, but Norfolk would. Who knows what purpose the courtiers would assign to his presenting you in his son's cast-offs."

FitzRoy blinked. "If every little thing can be made out to have meaning, I am not sure I am going to like being at court. I want to see my father, but . . ."

"Each day as it comes, Harry," Denoriel advised. "Take each day as it comes. Likely as not Norfolk has a perfectly innocent purpose—and one that may have nothing to do with you at all. Say, for example, that he does not want the king diverted from his meeting with the ambassadors."

"You always say one day at a time, and it's mostly you're right, but I still want to see my father." Somehow the boy sounded plaintive and imperious, all at the same time. "Could I insist that tomorrow a messenger be sent to him?"

Like father, like son, Denoriel thought. Harry had as little use for state duties as King Henry, who, he was sure, would be delighted to put the ambassadors off while he greeted his son. He shook his head.

"I don't know what to say about that, but surely you can wait until this afternoon, after we look at the city. I—"

The door opening interrupted him, and Gerrit put his head in to say that the horses were ready. He and Shaylor preceded FitzRoy out. Ladbroke was already mounted. Denoriel put FitzRoy up into the saddle of a fine-looking black and himself mounted Miralys. Shaylor mounted while Gerrit watched; then Gerrit mounted. Dunstan had excused himself, his oversight of the tailors currently more important, as he foresaw little threat to FitzRoy in Denoriel's company.

They rode north along the King Street to Charing Cross where they bent right into The Strand, on the way passing the grounds of York House, which had been Wolsey's and was now the king's. Denoriel told Harry that it seemed now to be Lady Anne's favorite place of residence and there was talk of the king enlarging it. Other large noblemen's houses—almost palaces really—could be seen through trees. The houses fronted on the river which actually made quicker and easier transportation to the city than horses.

FitzRoy showed no interest in those great houses until they passed Temple Bar and saw the buildings of the Temple. He drew rein as they came to the gate and asked Denoriel if the law students allowed visitors to see the tombs of William Marshall and his family. The request being readily agreed to by the porter as soon as he heard who was making it, they were escorted to the church where, in the west part, outside the choir they found the monuments.

After examining the tombs of William Marshall the elder, his son, also William, and the next brother, Gilbert, FitzRoy quietly shook his head. "It's very strange, isn't it? He was a great man and had a large family—five sons—and yet his house and name failed with that second generation."

"That's a grim thought," Denoriel said, putting his hand on the boy's shoulder and steering him gently toward the door. "The younger William was certainly murdered and Gilbert probably was too—"

FitzRoy looked surprised. "Master Palsgrave never said anything about murder."

Denoriel didn't answer until he had distributed the proper largesse to those who had accompanied them and they were remounted. Then he said lightly, "Likely because the murders were the king's doing. The third Henry would take no prizes for virtue, although he was a great patron of the arts. He should have been an architect instead of a king. He did so love—"

"You sound as if you were there and knew him," FitzRoy said, laughing.

Denoriel laughed too, although he was shocked at the slip. It was too easy to talk to Harry; he must be careful. He said, "Our teachers are a bit fairer minded, not having any need to be wary of what a royal official might think if he heard a tutor declaring a past king a murderer."

"Pooh," FitzRoy responded. "Who cares about a king who's been dead over two hundred years. Still, it makes one think . . . Five sons and not a grandson with his name. And even the son of the eldest daughter was murdered. Are you *sure* it wasn't a curse?"

"Not of mine," Denoriel said lightly and picked up the pace so that they passed the remainder of Fleet Street quickly.

He noticed that FitzRoy was looking curiously at some of the shops, but he did not suggest stopping, because he was sure the greater market along Cheapside would be more interesting. Thus he turned north at Ludgate and east again on the narrow street that ran along the north side of St. Paul's church. The lane met another running north and south—south was the entrance to the church; north debouched into the market.

FitzRoy probably knew from the hubbub of sound when they reached the cross-lane that the market was to the north. He hesitated briefly, cast a rather guilty glance southward, because he must have suspected that the "proper" thing to do was to visit the cathedral, and then rode north. Where the lane entered Cheapside, the party perforce stopped because the street was thick with people.

Noblemen had considerable privilege. They could and sometimes did drive their horses right down the market, knocking people down and trampling unfortunates and goods. They seldom did it more than once, for none ever made it through the market without being liberally bedewed with rotten fruit and vegetables and well bruised by harder objects like pits launched by slingshot. A few had more violent accidents; staves had been known to be thrust between a horse's legs or a rotten melon to fall from above so that a beast was blinded and stumbled, throwing his rider.

Only very rarely was anyone brought to book for such crimes; there were too many people, too many shops and alleys into which any suspect might melt away and mingle with the crowd. And it was impossible, no matter how powerful the nobleman, to arrest hundreds of sober citizens of London. The commons and burgesses of London were not known for their docility—even to kings.

FitzRoy had been to markets before, but nothing in the mortal world—nor even Underhill which had been much larger but much less concentrated—had prepared him for Cheapside. "Is it always like this?" he shouted over the general hubbub.

"Yes," Denoriel shouted back. "We can go round if you want—"

"No, no," the boy said. "But I think we'd better dismount and go on foot. We'll never get the horses through. Ladbroke can go around leading the horses and we'll meet up again at—at the end of the market?"

He looked at Denoriel who nodded, slid down from Miralys and went back to Ladbroke, carefully handing him the reins which were not attached to much of anything.

"Go back down the street past St. Paul's, which will take you to Watling Street. You can come north again on Dow Gate to the lane that leads to Bucklersbury."

"I know it, m'lord. Shall I wait at your house?"

"Yes. I think we'll all be ready for a nuncheon, a chair, and a drink by the time we get to Threadneedle."

"Right you are, m'lord. I'll warn the servants that you'll be coming with a guest."

When he returned to them, FitzRoy and the two guards had also dismounted. Shaylor took the reins of all three horses and led them back down the street to where Ladbroke could arrange them so he could handle them. Gerrit was forging a way into the crowd with Denoriel and FitzRoy just behind him and, a moment later, Shaylor brought up the rear.

They moved slowly into the center of the street which, while crowded and made more hazardous by the peddlers carrying meat pies and hot buns and roast chicken on skewers and all manner of small goods like ribbons and laces in trays and baskets slung round their necks, was still less clotted with folk than the sides of the street. There the stalls of the merchants who had shops in the market displayed a variety of goods.

In front of each stall generally was a small crowd of unmoving people who were examining the merchandise. To try to make one's way through the customers brought cries of rage and threats or even blows, not only from those whom one necessarily displaced, but from the apprentices and occasional journeyman who were manning the stalls.

In any case FitzRoy was content to make his way a few steps at a time down the less-crowded center, the slow pace giving him plenty of time to stare right and left while the bulk of his guardsmen and Denoriel kept him from being battered. In short order—never mind having finished breakfast less than an hour past—he had eaten a meat pie, a sticky bun, and a chicken leg, which he pronounced the best he had ever had. The seller was long gone, or he would have bought the lot and carried them back with him to the great detriment of all their clothing.

Fortunately he was distracted from trying to go back and find the chicken-leg seller by a sweet metallic chiming. Twisting and rising on his toes to see, he grasped Denoriel's hand and tugged him toward a

silversmith's counter. There he wriggled his way past
two men who were considering a handsome silver bowl
and seized on a round silver ball, slit open and chased
into a design of baby animals, which held another much
smaller silver ball. It was this which made the sweet
chiming when shaken by the attached straight stem.

"A rattle?" Denoriel said faintly. "Were you deprived
of rattles when you were a baby, Harry?"

FitzRoy laughed until he nearly doubled over and
dropped the rattle. "Don't be silly, Denno," he chortled.
"It's for Dickson's little girl. Didn't you know he had
a new baby?"

"I didn't even know he was married," Denoriel said.

"To one of the baker's daughters." FitzRoy chuckled
again. "I think her father threatened to bake him in the
castle oven if he didn't marry her, since she was baking
something in her own oven—"

"Harry!"

"Well, anyhow, he seems to be very happy now. Told
me it was nice to come home to a clean bed and a
willing wife."

Denoriel didn't know what kind of comment to
make to that. He couldn't present a moral lecture;
FitzRoy knew what he was. On the other hand he
didn't want Norfolk or anyone else to claim the boy
had come under an immoral influence. After all,
because he was a foreigner, he would be the first to
be blamed. He would have to speak to Harry about
that, but not now. The boy attending the counter
arrived at that moment.

FitzRoy asked the price of the rattle. The boy, who
was perhaps a year or two older than FitzRoy looked
at his clothes, at Denoriel's, at the two guardsmen, carefully watching the crowd and blocking access to the boy,
and named a sum. FitzRoy laughed and named another,
about one-third what the apprentice had suggested and

added some pithy comments about not thinking him a lamb fit for fleecing.

The apprentice blinked in shock. Noblemen did not chaffer—although they were not above seeing something they wanted and sending a servant to bargain for it. That was the safest way to do business.

Dealing in person with a noble was chancy. One could ask a fair price and hope he or she would recognize that and pay without argument. But noblemen were suspicious and might demand a still lower price. One could ask too high a price and hope the customer would pay, being too ignorant—the mistake he had made with this boy—too proud, or too careless of money to care . . . and not vicious enough to complain to the alderman or guildmaster. But chaffer?

The apprentice's mouth opened and closed. He glanced at the older man, who was standing by, his face expressionless and his arms folded across his chest.

"You needn't look at him," FitzRoy said with a grin. "He'd give you that ridiculous price, but I won't, so either take my money or name a price you'd like better."

Spurred into action by the amusement in FitzRoy's voice, the apprentice took a chance of scorning FitzRoy's offer. He said he could see that FitzRoy wished to drive his master into beggary so that he and all the other members of the merchant's household would starve. He moaned and complained, inching down in his price, and FitzRoy pointed out imperceptible flaws in the rattle, complained of its tone, belittled it in every way he could.

In just over a quarter of an hour, with the participants flushed and invigorated, a price was agreed upon. FitzRoy pulled his purse out of the bosom of his doublet and paid. The rattle was carefully wrapped, a slip of cloth passed through the slits so it would not chime, and Gerrit put the packet into his gown, tied to his belt for security.

When they were clear of the shop, Denoriel asked, "Where did you learn that?" and gave in to the laughter that had been struggling for release.

"Mostly from Ladbroke. I often go with him when he buys for the stable. Sometimes from Dunstan and Bethy. They used to take me to the faires that came to buy me toys and some other things. Was it wrong, Denno?"

Denoriel laughed again. "Not when you are with me or just with your servants, but if you do that in Lord Henry's presence or George Boleyn's or most other noblemen, they will look down their noses at you for being common."

FitzRoy sighed. "I had a feeling from the apprentice's face that I was doing wrong. But it was so much *fun*, Denno. Much more fun than just paying and knowing I'd been cheated."

"Have your fun, my lad. I won't betray you"

Having surreptitiously squeezed Denoriel's hand, FitzRoy took full advantage of the permission given. He bought a handsome brooch and gold and silver embroidery thread for Mistress Bethany; he bought silver buckles for his guardsmen's shoes; he bought silk kerchiefs for the maids who served him in Pontefract and Sheriff Hutton; he bought a truly beautiful gold chain for Dunstan, a magnificent belt for Ladbroke, and a fine one with a silver buckle for Tolliver.

They had stopped for dinner midway. Shaylor had cleared a table at a cookshop for Denoriel and FitzRoy and they had eaten roast fowl, pork pasty, and beef stew and drunk mugs of ale sitting on rough wood benches at a splintery table in glorious vulgarity. The guardsmen ate standing even though FitzRoy invited them to sit with him and Denoriel. It was too hard to leap to one's feet and draw one's weapons, Gerrit explained, when one had one's legs under a table.

FitzRoy protested that an attack was extremely unlikely. Gerrit agreed, but, laughing, pointed out that life's way was seldom to afflict the prepared, but let a man put his legs under a table when he should be standing, and a riot would surely erupt.

Denoriel also laughed, but agreed, and the guardsmen ate on their feet, watching the crowd. But there was no attack. Nothing at all happened to spoil the day, and FitzRoy was shepherded to Denoriel's house where they all rested, drank more ale, and finally rode back to Norfolk's house exhausted but happy.

Shopping, however delightful, had not distracted FitzRoy from matters of more importance. The first words out of his mouth when they entered the withdrawing room where Norfolk awaited them had been to ask whether his father had sent a message. At that point, Norfolk had to confess that King Henry did not yet know his son had arrived. FitzRoy promptly demanded a message be sent, and Norfolk had to explain the plan to have FitzRoy come out of the "Fairy Mound" that was always presented by the first Lord of Misrule to the king.

Norfolk had not liked having Denoriel present when he explained, but Denoriel reminded him that he, Lord Denno, would be the Lord of Misrule that presented the Mound. When FitzRoy had reluctantly agreed to wait another five days to meet his father—after Denoriel had promised to take him to the East Chepe and the shops on London Bridge—he had asked for a refilling of his purse. Norfolk began a lecture on foolish expenditures, but had to acknowledge that FitzRoy had a good price for what he bought, and Denoriel completed his rout by offering to fund FitzRoy's future purchases.

Thus, the next day—Lord Henry still having not arrived—Denoriel took FitzRoy by boat to the foot of Gracechurch Street, from where it was an easy walk to the East Chepe. Another halcyon day passed, but Lord Henry was waiting for them, sour from a furious lecture by his father and irritable because FitzRoy had obviously had a wonderful time. He sneered at FitzRoy's "common" entertainment and promised to show him some gentleman's diversions the next day.

Denoriel warned Dunstan and the guardsmen. He did not really think that Lord Henry would take a boy not yet thirteen to a whorehouse, but he suspected that Lord Henry would know where all the cock-fights, dog-fights, bear-baitings, and less-than-pure masques would be shown.

However, what Lord Henry offered the next day was on its surface harmless. He took FitzRoy to the tennis courts—where FitzRoy was soundly trounced, tennis not being a popular sport in the northern counties. Lord Henry's purpose was to reestablish his dominance over his richer and potentially more powerful "friend." Having dried their sweat, rested, and had an elegant nuncheon—nothing like the crude food available in the markets, which to speak the truth FitzRoy had enjoyed much more—Lord Henry suggested some bouts of fencing.

In pursuit of the purpose of bringing FitzRoy to abject admiration, that was a major mistake. Lord Henry had had good fencing masters, but they were always aware of the exalted rank of their student. Their corrections had been gentle, their exhortations to practice mild.

Denoriel had been more concerned that FitzRoy might find himself fighting for his life. There was nothing gentle at all in the slap and prod of his sword when FitzRoy failed to guard himself adequately.

FitzRoy ended with painful bruises to urge him to greater skill. Denoriel was a brutal taskmaster, but FitzRoy had become, for his age and size, a remarkable swordsman.

He disarmed Lord Henry in five minutes in their first bout. The older boy laughed, putting it down to a freak accident. Still Lord Henry was more careful when they crossed swords again, displaying the most elaborate of his bows and flourishes. If they were supposed to engender fear or amazement, they failed. FitzRoy merely came forward and raised his sword to show he was ready. Bows and flourishes notwithstanding, Lord Henry's sword lay on the ground some feet away where FitzRoy had kicked it—as he had been taught to do—in only a little more time.

Lord Henry was glaring and red in the face; FitzRoy's sword, when he stepped back, was held carefully en garde across his chest—no threat but able to lash out in defense if necessary. The swordmaster hurried forward to pick up Lord Henry's weapon and hand it to him with a bow.

"Your Grace," he said, turning to FitzRoy and bowing again, "I have never seen the like in a boy your age. Would you do me the honor of giving me a match?"

FitzRoy grinned at him. "Only if you promise not to make me as black and blue as Lord Denno does. I may have to wear a costume during the twelve days of Christmas, and I do not want to need to explain my bruises over and over."

"Lord Denno, I gather, has taught you swordplay?"

"Yes." FitzRoy could not help but feel proud that he had been so good an example of his friend's tutoring. "Lord Denno, and the guardsmen, and sometimes Sir Edward, when he has time. I've fenced with Lord Percy too. I don't think he's as good as I am, but his reach is much greater so I seldom get a hit."

"Ah, let me show you how to come in under the reach of a taller man."

FitzRoy agreed eagerly and the swordmaster, as he had promised, taught him that trick and another, and tapped FitzRoy only lightly when he made a hit, but FitzRoy acknowledged each one punctiliously. And when the match was over, he bowed deeply and thanked the man—and did not fail to put a golden guinea in his hand.

Lord Henry watching rather sullenly from a bench at the side of the room, came forward as the servant was bringing their cloaks and said sourly that FitzRoy hadn't needed to reward the man quite that lavishly. "He gets paid, after all, for my lessons . . . which I now see were ill enough taught."

"Not at all, Henry. You know all the moves. You just don't make them quickly enough, probably because the swordmaster didn't think it wise to really thwack you the way Lord Denno thwacks me. When it hurts enough, you move faster."

"How dare he strike you! You're a duke, the first duke in the kingdom. He's nothing, just a rich merchant, likely he's not even really noble." Henry was so astonished that he let his indignation show clearly.

"He's my friend," FitzRoy said, stopping in the middle of the street. All trace of his usual good nature was gone from his face, and his voice was hard and cold enough to go ice-sliding on. "He's my dear, my beloved, friend, and he dares strike me because he does not want me to be a *dead* duke. Denno's saved my life more than once, but the older I get, the more freedom I have, the more afraid he is that he won't be with me the next time I'm attacked. He's trying to make me able to defend myself."

Dunstan, Ladbroke, and the two guards had closed in, providing further proof there was real danger.

Lord Henry swallowed. "I forgot," he said honestly remorseful, and shuddered slightly, remembering the attempt to drown FitzRoy. "Sorry, Harry, but it's just crazy that anyone should try to harm you now. The king is going to marry my cousin Anne, and she'll surely have a boy child. That will put you right out of the succession." He hesitated, studying FitzRoy's face. "Do you mind?"

FitzRoy shook his head vigorously as they commenced walking down the street again to where their horses had been stabled and explained, as he had explained to Anne, why he did not wish to be king, only leaving out his desire to be a diplomat. Since Lord Henry was equally desirous of avoiding dull responsibility, he truly understood. Thus, they were on better terms by the time they reached their destination some miles west of the city, and fortunately Lord Henry's third diversion, shooting at butts, did not reawaken any conflict.

FitzRoy was as good a shot as Lord Henry, but he pulled a much lighter bow so his arrows did not penetrate as far and sometimes even fell out of the target. The match was judged a draw, and Lord Henry had the pleasure of loftily promising FitzRoy that when he had his full growth they would be equal.

Since they had ridden out a mile or two past Westminster to try their archery and on their return had to thread their way through increasing traffic, Lord Henry had sufficient opportunity to measure FitzRoy's horsemanship. He judged correctly (although he did not acknowledge it), that FitzRoy had a superior seat and, lighter though he was, better control. Thus, as they neared Norfolk House he commented rather sourly that he wondered what his father had been talking about when he said the duke would need his help and instruction.

"Instruction in what? You can beat me with a sword or a bow and probably on the hunting field."

"Well, of course," FitzRoy said, opening his eyes wide. "What else have I had to do? Sword, bow, and riding are things one does in the country, so I've had lots more practice than you. But your father is quite right. There's lots of things I hope you'll teach me—to dance for one thing and how to talk and not *say* anything for another."

"To dance? Who's going to dance with a boy of twelve, even if he is the duke of Richmond?"

"Your cousin Anne, for one," FitzRoy began.

Lord Henry slapped his forehead with his open palm and let out a muted howl. "Right. Right. I forgot that too. Father told me and I swear, I clean put it out of my mind because you'll only have to learn one dance."

He dismounted in the court in silence, watching FitzRoy slide down from his saddle, then put a hand on the younger boy's shoulder and said, rather grimly, "As for talking without saying anything—" he sighed "—don't worry about it. Whatever you say or don't say, even if you stand mute as a stone, the ones who talk to you will decide what you mean, like it or not. We'll stick to the dancing. I *can* teach you that."

CHAPTER 28

Norfolk and his family-party arrived in Greenwich several days before Christmas and hustled FitzRoy into a cold apartment at the very end of the east wing of the palace. To his surprise, by the afternoon of the second day after their arrival, he had Lord Henry to keep him company, and not a sullen Lord Henry who had been ordered to do an unpleasant duty but a Lord Henry who seemed to regard their chilly and under-furnished apartments as a haven.

That afternoon soon after he arrived in the apartment, Henry announced that they had better concentrate on dancing. He played for his pupil himself, saying that he wished to spare FitzRoy any embarrassment from strange watchers, and since FitzRoy was in complete agreement with that sentiment, he readily agreed. Although FitzRoy was aware that Lord Henry wanted to be "better" than FitzRoy himself, he also sensed that Henry was really rather fond of him, and would protect him from the scorn of others. Fortunately the swordplay that had made FitzRoy graceful and quick

on his feet had also taught him to memorize movements and hand gestures, so Henry had an apt pupil.
Still Henry's brow was creased with a frown and his
mouth down-turned with dissatisfaction, even while it
uttered praise.

"What's wrong, Henry?" FitzRoy asked, when Henry
had said FitzRoy had the dance thoroughly mastered
and started to turn away. "Am I so utterly hopeless?
If I am, I'd better tell your father. I suspect it would
be worse to embarrass Lady Anne by tripping over her
or stepping on her feet than to change the plan. Maybe
I had better go to my father at once and allow Lady
Anne to come out of the Mound—"

"No!" Lord Henry exploded. "That would make
everything much worse. And you're not hopeless. You
do that dance as well as I could. Why do you say you're
hopeless?"

"Because you've been frowning and shaking your
head and looking like you've bitten into a sour apple
all afternoon and it's gotten worse and worse."

"That's nothing to do with you, Harry." Lord Henry
was silent a moment, and then added, "You don't know
what it's like in the public rooms and at the public
feasts."

"Why? What's the matter?" A thrill of apprehension
ran down FitzRoy's back. "The king isn't sick, is he?"

"No, no. King Henry is very well. It's just . . . just . . ."
His lips tightened and his jaw moved as his teeth
clenched. Then he moved closer to FitzRoy and bent
to speak in a murmur directly into his ear. "Everyone
misses the queen."

"Everyone?"

Lord Henry nodded. "Even my father and I and
Lord Wiltshire. . . ." He bit his lip. "It's like there's
a big hole in the middle of the floor, and everyone
walks around it without mentioning it . . . but it's *there*.

She . . . she wasn't bright or gay or really part of the fun, but . . ."

"I see." FitzRoy nodded understanding. "That was why your father said I was supposed to come out of the Mound, so that my father would be surprised enough to forget everything else and have someone of his own family to be with him."

"Yes, well, I think it would have been better if you went to him as soon as you arrived, but Anne . . ." Lord Henry shook his head. "It's all of a muddle, I fear. Politics is only part of it. I want the king to have a male heir as much as anyone and, naturally, it would be greatly to my benefit if Anne were queen and brought him that heir, but just now there is such an atmosphere of discomfort . . ."

"Come into my rooms," FitzRoy said, "they're a little warmer and Dunstan managed to get me some really good wine. I know I won't be able to help, but I won't talk to anyone about what you say—I swear it—and talking might make you feel better."

Lord Henry sighed, looked for a moment as if he would refuse, and then said, "For this, my thanks. And maybe these are things you should hear."

He began by talking about Christmas at court, beginning with Queen Catherine's piety and her reluctant yielding to her husband's desire for pleasure. Thus in the court, the eve of Christmas had always been given over to religious celebration in which the king took enthusiastic part, but the next twelve days were for making merry and giving gifts—about which the king was even more enthusiastic. The queen never cared much for the Lords of Misrule and the coarse games they played, but she accepted the bawdy merrymaking as she had always accepted anything the king desired.

Now for the first time in over twenty years, the

queen and her ladies were absent. That absence left an uncomfortable void, and one that Anne Boleyn could not fill. To put her in the queen's place would outrage many in the court. But there was a further danger for Anne, for to put her beside the king would also imply that she was "wife" in terms of consummation. And above all, that was an impression she must not give publicly.

They talked about it and FitzRoy explained what he was supposed to do when he came out of the Mound. Lord Henry hmm'd and bit his lip and finally advised that, regardless of Anne's feelings, FitzRoy had better go first to his father. "You can then beg him to let you dance with the worthiest, the fairest, and purest maiden in his court, and then you can go to Anne and ask her to dance."

FitzRoy looked admiringly at Lord Henry. "I' faith, I like that much better than what your father told me to say. It doesn't sound so made-up. I can make that sound as if I truly mean it. But do you think Lady Anne will be angry enough to refuse to dance with me?"

Lord Henry laughed. "After you've publicly called her worthiest, fairest, and purest? And with the king watching, filled with joy over being newly united with his son? Not likely."

FitzRoy, although none too happy about incurring Anne's anger and, perhaps, a lasting spite, agreed. He thought it wrong to ask Anne to dance before he greeted the father he had not seen for so many years. Still, he had little enough appetite for his evening meal and he slept restlessly, twice waking in a cold sweat from dreams of being pursued by angry harridans.

He woke late and sluggishly and, unhappy with his own company, asked Lord Henry to join him at breakfast. Neither of them had much to say. Henry finally suggested that FitzRoy practice his dancing one more time. They were so engaged when Dunstan brought in Lord Denno, who wanted to know at once the reason for such glum faces.

"If you can't dance, Harry, you can't." Lord Denno said, warmly. "Don't worry. I'll think of something."

"No, Lord Denno, he can dance," Lord Henry said. "At least he can do the one dance he'll need to do with Lady Anne, but—" and then, despite his earlier disparagement of Denno, the foreign merchant, possibly not even deserving of his notice, he blurted out his uneasiness over the feeling in the court and what he and FitzRoy had decided to do.

Denoriel shook his head. "I am the last person to advise you. For one thing, I know little of the court, and for another, I've been far too busy to take the temper of the Lady Anne's feelings. But I should say, Lord Henry, that I would trust your instincts. If I were the king, no matter how fond I was of my lady, I would be hurt if my son ran to her instead of to me after our long separation. But put that aside. His Grace knows both choices. I am sure His Grace will know what to do when he actually steps out of the Mound. What I've come for is to show him the hall and the Mound and how the mechanism that opens it works."

He had instant and fervent acceptance of his offer and they all went down to the main floor and then trailed through the building to the Great Hall. This was closed with guards before the doors, but Denoriel led them to what looked like a stable off to the left. There were no horses within and the floor had been carefully cleaned. In the middle sat . . . FitzRoy gaped at what looked like a small grassy hill.

Lord Henry only gave it a single glance. He had seen it often before. Nonetheless, he followed eagerly when Lord Denno picked up a lantern, lit it, and then pulled at what looked like a small bush, which permitted him to lift away a panel through which they entered. There would be room for ten to fifteen people, FitzRoy thought, depending on how tightly they could be packed.

The curved ceiling and walls, which ran into each other, were painted dark blue on which appeared many silvery stars. Here and there hung light-green gauze curtains on which were painted trees with flowers at their roots.

Denoriel gestured to Nyle and Dickson to move right and left and directed them together to press down on the levers attached to the wall. When they did, a split appeared in the center of the Mound directly ahead and the walls slid back smoothly. Denoriel set the lantern down on the floor and beckoned everyone out, then told them to turn and look back.

FitzRoy gasped and tears stung his eyes. For a moment he felt as if he were looking out from the Gate at Elfhame Logres into the dim twilight in which one could make out only a distant vista of large trees, the ground carpeted with nearly colorless flowers. But he could not speak. Whatever it was that had touched him when he stood before King Oberon in Llachar Lle still bound him to silence.

Denoriel gripped his shoulder and explained that he would hold the place just before the central opening; Nyle and Dickson would work the levers and he would step out. There would be a loud bang and thick, colored smoke—the trick he had had Sir Edward copy, only the smoke would be thicker because he knew better how to work the trick. His eyes met Harry's and Harry nodded. He understood that true magic would thicken the smoke and enhance the color, but that did not matter.

FitzRoy was warned not to tear the gauze curtains, not to move until most of the smoke cleared, and not to fall down the steps, which were hidden in green cloth that had cut loops protruding from it so that it really looked like grass. The cloth also hid the wheels on which the Mound rolled. It would be pulled into the Great Hall by six royal guards dressed as wild men, their swords concealed in their fur robes.

Then Denoriel led them out, carefully closing the stable doors behind him. A guard stepped out of a small shelter and Denoriel nodded at him. The guards in front of the Great Hall, stepped aside for Denoriel, and he shepherded Lord Henry and FitzRoy and FitzRoy's ever-present personal guards into the chamber. All of them stopped just inside the doorway, staring first out and then upward and then around at the busy crowd rushing this way and that, carrying and dragging great bundles of greenery.

The hall was more than forty feet long and perhaps twenty-five wide and the arched and beamed ceiling soared up a full two floors. Large as the chamber was, it was well lit near the middle of the day by large glassed windows between the arches. And it would be as well lit after the dark of the short winter's day had fallen by the huge chandeliers that hung from every cross beam and the candelabra that were fixed to the walls.

Because of its height and width, it was not as noisy as one might expect from the activity. Men perched on high ladders attaching swathes of ivy and branches of pine and hemlock to the beams. Others hung precariously over the railings of the balcony that ran around the far end of the Hall over the dais, hanging bay and holm, more ivy and mistletoe, which would permit the king to steal a kiss or two from any maiden coming near.

"Your Grace," Denoriel said—apparently not for the first time from his tone of voice. "The Mound will be drawn forward to between that second pair of windows facing the dais. The king will be seated on a throne in the center. Lady Anne will be standing just to his right, at the foot of the dais."

"Yes. I was supposed to start toward the king and then, as if I caught sight of her and was irresistibly attracted, I was to turn aside and ask her to dance." He shook his head. "I won't do that—as if a pretty girl were enough to distract me from my father."

Although he had made up his mind and was not tempted to change it, FitzRoy was still uneasy about Lady Anne's reaction. He had gone to considerable trouble to make a good impression on her and had, he thought, succeeded. But it made no difference. It felt wrong to be turned aside from his king and his father to flatter a woman.

So the rest of the day passed and the next day was taken up with going to church and trying on clothing and costume. Still if FitzRoy had known the effort Lady Anne was putting into her appearance for that moment, he would have been even more uneasy.

On Christmas day, an hour before Lady Anne Boleyn went down to the Great Hall, Lady Lee and Lady Alana, both stood examining her from the crown of her head to the tips of her toes. Lady Lee merely looked with fatuous fondness. Lady Alana nodded curtly, and Anne sighed softly.

She knew she was pushing the limit in her dress. Her hair was not hidden completely beneath cap-and-gable headdress. The band and headdress were there, but had been pushed back to sit on the crown of her head, exposing the rich mass of her hair, parted in the center, smooth and shining. The gable itself was sewn with pearls on two golden bands and raised up on a base of stiffened buckram. That was normal, and when it sat forward on the head it merely framed the face; pushed back as Anne had set it, it hinted at a crown.

Her gown was rich nearly to ostentation, saved only by the color, which was a quiet mulberry. It was the only thing that was quiet. The square neck was bordered by a thin band of gold lace set with tiny garnets. Around her neck was an elaborate necklace of cunningly worked gold interspersed with larger garnets and from the center hung down a pendant, also worked gold, set with three dark rubies. A longer chain of garnet-set gold made a wider circle around her neck, dipping into the front of her gown to lie on her breasts. Around the outside of the square neckline, on her shoulders, lay three more chains of gold, and from the center of the neckline hung a heavy gold pendant, a conjoined *AB* with another large ruby dropping below.

Alana nodded again. "In a general way, I would say it was too much, but for today, when it is very important for the king's attention to be riveted upon you—"

"You think the boy is a danger to me?" Anne asked.

Alana laughed softly, which softened her otherwise solemn expression. "Oh, no. Not at all. I think he will be helpful and will put Princess Mary completely out of his father's mind. But—everything is different this Christmas, so if the king should think of Lady Catherine, let his eyes come to you and tell him how rich a prize he has in exchange."

In so much Lady Alana seemed to have judged correctly. When Anne entered the Great Hall it was too crowded already for the king to see her at once, but she saw the uneasy movement in those who approached the dais and when she reached it herself she saw the petulant droop of her Henry's mouth. She knew how to deal with his petulance, but there was something else, a kind of sadness for something lost, in his small blue eyes. Anne swallowed a sharp remark and smiled and held out her hand.

She was relieved when she saw admiration replace petulance, and she stepped up onto the dais and leaned down to kiss his cheek. Then, laughing, she kissed his other cheek. He looked surprised. Anne was not often so demonstrative. Then she looked up above his head and seemed to count, and at last bent lower and kissed his lips, explaining that there were no less than three bunches of mistletoe over his head. "I must needs pay the sweet forfeit thrice, you see," she explained.

King Henry laughed, and seeing him pacified, the parade of courtiers began again. Before those pressing about him with good wishes could thin, trumpets sounded, the great doors were flung open, and Denoriel came through, flourishing a golden staff from the head of which came a sizzling noise and popping little stars of brilliance. He wore a tall pointed hat, all hung with arcane symbols and a black robe on which glittered more symbols. Then he pointed the staff at the doors; there were gasps of surprise and a few small cries of fear when everyone realized that the courtyard was no longer visible. Beyond the doors was nothing but blackness.

Another flourish of the staff. The blackness was gone and the Fairy Mound appeared, drawn by groaning and cavorting wild men, each of whom were followed by another in fantastic garb, cracking a whip. Behind the Mound, the doors closed. The staff pointed. In the balcony above the dais, musicians struck up a lively melody. Denoriel approached the throne, his magician's staff lowered so that its glowing knob trailed on the ground in submission.

As the Mound approached, Denoriel backed away from the king until he stood near the center. He swung the staff, striking the Mound with a resounding crash.

A huge billow of smoke gushed from the broken head of his staff, enveloping him. Denoriel muttered the Don't-see-me spell and stepped quietly away. As the smoke dissipated, the Mound cracked open. Sighs and murmurs of astonishment passed through the crowd as they seemed to look into a moon-lit, tamed forest of great trees and pale flowers.

Before the falseness of that vision could become apparent, FitzRoy leapt out of the Mound with ten courtiers behind him. All wore leaf-green hose topped with tunics of various light and bright colors. The tunics, square-necked, worn over white shirts with high collars, came to mid-thigh and were double-sleeved, the undersleeve, tight to the arm, of the same leaf-green as the hose, the oversleeve wide and trailing with dagged hems.

FitzRoy paused and looked around; behind him the courtiers made a low, musical sound of awe and pointed. FitzRoy looked ahead at the dais and cried out, "Father!" and ran.

King Henry, who had been watching the performance with unalloyed pleasure, started at FitzRoy's voice. The boy had reached him and fallen to his knees before Henry could rise.

"Harry?" he said uncertainly.

FitzRoy looked up, tears marking his cheeks. "Yes, Your Majesty, Harry . . . your son."

The king pulled the boy up from his knees and into his arms. "Harry!" He bussed FitzRoy soundly on one cheek and then on the other, then pushed him a little away so he could look at him. "You have grown so much. I almost did not know you."

FitzRoy took the king's hand and kissed it without reply. What could he say? That it had been years since his father had tried to see him? He would sound resentful, and he was not, not really. Denno had told

him over and over that the separation was more for
his own safety than because of political problems.

"I was worried about you," the king added, frowning. "I knew when you started for London, and guessed
about when you should have arrived but when I asked
for you all my accursed councilors would tell me was
that the roads were terrible and you were delayed."

"They were. I was." FitzRoy grinned. "But I have
been here a few days. Everyone thought a day or two
more or less would not matter if you could have a
pleasant surprise for Christmas. Was it a pleasant
surprise?"

King Henry kissed him and laughed. "I was surprised
all right. That magician . . . My hair stood up when he
smashed that scepter and the smoke rose. And then
he vanished." He looked around. "Where is he?"

"It's all tricks," FitzRoy whispered into his father's
ear. "He is a very nice man and later he'll show everyone how the tricks are done. If you will be good
enough to grant me an audience, Your Majesty, I can
tell you all about him. And I have so much more to
tell you, but now—" FitzRoy straightened up and raised
his voice "—now I wish to beg you to allow me to ask
Lady Anne Boleyn, the most worthy, the loveliest, and
the purest maiden in this company, to dance with me
in your name."

The crowd had been hushed while FitzRoy clung
to and talked with his father. Now his voice rang clear
through the hall. The courtiers, who had followed him
out of the Mound and had been standing in graceful
poses, raised their arms, their trailing sleeves falling
back to show bright contrasting linings. With raised
arms, they circled twice on the floor before the Mound
and then opened their circle and flowed toward where
Lady Anne stood stiff and silent at the edge of the dais.
They bowed. They made an aisle through which, having

received his father's laughing permission, FitzRoy made his way to his partner.

He swept off his cap and flourished it as he bowed, its long, brightly colored plume sweeping the floor. For a moment he thought Anne would refuse him, but Henry, laughing still, begged that she would not refuse him, else he would be forced to die of shame, and she held out her hand. The musicians struck up just the tune Lord Henry had played. FitzRoy made a wide, slow circle in the space before the Mound, giving plenty of time for the watchers to bow to Anne.

They did the first figure of the dance alone, which gave FitzRoy time, when he and Anne came together, to apologize. "Lady Anne, I am so sorry," he said, "I know that I have spoiled what was planned, but when I saw my father—" Tears came to his eyes, and he blinked them away. "I have not seen him for so long! I was overpowered by my desire to greet him." Tears came to his eyes again as he begged her to forgive him.

She said she forgave him; whether her words had meaning or not, FitzRoy did not know . . . and did not much care. All he could think about was being with his father again, being with him in private to talk as a son did with his father.

The rest of the evening's revels—or as much of it as FitzRoy was permitted to attend—passed in a kind of hectic dream. He watched the dancers, listened to the musicians, even danced a bit more himself. He knew that he ate and drank, but could not recall the taste of anything. And long before the revels were over, Lord Henry was sent by Norfolk to take him back to his own chambers, where he dreamed that he was riding with his father through an elven forest.

Normally such a hope would have been doomed to disappointment, but in a fit of pique because some of his council were still resisting his claim to be supreme head of the English church, King Henry had put aside all business until Twelfth Night. His own slight uneasiness about what he was doing, made him reluctant to spend his time in religious reading or writing or disputation. Those two accustomed pursuits temporarily ended left a gap in his morning activities into which FitzRoy just fit.

His open joy at being with his father was very soothing to both of them. Henry asked questions and got answers that were very pleasing. FitzRoy was just the kind of boy that Henry liked—a hard rider in the hunting field, a good shot with a bow, and a serious student of the sword. The crown was set on the king's approval when FitzRoy admitted that he was no hand at tennis at all. They had not had a court in either Sheriff Hutton or Pontefract and his tutor had been reluctant, he admitted, to provide another distraction to his already reluctant scholar.

Although he was a fine scholar himself, Henry laughed heartily over his son's confession. He remembered being much less enamored of books and lessons when he, himself, had been the boy's age. Moreover the deprivation provided the king with the pleasure of introducing and instructing his son in one of his favorite games.

Again FitzRoy's practice in swordplay came to his aid. He was quick with eye and hand and soon mastered the correct moves. And again his age and incomplete growth saved him from winning against the older, more corpulent king. His aim was accurate enough, but he had not the strength to drive the ball far, so many of his strokes fell short of the net. He did not mind losing at all; the king praised him for learning so well, put the right reason on his failure . . . and had the joy of winning the game.

All in all FitzRoy spent a lot of time with his

father over the twelve days, and when the question
was raised about the boy traveling back north, the
king quashed the suggestion at once. No traveling
until the roads were dry and the weather settled,
King Henry said. He had been frightened enough
when his son had been so long in coming. He was
taking no chances on losing him on the way back.
The northern properties were in the capable hands
of the councilors. Harry should stay with the court.

For a month or so, FitzRoy was very happy. As the
king reluctantly returned to the business of ruling,
FitzRoy saw less of him, but he did ride with his father
on the almost daily hunts and was praised highly for
his horsemanship. Also, King Henry found pleasure in
an occasional game of tennis and a cozy chat while they
cooled off and drank some ale, and Harry was often
called to stand beside his father—with Anne on the
other side—when courtiers were received.

FitzRoy got along well enough with Anne. He was
deferential to her and showed that he enjoyed her
presence and conversation. She was bright and witty,
and even when he occasionally felt she had gone too
far in making one of the courtiers the butt of her wit,
he kept his disapproval from his face. She was less
satisfied with his company, he was sure, but he knew
it had nothing to do with him. She simply did not like
anyone, even someone who approved of her, drawing
away the king's attention.

Moreover, more of the courtiers than Anne had
begun to notice the king's growing affection for his
baseborn son. This man and that made excuses to talk
to or ride with FitzRoy, and most of them had ideas
they wished transmitted to the king. Now Lord Henry
was very useful and helpful—when FitzRoy could reach
him. Lord Henry had a group of friends and often went
off with them to pursue private amusements. FitzRoy

compromised by telling his father he had been approached by this man and that and repeating what they wanted. Mostly the king laughed, but it all made FitzRoy uncomfortable. He did not want to anger anyone, and yet, it seemed that no matter what he did, unless he was very careful, he would have to anger *someone*. That was the part of being a diplomat he had not sufficiently considered.

By the end of February, FitzRoy was heartily tired of the court and was aware that he had seen nothing of Denno. He wanted most sincerely to be back in the snow-heaped quiet of Sheriff Hutton or Pontefract talking quietly with Denno and drinking hot cider before a roaring fire, but he could not bring himself to tell his father he wanted to leave him.

Finally he caught Lord Henry, on a flying visit to court, who grinned and said, "Don't! Go tell Lady Anne. She wants to be rid of you as much as you want to be gone. She'll think of something."

When Anne agreed to receive him alone, he told her how tired he was of being at court. First she regarded him suspiciously and accused him of wanting to get her into trouble with the king. But after he had denied this vehemently, he could see that she was beginning to consider the benefits of his suggestion. Finally she said that she could not ask he be sent back to Sheriff Hutton, not over winter roads. That would sound as if she were hoping ill would befall him.

"And I don't," she said, stroking his cheek carelessly. "You are a very nice boy. I don't want any harm to come to you . . . but I would prefer it if I could talk to Henry more often without you right beside us."

"Could I have a house of my own, say, in London? If I weren't right here, so a page could run and fetch me . . ."

"A house of your own in London, close by nearly

all of Henry's favorite places, even Whitehall?" Anne pursed her lips and then nodded. "That is no bad thought. Then no one could say I was trying to keep you apart." Slowly she smiled. "Well, why not? There are several residences right here in the city that are too small for the king himself. He uses them occasionally to house diplomats on short missions . . . Why not?"

FitzRoy returned to his apartments, feeling that he had truly won Anne Boleyn as an ally.

Anne watched the boy leave, feeling that for now, at least, she had truly won the king's bastard as an ally. And the longer this went on, the less likely it was that he would change his mind, or be won over to another faction. She was still troubled, however, that the king would suspect her of trying to be rid of the son who was giving him so much pleasure. She talked that over with her two intimates and Lady Alana who was usually silent on every subject except clothing, lifted her nothing face and smiled.

"His health, madam," she suggested in her soft voice. "Speak to the king of the boy's health. Surely it is not common for boys of twelve to be so constantly at court, to have so many late hours and so few times of quiet."

Lady Anne smiled; she was beginning to treasure her odd lady-in-waiting for more than her expert hand with costume. Lady Alana had a shrewd mind, and was often able to concoct a means by which Anne could get something she wanted while casting herself in the best possible light.

This particular suggestion would not only allow her to appear concerned about FitzRoy's health, it would allow her to appear maternal. . . .

The ploy was so successful—FitzRoy having caught on the first time his father asked him how he was feeling and admitted to some fatigue—that by the end of March the king had signed over to FitzRoy's possession Baynard's Castle, near the river south of St. Paul's. And, to FitzRoy's secret delight, not far at all from Denno's house on Bucklersbury.

He was so profoundly grateful when the king told him, that Henry, rather hurt, said, "Are you tired of my company so soon, Harry?"

Whereupon FitzRoy threw manners and protocol to the winds and threw his arms around his father's neck. "Of your company, Sire? Never! When I am with you, I am always at ease and happy. I never need to watch each word out of my mouth for fear I will say something someone will misunderstand or, even worse, take as a promise. I love you, father, but I am wearied and yet I cannot sleep, when I am pulled this way and that and importuned . . ."

The king returned the boy's hug and then patted him on the shoulder. "I understand all too well," he said, but he was still resentful, and added, "but I do not see what good living in a house apart from the court will do you."

"My servants can say I am not at home," FitzRoy answered promptly. "To any except your messengers and possibly Lord Henry, mostly I will be denied. If I am not at home to *anybody*, no one can be offended, and if they can't get in, they can't talk at me."

The king stared at him for a moment, then threw back his head and burst into gales of laughter, and FitzRoy knew that all was well.

CHAPTER 29

Baynard's Castle was actually no longer a castle. The stronghold of a twelfth century rebel lord, it had been razed to the ground and a handsome, commodious house built over its old cellars by the seventh Henry, the current Henry's father. However, what had been commodious in the previous century was cramped in terms of royal guesthouses now; embassies from one king to another had grown far more elaborate.

Henry's council thus felt it would be a good thing to get the expense of maintaining the house off the king's rolls, and it would do well enough for a ducal residence. There were much grander ones—some on the council owned them—but Richmond was not quite thirteen years old. He could add to Baynard's or build a grander house when he was a man.

Long before FitzRoy had been gifted with Baynard's Castle, the remainder of his servants and his baggage had finally made their way to Greenwich. There was no room for them with half the nobility of the kingdom squeezed into the area and no need for them either. Under-grooms and under-valets and a bevy of maids had been appointed from the overflow of such servants on the king's staff.

Norfolk had found FitzRoy's own people various lodgings in London, but they felt idle and lost and feared they would be dismissed. When Ladbroke and Dunstan arrived with the news that FitzRoy had a residence of his own, they were all overjoyed and hastened to move into the castle to make it ready. If Norfolk had intended to appoint a new staff for FitzRoy, he never had the chance.

By then FitzRoy himself would not have cared if Baynard's Castle was a hovel, and he fled to the cold, empty house only two days after the deed was delivered to him. He had barely escaped from going with the king to Hampton Court. Henry had said the house could not possibly be ready—and he was right—but FitzRoy was now desperate for a safe haven. Fortunately an encounter with an aggressive, opportunistic woman rescued him. She was importuning him with so much warmth to come and meet her daughter, that in his efforts to escape he had backed up right into the king's arms.

That was enough. King Henry knew he could not watch his son every minute and he had no intention of allowing twelve-year-old Harry to be trapped into any compromising situation—not with his own situation being so ambiguous. He gave permission for his son to depart the court. FitzRoy found only two rooms warm and furnished, his bedchamber and the kitchen. He did not care a bit and he wept with joy as he was folded into Mistress Bethany's arms and again when only half an hour later Denoriel, alerted by Ladbroke, appeared in the doorway.

"I thought I'd lost you," he sobbed, holding tight

to the Sidhe. "I tried and tried to think of a way to invite you to come to me, but I never could. And when I asked for you outright, Norfolk said it was time to break our connection, that I had my father and you were no longer necessary. I was afraid you would think that, having been welcomed by the king, I no longer cared for you."

Denoriel laughed and hugged the boy hard. "No, no. What with all those under-grooms the king provided for you, Ladbroke had plenty of time to ride to London and let me know what was happening. Still, I missed you, Harry." He ruffled the boy's hair and laughed again. "But your father or his council could not have chosen a better place. Did you know there are deep cellars below the house, part of the old castle that was here?"

"Cellars?"

"Yes, my boy, and you are going to become an expert on wine, so no one will be surprised if you are occasionally met coming out of the cellar at odd times of day or evening. Nor will it be thought odd if a close friend, who buys wine for you, is seen coming and going from the cellar."

A Gate! FitzRoy thought. *Denno's going to put a Gate right into my cellar. Will he take me Underhill again at night when no one will miss me?* He could not say any part of his thoughts, but his rather dull brown eyes fairly glowed bright hazel, showing sparks of gold and green.

For two more weeks FitzRoy lived in a cheerful disorder, taking his meals in the kitchen and spending most of his time directing the placement of furniture sent by some deputy of the king's steward. Then, with his house clean and furnished, with every fireplace in the building flaming high, life returned to what FitzRoy considered normal. He was more comfortable, of course, able to sprawl on comfortable chairs in a withdrawing room and be warm away from the kitchen ovens or his down covered bed, but there were disadvantages too.

He was again dining in lonely splendor instead of having slapdash meals in the busy kitchen—until Masters Croke and Palsgrave returned from their leaves. FitzRoy sighed. He liked both Croke and Palsgrave; they were fond of him and did their best to make his lessons interesting, only their return meant that lessons began anew.

A small respite occurred when Sir Edward returned from his leave. At least that ended Master Croke's and Master Palsgrave's attempts to hold dinner-table conversations in Latin and introduced instead the subject of setting up FitzRoy's stable, which was enjoyable. Unfortunately, Sir Edward was too prone to defer to the tutors.

On the days when Lord Henry came, sometimes bringing a friend or two, there was further relief. Lord Henry would have none of Latin and little of court gossip too. He talked of the hunt and other sport. Some days Denno came too. It was amazing, FitzRoy thought with his experience at court behind him, how elegant Denno was. He made Sir Edward appear rough, Lord Henry look callow. Only the tutors, although not so elegantly clad, held up well by comparison.

Lessons or no lessons, FitzRoy was now happier than ever. He was summoned to court periodically so he did see his father, but living so near he only stayed for the event in which he was to take part. Anne was glad to see him for a day or two now and again. The king was pleased by their obvious ease with each other—his two dearest, he called them. The weather improved as April passed and May began, but no one suggested that FitzRoy should go back north, certainly not FitzRoy himself.

Time was set aside for his lessons—he could not avoid them and did not wish his father to hear he was so busy enjoying himself that he would not study. But he *was* enjoying himself; Lord Henry generally included him when he and his friends went to see a cockfight, or a bull- or bear-baiting, and Denno took him to the docks and showed him the wonder of strange people from distant lands and the cargoes their ships carried.

Truth was that, while May edged into June, FitzRoy was utterly indifferent to the open talk about the king marrying Lady Anne without the pope's permission. He had long accepted the idea; when he was pressed, he said so and added that his only interest in the matter was that Lady Anne made his father happy and likely would breed him a fine male heir.

There were other rumors, that after a period of coldness between England and France, the king was hoping to bring about a new rapprochement with King Francis—one that would include Francis's support for Henry's divorce from Catherine and remarriage to Lady Anne. The rumors increased with the growing weakness of Archbishop Warham, who opposed the king's statement of supremacy over the English Church and his divorce and remarriage unless sanctioned by the pope.

"So, what do your crystals say, Master Fagildo Otstargi? Do they agree with most of the court that the king will seize the Church and marry Mistress Anne as soon as Warham dies?"

There was some bitterness in Cromwell's melliflu-ous voice and the threat in his eyes to any other, who had not Pasgen's ability to reduce the man to a mindless puppet, would have been terrifying. Only Pasgen knew he dared not make a puppet of Cromwell. It was only by virtue of the man's knowledge of the king and court, of his devious mind and remarkable ability to manipulate people, that Pasgen was able to manage so much of what happened around King Henry without ever awakening a flicker of suspicion of occult influence.

Cromwell had been right and Pasgen wrong about how to save himself when Wolsey fell. Cromwell had been right about the result of trying to tax—no matter the tax was called an amicable grant—without Parliament. He had been right about a lot of things. It was galling to need to reason and wheedle, but Pasgen knew that if he did not succeed in getting Anne into Henry's bed so that the red-haired babe would be born a bastard, he was going to need Cromwell even more when they had to destroy Anne.

Unfortunately there were some things of which Cromwell was simply unaware. Because of subtle friction between Norfolk and Wiltshire on the one hand, and Cromwell on the other, for example, the duke and the earl did not always acquaint the still-common privy councilor with all their plans. They were glad enough to use him, but they did not consider him an equal. That was how that accursed bastard FitzRoy had been summoned to court before Pasgen could induce Cromwell to prevent the idea from being presented to the king.

So there FitzRoy was, as dutiful a son as any man could desire, healthy, strong—the ideal heir . . . except that he was not legitimate. His presence was a constant reminder to the king that he must not allow his desire to force Anne into his bed. And the stupid, mewling FitzRoy had Oberon's mark on him and could not simply be wiped away.

Pasgen restrained a sigh. Cromwell had been able to solve the problem of FitzRoy. When Pasgen pointed out that he must be got rid of and why and suggested that Cromwell order the boy back north, Cromwell had said flatly that his power did not yet reach so far. The king would never agree. What Cromwell had arranged through the council was for FitzRoy to be granted a house of his own right in London.

At least, Cromwell said, the boy was out of the court and not in his father's eye every hour. Pasgen agreed; the center of London had advantages for a boy just entering his salad years. All the taverns and arenas for sport would keep FitzRoy busy and introduce him to mortal vices. If FitzRoy took to gambling, drinking, and wenching, perhaps he would again be banished to the north.

Anyhow with that reminder of the cost of bastardy out of the king's way, Pasgen could again begin to direct Cromwell to making it worthwhile to Anne to yield up her virtue. Cromwell had been right again when he pointed out that ennobling and enriching her father and brother would not much influence her. It was time, Pasgen thought, to make grants to the witch herself. Surely when she was a noblewoman in her own right, not dependent on father or brother for her status, surely she would repay the king in the coin he desired.

A finger gesture had made certain that Cromwell was unaware of the long silence after his question concerning the marriage of Anne and Henry. Now Pasgen completed the gesture as he said, "My crystal shows Lady Anne wearing the mantle and coronet of a . . . of a nobleman."

Cromwell frowned. "You mean she was married to someone other than the king? I do not believe it!"

"No," Pasgen agreed. "I do not believe it either. And there is no man in my Vision. It is only of Lady Anne wearing a ermine-furred mantle and a coronet. Is it possible that the king could ennoble a woman in her own right? Is it possible?"

Cromwell's lips parted to say "no," but he did not utter the word. His brow furrowed. "The arrangements are all but made for a meeting between King Francis and King Henry at Calais and Boulogne. I know that the king plans to take Lady Anne with him and that she and Francis should meet. But would King Francis feel sufficiently honored to meet the mere daughter of an earl? Hmm. Perhaps I could whisper in the king's ear that it would be a compliment to King Francis if the lady had some title of her own to support her dignity."

Some weeks later Cromwell summoned Fagildo Otstargi again. He was very pleased with Master Otstargi. Far from being shocked by Cromwell's tentative suggestion that Lady Anne be raised to the nobility in her own right, the king had embraced his suggestion with enthusiasm. He complimented Cromwell on his clear perception of Anne's worth and said he would seek for a way to reward him.

By the end of July King Henry had found a suitable reward for his astute councilor. In addition to being master of the king's jewels, Cromwell was made keeper of the Hanaper of Chancery—a more powerful position. If Master Otstargi saw any more unlikely pictures in his crystals, Cromwell said, he should not hesitate to speak of them. Only that they would all soon go to France, Master Otstargi said, and that did not need a crystal to predict.

In August, Archbishop Warham died. The king was on progress and did not attend the funeral. The mourning in court was more like rejoicing among those who favored the king's remarriage. On September first, Henry met Anne in Windsor and conferred upon her the title of marquis (not marchioness because she held the title in her own right) and lands to the value of a thousand pounds a year to support her. Half the court believed that the creation and lands meant that Anne had yielded, but nothing in her behavior or the king's changed. Then toward the end of the month Henry demanded that all the queen's jewels be surrendered so Anne could wear them for Francis to see in France. It became apparent that whether or not Anne was warming the king's bed, Henry fully intended to marry her.

FitzRoy had turned thirteen in June. Denno gave him the most magnificent sword he had ever seen, made of a silver alloy that was harder than steel, its hilt ablaze with jewels. FitzRoy had no doubt that each and every one of the stones was invested with a spell, and despite the stones the hilt fit into his hand with a firmness that told him it would never slip, no matter if it were covered with sweat or blood.

Lord Henry gave him a handsome brooch, but more important to FitzRoy, Henry took him to one of the naughty masques in which the ladies—only they were *not* at all ladies—appeared in almost nothing. What more he introduced FitzRoy to FitzRoy kept to himself but Denoriel guessed and promptly countered by providing FitzRoy with a night in the company of a group of playful nymphs and dryads. The contrast with the drabs of London was enough, FitzRoy assured Denoriel, to keep him from becoming addicted to common whores.

In any case FitzRoy and Lord Henry, too, had little enough time to get into trouble. Almost as soon as the meeting with Francis was definitely arranged, the two young men were informed that they would attend the king. This would require serious study not only of the French degrees of nobility, but of the persons of the French court—and all of it had to be done in French. Utter fluency was required ... and correct pronunciation too. Croke and Palsgrave were rein-forced with a French *duc* from an impoverished but very old and honorable family.

There was scarcely time enough. By October tenth the court was at Dover; on the eleventh they took ship for France. When the meeting had first been discussed, there had been objections to the king crossing the narrow sea so near the evil storms of winter, but the crossing was perfect. In only four hours, King Henry was stepping ashore at Calais. It was only the third time in his life that Henry had been out of England, and Calais had mustered every adornment and entertain-ment it could find to welcome him and Anne.

FitzRoy and Lord Henry, fast friends now, were taking full advantage of what Calais offered. Knowing he would be far too busy to oversee his ward, Nor-folk had commanded his son to see that the younger boy did not get into trouble. With Lord Henry's con-nivance, Denoriel had been added to FitzRoy's usual household as gentleman-usher. Over two thousand people had accompanied the king to France; no one was going to question the appropriateness of one more gentleman-usher.

By the nineteenth of October, King Francis had reached Boulogne; the very next day the kings set out for their well-planned meeting. Every move had been discussed and calculated, planned so that neither Henry or Francis should outdo the other.

No such considerations troubled Lord Henry or FitzRoy. They liked France. They liked the French. They were relieved that no one made fun of their accents and that they understood nearly everything that was said and could make the French nobles who were assigned to accompany them understand what they said. The five days the king spent in Boulogne were pure pleasure to them.

Neither cared that one part of Henry's plan had already failed. The only Frenchwoman of high enough birth willing to meet and greet Lady Anne was of such light virtue that Henry had to refuse. However, when Francis rode back to Calais with Henry, he personally greeted Anne with great warmth and was noted to have spent considerable time in her company, not only with Henry present but often enough with only her ladies and his gentlemen in attendance.

Francis genuinely liked Anne. Denoriel remarked to FitzRoy that she had probably done her cause more good with her witty conversation than Henry had with all his pomp and flattery. For whatever reason, before the meeting was over, Henry had assurances from Francis that he would use his uttermost influence to urge the pope to agree to the divorce.

The entire meeting had taken place in perfect weather. All the jousts and revels had escaped interruption by even a mild rainstorm; however, as soon as Francis parted from Henry at the edge of the English pale, the skies began to cloud and the wind began to rise. That night there was intense fog, and that fog lingered all the next day. Then the rain came pouring down and the wind drove behind it. Several ships that had set out for England were driven back on the French shore; one ship was lost.

Lord Henry and FitzRoy neither knew nor cared. With King Henry's permission, they had ridden south with King Francis, now part of the French king's court. Both young men, although FitzRoy was scarcely more than a boy, were to be trained and polished, fitted for their important roles in European society. Without even hinting about it, FitzRoy was taking his first steps toward his avowed aim of becoming a diplomat.

Denoriel was as amused and delighted as FitzRoy and Lord Henry. Miralys soon found an entrance to

Elfhame Melusine and Denoriel went Underhill to pay his respects to King Huon and Queen Melusine. They were beautiful and powerful, both perfect representatives of High Court elven appearance, but not nearly so overwhelming as Oberon and Titania, and they were in greater accord with each other, which made for a more peaceful and happier court.

Aleneil was neither so satisfied nor so at ease. She and Lady Lee had fought a rearguard action to keep Anne out of Henry's bed, but they had failed. Twelve days of foul weather with nothing to do and nowhere to go had raised boredom to a peak. Twelve days of cramped quarters, which forced Anne and Henry into more proximity than they were accustomed to, which provided only their bedchambers for private talk at last overcame the barriers each had raised.

Anne had been accepted by the French king, and she knew he preferred her not only for personal but for political reasons, as she was not tied by blood to Spain and the emperor. She was reasonably sure Francis would make every effort he could to make the pope see reason. Moreover the king had gone so far— ennobling her, publicly giving her Catherine's jewels— not her personal jewels but the queen of England's jewels—bringing her with him to meet the king of France. She was sure that Henry would marry her. What a fool he would look if he tried to cast her off.

Henry also felt that political events were pushing the pope in his direction; Francis had offered to marry his second son to the pope's niece—a strong tie there. But even if Francis could not push the pope into agreeing to the divorce there was a lesser matter that he could forward. With Warham dead, an archbishop of Canterbury sympathetic to Henry's view that he, not the pope, ruled the Church of England was possible. And once that new archbishop was consecrated by the pope, Henry's marriage to Catherine could be reexamined by English clerics, in which case Henry was assured that the marriage would be declared null and void.

The king's party had finally managed to cross on the twelfth of November, although it was a horrible voyage of nearly a whole day and night. However, they arrived safely at Dover and rode back to London where there was a joyous thanksgiving in St. Paul's. Henry and Anne could each retire to their luxurious apartments to rest and think over what had occurred.

By then it was too late to preserve Anne's virginity, of course. Aleneil knew when Anne finally succumbed and knew too that the coupling had not been much of a pleasure from Anne's point of view. That, at least, Anne had sense enough to keep to herself, possibly even—as the soft-voiced Lady Alana advised as soon as she had a chance—had sense enough to cover with a false enthusiasm. In any case, Henry seemed happy enough and eager enough to seek more of the same even when there was no longer a forced propinquity.

By the middle of December, Anne was pregnant. That rumor flashed around the court like wildfire in a dry summer. Some said it was fed by Anne herself, or by her most intimate ladies, and Anne only laughed; she did not deny. On the twenty-fifth of January, in a very private ceremony, Anne and Henry were married. The marriage was kept secret for the time being, while Cranmer was proposed and, by the end of March, consecrated archbishop of Canterbury by the pope.

Only twelve days after receiving the pallium, Cranmer requested permission to examine the matter of the king's marriage and by the twenty-third of May Henry's marriage to Catherine was declared null and void, making his marriage to Anne valid and the child she was carrying legitimate. Six days after Cranmer's judgment was made public, Anne was crowned queen.

The coronation had been planned well in advance, of course. The archbishop considerately informed the king of each step in the examination of his marriage and an estimate of how long it would take. Thus it was possible to recall FitzRoy and Lord Henry from France in time to take part in the coronation. Denoriel had been about to slide away into obscurity as soon as his young companions were safe ashore, but to his dismay Norfolk was in the welcoming party.

Instead of a cold dismissal—which he was afraid would inspire an equally cold (or worse yet, a hot) rejoinder by FitzRoy—for at fourteen and with the experience of life in two sophisticated courts behind him, Harry was no one's boy any more—Norfolk seized upon him with expressions of delight.

"Lord Denno. Just the man I was hoping to see. I was going to ask Richmond whether he was still in touch with you—" those words caused a fleeting expression of dissatisfaction to flicker across Norfolk's face, but it was gone as soon as it came, and he continued "—so I could get your direction. I remember when you played King of Misrule the Christmas of '32. You are the man to create the spectacle we need to lead the water pageant for the queen's coronation."

Denoriel groaned aloud and without any pretense. "Your Grace, that was one small device to make a smoke. I am not a magician and the man from whom I learned the tricks is—"

"No matter. No matter. Then you made smoke. And I remember you made sparkles leap from the staff you carried. We need much the same—sparkles to fly from the torches of the wild men and flame to belch from the throat of a dragon. Come to me when you are returned to London so I can show you the boat that will carry the spectacle. You will, of course, let me know what help you will need."

Over the next two days as the party returned to London, Denoriel tried in vain to escape his fate. It was Lord Henry who saved his groats by introducing him to the producers of masques, who in turn led him to the artificers who created the spectacles for the masques. Fire-breathing dragons were all in a day's (or at least two weeks') work to them.

Since Denoriel could enhance the pitiful foot-long tongue of fire to several yards of brilliant pyrotechnic without even being near enough for the metal inside the mechanism to cause him discomfort, the show was a resounding success. His wild men waved their sparkling torches and their bellowing could be heard not only on the barges that followed his light wherry, but on both banks of the river. And the barges that followed, all fifty belonging to the great London guilds, were bright and glittering with bunting, gold foil, and silver bells.

They had four days of it, processions and pageants and people in the street. If there was no wild enthusiasm for Anne, there was no protest either. Free shows and free food were welcome on any account. It was, all in all, a much grander coronation than that of Catherine, and even more impressive than the celebration held for the visit of Charles V. To any observers, except perhaps the Imperial ambassador, it was clear that the king had had his way; Queen Anne had been crowned with the assent of the people.

Free of duty, after a few days' rest, FitzRoy and Lord Henry returned to France, but this time they knew they could not remain long. The queen was already big-bellied with the child she carried and it was said she would be delivered by the end of September. The ten weeks that the young men had were spent in a round of visits of farewell and hearty invitations to the friends they had made to come and visit them in England—FitzRoy at least had his own establishment in which to make them welcome.

FitzRoy also had a private reason for suspecting he would not soon return to France. He had become reacquainted with Lord Henry's younger sister Mary in Calais, where she had been one of Anne's ladies. And he had spent more time with her in London as they waited endlessly to rehearse their roles in the coronation events.

FitzRoy had found being with Mary very pleasant; he liked her soft voice and gentle manner and their ties as children made for easy conversation. She was pretty, too. Thus, when Norfolk had approached FitzRoy on whether he would be willing to have Mary to wife, he had asked for some days to think, had consulted Denno, and had agreed.

He understood that the marriage was primarily designed to declare publicly that he was no longer a possible choice for the throne. While there remained the possibility that his father would name him heir, marriages to French and Spanish princesses had been considered. To bind him to an English nobleman's daughter implied that he was no longer a bargaining chip.

A secondary purpose, which Denoriel pointed out, was to extend Norfolk's influence over him. The third duke of Norfolk was not particularly astute in his relations with people, but he had realized, Denoriel said, that he could no longer simply order FitzRoy to do anything. Harry had not only the king's ear but Lady Anne's as well. If Norfolk needed to direct Harry's behavior, it was easier to do so through a wife. FitzRoy had almost balked at that, but Denoriel laughed and said it was no bad thing, since messages could be transmitted both ways.

In general FitzRoy was not particularly enamored of the idea of being married—he was only fourteen years old and had been relishing his freedom—but he understood the political reasons. In addition he was as eager as his father, if not more eager, to see himself removed from the royal line.

As to the particular bride chosen for him, he was well enough pleased. He had seen most of the ladies of suitable birth, and Mary was the best of them.

Of course, no mortal woman could compare with the beauty of the elven ladies he had met Underhill. In truth, it was the elven ladies for whom he yearned, for whom, in dreams, his loins burned, of whom he thought when he needed to rouse his body. But he knew any hope of an elven lover was impossible. His life and his duty were here in the mortal world, and part of that duty was marriage to Mary.

It was not so terrible; actually it would be pleasant to have an agreeable constant companion in Baynard's castle to read with and talk with and play at cards with. FitzRoy said his good-byes in France and headed back to England cheerfully enough.

Lord Denno was waiting for him at Baynard's Castle and invited himself to dinner. They were alone, except for Sir Edward, who excused himself early to go out and notify some friends of his arrival.

"There is a plague among your wine casks," Denoriel said. "I will show you some surprising ways to amend it if you will come down into the cellars with me."

"With all my heart," FitzRoy replied, his eyes brightening. "Nothing is more of interest to me than learning more about my cellars."

In an arch behind one of the great tuns, the bricks were blurred by age and shadow and were quite solid—unless a Sidhe lord held one's hand. Then the shadow deepened to featureless black and if one's courage did not fail, one could step through. To Denoriel's eyes the black was not featureless. In it appeared a bright blue diamond with a round picture at each point. One was the silver trees and star mosaic of Elfhame Avalon Gate. That he chose.

Lady Aeron and Miralys were waiting. FitzRoy first bowed profoundly to the elvensteed and then threw his arms around her neck and kissed her muzzle. Denoriel suspected that Lady Aeron felt much the same affection for her rider; there was no need for her to have come. Miralys could have carried both of them the short distance to the great Mirror of the FarSeers.

Four ladies waited. FitzRoy slid down from Lady Aeron and bowed to each in turn. The eldest spoke to him.

"This is no new thing we are showing you, but a Vision that came to our youngest, the Lady Aleneil, more than eight of your years ago."

The lens rose and the first image that appeared was the face of the scowling red-haired babe. FitzRoy breathed "Henry" when he saw who held the child, but a sharp gesture silenced him and in the lens the different futures of the realm of Logres unfolded.

A breeze came up, seeming to blow away the pictures. It fluttered FitzRoy's hair so that the blue six-pointed star glittered and flashed on his forehead. Slowly the lens sank down again. Aleneil stepped forward.

She said to FitzRoy, "You understood?"

"That the red-haired child is linked to a golden future, yes. I understood that. And I understood, too, that without that child, misery and horror will overtake my country. What I do not understand is what this has to do with me."

Aleneil sighed. "Neither do we—except when I

Looked at England without you in the future, it was all smoke and screaming and burning, and Elfhame Logres itself was empty, Llachar Lle a tumbled ruin."

"No!" FitzRoy exclaimed.

Denoriel put a hand on his shoulder. "That was what won you a fairy guardian. You soon became precious to me for yourself, Harry, but I was sent to you because we knew you could not be risked. For the sake of England and Logres, both in the mortal world and Underhill you had to grow to be a man."

"So that was why those men tried to kill me and over the years . . ." He looked from Denoriel to Aleneil. "I will do what I can, whatever I can. Indeed, my life would be a very small price to pay to save the beauty of Elfhame Logres and Llachar Lle. Just tell me what I must do."

"We do not know," Aleneil admitted. "That is the danger in FarSeeing. It often tells you just enough to drive you to act but does not show the right action. I hope that when you see the red-haired child, you will know."

"The babe that will be born to Queen Anne?"

Slowly Aleneil shook her head. "There has been no Vision but—but my heart says yes."

FitzRoy's heart said yes too, and he settled down to wait for Anne to deliver her child. Not, of course, that he was not occupied with other matters. Although there was no possibility of going north to take up his duties there, he began to take an interest in them and to read the reports of the councilors. Norfolk invited him to discuss his forthcoming wedding, telling him with a sour expression that final arrangements would be made only if the babe lived through the delivery and was healthy. If it died, FitzRoy would be restored to his old ambiguous position as possible heir.

Although FitzRoy was no more eager for being a

married man than in the past, he infinitely preferred
that state to possible heir. His attention fixed even more
firmly on Anne and her offspring. Prodded by Denoriel,
he sent messages and presents to Mary, but the truth
was that he was he hardly thought of her. He was far
more interested in the birth of Anne's child than in
his own marriage.

Anne retired "to her chamber" as was the custom
for women about to deliver at the end of August.
Usually about six weeks were allowed before delivery,
but Anne surprised everyone by giving birth—with
surprising ease—to a baby girl on September seventh.

It was not only the king and court who were surprised by Anne's early delivery. Vidal Dhu had also
been caught unprepared. He and Aurilia had had a
difference of opinion about when to snatch the child.
Vidal insisted on organizing a force to abduct the newborn baby during the excitement and confusion of the
delivery. He insisted that Sidhe could be disguised as
maids and midwives. These attendants often carried
bundles of sheets, large covered bowls, and a variety
of other cloths, boxes, and garments among which a
changeling could be concealed and a mortal child
carried away.

No long elaborate preparation would be necessary
for this changeling. Newborns all looked pretty much
alike, wrinkled and red with eyes swollen shut and near
bald-headed. And it would not matter how long the
changeling lived; many of the king's children had been
dead within hours of their birth.

Aurilia continued to oppose the idea, pointing out
that "at the time of delivery" was very uncertain.
Exactly when the changeling had to be created was
totally unknown; were they to make one every week
until the lady went into labor? And how would they
know what sex? That, the midwives and attendants

would know for certain even as the child emerged from the womb.

Nor was replacing some of the attendants so easy as Prince Vidal implied. Yes, if the labor was very long, they would have time to detain and replace some of those assisting in the birth, but what if it were not?

So when Pasgen arrived with the news that Queen Anne was in labor before even the first changeling had been prepared, Vidal Dhu shrugged. Perhaps another chance to steal the child would present itself or they would simply wait until the queen was disgraced and the child discarded.

In fact the labor was not long. Even had the changeling been ready there would scarcely have been enough time to make the substitution of attendants. And the changeling would have been the wrong sex. Because of the strong influence the FarSeers had predicted the child would have, it was assumed it would be male . . . and it was not.

King Henry had excitedly summoned the greatest nobles who were available as soon as he heard that Anne was truly in labor. Among those able to answer the summons was FitzRoy. He as well as the king and the rest of the court were disappointed that Anne's child was female. All the soothsayers had predicted a boy.

However, as the powerful shrieks of a very strong, healthy, and enraged baby spilled out into the outer chamber where the most important members of the court waited to see the child, a quick recovery was made. The king was so relieved that his precious Anne had been spared and that the babe was alive and, very obviously, strong, that the sex became less important.

Anne had conceived quickly and would doubtless do so again; there was time enough. The next child would be a boy. So, when the chief nurse emerged with the

wrapped child in her arms, Henry received her with
good grace and held her up for all to see.

Forward in the crowd as befitted his status as first
duke in the kingdom, FitzRoy looked up. Both mouth
and eyes opened wide and he stared, utterly transfixed.
He was seeing in life exactly the image from the great
lens Underhill. A full head of brilliant red hair—far
more hair than was usual for a newborn—crowned a
little red face wearing a ferocious scowl. FitzRoy closed
his mouth and swallowed hard. Lady Aleneil was
absolutely right. He knew what he had to do.

CHAPTER 30

FitzRoy needed to exert all his willpower to prevent himself from rushing out of the chamber. He was swept by the most violent need to go home at once to get the iron cross that had lain for years now among his most precious jewels. He needed to bring that cross and hang it around the neck of this most precious child. He could almost feel the powers of darkness gathering around her.

Naturally he did not dare rush away. He could imagine the ugly interpretation that would be put upon such behavior. The king would be appalled, and the entire court would say that he was angry because a girl—a legitimate girl—would replace him in the royal line. However, he had not spent a year in the French court where the English were regarded *very* suspiciously without learning how to control his expression. He stood still, smiling at the baby—actually, that was very easy—as long as the king displayed her.

That scowl. With a leaping heart FitzRoy realized it was not bad temper—although the child had been furious enough at her undignified expulsion from her mother's womb. Clearly she had a strong will of her own, but that scowl marked a characteristic far more important than that. This red-haired babe was already trying to see, trying to understand what was happening.

Then the king handed her back to her nurse, but still FitzRoy could not leave. He had to congratulate his father and say all the right things, that he was sorry the child had not been male as prophesied but that she was clearly a strong and healthy babe. A boy would follow. Henry nodded and smiled, clasped his son around the shoulders, smiled even more broadly when FitzRoy expressed his hopes for Anne's and the child's continued well-being. And still he could not leave. He had to show his smiling face, his true gladness about the child to all those assembled.

Dawn was breaking by the time FitzRoy left Greenwich. He had an apartment in the palace and could have stayed, but the iron cross was in Baynard's Castle. He had only one guard with him—the close watch that had been kept on him for so long was no longer necessary—but he had kept the four men in his service. They were by now utterly devoted and much more useful than silly pages. Now he told Gerrit to see if he could hire a boat to take them back to London.

"Never mind." Denoriel's voice came out of the shadows. "I've a boat at the water stairs. Tell me!"

"It is she!"

"She? She?"

"The red-haired babe. She. Yes. Oh, Denno, I could sense the greatness in her."

The Sidhe was silent as they made their way to the water stair and then down to where the boat waited. FitzRoy was too excited to notice that the boatmen were very odd-looking, and Denno led him to the stern of the small vessel and bade him sit.

"You are sure?" he asked FitzRoy intently. "You are sure this is the red-haired babe? Is there some way you can bring me to look at her?"

"Not at once, no. But sure? Of course I am sure. Why do you think I did not even stop to piss after waiting all those hours? I must get back to Baynard's Castle to get the iron cross for her. Do you not think whoever tried to seize me will try to seize her?"

Denoriel blinked at him. "Yes, of course, but . . . but what am I to do? You were a little boy and I could find reasons to be near you. How am I to protect a little girl?"

FitzRoy turned toward him, his face alight. "Do you remember that Lady Aleneil said I would know what part I had to play in the saving of Logres? She was right. It is true. I knew the moment I saw the child. My part is to do for her what you did for me. She is my sister. I am her older brother. She is an enchanting child. What more natural than that I should be enamored of her and wish to watch by her and, when she is a little older, play with her?"

A cold wash of fear passed over Denoriel. It was mad for a fourteen-year-old mortal boy to try to stand between Vidal Dhu and a child whom the dark Sidhe was determined to take. Danger . . . death lay that way. He leaned forward and took FitzRoy's hand.

"Harry, have a care to yourself, too. I . . . I feel you are right and that you, the only one who knows of the kind of enemies who threaten the child, the only one with status enough in the court to come close to her, must watch over her. But do not be so proud that you refuse me a part in your duties. There are helpers I can obtain for you and, if necessary, spells."

FitzRoy gripped Denoriel's hand. "Thank God for that, Denno. I know I will need all the help I can get."

"Indeed you will," Denoriel sighed, "and this I suspect will be no short task. She is a *female*. That means if Queen Anne bears a boy, he will come first in the succession. Even if she does not, there will be many who insist that the elder princess, Mary, should come first to the throne . . . and with Mary come the fires of Inquisition." He shuddered.

FitzRoy hardly heard him. The gentle rocking of the boat as they moved upriver was reminding him that he had no sleep at all the previous night and his eyes were beginning to close. He sighed and his head sagged back against the cushions of the seat in the stern. He still held Denno's hand, trying to think of a way to present the iron cross to those who cared for the baby. He knew that any gift he offered would be accepted, but the chances were that the iron cross would be relegated to the bottom of some chest and immediately forgotten. It was only iron, plain cold iron.

The trip downriver back to Greenwich the next day, with the cross where he could easily reach it in his sleeve, was much quicker than that the previous night upriver to London. It made no difference; he still had not thought of a way to arrange for the baby to wear the iron cross. Beside that, he had conceived the fear that the child had already been snatched. She was a princess and would have every attention, but no one but he could realize how precious, in how much danger she was.

He tried on three separate occasions that afternoon to get in to see the child. He would know at once if any exchange had been made, whereas her attendants might only think she was sickening, as several of the king's children had before. But he could not say that to anyone. Who would believe him? They would say he was mad.

Lady Margaret Bryan, who had been nurse to Princess Mary and was now appointed to care for the new princess, had come out to speak to him herself on his third visit. He smiled at her and asked eagerly, "I . . . is she well? Does she cry lustily? Is her color good?"

A dying changeling had no lusty voice; it made faint mewling sounds and its skin was like potter's clay, gray and moist. There was a moment of silence while Lady Bryan stared at him, and then FitzRoy blushed hotly, realizing that her gaze held a kind of horrified suspicion. Her charge was only a girl and had bumped him off the line of succession. Could he be hoping the same fate would overtake this child as those of Queen Catherine and the king?

Finally she said, "Those are very particular questions, Your Grace. How is it that you are so intent on the princess's health?"

FitzRoy swallowed and then, hurt and flustered, made everything worse. "I would not hurt her," he said. "I love her. I think she is the most adorable baby I have ever seen—"

Lady Bryan's lips thinned. "Yes? A quick-found love. And how many newborn babies have you seen, Your Grace?" She looked him up and down, sniffed, and turned away.

Appalled at what he had done, FitzRoy stood looking after her, biting his lip. He knew he would make things worse if he pursued her, and he nervously ran a hand through his hair, pushing it off his forehead. A maid who had followed Lady Bryan through the hangings that separated the inner and outer chamber but had stopped near the entrance when she saw Lady Bryan engaged, uttered a small gasp.

FitzRoy jerked his eyes away from the spot where

Lady Bryan had passed through the hangings and looked at the maid. He saw that she was carrying an armful of cloths that must be for diapering or swaddling. She would be one of the women who actually tended to the child physically and a hope rose in him.

"Should I know you?" he asked, beckoning to her.

She was of an age to have attended him when he was an infant. She might be one who was regularly employed in the king's household for such a purpose. If only it were so . . . he almost held his breath. She shook her head, but a little to his surprise, she came toward him, her eyes still fixed on his face.

"I do not know how you could, Your Grace," she said very softly. "I was a nursemaid to Her Grace the queen when she was an infant, and she remembered me and did me the great honor of offering me a place in Her Grace the princess's household."

Made uneasy by the woman's stare, still fixed on his forehead, FitzRoy raised a hand to pull his bangs down. He knew there must be some mark there that could not be discerned by mortals because when his hair became disarranged Underhill, everyone stared at him just as this woman was doing. To his astonishment, the maid put out one hand and caught at his wrist.

"Who are you?" she asked in a murmur.

"I am the duke of Richmond, the child's half-brother."

The maid nodded. "I heard Lady Bryan call you 'Your Grace' but I didn't know . . . It was true what you said to her? That you love the baby and would not hurt her?"

Her eyes did not meet his; they were fixed on his forehead. FitzRoy wondered what she saw there, but he would not ask her. He was cold as ice with fear. If she were Unseleighe Sidhe, he might be too late to save the princess. His free hand slipped into the sleeve of his gown and he gripped the cross. At least he would have some revenge.

"Yes, it is true. I love her. I would gladly give my life to protect her, but Lady Bryan suspects that I wish her harm because she is now the king's heir. It is not true. I fear for her and would offer her what little protection I have to give, this good-luck charm."

He pulled the cross from his sleeve and slapped it into the hand that still lightly touched his wrist. The maid started slightly, but did not cry out and instinctively closed her hand instead of flinging the cross away. *Not Sidhe, then*, FitzRoy thought. So how could she see whatever marked him? A witch?

She was looking down at the cross, then raised her eyes again to look at his forehead. "Iron," she breathed. "You want the babe to wear cold iron?"

FitzRoy nodded. He could not speak of anything pertaining to Underhill, which meant he could not warn against the Unseleighe Sidhe. And what if she were their agent? She could be a mortal enslaved to the Unseleighe. She would take his cross and throw it into the deepest, darkest privy she could find.

He almost snatched the cross back from her hand and then remembered what she had said about being Anne's nursemaid. And Anne, Denoriel had told him, was a witch herself—untrained and utterly rejecting of her Talent, but still a witch. The maid had swiftly secreted the cross within the bundle of cloths she carried. Now she curtsied and smiled at him.

"It will be done," she said. "And you are in time with it. The child is strong. She suckles well; the wet nurse complained of the grip of her jaws, young as she is. She is rosy and warm."

FitzRoy sighed with relief. "If you need anything or if you see anything that is alarming to you, send for me. I will be staying in Greenwich as long as the child is here, but my home is in Baynard's Castle in London, hard by the river Thames. I . . . I have friends who might help if there is a threat."

"My name is Blanche Parry," the maid said, "and if you want news of the child, you had better ask for me. Also you had better not come here again, at least not until there are other visitors, or Lady Bryan may mark you down as suspicious and unwelcome."

FitzRoy had been feeling better, not quite such a fool for giving away his precious cross, until that last sentence. His heart sank. Who knew what the maid was. He should have brought Denno—somehow he would have to arrange for Denno to see her, but he knew that would be very difficult.

He left Anne's apartment and went to find Denno near the stables where men came and went constantly. He told Denoriel his fears and suspicions, but did not receive the reproaches he expected. Instead Denno said, "Queen Anne's nursemaid, was she? Very interesting. No, I don't think she could be an Unseleighe slave. That would mean the Unseleighe FarSeers had Visions almost thirty years before ours and arranged to place one of their own in the Boleyn household. Unlikely. I'll ask Aleneil, but I don't think the FarSeeing works that way when it affects both the Seleighe and Unseleighe Courts. How come she spoke to you?"

"Because I pushed back my hair," FitzRoy said, his voice suddenly hard. "Denno, what did she see on my forehead?"

"She saw King Oberon's mark?" Denoriel whistled softly. "That is most unusual, most unexpected. She must be a strong witch, very Talented."

"You never told me there was something on my forehead."

The cold anger in FitzRoy's voice finally pierced

Denoriel's concentration on the maid. "No, I didn't," he admitted. "I'm sorry, Harry. Because it was my fault, you see. That cross is so strong that it made my bones ache even when it was in its pouch. You were marked to protect you, so you wouldn't have to wear the cross any more. No one from . . . from anywhere would dare hurt you or try to abduct you. Then when the danger was past, I was so used to seeing the mark upon you that it simply never occurred to me to say anything about it."

Having been skillfully led away from the question of whether the mark was what also prevented him from speaking of Underhill, FitzRoy shook his head. He could never be angry with Denno for more than a few moments. He owed him too much, loved him too much.

"What is the mark?" he asked.

"A six-pointed star that glows bright blue."

FitzRoy's eyes widened; he sighed. "I guess I'm glad no one can see it but your people . . . and a witch or two."

"Witch, yes." Denoriel's mind returned to the problem of Blanche Parry. "Why would the Boleyns hire a witch—and strong as she is, it is likely she was known to be a witch—to be a nursery maid? And why would Anne send all the way to Hever for a nursery maid? Is it possible that odd things happened in the nursery when Anne was a baby? Did they need someone who would understand and could control the events? And was Anne afraid her child might exhibit her unwanted Talent and be thought unsuitable to rule? No, I don't think Mistress Parry is of the Unseleighe—but I will ask."

In fact FitzRoy did not need to wait until Denoriel's questions about Blanche Parry were answered. Only three days later, when he took part in the magnificent christening ceremony that named the child Elizabeth, he saw that the iron cross was pinned to the inside of the chrisom, the robe in which the child would be wrapped when she was taken from the baptismal font. More important, he saw Elizabeth herself, red-haired and rosy and with a pair of lungs that produced shrieks that made the church of the Grey Friars echo when the cold water struck her.

Now that the child was baptized and Anne was almost fully recovered, although she was still confined to her apartment because she had not yet been churched, visitors were encouraged. FitzRoy was among the first. Lady Bryan watched him suspiciously, but she soon softened toward him.

He spent hours by Elizabeth's cradle, just watching her. There was devotion on his face, gentleness when he cautiously touched the baby's down-soft cheek, and a marked quickness to come between the cradle and any person not in Elizabeth's own household that approached her. Anne noticed and laughed, complaining that her erstwhile friend was faithless and had abandoned her for a younger and more beautiful woman.

"Perhaps not more beautiful," FitzRoy temporized with a sigh and a laugh, "but I certainly have been ravished away. You are still the most witty and lovely lady of my acquaintance, but it is Elizabeth who has a tight grip on my heart."

"For shame," Anne said. "Are you not about to marry Lady Mary Howard? It is she who should hold your heart."

"Yes, and I love Mary dearly, for she is pretty and clever and sweet. I look forward to our marriage. Only—" his eyes drifted back to the cradle and the sleeping child within "—only Elizabeth must come first."

Actually Anne was rather shocked by FitzRoy's fixation on her child and she told Henry, who laughed heartily. "Our child is his salvation from a fate he could barely tolerate," the king said. "I remember how I felt when my poor brother Arthur sickened and then died. Harry has no taste for power . . . yet. Now he sincerely hopes for a boy to be my heir, but meanwhile he wants to make very sure that Elizabeth survives to stand between him and the throne."

His affection and well-meaning accepted at the highest levels, FitzRoy was free to spend as much time with Elizabeth as he liked. However for the next few weeks he did not have all that much free time. There was the matter of his marriage. He pleaded that Elizabeth's need was more important; Denoriel countered with the fact that all doubts had been put to rest about Blanche Parry. She was a strong witch, a white witch, and for a few weeks, she and the cold iron cross could protect the child.

Fired with the purpose that had consumed him with his first sight of the red-haired babe, FitzRoy protested. Denoriel lectured him on the need to make his bride happy. He and Mary were making a life union. For the sake of the long years they would spend together, he must show her that he cared for her. He reminded FitzRoy of the misery of Mary's own mother, who had separated from Norfolk largely because of his mistress, and pointed out that Mary might fear her own life would go the same way.

Partly out of liking, partly out of pity, FitzRoy pushed his obsession with Elizabeth aside and began to pay attention to his future wife. He found her warm and pleasant and was definitely looking forward to their union . . . only that was a grave disappointment. He and Mary were married quietly with no royal pomp or celebration . . . and then told that they were not to live together because they were too young to cohabit.

FitzRoy thought back to his year in France and laughed aloud rather raucously, but when he looked at Mary he saw that relief predominated over disappointment in her face. He realized that she was afraid, and took her hand. Looking into her eyes, he said he was sadly discontent, that he had been relishing the thought of her company, that he had envisioned quiet evenings where he would read to her as she embroidered or that she would play for him on the virginals and sing or they could play music together. They could go together to a masque or to a friend's house to dine and then talk about their experience when they returned home. He looked to Norfolk and said that if he promised there would be no more to their marriage than that until permission was given for more, could he not have Mary's company at Baynard's Castle?

"Next year, perhaps," Norfolk said firmly.

So FitzRoy hugged Mary and let her go and her father shepherded her away. However, once the immediate sense of deprivation was overcome, FitzRoy was glad of Norfolk's stricture. He was able to move to Greenwich—his father always welcomed his company and Anne did, too, now that she was safely married. Since he no longer needed to be with Mary—although Dunstan took on the duty of reminding him to send his wife trinkets and tokens; several times a week one of his guards carried to her a book, a pretty comb, a lace kerchief—he could watch the little princess become more awake and more aware day by day.

He was not the only one who watched her, of course. One at least of Catherine's children had lived six weeks before it died. But Elizabeth gave no cause for alarm. She continued to nurse greedily, and her

shrieks when anything displeased her were evidence
of her will and strength.

Anne was churched after six weeks, according to
custom, but she kept Elizabeth by her another six
weeks. At the end of that time the king began to grow
impatient with the mother instinct that wanted to keep
the child close. It was a girl; he and Anne had better
set about making a boy. Elizabeth and her entourage
of servants were moved to Hertford by the king's order.

FitzRoy followed, found lodging in the area, and
continued his visits to his half-sister. She was old
enough at three months to be tickled and made to
laugh, to be gently swung back and forth in his arms
and soothed when she was fretful. And now, well away
from the king and queen, he brought his dear friend,
the man who had thrice saved his life, to see the baby.

Lady Bryan was stiff with disapproval at that first
meeting, but that did not last long. Denno was as much
of a charmer as King Henry, although his use of that
talent was never so selfish, and he regaled her with
tales about FitzRoy's childhood. He glowed with love
and Lady Bryan recognized a kindred spirit. Before he
left, Denoriel had held Elizabeth in his arms under
Lady Bryan's watchful but approving eye.

"She is, indeed, the red-haired babe of the
FarSeeing," he said to FitzRoy as they rode back to
the house FitzRoy had let two miles down the road.
"I did not really doubt you, Harry. I just . . . I hoped
you might be mistaken, merely enamored of a beautiful baby."

"Why?" FitzRoy asked sharply. "Is she not all that
was promised? Is there not a spirit in her that can . . ."

"Yes! But she is *female*, Harry."

They entered the farmhouse, where FitzRoy shouted
for a servant to bring mulled ale, and hurried into the

parlor where two cushioned chairs stood before a large hearth holding a bright fire. The night air was cold at the end of November.

"So what if she is female," FitzRoy said, harking back to Denoriel's last remark. "Thank God there is no Salic law in this realm as there is in France. There is nothing to prevent her from taking the throne. And once she has it—"

"Yes, Harry, but taking the throne is the rub. Not only will any male child precede her but also her elder sister. And if Elizabeth does not yield there will be civil war. Perhaps it is from that rather than from the Inquisition that the burning and misery come." Denoriel rubbed his temple; arguing with Harry made his head ache. "But what I am trying to say, Harry, is that there will be no quick seating of Elizabeth on her father's throne as there would have been if she had been male. There will be long years of danger through which we must guard her if the bright future promised is to come."

"Long years," FitzRoy echoed, looking troubled. "But . . . but once she is a maiden, not a child, I will not be able to . . . to watch over her bed or be with her as constantly as I am now."

"We will cross that bridge when we come to it. There is always Aleneil, who can become an intimate, and likely we will be able to find a way for Blanche Parry to remain with Elizabeth." Denoriel nodded thoughtfully as he said that, and indeed, getting Aleneil placed in Elizabeth's household was indeed the best solution. "Our business is to give her enough protection now to ward off any attempt on her that neglect might encourage. For now your care and Blanche's will be enough. The real danger to her will be if Anne conceives soon and births a strong son."

"But why? Surely that will make her less important."

The mulled ale came and Denoriel was silent until both had tasted it and approved and the servant had withdrawn. Then Denoriel said, "The one who wants her does not want her for the power she will have over England. He wants her for her inventive mind and strong will. And he wants her while she is still very young so that she can be bred up to believe what they wish her to believe, to relish cruelty."

FitzRoy looked appalled. "It would be terrible to so pervert her bright spirit. What more can we do to protect her?"

"Fortunately right now I doubt we need to do more than not invite an attack by neglect of the precautions we are taking." He sighed as he said that; now his beloved Harry was safe—or safer—but at the moment when he should be able to breathe a little, now there was a new danger to a new child! "For the moment we have one advantage. There is a prohibition against harming or abducting anyone really close to King Henry. That was what protected Anne, and I think it will be of some protection to Elizabeth while she is heir to the throne. However, the less important she becomes to the king, the more danger that she will be taken."

"You said that before," Harry replied, looking confused, "But I still don't understand."

"Harry, say Elizabeth be taken and someone—say, Blanche—cries that the true child was replaced by a changeling and it was the changeling that died, not the true Elizabeth. That might be believed. King Henry is tired of dead children. Other men's children live, his die. He will want to believe the child's death was not his fault nor Anne's." He waited to see if Harry understood.

Knowing his father now, FitzRoy nodded.

"So, Henry will give order that a hunt be made for

the source of the changeling. What would they look for?" He paused.

"Elves," FitzRoy said flatly.

"Exactly so," Denoriel agreed. "And even if they did not find me, nor Aleneil, the danger is not over. There are human sorcerers and some are strong, like Blanche Parry. If such a one should seek, he will find Gates like mine, and breaks in the mortal world through which those of Underhill can come and go. We are strong and we have magic, but we are few. Mortals . . . thousands, even hundreds of thousands all garbed in cold iron and carrying iron weapons. . . . We would be overwhelmed."

Queen Anne was pregnant again by February of 1534, and Denoriel's predictions seemed all too likely to come true. In April Blanche reported that she thought "something" was watching Elizabeth, something she could not see but that made a sour smell in her mind. She admitted it did not come close to the child—perhaps the cross always pinned to one garment or another was the reason—but it frightened her.

Denoriel brought her several amulets of Aleneil's devising that she could invoke with a word. Invoked, the spell would cover the baby and the crib. FitzRoy increased the frequency of his visits, and the next time Blanche sensed an intruder, FitzRoy was there, dandling the eight-month-old Elizabeth in his arms.

As usual the child was reaching eagerly toward the star on FitzRoy's forehead when suddenly her mouth twisted and she began to wail; almost in the same moment, Blanche cried out and pointed. Since he could see and sense nothing, FitzRoy could only clutch Elizabeth tighter and let the baby push the hair off his forehead while he stared in the direction the maid had pointed.

In a moment Elizabeth began to laugh again; simultaneously the maid sighed and said the noxious thing—whatever it was—was gone. FitzRoy stayed a little longer to make sure it would not return and then began to pray for Denoriel to come. There was some tie between them; FitzRoy did not know how it could work, but when he was really distressed and *needed* the Sidhe, mostly he soon arrived—as he did early that evening on a Miralys who, for once, looked tired. Ladbroke hurried the elvensteed off to the stable and FitzRoy hurried Denoriel into the house for a glass of wine in the parlor with the doors closed to everyone else.

"What am I to do?" FitzRoy asked after he had described what had happened. "Lady Bryan is most accommodating, but I cannot believe she would allow me to live in the house and sleep in the princess's chamber. And worse than that—" tears stood in his eyes "—I cannot see it or feel it. Even Elizabeth knew it was there. She—"

"The princess knew?" Denoriel breathed.

"She burst into loud wails the moment the maid cried out and pointed, and she began to laugh when it was gone." He was beginning to feel as weary as Denno looked. "Yes, and she constantly tries to touch my forehead. I am afraid she will disarrange my hair before the wrong person."

"You should not be holding her if a wrong person is in the chamber," Denoriel said, but absently, as if his mind were elsewhere, as indeed it was, because he added, "She is Talented, like her mother and her grandfather."

"But I am not!" FitzRoy exclaimed bitterly. "How can I protect her when I cannot see what I am to fight?"

Denoriel put his wine down on the polished table

that stood against the wall and came forward to embrace FitzRoy. "It is hard for you, I know, but I promise you will be able to see anything you need to fight. This thing that came into the princess's chamber could do her no physical harm. It was most likely one of the minor creatures, which has no physical reality in the mortal world. I am sure it was sent only to spy, to carry back word of the defenses we maintain."

"But I think it was the mark on my forehead that sent it away," he protested, "and I cannot be with the child every hour of the day and night."

"I will obtain more amulets," Denno said firmly. "Blanche can invoke one each night. During the day, I think there is too much going on in Elizabeth's apartment to invite any secret attempt to steal the child."

However extra precautions were not necessary for long. In July Elizabeth became the sole heir to the throne again when Anne miscarried. Anne was devastated—and with good reason. The king did not take this loss well. He had accepted a daughter instead of a son because the child was strong and healthy and confirmed his belief in his virility.

That robust child, with her strong will and the voice to enforce it, with the fact that she had already survived two of the illnesses that often carried off weaker babes, ensured in the king's mind that the failures of Catherine's pregnancies were her fault. The fact that Anne conceived again so soon after Elizabeth's birth also soothed the terrible fears of inadequacy that had been aroused by the long periods between Catherine's conceptions and Catherine's inability to bear more than one child that lived.

Anne's miscarriage was a poisonous reminder of all those dead or too-early-born babies. Worse, it pointed the finger at *him*. That Catherine's children had not lived was as likely to be her fault as his, but when a second wife also dropped children too early . . .

Anne was not only grief-stricken but badly frightened. It took weeks for the soft-voiced Lady Alana to get through the queen's self-absorption and convince her that her safety lay in soothing the king, in convincing him it was no fault in his seed that brought the child too early, that she would conceive again . . . as soon as he was active in her bed. Henry was shaken, but Anne's magic did not fail completely. If he found it almost impossible to rouse himself to couple, he soon was finding pleasure in her company again.

Underhill, Vidal Dhu and Aurilia were again having discussions about when to move to seize Elizabeth. Although they had a plan for destroying Anne, they had been well pleased when she conceived so quickly and had done nothing at all to interfere. It was Elizabeth they wanted, not the queen of England. If Anne had a son who lived, the watch on the red-haired babe would be much reduced. It would be much easier to replace the child with a changeling. And when that changeling sickened and died, there would be some grief, but a living son would compensate.

Vidal Dhu, always impatient, felt they should take Elizabeth while Anne and the king were still grief-stricken. One more baby was dead and the king was wondering whether he would ever have a living child beside Mary—who was constantly sick and ailing. It would be no great surprise if the other baby died. No one would look for otherworld causes.

Except perhaps Oberon, Aurilia pointed out, and counseled patience. Anne would conceive again; she was so fertile that even the king's feeble seed could take hold. There was no great hurry. Elizabeth was not yet a year old, young enough to bend to their ways easily. Let Anne try again. If she was successful and bore a live and healthy boy, they could take Elizabeth as soon as the boy was well established. If this pregnancy failed, it would be very easy indeed to destroy Anne in such a way that Elizabeth would be totally cast off. No one would care whether she lived or died.

Reluctantly, because he did not enjoy waiting for something he wanted, and he wanted to start work on that child, but almost relieved, too, because he knew abducting Elizabeth was coming close to violating Oberon's orders, Vidal Dhu yielded to Aurilia's arguments. Later they quarreled over the agreement more than once, because it took almost a year before Anne conceived again. Elizabeth, with her strong will and quick mind, was getting beyond the stage when she would accept Caer Modrun as her natural home and the ways of the Unseleighe as the only right ways.

In that judgment, Vidal Dhu was correct. Elizabeth now walked and talked and knew her own mind very well indeed. Beyond that, she often said and did things that left Lady Bryan, who had nursed Mary and not seen such precocity, amazed.

Elizabeth had called FitzRoy "da" with her very first word. Everyone had laughed heartily and FitzRoy explained that he was not her "da" but her brother. Elizabeth could not say brother; her little face drew together in her well-recognized scowl and she said "da" again . . . at the top of her voice.

From time to time FitzRoy tried other names for himself, Henry, Harry, Richmond. "Da," said Elizabeth, fixing him with eyes that had changed from a baby's unformed blue to honey-brown but could flash brilliant yellow, like a lioness's.

He was relieved to learn that Elizabeth also called King Henry "da" when he visited, and so long as she did, he put the matter out of his mind. However, when she was nearly two and very articulate, speaking in full sentences that were nearly adult so that she could easily have called him brother or Richmond, he set out to tease her by telling her once again that she was a big girl now and should give him his proper name, reserving "da" for her father.

"I know the king is my father," she said, her eyes dark and quiet, "but you, you will always be 'da.'"

CHAPTER 31

It did not seem as if Princess Elizabeth would have
any need for a special "da" during the remainder of
that year. Her second birthday was celebrated very
happily, although her father and mother could not be
present because they were together in Hampshire
enjoying a particularly pleasant progress. It mattered
little to Elizabeth who had around her all those to
whom she was accustomed and held dear.

Lady Bryan who was sensitive to her charge's willful ways and was curbing them with gentle firmness had,
as a reward for dutiful and unargumentative behavior
over the previous week, invited a select party to celebrate with the household. Not only was FitzRoy (who
would have come invited or not) summoned but Lord
Denno and Lady Alana, too.

Lord Denno had become quite a favorite with Lady
Bryan. She now knew his supposed background and
understood his special relationship with the duke of
Richmond. Considering his wealth and his discretion, she
was willing to encourage his interest in Elizabeth, too.

Lady Alana was invited because Lady Bryan wanted her. She was the queen's lady who most frequently came with messages, gifts, and garments of all kinds, and she was not on duty during the summer progress. And, if Lady Bryan had information or a question she wanted addressed to the queen, Lady Alana was always successful in carrying the message.

Lady Bryan also liked Lady Alana for herself; she was particularly gentle and soft-spoken—but would stand no nonsense, as would the two besotted men, from a naughty two-year-old. Moreover Lady Alana was no court beauty; one could hardly remember her face from one visit to another. Her gowns, however, were utter perfection, not only in fabric and design but in suitability, and she was generous with her suggestions on how anyone else's gown could be improved.

Elizabeth's health remained good, and Lady Bryan should have been perfectly satisfied; however, in the autumn and beginning of winter there were incidents that alarmed her. Twice Elizabeth woke screaming from a dream of something horrible looming over her. The diaper-changer Blanche Parry had been kept on as general nursemaid because she had the queen's favor and Elizabeth was attached to her; she was the one who slept in Elizabeth's room and she woke and calmed the child.

Lady Bryan was sure it was nothing but a nightmare; still she had the room searched both times. There was nothing untoward in it. The guard suggested changing the position of the night candle, which might have cast a shadow where the child could see it. By the time that was done, Elizabeth was asleep again. But one afternoon she had another screaming fit and began to gag, holding her nose and weeping over the terrible, terrible odor.

Lady Bryan smelled nothing and was open-mouthed

with surprise and fear that the child was sickening, but Blanche, who had been in the bedchamber, came running and shouted at Elizabeth to take out and hold up her cross. In a moment the child had calmed, saying the bad smell was gone.

Lady Bryan felt Elizabeth's head, asked nervously about her appetite, and then tried to forget the incident. However, she approved of Blanche's remedy. The cross was an excellent notion, she said; it was the right thing for Elizabeth to trust. In fact, she sent for the local priest and had him bless the cross.

She could have wished that Elizabeth had not chattered about her fright, but there was really no way to stop her. And, anyhow, she herself was not sorry that the tale brought FitzRoy to the house more often than ever.

But Lord Denno, came too, and that troubled her a little. FitzRoy was Elizabeth's brother and entitled to play with her and spoil her, but Lady Bryan was beginning to be concerned about Elizabeth's great affection for Lord Denno.

The child had wonderful times whenever Lord Denno visited. Her favorite game was playing pick-a-back—he was incredibly strong and would carry her about at considerable speed far longer than any other man. Another game made Lady Bryan so nervous that she had to put a stop to it. When Elizabeth rode Denno's shoulders, she would insist on clutching at the air over Denno's head. Lady Bryan was sure the child would be shaken loose and fall even though she insisted she was holding tight to Lord Denno's ears. That was ridiculous; there were no ears to be seen.

Another matter troubled Lady Bryan somewhat. She felt that neither man was as glad about Queen Anne's new pregnancy as he should have been. She could not help wondering if their passion for the princess would make them less loyal to a prince, should he be born.

Unfortunately the question was never to arise. The new year began with grief—at least for Lady Bryan. Catherine of Aragon died on the seventh of January. Having heard of how the king had celebrated in yellow garments of rejoicing and loud denunciations, Lady Bryan kept her few tears for private moments. She had learned to love Queen Catherine when she served as nurse to the Princess Mary.

The memory of Mary distracted Lady Bryan from grief for a moment. She smiled and sighed. Mary had been a sweet child. She sighed again and then laughed; Mary was nothing like the red-headed hellion she had to manage now. Mary had wanted to be good—and she had been, although it made her a little dull too—unlike Elizabeth who wanted first to be *right,* and then to have her way, and then to be good as a very poor third choice.

The sorrow over Queen Catherine had been private. But January continued with one disaster after another. On the evening of the twenty-fourth, a rider on a near-foundered horse came to give Lady Bryan the news that King Henry had had a terrible fall from a horse while jousting and lay unconscious, possibly near death.

Lady Bryan sat by Elizabeth's cradle herself all that night, swallowing and swallowing and wringing her hands. If the king died, by his decree and Parliament's vote, Elizabeth would be the next queen . . . if Mary's supporters did not begin a civil war or rush the indefensible house at Hatfield and kill the child.

By late morning the next day she was not alone. Richmond had arrived as soon as the news came to him. He was a skilled swordsman and he brought six more men armed and in armor. By the second night— after a somewhat less exhausted messenger arrived with the news that the king had regained consciousness but was still in great pain—Lord Denno arrived too.

How he could possibly have come so fast Lady Bryan did not know, but that was a thought that passed through her mind long after the event. At the time, she had been so glad to see him that she did not wonder. Later she was surprised also at the feeling of confidence he gave her. Then she was only glad that the constriction in her chest, the pounding of her heart in her throat was gone. She was so relieved, in fact, that she agreed to go to bed soon after he kissed her hand and assured her all would be well. She slept soundly, too.

"What now?" FitzRoy asked when Lady Bryan was gone, staring down at a sleeping Elizabeth and clenching and unclenching his hands.

"Now we wait," Denoriel said, flatly. He was at least as nervous as FitzRoy, but he had no intention of showing it.

"How long? Should I hire more men?" FitzRoy looked a little wild-eyed. "We cannot remain on guard forever. I am willing, but I am mortal and must sleep."

Denoriel embraced FitzRoy's shoulders and gave him a rough hug. "No more men, they would be useless. Your guards and Dunstan and Ladbroke are all warded against spells, specially those of sleep. The new men would be defenseless."

"Shall I set watches so the men can take some rest?" he persisted.

"I think what will happen will happen soon . . . tonight, I expect." Denoriel had had plenty of time to think out his plans as he sped to Hatfield. "Those who want Elizabeth know that they have only a short time to act, this night and possibly tomorrow, but I doubt they will act by daylight."

FitzRoy blinked. "Why?"

"Think, Harry," Denoriel urged. "If the king should die, royal guards will be sent to protect the new queen, dozens of them, all in steel and armed with steel. Even if Henry lingers but is like to die, the guards will come. And once the king is recovered, if he is recovered, Oberon's order again protects the king's heir."

FitzRoy nodded. "Very well. First we rid ourselves of any servant not quartered in the house, then we lock and bar each door. The shutters are already all closed to keep out the cold."

Denoriel glanced down into the cradle and smiled despite his anxiety. "Elizabeth is asleep and covered with a warding spell. I hope it will keep out the sense of evil that frightens her."

"I hope so too." FitzRoy smiled. "Although she yells so loud that she might frighten them off." He sobered very quickly and continued, "I think I will order that Ladbroke, Dunstan, Nyle, and Shaylor stay by the princess. They are armored in steel and armed with it. They will have Blanche to guard against magic and call for help if needed. Gerrit and Dickson can patrol the house. You and I—" FitzRoy patted his sword hilt and touched the strange metal gun, which for once he wore openly on his belt "—will hold the front door."

They could be overrun by a rush of Unseleighe creatures who were more resistant to cold iron, both knew, but Denoriel had alerted a number of the Sidhe who guarded against Unseleighe attack, and they assured him there had been no troubling of the lower planes. Denoriel himself felt that even Vidal Dhu would not dare bring a large force against the princess's house.

There was considerable local interest in the princess, and when the news of the king's accident spread, attentions fixed on Hatfield. It was expected that attempts would be made to conceal the king's death, if he should die. Thus, many watched to see if the queen would come to take her daughter or if any other large party arrived—such activity might well indicate that the king was dead.

The belief and the curiosity made Denoriel reasonably sure the Unseleighe would not dare bring an army of horrors, which would be sure to be seen by so many watchers. If the princess then sickened and died, the priests would take over for the king and begin to preach against the unholy.

Such guessing made Denoriel uncomfortable; disaster would follow if he were wrong. But he was not. He was right. The assault was signaled by an urgent knock on the door. Denoriel and FitzRoy hurried to the entrance of the first withdrawing room while the steward went to open the door.

The person revealed was mortal to Denoriel's witch sight and was wearing royal livery, so he did not rush forward. The steward backed away to give one whom he assumed to be a messenger room to enter—and in the next moment dropped to the floor. Before Denoriel could react, Pasgen followed the enslaved and corrupted mortal through the front door. FitzRoy, sword drawn, leapt to intercept the man, who was hurrying toward the stair that led up to Elizabeth's chamber.

Denoriel stepped forward to intercept Pasgen, who had clutched in one arm a dead thing that, aside from its red hair, hardly looked human. Behind Pasgen were two dark Sidhe, one of whom contemptuously raised a hand to cast either a spell or a levin bolt.

"No lightnings!" Pasgen snarled, and cast his own spell.

Denoriel did not even shake his head as the command to freeze rolled off his shield. Behind him,

Denoriel heard a frightful squall. Pasgen uttered a violent obscenity and drew his sword, but he made no attempt to attack. Another spell hit Denoriel's shield, much weaker; Denoriel drew his own sword and was amazed to see that Pasgen was already retreating.

Pasgen was not the swordsman that Denoriel was, but he was not so inept as to need to flee before they were engaged. Then Pasgen suddenly ducked sideways and threw the thing he had been carrying directly at Denoriel. Instinctively, Denoriel jumped back out of the way. In the same instant, the corner of his eye caught the second dark Sidhe drawing his bow and an odd hissing sounded almost in his ear.

Denoriel thought that the hiss had been the elf-shot missing him and gasped with fear that the missile had been aimed at Harry. But before the thought had time to form, before he had a chance to turn his head and open himself to Pasgen's sword-thrust, the Sidhe with the bow had screamed, dropped to the ground, and went on screaming. The other Sidhe had disappeared.

Pasgen shouted some curse and slammed his sword into its sheath. Denoriel knew he should act—but he could not think what to do. He dared not turn away to see what had happened to Harry. To rush at Pasgen and run him through was simply not possible. Whatever he thought of his half-brother, Pasgen *was* his brother, blood-kin. He could defend himself against him, but he could not attack him.

Neither attack nor defense was necessary. Pasgen lifted the fallen, screaming Sidhe to his shoulder, raised a hand and pointed. Instinctively, Denoriel jumped back, gesturing for protection, but the spell was not directed at him. The door swung forward and slammed shut. Denoriel whirled around, unable—even if the closing door was an illusion and harm would befall him—to resist seeing if Harry had fallen.

No harm physical had come to FitzRoy. He was standing just behind Denoriel, his mouth fixed in a grimace of horror, his throat working as he swallowed and swallowed to ward off sickness. His right arm was extended, and in his hand was the weird gun he had insisted that Denoriel buy in the Bazaar of the Bizarre.

Denoriel turned to look at the door, but it was no illusion. It was solidly shut. He stepped forward and shot the heavy iron bolt, hissing as it burned his hand. Then he sheathed his sword and went to take Harry in his arms.

"He was ahead. I couldn't reach him with my sword. I yelled for him to stop. I couldn't . . . I couldn't let him reach Elizabeth, so . . . so I shot him. He . . . he made that terrible noise and . . . and then . . . he . . . he fell in on himself and he . . . he turned . . . he turned to dust." FitzRoy's eyes were staring with horror. "The . . . the bolt. It's lying there in the dust."

"Oh, what a fool Pasgen is," Denoriel muttered. He patted Harry's back. "He was very old, Harry. He would have been dust long ago, except for living . . . where he was living. Pasgen set a spell on him to keep him from . . . from going to what he should have been when he came here, and your iron bolt broke the spell."

The boy shuddered in his arms. "That . . . that won't happen to Dunstan or Ladbroke, will it?" His eyes were sick with dread.

Denoriel pushed FitzRoy back far enough so he could see his face. "No, of course not. They are both young men—at least no older than they look. That poor fellow must have been living centuries Underhill as a slave. We Seleighe Sidhe bring the children we save back to the mortal realms—if they wish it—as soon as they are grown. And if they do not wish to return, we never let them cross the wall between the worlds again." Then he realized just what FitzRoy had asked, and stared at him. "How did you know Dunstan and Ladbroke had been to my homeland?"

"Ladbroke knew about Miralys, and Dunstan . . . the way he just accepts a lot of the things you do." FitzRoy sighed. "The way you never try to hide anything from him." Then he shuddered again. "The baby is dead, isn't it?" Tears stood in his eyes.

"Baby?" Denoriel echoed, his glance leaping to the stairwell, but it was empty, Blanche and the guards keeping tight watch on Elizabeth; they had been instructed to ignore any noise or disturbance and they had obeyed.

FitzRoy had gently pulled free of Denoriel's hold and gone to kneel by a small, cold body.

"Don't," Denoriel said.

It was too late. FitzRoy had already turned the poor thing over and he gasped and snatched back his hand in horror. Denoriel ran into the eating parlor and came back with a tablecloth. There was nothing recognizable except the red hair. The features had already melted into a vague pudding of rotting flesh—pits for eyes, holes where the nose should be, and a sunken black hollow for a mouth. The limbs looked soft, boneless. Denoriel threw the cloth over the poor thing and wrapped it firmly.

"How could it rot so fast?" FitzRoy whispered, his voice shaking.

"Because it was never given life, only formed roughly." Denoriel pulled FitzRoy to his feet. "I'm sorry you had to see that, but it was never a living person, Harry. It was just molded out of the mist of one of the places you know. It was as if you made a clay horse, didn't fire it, and then left it out in the rain. Only enough power was used to hold the mist together, and when it drained away the form began to dissolve."

FitzRoy breathed deeply and raised his eyes from

the wrapped bundle to meet Denoriel's gaze. "Will the Sidhe I shot fall apart too? God's Blood, how he screamed!"

Denoriel snorted. "No, he's just more used to hurting others than to being hurt. He'll go on howling until they get him to a healer who will soothe away the pain." Then Denoriel smiled. "You probably saved my life, Harry. If the elf-shot had hit me, I would have been badly injured if not killed."

FitzRoy was rapidly regaining his composure, far more quickly than Denoriel would have thought. "I was afraid of that. That's why I shot him. I had just almost vowed never to use the gun again when I saw what it did, but I couldn't let him shoot you, Denno."

"I'm glad you didn't. Elf-shot is not to be dismissed lightly. And I never thought about it because . . ." He shook his head. It was too unpleasant to admit aloud that he had counted on his brother not wishing to inflict any permanent damage on him . . . and been wrong. He forced a smile. "Don't worry too much. I just had forgotten to tell you what to do if I am hurt. All you need do is see that I'm loaded aboard Miralys. He'll make sure I don't fall off and will take me to a healer."

FitzRoy breathed out, a long, relieved sigh. "Miralys knows where to go?" He laughed shakily. "Of course he does."

A soft groan drew Denoriel's attention and he bent and scooped up the swaddled form. The steward was stirring. A gesture brought Harry's attention to the man.

"Pick up your bolt and scuffle that dust around, it's too man-shaped," Denoriel said. "I'm going to slip out and . . . and take care of this poor thing. And, for the sake of all the gods, don't dare mislay that gun. I had no idea it was going to be so effective. We may need it again."

For a time, however, that likelihood continued to recede. The next afternoon brought the news that the king was no longer in danger and would soon be recovered completely. That put off the need to be specially watchful—or at least, FitzRoy and Denoriel thought, until the spring when Anne's baby should be born . . .

And then tragedy struck again. Queen Anne miscarried of a boy child long enough in the womb to be identifiable but too unripe to be saved.

Early morning on the twenty-ninth of January, a message arrived summoning Fagildo Otstargi to attend on Privy Councilor Cromwell *at once*. The ugly manservant who had met Cromwell's messenger at the door took the message, nodded his head, and closed the door in the messenger's face. He went down into the cellar rather than up to the magician's bedchamber, and walked into a dark corner, from which he did not emerge.

Pasgen cursed fluently when he heard the alarm that heralded an arrival from the London Gate into the prison room below his house. He Gated into the room, took the message and read it, and cursed more fluently. The manservant cringed away, trembling. Pasgen hardly noticed, but he waved at the wall and the Gate to London reopened. The bound being sidled through, weeping with relief.

Barely a quarter hour later, Pasgen himself disguised and dressed as Fagildo Otstargi, stepped through the London gate, but to the terminus in his bedchamber rather than in the cellar. He came down the stairs, swinging a heavy furred cloak over his shoulder. A horse—not Torgan—was waiting, being walked up and down the street. Pasgen did not even glance at the manservant, who held the door open, plastered flat against the wall.

A few moments later, he was at Cromwell's door. A groom rushed out to take his horse, the door opened at once, before he knocked, and the house steward himself ushered him through the cold withdrawing rooms and into a small private chamber. There a bright fire burned in the hearth and Cromwell, wrapped in a furred robe, looked up at him with a tight, drawn expression and informed him that Anne had miscarried.

Pasgen's heart leapt up with relief. He had known that his attempt to abduct Elizabeth would fail, and he had protested about the half-formed changeling that Vidal had thrust upon him. If he had been successful in snatching the child and left that thing behind, even the most lack-witted would know it for a magical construct. Pasgen feared that King Oberon would kill him, or, worse, dismind him.

As the thought came to Pasgen, Vidal had smoothly offered to summon a selection of bogans to help him if he wanted them. Bogans! To add to the chance of exposure. Pasgen realized that inciting Oberon to fury was exactly what Vidal hoped for. As a spell worker Pasgen knew he was rapidly approaching Vidal's power, and even if Vidal did not guess that Pasgen was considering challenging him for control of Caer Mordwyn, Vidal wanted no rivals in power. If Oberon destroyed Pasgen it would be no insupportable loss to Vidal Dhu. In fact, Pasgen assumed Vidal hoped he could still control Rhoslyn, control her better with her support gone.

Pasgen was about to refuse flatly, but to his surprise Aurilia raised a finger and waggled it. It was a signal that if Vidal took Pasgen's refusal as a challenge, she would support Vidal. Pasgen knew that even with Rhoslyn to back him he would not survive a confrontation with both Vidal and Aurilia—and neither would Rhoslyn.

It was entirely possible, Pasgen had thought, that Aurilia also wanted him destroyed because she did not think she could control him as well or as easily as she controlled Vidal. So he would do as Vidal ordered; he would make the attempt, knowing he would fail.

It had been easy enough to make the decision, but the taste of defeat was no pleasant thing. And the shambles produced was worse than Pasgen had expected. One of the few mortals the Unseleighe could trust was dead beyond recall, one Sidhe very near death, one Sidhe that hated him with a terrible icy fury for seeing his cowardice exposed. Bitter in the mouth and bitter in the mind.

Pasgen had been soundly castigated for his ineffectuality, which did not improve his temper even though he had had no intention of succeeding. He had returned to his domain and brooded furiously. His mistakes were clear enough now. For one thing, he had misjudged Denoriel again. He suspected he had been right about the greatest force being concentrated right around the child—Pasgen ground his teeth—but he had no proof of that because he had never got past the front door.

There was the first mistake. He had expected his "heroic" half-brother to be vainglorious enough to confront him alone. His second error was to believe that Denoriel would count only on his swordsmanship; he had not expected his half-brother's shields to be so strong. The third mistake was still to think of FitzRoy as a child. Pasgen snarled silently. FitzRoy acted like a child, always playing with toys with the baby princess. But the weapon FitzRoy wielded was no childish toy.

Remembered rage tightened Pasgen's jaw, a happy accident so appropriate it was like an omen that events would now conspire to help him. The news of Anne's miscarriage might not be welcome to Cromwell, although Pasgen was not sure he could always read the man aright, but it was a soft consolation to Pasgen's ears and light to his eyes.

Now Aurilia could loose the toy she had so carefully prepared; Anne Boleyn would be destroyed, her daughter would be despised and abandoned, and Oberon would have no further interest in the child. It would even be possible that Denoriel and FitzRoy, realizing that she would never be queen, never bring in the age of puny mortal beauty and invention, would give over their ferocious protection of Elizabeth.

Thought is swift. Pasgen's grimace looked like shock while actually relief and conjecture had flashed through his mind. Now he need make no reply to Cromwell's announcement; he merely bowed stiffly.

"Why did you not warn me?" Cromwell snarled, his mellifluous voice for once harsh and uneven.

"Because there were ten futures in my glass—in three the king died; in three the queen bore a fine healthy son; in three more she lost the child; and in one she lost her head! Which of those did you want me to describe to you? On which do you think it would have been safe to plan?"

Cromwell hissed between his teeth. "Then you say you can be of no use to me?"

Pasgen shrugged. "I can look again in the glass. Now that we know only three of the futures I saw can apply, I can try to make sure which of those is most likely. Even so, what you do can take into consideration all three."

"And when will I know which way to direct my efforts?" Cromwell sounded desperate; well, he should. He had hitched his wagon to a star that fell, not once, but twice now. He had managed to survive Wolsey's fall; he must be scrambling to think of a way to survive Queen Anne's.

"A few days, a week, perhaps even two weeks—but there is no hurry. The king is still convalescing; the queen must be nearly insensible with sorrow and fear." Pasgen forced himself to sound soothing. "For now, only the most formal expressions of grief and regret need be dispatched. But in that one image . . . the one where the queen lost her head . . . there was another woman standing with the king."

"Jane Seymour," Cromwell said. "Soft and sweet on the outside, but a Seymour for all that."

"Nonetheless—" Pasgen moved closer so that he could murmur very softly into Cromwell's ear "—think on a way to suggest to the king that his second marriage was also accursed because he had a living wife."

Cromwell's jaw tightened. "That will be no easy thing without also touching on the king's assumption of supreme power over the English Church."

"No, no," Pasgen said. "Those two things are totally separate. That one led to the other, is irrelevant. Leave all matters of the Church aside. Now Catherine is dead. If *no* wife were alive, any new marriage would need no intervention by the Church. Such a marriage must be perfectly clean and holy and the children will be blessed."

Cromwell stared at Pasgen, his face expressionless. Somewhere within, however, Pasgen sensed a kind of satisfaction and was content. Although the mortal had worked assiduously to rid the king of his first marriage to make way for his second, that was largely to advance his own interest with the king. He had never really liked Anne or her family.

Possibly Cromwell blamed Queen Anne for his old master, Wolsey's, downfall. Likely there were political reasons, some possible rapprochement with Imperial interests and a drawing away from the French. Pasgen was not interested; he cared nothing for England. All he desired was the downfall of Anne so that he could abduct her child. So far Pasgen was satisfied. Whatever the reason, he believed Cromwell was ready to turn on Anne; that was all Pasgen cared about.

Both were silent for a moment. They had been talking treason, and for entirely different reasons both were uneasy. Pasgen bowed.

"When I have news, I will come again."

He took care that no one in Cromwell's house saw the grin that stretched his lips for a moment, but he was grinning again all the way back to his own residence, and still grinning when, Underhill, he summoned one of his dead-eyed servitors and gave him a message for Aurilia nic Morrigan.

"Dannae favors us," the servant repeated when allowed into Aurilia's presence. "The queen has miscarried. We can be rid of her and see her child discarded within six months."

Early in February Pasgen was directed to meet Aurilia in the pleasure gardens of Caer Mordwyn. There she handed him a small wriggling bundle, a very pretty little dog, a friendly, happy, little dog, wearing a handsome collar inscribed: *My name is Purkoy, my mistress Queen Anne*.

Pasgen took the dog but said, "Anne still has Oberon's protection. If the dog or the collar are bespelled to her hurt, we could be blamed."

Aurilia laughed. "I am not a fool. The collar is indeed bespelled, but no blame will attach to the Unseleighe Court even if it is detected. First, all the spells are beneficent. All support calm and good feeling—and, second, every one of them is a Seleighe spell."

"How did you come by Seleighe spells?"

Aurilia laughed again. "Some, bored with milk and honey and seeking a sharper flavor to life, come to us from the Seleighe Court. Such a one, disgusted as he was, remembered enough of the spells taught him to cast them onto the collar and to add a dampening spell so that only the person holding the dog will be affected. That dampening spell may also dull the queen's power over her husband."

The little dog's head turned from one speaker to the other, then he licked Pasgen's nose. Pasgen couldn't help smiling, and he was impressed with Aurilia's thoroughness. Vidal in his pride occasionally scoffed at Oberon's power. Aurilia never did, but still she was willing to try to circumvent that power by sly cleverness.

As if to prove that conclusion correct, Aurilia added, "But here—" she pressed into his hand a small gold stud "—is the final spell, another bit of protection. When you deliver the dog to a mortal, press this stud into his collar—but do not do it a moment before you are ready to leave. As soon as the spell is invoked—the collar will do that itself—Purkoy will sense and be terrified of all Sidhe. Thus, if there is a Bright Court spy near Anne, the dog will run and hide."

The spell was so effective that Cromwell, to whom Pasgen had been forced to hand the dog before he was ready, nearly lost the creature. Purkoy leapt from his arms and rushed, howling, to the farthest corner of the room.

"Some gift for the queen!" Cromwell snarled. "A dog that hates people."

"No," Pasgen said, raising his voice about the dog's howls. "Come away, leave it to itself for a few minutes. It was just frightened by you grabbing for it and my holding it back. I am sorry."

Fearful of driving the little dog completely mad, Pasgen did not wait for Cromwell's reply but bowed stiffly and walked out of the room. That did nothing to pacify Cromwell, who bustled after him. Seeing disaster for his support of the Boleyns—whom he didn't even like—looming over him, Cromwell was seeking someone to blame and was already furious with Master Otstargi.

He caught Pasgen in the corridor and dragged him into another withdrawing room. Slamming the door behind him, he began to berate his tame magician, complaining that when he really wanted advice Otstargi was missing.

Pasgen was so delighted at how well Aurilia's spell had worked, that he found it easy enough to keep his temper. He was pleased, too, at how dependent on him Cromwell had become because he was about to urge the man into a very dangerous game. And it was likely that he would play it.

For once Cromwell was not certain which way to jump or how. Anne was totally distraught, openly blaming her husband for her miscarriage because of his dalliance with Jane Seymour. Anne would take no advice of his. Henry was almost equally distraught. Instead of offering comfort to his wife for her loss, he had said to her only that she must put up with his behavior as her betters had done, and then added threateningly, "I see that God will not give me male children."

"Encourage that thought," Pasgen murmured, and then said more briskly, "I have brought better than advice. See that the queen gets Purkoy—that is the dog's name—and you will have time to think and plan. When she has the dog in her arms, the queen will grow calm and happy. She will talk of another conception and see no pitfalls in her path to it."

"And win back the king again so we will just begin all over?" Cromwell muttered under his breath.

"No, I think it has gone beyond that," Pasgen said, "but my readings are still not clear on whether the king will put her aside . . . or find a more permanent solution. Perhaps the dog should not come from you directly. But be sure she has received it and kept it."

"I think I may by accident have destroyed Queen Anne," Aleneil said to Denoriel.

Her skin, always fair, was now near transparent and the flesh beneath it seemed almost drained of blood. She had arrived in the dark, hidden in a deep-hooded cloak, and she was shaking so hard when Denoriel came out to meet her and help her dismount from Ystwyth that, without a word, he carried her inside. Now they were sitting side by side on the settle in the well-furnished parlor of Denoriel's London house.

Although it was April, the evenings were chill. A comfortable fire burned steadily in the hearth and candles cast a warm glow over the glimmering satin of "Lady Alana's" soft golden gown. Denoriel leaned forward and took his sister's hands in his own.

"How? What happened?"

"I killed her dog."

"You? You killed a dog? Oh, it was a construct? You have been saying for two months now that something was wrong with Anne, that she was not her usual self. How came you to miss a construct for so long?"

"Because it was not a construct." Aleneil swallowed and tears ran down her face. "It was only a very friendly, very silly, very sweet little dog."

"And you killed it? For what?"

"I did not kill it apurpose." Aleneil sighed deeply. "Lady Lee kept telling me about this adorable little dog the queen had, how when Francis Bryan had given it to her, it cured her grief over her loss. At first I paid little attention, but after a while I began to wonder because *I* had never seen this dog. Then I began to notice that the queen was very calm and that when something troubled her, she held her arm as if she were carrying something."

Denoriel lifted his brows. "Peculiar, but it is the calm that troubles me. From what Harry told me, calm is not a common state to Queen Anne."

"But she has been calm, yes, even happy, which seemed stranger and stranger because I do not believe the king has come back to her bed and Jane Seymour is more a favorite than ever. The only bright spot is that clearly the king finds her useful for some political purposes. He got the Imperial ambassador to bow to her and thus recognize her. If he can make the emperor recognize her, that will tacitly mean acceptance of Henry as supreme head of the Church. But—"

Her voice shook and Denoriel said, "Wait, love, you are whiter than milk. Let me get some wine for you."

Aleneil nodded and raised a hand to wipe away the tears. She sipped the wine when Denoriel had carried it to her and sighed. She went on to tell him of her growing suspicion about the dog and her growing doubts about Anne solacing herself for the lack of Henry's company with that of a number of gentlemen. She had even broken her usual silence to warn Anne that it was not wise in the king's absence to be closeted with this or that gentleman. But Anne had only laughed at her and pointed out that the gentleman most frequently with her was her own brother.

"And then this afternoon Anne complained to Cromwell about his giving up his rooms to the Seymours. The secretary was angry because it was by the king's order and he did not like it any better than she did. But he does not quarrel with her and turned on his heel just as I entered the room. He came toward the doorway, blocking my entrance. I just caught a glimpse of Anne, standing near the fire and clutching the little dog to her. I had to curtsey to Cromwell, but when he passed me, I began to walk toward the queen. I heard her call the dog's name reprovingly, then cry out in pain as the dog leapt from her arms."

Aleneil had finished the wine in her glass and Denoriel reached for the decanter on a side table and refilled it.

"When I reached her, the queen was rubbing her arm. I could see that the dog had torn her sleeve and scratched the arm beneath and I said I would get some salve for it, but the queen sent me instead to retrieve the dog, which had run into the next chamber. So I went to fetch it. The little thing was crouching in a corner as if I were going to eat it alive—" Her lips trembled and she bit them. "Oh, the poor thing. But I meant no harm. I spoke soft as I could and stretched out my open hand for it to smell and . . . and it leapt on a chair and out of the window rather than let me touch it."

"That is not possible, Aleneil," Denoriel said flatly.

"What do you mean not possible," Aleneil sobbed. "I saw it happen myself."

"Not that the thing did not happen, but that the dog, who everyone else said was sweet, friendly, and foolish, should jump out of a window to keep you from touching it. I have never known any animal—even the wild ones in the woods—to flee from you. They are more likely to run to you than to run away."

Aleneil put her wine glass down on the broad, flat arm of the settle and extracted her kerchief from her sleeve to wipe her eyes. Then she admitted what Denoriel said was true, that fortunately before she could rush to Anne and confess what had happened, another lady had entered the room and commiserated with her on the difficulty of catching a small agile dog.

Clearly the other lady believed the dog had darted by her and got away. And, of course, it should have . . . only that would have meant running closer to her, and apparently the dog could not do that. By then she had realized the oddity of the dog's behavior, and she slipped away to run outside before someone else found the body.

She wept again, remembering the limp, broken body of the little animal, but she swallowed back the tears and admitted to Denoriel that as soon as she actually touched it, she felt the spells in the collar.

"The dog was bespelled to run from Sidhe?"

"Yes," she sighed.

"Then you did not kill it," he said firmly. "Whoever put the collar on it killed it."

"Everyone said it was such a happy, pretty little thing." Aleneil sniffed and wiped away more tears.

"And a great comfort to its mistress," Denoriel said, his mouth set grimly, "inducing her to live in a fool's paradise. Well, now it is gone and Anne is awake again, can she—"

Aleneil shuddered. "No," she whispered. "That was why I first said I had destroyed the queen. It is as if all the terror and ill feeling and jealousy and spite that the spells in the collar held at bay are now pouring out."

Denoriel stared into nothing for a moment and then said, "I'll need to tell Harry to double his watch on Elizabeth who, fortunately, is in Greenwich now. Do you feel well enough for me to accompany you back to the queen?"

Aleneil sighed. "I am not going back. I am dismissed.

She blames me for Purkoy's death, which is fair enough, although I did not intend it. And there is nothing more I can do for her." Aleneil looked at her brother with wide sorrowing eyes. "To FarSee is useless. I Saw three paths and I, intending only the best, have driven the queen down the one that leads to the headsman's block."

CHAPTER 32

Although Denoriel cried out in protest against Aleneil's prediction that Anne would die, his sister had Seen true. He did not realize then, that the clarity of the Vision was owing to its imminence. They thought they would have time; Seeings were only possibilities and by actions could be changed. Denoriel did try to warn George Boleyn, offering to help with money if he would leave England.

Obviously he could not tell George that his sister had had a Seeing, but George was only annoyed with him, pointing out haughtily that he could not leave his sister when so many harpies gathered to tear at her flesh. But George could do little to control her. All through April, Anne alternately raged and laughed; she seemed to have lost all balance and it was clear she knew that many were pressing the king to be rid of her. And then she made a fatal mistake.

It began simply enough when Anne began to chide Henry Norris for not completing his marriage to Margaret Shelton, a cousin of Anne's. FitzRoy, who happened to be near, made a jest of men desiring not to answer to a wife, but Anne only irritably waved him silent. Clearly she suspected that Norris did not want to make a commitment to her cousin because of the campaign against her. Norris denied, tried to make some light remark, which only infuriated Anne further.

"You," she cried, oblivious to far too many heads turned in her direction, "you look for dead men's shoes; for if aught came to the king but good you would look to have me!"

"Anne!" FitzRoy gasped.

Her eyes widened and her lips parted, likely to change the words into some jest or excuse them, but Norris was so horrified that his voice overrode hers, crying that if he had ever had such a thought, he would rather his head was off.

And that it was on the seventeenth of May. Considering the many factions that wanted Anne repudiated, it was no surprise that Cromwell had news of Anne's outburst and Norris's response. Cromwell, amazed at the accuracy of Master Otstargi's prediction—although he had not been specific about what mistake Anne would make—went right to the king with an accusation of Anne's infidelity, and he had half the court as witnesses to support him.

Even FitzRoy was forced to repeat what he had heard, although he tried to insist that it was half jest and half temper—something the king should know well about Anne. He was dismissed with angry words, dismissed from the court entirely for his attempted defense. And by the time the week was out, five men had been arrested for adultery with Anne and she, herself, was in the Tower.

"Evidence" was found, trials were held with indecent haste, and every man—including, incredibly, Anne's brother George—was found guilty. Whether the judges actually believed the verdict they gave—Norfolk was weeping when he pronounced it—no one would ever know, but Anne and her "lovers" were sentenced to die, and so they did, the men on the seventeenth, Anne herself on the nineteenth.

FitzRoy was ordered—perhaps as a punishment for his attempt to defend Anne—to attend the beheading. At first he said he would defy his father and absent himself; however, on the seventeenth of May, Anne's marriage to Henry had been declared null and void and Elizabeth was declared a bastard. FitzRoy had to go to the Tower, had to speak one last time to Anne to assure her that he would care for Elizabeth and protect her, as long as they both should live.

His attendance at the execution was now necessary. To refuse—in King Henry's present mood—would be dangerous, even to his son. FitzRoy saw, at least, that Anne did not suffer. She was praying quietly when she laid her head on the block, and the stroke that ended her life was sure and swift.

"That was a piece of work very well done," Aurilia nic Morrigan said, smiling at Pasgen. "It was as if those fools of the Bright Court were our lackeys." Aurilia giggled softly, her green eyes bright with amusement. "Imagine them arranging for the dog's death! I could not have done it better myself."

Pasgen, who stood beside Rhoslyn before Aurilia and Vidal Dhu, who occupied a pair of magnificent gold-wrought chairs in a private, red-walled chamber in Caer Mordwyn, bowed slightly.

"You also manipulated that servant of the king—Cromwell, is that his name?—very well indeed. No one will ever suspect our role in bringing down the queen."

The words were complimentary, the tone was not. Pasgen wondered whether Vidal Dhu was as unaware as he seemed of the ability of others to read him or whether the subtle insults were designed to expose opposition.

"Thank you," Pasgen said. "And the quick declaration of Elizabeth as a bastard ensures that the child will be of no interest to anyone very soon. We will be free to take her whenever we like."

"I would not be so sure of that." Vidal's lips twisted in scorn and he shifted in the taller of the two chairs. "So far you have been remarkably unsuccessful in seizing *anything* the Seleighe wish to keep. The FarSeers tell me they still See a possibility of a future bound to that blasted child. I am sure those of the liosalfar receive the same Vision and may think it worthwhile to guard her."

"That is true," Pasgen said. "And beside that the boy FitzRoy—" an unpleasant memory, a memory of FitzRoy's grim face as he shot down a Sidhe, made him grimace "—no, I must not forget he is a boy no longer, and he is most unnaturally attached to the little girl. Moreover, what FitzRoy wants, Denoriel wants."

"And what Denoriel wants, Aleneil wants," Rhoslyn added.

Vidal waved a hand dismissively. "The child is no longer an adorable baby. I think FitzRoy will soon tire of her willful ways. We can wait."

Aurilia shook her head. "No, my lord, we cannot. Possibly FitzRoy will tire of her, but by then she may be useless to us. Remember that she is absorbing stupid mortal values with each day she is in her governesses' care. We can make any mortal obedient by breaking its spirit, but that is useless in this case. She needs the full range of her mind and heart to be able to dream of power and the ways to use it and to bring others under our hand."

Rhoslyn's eyebrows twitched—Pasgen thought it was in patent disbelief at that statement. It seemed that Aurilia knew what Elizabeth was by her reaction to their demon spies, and probably Rhoslyn could not accept the idea that Aurilia would welcome another attractive female with as strong a Talent as Elizabeth displayed with free will within Vidal Dhu's household. Even to Rhoslyn it must seem that to leave Elizabeth entirely in possession of her will might be dangerous. Pagen wondered what scheme was working in the back of Aurilia's mind.

Vidal, however, had nodded and shrugged, saying, "Oh, I am willing to take her as soon as Rhoslyn has made an adequate changeling."

"Two weeks, perhaps three," Rhoslyn said, "but I think no more than two."

A black frown replaced the bland expression on Vidal's face. "It took you months to create the changeling that was supposed to take FitzRoy's place," he snapped. "How does it come about that this changeling will take only two weeks?"

Rhoslyn's lips thinned. Pasgen suspected that there was still a small sore place in her heart where FitzRoy's changeling had lived. All she said, however, was, "You wanted that changeling to live for some weeks at least and be able to pass for the living child. A boy of six, already taught several languages and the history of his family . . . If he suddenly no longer knew those things surely a replacement would be suspected. I had to teach him. I had to instill enough power in him to keep him alive. I—" Her voice was rising.

Pasgen put a hand on her arm and she fell silent. "This child is clever," he said, but to Vidal Dhu, not to his sister, "but she is not yet three years old. If the changeling can walk and talk about common things, it will be enough."

Aurilia nodded. "Yes, and the dullness of the changeling will doubtless be thought owing to confusion and missing her mother if we take the child soon. Two weeks seems about right to me."

"Very well," Vidal agreed.

"So," Aurilia said, "Pasgen and Rhoslyn should be able to manage this abduction on their own. The household will still be in considerable confusion, and I think almost all of the guards and many of the servants will have been dismissed or assigned elsewhere. And Pasgen and Rhoslyn are so accustomed to the mortal world that this should be easy for them."

Beneath his hand, Pasgen felt his sister shiver. Elizabeth was less important, but she was still the king's child. To send Pasgen and her alone to take her was a prescription for failure, possibly a disastrous failure. Could Aurilia want the child *dead*? Fortunately before she could protest, Vidal Dhu turned toward his lovely companion.

"No, I think not." Vidal Dhu smiled slowly. "Perhaps Pasgen's and Rhoslyn's many failures at abduction were owing to bad luck, but they nearly brought the wrath of King Oberon down on us. I wish to have something to show for our effort this time. I think this time you and I, Aurilia, should accompany them to make sure, not only that no more bad luck occurs but also that the child does not slip through our hands into some private domain."

"That was never intended," Pasgen said, trying to sound indignant, although it was difficult because he was ready to grin with relief.

He certainly did not want Elizabeth, and he thought it better that Rhoslyn should not even think about keeping the child. Rhoslyn had been . . . different . . . since she had made and lost FitzRoy's changeling.

Moreover, Pasgen had not been sure until Vidal said

he and Aurilia would accompany them to seize Elizabeth that the prince still wanted the child—and he was still not sure *why* he wanted her. Of course, Vidal might have been seduced by Aurilia's vision of what Elizabeth could accomplish, but usually Vidal was shockingly lacking in a long vision of the future. Mostly his purposes were immediate. And now that Elizabeth had been declared a bastard, Mary's right to the throne definitely superceded hers. If Mary became queen, the Inquisition would follow and pain and misery would fill the wells of power of the Unseleighe Court.

That had been what Vidal originally wanted and he did not need Elizabeth for that . . . And then Pasgen remembered Vidal's passing comment that the FarSeers still envisioned one future in which Elizabeth reigned. That made Pasgen decidedly uneasy. Vidal had not commanded him or Rhoslyn to clarify the Seeing, which was usually diffuse and confused in their absence.

So, what else had Vidal's pallid FarSeers Seen? Pasgen controlling Elizabeth? Was that why Vidal suspected Pasgen of considering rebellion? If Aurilia and Vidal were in the party to take Elizabeth, why did they need him and Rhoslyn? Was this a different kind of trap than the last, intended to bring Oberon's wrath on his head? Was this a death-trap to be sprung by FitzRoy's terrible toy—such healers as the Unseleighe had had not been able to save the Sidhe FitzRoy had wounded.

"Very foresighted of you, my love," Aurilia said, and her glance flicked toward Rhoslyn. "It does so often happen that when many use a Gate, a few get cast out unexpectedly who knows where."

Rhoslyn barely prevented her lips from twitching toward a smile as Aurilia implied she and Pasgen would try to escape with Elizabeth, and Pasgen squeezed her

arm in warning. Pasgen was known for his skill with
Gates. But was Aurilia's remark a warning to Vidal or
a hint to her? Despite her efforts to hide her feelings,
it was not unknown that she had mourned FitzRoy's
changeling. Was Aurilia hinting that she could have
another child, even younger and more attractive than
FitzRoy?

If so, she thought, *I was right. To steal Elizabeth
would certainly bring Vidal hunting her . . . and me.
Aurilia would like to be rid of me—I have too much
power. But then why does she want Elizabeth here?
Because Elizabeth is a child and it will be many years
before her potential is reached? And in those years
what might happen to her?* One of Rhoslyn's hands
twitched nervously, but further thoughts were cut off
by Vidal, who rose to his feet.

"Yes," he said, "we will not fail this time, but the
act will need some foresight. I will send out several
spy demons to count the household and make picture
memories of those who guard the doors and such."

"Be sure your goblins and bogans do not go near
the child," Aurilia warned. "She can see them or sense
them . . . I do not know which, but she screams whenever they are anywhere near her. If she does that, it
will surely be reported to FitzRoy—once he was
actually in the room when it happened and he turned
Oberon's mark on the invader, so that it had to flee
and lost its memory too. If FitzRoy is warned he will
surely set a watch."

Vidal Dhu nodded, and held out a hand to help her
from her chair. "For now I only want a report of who
watches and when. Over the next two weeks, while
Rhoslyn makes ready the changeling, I will remake the
face of one of our bound mortals to replace the guard
on a side or back door so we will have unchallenged
entry. I will also need a replacement for one of the

menservants who carries meals and messages and such to the child's apartment."

"You must not kill the mortals you replace." Aurilia offered another warning. "We can put them in Gateways, from where it will be easy enough to retrieve them, and I will give them false memories of a quiet night with no alarms."

"Also," Pasgen offered, "it will be better if the disguised guard is not in place too long. Otherwise he might betray himself. Do we really need another? What if Elizabeth feels the difference in the servant and recoils from him?"

Vidal Dhu had offered his arm to Aurilia and started to turn away, but he looked back over his shoulder, his expression very cold. "That servant is necessary. We need him to take the child and remove the iron cross."

"The iron cross," Rhoslyn said hastily, wishing to remove Vidal Dhu's attention from Pasgen. "We cannot put the cross on my changeling. That would kill it at once, perhaps even dissolve it. But if the changeling is not wearing the cross, the nurse will notice. Elizabeth never goes without it."

"I will make one of blackened silver," Pasgen said. He still did not like the idea of a bespelled mortal coming so near Elizabeth, who was dangerously sensitive, but he also wished he had not awakened more suspicion in Vidal Dhu. "Has anyone seen it close enough to tell me what it looks like?"

"I've felt it—" Rhoslyn shuddered "—but never seen it."

"Never mind." Pasgen waved the problem away. "I will entrap one of the women servants who attends the child's bath. She will know and I can take the description from her mind."

Vidal, scowling, started to take a step, but Aurilia

held him back. "Our party, even with free entry to the house, should not be too large. I know you are very strong in magic, my lord, but it would be a great waste of power to try to put the outside servants to sleep as well as the whole household within, and if we were many, one or more of the outside servants might be awake and notice too much coming and going."

Vidal Dhu shrugged. "I will have reports from my spies about who is likely to be where, but there need not be many of us. As you say, the household will be asleep. We need the mortal to carry the child and a Sidhe to carry the changeling. You, me, Pasgen, Rhoslyn, perhaps two more Sidhe as guards—just in case they are more sly than we expect and have some magical protection in the child's nursery."

Pasgen nodded slowly and bowed as Vidal and Aurilia left the room. He felt that this foray would be successful. He had tried stealth and trickery and both had failed. Likely sheer force would be successful. He hated that the success would be Vidal Dhu's, but they had to remove all possibility of the red-haired child coming to the throne, and it was only good sense to get her young enough to train up in their ways.

FitzRoy had retreated from the scaffold as soon as the executioner's sword fell. He had wanted to slip away sooner; he had not wanted to see Anne die, but he had not been able to move, not even to close his eyes. When her head fell, blood gushing from the truncated neck, however, he wrenched himself backward, almost falling down the steps. Ladbroke, who had taken bold advantage of being servant to the first duke in the realm, had pushed his way to the very front and now held FitzRoy's horse and his own at the base of the steps.

He caught his blind and shaking master, and gave

him a leg up into the saddle. Seeing FitzRoy seated and trusting his horsemanship, even disordered as he was, Ladbroke slapped the horse on the rump and flung himself into his own saddle. Judicious use of his crop and his heels permitted him to come around in front of FitzRoy's horse, which was being given no direction. The crowd, mostly still staring at the scaffold, was forced by Ladbroke to make way for the horses, a few crying imprecations or growling curses.

FitzRoy was stonily unaware of anything beyond the turmoil in his guts, fed and renewed by the horror in his mind. When they reached Baynard's castle, he gave up the battle and was violently sick—although he had eaten nothing that morning. He brought up the wine he had drunk, but even long after he was empty he could not stop retching until Dunstan hurried to him and forced a small cup upon him.

"Drink," he ordered so forcefully that FitzRoy tried. Fire seared his mouth, his throat, and his belly. He gasped, eyes bulging, hardly able to breathe.

"Drink," Dunstan insisted again.

Still gasping, FitzRoy emptied the cup. The conflagration in his insides was renewed, but the sickness was gone. From his belly, but not from his mind. Tears ran down his face and he sobbed uncontrollably. He had not really liked Anne much—she was too self-centered, too selfish—but she had been so vital, so alive, one could not be dull in her presence. And now she was gone—never to laugh again, never again to utter another pointed, witty remark—just gone. He closed his eyes and shuddered.

"That's enough, Your Grace," Dunstan said. "We have to be going. Lord Denno's alone at Hatfield. He's a good man, but there's not enough of him to really protect the princess."

"Lady Elizabeth," FitzRoy said. "We must remember

to call her Lady Elizabeth. It would be unwise to be overheard denying the king's declaration of her illegitimacy." Tears ran down his face again and he dashed them away angrily. "Yes, we must go at once. I swore to her mother—" his voice broke and he cleared his throat "—I swore I would care for and protect Elizabeth as long as we both lived."

He turned toward his horse as his four guardsmen emerged from the stables. Tolliver followed leading several packhorses.

"Packhorses?" FitzRoy said. "But—"

"I told the steward, Your Grace, that we were going to visit Lord Denno in his house near Windsor for which, presumably, you would need a full wardrobe. Fortunately Sir Edward is still . . . at the Tower."

"Windsor?" FitzRoy repeated stupidly. "Does Denno have a house near Windsor?"

"I doubt it," Dunstan said, coming closer on the pretext of adjusting an article of FitzRoy's clothing. He lowered his voice to a murmur that would not carry beyond FitzRoy's ear. "But you did tell me, Your Grace, that you did not wish it widely known that you intended to be with the pr—with Lady Elizabeth for a time."

The valet stepped back, plucking an imaginary thread from FitzRoy's doublet, and FitzRoy said, "Yes, of course, Dunstan, thank you. I—I am not quite myself."

"It is to your credit, Your Grace." Dunstan's words seemed to squeeze unwillingly through tight lips.

It was a long, silent ride to the merchant's house in the village of Hatfield that FitzRoy had taken over. Now and then he wept again, not so much now for Anne as for his image of his father. It could not be the same between them. FitzRoy knew the charges against Anne were false; that the evidence was ridiculous, particularly that against her brother George. Either his father had deceived himself or he, too, knew Anne was innocent. No, he could never feel the same.

Arrival at the merchant's house he had bought in the village of Hatfield provided a distraction. He looked at the comfortable brick building with relief, remembering how Denno had approached the man secretly and had offered him a small fortune if he would leave quietly and go to London. There, he promised he would be set up in business anew, which Denno's man of business arranged.

Meanwhile a cousin of Denno's man of business took over the merchant's work, claiming to be the merchant's cousin. The village accepted him. They had all known that the merchant was very successful and it was no surprise to them that he had moved on to a larger town and greater things.

For FitzRoy there were many benefits to living in the house of a busy merchant. No one was surprised to see men-at-arms lounging around—a merchant had to protect his goods—or to see well-dressed people coming and going, even at odd hours. There was a private lane from the edge of the village to the large yard behind the merchant's house. It had been built to keep the merchant's wagons from damaging the road to the palace; now it served to let FitzRoy come and go in secret. There were storage buildings behind the house and a good-sized stable, large enough to take wagons . . . large enough to house a whole troop of soldiers, if they ever became necessary.

Denno was waiting at the back door; when it closed, he folded FitzRoy into his arms as if the young man was a child again. "Sorry," he whispered. "I am so sorry. We were not vigilant enough. If we had removed the dog . . ."

FitzRoy rested quietly in Denoriel's arms for a while, then freed himself and sighed. "It did not matter,

Denno. If she could not bear the king a living son, sooner or later it would have come to this. The king would not again have a living wife while he married anew." Tears filled FitzRoy's eyes again for the loss of a father he had loved, and he angrily wiped them away with the heel of his hand. "No, I will not think about it. I must live, at least for a few years more, with my father, until I can induce him to send me abroad. What is more important now is Elizabeth. In how much danger is she? She will never be queen now."

"Do not be so sure of that," Denoriel replied as they walked into the house from the back, passing the kitchen and a small dining parlor before they entered the merchant's own withdrawing room. "Aleneil Saw many futures and in only one of them did the queen die. There are fewer futures now, all horrible except one—one in which a red-haired queen sits on the throne of England."

"But how could she possibly come to the throne?" FitzRoy stood before the fire, nervously clasping and unclasping his hands.

Denoriel sat down in a high-backed chair and shook his head. "Beyond much sorrow and suffering, hers and that of the people, but it is not as queen that the Unseleighe want her. Indeed, they would delight in every future *except* that one. They want her to grow up desiring mortal fear and pain and to tell them how to use the increased power that fear and pain would provide them to dominate many other domains— perhaps even Elfhame Logres and Elfhame Avalon."

The more Denno said, the more Harry's gut knotted; bad enough to discover what a monster his father could be, but to think of that dear, naughty babe stolen and educated to be a thousand times worse— FitzRoy shook his head violently in denial. *"No!"* he shouted, so that Denoriel started.

"No," he said more quietly. "I will not let that happen."

Denoriel pulled on his lower lip. "If she rules this realm, she will weave so skillfully among the other nations that England will be very great. If she uses that skill for the purposes of the Unseleighe . . ."

"They must not have her. But how can I protect her?" he asked, desperately, feeling his head begin to ache. "And for how long?"

"To the first, I agree. I would not like Vidal Dhu for a master. How to protect her?" Denoriel uttered a mirthless chuckle. "Carefully. And for how long? Ah, there is the worst problem of all. Perhaps for years, until she is seated on the throne."

He groaned, seeing his own freedom slipping away. "Then I would not be able to leave England. I promised Anne I would protect Elizabeth and care for her as long as I lived." But better that than the alternative—

"Time changes all things, even Seeings," Denoriel reminded him. "Actually the worst danger is now, while she is little more than an infant, while Vidal and Aurilia believe they can warp her heart and mind to accept the misery of mortals as a good. And again, I think they will strike very, very soon, while her household is in turmoil and a different person does a different thing every day. This is when it is least likely that a change-ling will be noticed—"

"But surely Blanche would know," FitzRoy interrupted.

Denoriel put a finger across his lips. "Not so much freedom with her name."

He glanced over his shoulder at the door behind him. "Can there be a watcher?"

Denno nodded his head. "Not in this house, but somewhere not far . . . perhaps at the palace . . .

something is listening, and I do not know how long its ears are."

FitzRoy closed his eyes for a moment, then opened them again. "I will go to the palace now."

"Not tonight." Denoriel shook his head. "Everyone is too wakeful, too frightened, too full of grief that they cannot show. They dare not talk of what happened this day but they cannot think of anything else. Unfortunately it is likely that Vidal knew when the queen would die so they could already have prepared a changeling; however, it is very hard to keep alive the constructs made in the likeness of mortal flesh. Thus, they may have begun that work only now, when the fact of Elizabeth's disgrace and Anne's death is certain. At least tonight we will be able to sleep in peace."

The next day FitzRoy went to the palace and provided a diversion for Elizabeth, who was well aware that *something* was very wrong but did not know what and was, as a result, fretful. Two days later, Lady Bryan rode to London to try to discover what provision was being made for the dead queen's daughter. FitzRoy went to sleep in a side chamber near Elizabeth's apartment with an air spirit nestled by his side. But he did not need it; nothing happened.

By the end of the week Aleneil rode in. She was pale and tired and merely shook her head at the men who greeted her. "Nothing," she said. "The same images over and over—a boy child, and a harsh and dour rule, but not the disaster of the Inquisition, at least, not immediately. No image of Elfhame Logres, no joy, no music or wonderful performances. That is one. Another you know, it shows the fires of the Inquisition and two on the throne, a sad, dark-haired woman, much swollen in the belly and a thin, fair, pallid-faced man with a small, pursed red mouth."

"The image of the red-haired ruler is gone?" FitzRoy asked anxiously.

"No. That also is as it was, but there was one new thing. In the second image—that of the two rulers—distantly behind those on the throne is the red-haired woman, but not as a ruler. There is a threat over her."

There was a brief silence while Denoriel and FitzRoy considered what that might mean, then FitzRoy reverted to their present problem.

"But no hint of any attack on Elizabeth?"

Aleneil shook her head. "Nothing. No image of the child at all."

"As if she did not exist?" Denoriel asked, his voice higher than usual.

Aleneil looked stricken. If the child had been abducted and was being held in a shielded domain to prevent any attempt at rescue, she might not be revealed at all with an attempt to scry her or FarSee about her.

"No," she said finally, her voice somewhat uncertain. "More as if I were asking the wrong questions."

But if those were the wrong questions, no one could think of the right ones.

The tension in the merchant's house increased, but nothing seemed to happen. At least Lady Bryan still had not returned from London, so FitzRoy and the air spirit could spend most of every day with Elizabeth and every night in the small side room. Mercifully the weather was terrible—sometimes FitzRoy thought the heavens wept for the bright spirit gone from the earth—but at least it kept Elizabeth indoors and eliminated any fear of being attacked by a large party.

Another week shuffled by on leaden feet. Denoriel was beginning to question his assumptions about what the Unseleighe would do when, on Friday afternoon,

Blanche Parry crept into the merchant's house by the back door, calling silently for help.

They heard that "call" long before Blanche reached the door, and their state of heightened alert sent a surge of energy into all of them. Both Aleneil and Denoriel rushed into the kitchen to meet her and draw her into a quiet corner.

"I cannot stay," she said. "I have sent him away on an errand, but I do not know how long it will keep him."

"Who?" Denoriel asked; he knew most of those who served Elizabeth.

"Jack Chandler," Blanche replied, her face pale with anxiety. "The serving-man attached to the pr—Lady Elizabeth's apartment. There is something wrong with him."

"A changeling?" Aleneil suggested.

Blanche shook her head. "No. No. I'm sure I'd feel that. The man's mortal enough but he . . . he doesn't act like Jack."

"Harry is there?" Denoriel asked.

"Oh, yes, with the—the whatever it is that lingers by him—it worried me at first, but Elizabeth loves it. She laughs and laughs and tries to catch it in her hands, so I am sure it is a good thing. If His Grace were not there I would not have dared leave." She took a shuddering breath. "He can keep Jack away from milady with his sword, but he has no magic. I must go back. And I fear—"

"Yes, you fear rightly," Denoriel told her. "Go back, and tell him tonight may be the time. I will send over Ladbroke and Dunstan and he is somehow to keep them with him. Aleneil and I will come soon. We will wait for him in the little chamber in which he has been sleeping."

The maid nodded and darted out.

"You think they will make an attempt on Elizabeth tonight?" Aleneil asked.

"Or tomorrow," Denoriel replied, with an inner stab of certainty that made him want to run for Hatfield that very moment. "I doubt Vidal would expose his servant for longer than he must. He would fear exactly what did happen, that someone would notice something unnatural about the substitute. Only we are lucky to have Blanche who knows we will listen to her. Most others, even if they noticed something strange, would hold their tongues at first, assuming that the man did not feel well or was troubled about something."

"There may be others in the house that no one has noticed," Aleneil said, slowly.

Denoriel nodded. "I will tell Dunstan and Ladbroke to go separately and as inconspicuously as possible and then find a place to hide. You and I will come in with a delivery wearing the Don't-see-me spell. Nyle and Gerrit are already on the premises, hopefully keeping watch on Harry."

"We will have to get them into Harry's room one at a time so I can renew the amulet that guards against sleep spells." Aleneil bit her lip. "Is there anything we can do to shield them? If not, they will be useless. I am sure Pasgen is perfectly capable of bespelling them into freezing or Dannae knows what else."

"I have shields on them already, have had for years," he said with grim pleasure. "I will strengthen them and my own to the fullest I can."

The plan worked with remarkable ease. Denoriel would have been more uncomfortable and suspicious than he was already, if the guard at the back door had not come alert as he and Aleneil sidled past the small two-wheel cart a farmer's boy was pushing into the scullery. The guard looked hard at the boy and the cart

and right and left of the cart—by then it was too late—
Aleneil and Denoriel were inside. He even looked
behind himself in their direction, but his eyes would
not fix on them.

So at least one of the guards was safe.

Through the kitchen into a wide back corridor where
servants carrying trays could pass in safety, through a
wide door into the front entryway. The guard there did
not notice them at all, and they mounted the stairs,
careful to tread near the wall so they would not creak.
Equally carefully along the upper corridor to the door
of the room FitzRoy had described. Safe inside the
chamber, Denoriel dropped the Don't-see-me spell. He
knew he would have many drains on his power that
night.

Then they waited. For what, they did not know.

Only that, whatever it was—the fate of Seleighe
realms and mortal depended on their success.

CHAPTER 33

When the light began to fail, FitzRoy read to Elizabeth while she had her bread and milk, then kissed her good night and withdrew to his chamber. How he had managed to keep a calm and cheerful face for her, he did not know, for his insides were all a-roil with tension. From a crack in the door, Gerrit watched the corridor. Once the false manservant came along it and scratched on the door of Elizabeth's outer chamber.

They all tensed.

Gerrit drew his sword and prepared to fling open the door and leap into the corridor. Behind him the soft slither of more swords being drawn surely gave him confidence. However, Jack Chandler did not enter the room; he merely called to Blanche for the tray. The supper tray was handed out, and he went back down the corridor to the stairs.

Soon after Chandler came up again carrying small lit torchettes, which he set into holders in the corridor. He glanced toward the door of FitzRoy's chamber, where Harry himself was watching, but Gerrit had left barely a crack, not visible to Chandler, and the man went downstairs again. Then, FitzRoy left his room as quietly as possible and went to Elizabeth's apartment where he scratched softly and was admitted.

Now it was his turn to guard the door.

After him, more carefully, more silently, one by one the others followed. As they approached the door, it opened and FitzRoy himself, sword in hand, let them in. Last of all came Denoriel and his sister. By now the tension among them practically made the air hum.

In low tones they discussed the best disposition of their limited force. Aleneil wanted to lock the door to Elizabeth's inner chamber and meet their opponents where they were, but FitzRoy pointed out that there was no lock on the door of the inner chamber. Moreover, there were windows in the room through which the Sidhe and their unsavory creatures could come and also there was a side-entrance that went to a dressing chamber, which opened onto an inner, servants' corridor.

Without more ado, they locked the door to the main corridor, left Gerrit and Nyle on guard, and withdrew to the night nursery. Locking the outer door was more to provide a warning than any expectation of defense. The steward had a key, of course, and if the night guard was now one of the Unseleighe, that key would doubtless be in his hand. So, if the key turned in the lock, an enemy was on the way.

And they waited, the sour taste of fear in their mouths, as the palace quieted and servants went to bed.

Even so, when, some hours later, the door opened and Nyle and Gerrit saw old, familiar faces—the footman who had served the princess for years and the night guard, also an old servant—and Gerrit hesitated . . .

For seeing people he knew, he could not simply thrust forward with the sword in his hand.

He was lucky he had drawn it when the lock turned, however, because the guard did not hesitate. He lunged, driving Gerrit back and away from the door, attacking in utter silence.

Jack Chandler rushed through the space provided toward the door to the inner chamber. "Chandler, you dog! Stop!" Nyle shouted, and followed at the run, but he was a few steps behind and Chandler wrenched open the door and dashed toward Elizabeth's small, curtained bed.

Nyle, slightly longer-legged, caught up, but he, too, hesitated, because Chandler did not have a weapon in hand. Thus, he did not thrust through Chandler's back and kill him; instead he slapped him hard with the flat of his sword.

Screeching an unintelligible curse, Chandler drew his sword and swung around, flailing at Nyle.

At that moment, they *all* made the fatal mistake of being distracted, and the rest of Vidal Dhu's party rushed unimpeded into the room.

FitzRoy howled a warning. Vidal, almost contemptuously, cast a shower of small knives at Denoriel, who had dropped the bedcurtain and turned to face him from the foot of Elizabeth's bed. Sword in one hand, strange silvery object in the other, FitzRoy stood at the left near the head of the bed.

Seeing that "toy," Pasgen hesitated and found himself pushed sideways to the right by the two Sidhe behind him. One simply glanced contemptuously at Pasgen and ducked away from him around the foot of the bed. His sword was still in its sheath, and he carried a blanket-wrapped bundle in his arms. The second Sidhe loped past Vidal, who had watched in some astonishment as the knives, which should have sliced Denoriel into a quivering lump of screaming flesh, had simply disintegrated.

"Damn you!" Vidal prepared another vicious spell, making preparatory gestures only to see Denoriel draw his sword and advance on him. Vidal laughed, and FitzRoy trembled; the closer Denoriel was, the more easily he would be made into a target.

But it was too late to do anything—that strange Sidhe had just discovered him. He drew his sword.

Aurilia had slipped into the room after Pasgen. Aleneil started forward to intercept her from where she had waited, half watching the door to the dressing room in case there was a double attack, but Aurilia was too quick. She sidled around Chandler and Nyle, who were slashing and hacking at each other, her gaze fixed on Elizabeth's bed opposite to where FitzRoy had engaged a very surprised Sidhe and was fighting him to a standstill.

Aleneil stepped away from the wall to follow Aurilia only to be confronted by Rhoslyn, who threatened her with, of all things, a sword. Thoroughly infuriated, Aleneil hissed out the strongest defensive spell she knew and pointed at Rhoslyn's sword. That promptly began to glow, bright red . . . orange . . . yellow . . . white. Rhoslyn shrieked a curse and dropped the weapon. She did not reach for the knife in her belt, probably knowing that any weapon she touched now would turn on her. Instead she leapt at Aleneil, nails growing into talons on hands crooked into claws.

Aurilia had paid no attention to the fighting, cursing men around her. She went directly to Elizabeth's bed and pulled aside the curtain. She saw the cross on Elizabeth's breast but felt only a slight discomfort. Brows drawn into a puzzled frown, she reached toward the child, only to have her hand stop. She pushed, but the shield under her hand resisted as firmly as a pane of glass—only breaking it would take a lot more effort.

Aurilia's lips folded tightly together and she extended her senses toward the shield that protected Elizabeth. She would have to find its key and open it before they could seize the child. Completely concentrated on the shield, she was not aware of a movement in the shadow of the dressing room door. A moment later she was not aware of anything at all, as a large, heavy candelabrum crashed down on her head.

Blanche Parry smiled triumphantly and quickly bent to pull Aurilia back into the dressing room. She glanced around, but saw with trepidation that there was little more she could do to help the others. She would have no protection against the increasingly virulent magics that the black-haired Sidhe was using against Lord Denno and no spell she knew would touch that Sidhe, she was sure. His Grace of Richmond was more than holding his own; the Sidhe fighting him was bleeding from several wounds. The blond Sidhe, who looked so much like Lord Denno, seemed to be no threat to anyone. He was staring at the wall beyond where the two Sidhe women were grappling like a couple of angry fishwives.

There were too many combating pairs for Blanche to do anything to help, but she would go to help the female who was Denno's and FitzRoy's friend when— or if—she could. For now, she had something else more important to do. She was going to remove one threat, at least, from her darling Elizabeth for a long time, if not for good. This Sidhe she had rendered senseless, had great power, almost as much as the black-haired Sidhe fighting Lord Denno. Well, soon her power would be useless.

Blanche sank to the floor and removed from around

her neck a black chain from which ten little iron crosses dangled. Smiling grimly, she sat squarely on the Sidhe's chest, holding her down, lifted her head, and wrapped the necklace tightly around her forehead. Even unconscious, Aurilia began to moan and struggle. Blanche held her fast. On Aurilia's forehead ten crosses began to redden and blister. Blanche began sing very softly, a spell that soothed the mind by wiping from it all complex and unsettling thoughts. But it was not a spell that could be hurried.

On the wall Pasgen had been staring at appeared a black spot, at the same time utterly dark and dazzlingly brilliant. Pasgen looked toward his sister, who had screamed with rage and frustration as Aleneil's skin turned dull silver and Rhoslyn's claws broke against it. The spot on the wall hesitated, began to shrink. Pasgen drew his mind from the battles around him and concentrated. The spot began to enlarge into a dead-black oval, but if one looked hard with witch-sight, one could make out the glints of red and gold of Vidal's throne room far, far back.

With one last word, Pasgen fixed the Gate he had built to carry Elizabeth away to hold until he terminated it. It would draw power from him, he knew, which would limit the magic he could do, but it would not limit his physical acts. Pasgen turned back to aid his sister, but hesitated, unsure of how to intervene. Rhoslyn was attempting to gouge out Aleneil's eyes while Aleneil had her hands wound in Rhoslyn's hair and was threatening to pull off Rhoslyn's scalp.

Dunstan and Ladbroke had been waiting in the darkened dressing room watching the door to the servants' corridor. When they heard the sound of fighting, they were torn between the need to watch for a secondary attack and the more immediate need to join the battle. It only took a few moments to decide because the door to the dressing room had an iron bolt. Dunstan checked to make sure it was shot firmly home, and both men rushed toward the fighting.

They barely saved themselves from tripping over Blanche, warned by her soft singing. Both shivered and parted right and left around the writhing, whimpering body and the shut-eyed smiling nursemaid. They emerged just in time to see a blond Sidhe who looked very much like Denoriel reach out to seize Lady Alceneil, who had grown a strange silver skin and was wrestling on the floor with another female Sidhe.

Two men burst into the room and Pasgen whirled to face them, backing away to cast a sleep spell, which had no effect, and then one of paralysis, which rolled off their shields. Uttering a string of obscenities, he drew his sword and blocked their thrusts, but he knew he could not hold both men off for long. He was probably a better swordsman than either, but together they were too much for him. He continued to back away toward the closest concentration of Dark Court fighters.

Denoriel was still fighting sword-to-sword with Vidal Dhu. The Unseleighe lord's face was sickly pallid with two crimson spots high on his cheekbones. His eyes were almost as red; his mouth was distorted by fury. He had his sword in hand, but had obviously been mostly unsuccessful in blocking Denoriel's cuts and thrusts because he was bleeding freely from a number of small wounds.

Those were less owing to bad swordsmanship than to a lack of concentration. Most of Vidal's attention was on throwing spells at Denoriel. Little shining knives, ribbons of light, threads of poisonous worms, balls of light that burst over Denoriel's head and ran down over his shields. Those shields were not what they were at the beginning of this fight, because Vidal's spells were not totally ineffectual. Each new assault wore away at Denoriel's protection and he had to renew it. And he began to wonder, at the back of his mind, which of them would run out of power first.

FitzRoy had managed to drive the Sidhe who had attacked him down the full length of Elizabeth's bed. He cursed in a fluid sing-song under his breath because the elf was just good enough that FitzRoy was unable to finish him off. He could have shot him, of course; the iron-bolt-throwing gun was in his hand, but he could not stop hearing the screams of that other Sidhe he had shot and he could not make himself pull the trigger.

There was a shriek of pain from the outer chamber. No one except Nyle cared. Nyle heard, but he could not finish off Chandler and go to help his friend. Chandler was far more powerful than he looked and a much better swordsman than any manservant should be. Nyle's moment of inattention was costly. Chandler beat his sword aside and thrust. Nyle twisted away, but the blade slid along his ribs and he cried out in pain.

"Coming!"

That was Gerrit's voice. Nyle could feel blood running down his side and he called again. Gerrit's blade beat aside Chandler's return stroke. Nyle slipped under his guard. Gerrit ran him through. They both stood for a moment, panting, and then guiltily looked for their master. He was still fighting gamely, although he was now dripping sweat. Both men looked for the quickest way to him.

Just beyond them a black-haired devil was holding

a sword in one hand and making throwing motions with the other. Things seemed to crawl over Lord Denno and then drop to the ground or disappear. Lord Denno had his sword out; he had wounded the other man. Beyond him someone who looked a lot like Lord Denno was fighting with Ladbroke and Dunstan.

Nyle and Gerrit consulted each other with a quick glance. They would never get through that way. Both looked toward the other side of the room and, simultaneously let out roars of rage. Another one of those blond demons was sneaking toward their master's back. He had a bundle in one arm, but the other hand held a bared sword and there could be no doubt that he intended to stab His Grace in the back.

Ten strides took them across to him, still shouting, and he whirled to face them, parrying the blows launched at him not only with his sword but with the thick bundle in his left arm. Nyle's sword slid along his opponent's and the tip touched him. He shrieked with pain, which startled Nyle so much—because he hadn't actually wounded the man, only touched him— that he jerked back.

Gerrit stepped smoothly in front of him, thrusting. Again the bundle was thrust into the sword's path; it stuck, and while Gerrit struggled to pull it free, Nyle attempted to stab his opponent over that awkward shield. He thrust so hard that his sword went right through and nicked the body behind. The long-eared creature squalled with pain, dropped the bundle, and began to shout the same unintelligible phrase over and over while slashing so furiously with his sword that neither Nyle nor Gerrit could close on him.

That Sidhe had been infused with great power, which he was supposed to feed to the changeling just before he placed it in Elizabeth's bed. But the changeling was

dead now, stabbed many times by steel swords. Doubtless he would be punished for that, but the pain of the
scratches he had already received was so great that his
master's punishment faded in comparison to his fear of
being wounded by steel. He took the power he had been
given and wrapped a spell of sleeping in it and cast it
at the men who fought him.

Nyle hesitated and shook his head. His eyes closed;
he fought them open, and they drifted closed again.
He fought it because he saw Gerrit wavering on his
feet. He tried to raise his sword, lest the person they
were fighting take advantage of this overpowering
lassitude and skewer them. Since he knew that in
another moment he would not be able to use the
sword, he gripped it near the hilt by the blade and
threw it. He never knew whether or not he had hit
his target, only that it squalled again, as the lassitude
overcame him and he dropped to the floor.

FitzRoy had been unaware of the Sidhe who intended
to take him from the back until he heard his men call
a warning. He turned then, so he could watch better
while still keeping most of his attention on the Sidhe
he was fighting. It was not a good plan, and he would
have been dead in a few minutes, except that the Sidhe
had seen something that distracted him as much. Vidal
Dhu was down on his knees and over him, with one
hand extended, stood a figure that glowed and crack-
led with white lightning.

Hastily the Sidhe disengaged and leapt back, actually
dropping his sword as he pulled his small bow out of the
spell-protected sheath in which he carried it. From a
pocket in the sheath, he pulled a shaft. He nocked the
short arrow with an evilly gleaming head and drew the
bow. FitzRoy saw that the elf-shot was aimed directly

at Denoriel. He leapt forward, shouting, and slammed his sword across the Sidhe's arm. The bolt flew wide.

Pasgen heard FitzRoy's shout of warning and turned his head. His eyes went wide as he saw the bow swing in his direction. He flung himself sideways, screamed as Dunstan's steel sword nicked his forearm, but it was not the pain of the iron touching him that wrenched the cry from him. To his horror he realized that the elf-shot had passed between the two mortals attacking him and struck his right shoulder, and the pain that screamed through him was unbearable.

Rhoslyn heard Pasgen scream. She launched a terrific blow at Aleneil and then thrust her away with all the strength she had. Aleneil, unable to avoid the blow completely, was rocked off balance and staggered back, raising her arms to guard herself and launch a blow of her own, but Rhoslyn's attack had ended. She rushed to Pasgen and fell on her knees beside him.

FitzRoy's cry had another, more disastrous, effect. His voice drew Denoriel's attention. The bolt of white lightning, that Denoriel had been about to loose on Vidal hung suspended for just a breath, but in that breath Vidal had lunged to his feet and muttered a spell. Poison now glistened along the blade of his sword, and that blade was only a few fingers'-breadth from Denoriel's throat.

Because he was watching to be sure that the elf-shot had not hit his Denno, FitzRoy saw the new danger. Without a regret, the silvery gun rose. The iron bolt hit Vidal Dhu with such force that it flung him backward. He began to shriek, his voice warbling with agony, but his head struck the floor forcefully, mercifully stunning him into silence.

The strange Sidhe with the crossbow cried out and, unthinking in his fury, nocked another elf-shot, turning the bow on FitzRoy. FitzRoy flung back his head to clear the hair from his eyes. To the Sidhe's vision, the blue star suddenly visible on his forehead gleamed, almost pulsing with energy against the threat of elf-shot. Simultaneously, FitzRoy raised his gun. The Sidhe cried, "No!" and tried to fling away his bow, but the bowstring snapped forward, the nocked shaft flew the short distance between the Sidhe and FitzRoy and the bolt struck FitzRoy full in the chest.

There was no force behind the bolt, it did not penetrate even past FitzRoy's clothing, but elf-shot was deadly stuff, and needed only to touch a mortal to harm.

The bolt fell to the ground. FitzRoy coughed once, wetly, tried to draw a deep breath, and could not. The air rattled in his throat, but the gun was steady, trained on the Sidhe before him.

"No, please!" the Sidhe cried, raising empty hands.

The room was almost quiet. Keeping the gun leveled at the Sidhe, FitzRoy looked around. There was nothing to fight for any more. The mortal who was supposed to remove Elizabeth's cross was dead. The Sidhe who had been fighting Nyle and Gerrit huddled on the floor, moaning with the pain of steel-poisoned wounds. Rhoslyn had lost all interest in Elizabeth; she knelt by her brother, trying to block both the poison of the steel-inflicted wound and the elf-shot. Blood gleamed wetly on Vidal Dhu's black doublet; he was unconscious but still breathing.

FitzRoy saw movement by the door to the dressing room. He stepped back so he could cover both the Sidhe and that doorway, but it was Blanche Parry, dragging Aurilia by the feet. He looked at the Sidhe.

"I can kill you all," he said, lifting the gun, fighting

the strange tightness and pain in his chest, "and remove your ears so there will be no hint you are not mortal. Then my men will bury you, and you will be no embarrassment. Or, you can remove the living—and go—"

Rhoslyn had turned her head to listen and rose to her feet. "Quick. Help me with Pasgen and I will help you with the others. We can use the Gate Pasgen built, but hurry. I don't know how long it will last with him unconscious."

The Sidhe cast a nervous glance at FitzRoy, but he nodded and gestured with the gun. Pasgen was quickly moved through the Gate, then Rhoslyn and the Sidhe carried Vidal Dhu through it. The Sidhe moaning over his steel-poisoned wounds was dragged to his feet by his unsympathetic companion and shoved through the gate. Rhoslyn returned, stood beside the sole unwounded Sidhe, and looked to see if there were any more survivors.

"Here," Blanche called, "don't forget this one," shoving the limp, softly moaning Aurilia in his direction. "Nor this." Her face hardened as she picked up the still-covered bundle and thrust it at Rhoslyn. "Remember," she added, as Rhoslyn took the blanket-wrapped changeling, dead before it had ever been awakened to life, not ungently into her arms. "I can smell them at twenty feet, and there's always this." She lifted the black iron necklace with its dangling crosses. Rhoslyn shrank back. "Look at that other one when she wakes up, if she wakes up, and decide whether it's worth it to try again."

"To me she is not," Rhoslyn snarled. "But I do not rule."

Rhoslyn turned on the words and ran through the Gate, following the Sidhe with Aurilia. Blanche's eyes following her, widened as she saw the empty blackness.

She wrenched one of the crosses from her necklace and threw it into the void. A moment later there was a violent flash. Plaster rained down from the wall and a blackened area of lathe showed behind it.

Blanche bit her lip. That those who wished ill to her princess could come through solid walls had not before occurred to her. The cross had solved the problem. She would need to have more made, larger and heavier, since she would not need to wear them, and she would need put some kind of warning spell, possibly a warding spell too, on the wall. But it was no immediate problem. The demons would need time to lick their wounds. And meanwhile . . . Blanche went to kneel between Nyle and Gerrit and began to whisper the spell to wake them.

Denoriel was dying. He knew it. He was only dimly aware of Aleneil kneeling beside him, her hands on his chest, holding back the worst of the agony of burned-out channels of power. His whole body burned. He had been full when he confronted Vidal Dhu and his shields had been layer upon layer, the strongest he could build. But Vidal was strong, stronger than he thought—having assumed wrongly that the dark magics were weaker than the bright—and his shields had melted away under the repeated assaults.

He had had no choice but to draw in the white lightning magic of the mortal world, but he had been careful at first, taking only enough to keep his shields high. He knew he could not fight Vidal with spells and did not try. He had hoped to distract him and defeat him by the sword.

He had not feared for Elizabeth. Vidal wanted her alive and well to twist and corrupt. Moreover, she was well shielded, which should protect her against any casual or deflected spell, and even keep any Sidhe brave enough to try to lift her while she was wearing the cross from touching her. However, when Vidal had been thrice wounded and realized his spells would never penetrate Denoriel's shields, he began to throw those spells at Elizabeth.

The shields Denoriel had devised to protect the child were not meant for that. One, two more castings and Elizabeth, all her brightness, all her sweetness, all her intelligent ferocity, would be gone. Denoriel reached out and drank lightning, drawing the terrible power through his body to cast out again as bolts of raw power at Vidal Dhu.

The first blast had staggered the prince of the Unseleighe Court, the second had beaten him to his knees, the third would have maimed or killed him— but then Denoriel had heard FitzRoy scream a warning. The bolt he had fashioned had lashed back . . .

"Denno. Denno."

Slowly, painfully, Denoriel opened his eyes. "It's all right, Harry," he whispered. "Elizabeth will be safe for a long time."

"Denno, don't die. Don't."

Tears dripped down on the hand FitzRoy was clutching and he coughed wetly as he bent his head to kiss Denno's hand.

"No," Denoriel lied, trying to smile. "I won't die, but I'll be a long, long time healing, my brave lad. Take care of yourself. Take care of Elizabeth."

FitzRoy's hand tightened on his so hard that Denoriel could feel it through all his other pain. He blinked, made an effort that nearly wrung a whimper from him, and saw more clearly. He did not like what he saw. Harry was white, his face slicked with sweat as well as tears, and there was panic in his eyes, the kind of panic a person feels when he knows it is impossible for him to complete a desperately important task.

"He mustn't die. He mustn't," FitzRoy gasped. "Lady Aleneil, he told me that if he were ever badly hurt and not near any Gate, that I must put him on Miralys. He said Miralys could take him to a healer."

Aleneil leaned forward and kissed FitzRoy's cheek. "Thank you. Thank you for keeping your head. I had forgotten all about Miralys."

"Ladbroke. Dunstan," FitzRoy called, coughing again. "Let's carry Lord Denno down to the back door."

"Miralys will be there," Aleneil promised.

The first thing Mwynwen did was to strip the power-drinking spell from Denoriel. Then, for a month, she kept him under a healing sleep spell, which allowed him to eat and drink and perform other natural functions without really being conscious. After the second week, she had sent messages to the Magi Gilfaethwy and Treowth. Both grumbled, but both came, and separately examined Denoriel. Both agreed that Denoriel might be healed, but that he must not touch any power. "Not for so much as lighting a candle or passing through a gate," Treowth said.

By the middle of the fourth week, however, Mwynwen felt that Denoriel was resisting, fighting to come awake, fighting the pain it cost him to fight. At first he had been soothed by his sister's visits, but for the last few days his struggle seemed to increase in Aleneil's presence. This time even Aleneil noticed, and when her soft urgings to rest only brought new struggles, she left the room.

Mwynwen drew her aside into her private apartment and when Aleneil asked anxiously what was wrong Mwynwen admitted that she did not dare make the sleep deep enough to truly blank Denoriel's mind. Then she asked whether Aleneil knew what could be troubling her brother.

Aleneil bit her lip. "I hope it is his concern for Lady Elizabeth. If so you could bring him to consciousness and I could reassure him in a few moments. I hope after that he will rest easy again."

"You hope. But?"

"But I fear he is worried about young FitzRoy," Aleneil sighed. "And if he is . . . I do not know what to tell him." She lowered her gaze to her hands, wringing together. "I fear FitzRoy is dying," she whispered.

"Dying?" Mwynwen's voice rose in shock. Then her voice, too, dropped to a whisper. "Could their lives be linked, my Richey and his mortal original? Richey . . ." she tried without success to hold back a sob. "Richey is failing."

"I am so sorry," Aleneil said.

She had thought when Mwynwen took the changeling into her care that it was a sad mistake, that Mwynwen was simply borrowing grief. On the other hand, the poor little thing was living, had a sweet personality and a bright mind. Not to help it would have been near to murder. No one had expected it to live more than a few months, possibly a year or two. But Mwynwen had loved it desperately, and driven by desperation had devised a spell to feed it power constantly.

"How long has FitzRoy been ill?" Mwynwen asked.

"He wasn't ill at all. In the battle that nearly killed Denoriel, FitzRoy was touched by elf-shot. He wasn't pierced by it, but somehow damaged. His lungs are full of liquid and he cannot breathe."

"Elf-shot? FitzRoy was harmed by elf-shot?" Hope lit Mwynwyn's eyes. "If we could bring him here, perhaps I could heal him. Perhaps when he grows strong, Richey will grow strong also."

"I am not sure how we can steal FitzRoy away. He is a person of some importance. Also, King Henry had him moved to St. James's palace where his own physicians could care for him. King Oberon would be *furious* if anything about FitzRoy's disappearance hinted at otherworld influence." Aleneil shook her head sharply, annoyed with herself. "Never mind that. I will think about that later. For now, wake Denoriel and I will tell him that all is well with FitzRoy."

"No," Mwynwen said. "He will never believe you and it will make him fight his healing even more fiercely. You must tell him the truth. Tell him about the elf-shot and that we plan to bring FitzRoy here so I can cure him. Promise to have him waked when FitzRoy arrives." She bit her lip. "We will think of something. Surely, two such clever women as we can think of something!"

In that, at least, Mwynwen and Aleneil were successful. Denoriel sank back to rest and his healing proceeded apace. In another two weeks, his pain was so much diminished that Mwynwen allowed him to be fully awake for a few hours each day, and then a few hours longer. By the next week, he was awake at his own will, and on the second day of that week, as he was about to take a nap, he nearly fell out of bed when a young man with sandy hair and slightly muddy brown eyes peeped around his door.

"Harry!" Denoriel exclaimed, trying to struggle upright. "You are here already! Aleneil said they were having trouble reaching you." The door opened fully, showing the young man clinging to the doorframe, trembling. "Oh, my dear boy, come in and sit down. You are shaking. You should be in bed. I will come to you, I promise. Call for an attendant to take you—"

"No, please," the young man whispered, falling into a chair by the bed. "I am Richey, not your Harry."

"Richey . . ." Denoriel's voice faded as disappointment overcame him, and he allowed himself to fall back on his pillows. "I am sorry to see that you are not well . . ."

"I am dying," the young man said, his brow creased with such pain that he looked old before his time. "Inch by painful inch, and I cannot convince Mother to let me go. She feeds me power . . ." his eyes filled with tears, "and it hurts. I am so tired, so tired . . . I am too tired to sleep and I want to sleep, to rest . . . to rest . . ."

Denoriel forced himself upright again. "If I can help you . . . But how can I help?"

"I understand that much of the trouble in bringing your Harry here is that if he disappears without explanation the king will seek him and turn everything upside down to find him and that might breach the secrecy needed to protect Underhill. But if I took Harry's place, no one would wonder or look for him."

For a moment, Denoriel stared at him in utter disbelief. Surely the changeling—no, it was not a mere construct any more, and had not been for a very long time—the young creature knew that this would be a death sentence! "You would die, Richey!" Denoriel exclaimed. "There is power in the mortal world, as I know to my sorrow, but it would not keep you alive."

"Yes, I know." He smiled faintly. "And I would rest at last, really rest. Can you devise a way to exchange me for your Harry?"

"Mwynwen would kill me! No, of course she would not, but she would hate me forever. I would not dare mention such a thing to her." He stretched to touch Richey's thin hand. "Don't worry about Harry. Aleneil is clever and Harry's servants were once mortals Underhill. They will find a way."

"To save Harry? Yes, I don't doubt it. But will they be in time? I fear not." He lowered his head and a tear streaked his cheek. "And what of me? How much longer must I suffer?"

"Oh, Richey, Richey!" The door flung open and Mwynwen ran in and dropped to her knees beside the young man's chair. "My dearling, dearling. Why didn't you tell me you were in pain? I could—"

"Lull me asleep, Mother?" The tears were now flowing more freely down Richey's cheeks. "How many days, weeks, months have I lain in a near stupor, too tired to sit, too tired to read, too tired play a game or watch my creatures at play? I could not be ungrateful to you. I love you too much. I could not tell you and hurt you, but I am glad you were listening in case Denoriel called and overheard." He sighed. "I am glad you know. I am tired . . . tired. And . . . and I do not want to rot, to dissolve, while I am still living and aware. Look!"

He pinched his flesh and a piece came off, leaving a sore that oozed for only a moment but did not heal. Mwynwen watched, horror marking her face.

"Richey," she breathed. "My dearling. Richey." Tears began to pour down her face. "Oh my dear—what have I done to you?"

The fifteenth of July was a particularly pleasant day, clear and bright and not too warm. Shandy Dunstan lifted his master, gritting his teeth to repress his alarm. "Those stupid Sidhe have left it too long," he muttered under his breath, probably thinking FitzRoy couldn't hear him.

But there was nothing wrong with Harry's hearing, though the rest of him was failing. They looked down at a body weighing nearly nothing, and the movement was enough to set off a new spasm of coughing. Dunstan looked around in alarm. He had sent Mistress Bethany to procure fresh kerchiefs, but if she heard

FitzRoy coughing she might come back too soon and make Dunstan leave him alone.

Which, at the moment, was what Harry would rather have had.

A nearly transparent hand wearily raised an already stained kerchief to FitzRoy's mouth. He wiped his lips and whispered, "Let me lie, Dunstan. You say the sun will do me good, but you know and I know that nothing will do me good. I only wish I knew how Denno was."

To FitzRoy's intense surprise, Dunstan grinned. He had not really smiled in over a month. "Just don't order me not to take you out, Your Grace, and you're likely to find out."

"What?" FitzRoy mumbled, not sure he had heard aright.

"Yes, and there's a nice visitor wanting to see you, only she can't come in the palace."

"I don't . . ." There was a pause while FitzRoy coughed again. This time Dunstan took the bloody kerchief from his hand and put a clean cloth into it. "I don't think I really want to see even Mary," he added when he could speak again.

"Not your wife. It's a Lady Aeron that's looking for you, but she's a little too big to get entrance into St. James's through a door, so we have to bring you out."

"What?" His mind struggled to grasp what Dunstan had just said, but his body seemed to have figured it out already; his eyes were wide open, and he began feebly trying to help Dunstan pull a heavy dressing gown over his body. "Did you say Lady Aeron?"

"Yes, Your Grace. And here's Master Ladbroke to help carry you out into the garden. Just let me slide you to the edge of the bed and help you stand . . . just for a moment. Now an arm around Ladbroke's neck and another around mine. That's all you've to do, Your Grace, is hang on."

✦   ✦   ✦

Shaylor was waiting just outside the door. He bit his lips when he saw FitzRoy seated on Dunstan and Ladbroke's arms, trying gamely to keep his head up. But he had done what he was told to do, made sure the corridor was clear. If any of the nurses or doctors saw them carrying FitzRoy out, they might prevent taking him out into the sun and Dunstan said that might help.

However, they made it outside and then through the elaborate gardens near the house, each one guarded by one of his men—Nyle, who gently touched his hand as he bowed, Gerrit, with tears streaking his cheeks, who murmured, "Wish you well, Your Grace," and Dickson, who swallowed and swallowed and could not speak at all. Then they came out through a tall hedge to a less ordered garden with clumps of tall rose bushes. There was a well-cushioned chair almost hidden by the roses, into which FitzRoy was lowered.

For a while he must have lost consciousness, because the next thing of which he was aware was the blowing of a horse and a velvet muzzle touching his cheek. He tried to say, "Lady Aeron," but the coughing took him again . . . only this time the most beautiful woman he had ever seen—well, he had seen Queen Titania, and she was more beautiful of course, but this woman was dark and vivid and her eyes were kinder—put her hand on his chest, and the coughing stopped.

"Quick, off with that robe," she said

To FitzRoy's amazement he had strength enough to stand up and undo his robe, but he hesitated to remove it because he wasn't even wearing small-clothes underneath. It had been too much effort to get them on. And then he saw Dunstan and Ladbroke helping an equally naked man from Lady Aeron's saddle, while a second elvensteed waited.

"Off. Off," the woman said impatiently, pulling at
the robe, and when she had it off him, turning to the
wilting young man, who—FitzRoy's breath caught—who
had *his* face . . . She wrapped her arms around his—
twin?—but he had no twin—and sobbed, "Richey.
Richey." And tears ran down her face. But then she
helped Richey into FitzRoy's robe and set him in
FitzRoy's chair.

It was very, very strange to see yourself sitting in
a chair while you were standing elsewhere, FitzRoy
thought, but even the amazement he felt began to slip
away from him. The strength that the woman's touch
had given him was ebbing swiftly and sun or no sun
it was chilly to be standing naked in the garden.

FitzRoy wavered on his feet and looked around for
someone or something to hold on to. He did not need
to look far. Dunstan was on one side of him and
Ladbroke on the other. They had peculiar expressions,
broad smiles on their faces and tears in their eyes as
they lifted him up onto Lady Aeron's back.

His feet feebly sought stirrups. He knew it was
insane for a man in his condition to try to ride a horse,
but to be on Lady Aeron's back again was like a fore-
taste of heaven. He was perfectly willing to die trying to ride her. Besides, something warm and soft was
around him, and he hardly felt it when Lady Aeron
leapt straight upward into seeming nothingness. *Gate*,
he thought, as he felt the strange shivering chill, but
there was no Gate at St. James's palace. . . .

And then he remembered that Denno had once told
him that the elvensteeds didn't need a Gate. And it
must be true because Lady Aeron was down without
a jar on a lawn like velvet approaching a house that
seemed to flower from the land around it, and by the
door . . .

"Denno," FitzRoy gasped, beginning to weep.

"Denno. I thought you were dead. They told me you were healing but I didn't believe them. I couldn't believe you wouldn't come to me when I was dying."

Lady Aeron had stopped and Denoriel ran forward to reach up so that FitzRoy fell off into his arms.

"Harry," Denoriel breathed, trying weakly to hold his dearest friend up.

Then the invisible arms of a healer's servants, always alert for those needing help, caught at FitzRoy, and Denoriel had only to walk beside him, staggering slightly. Inside the house, FitzRoy was laid in a bed and a silken coverlet floated over him.

"I'm nearly well, Harry," Denoriel said, grinning like a fool with joy, "but don't tell Mwynwen that I came out to meet you or she'll burn off my ears. She told me not to."

FitzRoy touched his face. "I'm so glad to be with you Denno, so glad. And to have seen Lady Aeron again. I don't mind dying now."

"You won't die, Harry," Denoriel said, laughing softly. "Mwynwen said you wouldn't, and no one dares die when she says they'll get well. You'll be hunting on Lady Aeron's back before there's snow in the mortal world."

And so it was.

But, on the twenty-second of July, in the Palace of St. James a changeling, who had lived his life as Richey, peacefully died as Henry FitzRoy, earl of Nottingham, duke of Somerset, and duke of Richmond. FitzRoy's father was not there—King Henry was on progress, showing his new wife, Jane Seymour to the country. However Richey, who had never known the king as his father, did not care. Nothing hurt; power did not force its burning way in to galvanize his aching body; his "mother's" terrible grief no longer tore at his heart.

Nonetheless he was never alone and was tenderly cared for by three of FitzRoy's faithful servants—Mistress Bethany, Shandy Dunstan, and Kip Ladbroke. The men showed no horror over his disintegrating body—the woman never saw it, for she had been bespelled to see only her duke's wasting form. All talked gently to him when he was not too tired to listen. That morning a priest came; Richey pretended to listen because that was what Denno's Harry would have done, but he wept when the priest was gone because he had lived all his life in "heaven" and had no desire to return, only to be at peace. Afterward, in the outer chamber four silent guardsmen kept the young man they believed to be Henry FitzRoy safe from further intrusion—until nothing could intrude on him ever again.

"You know you'll never be able to go back, Harry," Denoriel said, and glanced uneasily at his companion.

They were sitting in the back garden of Mwynwen's house with Lady Aeron and Miralys grazing in the near distance. News had come the previous day about Richey's death and his strange funeral. They had heard that the duke of Norfolk, placed in charge of the funeral arrangements, had been ordered to wrap the body in lead and have it hidden in a farmer's wagon. It had been carried in secret to Thetford and buried quietly in the Cluniac priory there.

They had not spoken about the consequences of Richey's death then, but had concentrated on trying to console Mwynwen. She had wept bitterly for a while, knowing the reason for the lead wrapping and the secrecy, but when the worst of her grief and horror had passed, she had taken FitzRoy's hand in hers and kissed his cheek and called him Richey's gift.

Denoriel had breathed a sigh of relief. He had been

much afraid that when Richey died she would begin to resent Harry and not put forth her greatest effort to save him—and then he had been ashamed of himself. Mwynwen had loved Richey, but she was a dedicated healer.

In the week between Harry's arrival and Richey's death Mwynwen had struggled constantly to draw the poison of the elf-shot from FitzRoy's body. Fortunately what FitzRoy had absorbed was only an exhalation loosed by the mild pressure of the blow of the bolt. Had the elf-shot really touched him, she could not have saved him.

Even so, he would need to live with her so she could continue to draw out the poison as it slowly leached from his flesh and bone. At least he no longer coughed and he could breathe easily. He was still skeletally thin, but that would soon be amended by the meals Mwynwen's servants stuffed down his throat at frequent intervals.

"Yes, I know," FitzRoy said in answer to Denoriel's warning that his own world was closed to him forever. "You know I always wanted to live Underhill. Why should I repine when I've got my wish?"

"It's very dull Underhill," Denoriel warned.

Harry glanced over his shoulder at the house where Mwynwen was seeing another patient and then looked across the garden at Lady Aeron. "Not to me," he said. "Besides, I've had enough excitement to last me for a good long while." Then he said sadly. "I'll miss Elizabeth and she'll miss me, but I would soon have become a danger to her— the first duke in the realm and the king's bastard to boot, how long do you think I would have been permitted free access to the princess who had been declared a bastard?"

Denoriel frowned. "I suppose that's true. In any case,

you need not worry about her safety. Vidal Dhu is still hanging between life and death and Aurilia has not the sense of an infant. Both may recover, but it will be a long time, much longer than my full restoration. Aleneil will soon be established as a maid of honor to Elizabeth and Blanche has an air spirit to serve as messenger when Aleneil is not on duty."

FitzRoy was silent for a moment, but then suddenly he grinned broadly. "I will lay odds that Elizabeth will be a lot more trouble than I ever was."

Denoriel groaned softly, but he was grinning too. "Do not remind me, Harry. I cannot stop thinking of the color of her hair . . . and that scowl . . . My heart nearly fails me."

FitzRoy laughed, and the healer's garden was filled with the sound of unfettered joy. "She's more than a match for any mortal ever born, Denno, and that includes my father, I wager! No matter what he *says*, there will never be any doubt in anyone's mind that she's Great Harry's child. Not to him, and not to anyone else in or out of England."

"Nor Underhill, either," Denoriel sighed. "I fear it's myself that will be needing protection from her, and not her enemies, before she's much older."

"Believe it, my friend," FitzRoy said, grinning. "Oh, truly believe it!"

AFTERWORD

Henry FitzRoy, Duke of Richmond, died on the twenty-second of July, in the Palace of St. James, exactly as described in our story. And, as we described, for some unknown reason, though the official cause of death was stated as "consumption," his body was wrapped in lead and buried with almost obscene haste and in great secrecy. Henry VIII, his father, was enraged when he learned of how his son's body had been treated, and that he had not been told of the death until after the burial.

No one knows why FitzRoy was treated in this odd fashion, though there has been a great deal of speculation by hundreds of scholars over the years.

With the exception of the Sidhe and some underlings, all of the characters we have used in this book were real, historical personages. We have, however, for the benefit of modern readers, kept their language "modern" and kept "forsoothly" speech to a minimum. And we have done our best to work entirely within the framework of actual history.

This includes baby Elizabeth's amazing precociousness; she was, indeed, speaking in whole, nearly adult sentences by the age of two. One almost does begin to believe in Sidhe. . . .

The following is an excerpt from

Ill Met By Moonlight

by Mercedes Lackey and Roberta Gellis

available from Baen Books
March 2005
hardcover

PROLOGUE

The great gold and black banners of King Oberon and Queen Titania flew over the Palace of Avalon proclaiming to those of the Elfhame that the king and queen were in residence. And none too soon; never mind that the Elves and their Underhill kin lived long and slow lives, those lives still intersected with the mortals in the World Above, and in *that* world things were moving, and in directions that were—less than auspicious. Once again, there were choices to be made, and those choices would resonate Underhill for centuries to come.

Still, for this moment, Aleneil could only watch and wait, as her elders and superiors set the wheels of politics and progress in ponderously slow motion. Eirianell, who had been FarSeer in Avalon since Atlantis disappeared beneath the sea, summoned to her a young mortal servant and bid her go to the palace and ask Lord Ffrancon if an audience for the FarSeers could be arranged with the King and Queen. Then, once more, the four FarSeers raised the great lens and looked within.

They looked upon a mortal future far removed from the England of Great Harry's prime. The land of England in the World Above was dark, not black with horror, but gray with dullness and misery. No singing and dancing accompanied by hearty cheers bespoke the merriment of a masque. In ale-houses there was only silence or sullen exchanges where once raucous laughter greeted bright-eyed poets with overlong hair who stood on tables declaiming verses of varying quality to the left eyebrow or shell-pink ear of their latest mistress. In a Court that had once been almost blindingly brilliant with sparkling gems and garments of rich hues and cloth of silver and gold, there was only drabness. Suits of black, of gray, of flat, ugly brown bedecked the courtiers, and gowns of the same hues made plain the most lovely of women, who wore no adornment and kept their eyes always lowered. A young king ruled, fair enough of face but dour of expression—and of a mind and heart so closed that it permitted no new thoughts within.

What happened in the World Above was reflected Underhill; it might be slow in coming, but as life and liveliness drained from the world above, it would drain from Underhill. Still, the reign of a single king, the lifetime of a mere mortal, was insignificant—so long as the damage to the World Above was limited to what was displayed here.

But the trouble was—it would not be limited to the vagaries of a humorless king in love with austerity.

The next vision was worse, but the FarSeers did not flinch, for they had seen this one over and over, ever since Great Harry had sired his first living daughter. Now black horror ruled the land except for the terrible red of fires which ate screaming victims——men and woman and occasionally (the FarSeers moaned in pain as the images crossed the lens, for they never grew accustomed to this) children. Books burned, too, English Bibles and any other text that raised any question about strict Catholic doctrine and abject obedience to the pope, no matter how corrupt and venal that leader might be. A dull-haired woman sat on the throne, her belly bloated, her once-sweet face twisted with misery and determination.

And then the prize—at the end of the storm and the tempest, came the rainbow. Color and life so vibrant it nearly burst out of the lens into reality. Theaters rose on the banks of the Thames with bright flapping banners to advise that a play was being given. Music and dancing gladdened the hearts of all. The presses clanged and rumbled as volumes of poetry and plays and books of theology and wondrous tales were imprinted for all to read. In the vision were some dark blots——poverty, cruelty, ignorance——but the FarSeers were aware that this was the human condition and simply accepted them. The mortals had been granted free will, and with that great gift came the privilege to abuse themselves and others; the point was to see to it that the bright and goodly things outnumbered the dark and dismal.

And reigning over all of this was the red-haired queen, whose golden eyes were alight with curiosity and intelligence, and who strove to mold her subjects into a unified nation without making all alike.

Even though the vision was unreal, an ephemeral thing, there came right through the lens a taste and smell of sweetness of new thoughts, new beauty, vibrant excitement. And in this Vision only, behind the queen, unmistakably, stood the Sidhe lord, Denoriel Siencyn Macreth Silverhair, and his twin sister, Aleneil Arwyddion Ysfael Silverhair.

Aleneil, the youngest of the FarSeers, sighed at seeing her image in the lens. "I thought, perhaps, the mortal world would proceed without our help. I do not know if Denoriel ..." Her voice faltered, for her sibling had been sorely injured in protecting the red-haired babe who would be, if she lived, the queen of the joyous vision. She interlaced the long fingers of her supple hands together, to keep them from trembling. "It is possible that Denoriel will not be able. The channels through which his powers flow were burned and Mwynwen does not yet know whether they will heal or how they will heal."

"He *must* be able," Morwen, the next youngest of the FarSeers said, firmly, as if her own will could impose wellness upon Denoriel. "You saw what would come if you were not in the Vision. Dullness and misery we will survive. Other times like that have come and gone. But think what will follow if what is in the dark-haired queen's womb is born. Will Logres survive? Will Avalon?"

"Patience. Balance." The FarSeer with hair the color of old gold and a gown in the style of Periclean Athens held up a hand. "Eirianell has already requested an audience. Perhaps the High King has knowledge we do not." She lifted her hand, and the others rose with her, to fall in behind her. *She* led the way with head held high, and every sign of serenity as they bent their path to the High King's palace.

Aleneil wished that she had such serenity—then wondered if it really *was* composure on the part of their leader, or only a counterfeit. Aleneil was no older in true years than she would have seemed to mortal eyes; the leader of the FarSeers was as ancient in mortal years as the style of gown she favored. She had thus had many years to cultivate a mask of calm repose.

There was no sign of what the FarSeers had read in their lens as they walked beneath the star-bespangled, false-sky, between two rows of towering linden trees, covered with silver-green leaves and golden flowers. The path beneath them was of soft and springy moss, interrupted only by artistically placed stones and clumps of violets and bluebells. Ahead of them stood a palace of lacey marble and alabaster that had changed little over the passing of the years. Avalon looked as it had for countless centuries; dreaming in an endless, peace-filled blue twilight, as nightingales sang and crickets chirruped.

And unless the High King found some new wisdom, if Denoriel could not take up the task of guarding and guiding the young Princess Elizabeth Tudor, it all might end in fear and flame.

If Oberon had more knowledge than his FarSeers, he gave no sign of it. He greeted the ladies of the Visions not in his Throne Room where the entire Bright Court might listen to them, but in a private chamber. However, this was no intimate chamber where a king might shed his dignity and speak as an ordinary being with intimates, or even play for a time. They gathered in a room where gracefully arched openings perforating all four walls framed only blank alabaster panels. There were no places save the single door into it where this chamber was open to the palace or the grounds. This was where a king made arrangements and gave judgments he had no desire for his entire court to know.

The room looked cool and somehow as if it held apart from what happened within it. The walls were pale silver, slightly sparkling. There were no windows, which was somehow faintly oppressive, but light, the soft, silvery twilight of Underhill, suffused the chamber, coming from everywhere and nowhere. The ceiling was lapis-lazuli; the floor of blue-veined marble. At one end was a dais, and upon that were two thrones. They were not huge, nor encrusted with gems and ivory and precious almost-living shells as were the thrones in the Great Hall; these were made of a dark, shining wood twisted into strange seemings as if it had grown that way. The High King sat in one of these thrones, his Queen, Titania, in the other. Neither throne was larger than the other, mute testimony of their joint rulership, though Oberon had been High King longer than Titania had been Queen.

Having listened to the Visions of the FarSeers, High King Oberon leaned slightly forward toward them. Dark eyes—a black that somehow glowed—fixed on the four women who stood before the throne. They knew him of old, of course, but even so each stared in wonder at him. Power pulsed in him as if barely held in check, and he was beautiful . . . All Sidhe were beautiful, but Oberon was . . . different.

His hair grew from a deep peak on his forehead and swept back in gleaming black waves, the points of his ears showing through, enough to mark him as of elvenkind, if his beauty were not enough. His brows were equally black and high arched over the fathomless eyes. In contrast his skin was white, not pallid and sickly, but with the hard, high gloss of polished marble.

He towered over all other Sidhe, and not by enchantment. Physical strength almost immeasurable was his, and formidable muscles in shoulders and thighs strained the black velvet tunic and black silk hose he wore. He was all in black, only lightened by silver piping on every seam and the silver bosses on his belt and on the baldric that usually supported the long sword which now leaned against his throne.

"You know I cannot do what you ask," he said. "I am High King of all the Sidhe—Seleighe and Unseleighe alike. If I favor the Seleighe over the Unseleighe, the Unseleighe could rightfully deny my right to rule. I do not say their rebellion would be successful—it would not. But I would know that I had been unfaithful to my trust, and my power would be lessened. And they, feeling restrained and persecuted Underhill, would meddle more and more in the mortal world so that in the end we might be exposed for what we are."

"But if the Inquisition comes to England, it will rip and tear until Underhill is exposed anyway. Remember El Dorado and Alhambra." Eirianell met the black eyes with calm. She had known those who wielded power enough to sink a continent and dared reason with King Oberon.

But he showed no anger, only smiled and then said, "If. There are three futures. When we know more, I will examine my constraints more closely."

"But I have no such constraints," Titania said, her green cat-pupiled eyes glowing with challenge.

Her voice was sweet and rich as warm honey and her presence was the bright contrast to her husband's dark power. Titania was a wonder even to those she ruled. The Queen's lineage was pure High Court, Seleighe elven, except that she was even taller than most male Sidhe. Her body was, of course, perfectly perfect. Her hair was a rich gold, elaborately dressed in a high confection of tiny braids and curls, which showed off her ears; they were delicately shell pink, almost transparent—but the pointed tip of one ear was bent, which tiny imperfection made her somehow more perfect.

Oberon turned his head toward her, but he did not speak. Aleneil, who always watched the High King of the Sidhe as a doomed bird watches a snake, caught a fleeting glance from his dark eyes. She saw, or thought she saw, a kind of satisfaction in that glance. However, in the next instant there was nothing to be seen in Oberon's eyes but an avid sensual hunger, perhaps heightened by Titania's defiance.

The Queen's eyes glowed a bright, pure emerald, brilliant pools deep enough to fall into and drown. Her lips were pale rose, and through the ethereal light violet and white silk robes she wore, she looked . . . translucent, as if she were lit from within. The tip of Oberon's tongue flicked over his lower lip. Titania smiled.

"I desire greatly to see the red-haired child grow up to rule Logres," she said defiantly. "Do you forbid me, my lord?" The smile had not faded from her lips and her eyes, if anything, were brighter, almost casting visible sparks.

"No . . ." Oberon drew out the word and at last looked away from his queen toward the FarSeers. "I do not forbid, only caution. Do not act in your own person, my lady, and keep your favor for the red-haired queen secret." He shook his head before Titania could protest. "I say that more for her sake than for yours. She already attracts our Dark kin's regard; the attention of our Queen might well tempt them beyond caution."

Titania rose from her seat and Oberon rose too, more slowly. She gestured at the FarSeers. "I will see you ladies anon."

CHAPTER 1

The imp skittered sideways. Although it stood upright on its hind legs, it was no bigger than a mouse and looked much like one, with a round little body, and four thin legs and a long naked tail—except that it was bright red and quite naked. It had little beady black eyes, large round ears, and a pointed muzzle from which sharp little teeth peeked. Those sharp teeth and equally sharp, overlarge, claws on stick-thin front and rear limbs, from which a sick yellow-green slime oozed, curbed any desire to laugh in the one to whom the imp was squeaking. It might be small—but size was no measure of how deadly a thing was, especially Underhill. Most especially when the thing was Unseleighe.

Pasgen Peblig Rodrig Silverhair frowned and moved a finger just as the imp leapt toward him, and the creature squalled and made a convulsive movement to retreat. It was held suspended midair, its struggles quickly subdued as if a heavy, invisible blanket had been wrapped around it.

If anything, the creature looked more comical than

before, hanging helpless as it was, squirming and writhing. However there was another, more pressing reason
not to laugh than the imp's poisoned claws, which in
any case had been neutralized for now. It carried a
summons from Prince Vidal Dhu.

Pasgen did not frown, but he was—perturbed. Prince
Vidal Dhu. Vidal summoning him. For the past four
years Vidal had been hanging between life and death,
saved from perishing of iron poisoning only by his
Healers, who, constrained by blood oaths, died draining the poison out of his blood. Now it seemed that
Vidal had at last recovered enough to emerge from
hiding. And he should not have been able to find
Pasgen.

"So Prince Vidal wants me," Pasgen murmured. "How
interesting." His frown grew blacker, and he raised his
eyes to stare at the little monster. "How did you find
me?"

The imp squeaked "Let me go. Let me go. Prince
Vidal will punish you if you harm me."

The invisible blanket tightened around it. It tried
to struggle, could not. The power that held it tightened more. A despairing squeal contained the word
"Token."

"Give it to me," Pasgen said, the edge of command
in his voice.

The creature's mouth opened and it disgorged a small,
coiled object, wet with slime. An immaterial hand slid
through the field that englobed the imp, seized what
it had vomited and carried it toward Pasgen. As it
approached, he could sense the drumming beat issuing
from it, a drumming that perfectly matched the beating of his own heart.

Another gesture with one finger and the imp was
dead, crushed to a formless lump of red, mottled and
streaked with green-yellow gore. The force that held

it then carried the mess outside to be consumed by the things that scavenged Pasgen's gardens. Its death had been quick, too quick for the creature even to squall. Pasgen could not allow anything that knew the location of his private domain to live, but all the years of Vidal's training had not been able to teach him to enjoy pain. He could be vicious when necessary, but he was never cruel just for amusement.

Cleaned and dried by other invisible forces, the brown scrap was clearly preserved skin attached to a thin layer of flesh. His own skin and flesh, Pasgen knew, from the vibration of congruence. He stared at it, appalled. He had always been careful about hair clippings and nail parings, making sure to burn them. And all the while Vidal Dhu had his skin and flesh. When and how had Vidal obtained so powerful a token? More important, was this the only one the Black Prince had? And now what was *he* supposed to do with it?

Pasgen held out his hand and the scrap of brown leather was laid upon it. Pasgen closed his hand. He was immediately aware of a feeling of constriction. He opened his hand again; it was trembling. If he could not close his hand on the thing without feeling choked, what would happen to him if he tried to destroy it? Had Vidal known he would kill the imp? Had Vidal hoped he would kill himself too, unaware of the token?

Nonsense, he told himself. He had not been aware of any sense of confinement when the token was inside the imp. Most likely it was only because he knew he was closing his hand over it that he felt closed in. Nonetheless panic still rose in him at the thought the token might fall into anyone else's hands. Yet if he could not test its properties himself, who could he trust to touch it?

That question was answered before it was quite complete in Pasgen's mind, and the answer calmed and simultaneously raised a new wave of panic in him. His twin sister Rhoslyn could be trusted to know about the token and to test its effect on him, but if Vidal had a token from him, it was all too likely that the prince had one or more from Rhoslyn also. He had to warn her—not that he knew what good a warning would do . . . or would it be worse if she knew?

Pasgen rose from the stark white chair on which he had been sitting, his hand held carefully in front of him . . . and stood irresolute—a condition that had not afflicted him for many, many years. Should he go to Rhoslyn at once or should he first go to Caer Mordwyn and discover what Vidal wanted?

What Vidal wanted. Pasgen brought his skittering thoughts to bear on that. The fact that Vidal was able to want anything was another shock. Pasgen cursed softly, his eyes on the token lest it fall to the floor. He had been inexcusably careless, assuming as the years passed that Vidal would die or remain a near-inanimate hulk.

Pasgen himself had recovered in two years from the wound he had received in the battle waged against his half-brother and half-sister and their Seleighe allies. But *he* had only been scraped by a passing elfshot; not exactly harmless, but nowhere near as deadly as Cold Iron to one of the Sidhe. Vidal had been shot with a bullet from FitzRoy's mysterious gun.

Well, FitzRoy was dead. He would shoot no one again. Pasgen's lips twisted. And if someone had to be shot by a mortal, Vidal surely deserved it more than anyone else. Unfortunately it seemed that Vidal had survived with enough mind and will to demand his presence . . .

Or was it unfortunate?

The idea that had come to Pasgen seemed to lift an enormous weight from his heart, and it removed his indecision. He would go to Rhoslyn, warn her about the token and leave his with her—obviously he could not carry it with him to Caer Mordwyn. It would be safe with Rhoslyn; more to the point, it would be safe being guarded by the creatures his sister had set about her to ensure her own safety. Pasgen shuddered gently as he thought of the big-eyed, childlike, girl constructs with their wire-thin fingers that could be gentle as a butterfly or cut right through flesh and bone. They guarded Rhoslyn's domain every bit as efficiently as his own burly male guardians—better, perhaps, because invaders were prone to underestimate them.

He looked down at the scrap of skin and flesh in his hand and went to the black lacquer desk under the window. The top was glass-smooth, the surface clear except for the low gold-wire stand holding three thin gold pens. No design marred the perfect surface of the drawers on each side of the kneehole. Only absolutely plain pulls—octagonal bars of pure shining gold—were fastened to the face of each drawer.

Pasgen opened the middle drawer on the left-hand side of the desk with his free hand. It held a variety of boxes of different sizes and materials. He removed a small tortoise-shell square from the front of the drawer, struggled for a while to open it single-handed, and then, grimacing—because he was reluctant to have even his near-mindless and totally enslaved servants in the vicinity of that token—moved away and summoned an invisible servant to separate top and bottom.

He bade the servant clean the box and then dismissed it. After a moment, he drew a deep breath, deposited the token inside the box, and closed it. For a while he stood with his eyes closed, just breathing deeply and evenly. Finally he opened his eyes and looked around at the white leather chairs and settles, the black-framed chairs for visitors (not that he ever had any), the black lacquer side tables and low, central table, the black-and-white tiled floor.

All were clear and bright. No fog or dullness, as if he were peering out through some obstruction, obscured his view. It *had* been his too-active imagination, after all. He uttered a deep sigh, tucked the box into the bosom of his doublet, and left the house.

Usually Pasgen took his time when he crossed the garden and park in his domain. The beautiful, symmetrical order of the flower beds, the hedges, the trees with their ordered branches and precisely placed leaves always soothed him. There was so much disorder in his life, in his mind, in his heart, that the rigid and mathematical precision of the place was a balm to his spirit.

Today Pasgen merely hurried down the lavender graveled path that branched off the main way, which led to a stark but plainly marked Gate. That Gate had six exits, all equally unpleasant; two of those six *could* be fatal. It was a trap for the unwary, a clever way of disposing of any who thought to spy upon him or worse, and make a quick getaway. The side path took several turns and even crossed the kitchen garden before it petered out. A few steps beyond the little square that seemed the termination of the path, two slender white-barked saplings stood about two feet apart, exactly like similarly paired birch-trees all along the path. Pasgen stepped between them, and was gone.

He emerged in a narrow alley that led to a quiet back street from which one could hear the sounds of a busy market. The alley was empty, as it had always been since Pasgen cast an aversion spell on it. The two doors that had once opened into the alley were boarded up. The street beyond the alley was not always empty; only a little of the aversion spell leaked into it, but people using it had a tendency not to linger and those whose houses backed on it tended to use their front doors.

Today the street as well as the alley was empty, and Pasgen strode toward the sound of the market.

It was not large, an open area perhaps three or four streets square, but then the merchants were diminutive, the tallest coming only to Pasgen's elbow, so each booth did not take up much space. The customers, however, were of all sizes, many of them Sidhe, and a few even larger folk, which made the market seem very crowded. Pasgen did not mind at all. He slowed his pace to a shopping stroll and was soon indistinguishable from the many other Sidhe. Seleighe, or Unseleighe? There was no telling. Anyone who came here was careful to make his—or her—costume as neutral as possible.

He even stopped at a booth displaying a wide variety of amulets. Most were simply small carved figures of everything and anything, even of every religious symbol—the Christian cross, the Moslem crescent, the Hebrew six-pointed star, and the symbols of every pagan god Pasgen knew . . . and a number that he did not recognize. Curiously, he touched the cross.

"Fine work," the little brown merchant said. "Won't burst if you put a spell on it. Sold a lot of them. Seem to like love-spells they do. Seen them glow a little with a love spell."

The little man had an inordinately long and pointed nose that drooped a bit toward his long and slightly upturned chin. His ears were too large, the lobes hanging a bit below his chin and his hair was thin and scraggly. Pasgen shook his head but smiled and took up four anonymous-looking ovals, a wooden rose, a ceramic coiled serpent with lifted head, a leaping horse of bone, and a glass Sidhe head, with open eyes and mouth, that clearly split apart just behind the pointed ears to hold something small.

"How much?" Pasgen asked, reaching for his purse. He spoke in the common trade tongue used in every marketplace Underhill that was not large enough to have a universal translating spell.

"Gold I have, Master," the gnome replied in the same language. "Bespell for me an amulet and you will have paid."

"Or overpaid," Pasgen said, still smiling, but with his voice turned hard. "What kind of spell?"

"Sleep. That should be easy enough for you, master."

It was easy. Pasgen looked down at the table, saw several more charming or frightening figures. "For what I have in my hand, one use," he said. "If you want an amulet that will always bring sleep . . ." Suddenly he realized that very few Sidhe were capable of creating such a spell. To do so would mark him in the gnome's memory. He shook his head. "I cannot do that," he said, "but for five uses . . ." He narrowed his eyes as if considering what he had offered. "Yes, for five uses, I will take these—" he marked the amulets with his finger "—as well as what I have in my hand."

The gnome protested and bargained. Pasgen allowed himself to be divested of three of the amulets he had marked because to fail to chaffer would also mark him as unusual; however, he was growing impatient and finally made as if to throw down the amulets he was holding and walk away. That brought the gnome to heel and he accepted Pasgen's last offer of the five-times spell for the handful of amulets.

"Which shall I bespell for you?" Pasgen asked, about to pick up any amulet the gnome indicated.

Instead the little brown creature pulled a box from under the counter and opened it. Inside was a very plain oval, lightly inscribed with a small tree entwined with a clinging vine. When Pasgen picked up the amulet, it was blood warm in his hand, but it was the material of which it was made, not magic that warmed it.

He bent his head and began to murmur. He could see the gnome straining to listen but ignored him. He doubted the creature could make his harsh and scratchy voice sound the liquid vowels and sweet tones of the Elven-mage-tongue.

"So." Now Pasgen was in a hurry, and he dropped the amulet back in its box. "You can give the amulet to the person you want to wear it all the time, or you can lay it on that person's forehead or breast at the time you want the person to sleep. Then, to invoke, you say 'Minnau ymbil' and when you want the person to wake, you say 'Deffro deffroi'."

"And to whom do I complain if the spell doesn't work?" the gnome growled as Pasgen picked up the amulets for which he had bargained.

Pasgen started to turn away, but then hesitated and said, "Cry for justice to Vidal Dhu at Caer Mordwyn."

"Vidal Dhu is dead," the gnome protested. "You know we are between the Bright Court and the Dark and we had that news from both sides."

"Oh, no," Pasgen said, with a lifted eyebrow. "Then I give you a gift, along with the price of the amulets. I assure you he is alive and well and will be holding court at Caer Mordwyn ere long—but the spell will work. Never fear it."

And he slipped away, weaving skillfully among the booths and the customers. Actually he made two rounds of the market in random fits and starts until he began to move into less crowded areas and finally slipped behind a booth displaying very small gardening implements. There he waited rather patiently, considering his urge to continue to his goal, but he neither heard nor felt any magic. Finally he took out the amulet of the snake and sang to it the spell that opened a small, one-passage Gate.

Clutching the amulet in his hand, he walked away

from the market into the narrow streets of the town. The houses were hardly higher than his head and after some random turns and crossings, he could see that no one was following him. Then he walked directly out of town until the open ground that faced him blended into a formless mist. He invoked the Gate and stepped through, although if he had not known that he had passed through a Gate, he could easily have believed he was still in Gnome Hold.

Here, however, the mists were not formless. They swirled and twisted, retreating from him and then billowing toward him as if an erratic wind blew. Only there was no wind. Pasgen set out into the chaos with a steady step. As he went, he turned his head sharply to sniff in a wisp of mist that was passing his shoulder. A sharp scent, but not unpleasant.

A little later, he stuck out his tongue to taste a cloud that had formed directly in front of him—and that was sweet, decidedly sweet. Pasgen smiled and began to draw into himself some of the energy Rhoslyn might have used to create a construct. By the time he came to the Gate he had sensed at about the middle of this Unformed land, he had restored all the power he had used to create the gnome's amulet and build his Gate.

The Gate in the Unformed land took him to another busy Hold, the next to a dead Elfhame. Pasgen did not linger nor leave the Gate. He turned his back on the crumbling Hall and averted his eyes from the encroaching "garden" of viciously snapping "plants" and putrescent flowers. Fortunately, this Gate had three unused settings. Quickly, he willed a new terminus in another Unformed domain where he built another Gate that, at long last, deposited him at the edge of Rhoslyn's holding.

As always he sighed, mingled exasperation and appreciation, because the scene before him was both untidy and, somehow satisfying. There were no long, perfect vistas; the view was broken by little ponds around which there were patches of trees, then meadows cropped smooth by dainty sheep. Sheep? What were sheep doing in an Unseleighe domain? When the Dark Court wanted mutton, they engaged in a riotous hunt on mortal flocks, left grazing injudiciously too near a Stone Circle, a Standing Stone, a Barrow, or some other passage into Underhill. Pasgen shook his head. Not that they often did such a thing, at least, not for the meat. Venison, boar, and pheasant were more like to grace the tables of elvenkind. Or peacock and antelope, had anyone a taste for the exotic.

Beyond was a patch of woodland from which emerged a babbling brook following a wavering course over stones of every size and shape. He sighed again as he invoked the minor spell that would in effect give him seven-league boots and take him in three steps to Rhoslyn's castle. A castle . . . Again he shook his head. It was a mortal child's dream, that place; a fairy-tale castle with pretty towers and turrets and bright flags snapping in the nonexistent breeze.

His last step took him to the drawbridge over the moat—the shining, clear moat in which one could see large, bright-colored fish swimming. That was new. The moat used to look like a moat in mortal lands, or one in Unseleighe Underhill—muddy, green with algae, and clogged with razor-sharp swamp grass. It had never held golden fish with trailing fins before. Those were Seleighe things. If Vidal saw . . . If Vidal had a token and found Rhoslyn's domain and saw what looked too much like a Bright Court palace, he would tear it apart and break Rhoslyn's heart.

Pasgen swallowed hard, clenched his jaw, and reminded himself that—*that was then, this is now.* Vidal would do no such thing. Pasgen knew he had been close to matching Vidal's power before the disaster, and he had spent his years in learning new magic and finding new sources of power, while Vidal had been lying insensate, unable to learn or do anything. Vidal could do nothing to harm Rhoslyn that he, himself, could not counter . . . unless Vidal had also spent the years in growing stronger. And how could he? Surely the time had passed in weakness and pain.

As Pasgen set his foot on the first step of the portico that enclosed the castle door, it opened and two of Rhoslyn's constructs barred the way, standing and watching him. He was surprised. All of Rhoslyn's constructs knew him and all had been instructed to let him pass without hindrance.

"Who are you?" one of the constructs asked. "What do you want here?"

"I am Pasgen Peblig Rodrig Silverhair, he replied. "I am Lady Rhoslyn's brother and I have free passage into the lady's home. Are you new-made that you do not know me?"

It was impossible to tell one of Rhoslyn's constructs from another, except by the ribbons around their necks. They all looked like starveling girl children with huge eyes and small mouths. But those pursed lips could open wide as a lion's maw and show teeth that were as long and pointed as any wolf's. And the long, thin fingers on their sticklike arms . . . Pasgen had seen those fingers slice up an ogre as if he were a cheese.

For a long moment the constructs stared at each other in silence and Pasgen began to debate in his mind whether he could destroy them before they wounded him . . . and what his sister might do to him if he destroyed her toys.

Then Rhoslyn was there, stepping out of a shadow as if she had been conjured.

"Pasgen," she said, and looked at her constructs. "What ails you? Do you not know my brother?"

"Yes, lady," the girl with the yellow ribbon whispered, flexing her hands, "but this one is not the same. He has two hearts."

As Denoriel passed through the door to Aleneil's house, he wondered whether Elfhame Avalon was not just a bit too open to passers-by. Elfhame Logres was open too—the gardens, woods, and meadows, but the palace Llachar Lle had defenses. Even his own apartment inside the palace had a door that would exclude any who had not been sealed into its memory.

Of course with the Academicia in Avalon where most of the Magus Majors lived and worked, an inimical intruder would not last long. Not to mention what King Oberon and Queen Titania could do should anyone be foolish enough to invade the place . . .

Denoriel found himself smiling, and relaxed; he was being foolishly protective. Surely he did not need to be concerned for the safety of his precious sister and Avalon. He was still smiling when Aleneil stepped from the doorway of her solar. She smiled at him, and then laughed aloud.

"I guessed you would be coming here as soon as Mwynwen told you, but so quickly . . ." She frowned anxiously. "Oh, you didn't make a Gate, did you?"

"No, no. I will go strictly by the rules. I remember all too well what happened two years ago when I carelessly tried to light a candle. I have no desire at all to feel again as if every vein in my body is afire." He grinned at her. "Miralys brought me by his own sweet ways without regard to Gates or other passages."

"Ah." Aleneil turned and led the way into her solar. "I suppose the elvensteeds use magic, but it is something completely unlike our own."

"I think," Denoriel replied, having had quite some time to actually think about such things *and* great need to actually do so, "that it is more that they are like otters that slice through the water of magic, and we are the poor ducks, paddling furiously across the top of it and doing as much splashing and churning as getting anywhere."

That made Aleneil laugh. "Oh, please. A *swan* at least! Well, thanks to Miralys, then. He must have felt your need."

He gave her a comical little bow.

She smiled at her brother as he sat in his favorite chair, fingering the mother-of-pearl design inset into the arm, but she still felt concerned. The blue-green pattern of the cushions no longer picked up gold highlights from his hair; that was pure silver now. And there were small lines graven by pain and tension around the emerald eyes with their catlike pupils, and around his well-shaped mouth.

"Are you sure you are well enough?" Aleneil asked. "I know Mwynwen must have said you were, and I suppose Treowth also approved, but——"

His lips thinned. "I hope they are right. As I said, I do not enjoy being afire. But four years, Aleneil . . . eight long seasons. I am beginning to think I would rather not exist than be imprisoned and powerless for much longer." He saw the distress on her face and reached forward toward the settle to pat her arm and smile. "I am sure Mwynwen erred on the side of caution rather than optimism."

"Unless your endless complaints wore down even Mwynwen's patience," Aleneil said, but she was smiling again.

"And you do not give Treowth proper credit," Denoriel said, grinning. "I know he is more concerned for his reputation and his skill in magic than for the welfare of any people, but it would reflect ill on him if his magic killed me."

Aleneil laughed aloud, making a gesture that waked a peculiar, invisible movement in the air. By the time she spoke again, a small table had appeared beside Denoriel's chair bearing a flagon of his favorite wine and a delicate glass.

"So, what is permitted you now?"

"Passive magic. I may go through a Gate and visit the mortal world, so I want to see Elizabeth—and Harry wants me to see her. He worries about her . . ." He hesitated and then continued. "I don't think Mwynwen likes his concern with Elizabeth. I think she fears he will want to return to the World Above and she does not want to tell him that he cannot, not really. Oh, for a few hours, even a day or two, but not to live. The elfshot still poisons him and she must drain it every few weeks. I hope if I see the child and can assure him of her health and safety he will be more content."

"You think he will believe you more readily than me? I have been visiting her regularly all this time and telling him that she is safe and happy. She has a most loving governess in Katherine Champernowne. Blanche Parry is now chief of the maids and a close companion."

Aleneil caught her brother's look of sudden concentration, and felt both alarmed and pleased. This was the first time in four mortal years that Denoriel had shown interest in the child they had all worked so hard to save.

"Does Elizabeth know what Blanche is?" Denoriel asked. "As a babe Elizabeth could see through illusion. Can she still do that?"

Aleneil sighed, for she had not been able to get as near to the child as she would have liked. "If she can, she does not speak of it. She is a strange, self-possessed child most unchildlike child and says very little . . . but I think she does know what Blanche is and values her accordingly. She has other safeguards too. Dunstan is still groom of her chamber. Likely in a few years the office will be given to some high-born nonentity, but the whole household depends on Dunstan. He will retain his authority if not his title."

"Remind me to tell him that Lord Denno will assure him his salary if he be superceded."

Aleneil smiled. "I think that just, but not necessary. He is besotted of the child, and so are Ladbroke and Tolliver, who keep her stable. None would overlook any danger to her and all of them swear that there has been no intrusion from Underhill in all this time."

He nodded briskly. "Good enough. Still, I need to become reacquainted with her. She liked me well enough when she was a babe, but nothing compared with what she felt for Harry. If your FarSeeing is true— and I have never known it not to be—you and I will be with her when she is crowned, so she must get to know me."

"Crowned." Aleneil's smile turned to a frown. "My brother, you must never forget that is only one of the Seeings. There are two others. One is only dull and disgusting, but the other is of the dull-haired queen with the swollen belly. We all feel it. The Great Evil will grow inside her. If that comes to pass, I do not know if Underhill will survive. We must keep Elizabeth safe and in the line of succession. We must."

But now Denoriel straightened unconsciously in his chair, looking more like his old self—and a Knight— than he had in many a season. And when he spoke, it was with all of the old certainty. "If we must, sister dear, then depend upon it. We will."